Kings of Shadow and Stone

also by Anastasia King

WORLD OF AUREUM SERIES:
The Sunderlands
Kings of Shadow and Stone

World of Aureum Series, Book Two

Kings of Shadow and Stone

ANASTASIA KING

Kings of Shadow and Stone by Anastasia King
World of Aureum Series: book two
Copyright © 2022 Anastasia King Books, L.L.C.
First printed in the United States of America in 2022.

ISBN 978-0-578-31887-5

Anastasia King Books, L.L.C.
Anastasiakingbooks.com

Ordering information: anastasiaking@anastasiakingbooks.com
Printed in the United States of America
Authored by: Anastasia King (Pen Name), Breanna Diaz
Cover & Illustration: Alcaino Illustrations
Formatting: Zachary James Novels
Editing: Mackenzie at Nice Girl, Naughty Edits

WARNING: This story is not sui age of 18. This book c

This book contains portrayals of consensual or dubious consent, and con well as explicit language; graphic viole of addiction and substance use; the bondage and blood-play/consumptic but with sensitivity.

National Suicide Prevention Ho
National Human Trafficking H
LGBTQIA+ Trevor Hotline (S
Deaf Hotline (Suicide) 1-800-
S.A.F.E. (Self Abuse Finally E
National Sexual Assault Hotlir
Domestic Violence Support 1
Alcohol Treatment Referral
Grief Share 1-800-395-5755

Your story isn't over. Don't
in the USA.

Things to look forward to: a ma
anti-heroine who's not afraid to
alpha males, and aggressive assh
    You don't have to like the
monsters. Everybody's got der
with them, turn back now. No
the freaks… let's play.

For those who prefer the music of the night

Where Book One Left Them:

Keres & Liriene— *Baore Province, Kingdom of Dale*

Darius—*the Moldorn Province, the Lydany military camp*

Osira— *fleeing the Temple of Mrithyn*

Silas— *Ressid Province, the Guild of Shadows*

Kings of Shadow and Stone

ANASTASIA KING

ISBN 978-0-578-31887-5

Anastasia King Books, L.L.C.
Anastasiakingbooks.com

Ordering information: anastasiaking@anastasiakingbooks.com
Printed in the United States of America
Authored by: Anastasia King (Pen Name), Breanna Diaz
Cover & Illustration: Alcaino Illustrations
Formatting: Zachary James Novels
Editing: Mackenzie at Nice Girl, Naughty Edits

<u>Things to look forward to</u>: a magical world teeming with secrets, a badass anti-heroine who's not afraid to be a brat or a bitch to get her way, broody alpha males, and aggressive assholes who'll melt your panties off.

You don't have to like the main protagonist and antagonist—they are monsters. Everybody's got demons. If you don't want to explore the dark with them, turn back now. Nobody's going to judge you. If you're one of the freaks… let's play.

For those who prefer the music of the night

Where Book One Left Them:

Keres & Liriene— *Baore Province, Kingdom of Dale*

Darius—*the Moldorn Province, the Lydany military camp*

Osira— *fleeing the Temple of Mrithyn*

Silas— *Ressid Province, the Guild of Shadows*

Pronunciation Key

THE GODS:

Mrithyn: *Mr-ith-een* | The God of Death

Enithura: *Ee-nith-oo-rah* | The Goddess of Life

Ahriman: *Ah-rih-mon* | The God of War and Chaos

Adreana: *A-dre-on-ah* | The Goddess of Darkness and Secrets

Oran: *Or-ahn* | The God of Light and Revelation

Imogen: *Ih-mo-gen* | The Goddess of Peace and Order

Taran: *Tar-ahn* | The God of Earth, Phenomenon and Disaster

Nerissa: *Neh-riss-ah* | The Goddess of Sea and Sky, Discovery

Elymas: *Ell-ee-moss* | The God of Wonder and Magic

Atys: *Eh-tees* | The God of Punishment and Affliction

Tira: *Tee-rah* | The Goddess of Knowledge and Debate

Attor: *At-tore* | The Goddess of Adversity

CHARACTERS:

Keres: *Kare-ehs, Keh-rus,* or *Keer-ees.* | the Coroner, servant to the God of Death

Berlium: *Bur-lee-um* | the King of the Baore

Hadriel: *Hay-dree-il* | Supreme Magister of the North

Liriene: *Leer-een* | Keres' elder sister

Thane: *They-n* | a Ranger of the Shadow's Guild

Darius: *Dare-ee-us* | Keres' lover

Silas: *Sigh-lass* | Keres' husband

Osira: *O-sigh-rah* | the Oracle

Cesarus: *Ceh-zar-us* | Osira's wolf companion

Rivan: *Rye-van* | Guild Ranger, Thane's best friend

Morgance: *More-ganse* | Guild Ranger, Thane's friend

Elix: *Ee-licks* | Guild Ranger, Thane's friend

Jareko: *Jar-echo* | Guild Ranger, Thane's friend

Indiro: *In-deer-oh* | formerly Resayla's knight, a guardian

Emeric: *Em-er-ick* | Headmaster of the Shadow Guild

Aiko: *Eye-co* | Guild Agent

Chiasa: *Chee-ah-sa* | Guild Apprentice, Aiko's sister

Geraltain: */G/ eh-rahl-tane* | former Coroner

Resayla: *Ree-zay-lah* | Keres' mother (dead)

Herrona: *Heh-row-nuh* | Keres' aunt (dead)

Ivaia: *Ih-vye-uh* | Keres' aunt (dead)

Hero: *Heer-oh* | the Queen of Ro'Hale, Keres' cousin

Rydel: *Rye-dell* | Elistrian Ambassador, Hero's lover

Vyra: *Vye-rah* | the General of Essyd and Lydany

Epona: *Eh-poh-nah* | Vyra's best friend

Adrasteia: *Ah-drah-stay-a* or *Ah-dra-stee-ya*

PLACES:

Baore: *Bay-or*

Bamidele: *Bah-mih-del-eh*

Ro'Hale: *Row-halay*

Ressid: *Res-seed*

Moldorn: *Mole-dorn*

Essyd: *Es-seed*

Lydany: *Lih-da-nee*

Ceden: *See-den*

Falmaron: *Fall-mah-ron*

Massara: *Maz-arah*

Allanalon: *Ah-lah-nah-lon*

Kryptag; *Crypt-ahg*

Ashan: *Ash-ahn*

Illyn: *Ill-yin*

Aureum: *Awe-ree-um*

PART 1

ALL THE BROKEN PIECES

"Know this, First Children and Second Sons,
By love were all things made,
And by hatred are all things undone.
By the Divine Order do we live,
Or by Chaos do we die."

—Haf'naar verses 75 & 76

1: SISTERS

Liriene

Day One, Tecar

Darkness could not hide what I was. In that cave, I huddled beside my unconscious sister and tried not to laugh. Delirious laughter bubbled up within me. It took me digging my newly grown claws into my thighs to suppress the troubled mirth.

I made myself bleed. The warm stickiness was running down my legs. Keres took a sharp inhale and began to groan, as if the smell of blood stirred her. *Wrong.* I shouldn't have claws. Blood shouldn't call to my little sister's senses. But she was cursed, and we were both claimed by Gods.

The irony was not lost on me. Growing up, I told myself I'd been the good one. The truth was, I'd done everything wrong. So, I laughed at myself.

I let Katrielle follow Hayes off into the woods—they were ambushed, and she died. Because it scared me to fight for her. She was supposed to marry him, to protect us. Our secret.

If I had been the good one, I would have stopped her that day. I should have asked her to run away with me. Instead, I cared too much about what others would think. Our kin would never welcome us back if we ever returned. Because of our "unnatural" relationship. I couldn't just cut ties with my family. She didn't want that for us either.

I had to be good.

It cost me the person I cared about most. Now, I was buried under the weight of my realizations. Katrielle was buried under the ruins of our home. I lost everything. Except Keres.

I was harsh to Keres as a child. She had mother's favor. Why did she need mine? When she and Kat became friends, I looked past my sister to the girl beside her. I found my own friendship in Katrielle, which evolved as we got older, and I excluded Keres more and more for it.

Mother would run her fingers through Keres' long black hair. Turning her head from watching Kat and I run off to play. They had the same shade of green eyes, but Keres' were bigger and glossier. I know she always looked back over her shoulder as mother led her to the river. She was waiting for me to turn around and see her. I felt her gaze prickling between my shoulder blades.

If I'd been the good one, Keres would not have been at the river that day mother died. She would have been with me and Katrielle, Hayes and Darius, Silas and Thaniel. Having fun. Safe from the killer, safe from the river, safe from the God of Death. I left Keres behind, and she died for it.

Wrong.

When I saw my father dead on the battlefield, I felt an eternal spring of supernatural power burst open, right between my eyes. His death was the final blow that would shatter my good little world like a crystal ball.

For years, I rebuked Keres time and time again for her cursed power. Sought to control her, to prevent her from being consumed by whatever Mrithyn had done to her. Sitting in the dark of that cave, plagued by the fascinations of the God of Light, I finally understood.

Katrielle worshipped Adreana, the Goddess of Darkness, above the rest of the Pantheon. She was our secret keeper. I laughed again at the irony. The Gods are cruel, but love is the cruelest trick on mortals by far: appears to many a window, while some see only shards. I found myself cut on the bit of love granted to me, bitterly severed from my soul mate.

The attack on our people feels like a distant nightmare. Oran was there and everywhere, and the world seemed to have this fabric stretched over it, the threads connecting all the facets of creation to one another.

Those interwoven threads were a force of energy I could feel within. Some threads seemed tethered to me, like the one I could feel tugging me toward Keres. She wanted me to follow her, but another thread was being pulled.

Far away to the east—to Thane. He was present without actually being there. It should have frightened me, but he told me he was coming to help.

I told my sister about him as she tried to lead me through the battle. I felt the strings all around us reverberating with the song of war. Like an orchestra of energy and emotion. I was so lost in it all, but Keres didn't let go of me.

When Ivaia and Riordan died, I felt and saw the threads snap. Their connection to me and Keres... unraveled. It hurt more than I expected it to. If this was what my gift would do to me for the rest of my life, I didn't want it. Amplify the emotions I so desperately wanted to avoid? I didn't know how much longer the rest of my life would be in that case.

Keres awoke. I heard the shift in her breathing and my body went rigid. "You're up."

She rolled over and stopped. "Are we in a cave?"

"Yes," I responded.

She sat up. Her hands reached for me and found my shoulders. We huddled together, her warm skin a shock to my system. I was so cold. We stayed like that for hours, and I felt every minute tick by, dragging us each into ruinous thoughts.

"Memories will destroy you," I whispered and sighed.

"Do you remember having visions?" she asked.

"Violence. Terror. Chaos. Those events come from the twisted side of my wildest dreams. What am I becoming?" I dropped my head.

Keres grabbed me, lifted my chin, and pushed my shoulders back. "Liriene," she began to reassure, her breath close to my face. "You are not becoming anything. I won't let the Gods—"

"How can you stop Him?" I asked. "I saw Him." Then the tears flowed. "He sees me even here beneath the earth. He is showing me ruination. War. Death."

She dug her fingernails into my shoulders, and it distracted from the pain in my legs caused by my claws. She shook me. "Ignore Him. Block out His voice, close your eyes."

"I can't." I latched onto her. "Everyone thinks Oran is a child-like God. That He is giddy and bright. It's not true. He's terrible. He sees all,

3

knows all. These visions are blinding." I tried to steady my breathing, lower my voice. "He is not a sun God. He is revelation, and He shows me such darkness. Adreana does not hide Him from us, she hides *us* from His truth."

"What does He want? Why claim you now?"

"I don't know."

She fell silent for a moment.

"The darkness was meant for me, not you, Liriene."

Wrong.

I leaned away from her, sitting up straight. I placed my hands on her face. She felt feverish.

"We all have both light and darkness within us," I said.

Our conversation was interrupted when Varic and his men came for us. As we were led to the castle, Oran's power was molten in my veins. Was this what Keres had felt? Was this why she boiled in her rage and steam fumed from her mouth?

I barely noted the change in our surroundings, following Keres' bare feet but getting lost in memories. I remembered that day Keres chased me through the camp. She was livid over my claim on Katrielle. Keres was no longer the little dark-haired girl with mournful emerald eyes. She was like an unholy ghost with a bottomless stare. Unlike anything I'd ever seen until I was brought before King Berlium.

The darkness in Keres' eyes was predatory. The King was paralyzing.

A raw and intense sensual prowess rolled off his body like water off oil. He washed me in a wave of that seductive destruction. I felt myself drowning in his blue eyes. When he held me captive with his gaze and touch, I sensed a synergistic force within him. His own power mingled with something else. Something veiled behind the impassable darkness of his mind.

It kindled something buried deep in the ashes of my spirit. An instinct that felt as foreign as it felt ancient. Like a golden eye opened in the core of my being, and a beast of my own awoke.

Keres snapped me out of it. She drew his attention to herself, and then he had her under the thrall of his seductive magic.

4

Wrong.

King Berlium looked between me and my sister, designing a rift between us. In that moment, Keres laughed, and the King of Stone quaked with fear.

2: SECRETS
Thane
"He stole her."
Day Thirty-Five, Present Day

"Then the day has finally come for us to confess our secret."

Rivan leans on his knees, his head bowed into his hands. He lets out a pensive sigh. My fingers play at the brim of my wine-filled goblet as I lounge in my chair. It feels like we've been here for hours. Perusing our options now that the Coroner was a prisoner in the Baore. How can we avoid the destruction on our path toward her? We've debated and exhausted every possibility... except this one.

"We're taking an enormous risk," I scoff.

"Everything will work out," Rivan counters. I roll my eyes at him. He smiles because he knows it irks me more.

"This is our only option. We both know it, Thane. We've taken too much time to think. Things are getting out of hand."

He's right.

In the Guild, we live our lives by a code of dishonor: to violate any secret as necessary for the sake of balance. Rivan and I are the darkest of shadows. We watch the world when no one wants us to. When others would look away.

Collecting the Aureum's memories as they form. Our duty is as simple as shepherding the stars into constellations. Secrets turn the world over. Like a currency, they make it go round. Secrets can be brokered. Secrets can be weapons. Which is why Rivan and I are not supposed to be keeping any from our brothers.

But we are.

Our men trust us. They cannot hide their true selves, so we are not supposed to hide ours. Our bond, a spiritual connection of power, depends on each of us being vulnerable to each other.

I have pulled Rivan into my secrets, my lies. Only he knows the truth and protects me. Until now, it's been our only choice. We knew the day was coming when our safeguards would fail. When our choice would be stripped from us; our secrets, unraveled. The day we finally found her.

My Spirit is part of the Void. My brothers don't know how I truly struggle, because I grin when they ask me what I need.

"*Nothing,*" I say.

How could they ever understand I was full of nothing?

I've told them about my serving the Goddess Adreana. They know the glory of my power. They trust in it, oblivious of my dark curse. When they learn the truth of what I've done to them—the abyss I've bound them to, they will realize the dangers ahead of us.

Secrets can be weapons. Knowing can leave you vulnerable.

They, too, will be dragged into my darkness. When I become what I'm supposed to, they'll be at my side with no more claims to innocence.

"Shall we tell them tonight?" Rivan asks.

I don't want to tell them. He doesn't want to tell them. It's our unspoken agreement, but things are different now.

"After dinner." I lift my glass to my mouth. Before taking a sip, I add, "If we change our minds, we can tell them we wish to discuss Daia." I linger before taking a sip.

What words will suffice our confession or earn us absolution for our lies? Even if the truth washes out the lies, how can I part with the guilt I feel about my true weakness?

How do I tell them our bond is second to my bind to Death? After a lifetime of watching and waiting. After years of uncovering and trading secrets. After all the killing, stealing, and brokering I've brought them into…

"They will not want to discuss your sister." Rivan kneads his hands. "They'll want to talk about this. We won't be able to avoid it. Not anymore."

7

"Daia is making too much noise in the Natlantine." I try to change the subject. "The men have asked what we're to do with her."

Rivan turns his mismatched eyes to me. "Maybe she'll turn back to the Darkness. Eventually."

"She ran from it." I shake my head and take a deeper swallow of wine.

"She ran from the darkness in your heart, Thane. Not our work."

I hear the hurt in his voice. He's loved Daia since we were children. From the moment she burst through the guild doors ahead of me, mousy hair a ragged mess and her hazel eyes wild.

She hated me. She hated Emeric. My sister hated everything about the guild, but Rivan loved her. She was not interested in the world of darkness within Rivan—not with a new world out there, glinting with golden treasure.

"Women are creators—too bad they create so many problems." I smirk at him.

He looks up to the ceiling, the shadowed corners. "Life would be worse without women."

I let out an exaggerated sigh.

"Listen, Thane. For Resayla's sake, our men will go after her daughters. They're confused why the King even took her. They're wondering why it's taking so long for us to come up with a plan—why we shoot down all their suggestions. Leading them in blindly is more dangerous for them than the truth."

"I know," I groan, and rake my hands through my hair.

The men are not questioning me directly, but I know they need answers.

"It doesn't help that her husband is so pushy. His unrest is stirring up such questions."

"Speaking of. Once Keres is ours..." Rivan crosses his arms in front of his chest and finally relaxes back into his chair. "I think we must keep him at a distance."

I can see Silas in my head as if he were sitting at the table with us. Just this morning, his amber eyes glowered at me from under his hood. Angry words flickered into his mouth, and he snuffed them out—but I know he

8

ached to curse us all. Because he felt helpless.

He and Indiro arrived in a state of desperation, asking Emeric for our guild to aid in rescuing them. Indiro and Silas don't know the gravity of their request or my concession.

"He's wasting time. I cannot wait! How do you expect me to sit idly by?" Silas fumed.

"I fucking hate him. He's so annoying." I drain my chalice and pour more wine. As I lean across the table to refill Rivan's chalice, I say, "Once we've got her, yes, keep him at a distance. I swear on my brother, if he so much as even makes me wrinkle my nose in disgust, you'll be keeping me at a safe distance from his throat."

Rivan's eyes darken as they return to mine. "He's angry because he's afraid and doesn't trust us. Which he shouldn't. Two people he loves are in the den of a beast."

I smirk. "And Keres is about to go from the jaws of one beast into the belly of the next."

Honestly, I could empathize. Silas was separated from his kin. That's not something I'd know how to tolerate either. I just didn't want to be reminded of that feeling.

Rivan shakes his head. "What if she's everything she was designed to be?"

I don't bother answering his question. It wasn't a *what-if*.

Keres was created to be a snare—for me. A sick joke on the tongues of meddling Gods. I had no doubts about what she was. I only wondered who would laugh in the end.

🔲🔲🔲

Our brothers join us at our round table, weary of the day. I lower my hood as their gazes train on me. Dinner scraps litter the table. Playing cards and tankards.

Their bellies are full, and they are relaxed, awaiting. What morsel of information shall I serve them for dessert? They wonder, scratching their beards and shifting in their chairs to ease the silence.

"Brothers," I look each of them in the eye. "You have proved your loyalty to me time and time again, but why are you loyal to me?"

9

Rivan leans forward and rests his elbows on the table, steepling his hands in front of his mouth.

"Because you do what's needed. You don't back down," Elix says as confusion swirls in his pale hazel eyes. An exquisite contrast to his dark skin.

"Aye, you deliver," Jareko agrees, raising a glass and a smile touches his brown eyes.

"You're the boldest, wildest bastard I've ever known." Morgance bares his teeth in a grin, and his blue eyes flare with viciousness.

"And our brother Rivan?" I ask. "Are you loyal to him?"

"As loyal as I am to my cock—as we are to any among us." Morgance laughs.

"What's this about, Thane?" Elix asks.

The men look at one another, smiles dwindling.

No use tarrying.

I hold their gazes. "My lying to you."

"You're not really a lass, are you?" Jareko raises a brow and smirks.

I chuckle, but my smile fades as well, and I can feel Morgance's eyes boring into me. "No, no. Though I know we're all thinking about a particular lass. Princess Resayla of Ro'Hale."

We all remember the first time we met Princess Resa and her knight, Ser Indiro. When I channeled Keres, it shocked me to see how strong the resemblance was between her and her late mother.

"Is this about her daughters? Have you finalized a plan? Or are you lying about—"

"Mor, I'll explain everything. Just give me a chance." A more fragile request than he knew.

Morgance, Elix, and Jareko look at each other and then at me.

"First, we must thresh the truth from the lies."

The corner of my mouth flinches. In all my years, I've never learned how not to smile when I'm under pressure. They don't miss my tell and shift in their seats again. All my years of lying and I've never learned how to come clean.

"Princess Resayla has been dead for thirteen years. Her daughters were raised in the Sunderlands' clan, Ro'Hale. They are now prisoners in the Baore. I underestimated the King—his obsessions. He's become more powerful. Hungrier than ever. The Coroner is a walking weapon, which he now holds."

Elix fiddles with his brown, thick curls. His face looks weary and rugged, more than ever at this moment. "We all underestimated him."

All the world underestimated him—even the Gods.

My men do not know the extent of my relationship with the King. They only know that I've visited him throughout the years—that we knew each other. They don't know how.

The King unleashed chaos on the Baore when he ascended the thrones twenty years ago. My men were never comfortable with this. I didn't care. I know the darkness that inhabits him. It never surprised me.

My men would never question me, but my affiliation with the King… I know they've always wondered why I did not bat an eye at his actions.

When he started attacking the Sunderlands, the Guild started paying more attention. The world did. He'd withdrawn from me.

Now, he's taken a powerful game piece. One I need—that he knows I need. I had been waiting to take her, but I waited too long. I never expected him to do this. They don't know how deeply his betrayal cuts me.

Today, I will tell them.

"Underestimated? Thane, the world has watched King Berlium's war unfold, amazed by the revolution that followed. He's been attacking the Sunderlands—fucking finally, the Heralds sought answers. But nobody has gone after him. He engenders fear and mongers war. I don't know about you guys, but I never trusted him. He has become a recluse. Do you think no one noticed him withdrawing from you? I never understood your relationship, but I know admiration when I see it. You've never spoken against him until now," Morgance rants.

I smile. *Observant bastard.*

"I knew you were smart, Mor."

He snorts.

I scratch the scruff on my jaw. "Admiration is an interesting word.

11

It's true. The King is... a genius in his own right. His games, his war—have I admired him? Perhaps I did. He amused me."

"Genius has turned to madness," Elix says.

"Not necessarily," Rivan replies. "We know the King takes time in private every so often, but his recent seclusion is different. He's set wards around the Baore—a response to the attention he's earned. We can't hunt his secrets and motives. He's so calculated and controlled."

"Stopped inviting me over for tea, then locked the doors and shutters," I scoff. "It's been guesswork ever since. We can guess Keres is only a part of his reasons for his attacks on the Sunderlands. However, his apparent attempts at conquering the Sunderlands are not absolute. As long as the Ro'Hale and Elistrian thrones have Elven asses on them."

"Keres is a descendant, an heir to one of those thrones," Rivan says.

"Should he control her, the Baore won't be the only Province he dominates," Morgance says, piecing it together. "It's a power play—a pretty brilliant one."

"We have our own power plays to make in this game. Keres is the Coroner, but history will remember her by a different name. We must ensure that name is next to ours."

"Liriene is a Seer, a servant of Oran. Newly reborn. We know this because Thane channeled her during the Dalis' attack on Ro'Hale," Rivan adds.

"So, what's the complication?" Morgance grunts. "Why have you been taking so long to decide on a plan?"

Here we go. Rivan and I exchange glances. I put my booted feet on the table.

"Keres and I are bound."

"What?" Jareko leans forward in his chair, his sunny blond hair shadowing his face.

"As in an actual bond like ours?" Elix's eyes widen.

Morgance crosses his arms over his burly chest. "How can you be tied to her *and* us?"

"It is entirely possible for one to be bound to multiple people. There are different bonds—soul ties. It is also possible that a powerful bond can disrupt, weaken, or even sever others," I say, watching their reactions shift from *oh* to *oh fuck* to *no fucking way*.

I can't be gentle with breaking this news. These men are not even wholly convinced the sky is blue. With all we've seen, they've become skeptical. Especially of anyone outside our bond.

Elix's brows shoot up. "The Coroner is your mate?"

"Mate... is an interesting word." I smirk. "Like I said, there are different kinds of bonds people can share. I deliberately created ours, brothers. My tie to the Coroner is a twist of fate—still, it doesn't make us helpless. There's always a choice."

"If you choose this bond, will it sever ours?" Elix asks.

I ignore how that question makes my skin crawl. "Even drawing close to her is a risk. Choice or not. That's just one of the many reasons I've been ruminating on this," I say.

"Risks? More like consequences," Morgance snaps.

Rivan interjects, "Need outweighs the risks."

All eyes are on the table. Scanning the empty places and half-full glasses, as if they can find more palatable answers there.

"A twist of fate? Are you saying the Gods orchestrated this?" Jareko chimes in.

"They have an interesting sense of humor." I sigh.

"I'm still not understanding. You're not telling us everything," Elix says.

I knew this wouldn't be a neat conversation. I try to keep my line of thinking.

"The Coroner was wrought in savagery. I've watched her throughout her life since I first learned of our bond. I have no intention of committing myself to her, but we need her—"

"You've watched her and we're hearing this only recently?" Morgance raises a brow.

"Timing, Mor, is a very important thing. Keres is cursed with blood-lust and trained as a battle-mage. She's a brutal work of creation. Yet with all that power, naivety is the thorn in her flesh. An insult to her design. The Sunderlands is all she knows. I have been awaiting the day she would reach maturity—not as a woman, but as a Godling."

"Rivan, you knew about this? You've been awfully quiet," Elix says, drawing Rivan out of his thoughts.

Rivan nods and pours himself more wine.

I open my mouth to speak, but Morgance holds up his hand. "You keep saying we need her. She's the Coroner, but we've never needed her. Why now?"

"Because War is coming. As you said earlier, the King has been moving pieces, and he just claimed the deadliest one. I don't know the breadth of his plans, but I've been going over all our years, sifting through his habits, the things he's said. I've deduced a few moves he may make. All of them, catastrophic."

"Beyond the Baore, things are changing in Aureum. More Instruments have risen than ever before. The Gods are also planning their next moves in this game. Keres is on the board, whether she's with him or with me. She's not supposed to be with him."

"Does anyone else know about this *fetter* between you and the Coroner?" Morgance snarls.

"That's an obscene word—I can never be fettered," I growl back at him.

"Are you so sure? You said you've watched her all her life—maybe you've secretly fallen in love with her and don't want to admit it," Mor guffaws.

"Thirteen years ago, Keres died. She was a child. Her black-haired head disappeared under river water, and she drowned. She became the *Carenar*. She resurfaced, ashen-haired. Her wings unfurled. But she was still a child.

"As she got older, yes, she became beautiful, but that's not it either. The Gods—she's Mrithyn's, but she's more than that. When I say she is a twist of fate, I mean we're connected in a way that is bad for me."

"Why was she bound to you?" Jareko asks. "You speak of her death as if you were there."

I pinch the bridge of my nose and sigh. There's no going back now. The truth—all of it.

"Once she died, Mrithyn's hand touched this world. To create her. The minute he changed her, her Spirit called to mine. The bond snapped in place. Keres is what she is because of what I am."

"Because of… the Goddess Adreana?" Elix asks.

Rivan and I exchange glances. I stand from the table, adjusting my jacket. I refill my wineglass and drain it again. Pushing my chair out, I step toward the wall and turn around. Their silence makes the hairs on my nape stand.

"Brothers, I base my bond with you on something very dark. You're not the first—"

"The King?" Mor interrupts. "You're bound to him, too."

I rake my hands through my hair. "It's not the same."

"Give him a minute," Rivan soothes them.

I straighten my spine and turn back to them. What's unknown is dangerous.

"All those years ago, the power of my spirit drew you to me—bound you to me. We shared commonalities. Our ages, for example."

"Aye." Elix nods.

"I created that bond with you, but I have known the King longer than I have known you. We also had similarities then."

"How is that possible? You said you met him along our travels. We were children when we joined you…"

"I lied," I say under my breath, and then again, louder. "But my need for you all was not a lie. I bound us—I chose you. My connection to the King was also a choice, but my connection to Keres is not. Hers is a consequence of my choices."

"So, when did you really meet him?"

I snort and think back to that day. "A very long time ago."

I look at Rivan for reassurance, and he nods. I fixate on him for a breath, composing myself. One eye sapphire, the other like honey. Somehow, they balance me. His thoughts meet mine in my head, and he tells me to be strong.

Elix, Jareko, and Morgance await, attuned to the fact Rivan and I are having a silent conversation. I have led them to believe that I can

15

communicate with him through the bond, the way I communicate with them, but it's not entirely true. So much of what they think they know is untrue.

Rivan's eyes widen, and his jaw tightens as he takes a deep breath. He will have to reveal his secret, too. His brows settle low above his eyes, the colors in them darkening. I can feel the shadows in the room shivering cold.

"Telling me to be strong while you're shaking, you bastard?"

I can hear his Spirit chuckle. *"Get on with it."*

My mouth moves to surrender to the smile that comes because I'm the most uncomfortable I've ever been, but I quell it by shifting my gaze to their hardened, lined faces.

"I am not what I say I am."

Morgance stands to his full height, rolling back his shoulders and puffing out his chest. His sky-blue eyes train on me, but Elix and Jareko's fixate on Mor. Slowly, they rise, and so does Rivan. Tension runs along our bond—if it could be plucked, it'd sing like a harp string.

"Let him speak, Morgance," Rivan raises his hand. His diplomatic voice never wavers.

"When I found each of you, huddled beside bodies and covered in blood, my energy called to you."

"We were there, mate. We know the story," Morgance chides.

"And do you not wonder why you hypnotically followed me from the massacre *I'd* created? Why, as children yourselves, you followed a boy who slaughtered hundreds of people in a day, alone. The only people you knew in this world?"

"You know as well as we do you called us into freedom, Thane." Elix tilts his head.

"You saved us."

"I stole you," I drop.

Their eyes widen, and their bodies stiffen.

"Even now, you defend me. I brought your world down around you and then plucked you out of it. Question it—this bond you believe in as if it were your God. Think about it."

"You're speaking as if you've possessed our free will. As if you're manipulating us through this bond." Mor holds his arms out at his sides, disturbed by my words but making himself vulnerable to me as I've taught him to. His voice is gravelly. I've hit him where it hurts and that cold, hard heart is grinding against his stone exterior.

"They're our brothers," Rivan reminds me.

"I have not influenced your will. Only drew you to me. I needed you, even if I had no right to you. I was alone in the world. I cannot tolerate being alone."

"Aye, as we've known and never scorned, brother." Elix smiles, as if he's relieved.

"I can't be alone because of what I am. I said you were not the first to be drawn to me. You did not know what you were being drawn toward," I say.

I lift my hood back, settling it down against the nape of my neck. They all instinctively step back when my energy surges through our bond. A rise in power they've never felt from me. They scan each other's faces but look back at me as I hold my palms up.

"Well, boys." My voice splits in two. "I can't seem to find the words to wash myself of these lies, so I'll just have to show you the truth."

Their faces contort into mixed expressions of horror as I smile, my fangs and tongue lengthening. My eyes, dark as the Void. I rise above the ground and bare my true form. Absolution still feels far away, but I know I've come clean when Morgance falls to his knees.

3: SCOUNDREL

DARIUS

In The Sunderlands

My twin brother, Hayes, didn't deserve to die.

Silas invited me to a secret meeting. After the last of the nine died, he said we were going to get revenge on the bastards that killed them. I was all in until I saw the Coroner sitting at the campfire next to him.

Through the leaves, I saw her moon-white hair. Their conversation was loud enough to hear from a distance. Idiots.

I was sweating even though a High Winter wind was threatening to overturn Low Summer's balmy nights. No chill in the air could suppress the rage boiling within me.

Rampaging through the bushes, I startled them all. Silas cursed and lowered his weapon when he realized it was me. He gave me one of his pissy glares.

"By the Gods, Darius," he'd said. "If that's your idea of meeting us for a secret meeting, you'll get us all killed."

Keres' eyes trained on me. Brilliant, wild green, reflecting the firelight. She said hi.

I wanted to lunge at her, take her by the throat, and hold her face to the flames. Listen to her scream, feel her body jerk and writhe in agony. Hold her helpless and kill her.

Why? Because Hayes died helpless and in agony. She had no right being at that meeting, planning revenge for something she could have prevented.

"What's she doing here?" I asked.

"I beg your pardon?" Her dark brows pinched together. Silas said she used to have black hair. People said a lot of things about her. I never cared to listen until I heard she was supposed to be the tenth member of the company the day Hayes died. If she had been there, it would have made all the difference.

Right? Isn't that what the fucking Coroner was supposed to do—kill bad guys and protect the good ones?

My footsteps crunched leaves and snapped twigs, egging me on to break her bones.

"I cannot pardon you for what you did!" I shouted.

My voice rang through the trees. If the Dalis heard—if they came— I would have handed her to them myself. No. That would have been too easy. I wanted to make her beg for forgiveness for abandoning the company.

"Speak that way to her again, and I'll rip your tongue out from beneath your chin." Silas held his knife at my throat. My friend... threatening my life over a witch.

They all tried to reason with me. Told me someone misinformed me. She opened her mouth and said my name, and it felt like she was mocking me. Silas flipped his blade in his hand, catching it by the hilt. Staring me down. Taunting me.

Keres was all he talked about since her birthday in Mid Summer. She was finally twenty years old—ready to wed. He'd been fucking Moriya for years, waiting for Keres to be of age. To become his. Once her birthday rolled by, he buttoned up his pants and left Moriya on her back.

Conversation about the girl who wet his dick turned to the one who'd never touched one. Keres was a virgin. Shiny and new, like a sheathed blade.

He didn't love either of them. He'd barely made any effort to get to know Keres. She didn't grow up hanging out with us like her sister, so I never paid attention to her.

He finally spoke for her. Now that she was fuckable.

I finally saw her. Now that she was to blame... or so I thought.

"Where were you?" I'd asked. "You were to lead the group of scouts. I saw the orders. I saw your name on that list."

I awaited a pathetic excuse for her skipping out on the mission—for them getting slaughtered.

In retrospect, my brother wasn't the only one among the nine. So was Kat. Her best friend. If I hadn't been so angry, I might have been able to put it together. She never meant for anyone to get hurt. She hadn't deserted them. I just wanted someone to pay. So badly.

Our eyes searched each other's, and I felt like I was staring into a looking glass, which angered me more. She wasn't at the meeting because she felt bad and was trying to make up for it. She was just as angry and in as much pain.

"I was at my mother's grave."

Realization dawned on me. Knocked me off kilter. "The full moon."

I never paid more attention to the Coroner than anyone else did, but there were things about her everyone knew. One of those things was where she went on the nights of a full moon.

As she stared me down, I realized just how fucked up the whole thing was. She wasn't with the nine because she was at the River. The vigil she held in memory of her mother's death... was the reason more people died.

Her eyes were driving me insane, burning into me.

We were seeing each other for the first time, and we were exchanging something in that stare. I was angry. She was angry. But we weren't angry at each other. Not really. It was this fucking world that was the problem. All I wanted was to burn it down.

With the way her eyes held that firelight, I realized she did too. My hatred for her turned to ash.

Still, I didn't like that she had such an effect on me. I was already fighting hard enough to suppress the fire inside, and her eyes were a mirror for more than the feelings burning within. Feelings I'd been trained to fight against.

Every time my father hit my mother, or me and Hayes, my mother stayed quiet. She looked past him, to us, and her eyes held a warning. *Don't give in to the pain.* We shoved the feelings down as best we could. Took every hit. Until we couldn't take any of it anymore.

I didn't give in to the pain; I gave in to rage. It came easiest to me.

Keres was a mage. Everyone knew it. She burned some shit down once in combat training with Indiro. I knew there was a fire in her, too. Real fire. I could see it in her eyes that night. Her power stirred. Mine was supposed to be asleep. Her gaze was stoking it.

Silas watched me staring at her. The thought of how wrong he looked next to her distracted me from the anger. Led me into thoughts of him fucking her and taking her virginity. The look in her eyes told me she'd chew him up and spit him out.

The things that came out of her mouth that night confirmed it. We talked about killing people, and she chimed right along with all of it. She was a strategist who didn't flinch about breaking the rules—about hunting the Dalis. She drank Silas' liquor like it was tea.

And she kept fucking looking at me with those verdant eyes. There was an animal in her. I saw it and it saw me. Her gaze was smoldering. It distracted me—led me into thoughts of *me* fucking her. Which meant I'd probably stared at her too long, but she didn't stop either. I should have.

Maybe it was the emotions that spiked my blood, or the liquor. Or just the way her mouth looked so gods-damned delicious when she said the word *fuck*. Fangs and all, there was no looking away from this girl after that.

Silas walked her home that night. She was drunk. Giddy. Looking at him and Thaniel like she'd eat them alive. Indiro made me stay behind with him, and I watched her walk away.

"Alright, lad." Indiro passed me the last canteen. "I see what you're thinking. It's been plain on your face for most of the night."

I looked at his drawn face but didn't speak. Instead, I took a swig.

"Keres and Silas." He leaned his head back and looked up at the stars through the trees. "Their marriage has been arranged since before her birth."

I let out an exasperated sigh, disinterested in one of his lectures.

He sat up again, pointing a finger in my face. His long hair fell forward, shadowing his jawline. His eyes dug right into mine.

"Now, listen here. Whether you like it, I'm still a Knight of Ro'Hale.

Acting on orders from the princess I swore to protect."

Then he pointed his finger in the direction Keres had gone.

"That girl's mother charged me to look after her and her sister. To ensure everything went according to her wishes. Namely, Keres marrying a knight."

"And what about her wishes?"

"What about her wishes?" he echoed. "What do *you* care about her wishes? You were lookin' like you'd run your blade through her at the start. Now, you're thinking about shoving your cock in her instead. You think I don't know it, lad? I was a boy once; I know that look."

I shrugged.

"The girl is cursed," he said, lowering his voice. "Wicked and dangerous and fucked."

He held up his hands and sat back. "Now, I love her dearly, as if she were my daughter, but she's troubled. And your kind... doesn't do well with trouble."

I glared at him, locking my mouth shut. *My kind.*

He always beat around it. He took us in after we left Massara and schooled us into warriors. Gave us books to read, so we could learn about it. That's as far as understanding went. Not knowing how to handle what we were was dangerous. If we didn't control what we were, he'd make us leave. That was the deal.

After what we'd endured in our childhood home, we didn't want to leave. Mother came to Ro'Hale with us and then went back. We couldn't follow her, watch her keep getting hurt. She didn't listen. It made me want to burn Massara down, so she couldn't leave. But she was broken. Setting her world on fire wasn't the answer. Again, I suppressed every instinct I had. You can't help someone who doesn't want to help themselves.

Hayes and I read the books and pretended they were fairy tales. Closed the books and closed the door on what we were. Looked forward. We made time to check on mother. And to threaten father. I was in Massara before that meeting around the campfire.

"Did you tell your parents about Hayes?" Indiro asked in a softer voice.

"I told my mother."

"And your father?"

"My father would be glad to hear Hayes is dead."

Indiro's brow creased, and the lines around his mouth deepened. Pity. That's what that look was. I didn't need or want his pity. Or anyone's. He never let us talk about shit, but he asked so many questions and always had an opinion.

"Are you done now?" I asked and stood.

He shook his head and extended his hand so I could help him stand. We put out the fire in silence. Two scoundrels in the dark, we stole our way back to camp. Him, on his way to sleep off the alcohol. Me, on my way to lay awake and think about Keres.

It was better than thinking about Hayes or the fucking war.

A girl with power. A girl in pain, who felt the way I did. Who burned as hot. The smallest flame of my power woke up and stretched inside me under her stare. She could see the fire. She could handle it. It felt good not to have to hide it—better than it should.

Thoughts of her coaxed me away from the painful ones. So, I followed where they led.

In the Moldorn

Every night since, I've done the same: lay awake, thinking of her. Only now, I'm trying to lull to sleep what she awakened.

I've lost count of the sleepless nights since I left her in Ro'Hale. Tonight, I just want to rest but can't. It's like she calls to me. Around the same time every night, I look for her through the dark and memories. Stumbling with stars in my eyes. Moon until sun. I chase her shadow through my thoughts. I think about the way she moaned my name and the way she said goodbye.

It's still better than thinking about the fucking war, but when I get up and walk out of my tent—I'm in the middle of it.

Everything is fucked up. That Oracle kid told her we'd die if we stayed together, but what was that warning good for? Keres went home, and our people were attacked. Then she got abducted, and I was here, in the middle of chaos. How were we any safer apart than we were together? Dying isn't nearly as scary as living already dead inside.

When I sleep, Hayes cuts through my dreams. My mind conjures him when I feel at my lowest. He repeats the thing he always said growing up. Filling the silence his death created.

"Don't wake it up. That's rule number one for Daemons."

I tell him I'm breaking rule number one. It's gotten harder and harder not to become what we've suppressed for so long. I never thought I'd have to face the Daemon Call alone—without him. I'm slipping further into the fire every night.

Then he reminds me of rule number two. *"Don't let it win."*

My journey to the Moldorn was too quiet, despite the way my feet crunched the fallen leaves. The way my heart pounded in my head. The words Keres said took up space in my thoughts.

"We can't. Not like this. You have to go… We will never get the chance we deserve. I will never take a chance on losing you." I was able to change her mind about Silas, but not about this. Not about me. I wanted to kiss those words out of her mouth. But I couldn't. I argued with her in my head. Every step away from her was a debate, and Hayes kept interrupting with his rules.

It was a miracle I made it to the Moldorn without burning the forest down around me. When I arrived, I went straight to the Gryphon King, Arias. Just like Keres asked me to. Arias took my message and sent me here. To Lydany. A clan of Humans and Elves that dwell even farther south, beyond the wall that joins the two kingdoms.

As the Gryphons sought more information, they kept the General updated. Vyra kept me in the loop, letting me know when Ro'Hale fell. When the Coroner fell with it.

General Vyra tries to get on my good side, but she will be the first to push me over the edge. I'm restless and she's tireless. She wants me to fight alongside her and her men. Illynads fight her forces for a fortress on the tip of the Moldorn Province's coast. The Horn of Ceden.

All I know is I'm on the wrong fucking side of this wall because Keres is somewhere out there. I'm expected to just pick up and fight for this cause? This isn't my fight. These aren't my people. *My* people are in enemy territory.

As if General Vyra's pestering wasn't bad enough, her right hand, Epona, watches my every move. Neither of them like me, but Epona doesn't trust me. That's different. When you're disliked, you're ignored. When you're not trusted, you're stalked.

It's fine. I don't feel too warmly about either of them.

Epona is from a tribe of people governed by one word: survival. She's different from the general in so many ways. Her skin shines like bronze, and she has waist-length, doe-brown hair. It's so long, she has to tie it up when she trains. She flips her head over and gathers her curls with a ribbon in a way that makes no sense to me. Then it somehow ends up in a bun on top of her head, accentuating her sharp features.

She's more mountain than woman. I shudder every time her violet eyes land on me. They don't match the rest of her, and she caught me staring the first time we met. General Vyra called me out for gawking and explained that eye color is unique to Rift Dwellers. Asked me whether I liked it, with her flaxen brows raised over her own dark brown eyes. I told them both I prefer green.

The General is an attractive woman. She's just not the one I want to go to war for.

Today, at least, we're out walking. It's the only thing that helps. Of course, they don't let me out of their sight entirely, which is why I'm forced to go with them. But the cold helps... barely.

The men talk of the Gods-abandoned creatures that plague Aureum—Illynads. All I know is, if a monster gets in my face, I'll go fucking berserk. I'm one bristled hair away from snapping, but my thoughts continuously return to the things that have me wound up so tightly.

"Ah!" I fall into the snow. A pulse of energy blasts through me, and it feels like someone's poured hot oil into my blood.

Oh, fuck.

I open my eyes to see the snow beneath my hands melting and

steaming. Eyes and weapons train on me. The power in my blood bursts through me again. I feel the pulse in my skull, and everything I see goes red. Like the world's been painted in firelight.

I focus on my hands as fire crawls under my skin, through my veins. From my fingertips to my wrists. In the fire's wake, my veins blacken. I shove them deeper into the watery snow. Trying to focus, balling my burning hands into fists.

The fire's not painful but trying to suppress the overwhelming desire to *burn* hurts.

For a moment, it stills under my skin and seeps down back toward my fingers. Dragging against my nerves like fingernails. Slowly. Another pulse shoots up my spine, and I grunt. The fire and darkness race back up my forearms. My sleeves smoke as holes burn through them. Then my furs and my leathers. I can't stop it.

"Darius," Epona snaps. I find her eyes—they're the only thing that isn't tinted red. Violet and glowing. With the flick of her hands, the snow around me ices over. The frost crawls toward me.

Is she doing that?

"General, how do you want to proceed?" another soldier asks. I can hear their gasps puffing into the cold air.

"Wicked. Dangerous. Fucked."

That's what everyone said about Keres, but never knew about me. If I cared, would I have hidden it better? I hit the ground with my burning fists.

Everything I care about either goes to shit, dies, or leaves. Might as well beat fate to the punch and just stop giving a fuck, right?

Finally, someone's going to see what's been hiding inside me all along. I just wish it could have been Keres because she would have loved me through the hell of it all.

4: SUNKEN

SILAS
After the Wedding

"Forces beyond our power, or Mrithyn's, brought you two together. They bound you to each other. Do not abandon her over this foolish dalliance. You cannot walk away."

That's what Liriene told me after I found Keres with Darius. So, I married Keres. Neither of us had any real choice, right? It was arranged, and we just needed to honor our mothers' wishes. We'd both dishonored each other in the end. I'd never been true to her before the wedding. She wasn't true to me after it.

Liriene and I... we both believed that fate brought people together or tore them apart. Now I know it isn't fate. It's choice.

On our wedding night, I promised Keres I'd never hurt her. I tried to claim her body, heart, and soul. I could tell she still didn't trust me. I knew she would leave.

When she gave me her virginity, I put all thoughts out of my head. All thought that wasn't her. Her pleasure was my only focus. I tried to make her feel me, that I was sorry. When we were done, she lay there staring at me. Neither of us were convinced that this is what things were supposed to be like.

She'd gotten a taste of rash passion with my best friend. I'd gotten more than a taste of that with Moriya.

Moriya was... superficial, but she clearly thought it was deeper. I never spoke of Keres to her, because honestly, I liked the way she fawned over me, like a pet. Such a delicate little thing. So opposite Keres. So submissive and always anticipating me. The more I shrugged her off, the more she took me in. Moriya made me feel wanted. Keres didn't know how to make a man want her.

Somehow, that worked on Darius.

Keres *is* beautiful. People talked about her. They didn't always say nice things, but they were never wrong for comparing her to divinity. Moriya wasn't really a fair comparison. Keres was a virgin, but she was never innocent.

Knowing I could have the normal girl who was into me, it was good for a while. But in reality, I looked forward to being with the girl who was more like a Goddess.

Admittedly, I barely knew the *real* Keres. I trusted I'd get the chance to as her husband. Obviously, that didn't happen. Still, I knew more about her than Darius did. Even if what I knew was mostly from Liri's perspective. Darius barely ever looked at Keres until that night around the campfire. I'd grown up aware that one day she'd be mine.

Faced with two options, me or him, she chose him. Proving to me that connections between people aren't always what they're supposed to be.

The morning after our wedding, she was gone. I expected her to go. Whatever I'd poured into her that night, she'd taken and run with. Could I blame her? I did. Why did she have to be so damn predictable?

I saw her red lace undergarments on the floor beside our bed, and I could still smell her fragrance mingled with the sweat on my skin. I found her note on the pillow that read:

Silas,

After you promised never to hurt me again, I'd like to believe you wouldn't force me to be something I am not... and I'm not ready to be your wife. I have to go to the palace, as the Coroner. To find help for our people. Please try to understand.

-Keres

Of course, I could understand, but I didn't want to.

Me or her calling. One fate or another. Again, choice proved more powerful.

Infuriated, I burned her letter. Then her red lace undergarments. All

I could see was red. I didn't need more of it.

I set off to find Kaius or Liriene. Whichever I could find first to tell them about my run-away bride. What I got instead was Indiro.

"Where you headed, laddy?" He clapped me on the shoulder and drove me toward the war tent. I shoved aside the entryway flap and shrugged him off me. My heart was still kicking like a mule.

"Now, this is why I told you of her plans, Silas," Indiro said. "So she wouldn't catch you off guard——"

"She should have talked with me about it. She's my wife."

"You're just angry——"

"I have a right to be," I snapped.

"Darius told me what you did by the river." He folded his arms and focused his cold eyes on me. I leaned my head back and looked at the ceiling. Then I reached into my pocket for my flask. Indiro rolled his eyes and held up a hand.

"Now's not the time to be drinking. It's still early, and there's work to be done."

"I'm angrier when I'm sober, Indiro." I flipped the cap off and took a deep drought. The liquor wrestled the acid in the back of my throat and burned it away.

"You're not ready to be a husband as much as she's not ready to be your wife. This whole affair was out of order."

"We would have been married soon enough anyway." I turned and held the next sip in my mouth, puffing up my cheeks and feeling my gums and tongue tingle in the liquor.

"You're a damned fool threatening the lives of your betrothed and brother in arms, then rushing the girl to your bed. Did you expect her to love you? Death may be cold, but Keres' blood is as hot as her mother's was. Mrithyn made a Coroner out of an Aurelian lass, and you expected to domesticate her?"

I swallowed the liquor to keep from spitting it out. "I expected her to at least——"

My skin flushed even hotter, and I looked away from Indiro's eyes.

"Maybe our marriage is as cursed as she is."

Indiro scoffed. "The only curse on you is your thirst for the drink and your jealousy. You'd be better off filling your head with my lessons, filling your belly with some good food, and emptying that flask, boy."

"Don't pretend to be better than me."

"Aye, I may not be a better man. At least I know there's only one time in a man's life when he should be latched onto a drink, and that's when he's at his mother's tit for milk. Now, give me the damned flask."

He lunged for me. I swerved and was clipped only by his shoulder, then I took another large swig while he regained his balance. He swatted at me again, this time knocking the flask from my hand.

Liquor dribbled down my chin, and I threw myself at him, tackling him to the floor. His oily hair was in my eyes, and my hand was pushing against his face, our feet pawing into the earth as we wrestled.

"This is how you've chosen to train my heir?" Kaius' voice broke through our grunting and cursing. We both stopped and looked up. I jumped up to my feet and swayed as I jabbed my finger in my father-in-law's face. "Your daughter, Keres—"

"She's a good lass, Kaius. Stubborn but a good lass. Mostly," Indiro cut me off as he got up to his feet and dusted off his trousers. "She went to Ro'Hale on behalf of our people."

Kaius pursed his lips, looking us both up and down before proceeding to sit at the war table. He appraised the map and then finally gave us back his attention.

"Yes, Liriene already informed me that Keres had threatened to do as much. So like her mother, a rebel."

"Oh, so we're tolerating her behavior because it's *expected*." I held my arms up and clapped them against my thighs. "Lovely. I've taken a wild mare to my bed."

"Lad." Indiro's voice sounded a warning.

Kaius watched me, looking me over. "Is it true you tried to kill Darius?"

"To frighten, only." Indiro held up a hand. "A pissing contest was all. A show of feathers from one male to another."

"Hm. A brawl with a soldier of Massara would not do well for our clans' relations," Kaius said.

Indiro and I looked at each other. After too long a pause, Kaius spoke again. "Well, I don't see how it matters as she's married to you now, Silas."

"Keres never wished to be bartered," I said and wiped my mouth.

Kaius smiled. "She was not bartered, but gifted with a knight for a husband. Trust me, my boy. She'll come to see it as such, eventually."

"Will she?" I sneered. "Or—"

"Enough, Silas." Indiro silenced me. His hand found its customary spot on my shoulder. "We'll be leaving now, Kaius."

Keres' father waved us away, and I stumbled when Indiro shoved me forward from the tent. Liriene was waiting outside, arms crossed and a bare foot tapping.

"She's gone, then?" she asked, looking at us. We both gulped and hesitated. "Well?"

Her fiery hair was a tangled mess around her face. Her under-eyes were shadowed.

"Aye, lass, she is." Indiro nodded, looking down at her tapping foot.

"Agh!" She threw her hands up as she turned away.

"Liri," I called after her, stepping out of Indiro's grip. She didn't turn around or wait for me, lifting her blue skirts off her feet so she could storm off toward the edge of the camp. She walked right into the forest with the rage of a mother about to beat a disobedient child.

"Liri, where are you going?" I asked. Her hair trailed down her spine and wisped over her shoulders as the wind brushed through it.

Focusing on her long hair calmed me down a bit, as if the red inside me was leaving and taking up a place on her shoulders. Fitting. She often bore the weight of my cumbersome anger and confessions. Only the fiery Liri could soothe me in a fever-rage.

I trailed after her, farther into the forest. She never slowed her pace, until suddenly, she stopped. When I caught up, she took a deep breath, turned around, and punched me in the face.

The force knocked me off my feet, and I fell backward into the dirt, landing on my side. Head spinning now, the liquor disagreed with me.

"Fuck was that for?" I sat up and looked at her. My left cheek stung, and my teeth were singing in my skull. It was a surprisingly good hit.

"You bloody deserved it."

I blinked at her. I'd never seen a threat in Liriene before. It hung on the edges of her mouth. She aimed her finger at me as if it were a blade. Her gaze was sharper.

"For what?" I asked.

"You're her husband now. You're supposed to protect her, keep her in order."

"We both know she can't be kept, Liriene."

"That or you just don't know how to keep a woman, Si." A male voice came from my right.

I jumped up, recognizing it instantly. Steadying myself, I looked up at him, my stomach hardening and turning cold again.

I wasn't imagining it; his eyes were aflame.

"Careful, Darius." I smiled. "Without Hayes around to cool you down, you'll wake it up."

The muscles in his jaw tightened, and the fire in his eyes brightened. I could see how much effort it took him to control himself. Daemon or not, I'd fight him.

"Would you two put your cocks away?" Liriene growled and stepped between us. Her eyes, like muted stars, silenced us both.

"What's this about?" I spat on the ground.

"Day one of being married and you've already lost your wife. Idiot," she said.

Darius chuckled, earning my glare.

"And you—" Liri turned to him. "Who do you think you are, trying to bring shame on my sister and ruin a long-standing engagement?"

It was my turn to laugh.

"Honestly, you're both pig-headed sods, and neither of you deserve my sister."

We both looked at each other and then at her. She dusted her hands off on her skirts.

"Now, there's another reason we're here."

"Hopefully, not another ambush," I said.

"No." Yet another voice turned my head. Thaniel approached with his Human lover, Mathis, beside him. "Just a goodbye."

The five of us stood in a circle. Liriene made small talk with Thaniel and Mathis as any hostess at a meeting full of enemies would.

Darius and I seemed in silent agreement to pay little mind to Mathis. A Dalis Soldier stood so near to us. Smiling, laughing, looking at us intently.

It threw me off, but Liriene was happy at that moment. After losing Katrielle, she was content to see another couple getting a chance at the life she and Kat didn't get.

Thaniel was leaving with Mathis. After goodbyes, they'd turn around and venture off together toward the Baore. Maybe it was the drink, or maybe sheer curiosity, but that's when I asked...

"How can you love a Human?"

Thaniel looked at me and smiled. Liriene looked at me with storm-gray eyes, their expression like the threat of rain. Darius looked at the ground.

"I'm not wrong for loving someone who deserves to be loved," Thaniel said.

His statement spoke to Liriene. After years of secret love, she needed to hear it. None of it was wrong. Seeing Thaniel's determination to be with Mathis, Darius seemed determined to pursue Keres.

Keres was a blood-thirsty, raging little she-devil. She deserved to be loved, anyway.

Darius wasn't a cheap guy. He could get any girl easily, but he kept his head down. He didn't sleep around. The minute he noticed Keres, he saw something.

Something anyone with half a mind could see. I was the fool who looked elsewhere instead of showing her all this time that I saw it, too.

Darius believed in what he saw in Keres and that she did not want me. He believed he had a chance. I knew it. He'd leave next, following my wife. I was stuck in a place where I could see everyone else around me so clearly but could not see myself wholly. I knew I was supposed to be a knight. Noble.

Supposed to be a loving husband, not a jealous one who raised a weapon at his wife. To be sober. I knew I had the opportunity to follow Keres into Ro'Hale, be at her side as she sought her purpose. Really give her a reason to believe in us.

Still, I felt scorned and shallow. I wanted to believe in Keres the way Darius did. I wanted her to believe in me, but the more I wanted and wanted... the emptier I'd felt. Like the sheer wanting meant I couldn't have it.

After Darius left, I stayed wanting, watching. Drinking.

Thaniel and Mathis got to leave. Darius would follow Keres.

I was stuck watching others go after the life they wanted so dearly. Watching another go after the woman I wanted so badly. Watching, almost as if I were stuck inside a glass bottle, cast into the river and sunken.

I didn't expect her to come back without Darius—for us to be attacked and separated again.

5: SACRED

Osíra

The Kingdom of Ro'Hale, In Keres' Wake

The temple doors opened, admitting a gust of howling wind and a light-footed woman. Cesarus jumped to his feet beside me and growled.

"I've been expecting you," I stated from where I sat beneath the tree.

"You know why I'm here, then," the woman said in a sultry, warm voice.

"Because the Coroner did not heed my warning."

"Are you prepared to leave?" she asked.

"We are," Dorian said. He stepped out from the back room, and I listened to the swish of his cloak on the stone floor. He passed me and stood between the woman and I. Cesarus didn't move. I reached up and dug my hand into his fur. The tension in his body relaxed, and his tight, low growls subsided into heavy pants.

"The people riot, both within and without the castle. We have little time, and our escape route is narrow, but I can get you from the temple to the forest, as I helped Keres. Let's go."

I stood and placed my hand on the tree. Slowly, light trickled into my vision and blurry shapes took form.

"Come. Touch the tree, please."

Ever since Keres revived the Heart Tree, I could see when I touched it. When Keres had touched it too, I could see her. I believed it was because it grew out of the Godlands, here into our realm. I could see in the Godlands. The one place that made me want to shut my eyes and hide.

The woman did as I asked, and as she rested one hand against the tree, she came into focus. Her dark purple hood slid to her shoulders, revealing long wavy tresses of scarlet hair. Brilliant blue eyes. Her lips curved into a smile. I'd seen her in my visions, but she was even more beautiful in person.

"Now can we go? We don't have time to dally."

"Once I leave this temple, this tree, I won't be able to see again." I hesitated.

"If you don't leave and the Queen sends her men for you, you won't be able to do anything ever again. Please." She stepped closer and held out her hand.

Cesarus lowered his head and watched her.

I closed my eyes and took my hand off the tree. The world faded into black. Nothingness. I outstretched my hand toward her and walked with her.

"Can we go out another door?" she asked.

"Yes, this way," Dorian said.

They both guided me, and Cesarus stayed close by. Going downstairs was the trickiest part, but once we were in the basement, it was a straight path across to the second set of stairs. We climbed up, and Dorian pushed open the cellar doors, pulling me out after him.

My feet touched dirt and grass and stumbled a bit as we hurried into what felt like brambles. Cesarus was breathing heavily, excited to be outside. I tightened my cloak around my body and lifted my hood over my bare head. My feet burned from the cold of the mud. As we hurried along, the wind stung my face.

"I lead Keres to an exit on the palace grounds that lets out into these same woods. We're going to follow in her footsteps until we reach my accomplice."

"Accomplice?" Dorian asked, sounding a bit out of breath.

"His name is Rivan. He was here at court, under guise, sent to watch over Ro'Hale. When Keres arrived, our orders changed. We were both to stick close to her, help her in any way we could. She fled, but because of her concern for you, we'll help you too."

"The Queen is unhinged. I served as one of her ladies-in-waiting for the last couple of years alongside my sisters. The Queen has imprisoned them, though. Unlike them, my duty is first to the Guild."

"The Guild?" Dorian asked.

"Did you receive your orders from Ranger Thane or Master Emeric?" I asked.

"Both of them. They hardly ever decide without consulting one another. Especially regarding the Sunderlands," she commented.

"Are you speaking of the Shadow Guild in the Ressid?" Dorian asked.

"Yes," she answered. I heard her feet scuffle in the fallen leaves. "Oh, no."

Holding onto her, my body jerked as she lurched forward, but I steadied us both. "Be careful," I said. "I'm blind, and I'm not tripping."

She chuckled and caught her breath. "Right, thanks."

"So, you're an agent of Darkness," Dorian murmurs.

"A Shade," she added, annoyance lacing her voice. "Agent of Darkness is so morbid. Only the hermits in the guild call themselves that."

"Are we going to the Guild?" I asked.

"Unfortunately, no. Rivan will take you toward the Moldorn. You'll be safest there if you seek refuge in the Kingdom of Golsyn or Serin. I'm from Serin. My parents are nobles at court, and they're also Shades. Their names are Ser Bryon and Lady Isabelle. Tell them I sent you. They'll help you from there."

"The Moldorn is a warzone," Dorian stated.

"And the Child is an Oracle. If she wishes, she may help turn the tide of the war."

"The Child has a name," I said.

"Yes, right, of course. I'm sorry, Osira."

"You never told us your name, did you?" Dorian asked.

"My name is Nadia."

The wind shook the trees and my bones all the same. High Autumn promised we would fall into an unforgiving winter. Without hair, I feared I'd catch a head cold.

We walked as quickly as we could until we couldn't. I was sure my feet were cut from the rocks and twigs I'd stepped on. But the cold made them numb. My legs ached beneath my thin shift, and my cloak did little to keep in my body heat. My nose ran, my ears ached, and I all but hung onto Nadia's arm with exhaustion.

"We should be drawing close. Rivan left about two days ago but didn't go far."

"Why did he leave if he watched over Keres?"

"I watched over Keres in the castle. Thane told Rivan to fall back as a precaution. Trust me, he knows we're coming," she said.

"And so, I've waited." A male's voice came from somewhere up ahead, to the left.

Cesarus' footsteps quickened, and he ran past us toward the soft voice.

"Cesarus!" I shouted, but he didn't growl or bark.

"Good dog." I assumed the voice belonged to Rivan.

"I hope you've got a fire started. It'll be dark soon, and I'm chilled to the bone," Nadia said.

"Yes, follow me. Hello, I'm Rivan. I'm sure Nadia's told you."

"Yes. Dorian, and this is Osira."

Footsteps approached me and stopped short, a few feet away.

"Hello, Osira. Thane has told me about you."

"He's told me about you too when he channeled me. He said you would help us. Also gave me useless details, like the fact that your eyes are two different colors."

"Yes." He chuckled. "Well, usually, it helps people identify me. He must have not kept in mind that you can't see me the way others can. Come warm yourself by the fire. You look cold and hungry. I've roasted some rabbits."

"We don't eat meat," Dorian said in a tentative voice.

"If you want to survive out here and on your journey to the Moldorn in the grips of High Autumn, you'll eat whatever you can. Do you drink alcohol?"

"Not typically, priests of the Order of Tra—"

"Learn to. Alcohol warms the belly. I believe the Aurelesian doctrine permits it, within moderation, of course."

"Well, I, I—"

"I'd love to try some, then," I said and pushed past them.

"Cesarus." He came to my side, and I held on loosely to the back of his neck. "Help me to the fire."

I could hear the flames flitting in the wind, the burning branches snapping and popping. The smell of smoke and roasted meat. I followed my wolf toward that sound. Footsteps all around me told me we all moved toward the camp.

Rivan passed us food and drink. I had never eaten meat before. I picked up what felt like a small leg. The skin was crisp, and when I bit into it, my teeth stretched the meat away from its bone. The taste of char mingled with the juiciness of the meat.

As I chewed, it felt a little tough, but I got used to it. It was delicious. I ate like I hadn't eaten in days. Next, I tried the alcohol. It smelled bitter and sharp, but I took a sip and swished it around in my mouth. My tongue tingled. As I swallowed, the alcohol left warmth in its wake, which crept down into my belly. I took another sip and then another. Greedy for that heat.

"Alright, go easy. You'll get drunk," Dorian warned and took the flask from me.

"Is that so terrible?"

"You're only three and ten. It's a sin," he hissed.

"Oh, please," Nadia whined. "Let the girl drink. She deserves it after all she's been through lately."

"Will you accompany us to the Kingdom of Serin?" Dorian asked, brushing Nadia off.

"Unfortunately, I cannot. Thane contacted me just before you arrived. A battle broke out at Keres' home clan. The Dalis captured her along with many others of her kin."

"No." My heart jolted. "I told her to go home. I could sense something was coming and that her people would need her. I didn't know—" I felt like I couldn't breathe as panic gripped me. "It's my fault she was taken. I sent her back."

"Hey, hey," Nadia's cool hand touched mine. "It's not your fault. Besides, Keres would have gone back even if she knew it meant walking onto a battlefield."

My breathing steadied. "That's true."

"I must return to the Guild after putting you on the right path," Rivan said.

"You're going to help Thane rescue her." It didn't come out like a question.

"Yes, I will try."

That made me feel better. Finally, I relaxed on the sleep mat Rivan gave me. Cesarus lay next to me, keeping me warm. I couldn't sleep for a long while, thinking about Keres. I expanded my consciousness as far as I could, trying to let in the voices of the Gods. The wooing of the wind carried their voices to me, mingling with the distant cries of birds and howls of wolves. The low chanting and wistful chiming. They told me about the battle and warned me of those to come. Tears streamed down my face, stinging as the cold air hit my skin. I sniffled, and Cesarus twitched in his sleep. I think I fell asleep crying.

When morning came, I sat up on my sleep mat and tightened the blankets around me. Cesarus wasn't there and someone had put out the fire. I couldn't hear it crackling anymore, and I was cold.

"I've got to go," Nadia sighed.

"Couldn't you come with us? You said your family is in the Moldorn." I stood up, still wrapped in my blanket. Dragging it in the leaves as I walked in the direction of her voice.

"Step to your right or you'll hit the fire pit."

I obeyed.

"I'm going back to the castle."

"What? Why?" I stopped short.

"I told you. My duty is to serve the Guild. I have a role there."

"Your sisters are imprisoned. What makes you think Hero won't throw you in with them or kill you? You disappeared from her court in the heat of an uprising. It's too dangerous. If she hurts or jails you, you will have gone back for nothing," I argued.

"If that happens, I'll be with my sisters."

I shut my mouth and breathed out hard through my nose. I wished I could have that. A sister. Someone who'd rather sit in a cage with me than leave me behind. I felt that kind of... belonging when Keres came into the Godlands with me. Keres broke into the impenetrable darkness of my life, like a fist through glass. I don't know how I found her, but my soul cried out for her, and she reached out her hand. I scratched her eyes. Still, she came to see me.

Keres tried to stand between me and the Gods. She raised her fist and dared them.

"What more can they take from me when they already own my soul?"

I begged her not to anger them... but I'm the angry one now. When someone stands up for you like that, it teaches you how to stand up for yourself. The Gods had taken everything from me in one fell swoop, and I felt the urge to dare them.

Take another thing from me.

First, it was my sight. They replaced it with horrifying visions. My own father ransomed me, realizing I'd become valuable. Threatened my throat with a blade if Dorian wouldn't buy my safety. Next was my freedom. Confined to the temple and enthralled by the Gods, threatened by a mad queen.

Third, my hope. I'd go to sleep, my eyes would close, and it wouldn't make a difference. Darkness persisted. I'd awaken and open my eyes and never see the sun. I wanted to dive into the temple fireplace just to feel the light. Dorian tried to soothe me. Told me about the purpose of it all. But I felt useless.

I even lost my hair. It sounded childish, but it was salt in an already gaping wound. My head was bare, and my eyes were ruined. I felt like a worm. Undone. Like a cloth doll with all the stitches torn out. Plucked clean of my comfort, my liberty, my will, and then my self-esteem. I became smaller than my body, but I finally understood the Gods' chaotic, chiming voices.

Numbness washed over me when I was finally Unveiled. The numbness told me I was safe. Ready to stop feeling sorry for myself, ready to stop *feeling*, and maybe ready to serve. But it was a lie.

"No," I said. "You can't go. I can't let you."

"Let me?" Nadia giggled. "I told you—"

"And I'm telling you *no*." I stepped closer. "Ever since I became an Oracle, I've felt like the little girl that I was, has been withering away inside me. Everything that once sustained the child I was, has become ash. Daydreams, dresses, storybooks. My childhood is over. All day I listen to the Gods. The best I can do is try not to drown in the noise. I try to understand, to filter their voices and deliver their messages. For what?" I tightened my blanket around me.

"To warn people of omens and wars, just for them not to listen to me? You're walking into a trap if you go back there. You're endangering yourself needlessly. The kingdom is in shambles, and trust me, I only wish I understood your desire to be with your sisters; but if you go back, you might not even get to be buried next to them."

She didn't respond. It sounded like I was talking to the trees, to a world filled with wind.

"You've seen Queen Hero's madness. Keres was on a mission in Ro'Hale. Sent on behalf of King Arias. He's in the Moldorn, isn't he? What if we went there and told the Heralds what we know? Isn't that a better plan than walking into a crumbling castle?"

"She's got a point," Rivan said.

"We need eyes at court, Rivan."

"We have other eyes at court, Nat."

"Who?" she asked, incredulously. "Rydel? Are you serious?"

"Who's Rydel?" I asked.

"He's an ambassador from Elistria, the southern Elven Kingdom that lies near the Sunderlands' border with the Moldorn. He's been at Queen Hero's side," Rivan answered.

"He's been more than at her side. He's been *inside* her, too. What makes you think Thane would trust him? She might have turned him already onto her side. He's her lover," Nadia said.

"He serves his Goddess before Queen Hero," Rivan said in a low voice.

42

"His Goddess? He serves a deity?" Dorian chimed in.

"Yes," Rivan said. Nadia huffed, and it sounded like she dropped her rucksack on the floor.

"Come on, Nat. Rydel makes a much better spy than you," he teased. "He shares our goal. It'll be fine."

She harrumphed and stomped her foot.

"Fine." Her voice shot toward me. "I'll come with you. I wasn't prepared at all for this. I don't have my other favorite traveling cloak. I'm leaving everything behind. All I have is—" She started rummaging through her rucksack. "All I have is one hairbrush, one long-sleeved tunic, one pair of trousers, and my lip rouge."

"Oh, Gods," I sighed. "Sounds fine enough to me. I don't even have eyes."

Silence followed that... until Dorian cracked up laughing. I turned toward his voice and laughed too.

"I mean, really. We're on the run from a crazy queen, and you brought a hairbrush?"

Dorian and I laughed harder.

"Hey, at least I have hair," Nadia said.

Silence dropped over us again, a quick pause before I roared with laughter. Cesarus started whimpering, not used to hearing me laugh. I laughed so hard, tears ran down my face. Nadia and Dorian laughed, too. Her laugh was airy, tinkling like bells. His was hearty and raspy. I liked them both.

"Right!" I said and wiped my eyes.

"Right," Rivan said, as if he was worrying for our sanity. "Anyway, Nat. I'll tell Thane your new plan."

Our laughter broke down, but my smile stayed.

"Well, Osira, looks like I'm coming with you," Nadia cooed.

"Very good." Dorian clapped. "We'd welcome some humor into the mix."

Rivan traveled with us until the time came to part ways.

"Good luck, Osira," he said and clasped his hand with mine.

43

"Nat, behave. Tell your mom I said hello."

She giggled. "Bad girls never promise good behavior. I'm sure mother would love to know you think of her, though. She thinks you're charming."

"I *am* charming."

I shook my head and smiled. I heard hands clasp together. "Watch these two. Especially that one," Rivan said, and I wasn't sure which of us he meant.

"I'll do my best," Dorian said. I could hear the smile in his voice.

From there, we journeyed south, with the wind at our backs. I listened as Cesarus cantered around me. Since Dorian had given him to me, we'd both been locked up inside the temple, only going out a few times a day so he could relieve himself in the yard. It felt good to know he felt free.

I felt a little freer with every step away from Ro'Hale as well. I was walking toward the unknown, toward a future without form and ready to be molded by my choices. It was liberating... It was the first time I felt like I had a choice since the Gods blinded me. And we were going with purpose.

I wondered what Keres felt when she left the castle. Did she feel afraid of the path before her? Did her faith waiver? She told me the Gods cannot change who you are. They simply use you. As we walked, I made a commitment to myself in my heart, not to let Osira wither away, no matter how the Oracle tried to weed her out.

If the Gods want to use me, they'd have to get used to me and whoever I was going to become on this journey. Because I was someone before they made me something of their own.

If Keres could lose her life, in body and in service to the Gods, and still find the strength to raise a scythe, I could walk out of captivity with my bare head raised and my scaled eyes open.

But it would have helped if I could have seen the ambush coming.

6: SNAPPED

Keres

Day One

If I had King Berlium's blood on my hands in that moment, I would have fucking licked my fingers. He and I stood face to face, his expression like stone.

"Your Spirit for their lives, or your blood and their demise."

That was the choice he gave me. I laughed at him because he was ignorant of the images splashing across my mind: the spray of blood erupting from his throat beneath my blade. The light in his ocean blue eyes dimming forever.

His heartbeat knocked on my senses. Too slow and steady. Teasing. Inviting my fangs and claws.

"Make it stop," the Death Spirit purred in my mind. *"Make him beg. Make him regret this."*

The battle of Ro'Hale was only the beginning of my fight. I raised my scythe. His armies razed my people to the earth. Now, he demanded I bend my power, my Spirit, to his ruling. He wanted to make an exchange: he wanted the perfect weapon that I was and promised to spare my people in return.

All I wanted to do was trade places. He had me and my sister in his snare, had Elves corralled, but I was used to hunting men like Him. My hands were chained, but they were also trained for war. Mrithyn made me for this. The King would not shackle me for long. I was going to figure out how to free us without surrender. We could fight our way out of here.

King Berlium's jaw ticked as he raked his eyes over me, searching for weakness. His body was a wall. He rolled up the sleeves of his burgundy shirt, and the muscles of his forearms flexed. His gold and onyx rings glinted in the pale sunlight that washed the room.

The Goddess of Life Herself must have carved his face from ivory. His skin was smooth, and I noted only the faintest marks of age at the outer corners of his wide-set eyes. But I still couldn't tell how old he was. I assumed he was close to my mother's age or her sisters', but it didn't show where it should have.

The blue of his eyes was bottomless, shadowed beneath elegantly arched brows. He tilted his head, and if his skin had been made of diamond, the sunlight would have glanced off his wickedly sharp cheekbones. He had a chiseled jaw to match, which was darkened by days' old scruff. A delicate scar graced his left brow. Cutting through the dark, thick hairs like an insult. One I loved to see.

I could wound him like any Man... the only thing was, he wasn't really like any Man I'd ever seen before. Incandescently beautiful and absolutely brutal. My Spirit recognized his.

The reality of his presence dwarfed the stories we heard in the Sunderlands. Like a fist through the canvas that had been painted of him. His aura was heavier, darker than that of any ordinary, war-mongering king. There was music in his pulse that played against mine, a minor key in harmony. Darker. The darker side of divinity. He was native to the shadows I'd long stood in alone until I stood before his throne.

The Grizzly King was an animal in the skin of a man. But isn't that what all monsters are—just people wearing masks? I'd find a way to break his mask and uncover his weaknesses.

His pupils dilated, and I relished in the silent, visceral reaction. He didn't like the look in my eyes. It showed in the terseness of his voice as he barked out, "Do you laugh at me?"

"Do you truly expect me to fear you?" I asked in return. He could take me out of the Sunderlands, but he couldn't take the wolf out of me. We regarded each other, gazes crossing like blades.

"Pride is not something a prisoner can afford," he said. His voice was rich and dark as sin. As evenly paced as his heartbeat, and as arrogant.

I looked at my sister. "We may be your captives now, but don't misjudge me. You asked which of us is the servant of Mrithyn." I leaned back on my foot. "Congratulations. You've invited Death into your halls and welcomed Her foolishly with a kiss. But even a watery grave could not hold me, King Berlium. Don't expect to do a better job than that."

Those ocean eyes threatened undertow. I would not make the mistake of drowning twice.

"Lambs led to the slaughter, that's what he sees, but he will feel the fangs of his mistake," the Death Spirit simmered.

His fingers grazed over his beard as he assessed me. If my hands had been unbound, I would have planted a hand on my hip.

"Good." The word broke the tension in his body. He mirrored my posture. "Now we can begin our negotiations."

At that moment, I wanted nothing more than to unleash my wrath upon him. I did not want to make any deals with him, and I was sure he'd prove duplicitous, anyway. His gaze flicked over Liriene.

The way he looked at her made me want to drag him into the pits of Mrithyn's realm, even if it meant I'd be going with him. But then I looked at my sister, and even the Death Spirit knew not to disobey the command in gray eyes.

Wait.

Was it fear that froze her, or was it knowing that poised her? I had to trust the warning.

"I've answered your question. I am the Coroner, now give me something in return; what you promised."

He raised a brow, and the corners of his sumptuous lips curved.

"Let my sister go free, along with the Elves of the Sunderlands."

Liriene's eyes widened, and his smirk vanished.

"Loose ends turn into nooses. I'd be a fool to make that exchange. I can sense the power within her. I don't throw away bargaining chips. And besides, I never promised they'd go free. I said they would be spared."

I stepped toward King Berlium, and his guards shifted toward me. He waved them aside as I passed him and approached his throne.

The monumental stone throne looked like someone had carved it from the face of a mountain. Rough and misshapen, it weighed down the center of a stone dais, with carpeted stone stairs leading up to it.

"Spared? What does that mean?"

"It means they would join the Baorean Revolution," he said in a disinterested tone. "Just as all subjects of the Baore, they will contribute."

"They are not Baorean subjects. They are slaves. You are not their king." I turned and faced him. "But I am more than the Coroner. I am also an heir to the Mirrored Throne. Those who wear a crown do not bend to any man. Likewise, my people will not bend to you."

He strode forward to meet me, and my body reacted. Partly from anger, partly from an uninvited wave of lust. My chest puffed out as his did and grazed against him.

"You have no other choice but to bow to me. That is the bargain between us. Bow and you all live." He breathed on my face. His breath smelled like honey.

"I'm well aware of your blood ties. Queen Hero is your cousin. You are the daughter of Resayla, an Aurelian royal. Your people will recognize this, and with you at my side, we can bring them under the banner of the Baore. *Likewise*," he said mockingly, "I hold my own stock in power within the Sunderlands, and now I have half its clan-dwellers huddled up in a cave. You will bow. They will follow."

My jaw felt like it held all the tension in my body. His eyes searched mine, awaiting a response, as he inched even closer. His hand wandered up to my face, brushing my hair back behind my ear, and then he took hold of my jaw, forcing me to look up at him.

"Don't you see, Keres? These are all shards of the reason I've been looking for you. I've prepared for this moment. Now, you're finally mine. What I want, you will give. What you withhold is mine to take."

He gave me a smile, and a lie swirled in his eyes—the look of adoration. I knew it was obsession, which was worse.

"I expected—I hoped you would be as unnerving and unforgiving as you are, but I also know that you can be bent. Maybe even over my bed. There, I'll show you power. Break your body like a twig."

I moved to hit him, hoping the manacles might inflict some damage, but he caught me by my right hand with unnatural speed.

"Ah, ah, ah. Not a twig, then." He looked at the cuff around my wrist. It'd slipped down farther on my forearm as he held it up. Just a little too loose, but not loose enough. I tried to yank myself free, but it didn't even phase him.

He looked burly, but the truth of his strength seemed impossible. Hidden in the graceful trim of his frame.

Surveying my wrist, he said, "How slender and frail your hand looks. Deft hands made to kill. Callused from wielding a weapon, I presume."

He was right. My hand, even curled into a defiant fist, looked pathetic in his. The angry blue lines of my veins traced up the middle of my wrist. My pulse bucked against his touch.

His grip tightened. Pain shocked my arm, then pressure built in my fingertips. I yelped and struggled to scratch at him with my other hand held so closely but still frozen.

Too quickly, my right hand broke in his. The bones of my wrist, up to my knuckles, snapped with a sickening crunch. A scream tore from my throat, and I crumpled against him.

Liriene shouted. It sounded like her voice left her body in a drawn-out echo. The guards started moving toward her, lagging in their pace. Time slowed around us. But between the King and me, was an exposition of just how quickly my time to act had run out.

"You'll break like a dam. Cracking... slowly," he said as he held me there in agony. His stare latched onto me just as tightly as his hand. The timbre of his voice skittered down my spine. His vise-grip tightened further, and it felt like my bones were splintering into a thousand pieces.

"You will fracture like stone, and all that you've kept behind your walls will be bled."

My fingers contorted, and my hand purpled. Bone broke through the skin of my wrist and my blood heated his palm. He sniffed the air hungrily. Aroused either by the scent of my blood or violence itself. He dragged me closer, so I could feel his erection against my belly, and my throat ran dry.

I tried to pull free, and the pain became nearly blinding. Darkness cornered my vision, but I took another breath and focused on my hand, on my blood as it oozed. With the heat of my magic, the blood clotted and sizzled.

King Berlium dropped me. I clenched my left hand around my wrist and whimpered.

I sank to my knees, doubling over. All the ways I imagined killing him broke free from my mind. My stomach lurched. I focused on trying to stop the bleeding with my magic. Liriene rushed toward me, but the guard, Varic, held her.

"Call forth Magister Hadriel," Berlium ordered one guard, walking back to his throne. "Now!"

Another guard flew through the door obediently. Anger continued to boil my blood, but I resolved not to lie down and give in to the pain. I watched the King's every move.

"You're the Coroner, but what is she?" he sneered and pointed at Liriene.

"Some Elves were stirring up stories that someone powerful was hidden among the newly captured. When I found them, I knew that you'd wish to see them both," Varic said and pushed Liri forward.

Berlium nodded. Varic bowed slightly at the waist and took a spot at the long oak table to the side of the room.

My head was pounding, but the bleeding was slowing.... I was feeling heavier. I looked back to Liriene. Her gaze was on the door across the throne room.

"Hadriel."

I turned toward the Man entering the throne room, who answered to that name. King Berlium jumped up, grabbed Liriene, and snaked an arm around her waist. He knotted a hand in her hair and held her face up to the Magister. She didn't flinch. So quiet, so misplaced.

"You told me the Coroner was in the Sunderlands," he crowed, before pointing to me. "That one is the Coroner. What you failed to mention is that the Coroner had a powerful sibling." His voice echoed off the stone.

My mind numbed as my eyes met with the dark gaze of Hadriel, the Horseman who had led the attack on my people. Dark eyes, so deep a shade of gray, they were almost black, locked on me. His countenance remained unchanged as he scanned me and then my sister.

I tried to focus on the details of him, to keep my mind from slipping. He adjusted the sheath of his long black velvet cloak. Its collar was lined with gray and white fur. Beneath the cloak was a lean frame, fit as a soldier, but not nearly as impressive as Berlium's physique. Dressed in a black tunic with silver buttons, and black trousers tucked into black, buckled boots. His long chin and narrow jaw set. His hands folded behind his back, and he raised a soft brow at the King.

"I didn't know there was a sibling."

"Was it an unfortunate lapse in attention? Two servants reborn from a royal bloodline in the Sunderlands," Berlium said, then pushed Liriene to the floor. He whipped his attention down on her.

"Which God do you serve? What are you?"

She didn't answer.

"I'm amazed your men failed to bring her straight here. Gobbled up by Tecar—grossly negligent," Hadriel spat the words at Varic and then turned his attention to Liriene.

"It doesn't matter," I said. "You wanted the Coroner, and you have me. She's not a threat to you."

Liri's eyes were glossy with tears. She was afraid. I could hear her heartbeat trilling against her ribs. She must have been in shock.

The King returned to his throne, leaning back against the solid rock. His hands steepled in front of his mouth, and he shifted his stare between us. Hadriel crossed in front of him to come to my side.

"The Coroner needs healing. Immediately. We shall reconvene once I've tended to her."

Hadriel looked at my hands. I was dizzy standing there. As he took my arm, I leaned into him, or else I would have fallen over.

"What about the sister?"

"We can discuss her afterward," Hadriel silenced him.

"Varic," Berlium called. "Take the other to the holding cell until I call for her again."

"No." I jolted. Liriene and I locked eyes as Varic's men seized her.

51

"No, you can't have her."

Hadriel dug his fingertips into my arm, holding me back.

"Calm down, child. She will be escorted back once you're healed."

"It will be okay, Keres." Liriene smiled and didn't resist. "It will be fine." Tears streamed from her eyes as the guards shoved her. Hadriel's hand came down heavily on the back of my neck, and he steered me in another direction. I felt my body weakening, and the mana, the fuel for my magic's energy, was depleted. My control over the bleeding lessened. My steps drifted, so Hadriel lifted me into his arms. Over his shoulder, I watched the King sink into thought, his finger playing at his lips.

Then the door closed behind us, and my eyes closed with it.

7: SUNSET

Liriene

The Cell

All I could do was stand there. While they argued, he made his demands and threatened. I couldn't even think of a word to say.

This was the world Keres dwelt in—one of power. Clashes and curses. I was a flower caught in the brambles, and I hated feeling so weak and afraid. What could I have done? I wanted to be a better elder sister, and this was my chance to prove I could be. I failed. Again.

Because of fear. The King terrified me. Keres, next to the deadly beast, looked matched and rightfully placed in a throne room... it all was too much. I felt swarmed with Oran's promises and power. But then the King broke Keres' hand, and my confidence shattered with it.

The power in the King was unlike anything. The Otherness I sensed in him was a flicker of darkness in his eyes when he showed his true strength. He snapped her bones so easily. Sniffed at us as if that was enough for him to sense what was inside us.

He wasn't just a Man. He wasn't even a mage. I didn't know what he was, but it was terrible. What I could sense made my skin crawl. Like there were a thousand voices trapped within him. All of them were screaming. Tormented.

Could Keres sense it? How was she so unwavering? I had to commend her bravery, but she'd get herself killed. If the roles had been reversed and it was my bones that broke in the King's grip, she would have broken his stone throne in return. She probably wouldn't have even thought twice about it.

She was made like him, and he knew it. He wanted her. I was the question without an answer. I was the one he didn't plan on. And I had proved useless to her so far.

Now she was with the Magister. Wounded and dependent on him. Somewhere in this castle, he held her in privacy. What would he do? What would he say? Was she going to be okay?

Hadriel felt like a darkened mirror. No matter how I tried to See into him, I met resistance. My visions bounced off it, back into my head. He was shielded.

Would he be able to heal her? How could she fight without her dominant hand?

I watched Keres all her life. When she practiced her writing, her shooting. Her nimble fingers turning page after page. I watched her cook and enjoyed her meals. Her hands… she couldn't fight him with one hand.

But I still had two. Chained as they were. I would not let him get away with hurting her again. As long as we were together, I was going to do better. I have to trust my senses and my sister.

I steeled myself. Counting my breaths until this cell door opened, and they brought me back to the throne room.

8: SADIST

𝕳𝖊𝖗𝖊𝖘

Day Two

I awoke in a candle-lit chamber that smelled of incense and flower oils. My body was sore and so drained, but my hand...

It was heavy as lead at my side. Crippled. My bones were reset under the skin, and the wound was sutured closed. A thick glaze of ointments marinated it, and a loose cloth-dressing tied it to a wooden splint. I didn't dare move for fear of pain. My head was no longer throbbing, but my chest felt heavy.

"Yes, relax. Nothing shall harm you here." A rich, wizened voice hit my ear from somewhere behind me. Hadriel moved to my side. "Take a drink."

He held up my head and raised a cup to my mouth. I looked at it and up at him.

"It'll help with the pain," he said. So, I listened.

After a few gulps and a couple of minutes, the pain lessened—but I didn't feel better.

I watched him move around the room, his robes swishing on the floor.

"I know what you're thinking. Remembering, rather."

He caused Ivaia and Riordan's deaths.

"I know you have no reason to trust me, and I will not plead with you. Just know that here," he paused, gesturing to the room, "we are in a stasis of sorts. A reprieve. From the world, the warfare, our own ties to one another."

"Why should I believe that? Why would you help me? You led the attack on my people."

I tried to read the lines of his face, but I didn't understand him. His cold gray eyes were like a stone wall.

"Your sister is endangered here," he said flatly.

"*Elves* are endangered here," I retorted, sitting up again, but more carefully this time.

"Unless you do what's best for them…"

"And that's giving myself to King Berlium? What am I supposed to believe would become of my people if that were to happen? Which it won't."

"He will demand great sacrifices to get what he wants. He acted rashly in breaking your hand, but I don't apologize for him. I can only be the mouthpiece while he can be the crushing hand."

"He wants me to fight for him, but he broke my dominant hand. Make it make sense."

"He is a salacious man and a genius. However, sometimes his anger clouds his judgment. I'm sure you can relate, Coroner."

"What is he?" I asked. Berlium's anger caused my injury, but his apparent power to manipulate through desire may cause more pain. Lethal lust.

"He is man and monster in one. He is the Unbridled."

"What does that mean?"

"I can't tell you all these things now. We do not have time. You must listen only to my warning. Do as King Berlium asks. Do not give him a reason to injure you further. If you want to stand for your people, for your sister, for yourself, then stand by him."

"I could never."

"Do not spurn my warning. I am trying to be the voice of reason here."

"And why would you advise me regarding him?"

"Because I want the same thing as him—your cooperation. I'm willing to earn it, while he will simply take it. We have been searching for you, preparing for this. You are working against forces you don't understand, and your options are limited. The Sunderlands is in ruins. You either fight us, bringing down his wrath—his punishment upon you, your sister, and the enslaved. Or, you comply. Your actions can save your people… or condemn them.

"You and the King are alike. Two rams intent on clashing, but your people are between you. He doesn't care whether they live or die. He'd rather make them useful, but he can do without them. Do you want them caught in the tangle of horns? Think about it as we walk back to the throne room. We must reconvene with the King. You slept through the night." He rose to leave, and I looked down at my bandaged hand.

"Perhaps you can show the King your mind, instead of baring your teeth. Can you be more reasonable than him? He's only going to get angrier."

"Well, you don't know me. I don't just back down."

He rolled his eyes and folded his arms into his belled sleeves, turning to leave.

I pushed the blankets back and stood. "What will happen to my sister from here?

"Which God does she serve?" he asked as he neared the door.

"Why should I tell you that?"

He looked at me, his lips pressed into a thin line. "You are the Coroner, the one we've been searching for. We have no plans for your sister. If she cannot prove useful, he will assign her a purpose. Your compliance will ensure it is just."

We proceeded to the throne room. Liriene was standing before the King, silent. I ran to her, and she wrapped me in her embrace and squeezed. The guards did not try to separate us.

Hadriel moved to Berlium's right-hand side. Liriene and I locked arms and faced them. She was careful to avoid touching my broken hand.

"So, what now?" I asked, meeting the King's stare.

"Now, you tell me what I want to know. What God do you serve, girl?"

He directed his question toward my sister. She swallowed hard, and

I nudged her. She couldn't let fear rule her.

"I—" Her voice shook. She coughed, clearing her throat, then tried again. "I am a Seer, Oran's servant. I have a Spirit of Fire and Revelations. I can See into you, King Berlium. Does that make you nervous? Is that why you're looking at me that way?"

He schooled his expression at her maternal voice, her scolding. That was the Liriene I knew.

Berlium got up from his throne and walked over to us, watching me. He stopped and looked at Liriene. "I sensed something as bright as a thousand fires within you. Something just as dangerous," he said. "That is something I've never sensed as strongly in another servant of the Sun God. The Seers who visit my court to entertain me with their fortune-telling, they never show power like yours."

He turned back to me.

"When I received reports that my encampments in the Sunderlands were being attacked, we surmised there might be an Instrument in play. There were stories circulating about the Coroner. We didn't know whether they were true. Elves are superstitious people, and they were hardly singing your praises. They spoke of warnings and omens. Perhaps they had planted the stories to deter us from occupying the land. We couldn't know. Someone I trusted told me a story."

"Who?" Liriene and I asked at the same time.

"The story was confirmed when we learned the Coroner was at court in Ro'Hale. And my hunt was upon you. You are a weapon. I am a warrior. I reign supreme in the Baore. I am crushing your homeland. You are paramount to me, to the continuation of my revolution." His gaze washed over me again before lifting to meet mine.

"Back to your first question. What now? Mrithyn is more powerful than Oran. Although Liriene seems to be a unique Seer, it's hard for me to believe how useful she'd be. I'm not sure what I'll do with her just yet. Knowing more would help. When did your power manifest?"

She looked at me. "During the Battle of Ro'Hale. After I found my father, maimed and dying, something awakened in me. This power. It was like—"

He waved his hand to silence her. "I care not for the tragic details. Seeing as your powers are new and untried, I doubt you'll prove very useful."

"Sire." Hadriel raised his hand. "Might I suggest we keep the sisters separated? Together, they might be a threat."

"Very good point, Magister Hadriel." He turned his back to us and waved his hand again. "Varic, take Liriene. Seers are not of any great importance to me. There are more of them than there are uses for them. Besides, no matter how powerful Liriene is, I have Hadriel. A Magister, and now I have the Coroner. I think subduing you will prove enough of a task. Liriene will join her kin in Tecar until I can think of a reason to bother with her."

Liriene didn't resist Varic as he chained her. Was this Hadriel's twisted way of helping me protect her by keeping her out of the King's hands? I tried to remain calm, but it wasn't really working.

"Will she be safe there? She'll be sleeping in a fucking cave."

"She'll be given work and fed. That's all you need to know."

"And where will I go?"

"You will stay here in the castle," Berlium said, his voice dropping as if he was suddenly bored without a mystery to solve.

"Will I be able to visit her?"

His eyes narrowed on me. "You do not get to make requests."

"I—"

He held up a hand, interrupting me. "Only my wants matter in this kingdom. You will soon learn that." Berlium paused and looked at Liriene as Varic put her in chains. "Wait."

Liriene and I locked eyes, and I moved between them as he approached her.

He looked down at me and grinned. "Step aside, Keres."

I wanted to attack him. Even the Death Spirit rattled in my head in warning.

I dropped my gaze to the floor and stepped back, moving beside her. My broken hand ached, reminding me of its uselessness.

He inched closer. "Give me your hands," he said to her in a rough voice. She closed her eyes and took a deep breath.

"Please, don't hurt her." I stepped closer, raising my good hand between theirs.

"If you don't get out of my way, I will do much worse," he sneered.

We both obeyed him. He took her cuffed hands in his. So gently, and he smiled, sweet as wine. She met his gaze and lifted her chin. Her eyes lit up with silver light, like stars, and his widened. His smile turned vicious, and his grip tightened.

I shifted on my feet, trying to resist the urge to attack him. Flames crawled under my skin, searing and punishing me for not allowing them to bleed into reality.

And then the light in her eyes died, and her jaw dropped. The room suddenly felt colder, and her body felt colder beside me. Her eyes dulled and lined with tears. He gave her back her hands.

"Thank you," he said.

"What have you done?" I looked from him to her.

He nodded at Varic and moved in on us. I reached for her again, and she forced a smile, but tears rolled down her cheeks.

"What's wrong? What did he do to you?"

The room seemed dimmer, like the light beaming through the window had crawled back to the sun. It no longer reached her eyes.

"You are my blood. I love you as I love myself," she said.

"I love you. Please tell me——"

But she wasn't going to. Her bravery receded. She was retreating. Panic rose in my chest. I have had problems with my sister all our lives, but she was always there. Especially after mother and I died. When I came back, Liri's was the first face I saw as I opened my eyes. When Osira channeled me, hers were the hands tending my wounds. No matter how many times we'd hurt each other, whenever I truly needed her, she was there.

My sister was home to me. Blood and bone, tears, and even spit of my own. She's from the same place as me. She's from the same person as me. From the same love. The only thread left in this world that tethered me to my own origins.

I never had to look at her this way before, but now it was all I could see as the guards took her from me. Everything about her seemed surreal now. Every difference between us was forgiven as they pried her from me. I watched until the door closed behind her.

I turned to the King. "What did you do to her?"

"You'll see for yourself soon enough, but let's talk for a moment."

I clenched my good hand in a fist. My blood was boiling. My heart was pounding, and his was gratingly calm.

"Your people are in stasis. They do not live; they are not dead. They are stuck in between, and your choice is very simple. You make use of yourself, and we give them a new purpose. New freedom. You will become my weapon, and under that circumstance alone, you will get them to rally."

His words incited a riot within me, but I knew that even if I could get my people to trust me—to follow me—they'd still have no fighting chance against him. They'd always feared and ostracized me for what I am. It would be a miracle if they listened to me. It'd also have to be the coldest day in hell when I'd listen to him.

"Times are changing," Hadriel added. "War is at hand."

Berlium crossed his arms and nodded. "The Baore thrives under my reign. We are stronger than ever. Industry and innovation; the society I'm building is more advanced than any. Even Perl, the foothold of the Council, aspires to the Baorean evolution. Your people will be the dust of what I've crushed, or they can build new foundations. The Sunderlands' future rests at my feet. I have sought your hand… to help me mold it." I noticed the way he lingered on the word. His gaze dropped to my left hand, to the ruby ring that sat on my fourth finger.

"My hand?"

"We shall be joined in marriage, Keres."

"What?" I shouted.

"Did you think I was going to leave you unchained? No." He chuckled in a low, deep voice. "You shall be tied to me. But first, you will bow."

61

9: STRIPPED

𝔎𝔢𝔯𝔢𝔰

"You've taken enough," I said. "I don't owe you anything else."

He stood toe-to-toe with me, looking down at my mangled hand, and satisfaction settled on his shoulders. Berlium's face was a dreamscape, his eyes the nightmare.

I moved my hand behind my back instinctively as the fire inside me licked over my bones. The tempest in his stare woke those flames and made the Death Spirit sizzle in my thoughts.

Hadriel watched us with a stone-cold face. His body was so still, he looked made of stone. I wondered what they saw in me, then. Did they see the predator beneath my skin, poised until the opportunity to strike arose? Did they see my exhaustion? I felt it. I felt like it was hard to hide it.

"You've been interfering with my war. If you do not bow, you will break—more than just a hand. Your mind is not beyond my touch. I will make use of you if you do not offer it yourself."

I focused on his cerulean eyes, the tension between his brows. His breathing. Rage swelled in the depths of me. It was a force that matched the tempest within him.

The heat of my magic coursed through my body. It started in my chest, reached for my throat, and purged my lungs of the tight, labored sensation of anxiety that had crept in. Heat rose to my cheeks and ran down my spine. The fire draped across my shoulders and poured down my arms, down my legs. Steam poured from my pores and smoke rolled off my tongue. The pain subsided once more as my magic invigorated me.

"I will not be your plaything. I am not Herrona."

His hand was at my throat before I blinked, and he growled. The contact of his skin carried the cloying taste of his power. It barreled into me.

My left hand alighted on his hand that was wrapped around my throat. "I know you tried to claim her once too. I feel your power even now. You must have used it to seduce her. You sought to conquer her, to possess her. Well," I gritted out, "you will find I am not a prize so easily taken."

He bared his teeth, the tips of fangs drawing my eyes to his mouth. The inferno of magic within me surged. Flames coated my skin, but he didn't withdraw. Orange light danced in his tempestuous eyes. Like fire on water.

Berlium tilted my head back, bowing his head close to my neck and sniffing again. His other hand felt for my pulse. The heat of his touch drifted away, replaced by his breath, and my eyes fluttered closed. He trailed the tips of his fangs over my skin. My face flushed, and my stomach fluttered as his seductive magic pervaded me.

"He is just like us," the Death Spirit trilled. A shiver of her excitement reverberated in me, and he seemed to sense it. His cock hardened between us, pressing into my belly.

"No," I sent a scolding thought back to my little monster. *"He is just a devil, used to dancing in fire."*

"I've been hoping you would fight me. Listening to the rumors made me hopeful. I've been waiting a very long time for someone like you. And I can feel your mind—your curiosity reaching toward me like a gentle, tentative hand. I can touch your thoughts as easily as I can your body. I've been longing to."

His hand tightened, his fingertips digging into the sides of my throat.

The rush of a thousand wings broke the silence of the room. Black, flitting things burst into life as if they'd sprung from the far, shadowed corners of the room. Leaping toward us and whirling around us until everything sputtered into a shivering black void. I could feel the stone floor beneath my bare feet but couldn't see it. And that sound. It was a white noise that seeped into the hollows of the void. Whispering, hissing.

His eyes darkened into an oceanic storm. The only thing anchoring me to reality was his touch.

"Give it to me," he said in a low voice.

"Give you what?" I asked. Sparks dropped off my tongue. Like spittle, they landed on his skin, but his body absorbed them. I tightened my hold on him with my left hand.

"Give it to me, or I'll take it."

"What do you want from me?" I asked.

"Everything." The word rattled through his chest, into my mind. He lifted me by my throat, blocking my breathing.

Berlium suspended me over the abyss beneath us. I clung to his forearm, and I kicked my feet wildly. It didn't faze him. Claws pierced through my fingertips. My Death Spirit shifted through me, as if she was eager to meet him, to show him the executioner hiding beneath the mask of a condemned girl.

From the pricking pressure that built around my neck, it felt like he made a similar move.

"Claws like ours," the Death Spirit hummed.

Berlium and I dug into each other. "Listen to me now. You have no power here," he said.

It felt as if his touch reached under my skin. First knocking, then barreling through me. Driving into bone. The flames within me licked at his prying fingers but were devoured by his pull. Light flashed beneath my skin, flaring in his eyes. My magic's heat leaked into the space between veins and sinew. Sizzling, cooling and then hissing out in a chill that flashed through me.

The veins of his arms jumped up to the surface of his skin and ran wild. The blue of his blood brightened and deepened in pulses, crawling toward his heart. Dragging my magic from me into the depths of his Spirit.

Confused, I closed my eyes, retreating into the place in my mind where the fire burned. I called forth boiling rage, but nothing answered.

His hand tightened, and I was losing too much air again.

My body weakened when he drew me back to his chest. My feet touched down on the stone floor, and his hand loosened. The darkness fell like soundless shards of black glass that never hit the ground. Simply vanished.

I slumped against him. He pulled my head back by my hair, and his gaze traced every line of my face, his mouth barely an inch away from mine.

"Your chains belong to me now, little wolf."

I wriggled in his grip, but he had me by the shoulders. A crimson headache clamored into my skull, and nausea boiled my belly. I emptied my stomach, mostly bile, on his polished boots.

He moved to strike me, but Hadriel cut in. "Let me take her now."

Berlium pulled me away from Hadriel's reach and shook me. "Resist me anymore and I will take what you love next. I fucking own you. By the time I am done with you, you will believe it as deeply as you believe in your God. You cannot deny me."

Darkness played at the edges of my vision again.

"Fuck you," I said and wiped my mouth with the back of my hand.

He slapped me hard across the face. Hadriel lunged toward us, pushing himself between us. He took me in his arms. I was shaking, dizzy, leaning heavily into Hadriel. Once more, I tried to unstop the dam of my boiling power, but nothing happened. No magic. My skin crawled as if there was frost beneath it, biting into my bones. Berlium stepped back.

"What did you do to me?" I asked, as Hadriel pulled me toward the door.

The Death Spirit rattled my ribs, but there was stillness in my blood.

I met Hadriel's gray eyes. My body numbed; my mind disconnected from it. I felt like I was outside myself, a piece of me torn away and shredded before my eyes. No irritation under my skin, no scratch of clothing against my flesh. No more pain in my broken hand or bruised neck. No roaring pulse in my ears.

No fire.

No fury.

"Where do you want her?" Hadriel's voice broke the silence.

"Give her the black room. I'll send up servants and a guard."

10: SLAVE

Liriene

Day Two

In the slave corral, men shoved me to the ground and whipped my back. I tried to rise to my hands and knees as the air jolted from my lungs in pain, and my ragged blue-gray dress shredded under their lash. A heavy leather boot kicked me back down, only moving to make room for the biting ends of the cat's tail.

I lifted my eyes to Elven brothers and sisters. They winced as Varic's flogging drew blood from my skin, and cries tore from my throat. I dared not crawl away or cover myself. My kin dared not intervene.

They watched me, flinching. Their eyes locked on mine as I wept and dug my nails into the dirt, recoiling at every strike. Their eyes faltered and looked away as the skin was ripped away from my shoulder-blades and bone was exposed. They turned their backs when mine wept blood in steady scarlet streams, and I emptied my stomach on the ground.

The beating finally stopped after twenty-two lashes. I had done nothing to earn them, but I knew that my being born Elven was enough incentive to harm me. Could they have known each lash counted a year of my life?

This was my welcome to the slave den of Tecar. As if Varic was tilling soil, he opened lines in my skin, and sowed seeds of terror. They rooted in my core, weaving their thorny tendrils around my heart. Fear bloomed within me, poisonous as nightshade.

They left me on the ground. My fingernails stayed buried in the dirt until calloused hands lifted me up from under my arms. I was faint but made to stand. When I opened my eyes, I was met by a pair of eyes so green I thought they were Keres', but they weren't.

"Name's Shayva," the female told me as the male steadied me on my feet. "And this here's Maro."

It hurt to breathe. The rise and fall of my chest made me hiss with pain as the tatters of my dress chafed my open skin. They goaded me into walking, helping me keep my feet under me by moving forward arm in arm with me toward the cave. Just within the mouth of the cave, they set me down. Maro ran in to fetch the things she bid him to.

"They allow you to keep herbs and salves?" I asked, biting back tears as my muscles quivered with pain.

"I was a Vigilant apprentice of clan Hishmal. They require me to heal some of our kin when they're too liberal with their violence. To keep the strong alive for work. They never let me tend to the weak or dying. Only the broken and battered. You are not weak, so they won't stop me from tending your wounds."

Shayva tucked her blue-black hair behind her ears, which I immediately noticed had been mutilated. They had removed the upper ends of her ears with what looked like was a harsh slash that grazed and scarred her skull as well. Her eyes tracked mine, and sorrow flickered within them as I stared. I couldn't help it.

"They cut you," I said, trying to ignore the pulsing agony riddling my back.

She offered me a shaken smile and lifted her chin. "They don't like that our ears point to the heavens. That the Gods whisper freely to us and not them. So they take our pointed Elf ears, as if they're taking our crowns."

I followed her chartreuse gaze to a lone, free-standing wall across the campgrounds.

Elves moved like animated corpses between us. Numbed with grief and loss. Their bones pricked up against the fabric of their skin like threading needles. How they found the strength to stand, let alone tow stones to the monuments they built, astounded me.

The Dalis drove them onward with crops and whips, splitting the skin of their backs open when they fell from exhaustion. I recognized a few of them. People from my clan I was never close to.

Almost all bore scars of the lash. Scars I now shared with them. Some had been branded, and my stomach roiled at the thought of being scalded by iron. The air stunk of carrion, and birds circled over the two gaping pits where the Men were throwing our dead to rot. I noticed no one dared to near the wall Shayva was looking at. I winced as I realized what adorned the stone wall.

"They flog any who seek its shade or throw them in the death pits."

I bit the inside of my cheek to stop my tears at the pain shooting down my spine. Sweat rolled down my skin, careening through the valleys on my back created between the raised skin of my wounds. I turned my head and watched as two Dalis Men carried a dead Elf by arms and legs between them. They neared the brink of a pit and swung the body over its edge, tossing it onto the mound of carcasses within.

"If you try to escape or rebel, they break your legs and arms and throw you into the pit. Unable to climb out. Only able to writhe like a maggot in the mass of the dead."

Pinned to the stone wall were the pointed ends of my people's ears. They had hammered rusted iron nails through the torn, bloody cartilage into the stone. The most meaningful monument in this encampment. An iron ladder leaned against it, as tall as the stone wall. And an Elven child stood at the foot of it. Shayva noticed my eyes lingering on the boy. He held a large mallet and stood still as a statue beside the ladder.

"They make him pin the severed ears," she whispered.

"Why did they take yours?" I asked. Her eyes filled with tears, and I regretted asking. "You don't have to tell me," I whispered. "I'm sorry."

She straightened up at my touch and looked me in the eye. I took a deep breath, realizing how much she resembled what Keres looked like before Mrithyn claimed her. The raven hair and emerald eyes. Keres might have grown to be this kind of woman if she hadn't died so young. Shayva couldn't be much older than me.

"They cut my ears..." she paused and wiped her nose, "because I screamed when they killed my brother."

I pressed my fingers against her hand to steady us both. The stench of death wafting from the pits seemed overwhelming, knowing her brother was among the rotting dead. Limbs heavy and tangled in masses. Bodies that were once temples, now pillaged by maggots. Deaf ears harassed by the buzzing of flies, and mute mouths crusted with the dirt of their open grave.

"What was his name?" I asked.

She searched my eyes for a moment and then smiled sadly. "His name was Kit."

I prayed Keres would never step foot back in this camp. These Men saw us as lesser than animals. Because we look different from them and that our walk on this earth is different from theirs. Our culture, history, and magic. It was nothing to them. They've taken us to use us—to abuse us. To oppress us and end us. To send our souls crying to the Otherside.

I looked at the Sun and saw fire feathering around its edges. It didn't blind me or burn my eyes to look. I saw the gilded face of Oran in the fire of that star. He saw me watching him as he burned above. A light exposing all this darkness… and doing nothing.

Maro returned with Shayva's things. She started with strong-smelling, greasy salves. I bit down on the sweat and blood-covered fabric of my dress and allowed her cool fingers to press the salves into my wounds. I focused on the castle, on the sunlight reflecting off its windows. Trying not to close my eyes or cry from the pain. I bit down on the cloth harder when she touched the salve to the wounds between my shoulders.

Light glinted off the glass panes and paled the stone of King Berlium's castle. If I could set it on fire with my mind, I would, but he had stripped me of my power.

PART 2

KING OF STONE

"One who does not see the divinity within themselves,
Will never see the connectedness of all things.
As a worm within the apple is the contempt of your nature.
Your lapse in vigilance is its diligence:
To eat at your core, your seeds of truth.
That you'll never know they were there."

—Barathessian 9:21

11: SPIRALING
Keres

Hadriel led me from the throne room, up a spiral staircase—just one level. A door creaked as he pushed it forward and then held it open for me. I looked both ways down the long hall. To the right and to the left, it stretched on, dotted with doors.

"These are the living quarters," he said in a low voice. "Each of these rooms is dedicated to our servants. You'll be taken care of much better, though, of course."

"In the black room? Is that some kind of torture chamber?"

"Nonsense." Hadriel folded his hands. "It would delight the King to have you near to him. His chambers are just one floor higher. Come, I shall show you the way."

His long cloak swished against the stone floor and dragged behind him. My mind was reeling, and my face still stung from where Berlium struck me. I didn't turn my head to observe the things Hadriel pointed out. Mentally, I was trying to uproot whatever seed of magic Berlium must have planted in me to poison my magic.

Hadriel's voice was grating. Every flit of his fingers, every announcement of just how grand and generous they would be toward me if I complied... I couldn't marry these thoughts to the memory of my first time seeing him.

Should I be listening? Learning the castle? What had happened to my magic? Would I get it back? My mind couldn't pick a subject and stick to it.

Hadriel was both the warrior that killed Ivaia and this. A groomed and polite nobleman.

The end of the left hall opened into a rounded foyer. My awareness snagged on it, only because of the double staircase with black marble steps splayed out in the center. The floors above were all opened up the middle, making way for the stairs that wound up and up into a tower. Gold-banisters marked off their rounded edges, like balconies, and I counted eight tiers.

We ascended one level. A golden statue of King Berlium greeted us. Armored and equipped with a golden sword and shield. Poised mid-strike. The King's likeness wore a grimace on his gilded face.

This is what he thought of himself. A conqueror. In Elven culture, only idols were forged from gold. This didn't surprise me. King Berlium may have believed himself to be Godlike, but I knew he was just a man. Any man could bleed.

Beyond the arrogant figure was an ornate black door with gold accents. I looked at the other doors. To the right of the statue was a red door with identical gold markings, and to the left of it was a green door just as ornate.

"Which will be mine?" I asked.

"The red door, that's the black room. Go in and rest. I'll be back with the servants."

"Spies to watch my every move," I snorted.

"You're still a captive."

Dully, I looked over his shoulder at the golden statue before rolling my eyes. Just before I closed the door, I gave Hadriel a last glance. He simply nodded. I listened for the swishing of his cloak against the stone.

"Captive." The Death Spirit winced and then sighed. *"Clawed but caged. Careful now, don't let them see us lick our wounds."*

My broken wrist throbbed in its cast. I wiped at my eyes with my left hand and just stood there for a moment. As I pinched the bridge of my nose, the dull ache in my head seemed to lessen a bit. Just enough for me to notice the plush carpet beneath my bare feet.

It was black with swirls and strange characters woven into it. Depictions of battles, the skies, mountains, oceans. Horses and monsters.

All in red thread. My eyes followed the pattern as I turned to face the room.

It was difficult to feel anything remotely pleasant looking at the room. I was so tired. The bed was in the center, against the left wall, lifted onto a black wood platform. The sheets were black satin, and a fluffy fur pelt was strewn across it, along with an unnecessary number of pillows—most of which would end up on the floor.

Across from the bed, there was one door between a wide chest of drawers and a wardrobe made of black wood. I walked over to open it and found a bathing room. On the far end of the room was a writing desk under the latticed window. One which was too small for me to fit through, and it was locked, anyway. I couldn't see what was beyond the frosted glass.

The black wallpaper made the room feel as heavy as my eyelids. I didn't care enough to give it any more attention. I dropped onto the bed, careful not to hurt my hand. I slept a little. About twenty minutes later, I awoke to a heavy-handed knock on my door.

"Keres," King Berlium's voice preceded him as he opened the door. A short woman with generous curves, and a tall, armored man followed him into the room.

"Ceil." Berlium gestured, and the woman stepped forward, dropping into a low curtsy. The dip of her head revealed the ash-blond bun neatly coiled at the base of her neck. Straightening back up, loose pieces of her hair shifted to frame her full face interrupted by a flat nose.

"My lady," she said in a domestic, mewing voice, before lifting her russet eyes to mine and stepping back.

"Yarden." Berlium waved his hand. The man stepped forward, his greaves making a gravelly sound.

"Sire," he answered before bowing to me. "My lady."

He wore a full suit of armor. Like a knight in a picture book. A cutaway in his helmet permitted a narrow glance at his handsome face with skin the color of the earth, and hazel eyes.

"Ceil will cater to you. She may have the help of another maid named Minnow when needed. Yarden will guard your door and escort you throughout the castle when necessary."

I nodded. He turned toward them and lowered his voice into a stern, near-whispered command. "Do not let her out of your sight beyond this door. I want her looked in on every hour. Ceil, give her the tray."

She grabbed a gold tray from the cart that stood in the hall. On it was a teacup filled with a steaming hot, honey-colored brew, accompanied by a bowl of vegetable stew. On the side was a dinner roll, a cooked potato, and a small bowl of cherries. Beside the tea was a slender glass with what I recognized must be red wine.

King Berlium said, "Eat. Drink. The tea is from Hadriel. For your pain."

I said nothing as Ciel placed the tray on the writing desk and pulled out the chair. I was starving.

"Please eat while I draw you a bath. You must be eager to get out of those clothes."

I looked down at myself. I'd forgotten I was still in the blood-crusted, muddied clothes I'd battled in at Ro'Hale. From Tecar to the throne room, I hadn't changed. I was filthy. I smelled. My hair felt like a tangled mess. No wonder King Berlium hadn't been taking me seriously. I probably looked like a wretch, not a warrior.

I looked up to find the King watching me through narrow eyes, which traveled over my filthy clothing, my mess of hair, my broken hand. His upper lip twitched toward his nose. "Make sure that the bath water is hot. She smells like blood." With that, he left the room, Yarden following him.

"Yarden won't ever be too far from you. Posted right outside your door. A guard named Anselm will relieve him when he takes his breaks. Yarden will not treat you like a prisoner, but Anselm will," Ciel said.

She continued chatting as she filled the tub. I shoveled the soup into my mouth and finished both slices of bread. The scent of lavender filled the room, and the warm, honey flavored tea washed down my parched throat.

I picked up the wineglass and the bowl of cherries with one hand and carried them awkwardly into the bathing room when she finally called for me. She saw me struggling and took them from me, leaving the wine glass and bowl of cherries on a sleek golden tray that stretched from one edge of the tub to the other.

With my non-dominant hand, I tried to peel my disgusting clothes from my body. Seeing me fumble with that, she couldn't move fast enough.

"Let me help you undress," she said as she flitted to my side.

"No," I barked back at her. She didn't seem afraid or put off by my sharpness. Perhaps she was accustomed to being treated poorly.

"No, thank you."

She offered me a weak smile and busied herself. Steam lolled over the edges of the tub, promising to melt off the blood and dirt. I clawed at my clothing.

"Soak first. We'll drain the tub and then start again fresh."

Stripping down naked felt strange. Not because she was in the room, but because I was taking off my armor. In my enemy's castle. They left my weapons in the ruins. The clothes were holding me in a grave—on the battlefield. The last thing I remembered was Hadriel speaking into my mind. His word knocked me unconscious. I slept the whole way to the Baore. Obviously, Liri had stayed by my side all that time. She must have been terrified.

The pouch on my belt held Indiro's letter, the prophecies from my family's oracle. It also had the small potion bottle, Scorn, a gift from Famon; and the blood stone given to me by Iantharys. Of course, Katrielle's prayer beads were in there too. I placed that on the chaise lounge that took up one of the bathroom walls.

The first soak worked to remove most of the crumbs left by my home's ruination. Within a few minutes, Ciel managed to drain, scrub, and refill the tub. It might have been magic. I didn't care. Once more, I steeped in the hot, lavender-scented water. Marinating in my anger.

"My lady," Ciel tapped on the washroom door.

I sighed, sinking into the tub. "You don't have to keep calling me that. My name is Keres."

She entered. "Oh, I couldn't address you so informally, my lady."

She eagerly scooped up my soiled clothing, leaving my pouch. "I'll have these washed ri—"

"No, don't." Stretching my sore legs, I reached for the wineglass. I still couldn't believe I was in a fucking tub, while my sister was in a slave den. I drained the glass at the thought, then looked down at my body, keeping my bandaged hand on the edge of the tub. The scent of lavender clouded my senses, and I could feel the tension in my muscles subsiding. The tea was working against my pain—the wine helped.

Ceil stood there, awaiting my next word. I plucked a red cherry from the bowl.

"What would you like me to do with your clothes, my lady?"

I picked the stem off the cherry, popped it in my mouth, and chewed until I spit the seed into my palm. Staring at the red cherry juice on my hand, I imagined Berlium's heart beating and bloody, cradled in my claws.

"Burn them. And bring me more wine."

Three glasses of wine in, I'd scrubbed my skin raw. As if it could wash away the fury I felt at seeing myself so damaged. I'd picked all the dirt and crusted blood from under my fingernails, dug out dirt from my hair and behind my ears, and cleaned every scrape and cut.

I could still hear the screaming in Ro'Hale. As if every drop of blood shed that day had splashed into my skull, like a song of agony raining into my thoughts.

Ridding myself of the dirt and blood with one hand wasn't easy, and I could do nothing about cleaning my entire left arm without my right hand. I felt bad asking for Ciel's help. While I was in the tub, she'd sent for another female servant to help her find clothing for me.

"The wardrobe's been empty ever since Lady Vega's clothing was removed. I won't know where to find her some new clothes if you don't. Not like she can wear servant's garb."

"Well, how should I know?" the other woman retorted.

A pile of cherry pits filled the little porcelain bowl, and my wineglass was empty. I imagined a pile of severed heads and a bottle of blood in their place. I pushed the cherry pits around in the red, sticky juice at the bottom of the bowl. My vision turned the bathwater into blood too. It felt thick and hot, luxurious. How I imagined Berlium's blood would feel. The cherry pits pulsated under my fingertips, making music. I widened my eyes, watching them.

"I'm losing it," I said. Nobody heard me.

"*I heard you,*" the Death Spirit chuckled.

Listening to the ladies bicker about what to dress me in, I sank deeper into the tub until my chin was touching the water. I was in no rush. No matter what their distant voices were saying, all I could hear were the heartbeats of the cherry pits.

"What's going on in here?" A stern, cruel voice rammed through the cawing of the servants. Silence filled the air. I tried to pick myself up but was overly dizzy.

"Where is she?"

"In the tub, my lord," Ciel chirped.

Heavy, booted footsteps shuffled through the bedroom. "Why is the bathroom door closed?" he asked them.

"Is it?" I asked. My voice sounded disembodied, but a draft flooded the steamy bathing room, bringing me back to myself a bit. I looked up and saw sapphire blue eyes glowing back at me. The darkness of the candlelit room shadowed a handsomely drawn face and black hair. Those eyes poured over my naked body.

"Minnow, get out. Ciel, fetch the Magister. Yarden, close the door."

The sound of shuffling feet and "yes, sires" swam through my head. Stormy eyes absorbed every drop of my attention.

"Come here," King Berlium said as he rolled up his sleeves and knelt down.

"I'm quite comfortable where I am, thank you." I waved him away.

He reached for me, his hands breaking through the surface of the water and digging me out. I splashed him and he hissed. His callused skin grazed against mine, then he withdrew. We narrowed our gazes at each other. Heat banked in his.

I tilted my head back, lifting my leg up, watching the beads of blood roll down my skin. My mind was trying to convince me I sat in a tub of blood, but I wasn't so sure now that he was here. Either way, he drank me up with his gaze.

I pointed and flexed my foot and dipped it back into the water. As I lifted myself up, my breasts no longer underwater, his breathing quickened. His nostrils flared, and a low growl erupted from his chest.

My back arched and the air in my lungs softened into an answering purr as the sound skittered over my wet flesh. If I wasn't already sitting in a pool of water, I would have been. His jaw hammered as he raked his gaze over me.

"You don't scare me, grizzly bear," I preened.

He reached for me again, slower now. I watched the distance between his hands and my body close. His hand slipped under the water, brushed against my ribs, and curled around me. Then his other went under my knees. In one swift motion, he scooped me out of the tub. I held onto him with my left hand.

"I'm going to kill you," I whispered in his ear as he carried me to the bed.

"I'd rather like to see you try," he said. He was warm, and he held me against his body, which felt nice because I was shivering.

Why was I shivering if I'd been boiling in a hot tub of bloody water?

He lay me on the bed and threw the fur blanket over me. My head was pounding again, and all the lights in the room felt too bright. It felt harder to breathe, but I would not let him know that. Still, my vision darkened.

I heard him move through the room. The drawers of the wooden dresser creaked open and closed, and then the doors of the empty wardrobe. I saw him out of the corner of my eye as I stared at the ceiling. More footsteps shuffled into the room, bringing him to a halt.

"Ceil, go to my bedchamber. In the back of my wardrobe, there's a red shift. Bring it."

"Right away, sire."

"What's happened?" Hadriel's voice cut through to me. My senses were waning.

"Who's snuffing out the candles?" I asked no one in particular. The room was darkening. And spinning.

81

"What was in that tea?" King Berlium growled.

"Just the same herbal remedy I prepared for her last night."

With that, Hadriel was bent over me on the bed, forcing open my eyes and looking into them. The room seemed to be lit back up, even brighter than before, so I tried to pinch my eyes shut.

"Child," he said in a soothing voice.

I groaned in reply. Nausea rolled through me.

"What's on her lips?" he asked.

"There was a bowl of cherry pits and a glass of wine on the tray near her bath," the King said in his sexy voice.

"Wine?"

"Pretty sure it was blood," I said, trying to calm him down.

"Gods be damned, are you trying to kill this girl?"

"Of course not, sir. I just—" Ciel answered, moving back into the room.

"Hadriel, what do you need?" the King's voice was callused now.

"She shouldn't have mixed alcohol with my potion. It can cause hallucinations, intense fevers, loss of consciousness, and can depress her breathing. Water, get me water. And charcoal tablets. From my—ah, never mind. I'll get it. Stay by her side and don't let her sleep."

With that, another gust of cold air flooded the room, and the door slammed.

The mattress shifted underneath me as the King got on the bed and lifted me up by my shoulders. My head felt heavier than his stone throne, as it fell back.

"Little wolf," he said in a low, soft voice. "Wake up."

I strained to lift my head and find his oceanic eyes again. He placed his hand behind my head.

"Look at me."

I tried, but all I could see were cherry pits in his eyes and blood pouring out of his mouth.

"Ach!" I made an indistinct noise and pushed him off me. The movement earned a bolt of pain that sprung up through my right arm. Tears blurred my eyes, and the nausea ripped through me again.

"Fuck," I heard him say. "Lie still, dammit."

Visions of a masquerade played before my eyes. Courtiers dressed as animals, wearing masks. Nadia and Rydel. I was back in the pleasure gardens. Drunk on faery wine.

"Some kind of chamomile," I heard someone say, and I wasn't sure if it was me.

"Hold up her head."

Gods and devils, they're real. Fae and nymphs and spooky voices... they're just fun.

"I have to do it—" Berlium's voice reached me as his fingers threaded through my hair.

My senses were on a carousel of sound and color. Memories collided with reality. Berlium flashed into my mind, breaking through red and yellow firelight, and I realized I was in his arms. I could smell him. I could also smell blood.

Monsters aren't real, Keres. I heard Nadia's voice on his lips.

I heard Hadriel's in my head, too. "Drink."

Sapphire eyes held my attention. The world stopped spinning. Instead, it danced for him. Other memories played in my mind. As if he could see them, he looked around. My mind spun visions of my homeland around us like a web.

Elves dancing around the fire. The glint of Silas' helmet as he stood watch on the wall. The ground passing beneath my feet as I hunted the King's men. He followed winding paths through my mind until we reached a memory I didn't want to see.

They forced a sip of water past my lips. It was bitter, and I nearly choked. After I swallowed, it washed away the memory, but when I looked back up at him, he was looking at me differently.

A mix of emotions, just as bitter as the water, flooded his gaze.

"That should help absorb the wine and tea," Hadriel said. "It'll pass."

"Is she going to stop breathing? What are these marks from? She looks half-dead." Berlium's voice blanketed me.

"Liriene," I said.

Suddenly, she was there. In the garden, in her blue dress. Knees pressed into the dirt and hands busy with weeds.

"You haven't fooled me, Keres," my sister's memory said. *"I can see what's happening to you. And you're not fooling anyone."*

Berlium's eyes found me in my dream again. The visions blurred. He was the only thing in focus. A halo of light crowned his head. His lips parted, revealing a hint of his fangs.

"Hadriel, tell me she will not die." Concern creased the lines around his mouth and his eyes, making him less smooth—less like polished stone.

"I won't let that happen," Hadriel answered.

"Just stay awake. Focus on me," he whispered. "It's just a dream. It's not real."

But he was wrong. I was completely at their mercy, which was a nightmare. I lingered in it with him, trying not to let the scraps of memory float into the void we sat in. Trying not to let him see my world—the one he'd destroyed. It kept me awake; it kept me anchored in the arms that held me until he finally told me to close my eyes and sleep.

12: STRAINED

Keres

I awoke in bed, naked.

Discoloration on my arms and chest drew my attention. I pulled off the covers and stared down at my body. Nasty bruises had blossomed all over my skin.

"Drink this," a voice startled me. I looked toward the door, yanking the blankets back. King Berlium glided over the threshold, carrying a small tray with a teacup on it.

"Hadriel brewed it to lessen your pain. I swear it's safe. I tasted it myself."

He moved through the room, past me to the far window to the left of my bed, holding his head high, though no crown sat upon it. His spine was straight as a broadsword. His burgundy shirt was loose, almost casual. Tucked messily into his black trousers that ended in his black leather boots.

Even this far apart, I could feel the pull of his gravity. His power lured me closer. It was strange and reminded me of being in his arms before I lost consciousness. His scent brought my mind back close to him, into the feeling of his muscles tightly coiled around my naked body.

"What happened to me?" I asked in a low voice, seeing flashbacks of blood. "Why am I naked and covered in bruises?"

Berlium leveled a languid stare at me. I could hear his heart thrumming steadily in his chest, its hollowness. It drummed on slowly, disparate from my own. I looked toward the open door and saw Yarden's armored shoulder peeking out from behind the door frame.

Berlium laid the tray on the table. "You remember nothing?"

He leaned back against the table seated beneath the window, and his gaze reminded me I was naked beneath the sheets. I felt like he could see through to my heart—could hear it.

"I remember the bathtub filled with blood. You... you were in my dream. How did you do that? What are you?"

The lift of his brow and the curl of his lips should have been answer enough.

Arrogant. Powerful. Purely male. That's what he was.

"Part nightmare, part dreamer," he said. His rough voice did not match the romance of his words.

He was eating me alive with his eyes. Anger hardened my stomach and flushed my skin, which he seemed to notice and enjoy.

"What did you see?" The thought of him perusing my memories when I was vulnerable, I couldn't let it go.

Satisfaction glazed over his eyes. "Whatever I saw, I know it was more than you wanted me to."

His words were like a scratch on flint. If only my magic were still there to kindle. He'd found a way in. When I was unguarded. He cradled me through the fever dream and met things that lived in my mind.

"Fine," the Death Spirit grumbled. "Let him look. He can't touch those who live in our memories. Not anymore."

He frowned as he looked at me. As if he could hear my inner demon.

"Ceil added wine to your dinner tray, not knowing the alcohol and the medicinal tea should not be mixed. You were half-dead in the tub when I found you."

He pointed to the red linen dress at the foot of my bed. "We were more concerned with keeping you alive than dressing you. You were hallucinating, and your breathing was shallow. You hit me with your broken hand. I assumed the pain pushed your mind further under. Which was dangerous. So, I... lifted you out of the oblivion."

I shook my head. "I still don't understand how you can enter my thoughts at will."

"It's not for you to understand. As for the bruises." He raked his eyes over me, as if he could see them beneath the sheet. "They blossomed under your skin right before you fell unconscious. Hadriel said it was some kind of reaction in your blood."

I allowed my gaze to wander over him as he had taken the liberty to do with me. Scrutinizing. Glimpsing his collarbone, where his shirt was unbuttoned. The muscles of his jaw feathered, and he swallowed.

"Why help me?"

"Why?" He folded his arms, and his muscles bulged in his tight sleeves. "Because you're mine. You still have a purpose to serve."

I snorted. "And if I told you my power was cursed, would you still want it?"

"What's a demoness to the devil, but a servant?" He articulated every word so that I could see his teeth.

"What's a king to a God?" I leaned back against the headboard and crossed my arms. "I serve no one but Mrithyn."

A smirk claimed his mouth. "Be that as it may, your chains belong to me now."

"Don't underestimate me, Berlium," I said, anxiety pinging into my chest despite the words. I knew I didn't appear to be in any position of power.

Battered. Naked, clinging to my bed sheets.

"Your threats and demands will do nothing to dull the curse of my Death Spirit. There's no one in this world I hate as much as you. The only thing more dangerous than my hatred is my thirst for your blood."

He pushed off the desk, the sudden movement making my fists tighten on the bedsheets.

"You know nothing of thirst." Light and darkness shifted in his eyes. His gaze dropped to my mouth, and the corners of his own full lips dropped. His nose crinkled, and his black brows pinched forward.

Between breaths, he stepped closer.

"Naivety," he said in a strained voice and brought his thick-lashed eyes back to mine. "And divinity. Wrapped up in one young woman. It offends me."

His steps halted. Spine straightening, he looked down on me for only a few more breaths. He broke the stare, raking his ringed fingers through his raven hair. His shirt creased with the movement, the opening of his collar parting farther.

"And you're an arrogant, heartless bastard. Merely a self-proclaimed tyrant."

Shadows whispered over the edges of his frame, tightening around him like a dark cloak. He stepped closer, and they shuddered, like hundreds of thousands of black tiny wings fluttered against his skin. Leathery and shimmering in the pale sunlight. Like bat wings. Waiting to tear themselves free of his magnetic body.

Before I even registered the movement, he was on the bed. His hand swiped at the sheet and tore it from my body. It unfurled in the air between us like a banner—a black flag. Heralding that I'd just woken up a beast, welcomed in a trespasser, and teased a thief. It fell in a heap to the floor, and I crumpled. Cursing myself for the fear that bloomed in my chest.

A deep, guttural growl rose from the base of his core, as if it came from the shadow beneath him, striking up into his throat like an inverted bolt of lightning. It thundered into me. My pulse pounded as I sank into the bed, wishing I could sink through it and hide underneath. He crawled over me.

"I can smell your fear. It calls to me just as the scent of your arousal calls to me. You're excited, though you'd hate to admit it. Curious."

"Get away from me." I unleashed a kick at him, but he caught my ankle.

His gaze heated as it snaked down my leg. Like he was counting the bruises.

"I can even sense the broken blood vessels beneath your skin. The bruises, like purple flowers beneath a tender veil of flesh. A garden, tempting me to tear you open."

I was very naked, and the taste of his magic crept into the back of my throat. Berlium pulled me by my ankle, sliding my entire body toward him in a second with the slightest flick of his wrist.

My ankle burned where his nails dug in. Reflexively, I wanted to use my hand to get a grip, to fight him off, but I couldn't. He hiked my leg up around his hip and pushed me down with his other hand. Slamming me onto the bed and pinning down my good hand.

His cock strained against his trousers between us, begging to be set free, to ravage me. And I had to be losing my mind because a part of me wanted him to—no, it was his magic. Manipulation. The roiling in his eyes and the thrumming in his chest struck a cord of need in me connected to my inner monster. He wanted to play with her.

Dark magic pervaded the room, seeping under my skin. Running its icy fingers along the walls of my mind. I did not know how to resist, but I pinned my eyes shut and imagined a stone wall as tall and mighty as those of his own castle. I built it between us, and to my surprise, it worked. For a moment.

A sound of approval hissed against my senses, and the taste of his magic disappeared.

A knocking sound echoed in my ears.

"Let me in, little wolf. Or I'll break down your walls."

I tried to jerk my hand free. I planted my other foot on the underside of his hipbone and pushed with all my might, trying to create space between our bodies. But I was going nowhere. Without my magic, without two hands, I was helpless beneath him. My thoughts jumped between my anger and the thrill.

Berlium glowered at me, and his laughter hammered against my senses. Panic built in my chest, reaching up into my throat and dragging down the scream that wanted to break free. The touch of his chilling gaze pebbled my skin.

"You're going to have to do better than that," he said huskily.

I looked up at him. A sardonic smirk graced his lips, and his eyes were predatory. I felt his need to dominate me boring into my chest. The realization that he could was like a stake in the heart.

As if he could read every emotion coursing through me, his smile widened into a feral grin. His power slithered over my skin, pressing kisses of darkness, biting like millions of tiny teeth. His other hand traced my leg, careening over my hip and drifting up my abdomen. And then I felt his power again, like claws, scraping against the wall of my mind. Chipping away at it with a slow tap, tap, tap.

I heard him in my thoughts, a hissing whisper that made the Death Spirit purr.

"It seems you thirst for more than blood."

"As if you could sate me," the Death Spirit sighed, running her claws over the walls he threatened to batter. Taunting—much braver than I should have felt.

"Are you a virgin?" he asked.

My brows shot up and pinched together, and I opened my mouth to answer, but he laughed darkly.

"Didn't think so. Purity is useless. You understand what I want— what you want. You're just fighting it."

My blood ran hot, and heat pooled between my thighs. My breasts swelled and tightened beneath him, and he held himself with just enough distance above me to watch the frantic rise and fall of my breathing. I was aware of every inch of him that touched me, as well as the absence of his touch. Measuring the breadth of a winged chill that fluttered between us.

"From the way you're shaking underneath me, I'd say you've never been fucked by a real man. I guess that is a kind of purity. Only knowing the touch of a boy. I will not be sweet to you. I will devour you."

Callused skin grazed over the globe of my breast, flicking over my peaked nipple. He pinched, and a hoarse moan broke through my teeth, dissolving into a growl.

I jerked against him, and he tightened his grip on me, kneading my breast without mercy. My flesh burned, flushed with rage and heat. He dipped his head lower and his hot breath fanned against my skin. I strained to lift my head, to wriggle my shoulders, only bringing my chest closer to his mouth.

He took it as an invitation to close his mouth around my hardened nipple.

His lust planted seeds of desire in my core that rooted within my blood and sprouted into tendrils. Snaked up my bones and wrapped around my lungs, crawled up my throat, and flourished into another breathy moan. He nipped and flicked his tongue over the tender flesh before biting down harder.

A gasp shuddered through me as pleasure danced with the pain. He snapped his gaze up to mine. Shock flared through his eyes and was blinked away by amusement.

"Hungry little thing. Your body begs me to hurt you."

"Get off of me, you fucking sadist."

Another flurry of shadowy wings carried him to the foot of the bed. He was standing, not a hair out of place, and I bolted upright. Without another glance, he crossed the room. With one hand on the doorknob and his back toward me, he gritted out, "Drink your tea."

My eyes returned to the tray on the desk. Once the door clicked shut and his footsteps faded, I jumped out of the bed and snagged the sheet off the floor. I wrapped myself in it and stomped over to the desk. Hadriel's honey-colored concoction swirled within the porcelain teacup.

I grabbed it by the rim and pitched it at the window. The ceramic shattered against the lattice, and amber liquid bled down the pane.

13: SHOULD WE?
Keres

I looked at the broken teacup on the floor and questioned my resolve. There was a knock at the door.

"Come in," I said and began picking up the pieces with one hand.

Hadriel walked in and his eyes dropped to the mess on the floor, the splattered tea on the window. Annoyance crossed his expression.

"Has your pain gone away, then?"

I furrowed my brows. "No." In fact, it was making me feel sick.

"Leave the mess. Ciel will clean it up."

I dressed in the bathroom. Since Berlium mentioned it, I too could sense the blood under my skin—the bruises. I ignored it as I pulled clothes on.

Hadriel truly was living in the castle's belly, judging by the time we'd been walking and the number of staircases we'd descended. We turned down a long, narrow, and dimly candlelit corridor. At the end of it was a black door with etchings in another language. Silver and iridescent.

Yarden stayed behind as we crossed over the threshold. He gestured for me to sit and passed me a tiny vial full of what looked like water.

"This is fast acting. Drink the whole thing."

I swallowed it all at once and winced.

"It's alcohol," he stated.

"No shit."

Once again, I tried rectifying this worried face with the killer's mask he wore when we first met. All other versions of ourselves seemed paused in this room. As if the room made him just a man skilled in medicine, and me, an injured girl. Why, though?

"Last time you were here, you asked me why I helped you."

It was as if he read my thoughts. We locked eyes.

"I help you; you help me. Now, let me change the dressings on that hand."

He gently removed the bandages and dabbed at whatever grease from the ointments my skin hadn't absorbed. He moved so carefully, with the steadiest hands. Not even grazing the splints my fingers were stretched against.

"I'm going to need more to drink," I said, looking away from the gruesome injury.

He rose from his chair and reached up to the top of his bookshelf, pulling down a bottle and pouring me a glass. I held the glass up and sniffed. The sharpness of the liquor made me think of Liriene—how her face scrunched up after every sip of alcohol. I was never so sensitive. It was liquid fire, and I loved everything that felt like burning. Especially without my magic biting its heat into my cold bones.

While he continued his ministrations, I took swigs. Looked at the collection of oddities that littered his shelves. Besides the jarred medicinal supplies, he had a comprehensive library. Most spines had the words *history*, *method*, and *science* in their titles. In a far corner, there was a counter covered in what I recognized to be alchemy equipment.

I remembered it from an illustrated book I'd inherited from my mother. Mortar and pestle, a rack of small-corked bottles. Glass beakers that connected to each other. The neck of one extended toward the center of the counter, where a bowl was set to catch its contents. Vials set on metal stands, with candles set beneath them. Animal skulls and a book with black pages littered the counter, too.

Nothing fascinated me more than the large glass cloches that housed dead animals stuck in stasis in their containers. A moss green toad in one. A crimson snake curled around a black branch in the other. Stranger, a crow perched on what looked like a bigger bird's skull. Its wings flared upward, frozen in flight. A giant spider crawling over a clear and white chunk of crystal. And in the last, an ageless black rose.

I winced, giving his work my attention again.

"Sorry," he whispered. His lips pursed in concentration.

"What are those?" I tilted my head to the cloches. He glanced and then looked back at my hand.

"Tools."

After cleansing the broken skin, he took a flat wooden stick and dipped it into the same poultice he'd applied last time. It was thick and jelly-like, a burnt yellow in color, and smelled strange.

"So, what do you think I could help you with? Fuck, is that supposed to burn?"

"It should feel cooling in a moment." He reached for more gauze and unwound it from its spool. "You can help me with the King."

The poultice cooled my inflamed skin as he promised, and I tried to hold still as he re-wrapped my hand.

"Last time you were here, I told you the King is man and monster in one."

"The Unbridled, as you called him," I said.

"Precisely."

"And what precisely does that mean?" I asked, watching him wind the strip of gauze around and around my hand until he decided it was enough. He cut it and tied up the loose ends into a neat little knot. I took my hand back, and he started cleaning up his supplies.

"What do you think it means?" he asked.

"You know, you remind me of someone I met once," I said, crossing my legs. "He called himself an alchemist but seemed more of an acolyte or monk, with the way he debated theology. Are you a monk?"

A smile crept into the corners of his mouth. "I am a scholar of the world, a warrior, and an arcanist. I am not a monk."

"Because you've got the whole vague and wizened thing about you. It's as convincing as it is infuriating. The robe that swishes when you walk, the bald head. The tattoo... Well, I guess you're not a monk because I don't think they have tattoos."

It was noticeable if he turned his head. The head of a viper poised against the nape of his neck lifted as if to whisper in his left ear. It wasn't colored or bold, appearing faded from time. Its eyes seemed to watch you as he moved.

He touched it. "Ah, yes. That they don't."

"Does it mean anything to you?"

"It means many things." He stopped busying himself with objects on his huge shelf of books and beakers, potions, and trinkets.

I opened my mouth to taunt him again about his ambiguity, but he stopped me with just a look. His grey eyes were cold. Cold as they were on the battlefield. Such a shift—it took me aback. This, the version of him I knew, existed outside of this room.

"When you look at me, you see this face." His eyes darkened from the gray of clouds to near black. "You hear my voice in your head. From that day on the battlefield, when I caught you."

In a blink, his face shifted back to normal. His eyes were soft and almost friendly, his smile was warm. I couldn't see the viper creeping up over his shoulder from this angle.

"All you know is the Sunderlands, but you're a long way from home, Coroner." He walked back to stand in front of me. "I'm helping you because you need help. You may have been one of the wolves back home, but here, you're a lost lamb."

"I'm not completely helpless. What do you take me for?"

"A child," he said sternly.

I stood up and wished I could clench both fists.

"You're reactive," he said before I could speak. Not to prove his point, I stayed quiet.

"You're petulant because you believe in your power, your rights, and all that you've accomplished in your twenty-something years. The King and I have lived much longer than you have—"

"What does that even mean? I've heard stories about this land, him. I'm not oblivious to the fact that he is different," I interrupted, not caring much for his condescending tone.

I was thinking about Herrona's journal that Hero had shown me. How she insinuated he seemed undying.

He is like us, the Death Spirit said. I rolled my eyes, but it wasn't at

Hadriel.

Hadriel's look of disdain melted into a cooled appraisal of me.

He'd been helpful since I'd arrived, tending to me, defending me from the King's anger. Treating me like a lost lamb. Really, he was just trying to figure out what I knew and how easily I could be manipulated. A diplomat's ruse. I was attributing my own meaning to the serpent on his neck. I wouldn't fall for it.

"No matter what you think you know, Coroner," he said as he held his hands out to his side, "you're out of bounds in the Baore. No matter how self-important you feel, life in your clan carved out a very tiny mold for you to grow in. And now that mold is broken. You have no rights here, and there's nothing you'll accomplish as long as you're uncooperative. You may match the King in temper, which means you should understand how easy it is to anger him and the severity of his wrath. Here's the difference between you and him…"

We stared each other down for that silent breath.

"Anything the King threatens to do to you, fully expect it. Anything he wants, he will take. Being a monster of a man is how he became the sole ruler of the Baore. It's how he crossed a bloody 'X' over the map of the Sunderlands. He does not hold back. It's not in his nature to. He is the Unbridled."

I kept my body relaxed and my face hardened. But inside, my stomach twisted into knots.

"When you get your answer—when you learn what he is, you will realize what you aren't: Strong enough. Smart enough. Fast enough. With a marred hand and no magic, are you able to fight us?"

He stepped closer and closer. His eyes darkened once more, and he tilted his head, showing a bit of the viper on his neck.

"Should we fear you when you don't even understand what you are? Without your magic, you don't know. Because for too long you've been a girl playing in the dark of an ancient forest, with a taste for blood, and a tiny spark of power. This does not make you even near equal to what we are. A puddle that reflects the sky is not heaven. Without me, you will remain powerless. Your hand will heal, but I can remedy your ignorance.

"He took your magic because it was the only weapon you still had left to wield—the only one you truly know how to. With it out of the way, I can teach you how to wield your Death Spirit. That is what we both want from you. Not a little girl who spits fire. A reaper."

14: STAKES
Keres

"Dinner will be served soon, my lady," Yarden said without looking at me as we walked back to my room.

"Dinner with the King," I scoffed.

He touched my arm. I flinched at the contact, and his hazel eyes searched mine as his hand drifted back to his side. "I'm sorry, my lady. It's just—"

He searched the halls, and my attention followed. We were alone. Still, he leaned closer and whispered, "I'd ask you to be on your guard."

I furrowed my brows, not knowing what to say.

"There are things I cannot protect you from," he said so softly, it sent a chill running through my body. I took a step back from him and brought my broken hand to my chest. I looked down at the fresh dressing. Hadriel's words burrowed into my thoughts. *With a marred hand and no magic, are you able to fight us?*

I lifted my eyes to the knight's. Of course, he can't protect me here. Not from the King.

"Call me by my name," I said and lowered my hands at my side.

His eyes widened within the hollow of his helmet, and then his lips pressed together. Hesitantly, as if he were tasting the words, he said, "Lady Keres."

I nodded.

"Ciel and Minnow expect to help you change for dinner." We returned to my bed chambers. He was right.

Ciel and Minnow were waiting. This was my first time really meeting Minnow, which she was keen to mention in a sing-song voice.

"We've got clothing for you! A gift from his majesty," she chirped. She was cradling a stack of large parcels in her long, slender arms. Long-nailed, delicate fingers plucked the ribbons apart and spread the crinkly paper, revealing dresses of all colors. Deep to pale. Much like the contrast between Ciel and Minnow.

Ciel was fair, but Minnow's skin was a rich umber. Excitement lit up her tawny eyes, and her full lips parted in a brilliant smile. I noticed she took time to apply rouge to her lips and cheeks, kohl liner to her eyes. She made Ciel, although pretty, look plain. Every step Minnow made tinkled with the sounds of the bells on her twin gold anklets. Her frock was the same as Ciel's, but she'd embroidered flowers into it with plum colored thread. Two Humans, so different from one another. The one like sugar was cold, but the one like spice was warm.

They helped me change out of the red, thin shift dress and laid out a heavier one. It was a deep burgundy—the same as the King usually wore—made of velvet and silk. I obeyed their pestering for me to bathe. Let them have their way with me. It felt ridiculous, putting on rouge and a velvet dress. Being dressed up like a doll, a plaything.

The silk bodice fit like a bustier. I sucked in a breath as Ciel fastened its silk ribbons at the back. Holding on to the bedpost and my breath, I watched my breasts plump up with the support of the bodice's frame. Appliques overlaid the edges of the neckline. Red-brown pieces of velvet cut to look like flower petals, which perked up against my breasts.

The bodice overlaid the skirt of the dress, and its bottom had the same flower petals sewn at the edges as well. They blended in with the skirt, which was the same darker red, but it wasn't as delicate and shiny as the bodice. I swished my hand over it, following the trail of my hand against the velvet, before smoothing it back.

The sleeves sat off the shoulders, fixed there by ruched elastic, rippling down to where it tightened at the elbow. Fitted to the wrist. The applique detail repeated at the shoulder, but the sleeve ended in a soft, loosely pleated cuff that continued past my palms.

Ciel slipped a pearl bracelet over the cuff and laid a matching necklace at my collarbone, filling the ample space between my neck and the dress's dangerously low neckline.

Minnow set matching burgundy slippers in front of my feet.

"Elves don't cover their feet," I said.

She blinked at me, tilting her head. Her luscious black curls shifted, the longest pieces only reaching her jaw. She opened her mouth to speak but Ciel responded first, "Well, then let's just brush your hair and be done."

She did so and braided it back loosely. It would probably come undone, and that was the worst part of all of it. This dress was not armor. It could be torn.

The dining hall was probably larger than it should be, with a long dark wood table running up its center. I doubted Berlium ever had willing guests. Hearths with arched mantles held up each corner of the room, housing raging fires. Iron chandeliers held up black-waxed candles. Red light danced across the stone walls and lit up in the archways.

The sound of chains dragging on the stone drew my attention to a far corner of the room. King Berlium's massive frame emerged from the door beside the hearth, and as he passed it, the fire swelled and stretched. Shrouding him in auburn light.

His black sateen shirt, with a characteristically loose collar, was tucked into tight black trousers. It had laces at the front which were loosely tied. His wavy hair was brushed back, the length ending just below his ears. A stray wisp crossed his brow as he tilted his head forward. His too-bright eyes dropped to my chest and followed my dress to the floor. The necklace felt like a collar, the grating of the chains against the floor pulling at it.

The chains in his hand were iron. They scratched the stone as he advanced. In tow were two women. One with skin like porcelain and the other's like mahogany. Both wearing gray, sheer, lace dresses. I watched the sway of their hips as they followed him, the bounce of their breasts. The floral swirls of the lace did little to hide their softly puckered nipples, or the starks of hair between their legs.

Their attention glazed over the room with twin sets of empty green eyes. Despite their hands being cuffed, they reached for the King. Making small, pretty noises as he turned toward them and grinned. He locked their chains to a post on the wall near the head of the table and took a step away from them, which they resented.

"A feast," he said, gesturing to the still-empty table. He snickered. "Why do you look so confused?"

I moved to the closer end of the table and pulled out the upholstered chair.

"Afraid to come closer," he said, dropping his voice an octave. It wasn't a question, but a dare.

Closeness to him promised danger. His presence was as consuming as the fire that leapt in the hearth at his passing. Heat flushed my cheeks, mirrored in his stare.

I watched him, watching me, as I pushed the chair back in and rounded the table. Keeping it between us. The walk from one end to the other by which he stood felt like passing through a valley. As if at any moment, I'd be ambushed.

I startled as the doors opened and a team of footmen bearing golden trays flooded the hall. In a ripple, they laid their trays down one after the other, in cadence with my heart. I rubbed my left palm against the dress, shifting the skirt to hide how my fingers trembled.

The women writhed against the pillar, toying with their chains, and all the footmen pretended they weren't even there. They uncovered the plates and poured red wine, then left.

The King lifted his chin as he appraised me, and I realized I'd stopped walking. Focusing on the chair nearest the head of the table, I closed the distance and took a seat.

He sat at the head of the table and gave his attention to the women, who purred and mewed at its return. I swallowed and looked down at my plate. The dark meat on it oozed bloody juice. I held my utensil uneasily in my non-dominant hand, hesitating. His gaze followed mine.

I gracelessly speared a quartered, roasted potato. After minutes of silent chewing, he noticed I hadn't touched the meat. He coughed, wiped his mouth with his cloth napkin, and dropped it on the table.

"Is the steak not to your liking? I prefer it on the rarer side. Didn't think you'd disagree."

I met his eyes, a chill raking down my spine at the coldness of their color. The dark scruff on his jaw did little to mask the way he ground his teeth.

"I don't eat meat," I said, then picked up a piece of mushroom, coupling it with a flimsy sliver of cooked onion. As I took the bite, he watched my mouth and licked his lower lip thoughtlessly. Every mannerism was as sensual as it was predatory.

"You don't eat meat," he repeated and looked back up at me. The corners of his eyes creased, and he snorted softly. "Strange, for someone who speaks so much of blood thirst."

"It's something most of my people observe. Sometimes fish is acceptable, but—"

"Why pretend to be like them?" he asked with a lift of his hand. "Why not satisfy the craving?"

"Because I don't make light of it," I shot back.

Movement caught my attention—the women, now wrapped in each other's arms, began kissing. Slow, ravishing. Heat rose to my face, and I refocused on my plate.

He pushed his seat back, the wood abruptly scraping against the stone. I tracked his movement, noting his height, sitting there as he stalked toward the women. Their mouths parted, and they locked eyes with him. Their lips curving before they rejoined in the kiss.

His power speared out of his body into them. Their backs bowed, and they moaned into each other's mouths. As if they felt him without his hands on them.

I felt it too. Between my thighs, an angering need erupted in me. The grating of the chains, the chafing of my dress, the whining of the women. I wanted to rip it all apart—tear him down for making me feel this way against my will. For making them into what they were for him.

As he neared, the woman leaning against the wall pulled her partner into her arms, crushing the lace between their bodies. She opened her mouth hungrily against the other's and nested her hands in her hair, pushing back her dark brown locks to reveal long, pointed ears.

She massaged the other's breasts, pinching her nipples. I looked closer at the fairer-skinned woman and noted the rounded edge of her ears through her light brown hair. A short breath escaped me.

He didn't miss it. He raised a brow and smirked. The chains rattled as the women touched each other. Tinkling, tempting him closer.

He approached them. Angled his head, watching the dance of their tongues. They giggled and sighed. He came up behind the dark-haired girl and traced his eyes down her backside, before turning to me and asking, "Do you recognize her?"

I shook my head. "Just because she's Elven, doesn't mean I know her."

The women ignored me, like I wasn't even there. I clutched my utensil, wanting to stab him with it. This was all a trick of his seductive magic. I knew it was.

He grabbed a fistful of her hair and arched her head back. Her dark lashes fluttered, and she bit her lip, leaning back into him as her partner lowered her mouth to her neck. Licking and kissing down over her chest. Running her tongue against the fabric over her nipples and humming.

He brought his other hand to her throat and pressed himself against her backside. She rocked her hips back into him, grinding against him.

"See how she moves for me? Her body begs me to hurt her just as yours did."

He massaged her throat, her collarbones, her jaw. Then a fingernail lengthened into a razor-sharp point, and he dragged it down the side of her neck.

I shot to my feet, the scent of blood pricking at my senses. It oozed from the slit, and she leaned into the touch, as if she enjoyed bleeding for him. His tongue flicked out, swiping at the rivulets of blood that glistened against her dark skin. My throat ran dry as I watched.

Her gasp broke into a moan as he suckled at the cut. The other woman hummed ecstatically, kneading her breasts and her hips before running her hand down between her legs.

His clawed finger tilted her head to the side, allowing him better access to her throat. Sipping every drop. Then he twirled her around, backing her against her partner and pushing them both against the wall. Wedged between him and the other woman, she met his eyes with a feral grin. Tangled in her chains, she held up her wrists to him. He pulled a key from his belt, and he unlocked each one.

As the cuffs clattered onto the floor, she threw her hands around his neck and kissed him. Her blood still on his lips. The other woman wrapped her arms around his prey, playing her hands up and down the front of her. I felt frozen in place.

He took her hands from his neck and pushed them back down—into the other girl's control, who giggled as she restrained her. The dark-haired woman rested her head back on the other's shoulder, and he pulled away from them.

He ignored me as he returned to the table and picked up a knife.

"What are you doing?" I snapped.

The women glared. Once he turned back to them, he pointed the blade at his willing victim and asked me. "Would you take her place?"

She hissed in my direction as if she'd kill me if I tried. He brought the serrated knife she seemed to crave to her. Resting the tip at the top of her sternum. Wordlessly, she moaned, arching her back, pressing her chest against it. The other woman started kissing her neck and reached a hand down between her legs as she parted them. Opening herself the way she seemed to want his knife to.

He dragged it downward, and she bit back a cry as it tore the lace dress, leaving a thin, bloody seam down her middle—stopping at her navel. Grabbing her by the hips and bringing his mouth to her stomach, he licked his way back up to her neck. Blood continued beading and dripping down her abdomen with her movement, and his hands smeared it against her skin. She relished in it.

The cloyingly sweet fragrance of his magic, like honey and blood, saturated the air. I felt it sticking to the roof of my mouth, the back of my throat. My tongue felt heavy and thick with it. I moved from my side of the table, lifting my dress' hem above my feet.

His eyes shot open and shimmered, even brighter than usual. So unnatural, so enchanting. His lips, red and wet, parted to reveal his elongated fangs.

I stopped short, but the Death Spirit urged me forward.

He withdrew from her, and she whimpered, angling herself toward him and offering her blood. He straightened up, latching his eyes onto me as he ran his tongue over the edge of the knife and then reached out his other hand to me.

"You want to save your people, don't you?"

Again, they whined in harmony.

My mouth dropped open, but I couldn't find the words—couldn't will myself into his hand.

"We can handle him; we can make him bleed." The Death Spirit found this all too enticing. I took a step back.

He snarled and grabbed the woman by the throat, ripping her away from the other, and pushing her toward the table. She crawled onto it, losing whatever was left of her dress. With her long arms, she swiped the plates onto the floor and sat up on her knees. The plates shattered and the blood from the meat spattered the ground.

She moved, circling her hips and rolling her body, running her hands over her bloodied skin. Her head dropped back, and she sighed.

These women were mindless!

The other yanked on her chains, crying to be given the same treatment. He moved closer to the table, dragging the woman back to the edge. Ran his blade down the inside of her thigh. Ignoring the bleating of the other. I didn't know what to do. Would he kill her or fuck her? Both?

"Tell me again about the monster you think you are, little wolf," he said to me, "This curse of yours I ought to find terrifying."

Then, he rewarded my silence with a toothy grin. "After tonight, I don't think you'll forget that I am your ruler. There is no animal in my kingdom more powerful than me. You said there was nothing more dangerous than your hatred, but there is nothing deadlier than my hunger."

He raised the knife in his fist and hammered it down into her chest quicker than I could scream. The knife met bone—crunching and squelching. She yelped, falling back toward the table, but he caught the back of her head. A cry erupted from me, and my hands flew to my mouth to catch it.

He ripped the knife from her chest, widening the puncture, and blood boiled up. She made an animal-like noise in mindless agony, blinded by his magic. As he leaned down and lapped up the blood that cascaded over her breasts, I ran.

Flung the doors open and launched into the hall. Yarden followed, but I didn't look back. Trying to outrun the sounds of her strangled moaning and the giddy trills of the woman still chained to the wall.

Halfway down the hall, my vision went black, and I stumbled. Throwing my hands out in front of me to catch myself, I crashed down on my broken one. I howled in pain, and tears built in my unseeing eyes.

Was I being channeled? *Not now, please, not now.*

Hands were on me, trying to lift me. My senses told me it was Yarden's hands, but still I shouted, "Get off!"

He released me. I knelt there with my hand on my chest. Not daring to touch it—not daring to move. The sharp shooting pain sent bolts of red into my skull. Crimson light burned my vision, melting into a blurred view. I saw movement.

I blinked away the blood on my lashes. No, not *my* lashes. The woman lay dead on the table before me. The other beside her, with her throat slit and her eyes trapped in the back of her head.

No more sounds except his ragged breathing. As if I was in his head, I got dizzy when he turned toward the door. He was coming. I could hear his footsteps; I could see what he saw. I scented the blood on him. Thickening his breath.

We looked down at the blood on his hands, dropping the knife. The carpeted hall stretched out, with me at the end. I saw myself through his eyes, crumpled in my dress and wide-eyed. His hands reached toward me, and his touch gave me back my sight. It rolled back into my head as his bloody hands seized me by the shoulders. He hoisted me to my feet, and I focused on his face.

This close, his eyes were like a trap. Storm clouds passed through them, and lightning bolted across his irises. I stared, feeling almost as mindless as his other victims. The shifting waves of blue washed away my thoughts. When he tore his attention away from mine, I realized he'd been starting just as intently. His eyes ran down to my hand. I looked down at it between us. Fresh blood saturated the dressing.

"You thought you could run?" he growled in my face. I pulled back, pinching my eyes shut.

"Look at me," he roared. "Isn't this what you wanted to see? How far you could push me? Damn you, open your eyes."

I willed myself not to show fear. My hair was a mess around my face, loose from the braid. He brushed it back over my shoulder and looked down at my throat.

"You could have saved them. If you'd taken their place. Isn't that what you want, Coroner?" He shook me. I looked up at him from under my brows, taking my mind away from the pain. Swallowing the taste of his magic, like a hot iron branding the back of my throat.

"I would rather die than to be made mindless—your plaything."

Finally, the Death Spirit agreed, and her soft growl rolled through my chest. My gums burned, and I tasted blood as I forced my own fangs down lower into my mouth and bared them. His gaze dropped to my mouth, and his hands dug into my shoulders. Sticky. Crushing the velvet flower petals. I grabbed his collar with my good hand and pulled him down.

The warmth of our breath melded between us, his carrying the acrid smell of blood that lit my senses on fire. The strands of his jet-black hair that fell forward fluttered against his skin. I angled my mouth up toward his throat, inhaling the scent of him. A thick, metallic scent that whetted my appetite. He stood still as stone. Finally—fucking finally—his heartbeat raced.

"Afraid to come closer?" I breathed against him, watching his pulse shudder in his neck. I leaned into it, brushing my eyelashes over his skin, and planting my mouth on his collarbone. His head bowed against mine. I touched the tips of my fangs to his skin.

He jerked me back, shoved me away, but I caught my footing. His eyes bore into mine for a few breaths. The storm in his eyes settled, and he wiped his mouth. I dragged my gaze over him. The blood staining his hands and clothes was now on me.

I locked eyes with him again, and the Death Spirit hissed at him.

His lips parted, letting out a scant breath.

"Finally," he whispered.

For just a moment, I wondered what he saw.

15: So Many Questions
Ceres

After the King let me go, Yarden took me to Hadriel. He had to fix my hand and redress it, and he did so in silence. It was a great *I told you so* moment for him. The splint had basically saved my hand, but that didn't mean it hadn't hurt like hell. He told me to return to him tomorrow, sending me off with a cup of tea for the pain.

Back in my room, I sat with my knees to my chest in the bathtub. My arm rested on the brim of the tub to keep it from getting wet while Minnow washed the blood off my shoulders.

"Do you know what he is?" I asked her.

Her touch stopped between my shoulders.

"The King…" She hesitated and then started washing my skin again. "He's like a pendulum. Always moving between extremes."

"Do you serve him against your will?" I asked.

"No," she said, as if my question surprised her. "Above all things, he is my sovereign. His nature makes the Baore strong. When needed, he is quiet. He listens to his people. When needed, he roars. We are as devoted to him as he is to us—that's what he is. Ours. And we prosper in being his."

Strength. Devotion. Prosperity. That's what she saw in the King. Missing the fact that he was a monster. Was she ignorant of it?

I thought about him being like a pendulum. Shifting between extremes unimpeded. Unbridled. His touch was a hammer-blow that drew blood, or an aphrodisiac that sent my pulse racing.

I crawled into bed, under the heavy covers. Still, nothing warmed my blood.

I awoke the next morning nauseous. I couldn't pry myself from the safety of the bed or from the dangers in my memories.

Bloodshed. Violence. The screaming, the gurgling, the gnashing of teeth, the crunch of broken bone. None of it disturbed me anymore. But I could still hear his breathy suckling at her blood, felt the dryness of my throat. The sensation reminding me of my own blood thirst. The dullness of his heartbeat compared to the mangled moaning of the women.

The arousal and the horror I felt—the blend of them terrified me the most.

I rubbed at my eyes and rolled over, staring at the frosted window. White light was stuck to the other side of it. The sky must have been cloudy, from the way it shifted into gray, back to white. A black form shot past the window. A bird.

"Injured," the Death Spirit whined. *"How could this happen to me?"*

I held up my broken, splinted hand, blocking the pathetic sunlight. I've never struck and missed. For all the Dalis bodies I had piled under my name, not a scratch on the tally board for them. Only the Gryphon King Arias had landed a strike on me—he didn't count. He was a bird... thing.

I'd made it through every terrible battle of my second life, unscathed. King Berlium lifted a hand and was the first man to wound me.

I could hear my own bones snapping in his grasp. Cracking, splintering...

Silas had threatened to hurt me once. Then promised he could never. Darius promised me unbridled passion. How ironic. They were boys compared to Berlium, but the King wasn't a man either.

I missed Darius. Anger hollowed out a dark chamber in my heart. Against the omen that drove us apart. Against the miles that separated us. And the King.

I'd carve out his heart. I could see the dead women on the table again. *A feast.*

His thoughts infested my mind. How had he done that? He did more than that. His presence touched my Spirit.

The way I could answer his growls and hissing disturbed me as much as it excited me. In all my years hunting Dalis, I couldn't see or just summon the Death Spirit. I'd tried staring myself down in the mirror. Willing to see what Ivaia told me I looked like. An executioner with the abysmal darkness of Death in my eyes. Everybody else saw my power through my eyes—black holes as bottomless as his thirst.

"He is hollow in the same places as us," the Death Spirit said. He could hear her—call to her. She seemed to recognize him, but I didn't. How?

I wasn't any closer to understanding what he was, and it made me confused about what I was.

The door creaked open.

"Good morning, my lady," Ciel announced. "Time to get up and face the day."

I didn't move or make a sound. Ciel's footsteps shuffled around the bed, bringing her into view.

"My lady," she offered me a tender smile that faltered when I slid my gaze over her.

"How pale you look. You'll do better with some of Hadriel's tea, and a bit of breakfast."

"I don't have the energy."

She frowned. "Come, I shall help you, then."

She drew back the covers, and I sat up, begrudgingly. The bruises on my body were still tender. As she helped me wash up and dress, I felt numb. Stuck in a shell of disquiet.

She helped me into a black velvet dress that emphasized my hourglass figure and ended at the floor. Silver thread embroidered the neckline and flowed down the long sleeves along their seams. It was simple and warm.

Yarden was at the door, of course. I cast a wary glance at Berlium's bedroom door.

"The King left this morning," Yarden said gently.

I looked back at him, and he gave me an easy smile. The knots in my stomach unwound.

"I hope to see you later, Yarden," Ciel said timidly as she passed him.

His eyes tracked her, but that smile faded. She descended the stairs on light feet.

He tipped his head in that direction, like nothing happened. "Shall we?"

I lifted a brow at him and bit back a teasing smile. He shook his head, grinning sheepishly, and we followed in her footsteps. She'd walked fast, so we had the hall beyond the stairs to ourselves.

"You tried to warn me."

A strange emotion flitted through his eyes, swept away by his thick black lashes.

"I've already said too much, and still it wasn't enough. We probably shouldn't talk about last night," he replied.

"Why not?" I shrugged. "He's not here."

Despite it, he still looked over his shoulder.

"I'm not afraid," I said, convincing neither of us.

An enemy had never bested me, but that didn't mean I'd never felt fear. The Dalis were a force to be reckoned with. I knew better than anyone. It shouldn't have been a surprise that their leader was as evil as they were. I expected a king, cold and heartless. I didn't expect a devil whose presence screamed power. Not the obvious aura any war-mongering king would project, but something on the darker side of divinity.

In all the stories told in the Sunderlands, none spoke of what lurked inside King Berlium Gaspar. Except Herrona—she only hinted at something like near immortality within him.

My thoughts were waxing and waning through phases of anxiety and anger. Triggering so many questions.

"What *can* you tell me?" I asked. We still had a way to go to Hadriel's chambers.

He sighed. "We can talk about other things if you'd like. Although, I think you might find me boring."

"I doubt I would. Tell me about the castle. How long have you been here?"

"When I was knighted several years ago, they sent me to Dulin, the

King's other castle, to guard someone. But the dynamic between us... it was best I left."

"Oh? Another mystery."

"Nothing ominous, I assure you. It's not a secret, it's just not something I'm proud of."

"Did you fail in protecting this person?"

"No," he said, and his gaze lowered. "The only thing I failed to guard was my heart."

I looked wide-eyed at him. "Well, aren't you a knight in shining armor? Paramour."

"I was a fool. It was completely inappropriate."

"So, you ended it, then?"

"Certain people took notice and came against us. But ultimately, she ended it."

"I see."

He sighed. "That was three years ago. I've been here since. Dulin is... nothing like this place." His gaze traveled across the paintings that adorned the walls.

The paintings were masterpieces, really. Scenes of animals in the forests and mountains. Beasts of prey. Painted in realistic shades of greens and blacks, grays and blues. In gilded frames which were a striking contrast to the stone walls. Claws and fangs and beady eyes.

I pointed at one of a bear. "The King's portrait."

He chuckled.

"My family told me he killed his own father and his uncle to take both thrones of the Baore. They called those kings the brother bears. Now they call him grizzly. His own brothers, his cousins. Every contestant, he cut them down. I wonder, were they like him?" I looked at him.

His hazel eyes brightened. "No one is like him."

We started walking again, and I picked his brain. "Aside from murderous madmen and amorous knights, what else can you tell me about Baoreans?"

"Baoreans are like anyone else."

"Ha," I scoffed. "I'll believe it when I see it. I've yet to meet a Human

113

who was anything like an Elf."

He paused, his brows furrowing.

"Oh, I didn't mean to offend you,"

He shook his head. "Is that all you see?"

"That's all I've been shown."

He stopped and took off his helmet. He was handsome. His jawline wasn't overly bold, its curve softening just beneath his rounded ears. His soft hazel eyes and heavy brows were familiar, but no longer framed by a shell of metal. His hair was a dark brown, and it curled so much like Darius'. He had a pretty little mole off the right side of his full mouth. And beauty marks all down the left side of his neck too.

"You hate the Humans that hate Elves, but how does that make you any different from them? You say you've never met a Human who was like an Elf, as if being Elven makes you inherently better. When you look at me, you can see the shape of my ears. The color of my skin. My sex. You see something different from you, and you feel disdain or hatred?"

"I've only ever seen enemies in people like you. It's not personal."

"But it is, all discrimination is, and everyone is capable of it. It happens on all different levels. In some ways, I'm treated better because of my sex—a male. My status, a knight. Some men treat women poorly—considered the weaker sex. Beautiful women typically fare better than the unattractive. Then again, I've been mistreated because of my skin color by men who wear the same armor as me but look different in it. What makes any of it right? What makes anyone better than another? It's twisted thinking. You see that, don't you?"

"I do," I said, taken aback.

His gaze softened, and we walked on. "Our societies are very different, but you can only blame so much on it. Everyone develops prejudices and experiences different privileges. Me, you. But it's important to question these things. There is power in what we choose to ignore, and in what we choose to acknowledge. You can't see the goodness in the differences and similarities between people if you're constantly making an enemy out of what looks or talks differently than you. If you can't see the good, you'll be just as bad as those you hate."

Guilt bit into me. He had given me something to think about. I imagined a version of myself who wasn't so ignorant and hateful. Who had seen the world and knew more than the twisted thinking he called out. Considering an *army* propagated the prejudices I expected in Humans, maybe Yarden was rare.

At the end of the hall, there was a door. Behind it was a set of stairs, and then another. Step after step, we shuffled down and chatted about things we had in common, and I was happy that there were many.

Hadriel's door opened abruptly. "I could hear your raucous conversation echoing down the stairwell."

He looked from my knight to me, and back again. Yarden tensed.

"Oh, please, Hadriel. Everything's louder in a stairwell. It's not like we were cursing king and country—although I might have in my head," I said and crossed the threshold.

Both his brows shot up as he watched me move toward the chair beside the cot. He glared at Yarden and then closed the door.

"Are we going to have a tea party?" I asked, crossing my legs and leaning my arm over the back of the chair. The conversation with Yarden stimulated me, much to Hadriel's displeasure. He stalked over to the hearth, glowering.

He prepared and handed me a cup of tea. I took a sip and smacked my lips before giving my review of a satisfied, "Ah."

He huffed. "Drink it quietly. I have something to tell you."

I looked up at him. The coolness in his eyes was just as chilling as Berlium's.

He selected a book from his library and held it between us. As I went to take it, he snatched it back.

"First, listen."

I nodded.

"After last night, you must abandon all thought of retaliation against the King. Listen," he hissed as I was about to interrupt.

"He is the Unbridled. He's shown you only a glimpse of what that means. If you think it can't get worse, it can. A broken hand and a nightmare are the most blessed of the curses he can unleash on you. Hold on." He sighed, and I snapped my jaw shut.

"I told you I would teach you how to wield your Death Spirit. I have one condition, and I need to know what you know about it. Clearly, there is some level of ignorance."

I snorted. I was to be schooled all day today, then.

"I owned one book about the Gods. One my mother left behind called the *Hand of Gods*. It was incomplete, so I only know that the Coroner before me was Geraltain and he bore my curse. I know basic Aurelesian doctrine—the Elven version.

"Ivaia taught me about Elymas and his gift of magic to my family. I know very little about the Transcendants. Which I learned from a priest in the temple of Mrithyn. Other than that, I know what Mrithyn has told me about Himself in my dreams. His nature and voice. I have more questions than understanding."

"I'm sure." As he slowly extended the book, he added, "Your book was incomplete because your mother never finished taking her notes from this one."

"The Hands of Gods," I gasped.

"The one she left you, she wrote herself."

"What?" I gaped up at him. All the time I spent reading... It was her handwriting. I looked down at the book and opened it. In the margins were more notes.

"That's her writing as well." He scoffed. "She knew I hated when she wrote in my books, but she did it, anyway."

"You were friends?" I blurted.

"Peers. You know your mother was a Magistress for a time?"

I nodded.

"Before she married your father, she traveled. It's where she got all her books. For a time, she traveled with me. As all Magisters do, I led her through the Baore, teaching her what I know. She shared with me what she'd learned in the Ressid and Herda'al Provinces. It was necessary for those in the Ministry to share information periodically. She would have moved on to the Natlantine, but unexpectedly stepped down from the ministry. Returning to the Sunderlands to be mediocre. So, I stayed here."

"She wasn't mediocre," I snapped.

Looking down at the book, I thought about her sacrifice. "I never thought she would have wanted anything to do with the Baore after what Berlium did to Herrona."

"Why not?" He shrugged. "Your mother was very diplomatic. Unlike you," he said with a hint of a smirk. "She learned to see beyond the blood feuds, to the true dynamics between provinces. Sought to understand what made a people strong, what made a culture rich. She was an exceedingly gifted scholar. That little trunk of books could not contain the things she had or wished to study. It's a shame she gave it all up to marry into the clan. To appease Herrona."

"To heal the Sunderlands," I corrected. "The clans rely on the crown. After your King fucked everything up, the clans and crowns were at odds. Her marriage to my father, the establishment of my clan, was a grasp at peace."

"Yet the Sunderlands is still a mess. She gave up her dream; died in that clan, and it's ash now."

"She didn't die. She was murdered. In front of me. It was the day we both died."

"Semantics." He tilted his head and searched my eyes. "Tell me, was she there with you in Mrithyn's presence when he claimed you?"

"Yes." The memory hurt. It probably showed on my face.

"Interesting. Read the book. I'll give you one week. If you think you can study on par with your mother, read it in two days. Only after, will we discuss your powers further."

My fingers touched the leather, reaching hungrily.

"Now. My condition. If you do not heed my warnings, if you plot against the King, I cannot help you. Nor will I teach you."

I nodded and thanked him for the book. It was a promise I couldn't keep. I *could* put my plans for revenge on hold long enough to read the book. I would not walk out of the kingdom empty-handed. Whether he sensed the hollowness of my agreement, he said nothing more.

I left with the book under my arm. Yarden offered to carry it for me, but knowing it contained my mother's notes... I never wanted to let it go. This felt like the first reach toward that version of myself who knew more—who was stronger. I was not a lost lamb, but a wolf. I just needed to sharpen my fangs.

16: STUDY

𝕳𝖊𝖗𝖊𝖘

Day Seven

I read it in three days. Without the King around to bother me, I read day and night. Only stopping to eat. Even that was a chore. I didn't let Ciel or Minnow touch me, didn't bathe, though I desperately needed to. I just couldn't put it down. It was like holding a piece of her.

I never knew a book could change your life. My mother's notes were astounding. From the small book collection she left behind, I knew she was a studious woman. I just never expected her thirst for knowledge to include this kind of information.

She seemed more entranced by the Gods than Ivaia was. Knew things that weren't in the book that she added into its margins. Wrote questions and then pages later, wrote the answers she'd found. She also referenced other books in her notes, marking down their page numbers. I wanted to read those books too.

As I read, I took my own notes in a separate journal I'd found in the desk drawer. It was blank, red, and someone's name was embroidered into the leather. Lady Vega. I didn't care who she was—she'd never used it. So, I did.

Unlike my old copy of the book, this one had a complete section on Geraltain, the Coroner before me. It spoke more in depth about his relationship with Mrithyn. He favored swords. He was a world-renowned monster hunter. Apparently, he'd lived longer than two centuries ago. Not one, like my book said.

Considering the haste my mother seemed to have written our copy in, she must have misprinted.

I remembered what it felt like to fight the Gnorrer. It was jarring to fight something that didn't die so easily. I was so used to every strike being fatal unless thwarted somehow. Mrithyn guided my arrows. The Death Spirit made no mistakes. According to the book, Instruments were Demi-deities. Monsters were also closer to the Gods in power than mortals, making us evenly matched opponents.

There were words to describe Geraltain that haunted me.

Soul-Eater.

Blood Waker.

Godlander.

My people had always feared me, called me a witch or a Goddess. I always denounced their claims that I was anything more than an unlucky mortal girl who served a dark and twisted God.

But I was more than that. Realizations about my death were making sense, but still felt incomplete. Things Mrithyn has said that fateful day rang in my head.

"My love, Enithura, made you fair."

He was impressed with me, but He never told me why. It was like Mrithyn was withholding it from me, waiting for me to grow to a level of understanding before He would show me. At least, that's what the Death Spirit kept singing about.

"Little wolf, our jaws must open first." She rather liked the King's pet name for us.

This book raised new questions—better questions. Just how different were monsters and Instruments? Was Berlium a literal monster—was that why the Death Spirit felt matched by him? What kind of monster craved blood? I didn't think any other Instrument would. I thought it was a curse unique to Coroners.

The Death Spirit yearned to understand the Grizzly King. She wanted to play with him. I needed to understand the differences between him and I as much as she wanted to see the similarities. I just needed her to be quiet when he was around. She was so gods-damned obsessed with him. Bitch.

"No purring," I said to the Death Spirit, who was feeling more and more like something other than myself. She only chuckled at my protestation—a dark, tinkling laugh that echoed through my head.

When I put the book down to rest my eyes, ocean blue ones stared into me. I couldn't help but feel like he was watching, even though he wasn't in the castle. He had touched my mind, had tempted my Spirit, and I didn't think that was something I'd escape so easily.

I didn't want to be found lacking when I discovered Berlium's weakness. I wanted to be stronger. It was another reason to keep my thoughts on the book.

The thing that shocked me most in the book was an entry about a God I'd never heard of before. I never even knew there were more Gods in the Pantheon than the ones my people worshiped. My mother knew, though.

I'd heard over and over that my mother was brilliant, powerful, fearless, and respected. Indiro had only talked of their time there together with pride. Glazing over details of what they did but never in short supply of praises for her.

She seemed most intrigued by this nameless God, and details of His power were few, vague. She penned her ideas, questions, and best guesses. Highlighted things she must have thought could be clues. Mentioned a "promising morsel of information," being along the eastern border of Aureum. That was far away, and I had no chance of exploring that, but I wondered if she had in all her travels? Maybe she wrote the answers in a different book.

What made her want to chase this knowledge through pages and across borders? She pursued him. This nameless deity... the God of Fear. Why?

17: Sustenance
Keres

Seeing Berlium so clean, so bright-eyed, felt unnatural.

I had finally bathed and tore myself from the book. My hair was still damp, and I was hastily braiding it when I'd stepped into the foyer. Finding him on the other side of his golden statue, he watched as I circled around it. I headed toward the staircase. He headed toward his room.

"You're back."

"Missed me?"

"Terribly," I mocked.

He narrowed his eyes, and the corners of his mouth lifted. So clean-shaven, so soft-skinned. Other parts of him hardened. His stare, his cock—just as mocking. He watched my fingers finish the braid.

"Wear your hair down for me at dinner tonight," he said in a rich, sexy voice.

"Who's on the menu?"

He snorted. "A little calf named veal."

I didn't hide my distaste, but he didn't care. He continued to his room, and Yarden and I continued down the hall. We weren't going anywhere in particular. I just needed to walk. It was disgustingly early, but it was the only time I had to myself. Well, with Yarden. Ciel and Minnow hadn't come to my room yet. I insisted we wouldn't be there when they did.

Yarden didn't mind. He'd just switched places with Anselm, who was only there when I slept. He had energy. His steps seemed a little more directed than mine. We went through a door beneath the stairs.

Beyond it was a long hall that opened up on either side with several arches. To the right and to the left were grander rooms. One being an enormous room filled with sculptures that I wanted to revisit. He led me elsewhere.

In this hall, there was a cold, empty ballroom. A dimly lit parlor attached to it with couches and chaises. The last room on the right was a small dining room, and the last on the left was a bare alcove with another door.

It led into a shade-drenched courtyard.

Large, flowering trees scattered throughout kept nearly everything beneath their boughs protected. The cool, High Autumn air relieved my senses.

Despite the depth of the season, these trees weren't bare. They wore dark green leaves and thorny, black, thick-petaled flowers. Their bark was black, glistening with the dew that rolled down from the leaves.

The ground was mostly a rich dark soil with pebbles and steppingstones dotted in a hapless pattern. Large boulders stood in a circle at the center, with benches between them. Ivy and moss crawled along the ground in places, wandering up to the trees and scaling the boulders.

The flowers' sweet fragrance mingled with the scent of the lush soil. It was grounding. Among the standing stones, I stood with my face lifted to the sky, the light peeking through the branches. I yearned for home.

Yarden's armor creaked as he followed me. Beside the largest boulder were two ornately carved stone chairs, and between them was a round stone table. Small enough for a pair to play a card game or share a meal. I sat on one of them and pointed to the other. "Don't just stand there, sit with me."

His armor made too much noise as he sat.

"Are you cold?"

"I've got something underneath," he said with a smile.

"That you have to live in that suit is ridiculous in my opinion."

"Appearances." He shrugged, but he took off his helmet and placed it on the ground between his feet. I shifted in my seat and felt my dress snag a bit on the coarse stone.

"I've given some thought to what you said last time we talked. You know, anytime I've ever seen a Human, they were cruel, and their cruelty made them ugly. I hunted men in the darkness of the Sunderlands Forest. Murderers. I saw only darkness. Grimaces. Roaring mouths and hate-filled eyes. There was a bluntness to their faces. As I watched them die, their expressions changed a hundred times in a minute before finally relaxing. Even in death, they were brutish and ugly. Dull, even."

He leaned his elbows on the table.

"I see kindness in you, though," I said. "Thank you for helping me see something other than darkness."

He blinked at me, and a smile stretched lazily across his mouth.

The courtyard door flew open, and it banged against the wall. Yarden jumped up, and his hand landed on his sword hilt. I craned my neck, looking for the owner of the shuffling footsteps approaching.

"Breakfast is served!" Ciel sauntered toward us, holding a large, heavy silver tray laden with food.

"Oh, my," I said instead of *oh, fuck* like I wanted to. Yarden moved to help her with the tray, and I caught the tiniest glimmer in her eyes when she looked up at him.

As he laid the tray down on our table, Minnow came up beside him and set a smaller tray with a teacup and sugar in front of me. "From Magister Hadriel. He said this one is safe to drink with alcohol."

"Thank you," I said as I looked over the food. Yarden stepped aside as Ciel stepped up. She clasped her hands together and beamed with pride.

"Poached, peppered eggs. A pumpkin bread loaf glazed in honey butter. Fresh cherries with a glass of champagne, as I know you love them."

"Beautifully made, Ciel. Thank you. I just need one more thing, please," I said.

"Anything, my lady."

"One more place setting. For Yarden."

"Lady Keres, I couldn't—" he tried.

"Nonsense." I waved my hand at him. "Ciel, you said it yourself. I must befriend my knight. Your summation of him is true. He's very kind, and I need kind company."

Her smile lingered, but confusion dimmed the light in her eyes. She was very easy to read.

"Yes, of course, my lady. Best to make friends during your time here." She turned and walked back down the path.

"Yarden, sit back down, and Ciel," I called for her as she left. She turned with a plastered smile on her face. She quickly glanced at Yarden sitting beside me, but he wasn't looking at her.

"Don't forget his champagne, please."

Yarden and I sat in silence until only Minnow returned. She still beamed with pride over the elegantly delivered meal and chattered as she set Yarden's plate.

"It's amazing how Ciel can command the other servants. She's organized, and she has excellent taste. She specifically requested everything on this tray for you."

I smiled at her. "You are both earlier risers than I thought—very attentive. Thank you."

"Oh! My lady, that truly means so much." She curtsied. "Enjoy your meal."

Yarden still seemed shy, but I encouraged him to dig in. "There's no way I'll be able to eat this all myself, anyway."

"Thank you. I certainly wouldn't be eating so well in the barracks. Our food is the sustenance it's meant to be. Nothing so exotic as cherries and champagne." He smirked and took a sip of his drink. "Magister Hadriel sends tea for you daily. Does it actually help with the pain?"

"I think it helps with more than that. I've peeked under the bandages. My hand is healing better—faster than I expected it to." I took a sip.

"How do you know what to check for?" he asked, then shoveled another bite into his mouth.

"I worked closely with the Vigilants of my clan. They're our healers who practice ancient magic to restore both the body and spirit. In times of death, I'd perform the rites of passage for a soul as it left its body. Not as necessary as their healing skills, but more of a courtesy to my passing kin. Practicing alongside them, I learned about healing. It was comforting, knowing I could help in preventing a death as well."

His eyes were fixed on me, and he'd stopped eating.

"I'm sorry, I hope I didn't just ruin your appetite." I put my teacup down.

"Not at all. It's just..." He wiped his mouth and shook his head.

"Everyone is talking about you all the time. I hear it when I'm not at my post with you. They paint these pictures of you that make little sense."

"My people treated me similarly. But humor me, what do they say?"

He took another sip of champagne and moved his fingers toward the cherries. He paused and looked at me, his brow lifting a bit.

"Help yourself." I smiled.

He returned the smile and held it up.

"The King has many interesting things imported from other provinces. I've never had one before."

He popped it in his mouth before leaning back in his seat. After a moment of chewing, his expression jolted into one of shock.

"Bit the pit?" I laughed.

"What God would put such a hard thing in something so small and sweet?" He closed his eyes. "I'm sorry, that sounded wrong."

I laughed, and he gulped.

"You swallowed it?" I burst out laughing again.

His eyes widened. "Was I not supposed to?"

"No, you're supposed to spit it out, but it won't hurt you."

We both chuckled and then he told me, "Some say you're a witch. That you transform into a winged monstrous bird when you prey."

We both burst out with laughter. The Death Spirit liked that one, sending a tingle down my spine.

"Fuck, could you imagine?"

His eyes widened again. "Lady Keres." He touched his hand to his chest.

"Nobody guesses you use such language."

"Yeah, well, they don't know shit about me, anyway."

"True." Then he looked down and sighed, folding his arms against his chest. After a minute, he went on.

"I told you. Everyone has their prejudices. To many Baoreans, Elves can be two different people. A deer or a fox. Elves in the Eastern City, Falmaron, they're the vixens. They don't believe in the Gods or moral law or tradition. They put their trust in gold and trade. Those Elves are enterprising scoundrels. Thieves. Some say they traded their magic, heritage, and religion for economic power. They hope you are more, um, docile... like a deer. The way they see the Elves of the Sunderlands."

"Of course, they do. But Elves who don't believe in the Gods?" I asked. "How strange."

He held his hands up. "Everyone is capable of arrogance."

It was strange to imagine Elves in any position of power, outside of the forest, and taking advantage of Men. Some, if not most, Humans held the belief that Elves should be small. I guessed I'd also been trained to think of my people in a small way because of how others stifled us. Hearing we could be just as defiant and notorious.... it felt the same as it did to hear stories about the Natlantine's pirates as a kid. Cool but unreal in your world.

"Funny. Never could have imagined that one day, I'd be discussing dangerous Elves with a Man here to protect me. All while sipping champagne and choking on cherries. How fanciful."

He sighed. "Rumors are very entertaining. Some are worrisome, though."

"Oh, right. I'm a bird of prey. Can't forget that one." I chuckled.

He laughed again and ate another cherry, remembering to spit out the seed.

"Some say you'll do that to the King," he said, pointing to the cherry pit. "Chew him up and spit him out."

"Does that worry you?" I asked.

He looked around at the shaded windows embedded in the surrounding walls. He glanced toward the door before meeting my gaze again.

"Some of them say you will kill the King. Of course, that concerns me."

I leaned back in my chair. There it was—the difference between us that mattered most. Always on the other side of the door when we weren't similar. When I was a captive, he was a guard.

I schooled my expression. I desired to do exactly what they accused me of, and I wondered what would happen when I moved to do so. Would Yarden get in the way? Most likely. The thought soured my stomach.

"What do you say?" I asked.

He lowered his eyes again. "When others talk, I listen. I choose not to add to their enthusiastic cloud of rumors. What I'd say directly to you..." Amusement replaced the calculation in his eyes. "Is that you may very well shape-shift into a monstrous bird and scour battlefields for the dying." A smile played on his lips. "You're not a deer or a fox. I don't know what you are because I've only known you a very short while and under very unfortunate circumstances. I'm impressed by you, but I'm still trying to figure you out."

He looked up at the sky. "I do not speak against my King. You are smart. Some people fill their cups with poisonous thoughts which become their beliefs—people drink deeply of their beliefs. They'll refill that cup repeatedly with similar thoughts. Never bothering with other perspectives. Becoming dependent on their beliefs. It shapes how they treat people. It determines how they function. Like an addiction.

"It takes intuition and insight to break that cycle. Intellectual initiative. Which I think many people lack. Despite any drop of negativity that could poison your thoughts of me or someone like me, you've shown me you can be open-minded. That's temperance. I imagine you're in pain. As much as you want to live up to that rumor, you aren't a fool. I pray you don't drink too deeply of your thirst for revenge. That you exercise temperance; keep being open-minded. Because drinking poison will only get you killed."

18: SCARRED

Keres

"Oh, my lady, but look at this pink!" Minnow held the dress against herself and spun around, fanning out the skirt of the dress.

"Too wispy. I'm cold just looking at it."

Ciel combed out my hair and nodded toward one dress Minnow had hung up.

"That's a better choice. Emerald green to match your eyes."

It was that one, a cobalt blue one, or a deep burgundy one. Both of which reminded me too much of Berlium. I took another sip of my wine. Minnow had no problem making the bottles flow, even though Ciel said it would ruin my appetite.

"Having dinner with him is enough to ruin my appetite," I'd said. So, I drank.

Ciel didn't braid my hair. I wondered if he told her not to.

I couldn't even look at Yarden as he walked me to the dining hall. After his warning at breakfast, I was questioning whether my own life mattered more or less than what I wanted.

Was my desire to kill the King one edge of the blade? Was the other the risk that I could die in the process? It should have been scary, but it wasn't. Dying might be the price I'd pay, but if I was headed back to Mrithyn, I wasn't going alone.

Berlium stepped into the dining room as the doors closed behind me. Once again, putting that divider between me and Yarden. The King's eyes crossed clear over the heads of the footmen setting the table. There were no chains in his hands. No metal except the gold and onyx rings on his fingers. He'd worn blue. I was glad I didn't.

As the men dispersed, he pulled my seat out for me, keeping his hand on the back of it while I sat. His scent exuded from him—honeyed spice. Distracting from the aroma of the food.

His fingers reached into my hair and twirled a lock around his finger.

The hairs on my nape stood.

"Did you know that Baorean wolves have white fur?"

"They must be beautiful," I said in an even tone.

"Very." The timbre of his husky voice sent an uninvited shiver through me that landed between my legs and made me want to squirm.

He finally took his hand away and sat down. He hadn't lied. Meat littered the plate again. He made quick work of carving his into bite-sized pieces. I toyed with mine. Debating. Picking up forkfuls of vegetables in between moments of internal crisis. It was dead... what was I afraid of?

"I chose veal tonight because it isn't as bloody as beef," he said around a mouthful and shrugged. "One bite isn't going to kill you."

The words sounded so civil, but hearing 'bloody' and 'bite' from his mouth felt riotous, and so did my salivation. It smelled divine. It looked horrid.

"Oh, allow me," he said and reached for my plate.

He cut the meat for me as he had his own. I doubted it was in kindness but control. He enjoyed my reliance on him, as much as he'd enjoyed crippling me. I glared at him as he returned my plate with a smile. I stabbed a piece of the meat with my fork. His gaze followed as I lifted it to my mouth and paused.

"Keres, it's already dead. Would you dishonor its death by refusing to take its gift of nourishment?"

I looked at him. He worried his bottom lip as he watched me, his fangs glancing at me. I tore a piece of the flesh between my teeth. Chewed it slowly.

The flavor... was more delicate than I expected. Tender and succulent. I wanted more.

"See? Harmless."

It wasn't, though. I closed my eyes and sent a quick prayer up to the

Goddess of Life and the God of Earth for good measure. For forgiveness. Then one to the meat itself. A thanks for its life. Probably insufficient mental gestures, but it made me feel a smidgen better. Because it was delicious.

I thought about the Elves Yarden spoke of. The vixens who'd abandoned belief and tradition. Wondering what their first step downward was, but with every bite, I stopped caring. I cleared my plate.

"I love a woman with an appetite," he said.

I looked over at him. He'd long finished his meal and had been watching me eat. His stare was a soft pressure. The wheels of his so-called genius mind were turning.

"We want into his head," the Death Spirit chirped.

"How was your trip?" I asked, picking up my still-full wineglass and breaking eye contact.

"As they all are." He reached for a pastry on the dessert tray. "I went to my other castle, Dulin. Do you know about it?"

"I know your uncle used to sit on the throne and you killed him."

He chuckled and took a bite of the pastry. "Oh, that's good. Try one." He pushed the tray toward me, and I took one. Sniffing at its powdery crust before popping it in my mouth. It was filled with some kind of cream. He downed another, took a sip of wine, and continued.

"I take trips every so often. The most precious parts of my wealth are stored there. In my absence, my Marquis manages it. Still, I like to check on things."

I wondered if he meant that he kept a slew of women chained there as well. Is that where those two had come from, or Tecar? The thought brought up Liriene. My anger.

"This slave den you've filled with my people. What is it for? Why are you hunting and enslaving my people?"

He pursed his lips and wiped his fingers on his napkin. "Is that what you wish to speak of? Can we not enjoy our meal?"

He wiped his mouth and threw the napkin down.

"I think of nothing else when I look at you. Maybe you and your people live in a delusion, but I don't. You are a twisted creature who preys on my people—"

He slammed his fist on the table, and I flinched.

"Your people." He stopped himself, biting back his next breath and glaring. I frowned at him.

"I sent my troops into the Sunderlands years ago, and for a time, they were no threat. They bartered. I offered treatises to some clans. This may surprise you, but there are people of my own that dwell along that border. The Elves of Allanalon harassed them. The Massara clan has a unique relationship with the Baore—not always productive."

"Productive how?"

"The Sunderlands has resources I'm interested in. The Gods' Woods, for example, the timber of its native trees is valuable. Excellent for weapons. Massara also has mines in the Rift that connect with the Baore's."

"Allanalon is positioned along the River, at a point where certain plants grow. Something about the soil makes them medicinally unique. I offered the clans an exchange for shared resources. Massara agreed. Allanalon resisted. My orders were to subdue the people, and from then on, they did."

I slammed my left hand on the table. "Subdue us. By any means necessary. You let them steal, rape, and kill clan-dwellers. For what, plants and logs?"

He shoved his seat back and stood. So did I. He rounded the corner of the table and stopped before coming nearer to me.

He was an epicenter. My body reacted to him, and I hated it. My steps carried me to him, slowly. The Death Spirit wanted to lunge. Aching for the chance to go toe-to-toe with him. The irresistible aura he emanated permeated—dominated the room. I didn't stop until we were an arm's length apart.

The Death Spirit growled traitorous thoughts in my head, *"We can take him on. He is like us—he can handle us."*

"You're right," he said, leveling his gaze at me. "I did not stop my armies from their killing, raping, and stealing from the people of the Sunderlands. Not because I hate Elves, because I don't. Foremost, I'm a king. I can't go back on my word. My people's needs came before yours. I vowed to meet those needs. Which brings me to my other reason. Do you want to know why?"

"You honestly believe you have a good enough reason?" My voice came out louder than I expected. My chest felt heavy, but still I stood up taller as he closed the distance between us.

"Power." The word drummed into me.

Echoed in my mouth. "Power."

I knew it was true. It was the difference between us. He had it and I wanted it. He had the power to destroy and conquer. I wanted the power to stop him. It wasn't a worthy answer for his wanton murdering, but I understood it.

"Yes, little girl," he sighed and looked me up and down.

I sifted through my fury, searching for an intelligent response. But his eyes—I raked my gaze over him, returning the appraisal. He was hard. Once again, aroused by me. *Well, well.* I wasn't the only one fighting their body.

My hand moved before my brain thought it through. I threw myself against him, slamming my hand against his trousers, and taking hold of his cock through the fabric.

He doubled over, stumbling into me.

"Call me a little girl again," I said in his ear.

His hand went up to my throat, and mine met his there. He wheeled us around and shoved me back into the nearest pillar.

"You want to me to treat you like a woman, then?" He threatened in a thickened voice. He braced himself on either side of my head. My breasts rose and fell with every ragged breath, nearly spilling over the low-lying collar of my dress.

Softly, his fingers touched beneath my chin, lifting my face. Deftly, he swiped one over my bottom lip. My pulse was wild in my ears, I felt it in my neck, and I guessed he could see it. He took a sharp breath, as if he scented my arousal.

"I could crawl," he said huskily, "into the secret corners of your mind. And what would you do to stop me?"

My skin prickled and flushed as heat banked in my core. His eyes razed me, stripping me down. From my white hair to my toes. Peering into my Spirit while his reared back to batter through the mental wall I was trying to build. Berlium's power flowed through his touch. Tracing the curves of my neck with his fingers. Inch by inch, breaking down that wall, brick by brick.

I fisted his shirt in my hand. His eyes drove into mine, and a smile licked at the corners of his mouth.

"You're mad, my King."

His brow lifted at how I'd addressed him, and his gaze dropped to my mouth as if he wanted to see the words on my lips.

My King.

"There is no justification for what you've done to my people. You're cruel and crazed. You think you deserve power, but you're wrong."

"If that's what you want to think. Do you think you can stop me?"

Adrenaline coiled in my blood and muscles. I pushed off the wall, leaning closer so that our chests were touching. "I will."

He watched every word I said leave my mouth, reading the truth in them.

"I am the Coroner. The right hand of Death. I'm used to my armor being chipped away at by savage men. It's never made me weaker; it's made me jagged."

"Ah, yes," he replied, and met my eyes. "Mrithyn's hound. Unleashed on the earth, to dog down all the murderers and the monsters. The jaws of Death. Biting, biting, all the time. Your little fangs do not frighten me, Keres. They're exactly why I want you."

I shoved him, wishing I could put both my hands on him, and he backed up. I looked toward the door.

"You're not going anywhere."

There was nowhere to run in his castle. All that mattered was the precipice we stood on, and who would topple first.

"Did you expect me to hate you for what you are?" Berlium taunted, holding his arms out at his sides. "Because you are a broken shard of a woman? I plucked you from the Sunderlands, not because you were a rose, but because of your thorns. I'm not afraid to touch every sharp edge of you—not afraid to lick my fingers after."

He grabbed me again, impossibly fast. He placed his large, callused hands on my neck, skimming down to my shoulders, and then his skin grazed my exposed chest. Lust towed me into the wake of his hands.

To my horror, the air between us had no scent of his magic. My heart pounded in my chest and between my legs. This was a desire as visceral and natural as it could be—it was still wrong.

"I was looking for you, Keres. Another resource to be tapped."

I snorted, but it wasn't funny.

"Everything I'd heard about the monster in the forest called to me like a siren's song. My people were hunting yours—I was hunting you. Drawing you out."

"For power," I said.

"Now, you are here with me." He ran his fingers through my hair again. "Like calls to like."

"We are not alike," I growled.

"Does it frighten you? That I see you and I want what I see? That someone else understands your thirst?"

The Death Spirit luxuriated in the roughness of his voice. Leaning into his touch as he ran his thumb over the hollow of my throat. My head tipped and my eyes rolled back. My mouth ran dry. As if he touched the part of me where that cursed emptiness dwelt. The gnawing hunger.

I tried to push it back down. I should have felt vulnerable, but the Death Spirit felt naked and liked it. She wanted to be put on display, to show her colors and entice him. Wanted him to touch where we ached. He was unlike any prey we'd ever tasted—because he wasn't prey. He was every bit as much a predator as I was.

I opened my eyes and looked at him. His breath hitched. Had he seen the darkness within me? I blinked it away.

"What you feel right now. Beneath my hands. Imagine not having to be ashamed. Or afraid of what you are—what you could be. If only you submitted. Would you give me the chance to show you what was in the dark?"

He took a step back and that sound of pounding wings rushed into the air. This time it came from him and rose around us, blocking out the world until darkness settled, and we were standing in the void again. That flavor of his spell rose into my mouth, less assertive and bitter than usual. Just a hint of it lingering on my tongue.

He took another step back, his foot dropping behind him. Down a step into a pool of black water. The ripples ran away from him with a speed that matched my heartbeat. He held up an inviting hand.

"Why live a life that you had to hold in question? Isn't it exhausting, trying to figure out whether you are what you're supposed to be? Whether you're good and clean?"

Another footstep sank down.

"For people like us, it's impossible to be heroic. We weren't designed in a mold shaped like goodness or a mold shaped like evil. We were simply poured into the hollow spaces of a world that's made of both."

I took a step toward him and stopped myself. He tracked the movement and his lips curved into a tempting smile.

"Can you be molded into an instrument of power? Or will you continue trying to fit into the body that died so long ago? You're not a little girl, you're right. You're a Godling. I can make you a queen. We can be one and the same."

"We are not the same."

Dark laughter thundered from his chest. "Oh, but we are."

"I don't kill innocent people!"

"Show me a man that is innocent," he said, ripping his hand through the air.

Images flashed across the curtain of darkness. Visions of war. Of him on the battlefield. Slaughtering. Blood sprayed across the snow, and screams echoed through snow-capped mountains.

"Show me who is the judge."

The next vision was of prisoners standing in a line that led to the gallows. An executioner bringing down his axe on a guilty man. I realized we were in his mind. These were his memories. I looked at him as the world he'd lived in spun all around us, full of horror, with him as its axis.

I took a step backward.

"War is not about who is innocent or guilty—it can't be because that is gray. The only things that can be black and white are victory and loss."

"I didn't start this war. We don't want the same victories."

"But what would you be without war?" Berlium seethed. "Were you not made the Coroner because Mrithyn needed a playing piece in this game? He designed you to be part of it. How could you be part of this and be innocent?"

"No, I—I was made to be—"

"Do you even know?" He spat the question. "Or are you too busy suppressing your Death Spirit to listen to it?"

"You want me to stop suppressing it? Fine!"

"Good! Let's see who can punish who."

The vision crashed like a silent wave, and he lunged toward me. Again, he was faster, which was really starting to piss me off. He shoved me toward the table. I stumbled into the chair, righting myself as he stalked closer. My eyes darted toward the knife on his plate. I picked up the closest thing and threw it at him. He dodged, both of us moving with the same thought: the blade.

My claw clasped around it.

I whirled on him as he lurched toward me. We collided. My back hit the edge of the table and I instinctively raised my dominant hand, but the slightest graze sent pain razoring through my arm. I kicked out at his legs, and his body crashed into mine as I lifted the knife. He caught it by the blade.

I twisted it, and he hissed in pain. Even as it cut him and the blood ran down his arm, he held it there. Grinned.

I pushed against his weight, but he was fucking stronger. My shoulder ached as he pushed my arm back over my head. We held it there, at his eye level, each straining for control.

The power of the Death Spirit swelled within me—the King and I matched in strength that held for just a moment, both of us baring our fangs.

My mind dove for the scrap of Elymas' power I prayed lay within me but came up empty-handed. He forced my arm back, and I leaned onto the table with it.

He let go of the knife and latched onto my wrist, pinning it to the table. His palm was slick with blood. With his other hand, he knotted my dress in his fist and hoisted me up farther onto the table.

Berlium's eyes penetrated mine and his hair was a mess around his face. My broken hand was useless at my side, but I had an elbow that worked perfectly fine. I jabbed him in the ribs, and he fell onto me. Bringing him that much closer. I threw my arm around his neck, bringing him even closer. I'd rip his throat out.

As if he sensed my line of thinking, he pulled back as I snapped my jaws at him. I wrapped my legs around his waist and his other hand shot above my head.

He pried my fingers from the blade and threw it aside. Then he grabbed my arm that was over his neck and pinned both of my wrists against the table above my head.

Our chests heaved against one another. His pelvis ground into mine, the friction impaling me on a spike of heat. I lifted my head and looked at our bodies. He tilted his head, watching me, and thrust against me. Striking me dryly between the legs.

A cry broke my mouth open and Berlium silenced it—his mouth crashed into mine. His tongue tore through my mouth, sweeping against my own. A thread of resistance snapped within me, and I kissed him back. He deepened the kiss, stealing the air from my lungs. He was full of hunger and all-consuming rage that left fire and craving in its wake.

He tore away from me, and I met the tempest roiling in his gaze.

"Hate me all you want, little wolf. I love the way it tastes."

He took both of my hands in one of his and used the other to hike up my dress.

"Stop!" I shouted as his hand grazed my inner thigh.

"I could break this sweet body of yours open and wreck you from the inside out," he growled back. "Could you stop me?"

His head lowered, and the heat of his breath fanned against my neck. I could sense his fangs looming above my frantic pulse. My core clenched at his words, wanting to resist, wanting to feel the power of his touch inside me.

"You can't hide your desire from me. No matter how you want to resist me, I can scent the heat in your blood," Berlium said in a low voice that pebbled my skin. His hand skimmed down between my legs, pushing through my wetness, claiming it with his rough hand. He traced his fingers down my center and then ran them back up to my groin. He licked my neck, skinning me with his tongue.

A moaned purr broke free of my mouth. He growled his approval at the sound I made for him. He looked back up at me as he massaged my apex. Excitement riveted me down to the bone. My nipples were hard and chafed in the dress as I panted. I fought against his hold, but I couldn't fight the need that soaked me.

"Fight back, scream, bite. I want you to resist me because only then will you realize you can't win."

"Fuck you," I said breathlessly. I could see my reflection in his eyes. Mine flaring with anger, dilating with desire. He brought his fingers to my mouth, forcing them between my lips. I sank my teeth into him—and he fucking smiled.

His knee knocked between mine, forcing my legs farther apart, and I deepened my bite to protest. He went still. Only keeping me pinned by the weight of his frame. He pulled his hand away from my mouth. Blood oozed from the punctures my fangs created and shimmered on his skin. He licked his fingers.

Chills crawled over my flesh, up my legs. To the place where his erection pressed against me through his pants.

"No more," I gritted out.

He laughed again and then narrowed his gaze at me.

"What would you give me instead?"

I froze beneath him. "Give you—" As if he hadn't taken enough!

"Give me one thing, and I will spare your body. Although, I don't think you want to be spared."

My throat was tight and dry from breathing so hard. His eyes caressed my face, then my swollen breasts that had nearly escaped my dress.

"What do you want?"

The tips of his fangs sank toward my throat as he dropped his head closer. This was it. He wanted to drink my blood and was going to do it as adrenaline pumped through my veins.

"Give me your word," he said against my ear.

I looked up at him with rounded eyes when he pulled back. He rose, lifting me off the table to stand before him. I yanked my dress down. He reached for the knife again.

"You will never again attempt to harm me."

"I will—"

"Or Liriene will die."

My left hand clenched and my jaw snapped shut.

He smirked.

"You fucking bastard."

"Give me your good hand, darling."

"A blood pact?" I held back. "Are you serious?" Beads of sweat had broken out on my brow, but now nausea rolled through me. He was going to hurt me, again and again, until I'd stopped fighting him altogether.

He stepped closer.

"People break blood pacts as much as they break any other promise," I said, although I knew this would be no ordinary vow.

He reached out fast and grabbed my left hand. I kept my fist closed.

"This is a blood curse. One you will accept. Unless you want me to do my worst to you—to your precious sister after you."

I stopped resisting.

"My life, for your sister's. Should you ever raise a hand to me, you raise one to her as well. If you kill me, she will die. That is the promise I want from you."

"And then you'll let me see her? Will you let her stay in the castle? Or promise me she's kept safe and taken care of?"

"First, we'll see if you can keep your word. Spread your fingers."

I never took my eyes from his. Didn't cry, as he dragged the serrated knife across my palm, around to the back of my hand, between my thumb and forefinger, and back into my palm to complete the circle. Blood oozed out from my hand all around and dripped down to my wrist.

We both reacted to it, but he reveled in it. When he cut a straight line through his palm, I hissed with satisfaction. His cut was deeper, from the base of his fingers to the heel of his hand, so that it crisscrossed my cut when we clasped hands.

Red and yellow light, hot as fire, burst into life where we joined. His mouth started moving, and I heard a choir of voices swirling around us, speaking in the divine tongue.

My voice joined the multitude in the same language. My mind didn't understand what my tongue seemed to know by heart. I could taste his magic in my mouth once more. When he released me, it ended.

"Yarden!" he shouted. At that, my guard entered the dining hall. "Take Keres to see Hadriel. He'll need to tend to her other hand this time."

Yarden's attention snapped onto me, but I looked at the King.

"What did you do to me?" I asked.

"Blood for blood," was all Berlium said before turning and leaving.

19: STARK
Liriene

The pain seized me unannounced, and I cried out.

I thought it was my magic, awakening in the palm of my hand. How could that be when Berlium stripped me of it, or blocked it somehow?

Shayva and Maro didn't know what to do. I didn't know what to do. A red angry line erupted from under my skin, encircling my hand. It glowed like fire, lighting up the cave and scattering shadows across its walls. They hissed and sang in a language like Oran's, but I didn't understand it.

My skin opened along the line this magic traced, and blood oozed from it. I cried as Shavya and I both tried to smother the fire inside, applying pressure to the bleeding.

I did not hear Oran's voice in the hushed symphony of voices that surrounded me. And that's when I knew this was an attack. Someone had cursed me.

I ran. Dalis guards readied their weapons as I flew out of the mouth of the cave, but I looked beyond them, to the castle.

My hand trembled and stung, throbbing and bleeding. It felt as if someone had cut me with a hot knife.

From outside the castle, it seemed nothing was wrong... except me. I looked down at my hand. The light and redness faded. The voices faded. Still, it bled. I clutched it with my other hand and looked at the guard who eyed my injury with suspicion.

"Just an accident. I fell. Cut my hand on a jagged rock," I lied.

"You better not have anything sharp with you." The guard stepped forward and grabbed my hand. Observing the stark, bloody circle that wrapped around my hand, just below my knuckles.

"Strange mark for a rock. Search the cavern." Guards pushed past me. One barked at me to follow him. I walked alongside them and watched Shayva, Maro, and everyone else empty every rucksack and shake out every blanket. Proving there was no hidden weapon among us.

"We haven't got time to search under every pebble in this damned cave. Let it be." As they withdrew, one ordered Shayva, "Vigilant, see to her hand."

20: Surrounded
Keres

The castle blurred by as Yarden escorted me to Hadriel's chambers. I couldn't keep pressure on my bleeding hand with my broken hand, so Yarden had to hold it for me. Every step jostled us, making his calloused skin feel like a pumice stone against my open cut.

I could feel the magic still singing in my blood. The smell of my blood, sticky on Yarden's hand too. Even though every step carried me farther from the King, I could feel him. My body was a page to him, and he'd left his mark on it.

Yarden probably heard all of it, which was embarrassing, to say the least.

"Lady Keres," he started, but I shot him a silencing glare.

When we reached Hadriel's chamber, he knocked. Hadriel looked past Yarden to me. To my bleeding hand.

I forced a smile.

"God of Fury," he said and reached for me. I stepped over the threshold as Yarden stepped aside.

"What did you—" He paused and turned my hand over to see the entire wound before fetching a damp cloth for Yarden to wipe his hands. Hadriel closed the door without taking the cloth back.

"A scratch from a rabid dog," I said, assessing the clean cut. It was deep enough to scar. Not too jagged, considering Berlium made it with a dinner knife.

"The mark of the Beast." Hadriel raised his brows at me. "He cursed you. What happened?"

I averted his eyes. He dropped my hand and started flitting about the room. He gathered gauze and a basin of warm water, another poultice. Two marred hands.

"It's a cut. This hand will heal, but what about my broken one? I've been checking it and it looks better. Will I have full use of my hand in the future?"

"You'll have to exercise it when you're ready to. For now, it remains in the cast."

Hadriel gestured for me to sit. The cut bled with prodding. Hadriel placed my hand in the water and started mixing in tinctures. Blood lifted from my skin and swirled in the water, plain to see against the bottom of the white bowl.

His brows were knit together in frustration. "He's making a mess of you."

I sighed. "He's got to keep you busy down here in your dungeon."

He gently removed my hand from the basin and dried it with a clean cloth. I hissed at the pain. The skin around the cut was terribly red and it burned.

"Do you even realize what this means?"

Blood for blood. That's all he'd said.

Before I could answer, Hadriel pointed to my hand.

"For every ounce of contempt and rage you give him, he will give it back tenfold. Nothing bars him from hurting you and your sister, or your people. Nothing stops him from doing anything he wants. Likewise, anything he promises, he will give."

"Is he like me?" I asked in a low voice. "Does he serve a God?"

"He serves no one but himself. You'd do well to learn from him."

"Learn from—"

He held up his hand. "Magic, talent, or anything else the Divine can add to you does not make you powerful. It's what you're already created with. Adding one cup of water to a dried desert pool does not make it an oasis. Adding to a bubbling spring makes it overflow. Berlium is what he is, because he was born with a gifted mind." He pointed to his bald head. "He is a genius. The Baore truly prospers under his reign. His revolution is undeniable."

"Monsters aren't born, they're made. His magic is not like what Elymas grants to mages. I can sense his Spirit—it calls mine. The Death Spirit has been louder in my head since meeting him. That can't be just because he is intelligent."

"The King is a gifted and revolutionary thinker, yes, but you're right. He is so much more than that. He would show you." He pointed to my hand again. "What he gives you depends on what you give him. I can teach you things you won't learn anywhere else. Be willing to learn."

"Well, you don't have to worry about me making any attempts on his life now. This blood curse was an exchange. His life for my sister's. That I may never harm him without harming her."

He pursed his lips, mulling it over. "I see. So, you hold both their lives in your hand then." His eyes came slowly back to mine. "That begs a question. And please, I need your honest answer."

I awaited it.

"Are you willing to sacrifice your sister to kill the King?"

⌘ ⌘ ⌘

Yarden could barely keep up with me after I burst through Hadriel's door and stormed off.

"Oh, Lady Keres," was all he could get out. He cantered after me as I climbed the stairs, as if I knew the way back to my bedchamber. I didn't. I just had to get away from the Magister.

Sacrifice my sister? I knew what his question truly meant. He wanted to know I'd abandoned hope of hurting the King—if I was capable of evil. How far I was willing to go.

What pissed me off is that the Death Spirit was considering it.

"What's happened?" Yarden catches up with me.

"I'm fine. I'm just surrounded by madness."

"Do you even know the way back to your bedchamber?"

"Feel free to give me directions," I said over my shoulder without slowing.

All the flights of stairs exhausted me, but without the ability to fight anyone in the gods-damned place, I welcomed the burning ache in my muscles. That's how I made it back to the upper levels. Huffing and muttering and turning when told.

The Death Spirit was trying to reason with me, which was incisive.

"It would be for more than the death of a tyrant," my demented spirit whispered. A darker, unfeeling side of my conscience. *"But it'd be a shame to waste his life. He is like us."*

"He's not like us," I said aloud.

"Lady Keres?" Yarden asked, but I ignored him.

"One sacrifice for the good of the world?" the Death Spirit murmured.

Liriene's star-gray eyes burst into the dark of my mind. Filled with light and life.

I remembered her looking at Katrielle, the three of us sitting in my home tent in the peak of heat one summer day. Wearing our shirts knotted up and the skirts we'd cut slits into so that they opened nearly up to our hips. We spent that day lazing about, fanning ourselves, drinking cold tea to cool off. I never realized that the look in her eyes when she watched Kat pop grapes into her mouth was love.

All summer, Liri wore her hair up in this messy bun, and Katrielle was constantly pushing flowers into it. Kat knew better than to do that to me. One scowl and she'd laugh. Pick the petals right off, singing this ridiculous, nonsense song that was different every time.

I remembered one version:

"Keres is so scary, in her armor, with her powers.

She never does her hair-y, won't be caught dead with flowers.

If you're looking for a lady, better not look at Liri either—"

"Hey! I'm a lady!" Liriene said.

"She's fiery as a poppy, but she's nicer if you feed her."

I could still hear Liri and Kat bantering. Could still see Kat throwing grapes at her, telling her, *"Here, hungry. Be nice."*

Light pressure on my left shoulder brought me out of my memories. I stilled, slowly turning my head to see Yarden's gloved hand on my shoulder. I looked up at him.

"Thank you, Yarden," I said and moved away from him, toward the stairs. He followed me up to my room and stopped at the threshold.

"If you need anything, I'll be here." He put his back to the wall just, and I closed the door.

I fell asleep with my face buried in my pillow. Dreamed of Ivaia and Riordan, my father, even Attica. Relived the entire battle. Even Queen Hero appeared on the battlefield, wielding her axe. Darius wasn't there and I realized that maybe that had saved him. Osira told me that if we stayed together, he would die.

I woke up thinking about the fact that I sent him off right before I returned home. Maybe he would have died if he followed me into that battle.

Death seemed to follow me wherever I went. I wasn't a safe place for anyone. My Death Spirit reveled in it, but if I learned to wield—control her...

"We could be stronger," she said.

Midnight's darkness blanketed the room and moonlight shone hazily through my frosted window. I stayed sitting up in bed, looking at nothing in particular. Sitting there in the dark with no one around. I was what I was. Vicious.

"We can be powerful. We can take from them." The Death Spirit loved the idea of being strong and dominant. So, I made a deal with her. I would find the King's weakness and exploit it—while I grew stronger.

There was only victory or loss in this world. No innocence. That's what Berlium thought, and I'd have to think like him to beat him.

"Would you give me the chance to show you what was in the dark?"

Maybe it's where the Death Spirit would thrive. Behind these walls, the world could not touch me. I didn't have to be afraid of who I was or wasn't supposed to be. No more suppressing the Death Spirit. Mrithyn made it mine. Berlium wanted to play in the darkness. I wanted to win.

"You're a Godling. I can make you a queen. We can be one and the same."

I had enemies who wanted to make me powerful. To mold me. Who will take everything from me, strip me down bare, and build me back up. I could either take a step into the darkness they inhabited or die fighting.

I *would* die fighting. Liriene probably would, too. I looked down at my newly bandaged hand.

I could choose to be the broken and cursed captive. Or their weapon, a student... a queen. They tied my hands and offered me what lay in theirs. But no matter what either of them wanted... I still had my own demands.

I closed my eyes, and in my dreams, Mrithyn met me. Holding out his hand. Promising me I'd never go into the dark alone.

21: STEP ONE

Keres

Day Nine

This kingdom was mine for the taking, and today, I was going to stake my claim. I couldn't fight or kill the King, but I could orchestrate his downfall while I rose in power. I didn't have my scythe, but a crown—that was a weapon, too.

Ciel and Minnow took their time dressing me today, and I went with the pink dress. I could be the serpent hidden underneath a flower. Another thing I had at my disposal was my feminine charm. It was obvious the King desired me. What was the harm in playing on that? There was only one rule: no killing each other.

"I want to see the room full of sculptures," I told Yarden. His gaze snagged on my dress. I couldn't blame him. I looked delectable.

It was a soft, sheer pink. The shadow of my nipples pressed against the bodice. The shape of my hips shifted through the skirt. Ciel had twirled the locks of my hair and Minnow patted rouge on my cheekbones. It gave me a delicate, flirtatious flush.

He led me back down to the corridor that opened into multiple rooms. The southern courtyard was the last door, but the first left turn brought us through an archway and into the room full of sculptures.

An expansive collection of full-sized statues, stoic busts on pedestals, and shelves lined with statuettes and other oddities. The walls were some kind of white stone, and there were faces and people carved into them.

"Who are they?" I asked.

"These are the hallowed figures of great Baorean influencers. Kings, queens, sages, military leaders, arcanists, philosophers, and scholars.

"Oh, where's your statue?" I chided.

He smiled and turned in a circle. "Ah, this one."

I followed him over to a bust. "Wow, they've even captured your mole." I poked the stone face. He chuckled.

"This is Mathis Palades. I don't actually like him. He was a radical atheist. He spent forty of his eighty-four years traveling Aureum to visit royal courts. Trying to persuade them to forsake their religious practices, cast out arcanists, diviners or oracles, mages, even healers from the courts."

"Why?"

"Him and his acolytes believed Gods and Monsters were dangerous manifestations of the collective's imagination. That they proved the destructiveness of 'magical' thinking. He believed we could drive these beings from the world if we stopped worshiping and fearing them. If we focused on other schools of thought instead.

"He believed the 'natural order' was a lie. That we'd realize a new order. Basically, if we could create Gods and rituals and monsters and magic—we could create any reality we chose. Why choose subservience? He prophesied an era of purging and penance. The revival of logic and the dissolution of magic. We'd be paying penance to our own nature."

I furrowed my brow. "So, he wanted people not to believe in Gods... so that they could become like Gods."

He tipped his head back and laughed. "Now you see why I don't like him."

"Same."

I swayed on one foot, swinging my eyes around the room. A delicate sculpture made from a smooth, pale gray stone caught me. It depicted a lady in a flowing dress, with long locks of curly hair. Her eyes were enormous. So strange.

"Lady Vega." Yarden walked up behind me. "King Berlium's late wife."

I gasped. Her face was beautiful, but I couldn't get over her eyes, the way she stared down at me.

"I heard Ciel mention her, and I found her blank journal in my writing desk. Why are her eyes so wide?"

"She gouged them out, nearly bled out, then got sick and died..."

"What?" I spun around. "You're joking."

"Wish I was. It happened almost two decades ago. She was very young, very tall, and very beautiful. She had silver eyes, something Baoreans don't have. Born in the Herda'al Province, from the mountains. And if you look closely..."

My gaze followed his pointed finger up toward her face.

"She's Elven." The tips of her slender ears were nearly buried in the carved curls.

"I didn't even know the King had married anyone after Queen Herrona."

"Yup."

I didn't want to look around the room anymore. King Berlium's dead wife was also an Elf. "How old was she? You said she was very young," I asked.

"Seventeen. People say she started talking to herself and was constantly scratching at her eyes, crying that she'd been blinded. But anytime her ladies went to dress her, they'd show her all her dresses and jewels, and she'd only choose the red ones. So, she could see."

I wondered if it was Berlium's trick. Like when he stole my vision.

"The sculptor portrayed her with eyes that were larger as an homage to her paranoia and odd death."

Fuck. Lady Vega gouged out her own eyes to stop from seeing what he'd shown her, if my guess was correct. It was a start. It was a sliver of information I could turn into a greater understanding. Maybe it was something I could use against Berlium.

"Damn," I sighed. "So, you really learn all these things simply by listening."

"I listen closely." His eyes searched mine but filled with worry. "King Berlium has hurt you. With me standing guard." His voice sounded tight. He tore his eyes away.

"It's your duty. No one can truly protect me here, anyway."

His face turned to stone, and we just stood there staring at each other for a few breaths.

"I'm sorry that I am what I am sometimes."

"What's that?" I asked.

"Someone who can't do more than listen."

I nodded. It was the reality of our relationship. He was a knight, ordered by the King to guard me. To escort me and protect me from everything but my greatest threat here.

"If you can listen to me sometimes, when I need someone to talk to, you'll be doing a lot more for me than you know." I offered him a smile. "More than that, it's obvious you can teach me things about the Baore. The castle. Whatever I can learn is helpful."

"Well, I'm all for stimulating conversation." He smirked.

"How old are you, by the way?" I asked.

"I'm twenty-seven. You?"

"Twenty. My birthday is in mid-summer. The twenty-first day of Enith, in the Year of Strings."

He chuckled. "Ah, that explains a great deal. You're a Vertex."

"A Vertex?" I looked at him like he must be joking.

"It's a thing," he assured me. "According to Andretheoran Science. The study of celestial bodies and their influence on mortal births. It characterizes each of the ten months by one God's nature, ruled by a constellation, and also dictates our seasons. Do Elves not believe this?"

"My people connected the Gods to the seasons and to natural phenomena, but nothing like stars influencing births. What is a Vertex?"

"An Andretheoran Sign is a measure of your personality, your destiny, and it's all based on ordinances. A Vertex is a person born in Enith. Your sign is designed by the Goddess of Life, Enithura, and her constellation is the tree."

I laughed. "Sounds like nonsense."

"Ask Hadriel about it. Look at this." We walked over to a shelf that had miniature gold idols on it. "The Aurelesian Gods."

They were lined up in size order. Their faces were smooth, untouched, but their bodies and clothing were carved. The largest looked like a man with horns. His robe draped languidly over him, exposing most of his muscled chest.

"There's a pecking order in the Pantheon." He pointed at a smaller woman and man who were close together.

"The Goddess of night, Adreana, and the star God, Oran, are the Reigning Deities. Comprising the stars, planets, all that. When they created the heavens, they honored the Pantheon, by creating constellations for each God that would shine brightest at their respective turns throughout the year. Then the Life Goddess joined in the fun," he said as he pointed to a larger idol.

"Being a Fate God, she orchestrated dates and times of birth to also directly relate to the Gods, their stars, the planets, and to affect a mortal's life path. It turned the sky into a spiritual map for mortals, to help us connect to the Gods. The Gods of nature gifted the seasons for respective months. For example, Ahriman is the God of our tenth month, Aramarth, which is High Autumn. Our present month and season. His constellation is the Horn, and people born under it are called the Heralds."

"You say you only know a bit yet end up being, like, a walking book."

He laughed. "I admit, I learned what I know about Andretheoran Science in a book once. I could also be tricking you with elaborate storytelling skills…"

I shot him a look and tried to suppress a laugh.

"I'm not," he said and held up his hands. "But I could have been. And you'd have been eating it up."

"Oh, please. So, what does being a Vertex say about me?"

"Vertexes are often like Enithura." Her idol's hands were open. The idol next to her must have been Mrithyn, whose hands were closed. His was the largest.

"Creative, restless, curious, adaptable. Extremely sensitive to the influence of the spiritual world, closest to the Gods of all the archetypes. They need to feel involved in their world, too. They'd rather have one foot in the gold-lands and one in the Godlands. She's a God, right. But she's also dedicated to our world, its creation. Obviously. This makes Vertexes great catalysts of change. Doors between our world and theirs."

"Alright, know-it-all. What's your sign?"

He beamed at me. "I was born in Low Winter, in the third month, Tarinth. The Year of Drums. I'm a Ram. Typically seen as stable, perceptive, and a lofty thinker."

I laughed. "Fitting."

He smiled. "My ruling constellation is the Mountain."

"So far, you've taught me about a madman, a dead girl with gouged out eyes, and the stars."

He chuckled. "And you couldn't even warn me about cherry pits."

I laughed, but the laugh died the minute I saw King Berlium standing in the doorway. His eyes crossed the distance between me and Yarden, who took a step away from me. Berlium's stare seeped into my sheer, wispy dress.

"And you, King Berlium?" The look in his eyes lifted my confidence. I straightened up. "Do you know your birth sign?"

Yarden swallowed uncomfortably. Berlium's jaw ticked. He stretched out his fingers at his side. What's this? Anger or jealousy? I raised a brow at him and smirked.

Then he let out a snort and crossed his arms over his chest. "I was born in Morth. Mid Winter. My sign is the Twin."

"And what God rules Morth?" My brows pinched forward, realizing Yarden mentioned ten months. But the Pantheon I knew had only nine Gods.

"Why don't you tell her?" Berlium held his hand out, directing his question at Yarden. But it wasn't really a question. More like a taunt.

Yarden looked at me. "It sounds ominous, but it's ruled by the nameless God."

"The God of Terror," Berlium added. "And he's not nameless. He's just dead."

My jaw dropped. "Dead?" It shouldn't come as a surprise that he knew about the God of Terror, if it was the same God that fascinated my mother. Hadriel knew. Of course, the King knew too.

Again, his gaze traveled down my dress. "Come here."

Instantly, my feet moved to take me to him, stepping over the questions that sprang up to grab my thoughts. Yarden froze in place as I left his side. I could taste the magic in the King's command. I couldn't deny him and drifted across the room toward him. But I took my time, allowing the sway of my hips to affect him just as strongly as his words affected me.

In a room full of statues, no face was as cold as his. Rough around the edges, where dark stubble was growing again. His blue-eyed gaze was a bridge between us. One that pulled me across it.

As I stepped up to him, not afraid to close the distance, he unfolded his arms.

His hands careened over my shoulders, one stopping at my elbow and the other by my uninjured wrist. He glanced down at the cut he'd given me. The bandage didn't cover my ring—it hadn't ever been covered. His fingers trailed over my hand, and then pressed against the groove of my wrist, below my thumb. I'd seen the Vigilants touch that place in people they healed, to measure their heart rate. His touch commanded my pulse to run to him.

"I have a present for you." His eyes sparkled.

I took his hand in mine. "What is it?"

His fingers were surprisingly tentative in mine, tender even. He looked up at Yarden.

"I'll be taking her from here. You can take a break."

I didn't spare Yarden a glance, devoting my attention entirely to the King as he led me to a wing of the castle I had yet to see.

"You'll find I can be as generous as I am brutal, Keres." His voice was as dark as usual, but more delicate. He rubbed his fingers tenderly over mine as we walked hand in hand. It seemed my dress was working wonders, since he stole side-long glances at me. I kept my eyes between him and the steps as we ascended.

"I understand that there are things you want. Things only I can give you."

"Like?"

We reached the top of the stairs, and a pair of dark green doors lay ahead.

"The truth in our history—between the Baore and the Sunderlands.

Answers. Hadriel has agreed to teach you. I won't leave him alone in the task. There are things I can gift you."

He brushed my hair behind my ears.

"You've felt me. Running my fingers over your thoughts. You've tasted my power. It lingers in your mouth. It can be both bitter and sweet. One or the other. It depends on the energy you feed me. If you want me to be... unpleasant. I can make you choke."

As if he couldn't resist, his hands passed over my collarbone, meeting at my throat.

"Or, I can satisfy the thirst in you. What I am to you... is up to you. Every step you have ever taken has led you to me. You can either stand beside me or fall at my feet. The choice is yours and the consequence is inevitable."

I looked toward the doors. He took my hand again, bringing me closer to them. Watching my face as I squinted at the inscriptions written in golden paint.

"Can you read Elvish?"

I focused on the delicate lettering. "It's a story."

He hummed with satisfaction.

"About a Goddess... named Tira?"

He nodded.

"She isn't in the Aurelesian Doctrine."

"She is one the Illynads worship. The Goddess of the Writ and Wisdom," he whispered.

My brows shot up when I met his gaze. He pointed to a section of the inscription. "In Aureum, she was a lesser deity. She once served Mrithyn, as His scribe. Her task was to pen the good and evil deeds of the dead."

"*You* can read Elvish?" I asked. He only smirked and kept on proving that he could.

"One day, her hand ached from the writing. Because the good and evil deeds of mortals were endless. She stood from her podium and questioned Mrithyn. Why was this task required? His answer was that it was for the sake of both mortals and deities to understand free-will and its consequences. How it shaped the world. Then She saw how wise this was.

157

"Still, She did not understand why Mrithyn would keep this wisdom in an endless scroll. Who was going to teach it to the mortals? He favored Her for the question and granted Her a new task of ministry. Sending Her into the gold-lands to teach mortals the wickedness of their ways, and how they might please the Gods.

"Her words were both inflammatory and inspiring. Mortals are not so easily guided. Those who listened took Her words to heart, and she taught them in what She knew. Her gift to them was the written word. They hailed Her as the mother of doctrine, language, philosophy, poetry, history. Anything that could be recorded. The great storyteller.

"A new era of knowledge began. Men who wished to defend their ignorance rose against her. Texts were burned. Scholars, slaughtered. She returned to Mrithyn, asking what they could do, but He despised the consequences of Her actions. Mortals had found yet another reason to wage war on one another. They had learned to debate. So, He banished Her. As the Aurelian Pantheon did with all of Illyn, sequestering Her behind the mountains so that He did not need to look at Her."

"They erased Her from the story she wrote," I said, barely above a whisper.

He nodded. "But look at this. Now, only the earth keeps a record of mortals' evil or good. It shows in its surface, in its decay or in its flourishing. Those who wish to see the evidence of their nature must look to nature and study. This was the birth of the sciences."

His voice trailed off, and we faced each other once more.

"It goes on and on really, more than can be written on a pair of doors, but what's behind them?" He smiled and rested his hands on the ornate golden handles.

"There are many Forgotten Gods, Keres. The Forsworn, remembered by Illyn. I admire the Goddess Tira—knowledge. Wisdom. Her record of the glories and atrocities of man. Study is an endless pursuit of Her power. This is but a shrine to Her."

22: SCRIPT

Keres

An arena of books—that's what his shrine was. His gift.

My eyes followed the shelves that housed thousands of books, up to the painted ceiling. To a scene that seemed to be of Mrithyn and Tira. A dark, hooded figure and a naked woman wrapped in a long scroll that unrolled between them. He was brandishing a finger at Her, holding a scythe in the other hand. Banishing Her.

"This is my personal study," he said and led me farther in.

The size of the room was intimate, as a personal study would be expected to feel, but not a wall was bare. The wood shelves were the same dark green wood of the door, and a matching desk rested in the center of the room. An upholstered, wing-backed chair was pushed away from it.

Inkblots stained the wood between an inkwell and a sheet of parchment. Dripped carelessly or in haste. His black-feathered quill rested on the thick paper he'd been scrawling on. I skimmed my eyes over it, but it was written in another language. Not Elvish or the common tongue. The characters were unlike any I'd ever seen before.

"What are you thinking?" he asked, drawing my attention back to him.

"Oh, you're asking nicely now instead of barging into my head?"

He ran his fingers over his chin, his lower lip, and nodded.

"You are… quite the collector. I didn't expect you to be a scholar."

He looked up at the books with fondness, familiarity. As if they were his friends. I wondered how many of them spelled evil. Told the atrocities of men; whether that's why he loved them. Settled and dusty on their shelves, they looked innocent. But as I'd realized before, there was no innocence in his world.

This room was a reflection of him. Every book was a member of the army that marched through his mind. Every page he'd ever read, a weapon. And I had grown up reading the same unfinished book repeatedly. This room was the insult of my ignorance.

"All of this could be yours, Keres," he said. The lowness of his voice couldn't prevent me from startling at his words. The promise, the temptation. I craved it, yet I despised that I did. Why was this so difficult?

"In exchange for…"

"Your hand." His gaze flicked toward my left hand, my ruby ring. "If you give me your hand in marriage, I can bring you higher."

"Like Herrona? Or Lady Vega?"

His brows settled, his nostrils flared, and the muscles in his neck tensed. He withdrew his hands behind his back and threw his gaze up at the books.

"Herrona could have been something. She wasn't born with power. She created it with her intuition and with her words. Do you think when I first came to her as a grown prince, she was oblivious to what I was? I've never been a good man, but I've always been remarkable. A revolutionary."

He held his hands out and turned, taking in the room's breadth.

"This impresses you or intimidates you. This is nothing. Just a morsel of my wealth—my resources. Let me tell you something about myself, Keres. Take a seat."

I moved to the chair and sat, crossing my legs. He leaned on the desk and eyed me. A golden letter opener that looked very much like a knife was between us, but of course, it was useless with our blood curse.

"To this day, I want what I've always wanted: the power I deserve. If I cannot reach the next tier of power, if I cannot create a staircase to it, I do not deserve it. As you can see, I've never missed a step because I have devoted myself to this climb.

"Herrona understood charm meant nothing to me. I only had an interest in her mind. I can touch the mind. That is my power. Carrying brilliance, dreams, dullness, or nightmares. And more. She knew, and still she allowed me in.

"She had always been a good woman. Making herself useful to me was a chance to taste everything she was not. But that taste turned to hunger, and hunger to addiction. Although insightful, she was not impervious. Taking her as my wife would have been effortless. Until Ivaia interfered. The hold I had on Herrona was not meant to be pried open. Hadriel tried to help her, but Ivaia ruined that too.

"It left her empty. She could have been something alongside me, but you, Keres, could be everything. The energy in your Spirit is eternal. It comes from a God. It cannot run out—you cannot be emptied. My Spirit is an equal match for yours. A vessel for your out-pouring. I can return every drop to you. This exchange could be everything. I can *feed* you."

"And why would you? Why lay a crown and your wealth at my feet? Why be so generous?"

He looked at me and considered his next words.

"I want everything for the sake of wanting. I've drained resources more times than I can count. Everything runs out. A dry throat is a death wish. There is no life without replenishment. You are a well of power— you are fresh. And you need me just as I need you."

I shook my head.

"You need an equal. I don't have to be your enemy. But if you want to run or resist, I can be the villain just as easily."

The Death Spirit was simmering in his words, like they were a warm bath. His threats were just as arousing as his promises, and both were dangerous.

"You *are* a villain, and you want to be my master. You act like you're offering me freedom—free roam of your kingdom, but it's no different at your side than it would be in Tecar. You want me in your world. I'd be stuck there. A whore to fuck when you wanted. Your weapon to wreak havoc. Your pretty temptations are nothing more than lies. This—" I gestured to the room. "A snare."

"You want to go to Tecar to learn the difference? Fine," he spat.

"It's a hellhole, right? So is your mind, Berlium. There is no difference."

"Oh, darling. You don't know the half of it."

"I may not hold all the knowledge and wisdom, but I'm not stupid enough to play into your lullabies. Not without making noise. I have my own demands. You can't even meet those. I don't want your fucking books. I want my people freed. I want my homelands restored. I want my sister, safe."

He shook his head. His laugh showed me all his teeth but didn't touch his eyes.

"Do you think I care about your sister? I've determined her importance to me. It earned her a rightful place—beneath us. The same goes for your people. They were the spoils of the Sunderlands. I keep them because I conquered them. Gold, castles, people, weapons. It all goes to the winner. Your people are mine now. Your idyllic fantasies and affections do not move me, as neither are useful."

I stood from the chair. We came toe-to-toe with each other.

"Would you rather I made you obey me? I'll break your sister's limbs and then throw her in the death pits while you watch if I have to, to get you to submit. Because you can't lift a finger to me."

I grabbed him by the collar. "I'd rather kill her myself than let you torture her. You want to use her against me? Don't underestimate my boundaries. Because if you lift a finger to my sister and she dies, I won't hesitate to send you with her."

He blinked at me, and I let go of him.

"You can't hurt her, Berlium. You surrendered that card by tying your life to hers. One wrong move and your blood is mine."

And they call this man a genius.

He raked his scarred hand through his hair. "You try my patience. I'm giving you the choice and you're not seeing that. If you don't submit, I will find a way to break you."

I held up my hands, both bandaged. "You're running out of hands to bind. What's next? What you did to Lady Vega—is that what you'll do to me?"

He slammed his hands on the desk. "This is not the same. And you would do well to keep her name out of your mouth, because you know nothing about her."

The gravel in his voice, the sharp set of his jaw. Obviously, I'd struck a nerve. I lifted my chin and crossed my arms over my chest, digging my heels in.

"I'm not like any woman you've snared before. I'm not a fool."

"Your stubbornness and arrogance are dangerous, Keres."

I held my arms out. "To submit to you is to betray my people. I've been fighting their demons for years—"

"You've *been* their demon for years," he chided. "They benefited from what you are and punished you for it. Despised you."

"How could you possibly know that?" I asked.

"Because you suppress your true nature—that's learned behavior, Keres. Your people looked at you and saw something bad. That's why you're so insistent on being good. Maybe if you stopped fucking arguing with me—actually listened to the truth of what you are, instead of the lies ingrained in you, you'd see that. You've taken others' expectations to heart, and it only hurts you."

"So, what, you expect me to bow into the war you've waged against my homeland because I got *hurt*? I wasn't made to be loved, Berlium. People hate hard truths. I am the embodiment of Death—the hardest truth in life. People don't look in my eyes and thank me for the darkness that stares back at them. It doesn't change what I am, and it doesn't mean I won't be everything they can't be."

I stepped closer. "Their cruelty made my demon meaner. Stronger. Hungrier. It's dangerous. I couldn't just feed into that. You don't believe in innocence, but I do. You're right, I'm not among the innocent. They are. I'm between them and everything else. Where I was placed."

He planted his hands on his hips. The tic in his jaw hammered, and his sapphire eyes darkened to obsidian. Which was as incredibly sexy as it was infuriating. Another thing we shared.

I shook my head. "You want me to just turn on my heel and march against them? Just because you do not care about them, doesn't mean I won't stop trying to do what's right for them."

"Keres." He clasped his hands in front of his chest. "Do you want to be right, or do you want to be unbreakable?"

I stared at him, grinding my teeth.

"What?" he shouted, tearing his hands apart. "What do you want?"

"I want to be free!" I shredded the air between us. "How many times do you want me to say it?"

"Until you hear how hollow those words are."

Silence settled between us. In his mind, what he offered was an equivalent exchange, but our definitions of freedom were not the same and mine meant nothing to him.

Villain or ally. Enemy or equal.

What would he make of me if I gave him what he wanted?

He told me over and over that he'd make me a weapon, a queen. All I kept hearing was the one word that beat steadily under all the others. As steadily as his unrelenting heartbeat. I knew what he'd make me: his.

It terrified me more than anything, but the Death Spirit wanted what he offered. I closed my eyes and took a deep breath.

He said we could feed each other. I wasn't sure what that meant, but it didn't sound good. My curse married to his.

He was a death wish—as was everything my Spirit craved from him. He wanted to draw out what I'd shoved down my whole second life. He wasn't offering *me* freedom. He was offering it to my darkness. To unleash everything I've suppressed for all my second life.

There was no way out but through the darkness. He was trying to get me to jump. I didn't want to fall—I wanted to rain down on his world. I wanted to sink my teeth into vengeance. The Death Spirit was shaking my bones, willing me to jump. Telling me I'd fly.

And if I did? If my people could find safety under his banner?

I saw the dark water below, in which he stood. The void from which he held up a hand. If I didn't jump, he would tear me down. Make me his mindless servant. My fight seemed already to be lost... but there was still one bulwark I could lean against. One railing left between me and the plummet.

"I'm married, Berlium."

He turned around and gave me an assessing glare. His eyes traveled down my arm, down to my hand. His mark—and Silas' ring.

"I may not have power here, but you have no rights to me."

His lip quivered with the threat of a snarl. He opened his mouth to speak—maybe to roar, but Hadriel opened the doors and both our jaws snapped shut.

"You wanted to see me, sire," he said in his calm, wizened voice. He glanced at me, his frown-lines deepening as he swept his gaze over my dress.

It had been a pretty attempt, but all arrangements between me and the King were bound to be ugly. As he said, he had very little use for charm. In this pink, sheer, girlish dress, I only looked as vulnerable as I was. It was affection and flirtation. Both things he had no use for. Things he despised. Good to know. He'd probably respect me more in armor, or if I wore a robe like Hadriel's.

Berlium held out a hand, inviting Hadriel into the room. "We have a problem I hoped you could remedy." His eyes flashed at me, filled with contempt. "Keres is married. I'd seen her ring. Her husband isn't in Tecar. I searched through their minds."

"It's possible her husband died in the battle of Ro'Hale, sire."

"My thoughts exactly. I want that ascertained, if you don't mind."

"Certainly," Hadriel said with a bow.

"What?" I asked.

He couldn't be dead. I saw him fighting… I'd lost track of him, but he was strong. And smart—sometimes. He couldn't be dead.

"He's alive," I said.

"Oh? Can you prove it?" Berlium asked.

Stone walls stood between me and the world. If Silas was somewhere on the other side, I had no way of being certain. "I just know it."

"Yes, well, now *we* will know it," Hadriel said and took a book out from under his arm. The worn, black leather was embroidered with words I couldn't read. But I understood one thing clearly—the image of a skull.

Its jaw was unhinged, its hollow eyes staring upward, as if in horror. As if it were looking up at any would-be reader and screaming a warning.

Berlium ordered me to sit and took his place beside the chair. Leaning on the back of it after pushing me in closer toward the desk. This close, his power rolled off him in waves, crashing into me. I glared up at him and he glared back.

I wished I could do that—throw fistfuls of power at him. He smirked.

Hadriel unclasped the cover and flipped the book open, drawing my attention back. He skimmed his hand over the first page, and as he closed his eyes, every candle in the room flickered out. Except the one on the table.

It threw a feeble, eerie glow toward the underside of his face, climbed up the edges and curves of his jaw, his nose, and his brow bones. Barely reaching the gray of his eyes.

A chill ran through me, and the page hissed as he turned it.

"What's happening?" I asked.

"Hush, Keres."

Another page shifted against the one beneath it, scrolling, and then snapping into a turn.

"Speak his name," Hadriel said. I looked at him, then at the book. Another page.

"Speak it now."

My tongue loosened, compelled by something. "Silas."

Hadriel lifted his hand off the book, and the pages swelled. Fluttered, turning on their own. Back and forth, over and over. Splaying open, then hissing into another flurry. Something unseen thumbed through them. Hadriel's eyes were closed, but they moved beneath his eyelids, as if he were reading as quickly as the pages moved.

The pages whispered and seethed, sighing and shuffling.

"He's not here," a soft voice belonging to none of us said. The voice of the book sounded so much like my Death Spirit's. I shivered and Berlium's hand touched my shoulder.

"He lives still. In darkness, lost, surrounded," the book said again. Every word moved the flame on the candle's wick. The fire turned green, then black.

Hadriel opened his eyes and looked down at the book.

Still, the pages hurried. "She is here."

"Who?" I asked, leaning forward. A choir of voices echoed through the room as if all the books joined in the conversation.

"Hush, Keres," Hadriel snapped and tried to lower his hand to the pages. They repelled him, and then suddenly they stopped. Lying open on a page. I leaned in closer—it was blank.

And then something crawled up to its surface, curling and turning, diving, and rising. Like a pen scratched at it from the underside of the page. Words bloomed in a black ink that pulsed with red and green light.

A name.

Ivaia.

My skin broke out in goosebumps. Every hair on the back of my neck stood—just as I did. I placed my hands on the desk, on either side of the book. The voices hushed, and the words flourished.

"Keres," a soft, hoarse disembodied voice narrated. A breath by my ear, against my skin, in my blood. Darkness enveloped us. I felt Berlium's hand on my shoulder, anchoring me. The candle lent its light to the book, and it glowed. Pulsed like a heart between the pages.

"You gave him your magic..."

"Be gone, spirit!" Hadriel shouted.

Ivaia laughed, and the flame sputtered.

"Keres, greatness is written in the lines of who you are. In the ink of your blood. Do not fear. Awaken—"

The book slammed shut. Light flared into the room. Sweat beaded on my brow and my mouth fell open. I looked up at Hadriel. His hands on either side of the book. He was sweating too. As if our attention to the book had been competing.

"Give her back! Open the book."

He withdrew it. Once again, he'd silenced her. Rage boiled in my belly, and I moved out from behind the desk, but Berlium grabbed me by the shoulders. Hadriel only watched, his face placid.

"I need to know what she wanted to tell me. Let me hear it."

"You're not ready," he said coolly. "You don't understand the Forsworn arts or deserve its secrets."

"*Yet,*" I growled as I jerked free of Berlium's hold and stood there seething.

This was it. A taste of the power on the other side of their offers. Something forbidden, something dark. It held answers. Answers I needed. Knowledge was a dangerous thing. The Goddess Tira was enough proof of that. She was banished by the Pantheon, and he called this Forsworn magic. It belonged to these forsaken Gods.

Hadriel practiced it—it answered him.

Berlium knew this power.

I needed it on a visceral level.

My body shook with need, my palms sweating. I wiped my brow. That magic had touched something atavistic within me, and my claws slid out. Wanting to touch it back.

Hadriel noticed and turned to the King. "We have our answer, sire. Her husband lives."

I snapped my attention onto Berlium. He rubbed his jaw pensively. "Then we must leave."

"Where are we going?" I barked.

Hadriel nodded and turned to leave.

Berlium met my eyes. There was no light in them. Only darkness— the look of hunger. Only Silas stood between us now, and he had a resolution in mind. A new conquest, with me as the celebratory feast.

"We're going to the Sunderlands to see the Queen."

The memory of Seraphina, Silas' mother, flashed into my mind. Her attempt to annul my marriage by beseeching my cousin and accusing me of adultery. Hero could sever our union, and she probably would after my betrayal.

I wanted what he had, but I didn't want to marry him. My stomach twisted into knots, my wants warring against each other.

"When?" I asked

He stepped closer and pointed his eyes down at me. "Go to your room. Pack your things. We're leaving in the morning."

"No, I won't—"

He grabbed me again and shook me. "This is your last chance, Keres. Fight me and I will fight you. Give me the vile poison of an adder's tongue, and I will give you my venom as well. Is that what you want? For me to addle your mind?"

"No," I breathed.

"What do you want?" he repeated the question.

I looked up into his eyes, and realization shifted through his. He could see my answer. He could feel it boiling in my blood, singing the way his did.

"We want what you have, Grizzly King. Everything you have."

A deep growl of satisfaction rolled through him. The sound stopped my shaking, calling to me in a very similar way the Forsworn magic did. But his call was to subdue me. The magic was uplifting. I pulled away.

A dark smirk took his mouth.

It was a dance, taking from him, giving what he wanted, and resisting still. I couldn't help but fall into the steps. I wanted what he had, but not him.

"Then go to your room," he bit out each word. "Pack your things and get a good night's rest. We leave tomorrow. I have an audience to hold, and then I will come and get you. Be ready."

23: SOLITUDE
Keres

"Fuck!" I hit the floor with my left hand. I knelt in the middle of my bedroom.

Maybe he was right about us being well-matched. In the worst ways. Berlium is relentless and insatiable. His need for power and control truly rivaled mine. We could go toe-to-toe in our thirst and slake each other. Even though he'd hurt me, he had not broken me. I was angrier—more determined.

Was Ivaia right? I gave him my magic unwittingly? I was more than that though—a girl who spits fire. He wanted me to prove it to him and myself. Was Ivaia wrong about Hadriel spell-binding Heronna? Maybe she lied. Either way, my family's enemies had caught up with me.

It takes a monster to fight a monster. I could be that. Power can give you a cage or a crown—I didn't belong in a fucking cage. Whatever he was, we were both made in the shadows of divinity, and I knew it in my bones.

For too long, my world—my mold—was too small. Like they said. Now, my Spirit was waking up and stretching. I was alone in the Sunderlands. A cursed girl. My desires were for love and revenge then. Now, they were darkening.

I could be like the Gnorrer of Trethermore Glade. The strange, deadly creature Darius and I killed. Its power was illusive. Its toxic fumes altered our minds, made us believe the glade had rotted when it hadn't. Berlium's gift to manipulate the mind was the same. It was all I needed to understand to start taking control back, inch by inch. By giving him the illusion of power over me. I could learn to play that part. His wife.

The thought of my marriage to Silas being annulled... it didn't matter how I felt. My anger helped me over it. Berlium's hold on me would be uncontested, and if I was going to commit to this false surrender, I'd need to release that defensiveness. I'd need to cloak my hatred in honey.

Like him, a devil that tasted like heaven.

I'd convince him he'd won.

The freedom to leave this room was bigger than I realized. It was freedom to learn the castle, as I'd done so with Yarden today. Freedom to learn the King, learn his domain, his Province. I'd find the way to save my sister, our people, and myself. He *was* offering me a kind of freedom.

I'd be his, but he'd be mine. If he believed me, he'd give me more... he'd make me his queen. Being a rebel could not hold a candle to what being a ruler could do for my people.

It wasn't guaranteed he'd allow me to have much control over his armies or sway over his court, but isn't this what he wanted me for? To be his greatest weapon? The Coroner and legal heir to the Mirrored Throne of the Sunderlands... now Queen of the Baore.

"Fuck." I wiped the burning hot tears from my face.

"We weren't made to be weak," the Death Spirit encouraged me.

Like Hadriel said, my true source of power had to be who I was, not just what I'd been given. And as I looked at my ruined hands, the ring, I knew I was better than this. Ivaia taught me better than this. Mrithyn promised He wouldn't leave me. I had to make powerful choices.

I stood up and walked over to the mirror. I growled at myself, staring myself down.

"Keres Nyxara Aurelian." I pointed my finger at the mirror. "A warrior." I shifted my weight over my feet, squaring my stance and my shoulders. It felt incredibly awkward, but I had to do it.

"I am fire. I burn without fear." Just like Ivaia taught me.

I wiped my eyes and resettled my gaze on my reflection. The Death Spirit was staring back at me through abysmally black eyes. The rest of me remained unchanged... but my eyes. I leaned in closer to my reflection. In the depths of my eyes, rivers of electric blues and purples, like lightning, coursed.

"Hello, monster." The Death Spirit's hissing voice laced my own. Hearing it out loud for the first time since the battle for my clan.... It felt good.

I raised my chin and my voice. "I am an instrument of the Divine and I am going to bring this fucking kingdom to its knees."

"Curse your God and die," a voice whispered in my ear.

I jumped and spun.

"Who's there?" I shouted. "I've heard you before. Who the fuck are you?"

A chill clamored down my spine, so I stood up taller. "Who are you?" I asked again. "What are you, scared? Hiding from me like a little bitch."

I sensed in the pit of my stomach that I wasn't alone. I stood back-to-back with my reflection, scanning the room. Every shadow seemed to flinch; every stretch of afternoon light seemed to shrink from the room. And the quiet bustle of life beyond my window stiffened until all was silent. My heart beat against my ribs as the wind knocked against the window.

And then it made itself known.

Much like the presence of Mrithyn... but violent. It crouched in the corner, emanating rage. The presence grew stronger. I reached my left hand back against the mirror to steady myself and closed my eyes.

I could meet with Mrithyn when I dreamed. Whatever was here, it was with me, but I wasn't dreaming. With my mind's eye, I saw some distorted version of the room. It was dimly lit and burning hot. Darkness blurred the shapes of the furniture. Thick smoke burned my eyes. I peered across from the room. Where that presence felt heaviest.

Faceless... or shadowed, with its head tilted up at me. I knew it was tall by the length of its legs—crouched down with its knees next to its ears. Its hands were flat against the floor, and it had ten fingers on each hand. Four arms. Dark-red flesh tightly stretched over a disjointed body.

It rolled its head to the side and growled as another head erupted out of its shoulder. That one had the face of an old man. Crying, distorted with pain. It spoke in a guttural voice, unintelligible words.

Out of its mouth, another body crawled. Wriggling its shoulders through until the jaw unhinged, and I heard it crack. It threw itself forward, birthed out of its second head, and landed on the floor in a nasty splat. I jumped back, banging into the mirror. The body was wet, bloody or sticky, and it lurched itself toward me, crawling on its belly in jerking movements.

"Stop," I commanded.

It did. I looked back to the first body. It covered its face and shook its head. Sighing and rumbling as it crouched there.

"Don't you growl at me," I said.

Both bodies started laughing. The one nearest to me, prone on the floor, rolled over. It looked up at me and continued laughing. Its face looked like a dead boy's, bloated and smooth. They both changed their language to one I could understand, and each of their voices was different. The first was gravelly and deep. The second was tight and high.

"I have secrets to share. Do you want to hear them?"

The Death Spirit hissed.

"No, I don't want any part of you." I raised my hands. They weren't bloodied or broken.

The child-like creature bolted upright and crawled back to its original body, hiding behind its knee.

"I told you… to curse your God and die," the elder one groaned.

"Never." I stayed leaning against the mirror. "I do not want to know your secrets. You're pure evil. You're not like Mrithyn. I don't want you here. So, leave."

"You are right; I am not like Mrithyn. I am the God you fear. Bow like the servant you are," It hissed and stood up. The faceless head tilted toward me again and the second head with the old face tipped back, lax.

"I do not bow." The Death Spirit's voice rang out with my own. "Mahrena ath Carenar."

I am the Coroner. "You have no power over me."

"You have no power," It replied.

"That's a lie."

"Elymas has forsaken you. Your magic is dead and cold." The child reared its head around the leg of the elder. A snarl played at its blue lips, and its dark blue eyes glistened with hatred.

I couldn't compel it to leave. There was no running from it. I felt that if I opened my eyes, I'd lose sight of it—bad idea.

"Who are you?" I lowered my voice. "What do you want?"

"What do *you* want?" The voice snapped. The heat in the room intensified, and the shadows deepened, stretching between us. The creatures seemed to get farther away. I didn't budge from my mirror. Faces of my dead loved ones flashed before my eyes, but I shook them away. Instead of rising to it, I stayed quiet.

"If only you'd bow, I could grant you the freedom you crave."

I didn't speak.

"I heard you in your room. You said, 'I am,' and I came to tell you I, too, am what I am."

My mind was buzzing with questions, but the Death Spirit bristled within me. I could feel Mrithyn with me, His touch a warning chill. Pebbling my skin. Telling me not to speak. It echoed Berlium's words, but this wasn't the same.

It growled again, annoyed by my silence. It shook its head and body like a wet dog and moaned as more heads and limbs grew out of its shoulders and stomach. I didn't make eye contact with any of them. I stood silent and unwavering. So, it filled the silence with booming, screaming, and agonized voices.

I looked to the door, listening for any sign of life beyond, but I knew I wasn't truly in my room. I was in the Godlands, across the Veil. In the Other. Just like I'd been with Osira when I touched the tree. I had an inkling that keeping my hand on my mirror was tethering me to the mortal world somehow... or opening the door to this one.

"I am strife. I am the ruination of all. Havoc and corruption. The spark of all flames, the bringer of all wars. The God of destruction and chaos."

"Ahriman," I breathed.

"Yes! Bow to me. Swear to serve me, and I will spare you."

I furrowed my brow. "I serve Mrithyn and no other master."

"Lies," Ahriman says. "You had the power of Elymas as well,

Coroner. Double-blessed by the Gods. You've been stripped of your gift of magic. Still, you are so much more. Let me bless you with hands that can bring war, bring change."

My stomach hardened as I tried to absorb what it claimed. "What do you mean? Is my magic truly gone?" I couldn't stop myself from asking that.

"You will submit to my power, and I will give you the answer."

"No thanks," I said in a steady voice.

Fire burst into life, filling the darkness and illuminating its faces. "Choose who will be freed. Your beloved people or yourself. You will not get both if you do not bow to me."

Mrithyn's presence was stronger now.

"Where were the other Gods when your mother was killed? When your father fell in battle? Where will your God be when the King ruins you?"

Despite the fire raging around us, I shivered. I didn't know how It knew about those things. I didn't know how It had channeled me and heard me. Had It always been watching me and waiting for the chance to attack? It spoke against Berlium, which meant It wasn't him.

"It would be easier to curse your God and die."

"Look behind me, Ahriman. See Who is standing at my back now." I stepped forward.

In place of the mirror, I felt Him there. Cold darkness crawled along my skin. His shadow stretched out, cast by the flames. The silhouette of massive angelic wings sprouted from my small shadow.

At that, Ahriman retreated. The voices silenced, and the room was empty. I opened my eyes. Too soon, Mrithyn faded from the room. But I was still safe, knowing He was never truly gone... just like He promised.

Taking in a deep breath, I turned and looked in the mirror. My eyes were green again. I wanted nothing more than to leave the room, to run. I looked toward the door.

"Yarden?" I ran to it and knocked. "Yarden, are you there?"

"It's Anselm. Be quiet," a gruff voice said.

So, he hadn't even heard me? Anselm was an asshole, but his job was to protect me. If he'd heard me in distress, he would have had to respond. I huffed and walked toward my bed. The book Hadriel had given me was at the foot. I picked it up and flipped through the pages, and found what I wanted toward the end of the book.

Ahriman, The God of War and Chaos.

The ruination of all. The spark of all flames, the bringer of all wars.

Chills ran rampant all over my body. I sat down on the bed and pulled the blankets around me. The more I read, the worse I felt.

It's still unclear whether Ahriman chooses mortals to be His lone servant or if, like Oran, chooses many. It wouldn't be beyond me to think that all mortals are the servants of Ahriman, unwittingly. Is His nature the same as the chaos all mortals can breed?

If so, how can one ever hope to defeat the nature of mortals, or their divinely inherited nature from the Father of War?

Can mortals be taught not to war, not to cause strife, not to fall or err? Is chaos not our first instinct?

We come into this world screaming, fighting for air. We fight all our lives. We fight for air in our dying moments.

Is living not War against Death?

Death must be the eternal, natural enemy of War. Men do not fight to die. They fight to live, to conquer. War is the perversion of Death's power. For those who win the battles, end the lives of their enemies. They take Mrithyn's power in their hands when they reach for their swords. They outcry Mrithyn's voice with horns and drums. Heralding bloodshed. Does this make Mrithyn weep? For, where Death is the peaceful submission of a soul, War is its defiance.

I skim the page and find a description—this one written in my mother's hand.

If one has seen the face of their father, their brother, their son, they have seen the face of Ahriman. As War may begin in any heart, War wears any face.

That entry had me slamming the book closed. All its faces. Elder or child, anyone could wage war. Ahriman truly was here. He also fled at the sight of Mrithyn. Natural enemies. That made me feel both better and worse. I looked across the room to the full-length mirror and wondered at Yarden's words again. Vertexes, born under the Tree of Enithura, were the most sensitive to spirits. One foot in the gold-lands, one foot in the Other. I'd need to learn more.

I was a warrior. I'd been on the battlefield, in the blood frenzy. My wrath was real. My hatred was real. I couldn't forget that, only hide it. Like Herrona, I cared for my people. But where she was known for her beauty, I was known for brutality. If I could stand before Ahriman and watch Him tremble at the power in my corner, then I would no longer be afraid of Berlium.

24: Surrender

Keres

Day Eleven

The throne room was packed. King Berlium entertained an array of guests, from noble to plain.

On the way from my room, Yarden explained the purpose of this audience was for people to voice requests and problems for the King to resolve. It hadn't started yet, though. I glanced around the room, noting the fine dresses and suits some wore, and the worn, dirty clothing others wore. Everybody was Human. With my hair down, my ears were less noticeable.

This was a public appearance of the Coroner—in her enemy's throne room. I'd rehearsed my announcement.

Everyone kept to the outskirts of the room, making a space in the center. I assumed it was for people to step forward, to have a stage for their audience with the King. There were guards everywhere. One of which I recognized from the day they brought us from Tecar. They were holding up the edges of the room. I hesitated, hidden in the crowd, when I saw my target.

"Are you sure this is what you want to do? He hasn't seen us, we can go—" Yarden tried to recant my plan.

"I'm sure." I let go of his arm and walked forward, apologizing to people who moved out of my way.

This man told me to go to my room like I was a child. To sit and wait. Like a dog. Not happening. I was making the first move.

King Berlium lounged on his throne, speaking with Hadriel, who was leaning in closer to him. His eyes were distant, disinterested in the room full of people who seemed obsessed with him. Women stared and talked in groups, giggling and eying him. Even men watched him as they made conversation and awaited his attention.

The idea that anybody could look at him and think he was merely a king was impossible. Berlium looked like a God on his throne. He dressed in all black, still not bothering to button his shirt all the way up. The cold daylight breaking through the window behind the throne washed him in an ethereal glow. He drummed his ringed fingers on the armrest of his throne.

Physically, he was intimidating. But the way his power snaked through the room, coiling in the shadowed corners, and licking up the walls, it was as terrifying as it was exhilarating. The energy of the room was pulsating to the same rhythm of that steady drum in his chest. I locked my senses on him.

His nostrils flared, and he sat up, looking around. Hadriel pulled away, and their attentions shifted. Here we go.

I stepped out into the center of the room, and all attention trained on me. The room went silent, and my shoes clicked against the stone floor, drawing the King's ocean eyes down to my feet. He narrowed his eyes as they lifted, taking in the details of my blood-red dress. Hadriel looked at Berlium, but the King was focused on me.

I dropped to my knees in the middle of the room and bowed my head. My long white hair fell forward around my face, draping over my naked shoulders. The skirt of the ruby dress flared out around me, catching the sunlight on the gold beaded appliques. I watched my chest rise and fall, my cleavage on display with the low V-neckline. Hushed whispers fell over the crowd.

"My King," I said and looked up into his eyes. The corner of his mouth twitched, and his eyes sparkled with realization.

"I come before you as the Coroner. To make a request on behalf of my people and the Sunderlands."

"Go on," he said in his deep, dark voice. His eyes trailed over me again and grew hooded with desire. I felt heat rise to my cheeks. The rest of the room fell away.

"For too long, our provinces have been at odds. Our borders, broken. Our bloodlines, enemies. In the end, yours has prevailed. My people are now held by you, and you've offered me the opportunity nobody before me has taken. To become your ally."

The people murmured, and he waved a silencing hand.

"Fighting between our people is foolish when together we can be so much more. I do not hold a throne in the Sunderlands, but I have the favor of a God. Together, we can strengthen both our people. United. I will fight for them and for you, if you'd allow me to. Let me claim our place in your revolution."

I looked down at my ring. "I also come before you as a woman."

When I met his eyes again, he smirked.

"In you, I see more than an ally. I see a match," I said.

I looked around the room, taking in the expressions of the audience. Ranging from wide-eyed to grimacing to confusion.

"People look at me and see darkness. Their views have held me in my past and in contempt of what I am." I looked back at him, and his gaze softened. "In you, I see a future where I can be what Mrithyn made me to be. But also, one where I don't have to be alone. Tell me, my lord, how long have you felt alone?"

His eyes darkened, and the corners of his mouth dropped slightly. It was answer enough.

"Neither of us has to endure it any longer. I want nothing more than to..." I steadied myself. "Than to be yours."

"A change of heart," he said, his expression smoothing.

"Yes, my lord. To prove it... I will make you one more promise." I held out my left hand, showing him my wedding ring. The blood-drop of a ruby shone in the light. I couldn't take it off with my broken hand, so I held up my left hand to him. As if I were swearing. Which I was.

"I'll exchange this vow, this ring, for you."

The women and men around me chattered, but I ignored them, focusing only on him. His eyes lingered on the ring, and a smile crept into the corners of his mouth. I looked at Hadriel. He watched me, his face expressionless.

Berlium had intended to pry this ring from my finger, but I'd taken control. I was going to give it.

He stood to his feet, and the energy of the room lifted onto its toes. The sunlight gilded his frame, making him look even more unearthly. I kept my focus on his silhouette as he walked toward me.

"Yes," he said. He was standing before me now, but I stayed on my knees, looking up into his eyes. Desire flared within me, and it wasn't a lie. Even if I was giving him what he wanted to hear.

"Keres, you knelt before me, a girl. Rise now. For, I will make you my queen." He extended his scarred hand.

Slowly, the room filled with applause as I stood. He drew me into his arms, and I wrapped mine around his neck. Fully giving myself, greedily taking him. Our kiss felt as binding as the blood curse.

We kissed like we were going to war—not becoming allies. A hunger for him consumed me. This time, he did not taste of honey and blood. There was no manipulation, no tricks or illusions—except mine. A tasteless, secret.

Berlium didn't care that we had an audience. His kiss stole my breath, as if he thought I didn't need it. His hands cupped my face, grazed down the sides of my throat. I held onto him, keeping him as close as he could be, as need erupted through me. There was a promise of power in his kiss, and I was starving for that feeling.

He pulled back. Light swirled through his sapphire eyes, taking my breath away. He looked down at my hand and slid Silas' ring off my finger. Laid it in my palm for me to do what I wanted with it.

My reflection in his eyes looked like a new person. Without a trick of magic, I saw what he saw. And then he gave me what I wanted... his belief.

"I will give you more than a crown. I will give you wings."

Although I told myself not to be afraid, I wondered what toll I would pay for following him into the dark.

25: STRONG DRINK

SILAS

Night Eleven

From a young age, Keres and I were told we would wed one day. Our tutors and families said we'd be like the princesses and knights in storybooks. Then she died. I was nine years old.

She was only seven when she became the Coroner. The way I looked at Keres changed—she wasn't the storybook princess. She was the monster.

The first time I saw Moriya, I was eleven years old. I felt a boyish fascination with her. The color and length and smell of her hair. The softness of her skin. The lightness of her gaze. Her voice. I hadn't looked at Keres that way. I kissed Mo for the first time when I was fifteen. She let me touch her for the first time on my sixteenth birthday.

It wasn't really until I was about eighteen and Keres was sixteen that I saw something like desire flicker in her when she looked at me. It was a crush. Something I'd seen in Moriya years earlier that hadn't dulled since, but my interest in Moriya had.

It was the most normal thing I'd ever seen in Keres' eyes since she came back from the dead.

When I finally saw that change, I knew I'd never look at Moriya the same way again. Mo still took me to her bed, seeming to grow more obsessed with me. She could sense my attention slipping out of her grasp and was desperate to recapture me. I loved being wanted, but I never loved Moriya. I was waiting for Keres, still holding back.

The night the nine went out, Darius, Thaniel, and I were on guard duty on clan grounds. Instead of standing at our separate posts, we met somewhere between them and stuck together. We sat in the dark around a ridiculously small fire. Smoked and drank. Instead of actually guarding the camp. All there was between our sleeping people and the terrors of the night... was us, squatting amid the trees.

I laughed at the memory.

Drunk, I'd brought up Keres. Of course, I'd done so many things wrong before even marrying her. Thinking I loved her was one of them. That night, I'd told Darius I loved her. Darius must have seen through it, but he admitted something I didn't expect.

"I think I'd do just about anything to fucking feel that way."

He had fucked one girl in Ro'Hale and one in Massara. Neither of them knew about the other, of course, and neither truly cared about him.

"For way too long, I've burned with just... this rage. Toward my father, toward myself, toward this fucking war. And I'd like to know what it feels like to burn for someone for once.

"The females I've been with, I feel like they've looked at me like I'm a piece of meat. Which, I am a delicious piece of meat. But I just felt used. They like my hair, my eyes, my muscles—" He paused to flex, and I'd rolled my eyes at him, "but they don't have fire in them for me or anything for that matter. They're full of this fluttery light." He shivered with disgust. "I feel like they don't even see past the surface of me. Also... pretty sure that if they did, they wouldn't touch me. If they knew what the fuck I am."

Thaniel and I didn't know what to say to that. It made me realize I had kept my distance from Keres because I knew what she was. The Coroner.

I wouldn't just marry the clan leader's daughter, an heiress of the Mirrored Throne, or even just a girl from home. I'd be wedded to something I feared. Deep down, I'd known all along, but when Darius said that... he was right. We don't reach out and touch the things we fear.

Darius wasn't afraid to, though. Whatever darkness lies in Keres, it called to the fire that burned in him.

The last time I saw her was during the battle. She was standing on the brink of the clearing. Her face was pale with shock. I'd never seen her freeze before. The horseman was racing toward her. It surprised me I'd even made it to her in time to push her out of the way.

When Ivaia's pillar of fire erupted into the sky, I wasn't sure what had happened. Then we heard this... voice. It shook the earth and Indiro and I grabbed onto each other to stay steady. Screaming and growling, layered with high-pitched and deep tones. Speaking some strange language. I caught the one word I knew, *Carenar*. At that moment, my eyes found Keres.

The battlefield splintered at the wave of her massive scythe. Her white, long hair whipped around her in a windstorm of her magic. Her footsteps burned into the ground and left embers glowing in her wake. She was everything I'd feared she was... and I couldn't look away.

I thought I was crazy as I saw shadows playing around the edges of her body. Trailing over her shoulders and twirling through her hair. For a split second, I thought they twisted into the shape of wings. She was wildly magnificent. She was some dark angel of Death and all the living souls in her path paled.

In the next moment, I'd been hit over the head by a sword pommel that failed to knock me out. Indiro was no longer directly at my side but fighting someone far off to my left.

Her terrible voice was piercing through my throbbing head. Then it stopped. She went quiet and the shouts of victory rang through the camp. I didn't dare turn around, engaged with three soldiers who didn't seem to care about what was happening in the eye of that storm.

The climax of that battle had crested, and we were lost to the outer rings of its ripple. Where men fought for the sheer pleasure of bloodshed, where no one cared about victory or loss. Just killing.

That was the moment I realized what Keres truly was. She wasn't a depraved predator. Everything people said about her being God-like was true. She wielded Death. Her voice called Life into question. I didn't understand the language she spoke, but I understood her words were some kind of Death Law. Once she fell, everything sank back into chaos. And we all fell with her.

Now Keres had been swallowed up by the jaws of the Baore. Darius was Gods know where.

In the dark Shadow Guild library, I leaned back in my chair, enjoying the feel of the leather on my bare back. I'd broken into a sweat thinking about that day. There was no running after her, no saving grace left on that field.

I thought I knew what Keres was, and I feared her. I thought I knew what Darius was, and I judged him. But when I saw how beautiful she was, how divine her purpose was, whatever I felt for her turned to worship—except she wasn't here for me to show her that now.

I frowned against the neck of the liquor bottle before taking a swig. I wondered if Darius, in his true Daemon form, was something fearsome, too.

For a breath, I felt extremely small. Just a drunk guy, ruminating in the dark of a musty library. So, I swelled myself up with another draught of liquor. I'd been down here for hours, staring at nothing—feeling everything. Watching the memories like a play.

Torturing myself with the thoughts of what happened between Keres and Darius in Ro'Hale. About how she would have compared her first and only time in bed with me, with him. Liquor's burn couldn't dull that sting.

The deeper I drank, the deeper my imagination went into detail. I'd only been with her once. Had he been with her more times? Did he know more about her than I ever would?

They'd taken each other from me. He was like a brother to me all these years. His friendship had always been on my side of the wall between her and I. Until he determined to break down that wall himself and buried me in the rubble.

Exactly like he said. *I'd do just about anything to fucking feel that way.*

I deserved to feel the pain that bubbled up when I was sober—it dulled the frustration of watching Thane do nothing. Night after night, I drank deep of my feelings and drowned out the cruel truths in my thoughts. Just like tonight. This place was in no short supply of drink or darkness.

Every night I tell myself I'll spend tomorrow dry. When the morning comes, I'm dizzy enough. It keeps the memories at bay. As the day drags on, Indiro drags me back to reality. Forcing me to study books in the Guild library. I knew it was to keep me off Thane's back.

Another male who's supposed to be fighting for her.

When night comes, so do the daemons and dark angels. I'm no match for them or for my drink. Every night, I pour my feelings into the bottle until I'm empty. Tonight, the room swam, and someone materialized from the shadows.

"Get up and follow me," the man said, a strange accent tightening the syllables.

"No," I sighed and rubbed a heavy hand over my face. He approached as I placed an empty bottle next to my feet and picked up the next.

As I uncorked it, the darkness edged my vision. The dimly burning lanterns faded. I raised my eyes up to the hooded figure and rested the uncorked bottle on my thigh.

"Now," the man said again. His hood hid his face, and the dim lighting didn't tell me who he was. It wasn't Thane or one of his men. I'd never heard his accent before.

"Who the fuck are you?" I asked.

"Aiko," he said curtly. "Now, don't make me repeat myself."

"Where are you from?"

"Chiasa," he whispered.

"Chiasa? Never heard of it."

Two firm hands clamped down on my shoulders and pushed me out of my seat. The bottle hit the floor, spilling the last of my liquor and then rolling away.

"Aye!"

"Chiasa is my sister," Aiko corrected me as his sister shoved me forward. I stumbled toward him.

"Come," he said as he turned.

"Where are we going?"

Neither of them answered. When I drifted, Chiasa goaded me forward. If I turned to look at her, she stepped back into the darkness. I couldn't even hear her breathing, or either of their footsteps.

"Are you a Shade?" I asked.

"You are in the Shadow Guild, Silas," Chiasa answered. "What else would I be?"

I turned, and she finally met my gaze. Her eyes were golden, gleaming at me from under her hood. A smirk played at her lips. I tripped over my feet, looking at her.

"Keep going," she said, clipping her words. Her accent was like her brother's but sounded prettier coming from her mouth.

"Yes, ma'am," I muttered and turned back to find Aiko glaring over his shoulder at me, paused before a door.

Despite the alcohol, some deep-seated Elven instinct woke up. Knowing I was alone with Humans, following them into the underbelly of the Guild. If they even were Human. Most people here were.

"Beyond this door, you will no longer be a stranger in this guild. We're bringing you in," Aiko said in a softer voice.

"Huh?"

Aiko opened the door. Light and music leaked out into the cold, dark library corridor we lingered in.

I hesitated, staring at Aiko, and he stared at me. His eyes were like Chiasa's, but more bronze than gold, and they were full of a language I did not speak.

I was taking too long to move, to cross the threshold, but something in Aiko's stare told me I was allowed to feel unsure. He was watching my face as his words registered in my mind.

We're bringing you in.

Those four words... it was like I'd never heard them before. The light beyond the door felt brighter, the music that filled the silence between us, louder. The more I stared at him, the more I believed I had no right to enter. He waited anyway.

I was an outsider. A stranger. We both knew it, but by opening this door to me, Aiko was taking away the unknown between us. Between me and the Guild of Shadows. He was bringing me in, which meant he was bringing me out of something as well.

He gave my feelings an explanation when he said, "Tonight is not the last night you'll live in the dark, but it is the first night you won't be alone with your shadow."

Something twisted in my gut, and the feeling made me want to vomit. I didn't deserve admission into the Guild. I wasn't even sure if I wanted it.

Aiko finally turned and walked into the room, leaving my next step up to me. Chiasa brushed past my shoulder. I stood there stupidly. She turned her head, a smile sneaking into the corner of her mouth and her eyes shimmering gold.

"Well? Don't you want to know what it's like?"

What a question.

Without waiting another breath, I took my first step toward its answer.

26:SHIFT

Osira

The Ambush

We'd been traveling for eleven days without Rivan when our camp was ambushed. All I could do was listen.

Cesarus had tried to fight them off when they attacked. It was dark. They had dogs of their own. His yelps, barks, and growls got lost in theirs and the fight. It surprised me the way Nadia swore. Not just a lady with lip rouge in her bag. I heard her unsheathe a blade, and she grunted as she fought. I knew Dorian carried a knife as well. I couldn't fight.

In the end, we were bound and towed away in wooden cages on rickety carts. Jostled so bad my body hurt. Gods knew where they were taking us. We traveled for another full week.

They spoke a language unlike any I'd heard before. I wasn't sure whether they didn't understand us when we questioned them or were simply refusing to answer.

Every night they threw us dinner scraps. Terrain seemed to change the farther we went. The cart tilted and jostled worse, as if we headed uphill. The higher we climbed, the colder it got. Dorian and Nadia occasionally whispered to me about changes in our surroundings.

We were in the Moldorn, traveling up a steep pass into the Rift Mountains. They told me I was lucky I could not see how closely the wheels of our cart rode along the edge of the narrow path up the cliff-side. It didn't make me feel any better. I was nauseous and threw up over the side of the cart, sticking my head between the wide bars. The cold didn't help. Nadia offered me her cloak, which I refused, and she resorted to sitting close together. I wished Cesarus could keep me warm.

I hadn't left the temple since my father ransomed me to Dorian on its doorstep. Dorian sent letters to priests of the Transcendant Order in the Cenlands. One answered, arriving at the temple with three animals. He told me to choose one for a companion. A wolf, a fox, or a cat.

Cesarus was the only one that comforted me when I reached out my hand to touch them. We hadn't been apart since. Now, I heard the other dogs and kept my focus on their breathing. Dorian said he was among them.

Nadia shook me awake on the coldest morning yet. "I think we've arrived."

They pulled us from the carts, barking orders as they shoved us through what sounded like a bustling camp. Children cried, women questioned the men, the men grumbled. In the distance, I could hear music.

"Where are we?" I asked.

"I think—"

"Blind girl." A voice cut through the noise. I snapped my head in its direction.

"I have a name," I said. My voice, as tightly wound up as my body felt. "Who are you? Where are we? Why have you taken us?"

"Osi," Nadia's warning tone softened me.

Footsteps told me that he was nearing. I didn't budge from my spot, even though the person behind me nudged me to walk.

"What's your name?" the stranger asked. From the height of his voice, I knew he was taller than me, but his voice was smooth as butter and warmer now. He sounded young. "I didn't want to call you blind girl, anyway."

"Osira," I said and waved my hand out in the direction I'd heard Nadia.

"Wherever they are, these are my companions. Nadia and Dorian. Where is my wolf?"

"The beast is eating. He's getting along with our hounds. As for your other questions, our chief has the answers. I will take you to meet him."

"We were abducted, bound and caged," Nadia spoke up before I could, but her voice was much softer than mine would have been. "We deserve at least a morsel of information. Perhaps, on the way…" I heard her step forward. "You might tell us more?"

He cleared his throat. "Follow me."

Her hand reached back and grabbed mine. I tried to rein in my remaining senses while we walked. Not being able to see made me sensitive to sounds and smells. The camp's inhabitants were speaking an unfamiliar tongue. The fragrance of strange food mixed with the fresh air.

The ground beneath my bare feet was coarse. Solid stone and gravel or pebbles. Some spots were damp and all of it was cold. The thought of boots like the Humans wore made me want to break more rules.

"My name is Takoda," the stranger said as we followed.

"Pleasure to meet you, Takoda," Nadia said in a smiling voice.

"Yes, greetings," Dorian chimed in. His voice was shaken. I knew he was as cold and weary as I was. The knot of hunger was tightly wound around my stomach.

"You are in the Southern Rift."

Dorian said, "Ah," as Nadia said, "Oh."

"We do not call ourselves Rift Dwellers, as your people call us. We are the Ragnar, and we do not look kindly on strangers." His voice dropped off a bit. "So, count your steps and never forget your way. You don't want to cross any warriors."

"Are you a warrior?" Nadia asked, not hiding her admiration.

"I am a man and the third son of the Chief. Of course, I am a warrior."

"How many sons does the chief have?" Dorian asked.

"Twelve sons and nine daughters."

"A fertile people on the barren mountain," Nadia chirped, but Takoda didn't laugh.

"The mountain brings us closer to the Gods, closer to their blessings. Children are blessings."

"Yes, of course. I'm sure a warm bed is also a blessing in such a cold clime," she added.

"Nadia." I tugged on her sleeve. Takoda fell silent and his steps slowed, so ours did too. His foot ground the dirt—he must have turned around.

"You are a charming lady," he said in a lighter voice.

"Why, thank—"

"Charm does not keep you from falling off the face of a mountain. Strength does. My people respect only strength. Don't try your humor on my father."

"Right." She swallowed. "Thanks for the tip."

I was thinking it might be better if Dorian did the talking.

We followed Takoda into what I assumed was a tent, by the fabric we pushed through and the feeling of a rug beneath my feet. My body shuddered from the chill nipping at our heels, but I could hear a fire crackling and was already getting warmer.

Nadia steered me. Low voices muttered and grumbled in their distinctive tongue, closer now than before. The strong fragrance of incense mingled with that of burning firewood. The farther we followed Takoda, the thicker the air got. I started sweating. Silence shifted through the air, and we stopped walking.

The clear pang of a drum penetrated the silence, startling me. One dry, heavy thud quickened against another, until a rhythm racked the room. The voices returned, hissing and chanting. Some whining and climbing until they were shrieking.

I pulled Nadia closer by her sleeve. I would have guessed Queen Hero was there by the sound that crept into the strange song, like the rattling of bones in a basket. Nadia and I held onto each other through the waves of sound and vibration.

Nothing could convey dread like the drums and chanting did. It made me feel as afraid as I did the first time that I heard the Gods' voices clamor into my head.

My eyes teared, and I turned my face toward Nadia. Just as quickly, her soft hand touched my face, and another calloused one slipped into mine. Dorian drew closer.

I hated the feeling of searching the darkness, not knowing where to look, not being able to see my surroundings. I hadn't gotten used to feeling afraid and not being able to see a way out. If I squeezed my eyes shut, I'd at least keep them from spinning uselessly.

"Bow," Takoda said.

Collectively, we obeyed, and immediately, the Chief's voice burst from his chest, like a mare through a gate. Words galloped from his mouth with urgency, the cadence of wild hooves. His language borne on sounds as hard as the mountains he ruled, as curt as their edges.

His voice thickened the air, his words knocked against my understanding. It was cold compared to the chiming tongue of the Gods that filled my head. The Chief's voice drove theirs out. Defiant compared to the God's. And it was as beautiful as it was harsh.

I wanted to dig myself into the ground to feel the rumblings of it all around me. I wanted to lean my ear against the Chief's chest and listen to the words being forged in the bellows of his lungs, before he uttered them.

Takoda's voice followed. A warm voice which carried large, rounded words across the room. The same language, the same consonants, but delivered like a piece of warm bread to a starving child. His voice was smooth as milk, and the harsher words of their tongue curdled it. Still, I wanted to drink it all in. I kept my eyes closed as I listened, so tuned in I barely noticed when Takoda had shifted to interpretation.

"My father speaks of the many rumors that climb our mountain. We want to know about this child. We shall hear her story. Blessed Oracle, lift the truth from the rumor and present it to us."

Nadia nudged me. That was my cue.

"I-" My voice quivered. I swallowed and cleared my throat.

Where would I begin? Were they looking for me to play prophet? What truth did they seek? How did they even know who I was? Questioning them was not a good idea.

"Start with your name." Mrithyn's voice fogged up my thoughts.

"My name is Osira," I said. My voice felt like a small orb of light in the back of my throat. Flickering, timid. Instinctively, I touched my throat. I felt the reverberation of my voice. "These are my friends, Nadia and Dorian. We come from the Kingdom of Ro'Hale."

The audience murmured. I paused, trying to find my story in the mud of my thoughts. Takoda picked up the few words I'd offered and translated them for his father. When he'd finished, I continued.

"You might have heard about what's going on in my homeland… about Queen Hero and the Coroner—"

Takoda interrupted me to translate for his father. The Chief replied and Takoda asked on his behalf, "We hear many things about your queen. That she has lost her wits. She hunts and kills the people that she swore to protect. That the Coroner is her accomplice—"

"What? No," I stammered. I took a breath and weighed my words.

Lift the truth out of the rumors.

They were looking at me as the girl who escaped the Sunderlands. I straightened my spine and let my hands fall to my side. The tiny orb of light in the back of my throat became a steady beam.

"Children who grow up in peace are really lucky. They get to be children… and don't have to worry about war or religion, politics or prophecy. They see soldiers and queens in their dolls. I used to think that way. I'm sure your own children must feel that safety. They watch your warriors, you, as Chief, and they reflect what they see through play. The rumors you've heard are as simple as a child's version of their father's war. That the queen has lost her wits—it does not portray what her madness has undone in our kingdom. The false claim that the Coroner conspires with her against the people, paints her as a villain. Well, that's just ridiculous."

Takoda coughed, reminding me he had to translate all that. I held my hands behind my back and waited for him to finish, shifting the weight over my feet.

Dorian whispered, "You're doing great, keep going."

Silence invited my next words.

"Queen Hero wears the bones of the people she kills—brutally. She kills people who give her a bad feeling, who speak out of turn. Her grand crusade is a hunt for her mother's murderer. She claims she witnessed this murder, but a God revealed to me she actually killed Queen Herrona."

After some translation, he asked, "Which God accused her?"

I halted, trying to sift through my memory of the pantheon's many voices, their prattling stories vying for my attention. My brows furrowed.

"Elymas… I think."

"If you'll allow me." Dorian shifted at my side.

"Osira was newly unveiled when this revelation came to her. Meaning, her gifts as the Oracle were still newborn and untried. You must forgive her uncertainty of which deity it was that spoke. Translating and relaying the Pantheon's enigmatic messages is difficult."

"There are many Gods in your pantheon, yes?" Takoda asked.

"Nine, canonically," Dorian replied.

"Among these Gods, are there no tricksters?" Takoda asked and then translated his own question for his father. The Chief snickered.

"Are you implying that the Gods lied to their oracle?" Dorian asked incredulously. I stayed silent.

"It is our belief that words shape reality. Can the Oracle tell us exactly what this God said?"

Under pressure, I couldn't. "I can't remember."

"Can you not ask them again?" Takoda pressed.

"The Gods do not repeat themselves," I said softly.

He exchanged words with his father.

"We heed all that echoes through creation. Living atop a mountain, we listen to the valleys. Try to make sense of rumors. In everything, there are truths and lies spinning like threads on a loom. Different colored words, spinning a story. We pick which to believe and which to ignore. That is how we shape our realities. Words are the world."

I could hear a smile quicken his voice, as if he loved speaking about what he believed in.

"Gods do not lie the same way they do not tell the truth. They simply speak and we base our lives on what we choose to hear. The freedom to design our lives on interpretation of their words is like the ability to forge a sword out of metal.

"An ingot is just a material, but we can see the possibility of a blade in it. So, we create one from it. Someone else might see the possibility of jewelry or coins. Interpretation—words are elements, stories are everything they make. The ability to co-create with the Gods, through storytelling, is our birthright. This is our doctrine, and it's why we listen.

The more material you have, the more you can create."

"Whoa," I said.

"It is prudent to believe that some deities may speak to different... possibilities of reality. Perhaps one God says Queen Hero usurped her mother. Maybe another says Herrona took her own life. You listened to one, choosing to believe only one."

"Well, I—" I tried... but he was right.

"Osira is still learning to thresh, if you will, the many things the Gods tell her."

Dorian tried to defend me, but Takoda's words were enough to make me question everything. I'd heard the voice of only one God when I asked that question, but I couldn't remember which. Was it a God who could be trusted? I assumed they all were, but was that true? No one taught me to discern or to question the Gods. I wonder if Keres ever did—she certainly seemed defiant in most things.

"Whatever we believe differently, what I know to be true is that Queen Hero is dangerous. And Keres is also dangerous... but she's on the right side."

"What is the right side?" Takoda asked.

"Our side," I responded.

"Is it the right side because it is our side?"

"Alright, enough of the existential crises, please. You're all giving me a headache," Nadia blurted. I whipped my head toward her and a huge smile stole my mouth.

Thankfully, Takoda didn't bother translating that.

"Do you know the Coroner has allied herself with the Baorean King who holds her people captive?"

"What?" we all asked.

"Gods save us all," Dorian groaned.

I let out a deep breath. "I didn't know that, but what I know is that the Sunderlands is in ruins. Queen Hero hurts more people than she helps. She kills the people she swore to protect, and shelters Illynads in her court. People who may or may not be on the wrong side, but who historically are aggressive and who also hurt our people.

"She repeatedly ignored the cries of the Elven Clans, while the Dalis Armies attacked and enslaved those people. Keres, the Coroner, was the first and only person to confront her and when she did, Queen Hero threatened her life."

"I was there, I saw it," Nadia added.

"What matters is there are people—*my* people, seized in violent hands. The hands of their own queen, and the bloodied hand of the Baore, if what you say is true. If the bloodshed doesn't stop, it will consume our world. And I don't think any amount of listening to the echoes is going to stop it. Not unless we do something."

Takoda translated that, dancing through his words with what seemed like caution.

"You do not speak like a child," The Chief spoke through Takoda's words.

I smiled. "Because, I, too, have been listening. Like you do. And I hear threats of war. Race against race. Province against province. But nothing terrifies me more than threats of a war between the Gods and mortals. Another thing the Gods have told me... is that they are coming. They are raising an army of servants, of people like the Coroner. We are on the brink of an Instrumental War. Whatever choices the Coroner is making, I only pray it's to end the suffering of her people."

Takoda's voice sobered as he relayed my message.

After that, there was no more conversation. They ushered us to a designated tent. Takoda didn't speak to us again.

Women came to us with clean clothes and bowls of hot soup. Meat, which Dorian said, was some kind of bird. We ate in silence, my warning to the Chief weighing us down. I think it was the first time Nadia had heard the truth out loud.

She spoke as if she could sense that my thoughts had turned toward her.

"Living at court and seeing the horrors... it didn't feel safe to hope that the madness would end. But... I think what you might have meant to be a warning... this war that threatens our world." Her voice thickened as if she might cry. "I believe it will save us."

Joy rushed through her; her tears were not for sorrow.

"That the Gods would intervene—it will be a holy war. To finally restore the balance between the good and the evil that fights for our land. Everything. You know…" She took a minute before continuing, "I watched Hero go from youth to queen. She was a quiet girl, but there was always something off about her. Saw Queen Herrona in her last few years. I've seen the hands of malice wrap its fingers around our court. I heard every scream, every drop of her axe against the marble floor."

She laughed.

"Now Servants to the Gods are rising? At a time where the Baore is unchecked in power, they planted a sentinel in its midst. When the life of the Sunderlands has been stolen, when our enemies pour across our borders into our strongholds. We're being given a gift in this war—a real chance to fight."

Dorian didn't speak. Neither did I. In my mind, this was an omen. The promise of death and bloodshed, ruination, shift in power. Chaos. For Nadia, it was change.

It hit me—that's what Takoda meant. War was just a word.

To me, it was a threat. It painted a picture of reality in which I needed a fortress, because it meant a loss of safety. An attack on my life as I knew it.

To Nadia, that word was a key. War wasn't going to just break open the hand of evil, it was going to open this world up to a new beginning and healing. It shaped a different reality for her, and that reality was something she would be happy to fight for.

I felt like I was seeing the world through her eyes, like a vision cutting through the darkness. It was the first time I really felt like my eyes were opened since I went blind.

27: SIGHT
Osira

After our strange dinner conversation, we went to bed in silence. The small cots were an upgrade from carts, and my body felt at ease. My mind did not.

A meek fire hissed and snapped in the center of the room, warming the entire tent. But I still felt a chill in my bones. The Gods were silent in my head. Takoda's questions confronted my thoughts. As if my mind had conjured him, his voice cut into the silence.

"Osira," he whispered. I realized he was in our tent. Probably peeking his head in through the entryway. I sat up.

"Takoda?"

"Yes, follow me."

I rose, leaving my blanket in a heap. I followed the sound of his footsteps until he took my hand and led me down a winding path.

Halfway there, I realized I'd just left the safety of my tent, my friends, and followed a strange man into the darkness and cold of midnight. A familiar, deep voice greeted us. It was the Chief. We followed him into another tent.

"My father says welcome, Osira."

The Chief's voice grew nearer, more somber. Takoda passed my hand into the Chief's hand. His touch didn't match his voice.

Takoda said, "He offers you his name: Roth."

"Nice to meet you," I said.

He turned my palm upward and spread my fingers apart. He traced lines in my palm as he spoke again. I shivered.

As if he was reading something off my skin. It felt like his touch left a trail of something. Like he was following my life, past, present, and future, down a path etched in my hand.

I wanted to close my hand, close the eyes on his insight. It made my skin crawl. He let go, but I could still feel every line, every hill and valley of my hand. It felt like he'd placed some kind of energy into my hand that made my skin tingle.

"What was that?" I asked.

"He was reading your palm. He asks if he may see your other hand."

I hesitated, kneading my hands together.

"He says the reading will not be complete without the other. One hand tells a different story than the other will."

I offered my other hand, palm up, and again he took it in his soft hold. The same sensation crept along the planes of my hand. I wondered what kind of story he was reading.

How much could my palms tell him? He spent more time with my left hand, my dominant hand. His breath caught as he spoke its secrets into existence.

"What's he saying?"

Takoda simply shushed me. "Wait."

The Chief hummed a few more words and let out a sigh, then released my hand. I waited, watching the darkness. Footsteps told me one of them was retreating to the far side of the room.

"What—"

"Wait," Takoda silenced me again.

I heard a trunk opening, rummaging, and then the footsteps returned. The Chief said something, and not needing the translation, I held out my open hands.

A metal object met my palms, cooling the warmth of the energy he'd left there. I turned it and explored it with my fingers. It was a hand-held mirror. I traced its glass face.

"But I'm blind…" I said.

The Chief chuckled under his breath.

"Only as blind as you choose to be," Takoda relayed. The Chief spoke and Takoda translated.

"He knows you were not born blind, as no oracle is. So, he wants you to think of this mountain. Its name is Halo. Named for the way the sun hides behind its peak at dawn and causes a halo of light to crown it. Can you see it in your mind?"

I remembered the brightness and color of daylight. Growing up at the base of the Rift, I loved its mountains. The way dawn colored the sky and broke between the peaks. As a little girl, I actually believed that the sun rose and set every day to beam light through the spaces between the mountains, to keep them from fusing together into one gigantic wall. I used to play in the shadows they would cast. Pretended the moving light chased me from shadow to shadow. If it touched me, it would split me apart, too. Make my head into a boulder, separated from the cliff of my body's plateau. My arms and legs would root into the ground and grow big and fat into mountains of flesh with fingers at the peak. I smiled just thinking about it. My ridiculous, eight-year-old religion: imagination. But I could see the picture they had painted of Halo easily and my gut clenched with longing.

"I think so."

Together, the Chief and his son guided me through the visualization.

"A mountain, from afar, seems like a fortress, built by the earth to protect regions from each other. Impenetrable, harsh, cold, even lonely. All these things are true from a distant perspective. As people who dwell in these blessed mountains, we know how vulnerable a mountain is. We know how it weathers. From afar, the mountains may seem barren or treacherous. But we know the gifts of the mountain, its stability, both shade and access to the highest light, fresh water. It gives perspective.

"The face of the mountain looks stern, but we who lean against it know its curves and edges like the smile of a loved one. We know where the mountain is weak and where it cries. Where there are cracks and cliffs. We also know the animals that find safety in its clefts. When we look at the mountain, we see both sides of its true nature and we respect it for all it is."

Takoda led me into the most creative places of my mind. A place I hadn't explored in a while.

"I see."

"Our Gods go by different names, but their powers are very similar: Light and dark, the elements, life and death, peace and turmoil, even magic. All these things touch Halo every day. It exists as both a physical bulwark and a subject of the divine. Just as our own bodies. I want you to think deeper now.

"Halo, like all mountains, has its crown, its neck, its center. Even a heart and a root. Our bodies are like mountains in this way. There is a line you could trace if you allow your mind to notice each part of your body. Start at your scalp and travel down to your throat, to your chest, your stomach, down to your feet. These are the places you hold energy. Can you imagine this?"

"Um..." It was strange to think about, but I could sense these different parts of me. I noticed all the tension in my body. My clenched jaw, my hunched shoulders, my clenched stomach, a dull ache in my legs and back from walking on uneven terrain. The mirror in my hand—I felt its weight. "I think I can."

"Good," they said. "My father says that youth abides with magic. Because you are young, you could easily see what he has described. As you heard earlier, our people believe we shape reality with our minds. He believes that children have the keenest ability to do so. He also asks if you have ever heard of the Rift Crafter?"

"Who hasn't?" I laughed. "I grew up in a war-stricken land. In the Kingdom of Ro'Hale, there are many warriors. The legend of the Rift Crafter is as commonly heard as birdsong."

"My father asks if you would like to visit the forge."

My jaw dropped, and both men laughed under their breath.

"Tonight?" I asked.

"Yes. The Rift Crafter only works at night."

"Why?" I asked.

"I'll let him tell you that," Takoda said. He took my hand gently in his. His father said something quick and short, which he translated to, "Keep the mirror and come back here when you're done."

I took Takoda's hand with my right and clutched the mirror to my chest with the left.

As we walked, I skipped with excitement. "This is going to be so awesome!" I squeaked.

He quickly shushed me, reminding me that people were sleeping.

"Sorry," I whispered. "It's just there were these kids I grew up with. We used to play-fight with wooden swords. Pretending the Rift Crafter made them. I wished..." My steps slowed. Takoda stopped walking and turned toward me. Listening.

I snorted. "I've wished for many things."

"As you were born to do." His voice was gentle as he squeezed my hand.

"How old are you, anyway?" I asked.

"Five and twenty."

Still holding his hand, I imagined this might be what having an older brother is like. I swung his arm and said, "I wished I could be a warrior when I grew up. Have a sword made by him. I've tried not to think about it since I went blind." I laughed bitterly. "It hasn't been hard to squish the memory down since all those kids I played with stopped talking to me."

"Did you keep practicing with your wooden sword?"

"No," I said, turning my head slightly away from his voice. "That toy is gone now. It's under my bed in my father's house. He probably used it for firewood after he sold me to Dorian. Besides, I'm three and ten now. I don't have toys."

"I'm sorry to hear that, but—"

"What's that sound?" I jumped. We both stilled, and my pointed ears pricked up, chasing that sound into the following silence.

Clang!

"There it is again," I whispered. It rang like a bell, bouncing against the mountains until it fell into the valleys below us. "Is that—"

"Let's go." Takoda pulled me into a trot. My feet faltered at first, but then I fell into his pace, not paying attention to the ground or my feet. Instead, as I ran blindly with only his hand tethering me to our direction, my attention snapped inward.

To my chest, the air filling my lungs. Then to my legs, the tightness of my muscles. Air whipped through me and around me, and I kept my hand locked in his. Trusting him to be my eyes while my feet flew. After a couple minutes, we hit a steeply inclined dirt path, but I refused to slow down. I didn't fear a misstep for the first time in a while. We hunted the song of the anvil in the night with the speed of wolves.

I almost got dizzy from not knowing which way was which but didn't care. It was the first time I felt careless since I'd gone blind. I wasn't stumbling over my feet. And Takoda didn't let me down. He brought me somewhere high up, where the wind stung my face.

The anvil's song cut into my senses. Rising above my panting breath, my pounding heart. I felt it reverberate in the ground beneath my feet. I traced its echo out into the void. It made all the mountains of the Rift sing. And then it stopped.

"Master Gaian," Takoda said. He led me forward and placed my hand into the Crafter's.

"This is Osira. She is—"

"I know who she is." His cool, low voice swirled into the air. He moved closer, pulled my hand upward, and bent down... until my palm rested on his cheek.

His skin was soft under my touch, and I wiped away a bead of sweat. He puffed out a laugh. I traced my hand across his brow. His forehead was broad. So was his nose. His cheekbones were sharp and his ears...

"You're an Elf," I said.

"I'm from the Sunderlands, too," he said in a smiling voice. My heart swelled.

"No way." I giggled. I could feel my cheeks burning. I didn't even know what to say. He stood up quickly and took my hand as he walked away. He let go as he pressed my hand against something cold and metal. Not like the mirror. This thing was massive. The cold was biting. I knocked my fist against it and earned a full ding.

"No way!" I squealed again. "This is the anvil!"

I held out the mirror and waited for one of them to take it so I could put both hands on the anvil. It was so big I couldn't wrap my arms around it. It was just as tall as I was, and it was smooth as a polished stone. I pressed my ear against it and knocked once more. The sound shuddered down my spine until I laughed again.

I spun on my heel, and before I could fully ask, "Can I hit it with the hammer?" a heavy object was nudged into my hands.

"You're going to need help to lift it, so I will instruct you how to stand and hold it. Then, we strike."

I turned back around, and he adjusted me until I was facing the anvil again and in the right spot.

"Feet shoulder width apart, put one leg back a bit," he said. I obeyed. "Loosen your knees. Right. Good. Now..." He helped me get the hammer up over my shoulder, bearing most of the weight. It felt like the length of a sword and must have been fifteen times as heavy.

"Now, clear your mind."

I was buzzing. Too excited to do any such thing. I couldn't stop wanting to shift my weight over my feet.

"Clear my mind?" I whined.

"Yes. Make space for the sound of the anvil. Imagine your head is as wide and open as the sky."

I kept my eyes closed and did as he said. Maybe *this* was why he only worked at night. No distraction, only dreams. As if the Gods approved of his instruction, they withdrew from my thoughts.

"Okay."

"It's important to remember the anvil will sing, but you must give its words. Just as the Gods spoke, and the world was born, you will tell the hammer what you want, and the anvil will sing it into existence for you. That is how you Craft. Think of a word, an intention. Every blade is wrought with intention and imagination. Crafting is the most powerful thing you can do in this world. We do not hit the anvil until we are clear on our intent. Let me know when you are ready."

"Any word?"

"Any word that means something to you."

My eyelids fluttered as I searched the quieted space in my head for a word. I asked my memories to give me something, but the more I thought back, the more noise crept back into my mind.

Painful memories. Loss. The rumblings of the Gods, the threat of war. The sound of me crying.

Shhhh, I thought to myself. I tugged my awareness back, out of the grip of that noise. Back to the mountain I stood on. Back to the anvil, to the hammer in my hands. I just wanted to smash it down on the anvil.

Which startled me. I realized how tightly I was gripping onto the hilt. How my body had tensed at those thoughts. I furrowed my brows, noting my reflex to those painful memories. And with a deep breath through my nose, I released that tension. I released those thoughts. I relaxed into my stance again.

"I know which word I want, it's—"

"Sh," Gaian said, "Don't tell me. Tell the anvil. Through the hammer. Tell the blade."

"You're going to let me craft a blade?" I asked, a smile breaking across my face. I opened my eyes, opened myself up to this incredible feeling. Pure joy. I hadn't felt like this since… since, ever.

"Of course." Gaian chuckled. "You didn't think I'd let you hit a bare anvil, did you? Takoda, take that and put it there."

I listened to the grate of metal, the tink as he laid it upon the anvil. My palms were sweating and the shadows that danced in my eyes softened.

"Is the sun rising?"

"It is."

My breathing kicked up with the wind and I wiggled my toes into the dirt of the mountain.

"Is it beautiful?" I asked, tears unexpectedly pricking my eyes.

"Is it?" Gaian replied in a low voice.

I turned my face toward the warmth of daylight. Everything about this moment felt beautiful.

"What if I miss?" I asked, my voice cracking a bit.

"You won't."

Distraction washed away. My senses narrowed down to the feel of the hilt in my hands, the weight of the hammer. I took a breath and pinched it in. Feeling the stretch of my clothes around my chest. The strain in my body as Gaian and I lifted the hammer together. I could feel him helping me direct it as the hammer arced up over us. As the hammer fell, I let go of a grunt.

The bell struck the blade, and a shock rocked through my body. Like lightning up my arms. The world around me rippled into view. From where the hammer connected to the blade, light and shadows undulated, taking form in waves of white and silver and pale blue. Carried by the song of the anvil. I could see the hammer in my hand.

I blinked.

I could see the blade beyond it, the anvil beneath it. The echoes still ringing out into the valley took my sight farther and farther. I straightened up, never releasing the hilt, and stared out across the mountain tops. Glittering in silvery sunlight. Tears blurred my eyes, and I wiped them away.

Colors shaded the closest peaks and trees. The blade was red hot, sizzling on the anvil. And still that song carried. I could see through its sound.

I tried to say something, anything, but no words came. None... except the one I'd forged into the blade.

Gaian was right. I'd crafted exactly what I wanted. My heart memorized that song, that picture. Even as it faded into silence, along with my vision, I still heard it humming within me. I wiped my eyes again and laughed.

"It *is* a beautiful sunrise," I said.

Gaian clapped me on the shoulder, squeezing the muscle there.

I turned to Gaian and paused, not knowing how to thank him.

Instead, I told him a secret. "When I was living in the Temple of Mrithyn in Ro'Hale, the Coroner visited me. While she was there... a barren tree that had stood in the center of the sanctum for over a century... it came to life. She watered it with her blood and now its leaves beat like a heart. Crimson."

"Crimson?" he asked.

"Whenever I touched the tree, I could see. And when we fled, I feared I'd never be able to see again. Not without that tree. But I could with the anvil."

"Indeed," he sighed.

"There are things in this world that can connect us to the Other side," Takoda joined in. I had almost forgotten he was there.

"Connect us to the Godlands?" I asked.

"Yes. The gold-lands, our realm, and the Godlands, belonging to the deities, are two halves of the same world. Separated by a curtain of power. Some call it the Veil and say it is hung from the stars themselves. Some call it the Void, the space between realms. Some even call it the Rift, like this mountain range, the way it separates Aureum from Illyn."

"There are doorways that can be opened from our side to the Other," Gaian added.

"Opened how?" I asked.

"With magic," Gaian answered.

"Powerful, untamed magic, practiced by very few people in this world. Magic named Elyam."

"Elyam?" I tried the name out. "Like Elymas, God of Magic?"

"Yes."

"Another name for this magic is Ragnam, named for Ra, our God of Wonder. Elymas and Ra are the same. The source of creative power, the one who gifts mortals with the ability to co-create the world. That is why magic manifests in some mages as power over the elements and more."

"And your people, the Ragnaar, you practice this magic?"

"We do."

I turned toward Gaian. "But you're Elven, not Ragnaar."

"Being Ragnaar is not about what you were told you are when, you're born. It's about self-creation. Anyone can be Ragnaar. It simply means they are a person who is choosing to be part of a world and its miracles. A person who sees both the spiritual and physical in creation. Who honors both the world in which they live, and the world that lives inside them."

"Like the way your father talked about viewing the mountain."

"Yes. That is the way of Ra. Awareness. Wonder. To be in awe of All that Is."

"Wait, so does this mean you can see the doors? To the Other side?"

"When you attune to all that is, you learn everything is a door. You see the divinity in all creation. If you can connect to this, you can enter the Godlands from anywhere."

"So, I wouldn't need to touch the Tree or hit the anvil... I could simply touch... like, a rock?"

Footsteps drew closer. A hand gripped my shoulder. From the ground up, the world came into view. I nearly fell over.

Gaian's eyes were closed as he held onto me and showed me the world.

I studied every line in his face. He seemed as old as my father, but there was kindness there which was never in my father's face. His hair was silver and tied up in a bun on top of his head. His muscles had muscles, and his arms looked stronger than cobras.

"Whoa. Are we in the Godlands?" I looked around.

"We are always in the Godlands." Takoda smiled at me.

He was handsome. His long black hair was braided over his shoulder. His skin was like copper, and his eyes were violet.

"It's just a matter of whether you know how to step into awareness of it."

I looked down at myself and examined my hands first. My nails had grown long. I knew I was bony, but for the first time, I realized you couldn't make out my frame at all in the loose, tattered dress I wore.

"Wait." I shot my head up. "I am a door."

"You got it." Gaian smiled, opening his eyes, which were blue. His hand gently lifted away, and they faded from view.

I turned in a circle, looking into the eyes of Nothing again.

"What if..." I dared to wish. "If I learned to practice this magic, Ragnam... would I be able to make a sword into a door? Could I use it to see, to fight?"

"To become a warrior." Takoda finished for me. Pride resounded through his voice.

"Well done, Osira," Gaian bellowed. "You're seeing it—the power you have. The power to reclaim your sight."

"What about the mirror?" I asked. Takoda got up and handed it back to me.

"A mirror is much safer to start with than a sword."

28: SEIZED
DARIUS

In the heat of the moment, General Vyra ordered her men to seize me. They hesitated, seeing I was literally on fire, from my fingertips to my elbows.

Epona's hands reached for me. Her skin felt like frost. My vision pulsed with darkness. I was looking at the sky a breath later, on my back. Then I realized it wasn't the sky, but her violet eyes. Her hands were on my face.

"Focus." Her voice dripped into my head. I felt water beading down my brow, sizzling against my neck. Steam filtered through my vision.

I closed my eyes, trying to do as she said. My body was shaking, but her hands were holding me down. It was what I needed. I dove into my thoughts—felt like I was passing out. But her hands kept the fever dream at bay while I walked through the fire in my mind.

I saw Hayes. He was saying something, but I couldn't hear him. I could still feel my body. Pulses of power shot through me sporadically.

Focus. Her voice surrounded the walls of my mind. I looked through my thoughts for Keres.

"*No,*" Hayes said clearly, calling my attention back to him. "*You're in pain. Don't look for more of it. You need to calm down.*"

"How?" I asked, not knowing whether Hayes or Epona would respond.

"Focus," they both said. "You're a Daemon. Your power comes from your Spirit. Your Spirit is on fire, Darius."

It was her speaking, but it was Hayes I saw.

Panic was winning. Every jolt of power burned in my chest, my stomach, my throat, my head. It radiated down my legs, seeking an escape route.

The Daemon Spirit—I'd been crushing it down for so long. Finally, it combusted. It felt like every heartbreak, every disappointment, every loss I'd ever felt, every ounce of hurt I'd ever felt, all burst into flame again within me. The more I focused on the pain, the worse it felt.

"Darius," Epona's voice sounded frantic. She shook me. I opened my eyes and saw her standing above me. I reached toward her, and she stepped back. The flames engulfed me. I lay there, just burning. Like a fucking torch.

Her eyes were full of light and water. They swirled with shades of blue and purple. The red light of my fire lit them up.

"I'm not afraid of you," she hissed at me. "But you better not burn me."

I turned onto my side and pushed myself up. She didn't flinch. As I shifted, I felt myself slipping. The snow beneath me... was turned to ice. And it wasn't melting. I looked back at her. Her outstretched hands.

"What are you?" I asked. I didn't need the answer. All I needed was for her to drown me.

I sat up and tried to stand. Ashes fell off me. My clothes. I was wearing only fire now. The wind whipped bitterly at me, and my flames spat sparks back at it. I closed my eyes and tried to gather them back into myself.

"I don't know how to do this," I thought to Hayes. *"And you're dead. I don't know how you're supposed to help me."*

I could see him again. My twin. It was obvious focusing on the pain wasn't helping. I opened my eyes again and looked at Epona. Her face was unreadable. I looked down at myself. Light shone out of every pore. My skin was smooth and golden, drenched in red fire. From my fingertips to just above my elbows, my veins were blackened. I held my hands up in front of me and focused on the fire.

My vision shifted in and out of clarity and red-tinged light. The flames danced in the palms of my hand, growing with my focus and shrinking from the wind.

The pain lessened as I gave it purpose—direction. Allowing the fire to come through. I opened my arms, and the flames crawled up to my shoulders. Swirling and licking at my neck. I looked up, and they jumped up around me. Off my skin and toward the Sun, like wings sprouting off my back. Anger rose within me, too. I was afraid, and I didn't like feeling that way.

Soldiers crowded around me started shouting as the flames grew taller. General Vyra snapped at Epona. I looked back and found her poised. In a fighting stance. The surrounding snow answered the wave of her hands, melting down to puddles of water. I met her eyes.

The flames swayed and unfurled. I held my arms at my side. I felt like I was crying but couldn't feel my tears. All I felt was fire.

The water was in her control. It rippled and rolled at her feet. Her hands dictated its hypnotic movement. I was getting tired. Needed it to end. And the look in her eyes...

She wasn't looking at me with concern anymore. As she gathered the water, siphoning it from the meadow of snow we stood in, she stared me down. Her eyes promised she'd smother me. I wanted her to.

The water stretched out, forming tendrils around her. Snake-like, watery arms reached out of the snow, mimicking her own arms. Her movements were as fluid.

I caught one last glimpse of her eyes before she thrust forward, and the water gripped me.

⊟⊟ ⊟⊟ ⊟⊟

In the winter, my mother liked to cook broth or stew almost every damn day. She also insisted Hayes and I drink tea. Something hot to eat, something hot to drink. She wanted to keep us warm.

We'd wake up with the attitudes of disgruntled soldiers, despite being six-year-olds. Sulking from our beds to the wooden bench we shared at the table. The blue clay cup was Hayes' and the red one was mine. Both filled to the brim with steaming hot tea. She let us put as much sugar as we wanted into it, and that's the only reason we drank it. Neither of us wanted to be warm.

We were figuring out that we were different from the other kids in Massara. Our father had always treated us as if we were stray dogs that our mom dragged in. He beat her for it—for getting raped and bearing twins that were half monsters.

Our Massara kin looked at us the way General Vyra was looking at me now. As if they didn't know whether to side with my father or with my mother. Or whether they should simply pretend we didn't exist and send us somewhere else.

"You are a Daemon." It wasn't a question, but a statement that came with so many.

"You noticed," I said to her.

On the table between us was something hot to eat and something strong to drink, but our meals had cooled, and our cups were empty. Surprisingly, Epona hadn't joined us.

"What is Epona?" I asked.

"She's like you. A force of nature."

"What does that mean?" I asked.

Her laugh cut through the dramatic silence. "Oh, please, don't be that cliche: someone who has no idea where their power comes from or how much they have."

I glared at her. "I know what I am, but not what Epona is. If she's like me, why is she the exact opposite of me?"

"Have you never met another Daemon?" she asked.

"Only my twin brother. I didn't know there were other kinds of Daemons. I only learned about the ones like us, with fire. Is she a... Water Daemon?"

"Yup. But none of this is my area of expertise. You'll have to talk to Yona about it."

"Yona," I repeated.

"By the blades, Darius, keep up. Epona's short-name is Yona. You're going to have to keep calling her Epona though, because she doesn't like you."

"I've noticed."

"I'm also putting her in charge of you."

Fucking perfect.

"Why can't I just leave?" I asked lazily. I knew it wasn't a realistic option, but I still wanted it to be.

"And go where?" She cocked an eyebrow up.

"To Hell, I guess," I said. "I need another drink."

She got up and walked over to the cabinet holding all the liquor bottles. Took her sweet time picking one out. She looked at me from across the room, holding up a dark green bottle. I nodded.

Something in her gaze shifted, and she walked toward me. Too slowly. My heart rate kicked up. She was looking at me... looking into my eyes. Hers were dark brown like earth, the deeper soil you only see when you're digging a grave. She'd braided her blond hair into a tight, thick rope that was long enough to wrap around your hand at least twice.

She'd switched out her usual rugged leathers and boots for linen trousers and a thin long-sleeved top that was untied at the collar. Her bare feet were silent as she padded across the carpet toward me.

"Why are you looking at me like that?" I asked in a low voice.

She smirked. "Like what?"

"You're studying me."

She broke eye contact as she reached my side and poured my drink. I raked my eyes over her quickly. Her casual clothes welcomed me to make sense of her in a way her armor didn't allow. She was a beautiful woman. Her eyes met mine and a familiar pain shot into my chest.

She stepped back.

"Do my eyes change?" I whispered. Hers searched mine, softening. "Does my power show in my eyes?"

She nodded. I'd suspected it. I remembered Keres' eyes. When we went to hunt the Dalis, when she wanted to kill Mathis despite Thaniel pleading with her not to. When she turned on him. I'd seen that darkness flood her eyes again when we fought the Gnorrer together.

"They look like campfire," she said. "I've seen eyes like yours before."

I raised my brows at her.

"Epona had a sister. Her name was Anora. A fire Daemon named Takoda killed her. He was from a tribe in the Rift Mountains. The Ragnar, people who dwell high in the mountains. Epona and Anora are from a tribe that lives at the base of the Rift, in the caves. Her people are the Taranar."

"So, they were enemies and then he killed her sister. No wonder she hates me."

"No, actually. Sister tribes." She frowned. "Anora's death was a tragic accident. Takoda and Anora were engaged to be wed. Epona traveled here with them to fight in my army a few years ago. We suffered an attack. Takoda and Anora… they were caught up in a fight with an Illynad. An Ashan."

I didn't know much about Illyn, and even less about its monsters, but Ashan was a term I knew. It spiked my blood.

Ashan were creatures born of fire. Volcanic and evil. My father often called Hayes and I Ashan and threatened to sell us to slavers who would take us to Illyn.

With Indiro's silent education, we didn't talk about the Ashan either, but we had to know about them. He procured books from some guy he knew. Had them brought in from the East for us. Until that point, we'd grown up fearing we were going to turn into demented Ashan's. We weren't exactly relieved to know our natures weren't too far off from theirs despite the key differences.

"Sounds like there was a lot of fire involved. Is that how Anora died? She got burned."

"Yes, and she wasn't Water Daemon like Yona. Just a soldier rushing to her beloved's aid. The Ashan had Takoda trapped. Both were blazing, and the flames got out of control. Anora got too close. A ball of fire that shot out from where Takoda was had engulfed her."

"Maybe it was the Ashan's fault. Did Takoda die too?"

"No, he returned to his people."

"Damn." I rubbed the back of my neck.

The general was holding on to the liquor bottle, eyes faraway.

"Epona doesn't hold a grudge against him, and she doesn't hate you."

I met her eyes and snorted. "That's very hard to believe."

"She just knows… the dangers of being what you are."

My thoughts wandered back to my fight against the Gnorrer, beside Keres. She had used fire magic to fight when her arrows failed. We took the beast down together between her powers and my blade. I found comfort in watching her wield the flames.

It was something I never told her. How, watching her control that power, watching her bring down a monster, made me feel like less of one.

If I could learn to control the fire the way she had, the way Epona controlled water… maybe I'd be able to—I didn't know what I wanted to do with my power. I didn't even want it, the same way I didn't want to be here in the Moldorn.

I looked at General Vyra. She knew. We both knew. My hands were more than empty and idle. I bound them. I didn't want to fight alongside her soldiers. Didn't want to fight the Daemon within me anymore.

She looked deep into my eyes, and my anger melted into apathy. I let her see it. That I was just so fucking tired. The more burnt out I felt, the less control I had. It was a loop I was stuck in.

Exhaustion, rage, and numbness.

One and then the other and then the other.

Over and over again.

Every step I'd taken since I left the Sunderlands drove each feeling into the ground beneath my feet. Became my foundation. One step into anger, one into disappointment, one into pain, a descent into an emotional and mental prison. Until today, until one more step into the wilderness led me into chaos.

Numbness never lasted.

Tears blurred my eyes, and I didn't even bother fighting them or wiping them away. The General didn't withdraw or shift her attention. She stood there. I burrowed into the darkness of her eyes. It kept me from seeing red. Her face stayed soft, and it kept me from putting up the wall I'd been building all my life. She witnessed me, my feelings, and for the first time since Hayes died, I wept. She didn't even flinch. Just stayed with me and I think what hurt the most was I really needed her to.

29: SWORD AND SHIELD
DARIUS

Finally, I slept. For the first time in almost two weeks. Without dreaming, without waking up sweating. The whole night, I slept evenly. Only opening my eyes when the Sun was high in the sky. I was wrapped up in blankets, holding a pillow. Like a kid.

I got dressed and walked out of my tent, headed toward General Vyra's.

Two men stopped me.

"Darius," the one with black hair said. Everybody in the encampment probably knew who I was after yesterday. These men approached me without fear.

"Sir," I nodded. He reached out and grasped my arm. A sign of camaraderie that startled me.

"Call me Zevran. This is Crete." The other soldier also reached out his hand in greeting. At a double-take, I realized he was Elven.

"Well met," I said.

Zevran gestured for me to follow him. "General Vyra extends an invitation to you."

"Oh?"

Over his shoulder, Crete said, "She wants to fight you."

"Excuse me?" I stopped in my tracks. Both men turned back toward me. Zevran was smiling, but Crete squinted his eyes at me.

What the fuck had I thought was going to happen? Yesterday, I showed power. Dangerous power. Then, like an idiot, I showed so much weakness. The General had shown me a side of her last night that was simple and safe. It pulled feelings out of me. Now she wanted to draw blood?

"She's waiting in the pit."

"The pit," I repeated.

"Yup." They both turned again and headed across the threshold of the woods. I followed.

Lydany, this camp, was nested in a clearing leaning on the Rift Mountains.

The Essyd Tower they used as a landmark to signify Moldorn's many alliances was far behind us. We were heading south, back into a forested area, but I knew we weren't going far. Through the thick of the trees, I could hear men shouting and the clash of steel blades. Adrenaline kicked me in the gut. This was bad.

"They call her the Queen of Swords, you know," Crete tossed over his shoulder.

"Why is she doing this?" I asked. I stepped on twigs and fallen acorns, gracelessly, as if I hadn't been raised in the forest. "Fuck."

Birds rustled in the trees above us, drawing my eye.

"You're not allowed to be stupid here, boy. Yesterday, you were very, very stupid."

I grumbled.

"As a soldier, when you're stupid, you either learn or you die. So, that's what you'll do today."

"Fuck me," I growled.

The hollering got louder as we neared another clearing. This one was small, hogged up by a huge ditch.

"This is the burn pit." Zev gestured to it. Men lined the mouth of the ditch, sitting and standing, all cheering on the fighters down below. "We burned the trees here when we cut a clearing into the forest for our camp. The ditch is full of ashes and debris. You're an Elf, which means being bare footed. Also, very stupid."

I mumbled a series of curse words as Zev led me over to a rack of weapons. I looked through the crowd and found the General watching me approach the weapon's rack. She was dressed in combat leathers and holding her customary sword and shield. I scanned the rack and chose a promising broadsword. I could use an axe and shield, but I wasn't going to attack her with an axe. Broadsword meant distance.

I didn't want to fight her. That's why she gave me such a toothy grin. I certainly didn't want to roast her alive. The look in her eyes was a dare to try. Epona was at her side, brows pinched in frustration as she watched me and the men approach.

"Lovely day for a tumble in the burn pit, don't you think, soldier?" General Vyra sang. I knew right then she was crazy.

Her hair was knotted up in a braided bun and her face was dirty, as if she'd already gone into the pit a few times this morning. Epona glared at me.

"Just what I wanted to wake up to," I said, giving the general a fake smile.

She giggled. This was so bad. She sauntered over to the edge of the pit, and I followed her. Men were still scrapping down below.

"Aye!" she shouted at them.

They stopped fighting and looked up at her like two kids caught by their mother. Sunlight glinted off the silver hardware of her combat leathers and highlighted the dark blue sleeves of the shirt she wore underneath. Her stance made her shield look weightless. The sword looked as natural in her hand as the bottle of liquor she held last night— like it might make her just as drunk.

"Get out of my playground."

Both men nodded and then bowed their heads to each other. The men drew my attention to the rope ladder that was nailed into the sides of the pit in the far corner.

"You can climb out, but you have to jump in," Zevran said, tracking my gaze.

"Of fucking course." I rolled my eyes.

General Vyra teetered on the edge of the pit. She spun and gave me a wild flash of a smile. She tossed her weapons in before jumping down.

She hit the ground with a heavy thud and cursed. There was no pretending it didn't hurt. The jump wouldn't kill you, but it wouldn't be fun. It would probably only seriously injure you if you fell wrong or landed on your weapon.

I approached the edge. She'd already reunited with her sword and was waiting for me. She held up her hand in front of her face and hooked her finger at me, daring me to jump.

I followed suit, dropping my sword in. I glanced quickly at Zevran and Crete, my eyes catching on Epona. Her violet eyes were boring into me. I offered her a smirk before stepping off the edge.

I landed on my feet and caught myself with my hands. My soles stung and my ankles ached. The ashes were deep and there was a bunch of broken shit that made me afraid to walk without looking at where I was going. But once I got my sword, I couldn't take my eyes off her.

General Vyra's pretty brown eyes were as hard as the face of her wooden shield. In the pit, we were in shadow. The ground was colder down here. The cheering voices echoed. I tightened both my hands around the hilt of my sword and reciprocated the general's glare.

"Well, we haven't got all day, my lady."

She moved to close the distance between us, making the first move, but I couldn't let her get too close or I'd lose the upper hand. I became aware of her height, her weight, how fast she moved.

Unlike me, she could use her hands individually. She could attack with the sword or the shield, or use both at the same time. In my mind, she morphed from a woman to a weapon.

Years of training came back to me. How to think, how to breathe, how to move.

She came at me, vicious and relentless. I had to back up as quickly as she moved forward to keep her from getting too close. My sword argued mostly with her shield as I tried to keep her just within my reach. The length of my blade loomed between us.

I made sweeping moves, forcing her to use her shield. Landing heavy blows to slow her down, I needed to control her pace. But the roaring crowd set me on edge.

I didn't want to hurt her. I didn't have a goal for this fight—she did.

My mentality wasn't to win. She'd forced me into this. My instincts were all still there, my skill was still there. I just didn't want to fight her.

I'd just have to wear her out.

She parried my blade with her shield more effectively than I could parry her sword with mine. I struck out again and my blade glanced off her shield. She buckled but used the momentum to drop and roll. She got up startlingly fast, and by the time I recovered from my swing, she was closer than I wanted her.

From then, it was a fight for space. The walls of the ditch loomed around us, at least twice my height. She knew I wanted to take back distance, so she kept turning my back to the walls of the ditch. She was going to win, whether that meant skinning me or scratching me, I didn't know.

Between the grunts of effort, the slip of my feet in the ashes, and the blows of our blades, I caught her eyes.

She could see I was holding back. Worse, she could see I was giving up.

I jumped back from her and stopped. She paused, panting. It was over. Her eyes were shadowed, and her jaw was tight. She lowered her weapons and stood there. The cheering faded. The sound of my ragged breathing seemed louder. I lowered my weapon, too. I was sure everyone watching was confused, but we weren't.

"What's the point, General?" I sighed.

"The point is, you fight," she sneered and closed the distance between us.

"I will not fight you the way you want me to." I pushed past her.

"Then fight him," she said, grabbing my shirt. I stopped and turned as she directed my attention toward the farthest corner. Zevran and Crete ushered a man toward the edge of the burn pit. He wore black weathered leathers, and a burlap sack covered his head. His hands were bound.

"Hey!" I yelled at them as they pushed the man over the edge, and he fell into the unforgiving ground. A cloud of ashes puffed out from under his body. He groaned in pain. I moved toward him, but the General held me back.

"He doesn't even have a weapon," I said.

She looked at the faceless man with disgust. "Have you ever used a sword and shield before?"

I nodded. I've trained with many weapons. She ordered me to swap with her.

"Who is he?" I asked. The man lay on the ground, groaning.

"A nightmare," she said in a low voice. Her eyes were trained on him, filled with hate.

The man's groaning turned to gargled laughter. He pushed himself up to a kneeling position. His laughter grew louder, mottled with madness. The general and I exchanged glances before she turned to leave, taking my former blade with her.

I adjusted my grips on the sword and shield. The man was in hysterics. I could tell from his voice there was something else to him, besides the obvious craziness. I walked closer to him.

"Get up," I barked at him. The men around the pit stayed quiet. I scanned their faces and found Epona's. Her violet eyes were lit up with fear. And if she was afraid of this guy...

I looked back at him. He stopped laughing and stood up.

He was taller than me, which was a rarity in my opponents.

"Unbind me," he hissed. His voice was unnatural. It sounded like—

Laughter crackled in his throat and smoke whispered off his clothes.

I raised my shield and readied my sword just as he combusted. I fell back but didn't lose my footing or take my eyes off him. The fire had erupted from his chest. His clothes didn't burn away, but the sack that hid his face did. So did the rope at his wrists. How had they even managed to bind him?

It was clear what he was. From the books I'd read, from the words my father spewed. He wasn't a man at all. His eyes were black and lifeless, his ashen face cracked in places, revealing the glow of an eternal ember within him.

He burned like a candlewick. Orange and red flames kissing his skin, hissing over the black leathers, and snapping against the wind as he moved. He opened his mouth, and a black double-tipped tongue rolled out, dripping sparks.

"Fuck. Me."

He was Ashan.

He bellowed and the flames coating his skin answered, tightening around him like a cocoon before billowing out in plumes that reached above the edge of the burn pit. He ran toward me.

His arms seemed limp at his side, and he hulked toward me, leaning forward like he might tumble over. His head twisted and rolled as his feet clawed into the dirt. His lengthened tongue unrolled out of his mouth, and reared up like a snake, poised to strike out at me.

"Fuck!" I shouted as I swung my sword to deflect it. Close enough, I could see his tongue was scaled. My sword hadn't severed it.

He stumbled past me. His black eyes met mine, and his laugh rattled through him again. His tongue whipping through the air as he spun around.

"Shit." I threw my weight against him to pommel him with the shield. I got in two hits. One to his arm and one to his head. He fell back, but I followed him, bringing my sword down on him.

It connected with his fucking tongue again. Which speared out and then folded in ways my sword couldn't. Reaching around my blade and nearly touching my face. I shuddered as it hit my shield, leaving a notable scratch on the steel.

He crawled backwards, evading my next strike. He got to his feet and the flames around him expanded until they split off his body and twisted into cyclones of fire.

He thrust his arms, commanding the cyclones to spin toward me. The two pillars of flame towered over me, whooshing and whirling. The heat reached me before they did, and my body's own power responded. Everything the light touched turned shades of red.

"Fuck this," I said, dropping the sword and shield. For the first time in my life, I allowed myself to morph from warrior to Daemon.

I picked my arms up in front of me, bracing for the fiery cyclones' impact. Someone screamed before they engulfed me.

Amid the raging fire, I lost my senses. My mind filled only by the roaring of the flames within and without. I could feel it on my skin and under it. It lit me up like a pyre.

I clawed through the cyclones, pulling the flames around me like a cloak. In one breath, I sucked them into my lungs, absorbed them through my skin. Clearing the air, I got one look at the Ashan before I gave the torrent back.

It felt like I was yelling, but my voice was a blue inferno. My fire surged across the burn pit, swelling with my rage, and crashed into the Ashan. He disappeared in the barrage. I heard him screech, which meant my fire was different, and too much for him to handle.

Men cheered and cursed, stepping back from the edges of the pit as the flames kissed the brim again. I charged down the path my flames had created. My vision still ran red, but I could see through the smoke and light without an issue.

I saw him.

He'd fallen on his back from the blast but was recovering. He stood, but I collided with him before he could regain his balance fully. Tackled him into the ashes.

My hands found his neck, his eyes, his disgusting tongue. He lifted his head as he tried to push me off him, digging his foot into my hip and pushing the heels of his hands into my chest and jaw. I punched him in the face and his head jerked back, hitting the ground with a satisfying thud.

Fire consumed both of us. My body didn't feel it, but my spirit did. The scorching, searing need to overpower him. I got my hands around his throat and screamed.

Again, my voice was a flare. His body bucked beneath mine and he tried to cut me with his monstrous tongue. I caught it with one fire-bathed hand and pulled while pinning him down by the neck with the other. Ripped the black, devilish tongue from his throat and tossed it into the ashes. Then choked his scream out of him.

As he suffocated, his flames scintillated over his body with less ferocity. But I wasn't going to just snuff him out. I was going to devour him. My hands ached with the strain of holding pressure, so I relaxed them just enough to let him cough up smoke.

I punched a fist into his chest. Boring straight through—cracked him open. His blood was molten, his organs like coals and embers. He sputtered, his dark eyes rolling back as black, and crimson bled out of him.

I watched his eyes as I dug my hand in and gripped his beating, incandescent heart. I squeezed and allowed him one last hoarse scream. My fingernails bit into his heart, sapping the light and heat from him and diverting it into my own body. My blackened veins pumped, drinking in his fire.

My skin glowed brighter, my ragged breath shuddering with violet flames. I took every last spark from him until his body was only a charred husk.

I stood, pushing off his crumbling body. The crowd around the pit was silent. Blue and red fire emblazoned the debris lost in the ashes. My weapons were scorched and ruined. Smoke piled into the air.

Still, I was aflame. I made eye contact with Epona and then the General at her side. Both were pale faced. The men's expressions varied from awe to the same look Vyra had given the Ashan. Disgust.

I held out my arms, blue fire kicking up around me and trailing off my skin. This time, I didn't need Epona to extinguish me. I felt cold.

I bowed humorlessly toward the General.

As I lowered my arms and raised my eyes back to her, my power was only a shimmering second skin. I took a deep breath, closed my eyes, and gathered it all back into my core. I put up the familiar wall and felt relieved that my power was completely obedient.

I didn't bother saying anything or looking at anyone as I headed toward the rope ladder. I left all formality in the burn pit. Climbing out, no one offered me a hand or a word of congratulations for surviving. Alone, I headed back toward the camp—stark ass naked. Conversation picked up as distance between me and the soldiers grew.

According to her story, the General and her right hand both had experience with Fire Daemons. They knew what I was, and still, she insisted on bringing it out of me. It was clear my time of hiding was over. No matter how I felt about it.

I considered leaving the camp. Wandering east or north, till I found a city. I could steal weapons, food, and coin from the camp easily enough. Try to get past the wall. I just didn't know where I'd end up or what'd I do to survive. What I'd become to survive.

What kind of world would welcome a Daemon?

The Ashan was a creature I'd so often compared myself to. I knew we were different, but I had difficulty separating us. Both borne of fire. Learning there were other kinds of Daemons, like Epona, was startling. I had so many questions.

What kind of life could I live beyond this encampment? My home was in ruin, and my heart was the same. All I knew was war, and I was becoming this.

If General Vyra was seeing something in me, some purpose for my power, I could only guess what it was: to fight the Illynads alongside her and her men. More than likely, that's what this had been. A test. An exhibition. To show her, the men, and myself what I was capable of. How valuable my power was in this war. I'd taken down an Ashan, bare-handed. I knew she wanted me to find meaning in that.

Wanted me *to want* to fight.

I wasn't stupid.

"The point is to fight."

She wanted me to fight my demons, to fight these monsters. She wanted it for me more than I wanted it for myself. What pissed me off even more was that it had burned one question into my mind.

The farther I got from the burn pit, the louder Hayes' voice asked me the question over and over.

Are you capable of touching this world without leaving a burn mark?

PART 3

KING OF SHADOW

*"When you've walked your world over,
you shall be given wings."*

—Gilded Hymns 5:11

30: SOLUTIONS
Thane
Day Eleven

"She's left the Baore," I said as I opened the door to Rivan's room. He sat up in the bed, shirtless and still groggy with sleep.

"How do you know?" he asked.

"I can sense her, the thread between us—it was strummed the minute she crossed the border."

"Which border? Where is she?"

"The Sunderlands."

He sat on the edge of the bed and scrubbed his hand over his face. I paced the room while he watched me.

"I know what you're thinking, Thane. It's risky—dangerous."

"All of this is risky," I said. "I have to try."

With Keres and Liriene hidden in the Baore, I couldn't reach them. Couldn't channel either of them. The King was no fool. His rise to power was treacherous. He wrote his victories in blood. Not that I despised him for it. I'd never despised him until he took her. For many years, he's been calculated.

But he touched her—took what was mine. Very foolish, indeed. Still, his caution preceded the mistake. The blood glyphs that soaked the soil of his lands were spiritual wards. That and the actual runes that were planted in monuments around the province. There was essentially a dome over the entire Baore.

Its focal points were the castles and his precious city, Mannfel, but it was weaker near the border. The wards guarding the castles and city were—I couldn't breach them.

The King himself was a shield as well. The powers of his mind were extensive. I could sense Keres now, but as long as she was directly at his side, I couldn't touch her. For my plan to work, she'd have to be alone. He'd have to be distracted, and he was never distracted.

Still, I had to try. I needed to use my senses.

Silas was waiting for us to make a move, but my men and I were facing our own risks. This was one solution. If it worked, we wouldn't even need to leave the castle. Passing through the Veil was always dangerous for me in my current state. I hadn't been willing to attempt this in the past, but things were different now.

He wasn't supposed to have taken her—kept her from me.

31: STRUCK

Liriene

Day Eleven

Fever coursed through me, unrelenting for the next few days. Varic and his men forced me to still work but assigned me lighter duty. Shayva had been doing her best, but it wasn't helping. She said my body was already fighting so much and this curse was extra stress. I could feel it in my blood. Every day since the mark appeared on my hand, I'd watched the castle as much as I could. I scanned each window and tracked every face that came in and out of Tecar.

On the sixteenth day, I saw Thaniel and Mathis loitering beyond the gates. It shocked me to see them here. They admitted Mathis in, but Thaniel stayed outside, watching him. Watching me. I'd wondered what had happened to them when they left Ro'Hale. And here they were… but something was wrong.

"I've got business with this one," Mathis said to one of our guards and walked past him, headed straight for me. I laid down my palette and brush, then stood from where I sat on the stone steps of a monument my people had built. My new job was painting copies of strange characters detailed in scrolls. I was too weak, too sick to labor.

He walked past me to view the wall I was painting. Images and words in a foreign tongue. I didn't know whether he understood any of it better than I did.

"A story of war and conquest, your people versus mine?" I asked as Mathis approached, pointing to what I'd painted. He nodded.

The Sun hid behind the clouds, but the glaring light was enough to make him squint as he met my eyes. The air was getting colder, and the rags we wore would soon be insufficient. Mathis eyed me as if he thought about it. Dressed in leathers and armor, a warm tunic.

My dress was filthy and torn open at my back. My long red hair, tousled in the wind, tickled my scarred skin. I was filthy. The look on his face—I didn't know whether it was pity or disgust. Or both. I had to remind myself he loved an Elf, my kin. I tried to give him the benefit of the doubt. Still, there was nothing he could do for me or any of the rest of us here in Tecar. His gaze was as powerless as it was thorough.

"They've left the castle."

I knew who he meant. "Where have they gone? How do you know this?"

"I am friends with a knight named Yarden. The King assigned him as your sister's personal guard. I saw him loading baggage onto the King's carriage. He couldn't tell me where they were going but that they'd be back soon."

"Could you make any guesses about where they might have gone?" I asked.

"Liriene, I'll tell you where they went because Thaniel wants you to know. People talk loosely within the castle. I overheard two maids talking in the hallway. One of them seemed fond of Yarden and was complaining he was leaving with your sister and the King. Said she didn't know why he'd be needed in the Sunderlands, when Keres would be at her ancestral kingdom with family."

"Oh, Gods." I pressed my right hand to my forehead.

"There's more—Are you ill?"

I sat back down on the step.

"Liriene, you're pale. Have you seen a healer? What is this wound?" He held up my left hand, which was wrapped in linen that was now soiled from outside work.

"I've been treated by our Vigilant. Still, my fever won't break, but go on. Tell me."

He looked around and nodded at the two guards some distance away who watched us.

"Your sister made a grand gesture just days ago. The King was hosting an audience. I was there, but I don't think she saw me. She entered unannounced and made her way to the center of the floor."

He locked eyes with me, and that pity flooded his eyes again. "She has sworn to marry him. She will become Queen of the Baore."

What came next… felt like a bolt of lightning. I saw its light in the periphery of my vision, shooting out of the center of the Sun, stepping down out of the sky, and fracturing the clouds. It struck me between the eyes… a vision:

She turned her head, her white hair cascading down her back in a long braid entwined with flowers. Her ears were adorned with jewels. She turned toward a voice. His voice. I couldn't see him, but his presence was pressing against the edges of my vision. She smiled and opened her hands. One, scarred like mine, and the one that'd been broken, was healed. A silver cup appeared in them.

The vision spun out into smoke, and voices chimed in my head. Laughter whirled into screaming. Blood splattered the stone walls of the castle. The silver cup was dropped onto a black-and-white checkered floor, spilling red wine. Dizzying flashes of light in hues of yellow and blue glinted off mirrors. I tried to close my eyes or to make the vision end, but my head was filled with light.

Then I saw white snakes slithering over naked bodies. I heard a raven cawing and watched it shoot across an all-red sky. Colliding with a stained-glass window of the castle, it broke its neck and fell to the earth. Keres stood before me, and the dead bird lay twitching between us. The sky seemed too close. The ground felt far away. We were suspended for a moment. My stomach flipped.

And then she fell. I threw myself forward and grabbed her, only to be pulled down with her. We landed on a stone, checkered table, somehow farther apart than before. I reached once more for her, but my left hand burned and bled.

I looked up at a black sky littered with blue and yellow stars and saw a blade hovering above her head. From the sky fell thousands of dead black birds. They landed all around her and were swallowed by white snakes that writhed against her.

She tried to crawl toward me, dragging her body through the spilled wine. The more I reached for her, the farther she became. She reached for the silver cup that rolled toward her. It refilled as she held it up and she drank. When she pulled it away, her mouth was red with blood. I heard the voice once more, and she smiled, looking up. I followed her gaze upward and the sword above her finally fell.

32: SERPENT

Liriene

"Wake up, child." A furtive hand dabbed a wet cloth at my brow. "Release what you see."

The vision was in tatters, parts of it replaying and overlaying others. Sounds garbled and lines blurred; but a soft voice towed me back to the shore of consciousness.

"Release what you see."

I opened my eyes. He was leaning over my bed, a basin of water and a cloth in his hands. I felt sweaty, and the air felt sticky with steam and the aroma of herbs.

"Magister Hadriel." I tried to sit up. My head ached, and I instantly felt nauseous and dizzy.

"Hush now, child. You don't have to move." He dropped the cloth back into the basin and rested it on a nearby table. His eyes drifted to my hand.

I raised it. Some kind of jelly was slathered on it, and he'd applied a light woven dressing.

"First visions are never easy," he said in a low voice. I returned my attention to him but kept my hand up.

"I've been channeled before, and I listen to Oran, but this was different. And this? Do you know what this is?"

"Yes." He tucked his hands into his belled sleeves.

Slowly, I sat up. There were many candles lit in the room and though they weren't very bright, my eyes felt like I had been staring at the sun.

"Tell me. Am I cursed?"

"It is a Bind. Created between your sister and the King by an ancient magic. Tying your life to his. It seems the wound festered; always a risk of that. I've applied a salve to fight off the infection. It seems your fever is broken now. You should make a full recovery within a few days."

"Thank you... How did I end up here?"

"Your vision arrested you. You were convulsing and unresponsive. A nearby soldier called for help. I was just outside the gates of Tecar, speaking with Varic. I assume you know him."

"Unfortunately."

"Varic and his men didn't know what to do. You were muttering incomprehensibly and gasping for air one moment, then seizing the next. Sometimes the messages are too much for us to handle. It will get easier, I assure you. Your body will learn to be strong enough for what your mind must bear."

"The messages. You've had visions then too? Are you a Seer?"

"I have seen a great deal." The lines of his face seemed deeper for a flash of a moment. His eyes, the busy, blurred color of a riverbed, brightened only for a second. I wondered whether I should tell him. He might give me insight or lie. Or maybe his reaction could tell me something.

"Might you be able to interpret my vision?" I asked.

His mouth parted as if he might answer, but the two fine lines between his brows pursed for a breath.

Then he said, "I might. Though, you might not want to hear it."

"Better to know than to wonder." The right-hand corner of my mouth lifted. "I do not want to be blind to what I See."

His eyes found the floor between us and then rejoined with mine.

I gave him the bones of the vision. "Blood in a silver cup spilled out. Dead birds and wriggling serpents. A looming blade. My sister, crawling across a checkered floor."

He lifted one hand to his mouth and lowered his eyes. For minutes, he stood like that, looking like he was reading the lines between the stone tiles of the floor. Turning around, he faced his bookcases. Weathered spines. Faded blues, reds, browns, and blacks. Pale and yellowed parchment.

He picked one.

"Marked Unseeing, this is…" He thumbed through the pages. "No, no. This is about Instruments, not visions. Visions." The book slid back into place, and he pulled out three more.

"A book about Instruments?" I asked as his eyes poured over another text.

"Yes, the Blind Ones. Those who are chosen by a God can see visions in their dreams. These things come from their God. They can't control it, nor can they behold such things in the waking world. Unlike Oracles and Seers. Oracles are physically blind, but their mind's eye is ever open. Seers are different still."

"Like me?"

He turned toward me and studied me for a second. As if my truths might be written on my skin. His eyes lingered on my face for a breath and then he returned to his book. "Yes."

"Like you?"

He smiled at the page. "I am not a Seer, not as you are. Though, from your curiosity, I can tell we are not all that different."

"What are you, then?" I asked.

His smile broadened. "I am… proud."

I tilted my head, trying to see into his eyes, but he kept them lowered on the book. I knew he wasn't still reading it.

"Proud." I nodded. "Why are you proud?"

"Perhaps I will tell you. First, we'll discuss this vision of yours."

He continued skimming the shelves until he finally found a book that held his attention for longer than two seconds.

"The Drums of Dreaming, a Comprehensive Guide to the Underlying Rhythm and Symbols. Well, what an ambitious title. Surely, there's something in here to help us interpret it. I think I won this book in a game of cards…" He flipped it open to the index and showed it to me. "Recall the most significant images of your vision. Find their match here and then turn to their definitions."

The words on the page were just as confusing as the characters I'd been painting in Tecar. "Try Silver Cup," I suggested, not wanting to give away that I couldn't read.

He looked at me before flipping through the pages. "Silver, a precious metal, can signify an awakening. Silver appears to us when we are in search of justice or protection, when we lack either..." He continued to flip through the book. "To see a silver cup or to drink from it, omens trouble or avarice..."

"Oh Gods." I looked up at him from where I had been concentrating on the floor.

He continued, "Ravens... Misfortune. Betrayal. Death. Hatred. Magic. Hidden self. Alternatively, this death omen may be an awakening to a new life or beginning. Did you see a bird flying or perched? This says, to see a bird flying... if a bird lands on you..."

"I saw it hit a window."

He skims, then taps the page. "To see a bird hit a window may denote confusion or blindness, encountering obstacles or neglecting your reflection.

"I don't know if I want to hear the rest." I said it, but I couldn't really mean it. I needed to read it, if only I could.

He looked at me questioningly before continuing, "The white snake appears to us when we must harness our energies and embrace new beginnings. The snake often brings with it temptation or signifies ambition, a lust for power. It may come as a warning not to ignore wisdom when facing threats." He returned his attention to me, and I felt like he could see what I was trying to hide. I could at least read the look in his eyes.

He cleared his throat and leafed through the pages. "Consuming wine suggests desires that may lead to destruction. Consuming blood signifies a thirst for power, life. Absorbing the natural forces of life. Snakes consuming birds... hunger for power. Falling... powerlessness, inadequacy. Sword—betrayal. Loss."

"That's enough." I stood and closed the book in his hands.

"Is knowing better after all?" he asked after replacing it on the shelf.

"I could have guessed at most of those symbols' meanings, but this is more solidifying. Stringing them all together, it's obvious the vision was as negative as it felt. I don't see any light in it."

"Liriene," he drew my attention, "you are the servant of Oran, a Seer of Light. Your God is not just worshiped as a source of natural light, as the Sun or of fire. He is the God of enlightenment. Light is not just about casting out darkness, it is about revelation. In that way, visions are not about good and bad. They are about truth. As you learn to See, you will stop looking for light and dark, good and evil. You will find meaning, insight, and you will gain erudition. You will simply come to know."

I nodded.

He opened his hands and nodded. "Are you sure you don't want to keep the book? It is in my nature to be giving."

"Your nature," I repeated. "I don't want to bring it to Tecar, but thank you."

Inexperience pricked like a thorn. Looking at him, I could see glimmers of his concealed nature. It was deep and possibly dangerous. Something lurking within him, maybe waiting to strike. Something teasing at my Sight. I needed to know, to understand him. There was something just beyond my perception...

"Your proud nature," I said, reminding him of what he'd said earlier. "Will you tell me now what you meant by that?"

He turned his neck and ran a finger over the tattoo of a serpent.

"I told you I am proud. All vipers are. We lay close to the ground, so others think lowly of us. Pride helps us stand when others would dare tread on us. Serpents do not writhe in dust. They reach, they bite, they climb, and sometimes they strangle. It is the nature of an underestimated thing. When my life is over, I'll be proud that I shed many skins, and yet remained true to my nature—my beliefs and desires. I can see you as you naturally are. You are not what people expected you to be. I can help you. I can give you parts of my mind and skills. Like shedding scales, I can leave behind pieces of myself in others. This way, what little I am becomes more. That is what I am. A man who reaches, who hopes to touch the edges of expectation as if it were parchment posted on a wall and waiting to be ripped down. I want to create space for the unexpected and the underestimated. I am a man who lies low until I am ready to give or extend a hand. That's my power. Because when a viper extends himself, he either poisons or tastes. I am very capable of either. That is what I am, and I am proud."

"A scholar. An arcanist. A healer," I said, and he lifted his eyes to meet mine. I Saw him. "A visionary."

He straightened his spine, but kept his head bowed ever so slightly. His eyes flared with streaks of star-lit silver.

"When you See, the blindfold of reality is undone. Your mind can open, can enter the beyond. Your eyes see through and past, and you understand it because in your mind you See truth."

"Are you helping my sister to see a new reality?" I asked.

He let out a sigh and folded his hands behind his back. "Your sister is the maker of her reality. None other exists—"

"She's too easily and too often shocked that she can be wrong. Resistant to change. Too focused on the darkness. I think it blinds her."

He offered me a small, knowing smile. "Her eyes will be opened as yours have been."

"You'll see to that, I'm sure." I looked down. "Although, Magister Hadriel, I must admit, I'm not sure I want Keres seeing the world the way you do or the way the King does. The way I do now. I fear you'll teach her things that will steep her in the darkness she's already weakened by."

"I will show her this world is not to be underestimated, and neither is she. I will teach her the breadth of her power."

"And the King? What kind of education is he giving her? Marriage can be an alliance or a war. When the time comes, you'll stand with your King, and I will stand with my sister. Despite all your navigations, my sister is not easily led. She will forge her own path and it might lead into a darkness deep enough to swallow us all. All her second life, I've been warning her. Trying to make her see the dangers of indulgence in power. Now, the Gods have seen fit to seat her at the table of her enemies. Those who would dine on her and those who would teach her their gluttony. A feast of power and magic, politics, and sex. You want to know what I See? Keres... devouring the King, spitting out his bones, and then licking her

241

fingers. I'll see to it that she does," I said and stood, "Excuse me if I don't so readily see her or this world as you do."

He stepped closer.

"King Berlium and Keres are to be married. She is in farther than you know. He is very persuasive, and yes, even very alluring. True power is, first and foremost, seductive. You are chained still. She is breaking ties to form new ones."

I did not answer.

"Are you forgetting your vision, Liriene? Is this blatant denial of what you have Seen? Keres thirsts for power. Whether that will be poison to her, or an antidote is still to be seen. You have seen one possibility. This is only the beginning, and nothing is settled. There are many realities being spun like so many parts of a web. All connected, all diverted by choices. Keres is making choices and you will, too."

"Are you going to give me some options?" I tilted my head at him. "If I would accept your help, what would it look like?"

"You must return now to Tecar. You are safer there than you think, for now. But I will speak with the King, and I will call you forth from the den. You'll be brought back into the castle."

"How—"

He held up his hand and then walked toward the door. He opened it and Mathis turned around.

I looked at Hadriel as I passed over the threshold. Before he closed the door, he spoke. "Open your eyes. Try to see the possibilities. Try to look beyond the expectations—especially yours and Keres'. You were captured by your sworn enemy. You expected to, what? Destroy this kingdom from the inside out? Taste freedom once more? You both expected to hate us, to stand against us. You've underestimated us. Keres sees the truth of this new reality. Don't embarrass yourself by letting her prove you blind."

33: SOLIDARITY

Heres

Night Sixteen

The past few days, the King and I rode in separate carriages, having only brief exchanges when we stopped to make camp. I was given my own tent. He looked... angry. He was never far, but there was something between us—I didn't understand what or why. Yarden rode with me, and we spent a majority of the time reading.

It was difficult not to spend all the daylight hours looking out the window. Drinking in the beauty of High Autumn's transition to winter in the Sunderlands. Brown and orange leaves carpeted the earth. Those that clung to the mostly bare branches were shriveled. Trembling in the wind. The noise of the carriages shattered herds of deer. Breaking them off in different directions. I could see the River Liriene at some points. All too soon, the gates of Ro'Hale opened, and I closed my book.

King Berlium reached out a gloved hand. I slipped my left into his and stepped down from the carriage. My hand was missing Silas' ring but wore the scar Berlium gave me instead. He rubbed his thumb against it, drawing my gaze to his. My right hand was still wrapped, stiff against its splint, but the bandages were clean.

The cold, ocean eyes he showed others were blinked away. The eyes he had for me were sapphire, flecked with gold. His brows lifted ever so slightly as he allowed them to wander over my body. He beamed with what felt like pride. Strange, the anger had dissipated.

Queen Hero wasn't expecting us, so neither were her palace guards, and it was the middle of the night. I quickly noted the newly reinforced gates that embraced the palace, and the generous increase of posted guards. I was dying to know what changed since I was last here. We turned to greet the three officials that flitted down the marble steps to meet us at our carriage.

I recognized none of the Elves dressed in various animal furs that approached the King and me. The leader of the pack tightened his spotted fur around his tall frame. As if he might catch a chill from the King's attention.

I lingered behind Berlium's right shoulder. The official caught me appraising him.

"Allow me to introduce my wife to be." Berlium gestured toward me, noting the male's fixed attention. "This is Lady Keres, of Ro'Hale."

"The Coroner," the man breathed. "A woman capable of great atrocities."

"Oh, you know me, damned for greatness." I rolled my eyes.

King Berlium smirked, passing between me and the official to stand by my right side, my weak side. The official's gaze drifted from me to the King, having to look up to meet his eyes.

"And you are, sir?" the Elf asked.

The question was preposterous, as we were flanked by a horde of guards. The crest of the Baore was emblazoned on their shields, embroidered into Berlium's tunic.

"You stand before King Berlium Gaspar of the Baore, you fool," I said, touching my injured hand to Berlium's.

A current of sensation zipped up my arm from our connection. Ever since I'd surrendered, his touch felt charged with energy.

"King Berlium." The official shuddered. The women at his side exchanged glances.

"And you are?" Berlium asked. The officials remembered to bow.

"I am Mika," the male said. "This is Lady Zora and Lady Rin."

"Nobody of consequence, then." Berlium looked past the entourage to the palace doors. "We are here to see the Queen."

"She is not expecting—Coroner, you are not welcomed here."

Berlium looked at me with a raised brow and a languid smile stretching on his lips. "What in the name of the damned have you done?"

I mirrored his smile. "I leave little fires everywhere."

The frown lines around Mika's mouth deepened. Setting a rebuttal aside, he opened his arm toward the steps. Notwithstanding the urge to glare at us as we left him behind. The Ro'Hale guards tightened their grips on their weapons as we passed them. The line-up of carriages behind ours stretched far back down the road. Each carriage door opened. I listened for the distinct crash of metal boots into dirt, the clicking of suits of armor in motion.

Thirty men followed behind us, ready to defend us. The stayed on the grounds or approached Hero's guards for... friendly conversation. Their presence intimidated both Hero's guards and me. King Berlium's men who walked behind us, drifted off to invade the open spaces of the entry hall. They were insurance for safe travels, but they would invite themselves into the barracks.

"We brought our enemy home, now, didn't we?" The Death Spirit noted, but the way Berlium walked the halls, it seemed like he knew this place well.

Mika led us toward the empty mirrored throne, and neither of us denied our interest in it... in the perfect image staring back at us. My gown was an assault on the purity of the marble hall. A black velvet, strapless bodice with a plunging V-neckline that dipped below my breastbone. The bodice ended in a sharp point that overlaid the black chiffon skirt of the dress. A black cloak rested on my shoulders and was tied at my throat. With every step toward the throne, I imagined the train of it absorbing the blood Hero had spilled in this hall.

My hair was loose. My eyes looked a wilder shade of green, lined with kohl, which was extremely difficult to do in the carriage while Yarden held a hand mirror for me. The look was growing on me, though. Golden jewelry lit up the soft hollows of my reflection.

The only soft thing about Berlium was his clothing. His outfit complemented mine with a black tunic, embroidered with the gold Baorean insignia—a bear raised on its hind legs and clawing the air. His soft black jacket matched his trousers. Not a strand was out of place. The usual, domineering harshness fractured his gaze into the mirror. Until he looked from his reflection to mine.

There was no ignoring the fact that the Grizzly King and I made a devastatingly beautiful couple. Our attentions shifted from the throne ahead to the rulers we saw in each other. We exchanged approval.

"I like the look of power," the Death Spirit sighed.

Mika led us down a familiar hall, and I suspected we'd find the Huntress Queen in the Pleasure Gardens. It felt like so long ago that I attended an unusual tea party here. I hadn't told Berlium about what happened between the Queen and me the last time I was here. It felt strange coming back—it seemed like nothing had even happened.

Anxiety mingled with my curiosity when we passed the door that led to the gardens. No life stirred outside, and we continued down the hall. Instead, we approached a set of white double doors. Mika opened them, and music unwound into the hallway. An erotic rhythm pulsed against the walls.

"Well, well," Berlium said. "It's a party."

As we crossed the threshold, his power invaded the ballroom like the break of a dark dawn. Heads turned, whispers lifted into the air, the shadows of the room deepened and flared with the hushing of wings.

The Huntress Queen's stare soared across the room and struck us where we stood in solidarity. She bared her teeth in a sinister smile.

"The crazed queen, the blood-thirsty Coroner, and the Grizzly King. This ought to be interesting," the Death Spirit hummed with excitement.

We descended the steps into the room, which was deep-set. The floor looked like marble that had been painted with blood and it probably had been.

The walls were black and Berlium's power crawled over them, touching every inch like vines, reaching forward with our every step. Silver chandeliers dripped with crystals and fire danced on the hundreds of candles. My feet were bare, of course, but he wore boots, treading soundlessly.

Queen Hero watched my every move, our gazes like crossed swords, pressing the blades toward each other in competition. Her throne was made of black wood that reminded me of the trees in the Southern courtyard of Berlium's castle. There was nothing fragile about Queen Hero—except her mind, probably. The spikes of wood in which her seat was nestled were filed sharp and jutted in random directions. Like wings made of spears branching out of her back. She was a rose among thorns.

Her dress—if it could be called that—was crimson. Sheer mesh from top to bottom. Rubies encrusted the dress, sewn in to cover only what was necessary, yet still not even accomplishing that. She stood, and I absorbed every detail of her. The sleeves reached her wrists, and the hem fell over her feet. Like a second skin, but red. Her platinum hair was up in a bun, and a crown of pale bones sat atop her head.

The scent of blood thickly layered the air. It coated my senses. A decadent vapor that felt like tiny pins pricking at my thirst. The deeper we walked, the stronger it got. Berlium's body was tense, his breathing shallow, as if the feeling was a hammer-blow to his craving. Every hair on the nape of my neck stood when he bristled.

I glanced up and watched the firelight dance across the jewels of the chandeliers, looking like crystallized blood that dripped from them. Rose petals were trodden underfoot of courtiers, ground into a powder that dusted their bare feet. All of them were dressed as scantily as the Queen, gyrating against one another to the erotic music.

Drums, the crush of bodies. Strings sighing and winds moaning. Someone stroked the piano keys with a rhythm you felt under your skin. The air was thick with the smell of sex and blood, like copper and sweat.

Berlium put his arm around my waist, drawing me in close and turning his head to sniff my hair. I'd washed it with rose water. He breathed deeply, and it seemed some kind of relief to him, but I noticed the press of his erection in his black pants. He pulled me in front of him, stopping us in the middle of the floor, where the crowd danced around us.

"Don't look at me like you want to fight me," he said huskily and pressed his body against mine, so I felt the length of his hardness. Holding onto my hips, he swayed us to the music. I relaxed into him, fitting against his body the way shadows fit into sharp corners.

"Oh, but I do," I said.

"Let's convince her otherwise," he said in a playful, low voice. Looking at me through hooded eyes.

I'd seen people dance in my clan. To wild drums and wood pipes, never to music like this. I scanned his face for instruction. As if on cue, the orchestra flaunted a robust, romantic tune.

"Show me how obedient you can be."

The crowd parted around us, making way for the power that rippled from him. His hands lifted to my shoulders and pulled at the knot fastening my cape. It slipped off, revealing the smooth skin of my shoulders and prominent collarbones. He passed it into someone's unsuspecting hands. Not bothering to notice the way they looked at him incredulously, and then cowered.

Berlium's gaze plunged into the neckline of my dress, and he bit his lower lip with a smile.

"Hold this hand up," he said, touching my stronger left hand.

I lifted it to the level of my eyes. He touched my elbow and ran his fingers up my arm to my palm. Gently, bringing his fingertips to mine and then settling them in between. His other hand grabbed me by the waist, and he brought us even closer. His scent, the feel of him hard against me, overwhelmed my senses.

"Put your other hand on my shoulder. Good. Now," he said, smiling, "move with me."

His footsteps directed my own into obedience. The cadence of the song sharpened and sighed, edging out before curling back in. The King's legs moved with a grace that was a testament to his training as a warrior. Everything else about his movements felt like the testament of... other skills.

If this hulking Human could do this, I was sure my years of training would help me too. I fell into his rhythm, allowing my body to relax and sway. Our feet drifted in tandem, our chests pressed together, keeping us tall. We pirouetted through the crowd, a dark, distinct couple against the backdrop of a red floor. Until the melody turned into a decadent descent. He dipped me down, allowing me to lose my weight in his arms. The crowd purred, and that's when I noticed many had stopped to watch.

The song climbed back up as he lifted me and spun me away from him. My dress flared just as the brass wind instruments did, earning another sigh. The orchestra led our dance through a crescendo, as if daring us to take the entire floor. Uncertainty stole my footing, but the King didn't falter or even let it show that I had. We moved like we were one. The song rushed toward its climax and heat banked in his eyes.

He spun me again and again as the song fluttered at its height. Through every turn, I whipped my head around to find his eyes waiting for mine. Until the last, when he caught me. I was dizzy as he dipped me low once more and slid his hand under my dress to lift my leg into the air. Dizzy as he kissed me. Dizzy from the power his kiss shared.

He lifted me up as the song ended. The crowd sighed and hissed with pleasure. Then he bowed to me. I curtsied to him. My heart was pounding.

Queen Hero applauded, and we both turned, offering her a swift bow. She turned to the band and applauded them as well, which the entire crowd echoed. We followed suit.

We approached her throne as the orchestra's music drifted back into a romantic, but more subdued, song. Hero's eyes glowed with that characteristic ferality.

One look from Rydel and his voice slipped into my thoughts.

"What a pretty dance."

"For such a monster?" I sent the thought back to him.

"Are you referring to yourself or your partner?"

I smiled as he neared. *"It seems he and I are not so different in that regard."*

His pleasant smile faded as his eyes met with the King's.

Berlium cut him a quick, warning glance. Had he heard the thoughts?

"King Berlium," Queen Hero moaned his name, snapping attention onto herself. She offered a small, courteous bow.

"Queen Hero." He nodded. "We didn't mean to crash your party, but after that dance, I'm very glad we did."

"As am I," she crooned. "Gods, the way you two dance!" Heat flared in her eyes as she looked at him. She leaned in closer, pulling Rydel's sleeve so that he followed. "I'm tempted to invite the pair of you to our bed." She snickered.

"I do not share." Berlium smiled still, but his voice was devoid of humor.

Queen Hero fidgeted on the balls of her feet, her gaze flickering between us now with poorly hidden suspicion. "I wasn't expecting your visit—especially one from *you*, cousin."

"We'll only be here as long as it takes you to cooperate." There was venom in his voice, and she recoiled, recognizing the bite in his words.

"Where is your Viper?" she asked.

"Occupied. Attending to matters while we're away," Berlium answered. The memory of Hadriel's viper tattoo popped into my head. To think he was actually known by that nickname wasn't surprising.

"Well." She clasped her hands together and her eyes darted between us. "Enjoy the party. When you're ready to retire, you'll be given a room."

"She's dismissing us?" the Death Spirit gasped.

"We've had a long trip. We'll go up soon," Berlium said.

"Of course." She nodded. "Do as you wish. We'll chat in the morning." She sat back down on her throne and fixed her attention on the room. Rydel moved to her side, watching the King and me.

"I'm too tired to dance," I said. Berlium placed his hand on the small of my back as we passed back through the crowd.

"Hopefully, you have the energy for something else." His voice was at my ear. Chills skittered over me, and wings fluttered in my belly.

A bunny servant met us at the door. "I will show you to your rooms."

Last time I'd seen Faye, a nasty guard was hauling her away from her injured sister Moriya. Silas' Moriya, who was nowhere to be seen. Nor was Nadia. Faye acted like she didn't know me—or didn't want to. I was dying to know what happened here. Without a backward glance, she led us back down the corridor. We followed her down familiar halls, watching her bunny tail and ears move. She hurried. As if she wanted to run.

"Is Nadia around?" I asked.

She stopped and turned. Her eyes were restless, her brows pinched together.

"No." Her hands balled into fists, and she spun back around, walking even faster. We followed in silence after that. Faye stopped in front of my mother's room.

"Lady Keres, you'll have this room again," she said, and opened the door.

The King and I exchanged glances. I didn't think about whether we'd share a room.

"This way, my lord." And she left, expecting him to follow. He lingered outside my door as I crossed the threshold.

"Goodnight," I said. He stared at me... so I smiled tentatively. The muscles in his jaw hammered, and he narrowed his eyes. Coldness crept back into them.

"Goodnight," he replied.

Faye was well down the hall. He left without another word.

Well, that was awkward.

Looking into the room, I took a wary step. Candles burned in the room already, and it smelled like dust. The only difference was the new dead bouquet set on the table in the closet.

The first time I heard the strange, disembodied voice telling me to curse my God and die was in this room. Then again, in the Baore. Was Ahriman following me? What tied Him to me, no matter where I was?

I stood there, leaning on the door for what felt like an hour. Afraid to take another step. A knock startled me.

"Lady Keres, are you in there?"

I hurried to open the door.

"Yarden," I said.

He was carrying my travel trunk.

"Your belongings." He smiled. "Did you pack stones? This thing is far too heavy."

I chuckled. "Books. Can't go anywhere without them."

"Dragon's fury," he huffed. "May I?"

I moved aside, letting him into the room. "You can set it at the foot of my bed, if you don't mind."

"With pleasure." He lowered it onto the carpeted floor and turned back to me. Darius was the only other male who'd been in this room with me before. Not that it mattered.

His smile faded. "Are you alright, my lady?"

I forced a small smile. "I'm fine. And you—you look… normal." I gestured to his outfit. He'd changed since the carriage ride. Lost the armor for casual trousers and a tunic.

He rubbed the back of his neck. "Yeah, well. The King didn't think a hulking suit of armor trailing you would be well-received by Queen Hero. Besides, he'll protect you."

"I see."

Our eyes stayed on each other for a moment.

"Well, I'm sure the King would not like me idling in your room."

"Yes, I'm sure." I stepped aside again, and he passed me. "Will you be idling outside of my room?"

"I'll be in the room next door." He tilted his head to the right.

We closed our doors at the same time.

⌘ ⌘ ⌘

I changed out of my dress, washed my face, and crawled under the blankets. Dreams flurried through my head. A figure approached me through shadow, drawing closer, but when I tried to focus on him, he moved farther away. Back and forth, he walked, but got nowhere. There was a strange familiarity to him. As if he'd been in my dreams before.

Abruptly, the shadows that shrouded him scattered, flying around him, obscuring him, and darkening the dream. A hand touched me under my chin and turned my face until I met ocean eyes.

Berlium pressed close, resting his hands on either side of my throat, and bowed his head closer. Angling his mouth toward mine. His mouth promised the taste of power.

He stopped a breath away. Tilted his head so that the tip of his nose barely grazed against mine. My lips parted when his did, and he drifted closer. His breath fanned against my lips, carrying the scent of honey.

"Don't close your eyes," he whispered. I lifted my gaze to his heated stare. In this dream, my hand wasn't broken, and I ran my hands across his bare chest. I skimmed my gaze over the planes of his chest, the muscles of his abs.

He lifted my chin with a finger, bringing his mouth down toward mine again. Stopping as I lifted onto my toes.

"You've been avoiding me."

"You've been missing me?" He smiled.

"Kiss me," I whispered back.

He brushed my hair behind my ear. "No, little wolf."

My brows pinched together, and I looked up into his eyes. Wrapped my hands around his neck as his tightened around my throat. My pulse hammered against his touch. I tried to pull him closer. His mouth lingered teasingly close.

"Every time you touch me," he whispered, resting his forehead against mine. "The way you look at me, the way you danced with me..." He pulled back and lifted my hands off him, dropping them at my side. "I grow so tired of lying women."

"What?" My stomach dropped. "What are you talking about?"

He stepped close again, toe-to-toe with me. Planting his hands on his hips, he blinked at me. Pupils dilating, his eyes darted as he searched mine. Defiantly, I leaned in closer and lifted my weight onto the balls of my feet so that I could bring my nose nearer to his.

He grabbed my face and breathed against my ear. I held onto his arms.

"I told you. I can sense what lives inside you. The truth, the lies, your desires, and your fears. You can't hide from me. I saw your duplicity the moment you walked into my throne room and offered me your ring. It was a power-play. You're trying to take the lead. You want to dance with the devil, Keres?"

"I've given you my word," I said, pushing against him, but he didn't let go.

"I'm Baorean, darling. You'd have to be made of stone to earn my trust." His voice was gravelly.

"I'm here, cooperating, aren't I?" I shifted on my feet. His gaze bored into me.

"I have offered you things you clearly want." A wave of his power washed over me as a rumble built in his chest. "You reach for me with one hand while clutching a dagger in the other."

He grabbed me by the wrists.

"We will wed. Have you not considered that your vow to me will be as binding as the blood curse? You will believe it in your bones that you belong to me. There will be no games. I will not be made a fool of. The crown I offer comes with a collar and chains, little wolf. You cannot be wooed, and I am not the man to try. Did you expect me to believe in your ploy at tenderness? Looking at me with adoration. Lies. You do not *sigh* into me, you rage. You do not dance, you war. I know the truth of you. I want nothing less than the chaos of who you are. I will not accept docility; it's not why I chose you."

The imprint of his touch vanished, and I stood alone in the dream's darkness, shivering. Not from fear. It was the shiver of a bowstring that a powerful hand had strummed. Trembling now because it had lost its arrow and missed its mark.

34: SUCCULENCE

Keres

Day Seventeen

"You were in my dream last night," I said to Berlium, who continued walking toward me down the hall. Unbuttoning the cuffs of his dark blue sleeves and rolling them up before meeting my eyes. Waves crashed into me.

"Oh? What a beautiful nightmare it must have been. Come, darling." He took my hand and pulled me into his stride. Yarden followed behind us.

I lowered my voice and looked up at him, struggling to keep up with him. His hair looked like he'd slept fitfully and just pushed it back when he woke.

"It wasn't just a dream, Berlium. I know you were really there."

The corners of his mouth tugged upward, but I frowned at him.

"You accused me of lies while telling me I'd be chained to you, like a dog. Yet when I gave you my word, you said you'd give me wings. You can't promise me one, then threaten with the other. So, which is it? Are you a liar?"

Berlium jerked me to a halt. "Good question. You're hearing me, but you're still not listening."

"You're not making any sense. You want me to submit, but you enjoy the way I resist you," I hissed, straightening until my chest grazed against his.

"I may be many things, Keres, but a liar is not one of them. From the first, I've told you what I want and what you could have. Open-handedly. To wear my crown is to be chained to me. For me to lift you up, you must be in my hand. It is you who is not understanding because you are still plotting." He tapped his finger on my head and leaned down closer.

"You want to lie, to take without giving, which makes you beneath me. I will not stoop or bend for dishonest sighs and smiles. You're only truthful when you shout and scratch—"

"How can you pretend you're any better than me? You—"

"Do you know what the difference between us is?" His voice was rough as he articulated his words. "I don't wait for anyone to give me what I want. I take it. Everything I have taken; I have traded my weakness and unworthiness for power. I became what I am because I gave up what I was. You are not willing to do that, yet."

I scoffed. "I told you I will not give up fighting for my people. If you want me, maybe you need to give up something I actually want."

He grabbed me by the shoulders. "I do not drop crumbs. I hold the things you count dear, and you're too afraid to climb up here and take them because you're afraid of what it means to be mine." His grip tightened. "If you stop fighting and plotting, you'll realize we truly are a match. Neither of us are saviors in this war. I'm not interested in the hero you think you are. I want the wolf in you."

"You'd make me a monster," I growled.

"Darling, the Gods did that for the both of us, and I worship them for it. They designed your darkness for mine. Until you can give me the truth of it, I dare you—keep talking. Make your demands. They are grains of sand, thrown against a wall." He chuckled darkly. "I'd wager that if you went mute till you could start a conversation I'd find meaningful—we'd turn to stone sitting in the silence."

The clap of someone's hands drew both our attention.

"My, my. The sexual tension between you two, it's so thick I could bathe in it. King Berlium, Keres could count the teeth in your head with the way you speak to her... and such little razors they are. I wonder, cousin, does he bite? I so hope he does."

Belrium's huge hand closed around my smaller one again as we turned to face her. Her gaze lingered on him, and the Death Spirit snarled within me. He stood taller, as if he heard it. Hero clasped her hands, her attention now flitting between us.

"Mmm, I'll take that as a yes. Fitting though, because Keres has quite the appetite herself."

Berlium smirked back at her. "I'm well aware."

Queen Hero burst out giggling and waved her hands. "Of course, you are, beast. Come, bring your beauty to the dining hall. We'll break our fast." She rounded the corner, leaving us to follow the train of her all-white lace gown.

Behind her, I listened to the bones clattering around her wrists and ankles with every step. The dress she wore was just as revealing as the one she had on last night, with the white lace doing little to cover her ass. She swayed her hips. Berlium's eyes rolled over her. She turned once to look over her shoulder, trailing her hands over her hips as she locked eyes with him. He looked at me with a wolfish grin.

I rolled my eyes. Rydel walked beside her, not as pompous, but also dressed in an all-white outfit. They glided down the hall, and I was thankful she hadn't painted these marble floors or walls with blood. They were pristine. The people who walked them—anything but.

I was starving. We'd traveled all day yesterday, eating only a little. And had gone to bed without dinner. My stomach was growling. Rydel, as usual, sat beside Hero at the table, and I sat by the King. Nobody else would join our meal, and our respective guards remained outside the room.

"You look ravishing," Hero said to me and sipped on wine despite it being so early in the morning.

I was wearing a dark blue dress, matching my wretched darling. An unfortunate coincidence.

"And you look as ravenous as ever," I said, raising my glass toward her.

Berlium lifted his glass as well before tipping it against mine. We locked eyes, and each took a sip. The wine was sharp as a blade, and her eyes narrowed to slits. I let the flavor play on my tongue until it smoothed.

"What brings my enemies to my table?" Hero asked, before touching her red lips to the brim of her wineglass.

"Enemies?" Berlium asked. "What an elegant word."

She lowered her glass and drank him in. "You've brought Death into my halls, beast. Sitting beside her, yes, you are my enemy."

"You'll find Keres on her best behavior." Berlium smiled.

"Excuse me—I'm the problem here?" I glared at both of them, trying to understand their relationship.

"Your head would already be rolling across my floor if you didn't have his crown to hide behind." She snapped her eyes onto him. "Your pet made a mess in my halls last time she visited."

"I am not his pet—"

"Oh, hush, puppy." She leered.

"You will not speak to her that way," Berlium snapped at her. He placed his hand on the back of my chair.

Hero's jaw tightened and her eyes widened at his tone. "Might I remind you, this girl is of my blood and a subject of my kingdom. If I wished to have her removed from your side…"

She quieted at the sound of his laughter. He turned his mirthful gaze on me and tucked my hair behind my ear. "It's funny. Hero, you and your cousin have a stunning likeness in attitude. So entitled." He dropped his hand into my lap and rubbed his thumb over my thigh.

She watched his hand, running her gaze up to his when he turned back to her.

"Though a difference between you both is that Keres actually has a right to be."

She scrunched up her face at him.

"I'm going to marry her."

Hero's jaw dropped open with laughter. I'd thought through every outcome of this conversation since Berlium proposed we visit the Sunderlands. None of the scenarios played out well in my head.

She held up the delicate chain at her neck. As she lifted it, a pendant—no, a bone. Lifted out from under the neckline of her dress.

"This is the finger of Seraphina, Keres. Your dead mother-in-law." She smiled. "She pointed this finger at you, accused you of adultery, and demanded I annul your marriage to your precious knight. Don't you remember?"

I swallowed my wine. The memory of that day was a bloody mess. Berlium watched her intently. Rydel's face was as placid and cold as the marble floor.

Her smile widened. "I took her head for her malicious words. And then you pointed blame at me."

"We were both guilty, cousin. Did you defend me to ensure I'd do the same for you when I learned the truth?"

"The truth." A bitter laugh broke from between her teeth. "I thought you believed the truth, but you too fell for lies." She looked at Berlium. "The first time I laid eyes on Keres, all I could see was how much she resembled my mother. It seems she has more in common with her than I realized," she scoffed as her eyes drifted to me. "The same weakness."

The muscles in Berlium's jaw feathered. He looked across at her like he was ready to lunge for her throat. She lifted her chin, slightly exposing the slender curve of her neck. Her pulse thudded heavily.

"Hero." My voice was as tight as the air was thick. Adrenaline coursed through everyone.

She shot dagger-eyes at me.

"It's time to put the past to rest. This is about the future of the Sunderlands, of our kingdom."

"*Our* kingdom?" She rolled her eyes and leaned back in her chair. "The Baore is your kingdom now."

"The Baore belongs to him. This is my kingdom as much as it is yours. We were both born into it, and we've both shed blood for it. Our mothers—"

"Do not speak to me about my mother!" Her voice cracked.

"I'd like to know what happened to her," Berlium said in a voice so low it startled us.

Rydel's violet eyes narrowed. Hero's gaze slid over the King. I could feel his body tense, but heard his heart rate beating steadily, as always. Hers was livid, thrashing in her chest now.

"I saw her. In the gardens. A man was with her. I wonder whether you know him."

"What makes you say that?" he asked.

"Everybody knows someone evil," she said with a raised brow. Her voice dripped with venom. "I've never found him. No matter how many men I kill, they all break without so much as a bead of truth in their blood. I no longer believe my mother's killer is even in the Sunderlands. Nor was he from here."

"What did he do to her?" Berlium asked.

"He fed her an apple."

I remembered when Hero first talked to me about her mother's alleged murder.

"Lies," the Death Spirit churned.

"That is the story," Rydel finally spoke up. "Now, let's not dally on such a grim subject. Are we ever going to eat?"

"Interesting story," Berlium said before looking back at me. "And what is your side of it?"

"The Oracle child that lives in the temple—"

"Lived, dear. She no longer lives there."

My brows pinched together as I reasoned through her statement. Nadia said she'd get Osira out; she had to escape.

"What do you mean? Where is she?" I clenched my left hand in a fist at my side.

Hero smiled, enjoying my reaction. "Dead in the woods somewhere? I don't know. She ran."

I closed my eyes and sucked in a deep breath. Berlium's hand squeezed my leg. "Go on."

I met his oceanic gaze once more. "The Oracle spoke on behalf of the Gods, who accused Hero of killing her own mother to take the throne."

He touched his chin in thought and turned back to the Queen with a sardonic smirk on his lips. "Well, then. Dead is dead. Doesn't matter who killed her. It doesn't change your present situation, Hero."

"My situation?" she scoffed.

"You've been slaughtering people here in your kingdom. I have it on good authority that you've lost control of your army. I've been in contact with Paragon Kade. Your arrogance and insolence are tempting enough reasons to depose you, but if you can prove yourself still useful to me, I'll allow you to live."

She shoved her seat back, jumping to her feet. Berlium did not satisfy her with a reaction.

"My lord, you'd do well not to threaten the Queen," Rydel attempted.

"Hero, silence your pet," Berlium said sweetly.

"I am no pet. I am an Elistrian Ambassador, sent to be of service to the Queen during her bereavement. Our relationship, like yours—"

"Your relationship," Berlium spoke over him. "Cannot be compared with ours the way a doll cannot be compared to a chess piece."

"Yes," Hero sighed. "And is his the side of the board you've chosen, cousin?" She glared at me.

"You'd do well not to play against the winning side," I warned.

"My, my." She chuckled and took her seat. "Everybody wants to rule the world."

"What I want is for you to annul Keres' marriage," Berlium said after a moment of silence passed, attracting her gaze. "She is Ro'Halen, an Aurelian. Break the marriage, and we'll be on our way."

She lifted her chin defiantly. "I'll think about it. After our meal, we'll talk more, and I'll give my answer. I killed someone in defense of Keres' marriage. I'd hate to see life go to waste."

"*Another lie*," the Death Spirit grumbled.

A quartet of servants burst through the doors, bearing silver trays laden with covered plates. Their attire was simple, all black, but their faces and hands were painted with iridescent colors resembling scales. Fish or serpents, I wasn't sure it mattered. Our place settings were tidily filled with dishes and utensils. Once the servants had retreated to the corners of the room, Hero bid us to eat.

In tandem, the King and I lifted the silver dome-shaped lids off our plates and paused.

"Are these..." his voice trailed off.

"Bones," I breathed.

Hero's eyes darkened with grim satisfaction while she picked a piece off her plate and put it into her mouth. She held it there between her teeth, smiling. Berlium covered his dish once more, and I did the same after a last look at fragments on the plate. Rydel shivered in his seat, watching his lover suck and gnaw on the bone.

"It's cartilage, actually. From varying body parts," she said.

"What bodies?"

Berlium stood from the table, and Hero cracked a laugh. He grimaced as she bit down. The cartilage splintered between her teeth and crackled as she chewed. With her mouth full, she said, "It's not as hard as bone, but stiff. No marrow in the middle of it."

"You'd dare feed me this—are you mad?" Berlium bit out.

She threw her scraps back on the plate and folded her hands in her lap. "Life unto death, waste not. I drink the blood, too."

I threw my napkin down and stood. Berlium stalked toward her. Rydel jumped up between them, holding his hands up. "My lord, please, let's handle this civilly."

"Civility," Berlium snarled in his face. "We are beyond civility."

Hero rolled her eyes and stood. "Oh, please, beast. You waltzed into my kingdom with threats dripping from your fangs. The word civil is not in your vocabulary, nor is it in mine."

She gestured to the plates. "This was not an insult to you—this was for Keres. I haven't killed a man since her."

Shadows shivered against Berlium's frame, promising to plunge us all into darkness if she didn't explain herself.

I shook my head. "I don't understand. You drink blood and eat bones—cartilage. Whatever. What does that have to do with me?"

"You killed the monster in Trethermore Glade, collected its bones, and had them reduced in a broth for the Oracle. Did you drink the broth yourself?" she asked.

"No."

"Pity. I consulted with my court alchemist, Mormont. He said bone broth is nourishing. More than that, it is a gift from the Gods and something we can partake in to honor them. It's no surprise it aided Osira in communicating with them. It made me curious..."

"If you haven't killed anyone, whose bones are these?" I asked.

"They're from a pig. Now would the both of you sit down. You're really making quite a fuss over nothing and ruining my fun."

"I'm not interested in your ramblings. Have this taken away and bring a meal, or we can skip to the part where I drain what I came here for out of you," Berlium said.

"Dessert, first?" She wiggled her brows and then relented when she saw he wouldn't. With the clap of her hands, the footmen returned and removed the trays. "Bring us the proper meal, Jakon."

We reclaimed our seats. New plates were laid, and I suspected there might be eyeballs under the lids. To my relief, it was normal. Well, almost.

"You eat meat. Not surprising," I muttered.

"I'm no longer one with our people. I do not hold their traditions. It's roasted ham. Also, poached eggs, and roasted vegetables."

I passed Berlium the knife and he cut the meat for me. He lifted a forkful and fed it to me before giving my fork back.

"A rebel after my own heart," Hero purred.

I didn't meet her gaze. We chewed in strained silence until she drolled out a sigh.

"You didn't let me finish my story. I'm so starved for good stories. Silence overwhelms my halls... well, when screams don't. It's enough to drive a woman mad." She snickered.

"You torture people, then?"

"I get what I want." She beamed. "It's how I reasoned that my mother's killer is no longer in the Sunderlands. After you left, I had to silence people. I threatened to put down those who sided with you, which was more incisive—so I offered a bargain. No more killing in exchange for their obedience. With Rydel's help, I subdued them. Still, I hunt for my answer."

"So, you insist you didn't kill your mother?" Berlium questioned.

"I did not," she said without her former smile. "The Gods lied."

I stopped chewing and looked up at her. She blinked at me, mocking my expression.

"What do you mean?"

"No!" She threw her hands up and rolled her head to the side and whined. "You've ruined the joke. No punchline for you."

She brought her hands together and batted her eyelashes. "Besides, you're famished, aren't you? Maybe later I'll grow tired of keeping secrets. For now, I'd much rather watch you stick that succulent meat between your lips. The way your King probably does all the time."

35: SPARKS
Heres

"She's bloody, raving mad." Berlium chuckled as he strolled beside me through the pleasure gardens. After the meal, Hero insisted we busy ourselves while she and Rydel went to do whatever it was they did. Probably torturing people.

"A depraved fool," I agreed.

The perpetually gray sky threatened a bleak winter and an impending storm. His boots crushed the dew-kissed grass that tickled my bare feet.

"How dull this weather is," I grumbled, tugging my cloak tighter around myself. It was black wool with a fur-lined hood. He picked up the hood and pushed it over my head. Then pulled a smoking pipe from his coat and prepared it as we walked toward the garden maze.

"I rather like the gloom." He shrugged.

"Of course, you do."

Again, he chuckled.

"If you gave me my powers back, I could light that for you," I taunted. He looked at me, a devilish grin on his lips. He snapped his fingers and blue sparks flew into the bowl of the pipe, lighting the tobacco.

"You *do* wield magic."

He pulled and then puffed out smoke that matched the clouds in color. Watching as they dissipated.

"I'm very good with my fingers, little wolf."

"Yeah, back home we call you the faceless terror with many merciless hands."

"I rather like that." He smirked when I rolled my eyes. He held the pipe out for me to take a pull.

"Don't inhale," he said softly. "That's it, just let it out." The smoke passed my lips and rose between us.

"I know how to smoke a pipe, you ass."

He smiled and took it back when I was done. "Of course, you do."

The smoke tasted earthy… or nutty.

"Do you like it?"

I nodded.

He licked and then bit his lower lip.

"And she's *my* girl," he said, turning his head to the side as if someone else stood there listening.

"You're just as weird as Hero, and your mood shifts like the moon." I shook my head and kept walking. He laughed and caught up to me. We drew closer to the entrance of the maze.

Berlium leaned down and whispered in my ear, "I was talking to the devil on my shoulder. He's taken a liking to you."

"Well, tell him I've already got one too many devils to deal with."

He passed his arm around my shoulders, pulling me into his languid pace. "I think we've made a wonderful deal, you and I."

"Hmm," I touched my chin. "My soul to break, your kingdom to take?"

He looked down at me, taking in every detail of my face. Like he was trying to read my thoughts—which he probably could. His gaze brushed over my lips and a half-smile crawled over his mouth.

"You be the dark angel on my shoulder, and I'll be the devil on yours."

It was my turn to study his face. I tilted my head and smiled with narrowed eyes.

"You think strange things, my lord."

We continued walking, and he sighed. "To be alone in my mind is a terror all its own, believe me."

"I do believe you."

He swallowed his response, and his gaze fell. "Keres, the next taboo you'll try will be shoes. Tell me how you're not cold."

"Cold-blooded. Can't you relate?" I flashed my eyes up at him.

His gaze dipped to my mouth again. "Not always."

I looked away from him to the entrance of the maze. We paused where the maze's path diverged.

"Want to play a game?" he asked, mischief touching his voice.

The hedges towered over us, some of which had bare patches where the season had stolen their coats. The path to the left cut into a sharp turn a few paces away, while the path to the right sprinted toward a stone wall in the distance.

"The wolf versus the hunter?" I replied.

He turned to face me and leaned in close. His eyes had stolen all the blue from the sky, leaving the daylight gray. Took its heat too, leaving me with a chill.

"I'll give you till the count of sixty, and then I'll come after you."

I looked past him, down the pathway. My heartbeat started running. Ready to flee. I knew somewhere in this garden, there was a gate... that let out into the forest. I'd escaped through it before when Nadia showed me the way.

"If you can hide for another count of sixty, you win."

"What would I win?"

"I'll teach you a trick." His smile showed me the tips of his fangs.

"And if you catch me?"

"If? I will catch you, my girl. And when I do... well, that is my prize."

Warning bells went off in my head. It was a game of chase between us. Two deadly creatures, neither intending to let the other run faster.

"Alright, grizzly bear. You're on."

"I hope you run as fast as your mouth does." He stepped back.

I snorted and started running in place, ready to speed off.

"One."

I launched down the path to the left, careening around the corner. My cloak billowed out behind me, slowing me down, so I tore the knot at my throat apart and let it fall behind.

"Two. Three. Four." His voice got farther away.

I spun wildly in a small clearing with three paths to choose from. A raven soared across the sky, and I chose the path it passed over. My feet pounded into the earth; my pulse pounded in my ears.

"Eight," his voice hissed against my ear. I whipped my head around and heard him laugh, but he wasn't there.

"Watch where you're going. Ten."

"Get out of my head, cheater."

"Eleven... twelve... thirteen."

I growled as I skidded around another turn. Thoughts of the gate popped into my head with his counting. He'd know. He was stronger, faster. I just had to find a place to hide. But I knew the point of this game was to prove I couldn't.

The feeling of being watched prickled between my shoulder blades. I looked back and knew he wasn't there but felt him.

A cold-blooded devil with a mind that birthed terrors—that was the man nipping at my heels. It was a reminder that I should feel uneasy. Instead, my inner demon felt some longing, which was, in itself, deathly frightening.

Turn after turn, I was getting dizzy. I'd spent my life running through the forest in the dark. Not a single reaching bramble could touch me, not a stone could trip me up. But the thought that Berlium was going to catch me was enough to make a mapmaker feel lost. Each choice in my path seemed more difficult to make than the last, more senseless. Hadn't I been this way before? *Ugh.*

I turned back and took another turn. A dead end.

"Fuck," I hissed under my breath.

"Forty-nine. Fifty."

I steadied my breathing, slowed to a canter, and retraced my steps until I came to a turn that I was half-way sure I hadn't taken before. Another clearing sprawled out ahead of me, but this one was large. Stone angels with ash-colored blindfolds danced in a circle. Slender, pointed ears stuck out from beneath the crinkly, carved cloths that covered their eyes.

"Sixty."

The word dropped into my thoughts like a stone into water. Red light splashed the sky. I nearly fell over as the world darkened. The sun was a blood-drop, drenching the maze in a crimson haze. It washed away the sparse green of the thicket and deepened the color of the bare earth.

A flock of ravens burst into the sky behind me. I stumbled as I wheeled around. Their voices were too loud, like they were in my head.

"Hide!" the Death Spirit squealed.

I dashed behind one of the stone pedestals that exalted its angel. Counting to myself now, I looked up at its grave face, finding black beady eyes staring down from the upturned hand of the statue. The raven opened its beak and shouted at me.

"Oh, hush," I hissed at it and peered around the edge. I had to stay hidden until the count of sixty. He still had to catch up. The time it took me to get here was the time he had to find me. To guess every direction that I'd chosen correctly.

Nineteen. Twenty. Twenty-one.

I pressed close to the cold stone and admired the maze drenched in the ruby light. More ravens settled on the angels, lending them their black wings. Maroon shadows filtered through the air as the rose-gold clouds breezed by overhead. I knew it was him painting my senses.

"Tricky bastard."

"Not nice."

My scream startled the ravens into flight and shattered into laughter as Berlium's hands shot to my waist. He wore a wicked grin. Against the crimson backdrop, he was a shock of black hair and flushed porcelain skin. The red light mixed with the blue of his eyes, turning them from sapphires to amethysts. He was so handsome it hurt.

He backed me up against the statue, so that she and I were back-to-back.

"You cheated."

"I never said I'd play fair. Only that I'd catch you, little wolf." His gaze never left mine as we nestled between the angel's frozen wings.

"And now?" My heart was a caged bird, and Berlium was the black cat that peered between the bars.

"Now... I get what any hunter does when they've caught their prey. I get to eat you."

I grabbed onto the lapel of his jacket with my good hand and pulled him into me. His hands threaded through my hair. Angling his head down, he brushed his lips against mine softly. The look in his eyes was the color of wine—just as intoxicating. His thumbs ran against my jaw. He closed his eyes and pressed his lips to mine.

My eyes fluttered closed at the tenderness of his kiss. Then his tongue traced between my lips, before he sucked the lower one between his teeth and worried it. When he released the tender flesh, I opened my eyes and looked up at him.

He parted my knees with his and shifted his weight against me. Brushing my hair back behind my shoulder and tilting my head to the side. His gaze found the artery in my neck. The muscles in his jaw feathered as he swallowed. Again, he closed his eyes and planted a tender kiss on my jaw. Turned my head the other way and pressed his mouth against my throat.

My head relaxed in his hands. I ran my hand under his opened jacket, following the buttons of his shirt down to his belt. He was hard between my legs, and his tongue deftly traced the curves of my throat. I passed my hand around his waist, grabbing onto his belt. Dragged my hips against his and moaned at the friction.

He caught the sound with his mouth, covering my parted lips so that I moaned into him. His tongue swept in, tasting my pleasure as he gave me the friction again with the slow movement of his hips. His tongue beckoned mine into the dance, and we joined in the rhythm his body set.

I pulled him by the waist, wanting him closer, as heat ignited between my thighs. He lifted my face to his, deepening the kiss with his hands in my hair again. I ran my hands up his back, luxuriating in the warmth of his body. His tongue twirled against mine, unraveling me.

I sucked his bottom lip into my mouth, running my tongue over it and biting when he pulled back. When I released it, he ravaged me again, bracing himself on the statue at my back. Our breath was heavy, and the carmine daylight was cold, but his heat soaked me. His thumbs pressed against the sides of my throat, but never wandered farther down—like I wanted.

The King's kiss was potent and disheveling. An argument of

ownership. He kept me pinned there, as close as he could be without being inside me. Stealing the air from my lungs, giving it back, like an exchange of power. I heard the flutter of ravens' wings around us but felt it between my legs. Where his cock was hard against me, moving teasingly slow. Denying me the pressure and speed that I wanted. Still, the slow, steady stroke of his movements threatened to undo me, and my breath staggered out of me when he pulled away. My eyes sprung open, and the world was colored exactly as it should be. The rich color in his eyes darkened, though. Obsidian.

"What's wrong—you've stopped?" I tried to pull him in again, but he rested his hand on my chest. The brilliance of blue washed away the darkness in his gaze.

"That was the taste of your honesty. If you're still hoping to win this game by trickery, know I don't play on turning tables," he said in a voice still husky with desire, and he wasn't talking about the game of chase.

"The dice always return to my cup. When I pour out my desires, they return to me. Every drop." He reached into his inner jacket pocket and pulled out a tiny black velvet box. "It's time to play your hand." He opened the box.

An emerald-cut, canary-yellow stone caught the light.

"Believe it or not, it's a sapphire." He plucked it from the box and held it up. "Set between two white diamonds. I hope you don't mind gold. I hate silver."

"It's beautiful," I murmured. It was. The gems were also huge and sparkled brilliantly. "Shouldn't we wait? For Queen Hero—"

"I don't wait for anyone to give me what I want." He took my hand and guided the ring onto my finger. Our eyes locked as it slid into place, and I swore flecks of similar yellow-gold swirled in the blue of his eyes. I blinked stupidly at him and at the ring.

He leaned in close enough to kiss me again. "Wear it to convince her that your play at surrender isn't a game."

"Her or you?"

He smiled and tucked the box back into his pocket. "You can't hide from me, Keres. Not your truth, not your lies. I'll always sniff them out."

He pulled out his smoking pipe, and before he lit it, he looked at me. "Hold out your hand again."

I held it up, thinking he wanted to see the ring—his mark on me.

"Palm up."

I turned my opened hand over, and he held his over it. He snapped his fingers, and the sparks skittered out, sizzling on my skin.

"Ouch!" I pulled my hand back and rubbed it where they'd stung.

He chuckled and held his pipe out to me. "Now, light this the way I did."

I stared at him, rubbing my hand.

"Go on."

I pressed my middle finger to my thumb, and then snapped it. A cold green flame took its first breath in my hand.

36: SHE

Keres

I returned to my room to get ready for dinner. Every move I made reminded me of the ring. I was used to wearing one, I just wasn't used to it being the King's. Guilt gnawed at my stomach, tugging my thoughts back to Darius. Even Silas. We were here to sever the marriage, after all.

Berlium held everything else that mattered to me, and I could no longer have the things I once wanted. By his hands, the power of his mind, my magic had been stolen. And with the snap of his fingers, I got a taste of it back.

The fire he gave me, of course, was no longer a threat to him. It was also different from the elemental magic that had coursed through me since childhood. These flames were cold to the touch. They felt like whispers under my skin. And the green... as if they were the breath of the Otherworld. Unholy fire. The color of my eyes.

At will, they burst into life in my hands. I allowed the flames to lick at my skin, crawl up my arms. Pale green shades shifted into colors dark as moss or the forest I called home. In places, they burned blue as his eyes, and golden as my ring. Their tendrils danced together, melding into green again.

A smile stole my mouth. He'd taken my magic but gave me something that felt better. This fire was raw and entrancing, but I had to get ready for dinner, so I let it soak back into my skin, leaving a tantalizing chill in their wake.

My travel trunk was made from black leather and gold. It reminded me of Berlium's boots. Minnow and Ceil had insisted I take the new dresses they'd had ordered for me. A collection split down the middle by their respective understanding of me. Minnow had chosen pastels and lace, while Ciel had selected jewel tones… and black. Berlium didn't want them coming with us, saying the fewer of his people along for the ride, the better.

The ladies included tons of small boxes filled with gold jewelry, and I found a simple chain to complement the ring. They heeded my request not to pack shoes, thankfully, but provided kohl, colored cheek balm, lip rouge, bath salts, and perfume oils. Things they insisted a Queen have at her disposal at all times.

All I cared about were the books and my small pouch full of personal items. Namely, Iantharys' bloodstone and Katrielle's prayer beads. I liked to sit with them some nights and think.

In hurried silence, Hadriel had packed me the medical supplies I'd need for the trip, but Yarden or Berlium would have to help me. He piled three more books in my arms and told me to take them with me. To have them all finished before I returned. It sounded more like a threat than anything when he said, "You'll begin training the moment you come home."

There was no reply for that. Home: The Baore.

Queen Hero told me Ro'Hale was no longer my kingdom. That the Baore was. My thoughts wandered back to Liriene, to Tecar, obsessively. Interrupting my efforts to stay calm and focused. I set the four books of my growing collection on the writing desk under the window. I balled the dresses up in my arms and lugged them into my mother's closet.

Her glass slippers glared at me from the center of the room.

"Right where I left you." I was tempted to put them on, to run toward any further understanding of my mother. Since reading Hadriel's books and her notes, I craved it. But I resolved not to put the shoes on. Not to go running into her memories and ghosts. Not yet.

I looked around for some empty hangers and mannequins for my dresses, finding none. My mother wasted no space. Her library of clothing was just as meticulously selected as her collection of books.

I dropped the dresses on the floor and stepped over them toward a rack of all black dresses. The fabrics varied from mesh to silk, wool to cotton, and others I didn't know the names of. A gauzy, long gown lingered under my fingertips.

A gasp left me as I pulled it off the rack.

All ideas of war and mothers, kings and queens, fell out of my head. I held the fabric up to my face and inhaled deeply. Spice and lavender. It gently grated against my cheek, and I closed my eyes.

I was back in the clearing, crying on Ivaia's shoulder the night the last of the nine died. The night I hunted alone for the first time. A dress that seemed to be made of cobwebs. The same narrow straps and plunging V-neck. The slits cut along the sides that stopped nearly at the waist. It'd only cover what it must. It was the same dress in a different color.

The very threads of the dress told me it had once been my aunt's, convincing me my mother had borrowed it as sisters do. I wanted to believe she kept it after Ivaia was banished from Ro'Hale, to have a piece of her sister. She probably had never worn it because it still smelled like Ivaia. My mother smelled like lemons and river water. I would not leave this piece of her in this closet to be eaten by moths.

By dinner time, I was ready. I'd scoured through my mother's jewelry and forwent any. Hero had to see my engagement ring. I also refreshed my makeup.

Ivaia was dead only in body. She was with me. After Hadriel invoked her, more or less by accident, I realized Death is only a new beginning. As I looked into the long, standing mirror, I realized Death was just like it: a mirror. Like my mother and Hero's mother, Ivaia was dead. Untouchable, like my reflection, but she was still with me. She was in my blood.

A knock on the door told me it was time.

Once more, we would join my crazed cousin and make our demand. At a table set for sinners. I felt like I was stepping out of an old skin as I crossed the thresh-hold to join Berlium in the hallway.

The Keres I was before… she wasn't dead. She was still inside me too, but she was a part of who I was becoming. All versions of me prior were like dresses I'd once worn. I could keep them in my closet.

Now it was time for this. The version of me that would make the noble women before her proud. Who would make herself proud. With every step, memories of my mother, Ivaia, Liriene, and Katrielle flashed through my mind. And I knew all I needed to hold on to was a singular belief.

She is with me.

37: SINNERS

Heres

"Did you two enjoy rutting in the garden?" Hero crooned.

"We were not rutting." I glared at her as I took my seat.

Berlium's gaze skimmed over my cobweb thin dress before he sat next to me and put his arm around the back of my chair.

"Pity. At least we have this. The wicked gathered for one last supper. A war-mongering king, the harbinger of Death, and little me. A mad huntress queen. We must indulge in some stories."

As the footmen served our boneless dinner, a quartet took their place in the corner of the room to serenade us. They played softly, not to disturb what I anticipated would be a disturbing conversation. We were each given our own bottle of wine and I knew I'd need it.

"How about you go first, beast?" Hero waved to Berlium.

"History tells my stories."

"I do so love notoriety," she preened.

He picked up his spoon. "I killed most of my family. What else do you want to know?" he stated around a mouthful of stew. We all looked at him and chewed our food in silence. He swallowed and dabbed at his mouth with a napkin.

"I want to know why." Hero smiled.

"Everyone knows why. Power. Everything I do is in pursuit of power."

"Even tear down a bloodline," Rydel said under his breath.

"Victory happens on the high ground. You will not reach higher than any other raised hand, unless you're not afraid to climb." He shrugged.

"Sometimes, to climb, you step on others. I have no regrets."

"You slaughtered your entire family and feel no remorse?" Rydel's face paled.

"Not my entire family. I spared only my youngest brother, Oraclio. I banished him. I was second youngest, so we were very close. I couldn't kill him or even order him to be killed. My father, King Myromer, however, was the worst man I've ever known. Gods, torment his fucking soul. Myromer didn't deserve the throne of Dale, and neither did my elder brothers. They were witless and crude. Wanted to eat, drink, fuck, and spend every coin they could.

"Our mother was long dead, but she was the first one who saw greatness in me. She helped me see not only my potential, but the potential of our province. I could do things for the Baore the men before me never even dreamed of. They were dreamless fools destined to inherit every resource a mind like mine needed. A mind like mine would not squander being king. So, I plotted against them.

"I had people on my side who were ready to overthrow everything for me. We devised an ambush. While my father was on one of his many trips, a group of men... furthered my cause. I ascended the throne. My brothers contested, but I conquered. I gave them the chance to renounce their claims, but they refused, so I executed them. Except Oraclio. So, I do not regret a thing."

"Your uncle, the King of Dulin, he was next?" Hero leaned forward and rested her chin on her hands. Her eyes were as round as her clean plate.

"The law the Council has made about having two rulers per province is ridiculous. Then no one is truly sovereign. Rulers serve the people and collaborate and then answer to the council. It's blabber—a broken chain. When there is discord between rulers, the province suffers. If they do not share the vision, how can they evolve? They rely on the council—that's the point. It isn't efficient."

"But it's a failsafe. In case one ruler is... notorious," Hero said with a smirk.

"And if both are corrupt, then what? The Council hasn't opposed a rule in ages, despite many being unfit. If they would, it's easier to depose one madman than two. Aurelian government fails to consider that. Hero, you yourself are an example. You rule ruthlessly. You murder." He turned his hand over, gesturing to Rydel. "The Elistrian King is lazy. Disinterested. Harboring grudges that blind him."

"Grudges against you," Rydel said, narrowing his eyes.

Berlium waved his hand. "He knows better than to act on them. Proves my point. Hero is a power in the Sunderlands. King Gemlin is not. No one cares that his throne is wasted space. My father and Uncle Leto were called the brother bears, but drinking and fattening quelled the ferocity with which they ruled in their youth.

"After claiming my father's throne in Dale, I traveled to Dulin. Alongside my men, I entered Leto's court and killed him. His three sons fought. I killed them too. I planted flags and made grand announcements. The Baore was mine. That's the story everyone remembers, the one in history lessons. No one ever talks about how far that list of names goes though: those killed during my ascension. It wasn't just my immediate family. Even the bastards, the wives, the women they lay with. There was no room for two rulers in the Baore anymore.

"At first, my people feared me. Over the last twenty years, I've served them as if they loved me. Now, go to any city of mine, Mannfel especially; nobody ever repeats the names of those who were killed. They sing my praises. Thank me for deposing the brother kings. My ancestors had also taken the thrones by force. It's the game some forgot how to play and which few win. If anything, I look back at my younger self with a strange sadness. That they forced me to be alone in my ambition. Unmatched. It made me unforgiving."

He moved his arm from my chair to rest his hand on my thigh. "On occasions, I look back. To learn from mistakes and relive the internal celebration of successes. I can't say I haven't thought about whether I'd do things differently. Not from regret, but because of the sharper thinking I now have."

I looked at him. For a minute, I imagined him as someone else. Not as the King with the blood of my people on his hands. Not as an enemy.

As whom he might have been if he'd taken a different path entirely. I wondered whether there truly was anything good in him. Maybe if given more chances, he might choose differently. It was a dangerous thought— one I quickly dismissed.

"In the end, this is the outcome I would have wanted, anyway." He smiled at me.

"What about *Prince* Berlium? The you that loved my mother," Hero said in a low, tenuous voice.

The pressure of his hand on my leg softened. He let out a sigh and looked up at the ceiling.

"When my mind goes backwards, it rarely revisits her. People believe my motivation to conquer the Baore and attack the Sunderlands was dejection. Scorn. They say Princess Herrona was my first dream, and that dream was dashed to pieces. Maybe there's some truth in it, but it's hardly as romantic as people think it was."

🔲🔲🔲

We all poured more wine and Hero insisted we migrate to a lounge room just beyond the eastern doors of the dining room. Upon entering, I noticed the small bookcases that lined the far wall. A modest reading collection. A fire was lit in the hearth and to the right of it sat a large amber-gold harp. I noticed the harp had an audience in the King. His face smoothed as his eyes played its strings and traced its curves.

Hero and Rydel cuddled up on the sofa and we took our seats on the one facing theirs. The servants brought us hot drinks and pastries. More wine. King Berlium and I relaxed. A strangely comfortable silence ate up the room until the King gave us the next story.

"Herrona was brilliant. At one point, way back when she was a child, our kingdoms were not muddied by so much strife. My father and uncle, your grandfather, King Adon, and the Elistrian King, Gemlin, were all at a banquet. This woman, more like a hag, dressed in tattered robes and stinking of filth, threw open the doors into the dining hall and screamed unintelligible curses. The armed guards who had been standing watch were frozen like stone. Paralyzed by a spell she cast. She ran hunched forward, her left arm dangling limply at her side and smacking against her thigh. Guests jumped from their seats and crowed insults and complaints at her. At the edge of the table, she stopped. She flipped over a chair with her right arm and then punched the air, shouting." He smiles.

"A storm was raging outside, and the thunder seemed to answer her cries. All the royal children were seated together, you see, on one long bench. The bench of blessings, my grandmother called it. Herrona sat there, staring at the hag. Keres, your mother was there too. All squirming—except her. Guards drew closer, but I just sat there watching Herrona. She watched the hag with such calmness. As if a storm didn't war against the castle walls, as if a madwoman wasn't shouting incantations at our families. As if she understood what she was saying. She then scooted off the bench, taking a dinner roll off her plate with her. She slipped between the adults and made her way to the troubled end of the table. Even the storm seemed interested in what she held up to the hag. The winds held their breath and the shadows from the candlelight craned their necks to see. The hag reached out her hand, and her voice trembled. As her fingertips touched the crust of the bread Herrona offered, light beamed out of her eyes, her mouth, and every pore of her body. This intense whistling sound lifted out of her throat until she burst into an explosion of colors and light. She shifted into her true form. Her shrieks became a song of praise for Herrona. I could finally understand her. The paralyzed guards jumped into motion and the storm settled. The crowd's angst turned to awe. I still dream of her song from time to time."

"What was she?" I asked.

"She was a Spirit of Famine. Come to plague the royal houses and our kingdoms. Unafraid, even as a child, Princess Herrona listened, and she understood her garbled tongue. And then she changed our fates with a simple offering. The Spirit shifted back into one of Harvest. The greed of our land and our people had twisted her nature. We were humbled and that season, we remembered her. Food was delivered to the hungry in hard winter months. No tables were barren."

"Sounds like something she'd do." Hero smiled. "She had a talent for listening, observing, and creating change for her people." I watched the sadness flicker through her eyes.

"I went away for a time, and when I returned, she was older. My admiration for her matured. She was fit to be a queen, and my ideologies about my kingdom were developing. I saw a brilliant match between us. But our brief time together changed her. What I am was a darkness she did not belong to. It cast shadows in her mind, dulled her spirit. Your people would have benefited from our match, even if she didn't anymore. My kingdom would have too. I was still prepared to marry her. I had use of her mind, not her heart. Our kingdoms developed quarrels. Quarrels turned to battles or to impasses. The dynamics between the Elven Kings and the Baore would never be the same. I offered Herrona marriage; a Prince of the Baore could wed the Queen of Ro'Hale. Ivaia tore it out of her hand. The bond was broken. Then, she married your father."

"Prince Tamyrr," Rydel noted, sadness touching his voice.

"Word traveled quick as arrows, and the news of their marriage struck me. She would waste away with that prince. I despised her choices. And then she was pregnant with you."

King Berlium and Queen Hero locked eyes.

"The ambush on my father was not the first I'd plotted. The first was the one that killed Prince Tamyrr."

Hero's face paled. Her body stilled. Rydel leaned forward to the edge of his seat, and he held up his hand. "There's no need to talk about such things."

"It's the truth. However dark it is. He offered an alliance. I didn't believe him but invited him to a banquet, much like the one our parents had enjoyed in days past. He painted the picture well. A bright future with no storms or curses. So, he journeyed out to my kingdom. Leaving Herrona at home. She was far along in her pregnancy and was lying in. He was duplicitous, plotting to attack me. I had more experience with treacherous people than he did—so I killed him."

Rydel jumped from his seat, and Hero's gaze dropped to the floor. I sat up with Berlium and put my hand on his arm.

"You admit it, then?" Rydel pointed his finger at the King. "You would admit you caused the death of our prince so blatantly?"

"It's been a little over two decades, Ambassador, and everyone knows it," Berlium stated in a bored tone. "Even Hero has been told the story. Does me saying it make it more real?"

"Yes," she said. "I've read my mother's diary. She thought she truly loved you—she learned you poisoned her thoughts. She was a good woman, and you ruined her. Then you killed my father."

"Brutality is real. I'm guilty of it. You're guilty of it, Hero. Even Keres' hands are unclean. If you're so incapable of being confronted by it, Rydel, why do you stay here? Why stay at Hero's side?"

"I am not without understanding of darkness, King Berlium. My reasons for remaining here are also my own." He sat back down and folded his arms across his chest like a petulant child.

"Should we cry now? Tamyrr played against himself. Hero, you kill for your own version of justice. I have killed for self-preservation or my own sense of justice. For revenge or power or because it *feeds* me. I don't apologize for it."

"I've killed for selfish reasons," I said and poured myself more wine, having drained my cup while listening to him. "I've been hunting the Dalis soldiers since I was thirteen. For every Elf they killed, I killed one of them. On and on. I was supervised. Schooled into thinking it was just. That it was what the God of Death wanted. Deep down, I knew it was more than that. It was what I wanted. That desire took root when Mrithyn claimed me and bloomed the day I faced my first decision to kill. I was seven years old, had died days earlier, and was newly reborn. Ivaia had all but torn me from my bed and dragged me into the forest. I stayed with her for a while and then she said we were going to take a trip. The first night out under the stars, we sat in front of a campfire, and she presented me with a scythe. She told me a story about the legendary Scythe of Mrithyn and said this weapon would be my first, but that legend would be mine one day, too. I slept with it by my pillow.

"The next day, we walked. I had no clue where she was taking me, but she just kept talking. My Gods, she went on for hours. She told me about random people she'd met on her travels, places she'd seen. Asked about my sister and my father, then went back to talking about magic. She talked so much it allowed me not to respond. I had so many thoughts boiling inside me, so much rage and confusion. Pain. My body felt like it could just fall apart. The walking helped because it was a different pain to focus on. I let my bare feet stomp into twigs and rocks. Every night we made camp. She'd wash my feet, tell me to be careful, and the next day, went on talking."

I looked at Rydel and then Hero.

"Go on," Berlium said. I looked at him too.

"When I was dying, sinking in the river, it was so quiet there. In between Life and Death, was this expanse of silence. My mother's voice had broken through that, as she prayed to Mrithyn to spare me. Her voice, His voice, Ivaia's voice, my kin talking about me and what had happened. Curses and prayers were on the tongues of everyone around me, in all the different ways they said my name. Keres—Death Spirit.

"Ivaia led me on a path following the river. The water showed me my reflection. My new white hair. Dullness in my eyes. I didn't recognize myself. My head felt like it was wrapped in layers of skin, and that my face was buried beneath masks. My mother's face. Ivaia's. My sister's. This resurrected creature I'd become. The excursion wasn't helping me escape the new reality. It was steeping me in it. Through the thick of it all, slid a sharp voice. It sounded like a multitude in one. Hissing, whispering. It cut other thoughts out of my head. And it was talking about all the things I felt."

The Death Spirit perked up inside my head, simmering in the memory of our first conversation.

"One morning, I heard voices. Others were traveling too. A Human family. I don't know where they were going or why they were in the Sunderlands. I wasn't even sure where we were. All I knew was I was tired. All I wanted was silence. I jumped up from my blankets and grabbed the scythe. I ran toward the voices. Exhausted from all the walking, but power was coursing through my veins. And that voice within was telling me to do things—"

I took another gulp of wine to steady myself and then looked at the King.

"I stalked them. Wandered away from Ivaia and followed them. There was a man, woman, and a child." My voice caught in my throat. Berlium's hand brushed against my thigh again.

I put down my wineglass and dropped my head into my hand. Nobody spoke. I took a deep breath, thinking back to that day.

"I was seven years old. Primed with Death Magic. I had a weapon, and I had hatred in my heart. The child lagged behind, wandering a little, following his parents. He was smaller than me, much younger. Slower. Witless. He'd stopped to pick up a rock and was about to put it in his mouth. His mother turned and said something to stop him, and then she saw me. I was right behind him. Voices echoed through the trees and the world blurred. Fear coursed through me, but the voices urged me. *They will kill any Elf they see. Everything has been taken from us. Our blood cries out.*

"I didn't know where the thoughts were coming from. Visions of blood and war. I heard screaming, the ring of sword on shield. The cracking of whips. Horses, battle cries, the raging of a mob. Calling out for justice. Calling out for war. Underneath it all, the strange voice ran rampant in my thoughts. *Just kill them like they do us. Make it right. Make it quiet.* My hand shook as I looked down at the scythe. The little boy's eyes followed my movements. His mother called him, but he and I were fixated on each other. She addressed me, but I ignored her. He was so young. Just like I was. He was alive. I had died. I envied him… I considered killing him—and his parents."

"But something stopped you?" Berlium asked.

"Mrithyn," I said. "It was like a war for my soul was happening inside my body. Like I was in a frenzy. Smoke swirled out of my mouth with my breath. I was on fire, on the inside. Mrithyn's voice blew through my thoughts, and I felt the stinging chill of a blizzard wind on my skin. He said He made me to be a sentinel, not to hunt the innocent. I knew I had a choice, but I also felt an unshakable, eternal thirst. I had fangs and claws. The family tried to back away. I pursued them. Every step was a choice. I knew I could choose to walk away just as easily. But the blood coursing through their veins—I could hear it singing. The ground beneath my feet seemed to shift, carrying me toward them. Like every drop of blood that had ever been shed in the Sunderlands, flowed in an underground river.

A path that we were on together at that moment. I saw the world would never be without bloodshed, injustice, and war. Mrithyn's voice was cool and calming, ringing out from deep beneath the earth, from some Underworld. I felt like if I dug a hole right there, between my feet, I'd find a red river running beneath it. And beneath that, Him.

"I think when I drowned, my body was there in the water, but my Spirit was in that other river. I could have sent that Human family down to Mrithyn. Added their blood to the song of the Sunderlands' damned. It was my choice. He wanted me to choose to do His will. So, I let them live. I looked at the child and saw innocence. If the man who killed my mother had looked at me—had cared about innocence, he wouldn't have killed her in front of me. I wouldn't have died. Still, it made me sick. I had the capacity to do the same to another child. To want to attack someone as innocent as I once was. Being Human didn't make him guilty. The same way being Elven didn't make me and my people worthy of being attacked. To this day, I still struggle with the choice because of my thirst. Who to let live, who to kill. One is always easier than the other. In a time of war like this, I see more guilt than innocence."

None of them said anything, but I knew we all understood each other. Clearly.

"I'm very easy to hate. Somehow, word got around my camp that I'd attacked the family in the woods. It wasn't entirely true, but that didn't matter. To them, I was some kind of monster wrought in the river's belly by an unforgiving God. People cursed me for it. Ivaia turned my bloodlust into something... justifiable. Hunting the Dalis soldiers. The reality of that, though, is that I couldn't live without killing. Without thirsting for their blood. I still hear the voice of my Death Spirit, hunger. It's what I've hated about myself for so long. I've told no one about that. There had never been a need to."

Berlium said, "If you can't face the monster inside you, you will always be at war. In fact, it's just nature. Whether you've committed atrocities or achieved greatness... every being can raise war upon others. I do not shy away from war. It is part of life—the way of life. War is ugly and twisted, but it is the truth of mortal existence. That reality can make you fearful and weak, or empowered and ruthless. To fight your own nature—is to make the wrong war. Unless we make peace with ourselves, it's a war we'll keep on losing."

"What about your first kill?" Hero asked.

"I'm afraid that's an even worse story." I paused.

"Being isolated because of what I am made me feel… lost. I was supposed to *be* something. A Coroner. Without being supervised like a temperamental child. I didn't know what that meant, but I wanted to feel in control. Maybe giving into my nature was the first step to figuring it out. Following the voice inside my head. I didn't know where I was going or what I was doing. Told myself I was scouting—that I'd find a reason."

I straightened up and took a deep breath. "I found a man. A traveling merchant. When I saw him, my stomach churned. I could smell his skin, hear his pulse. I followed him. Sniffing the air, the scent of his fear whetted my appetite after he noticed I was following. He was confused. A thirteen-year-old girl in a red cloak was trailing him. He turned and offered me a look at what he was selling. It was my chance to take what didn't belong to me—his life. I easily overpowered him. I tortured him. There was no right or wrong. Just instinct—just thirst. I was fulfilling my Spirit's sick desires with his blood. Eventually, I confessed to Aunt Ivaia. It's another reason why she kept me in the dark, feeding the grief and thirst in a way that made sense. That way, she didn't have to worry about me losing control with someone's child or a wandering merchant. But I never felt in control, not even when I gave into the Death Spirit that day. I still wanted—"

"Yes," Hero breathed. "I know."

"You know." I shivered.

Envy. Rage. Shame. Avarice. Guilt. Trauma and all its comorbidities. Mortal experiences. We sat there, experiencing the filth of feelings we harbored.

This was the worst of us.

We empathized with each other. Not with pride. But in some sick, safe, simple understanding. A silence pervaded the spaces between our confessions. Silence that couldn't be apologized away. A silence just to sit in until we knew how to move forward.

38: SIMILAR

Keres

Berlium poured me more wine from his bottle and clinked his full glass against mine. My head was swimming. Getting the wretched truths off my chest made me feel lighter. Not being judged made me feel... it made me feel things I couldn't name.

Hero's eyes slid over Berlium, appraising the way his arm draped around me, the way he crossed his legs. I wondered how tiny I looked beside him. Hero and Rydel were so different. She was cold, and he was caring. I didn't understand them.

"Such wonderful storytellers, the pair of you," she said. "But I think it's time I make my confession."

She stood, stretching. Twisting and turning and yawning.

"Cadathan," she called. The door opened and an armored guard that stood even taller than Berlium entered. I'd seen him before. He was the guard that took Moriya and Faye on my last day here. It felt so long ago— but warning bells were going off in my head now. As if Berlium sensed the same thing, he sat up, looking Cadathan over from head to toe. Hero tilted her head and smiled.

"I watched my mother die, King Berlium. I kill those who I suspect. Her murderer has not been in the Sunderlands since he killed her... but I think he is now."

He snorted and swirled his wine in his glass, watching the red spin until it nearly touched the brim.

"What makes you think I killed her?"

"You killed my father. You grew to despise her. I wonder... if you'll finally feel a morsel of regret now."

Cadathan drew his sword, and Hero threw her hands in the air, twirling in a circle. Berlium and I both stood. Hero stopped and jabbed her finger at the King—madness glazing over her eyes.

"You've captured my cousin. Though I hate her, she is still blood of mine. You've claimed one too many women from our family. Come, Keres. Stand by my side."

I felt frozen. So many reasons to do as she said, and just as many not to. Yarden appeared in the doorway, his hand on the hilt of his sword. His nose wrinkled in disgust at the sight of Cadathan, whose armor was pale as bone. His coarse face and long greasy hair made him repulsive—but he was formidable.

Yarden's eyes flared with bronzed light. I couldn't hold in the gasp. The sclera of his eyes and the beautiful hazel of his irises burned until his eyes were glowing orbs of ocher fire. He moved to draw his sword, but Berlium held up his hand. The light in Yarden's stare blinked out, but he didn't remove his hand from the hilt.

Berlium turned toward Cadathan, who sneered at him and readied his blade. Berlium was unarmed, but I knew the dangers of his power. It seeped from him, filling the room. Cadathan's brows pinched together. Shadows stuttered in the corners of the room. Everyone's heads whipped around, looking for the source of the sound of rushing wings.

Except me. My eyes were fixed on the King.

He raised his arms at his side, taunting Cadathan.

This room was far too small for a fight. Two hulking men, only one armed. And a crazed Queen egging them on. Berlium smiled at the man before him—because that's what he was. Just a man.

"Keres," Hero hissed. "Come here." She pointed at the ground. I took a step toward her and froze again. My Death Spirit growled at her.

Cadathan raised his blade and brought it down.

Winged shadows erupted out of Berlium—his figure lost in the blur of them. In a frenzied flight, the vortex of shadows shot across the room. Behind Cadathan. Berlium appeared amid them again, and I realized what they were. A shroud of black bats.

They came out of him, lingering on his skin. Matching shadows danced in his feral eyes. Cadathan wheeled around, bringing his sword up in another arc. I stepped toward him and stopped.

Berlium raised an arm, and with his sleeves rolled up, I could see the darkness that crawled over his skin until it reached his fingertips and encased his arm.

His hand morphed into a taloned claw, dressed in a black and leathery skin that looked like dragon scales.

Cadathan's blade glanced off the scales with a screech. Berlium waved his arm, turning the blade over, and grabbed it with his protected hand. His claws scraped against the blade, and he growled, ripping it out of Cadathan's hands. The brute faltered, stepping backward as Berlium turned the sword over and wrapped his hand around the hilt. He swirled it through the air and sank into a ready stance. A smirk graced his lips.

"Enough!" Hero shouted, running forward.

"Enough?" Berlium laughed. "What a cursed word."

The room went dark—pitch black. That sound of rushing wings filtered through the air. The bats screeched. Cadathan howled as the slash of a sword met flesh. Hero screamed and Rydel shouted.

I could hear their pulses raging. Only Cadathan's was silenced after hollow moments. Then footsteps. Berlium's footsteps. Hero stumbled over the furniture.

"Why can't I see? Give me back my sight!"

Another footstep.

I could sense him—the predator prowling in the darkness. Every part of me knew him. Where he was—that he moved to attack my cousin. I debated on whether I should let him. The scent exuding from his pores, the ripples of his power emanating from a focal point. The sound of his breath, the rhythm of his pulse.

I moved between them and lifted a hand to his chest. Feeling the armor of scales, the fluttering shadows that surrounded him. The rumbling growl beneath his ribs. I reached for his face. Feeling the hardened skin, the sharpness of his jaw. He sniffed at me and hissed in a breath.

291

Hero and Rydel whimpered and cursed under their breath behind us.

I brushed my finger over his leathery lips, which felt wider. Fire-hot breath fanned against my skin. I touched where his brows should be, reached for where his raven hair should be. Only cold, thick scales met my touch.

"What are you?" I whispered.

A clawed hand found my waist. The power that I usually felt underlying his touch had surfaced with his transformation. It rolled through me, utterly inhuman.

"Are you afraid?" His voice....

When I hunted, my voice split into a multitude. Its tones fled from one another to different ends of an octave. Some soaring into your skull, and others burrowing beneath your feet, shaking the ground. The rest fraying apart in the middle ranges.

His tore into two that rang in harmony. Thunder and its perfect companion, lightning.

"Yes," Hero whimpered.

Berlium lifted his hand to my face. The tips of his claws grazing the underside of my chin. The Death Spirit answered him. Her multi-tonal voice purred in my chest, slid up my throat, and sighed. He could touch the Other side of me and my Spirit leaned into that touch.

That part of me didn't fear him, but every mortal part of me did. It sent chills coursing through me. I shivered. He dropped his hand, and the light seeped back into the room. He stood before me, a man again. Blue-eyed and smirking. Dripping elegance and seduction that masked carnage.

I'd known of him my whole life—the Human King. He was anything but. He was shameless. Fearless. Brutal and powerful. Dedicated to the nightmare that dwelt beneath the fever dream he embodied in his Human form.

His power could inflict unbearable desire, mind addling need. Could blind you or make you see what he wanted you to see. He'd made me taste his imposed lust, but now touching his hidden truth brought a different, darker desire out of me. I wanted to feel shameless and fearless, too. Untouchable and understood.

I shouldn't want to see parts of myself in him. The blue of his eyes was a pool, an enticing reflection within. Promising me I wouldn't drown, drawing me in to drink from it as if it were a well of power and pride I'd never felt before. It wasn't wrong to desire feeling seen. It was wrong to want to be seen by *him*. Berlium looked at me the way I wanted to be seen. I didn't know how to look away from the enemy whose war was the reason I was made.

Darius had looked past the truth of what I was. He loved me despite it. Berlium wanted me because of it.

Hero was right, too. He'd broken another woman in my bloodline. Someone older than me. I didn't know how old he was. Logic told me one thing, and a gut feeling told me something else.

If he wasn't beautiful, if I could see the horror indwelling him outright, would I feel differently? I knew he saw me as beautiful on the surface. He could see the ugly truth of my Death Spirit, too. Still, our likenesses called to us. Shamelessly, fearlessly, our Spirits answered one another. But I couldn't bring myself to admit it. Because I shouldn't. This was war. It was sick, but I was not immune, and that terrified me.

We could see the disease in each other, and there was no remedy for that.

His gaze flicked toward Hero, and he threw the sword down beside Cadathan's body. He was... shredded. Decapitated. Dismembered. His skin torn open in gashes. I'd heard one swift swipe of the blade, but Cadathan's body... it was like Berlium had blasted through him.

Shredding him with the teeth of the shadows that protected him, his claws, his fangs, and the blade—he hadn't needed it at any point. I turned and looked at my cousin, where she clung to her lover. Hero looked at Cadathan and back at me. Rydel looked near to passing out.

"You'd marry this—this monster, Keres? Your soul will be damned."

I looked at her, listening to the sound of her pulse, listening to Berlium's. They were both monsters, but they were very different. And there I was between them. On one side, I saw someone of my blood. With similar sins. On the other, I saw someone whose Spirit was akin to mine.

"Hero," I breathed. "Annul my marriage to Silas. Tonight. We will leave in the morning."

She looked at Cadathan again. The smell of his blood soaking the marble floor was pricking at my senses. The King was still as stone at my side. Hero's eyes found mine again, and she pointed at him.

"He will make a nightmare out of you, Keres."

I frowned at her. "Blessed is the soul whose waking life is not shadowed by dread. Whose dreams are not full of the whisperings of Death. I am not a perfect or pleasant woman. I am cursed, but I am not alone in my darkness. Neither are you, cousin." I turned and looked at Berlium. "To be alone—it is a nightmare all its own."

He closed his eyes and drew in a breath. The muscles of his jaw and neck strained. It was the blood. Resistance and need competed within him. He spun on his heel and stepped over Cadathan. Raking a hand through his hair as he stalked down the hall.

I wanted to follow him but felt frozen again. My curse was never weak. It was the strongest, most volatile part of my being. Overwhelming. The scent of blood, the sight of Cadathan's butchered body, I knew the thirst Berlium felt. But it seemed worse for him than it was for me. Or different. Just similar.

39: SEVERANCE
𝔥𝔢𝔯𝔢𝔰

"Go to him. Go to him," the Death Spirit chanted.

I went to my room instead. My mind was spinning. Being around him was only going to make it worse. Hero just tried to have the King of the Baore killed... I still couldn't wrap my head around that. He actually held back from hurting her. Listened to me. I couldn't process that either.

I readied for bed, but I had a feeling I wouldn't sleep easily. Instead, I perused my thoughts as I lay there, running my fingers over my prayer beads. I touched the white one—Mrithyn's.

Being made the Coroner made me dark and vicious, and the hunger for souls that ached within me seemed eternal.

"Does the God of Death ever feel heartbroken over the souls He takes?" I asked my Death Spirit.

"Do we?" she replied.

As more and more of my kin suffered and died at Human hands, I indulged in rage and blood thirst. I feared how it made me feel... because that feeling was not heartbreak.

"No."

"Death does not hunger for souls," she sighed. *"He consumes them because it is the natural order. A river does not hunger for a rock but would swallow it all the same once it passed through the surface of the water. However, we hunger."*

"Is it because we are what Mrithyn can't be?"

"He cannot be hungry. Mm, but we crave delicious things—like the King."

"Why is he like us?" I asked.

"He must show us."

"And our curse... Why does grizzly bear have it too?"

"It comes from the same place."

My heart rate kicked up—she answered me! A solid answer. Well, almost.

"Where?" I pressed.

She laughed. *"He must show us."*

Yarden knocked on the door sometime later, delivering a letter from Hero. It was done. Her signature at the bottom of the document confirmed it. Silas and I were no longer married. The last thread tying me to my past was severed. I was free to jump—to fall.

"Free to fly," the Death Spirit insisted.

Darkness loomed below me, and even if I shouldn't want to, I wanted to dive in headfirst. Didn't I rise once before? I would again, I wouldn't break. Hadriel held the knowledge I wanted. Berlium promised me wings. And I'd fight to earn them—they'd be my own design. Not because of what he wanted to make me, but because of what I wanted to become.

"Unafraid. Unashamed. Untouchable... but He can touch us," the Death Spirit chanted.

I took Berlium's ring off—not without effort. Just to look at my naked hand. Save the scar he'd wrapped around it. I clenched it in my fist. All the promises this hand made... before another claimed it, I just wanted to feel the weightlessness of not wearing someone else's mark.

I made a promise to myself, holding that hand against my chest. I'd make my mark on this world.

$$\boxed{G} \boxed{e} \boxed{e} \boxed{G}$$

I barely slept, as expected. The candlelight grew tiresome, so I blew out each flame. The bedsheets were sticking to my skin, so I paced my room. Journaling seemed promising. My non-dominant hand couldn't keep up with my thoughts. My mother's closet seemed inviting. I remembered her shoes.

The closet door creaked open. I crossed one foot over the threshold and halted when a chill touched my back. My skin pebbled, and I lingered in the doorway. I opened the door wider and some moonlight from my bedroom window trickled in. The glass shoes glinted in the shadowed center of the room. Tempting me.

It felt like a trap.

If only I hadn't blown out the damn candles. I wanted to turn around. I could just relight the candles, and venture in without fear. But the sensation that I was being watched, that my movements were being predicted, gripped me. I didn't want to take my eyes off the darkness in the closet, half expecting it to reach out for me. If I moved, it would move. I knew it.

My heart felt frozen, and beads of sweat formed at my hairline. As I stood there, my heart thawed and remembered to beat. Frantically, as if it was making up for lost time. I couldn't see or hear or feel or even smell anything else in the room with me. Nothing was here but me... except someone was.

A crow outside my window cawed, and I flinched. "Oh, fuck."

My broken hand went to my chest, as if I could keep my heart from bursting through it. My eyes slid toward the window. Again, the crow cawed.

"Keres."

I jumped back and slammed the closet door shut. I braced myself against it. Afraid to move, afraid to even breathe too quietly. If it got quiet, I'd hear the voice again.

"No, no, no." I shook my head and started humming. This wasn't Mrithyn. It didn't even sound like the hiss of Ahriman.

That is not the growl of our grizzly bear, either.

"What are you afraid of?" The voice was low and husky. A deep timbre that rolled out of the darkness and echoed in my head. I spun around and pressed my back against the door.

"I don't bite."

"I do," I snarled and covered my eyes.

I couldn't stand that I was this scared, that I was talking to someone I couldn't see, but who could see me. Was I going mad? Is this what made Hero go mad?

The voice chuckled—it was laughing at me. I opened my eyes and scanned the room. The meager tendrils of moonlight crawled along the things nearest to the window but didn't reach very far. My bed was a shadowed bulk in the middle. Orange light seeped in through the crack under the door, but not enough to chase away my fears.

My mind knew only a few things at that moment. One, I wasn't alone, no matter what my natural senses told me. Two, I wasn't safe from these watchful, invisible eyes, as long as I was in the dark. I don't know how I knew it. But somehow, this thing lived in the shadows. It wanted me in the dark. It *was* the dark.

I tore myself from the closet and fumbled toward the door. Some force weighed heavily on me, like a net or a blanket. It felt like I was running through a dream, lagging because of an intangible force. I pumped my muscles and pushed my feet into the floor, willing myself closer and closer to the door. I reached for the handle and as the light beneath the door found my feet, I felt myself getting lighter. Faster.

The door swung open before I touched it.

King Berlium's hulking body cast a gigantic shadow over me, nearly blocking out the light in the hall. I didn't stop moving. I ran right into him—into his muscled chest. I shuddered as his arms wrapped around me.

Yarden emerged from his neighboring room, squinting in the light and shirtless.

"My lady, what's wrong?"

As Berlium stepped us both back into the hall, I looked at Yarden. A long sword hung limply in his hand, the tip of the blade touching the carpet.

"My lord, what happened?" He walked up to us, and I looked up at Berlium.

"Did you hear him?" I asked.

His eyes held no answer. His mouth only tightened, and his jaw set as he flicked his gaze back into my room. He released me from his hold, pushing me behind him. Yarden met his eyes, and a wordless exchange passed between them.

"No, don't go in." I latched onto Berlium's wrist, but I couldn't even fully wrap my hand around it. He looked back at me, and the look in his eyes softened my hold.

"There are candles. Matches on the nightstand," I said.

He smirked and snapped his fingers. Blue Fire danced in his palm. *Oh, right.*

They walked in without trepidation. Only caution. No hesitation. Only purpose. I stood peering in after them. I was afraid to look at anything but their backs. If I looked anywhere else in the room, I was sure I'd see some face or figure that they couldn't. I could still feel it watching me from the darkness.

As I listened to Berlium's heartbeat, I tried to steady my own. *Two. Four. Six.* Heavy beats. Drumming evenly. His breathing was near undetectable. No trace of fear, no scent of sweat. He was solid muscle, gliding into the darkness. The further he walked into the room, the further the presence receded. He reached the nightstand and made no drama about lighting a candle. Instead of lighting another, he spun around and held his hand full of fire up. Brightening the flames until the room was full of light.

Two. Four. Six.

He chased away the Shadow. The light chased away the cold sweat that had broken out across my back. They combed the room. Including the closet. My head felt dangerously empty from the silence as I waited. As if every moment I waited was an invitation for the voice to speak again.

Reeling, I tried to figure out why I couldn't shake this fear. Humming the song Katrielle often belted while she did little mindless things. Liriene also employed the tune when she was in the garden. I thought of their voices. Kept humming. Tapped my foot and laid my left hand flat against the wall behind me.

"Alright," I heard Berlium say. He pinched the candlewick, and then extinguished his fire as they emerged from the room.

"Keres will be with me in my room tonight," he said, meeting my eyes. His stare was still ice cold.

"Do you want me to stay here?" Yarden asked, pointing at his room.

"That's fine."

I looked at Yarden and nodded. He lowered his eyes and returned a curt nod.

The King led me by the hand back to his bedchamber. His steps were unhurried, but we didn't speak. I felt as if his pace was daring whatever had been in my room to follow us. I didn't want to entertain the thoughts further but felt calmer with him there.

Refusing to look over my shoulder, I kept my eyes on his hand holding mine. I realized I wasn't wearing his ring and wondered if he'd noticed.

After a few minutes, we reached his room, and he pushed the wooden door open without a sound. Dawn was still a few hours off. An old fire yawned and stretched in the fireplace to the right side of the room. He threw another log in, waking it back up. Light flared into life.

"I feel better now. With the door shut, with the fire going, with... you here."

"Good," he said coolly.

"You weren't sleeping?" I asked, gesturing to his outfit. The same dark blue shirt and black trousers he'd worn all day. Only missing his boots.

"Neither were you," he said and looked me over.

Unlike him, I was dressed for bed in a satin shift that cut off just above the knee. It was a shiny black and flowed out at the hem. Details he didn't miss.

His gaze assessed every stitch before he met my eyes again. I felt stupid standing there in the center of the room, not sure where to settle. There was something stirring in him. Something dark. His eyes wandered over me again, from my head to my toes. I busied myself with looking around the room.

The walls were forest green, trimmed with white. The bed was big enough for two, topped with white sheets and gray blankets. He'd tossed the pillows on the floor—just like I usually did.

"This room is very grand," I said. *Stupid. Stupid. Stupid.*

"Mmhm," he said and turned to stoke the fire. Relieved his attention was off me for a moment, I lifted a foot to walk toward the chair near the bed.

"Come here," he said before my foot could touch the floor again.

I redirected my steps and moved toward him. He looked back up and watched me walk. His eyes scanned me from top to bottom; seemed to look through me. Behind me.

I stopped in my tracks. My skin turned to gooseflesh. Was there something there? Should I be so trusting that he'd keep me safe if something was?

He looked at me once more and pushed off the mantle. Crossing his arms in front of his chest and straightening his back, he repeated himself. "Come here."

His command crashed into me. The fear that rooted me to that spot withered, and I closed the distance between us. Toe-to-toe. Before the fire, he looked down his strong nose at me. The firelight did wonderful things to the blue of his eyes, gilded the contours of his chiseled physique.

I felt tiny for the first time before him. How many times had I thrown myself into this spot? Shot up onto my toes and barked in his face? This time was different.

He relaxed his arms, and I thought for a moment he might embrace me. Or strike me. His eyes, gold-ridged sapphires, threatening to turn to jet. Wild and unpredictable.

"Are you angry?" I asked.

He took a step closer. Shifting his weight toward me and bowing his head even closer to my face. "Very."

The roughness of his voice brushed against my ear. Set my heart pounding. Another step and then another. Until he was behind me. I didn't dare move.

"Because of Hero? I don't think you have a reason to be angry at *me*," I whispered thickly.

"Don't I?" His breath softened against my other ear this time.

My pulse betrayed me, hammering against my chest. The heat of his body warmed my backside enough to make me aware of the chill that still gripped my spine.

He took another step and came around on the other side of me. Standing between the fire and me, there was no light to forgive the harshness of his eyes. Shadow undid the seduction within them. What I saw when I looked up was terrible, raw fury.

40: SAY IT
The King

Her heart beat so hard it shook her frame. Like a moth trapped in a glass lantern with no light, with no way out. Fear made her unlike herself. How many times had she stood in this very spot, right before me, and forgotten her size? She was always this close, this small, but never this afraid.

When I'd opened her door, admitting the light from the hallway into her bedroom, I saw something I didn't know how to explain to her without making her more scared. She was wrapped in heavy vines of shadow. Around her ankles, her wrists, at her throat, tangled in her hair, laced through her fingers, and curled around each knuckle.

Light shattered the darkness' hold on her. His hold.

Of course, he'd found her. Now that we were across my border, his attention was on us. These were the kinds of secrets he listened for—lived for. He'd turn the world over, looking for this kind of secret. For her. One thing I swore I wouldn't let him have. Even if it meant war between him and me. If he wanted her, he'd have to get through me to take her. She was mine now.

But she wasn't wearing my ring. It hadn't escaped my notice, and it made my anger quicken. Like a gage ticking near its limit. My thirst was making it harder to discriminate between reasons to be angry. I could gorge myself on reasons.

Because of Hero? No, little wolf.

The Queen's laughable attempt to have me taken down by one man—it would take an army. I should have ripped the Queen's head from her shoulders, but Keres stopped me. I stopped at the touch of her hand.

That is why I was angry at her. She moved me. No woman has ever done that.

Thane had almost taken her from me in his darkness. If he had the opportunity again, even a moment to catch her in such darkness, he wouldn't waste it. By that, I was infuriated.

Circling around her, I found nothing wrong, save my missing ring. Yet she shivered. The chill of his touch lingered in her bones, whispering over her skin. She didn't rise to match my wrath. She looked up into my eyes as I came to stand before her, and the smallest sound escaped her. Not a curse, not a scream, not a biting remark. A frail whimper.

By that, I was absolutely maddened.

I reached my hands out and touched her collarbone, tracing my finger along the lines and curves. Her ribs shuddered beneath my touch as her breaths shallowed. Her emerald green eyes seemed sallow. Her face paled, haunted by the firelight.

I rested the weight of my hands on her shoulders and looked into her eyes. So small beneath my touch. Her delicious lips that often curved into mocking smirks and usually parted only for foul words... opened and nothing came out.

I ran my hands back along her neckline and rested them at the base of her throat. She closed her eyes. As if resigning to let me do as I will.

"No," I growled and shook her. Her eyes popped open.

"He's gone. He's not touching you."

Her left hand shot up and grabbed onto my forearm.

"I am touching you." I rubbed my thumb against the underside of her jaw, turning her face toward mine. Her grip on my arm mirrored that pressure and reality flared between us.

"He's gone," she murmured, and her eyes welled with tears. I couldn't handle another reason to be angry. I'd rupture.

"Don't cry," I commanded. I pulled her into me and held her face up, letting my fingertips sink into the soft flesh on the sides of her neck, giving her enough heady pain to distract her. Her pulse punched into my fingers.

"He can't have you. I won't let anyone ever make you feel that way again."

With my other hand, I wiped her rebellious tear away. I couldn't help myself. As she looked up at me like that, I swiped my thumb along her bottom lip. She held onto me still. Her body relaxed, leaning into me. I softened my hold on her. Her breath caught as I lowered my head down to hers.

She had questions. I knew she did, but I didn't want her to ask them. Not now. The things I wanted to come out of her mouth—the sounds I'd make her release. Not frightful whimpering, not questions.

I made a slow descent toward her mouth. Listened to the change of pace in her breathing, in the beating of her heart. I waited till I could feel her breath on my face, basking in its warmth. I brought both my hands to frame her tender, elegant throat and she kept her head tilted up toward me. Her eyes fluttered closed as my breath passed over her lips.

"You're mine," I breathed against her.

She swallowed hard.

"Say it."

Her eyes opened again, and I drew my face back just enough to look at her. Light and shadow danced across her features. I could see reasons flying through her mind. Reasons she wanted to say it, reasons she didn't. They passed through her thoughts, in her eyes, like visions. Hundreds of them, if not thousands, like a flock of birds against a clear sky.

I pressed my body against hers and lowered one hand to her hip. Drifting down, cupping her backside under her dress, and pulling her closer to me. Now, her other hand was resting against me. Her mouth was that much closer. She lifted onto her toes just an inch higher, to be closer.

That's more like it.

She wanted to say it. Also wanted not to.

She desperately wanted to kiss me.

I dropped my head to the side and sniffed her hair. Her pulse beat wildly in her neck. I licked at the base of her ear and caressed her backside. My hand on her throat wandered lower and traced the neckline of her thin dress. She turned her head, leaning into my breath and my tongue. I nipped at her neck and her ear, and passed my hand over her breasts.

304

Another small sound escaped her… but this one I rather liked. My cock was always ready for her encouragement. Her nipples perked underneath the silk as her breasts readied for more, aching to be touched. They were luscious and warm beneath my hand. Her skin pebbled where I traced it, and I knew the chill that shook her now was not because of anyone else but me. How it should be.

"Say it."

She threw both her arms over my shoulders, turned her face into my neck and gave me similar attention. I let both my hands wander along her hips and up her back, massaging her along the length of her torso. Relishing the feel of her silken tongue darting against my skin. Her plush lips played against my pulse.

Tired of bending down, I made one more pass over her ass, and reached down to pull her off her feet and wrapped both her legs around my waist. Her short nightdress made room for me between her legs, and I walked her back against the nearest wall.

"Oh," she sighed as her back hit the cold surface.

I chuckled. Her left hand gripped onto my shoulder and her right arm draped over my other, pulling my weight into her. I was at the perfect level to lick and bite her throat. Her head leaned back against the wall as I held her there. Her hips were at just the right level with mine for me to grind against her. She moaned, and I felt it down to my bones.

"Mm, say it." I made a slow, circular movement against her. "You're mine. You know it. I want you to say it to me. Tell me you're mine, little wolf. Tell me no one else can touch you or take you."

She looked into my eyes again. "I'm…"

Lust swirled in the depths of her green eyes; her pleasure awakened. She closed them again as I moved against her, as if she were afraid that I'd see the truth in her eyes. I pulled her from the wall, and she tightened her hold on me as I moved us toward the bed. Not giving her time to react before I had her on her back.

She leaned up on her elbows and watched me take off my shirt. Her eyes noticed my erection pressing against my pants, begging to be set free. I ached to unleash myself on her, but I was holding back—awaiting my

305

answer. I leaned forward and crawled onto the bed over her.

She reached up, wrapped her arms around me, and pulled me down onto her. Her mouth met mine hungrily. Surprising me, letting my tongue in to taste hers. Lashing mine into submission and then demanding more.

She sighed again, and I lowered my hips, grinding my cock against her softness. She moaned into my mouth and rocked her hips back against mine. She clawed at the tattoo on my back she didn't know was there, wandering up the nape of my neck and making a mess of my hair. She held our mouths together. I rested on my forearms, on either side of her head, and allowed her to hold me in that kiss.

I gave her room to let her body grind against mine the way she wanted, desperate for the friction. She opened her mouth wide, letting my tongue in to twirl against hers. She opened her legs wider. So, I reached down and lifted her dress, baring her sex. Holding myself over her body, I met her tender flesh with my rough hand.

She stopped kissing me and looked down at where I touched her. I sat up between her legs and massaged her wetness. The space between her brows puckered, and she bit her deliciously swollen lip. She looked up at me when I used my other hand to lift her shift up above her breasts and held the hem at her throat.

Leaning over her, I pushed her back down into the bed and grazed my thumb against her swollen clitoris in circular motions. I watched her eyelashes, like two dark fans, flutter open and closed. I slipped my fingers down her center and slowly stroked my way back up, spreading her. Playing, rubbing my knuckles against her so she could feel the cold metal of my rings. The green in her eyes flashed at me again.

"Say it," I whispered.

The lines of her face softened, and her eyes lowered. I dipped one finger down into her and drew her gaze back up to mine.

"Keres." I smiled.

She was fighting it. I could see it. I could see *her* again. Her mouth answered my smile with a demoness' smirk. She knew I wouldn't give her what she wanted until I got mine. Saw through my game the way I knew she would, but she still wanted to play.

I withdrew my hand, and hers rushed toward me. She grabbed me by the edges of my trousers and pulled herself up until she was kneeling in front of me. One handedly, she fumbled with the buttons, carelessly grazing against my eager cock as she pried at them.

I caught her wrists and brought them to my mouth, licking each one along the prominent blue veins that lined their undersides.

"Do you think you're hungrier than me, little wolf? No."

She leaned closer and smiled against my mouth. Denying me a kiss, she moved her head to the left. Her breath closed on my earlobe and drifted down my neck before returning with the simplest, most necessary words I needed to hear...

"You never asked me to be yours. In fact, you simply handed me a ring, and all but dared me to wed you. I will not answer unless you ask civilly, you brute."

Dammit.

I pulled away from her and reached into my pocket. She'd put the ring on her nightstand, right next to the box of matches. The two most inflammatory things in her bedroom in one spot.

Then, I pushed off the bed. Between the bed and the fire, I knelt down on one knee and offered the ring to her.

She pushed a wisp of hair behind her ear as she stood, and that taunting smirk never left her reddened mouth. Right then and there, I wanted to toss the ring aside and take her on the floor. Roughly, with or without an answer. She was mine. She just needed to say it to herself and then to me.

"Keres," I started.

"Nyxara Aurelian. That's my full name."

I cocked a brow up at her, which only made her eyes brighten more.

"Keres Nyxara Aurelian." I couldn't keep the corners of my mouth from twitching upward.

"I know the power of promise in you, and I want to feel it. Everything we've already established would be possible for our people. I've been ready for it before I even met you. But ever since you marched into my throne room, I've been attracted to your conviction. I've studied you—

the way you fight for your beliefs. Even when you're stubborn, it's based on that conviction. There have been too few people in my life who offer that. In a short amount of time, I've watched you tumble through doubts and come up swinging. You tried to beat me at my game—even in chains, you challenged me. You tried to kill me with a dinner knife, woman."

She chuckled.

"I want the chance to know you better, but I already know I want you to be mine. I've said it before. I don't have to be your villain, but I'll never be the hero. Which is fine because even if we're damned, beautiful, we certainly don't need rescuing. I've told you the truth of it from the beginning. You can't be wooed, and I'm not the man to try, but I think you know our Spirits have been conspiring together. I love the way you purr, and I plan to make you do it until you're hoarse."

She let out another laugh, which cascaded down my spine.

Wicked, teasing thing. "Bloody Gods, Keres. Stop laughing and please just say you're mine?"

Every bone in my body ached for her to say it.

After I saw her in the grasp of that Shadow, I knew I couldn't let her slip away. No, never. I needed this viscerally, in the depths of my dark Spirit. I hadn't felt need like this before. I didn't expect it, but that was the truth and it had swallowed me quicker than I wanted to admit. She became something I needed, and I would not deny that truth. She needed me too—she just didn't know it the way I did. She'd be safer with me. The world would be safer if she were with me.

I just needed her to say it now. So, I could protect what was mine.

She plucked the ring from between my two fingers. Her eyes wandered over to the fireplace. Contemplating all those reasons once more. For a second, I feared she'd throw it into the flames, and I didn't know what I'd do if she did. If I couldn't have her—no. The Beast in me would not be denied.

Finally, she returned her attention to the ring, to me, and slid it onto her finger. Smiling as my heart raced in my chest—an effect only she had on me.

"It takes a bit of darkness and damnation to be my match. Though this isn't love, something in you calls to me. For so long, I've felt lost in shadow, cursed, and alone. Nobody truly understood what I was, not even myself. You don't see a nightmare or an omen when you look at me. And though there are many harsh truths I see in you, one of them is that I am not afraid of you either. A piece of me has already chosen you, but don't think for a second, I won't keep fighting you."

I laughed this time and stood.

"There, I said it. Are you happy now?"

I needed only that. There were only two necessary words left for me to say.

"Thank you."

She smiled and looked at me through hooded eyes. She ran her fingers along my bared chest, my ring sparkling in the firelight. I caught her left hand and lowered it. Smoothing her palm over the planes of my abs. She traced each ridge... down to the buttons of my trousers.

"Now," she whispered. "I'm going to taste you."

My pulse throbbed in my cock at her words. She looked down and tugged at the buttons of my pants. I helped her—because I had hurt her. I'd never felt regret before. The way she smiled up at me, despite the pain I'd caused her—she could take it. She could make me feel for her. Anger. Regret. Painful need.

I could destroy her for it. Worship her when she fought back.

She helped me push my trousers down to my ankles because she wanted to.

I grabbed her collar and tore her dress with both my hands because *I* wanted to.

A gasp escaped her. She was mine, and I was going to rend her open to bury myself in her. I threw her dress aside and grabbed her by the throat. Pulling her into me again. The scent of her arousal was thick in the air, and I could taste it on her tongue.

Keres' mouth claimed mine as hungrily as I wished to possess her. Her hand found my cock and stroked me between us. She couldn't even wrap her whole hand around me, but her grip was unforgiving. I growled a moan into her mouth and pushed her down to her knees.

She placed her cast hand against the side of my leg and used the other to work teasingly slow. Her gaze was heated, and her mouth curved before she ran her tongue along the underside of my cock. She lifted my shaft, angling her head to repeat the stroke, licking up the side until her opened mouth grazed over the tip of me. She alternated between licking me softly and jerking me hard.

She sighed against my skin with wet heat. One hand gripped me firmly at the base as she pursed her lips and rubbed my cock over them. I pushed against her delicious lips, and she parted them, allowing my cock in deep. She wrapped her mouth over me and took me deeper. I felt the back of her throat—somehow her jaw opened for me. She sealed her lips around me. Moaned as she drew back and then pulled me into her again and again. The trill of her unearthly voice reverberated through me as she drank me in.

Her Spirit was rising. This was the real Keres, looking up at me the way only she could, with obsidian eyes that promised oblivion.

"Fuck," I groaned.

Her tongue flicked out, lengthened and more pointed. Her fangs grazed my skin, and I hissed from the pleasure. I nested my hand in her hair and forced myself deeper into her throat—and she took it. Sucking me deeper, turning her head to twist her tongue around me. It was glorious, the way she took my cock deep in her mouth. Working her tongue to stroke me as she let me thrust into her.

My body tightened with the need to release as she fucked me with her mouth. Her delicious lips dripping with saliva, tasting my pre-cum and lapping it up. She spit on my cock and then swallowed me hungrily. Moaning, purring against me with a layered voice. Hers and her monster's together.

"If you keep letting me fuck that pretty little mouth of yours like that, this is going to end before either of us wants it too." I pulled her head back, and she smiled up at me, licking her fangs, her lips. "Get on the bed."

She kept her eyes on me as she obeyed. The color within them shifted between black and green, devouring the firelight.

"Your eyes," I breathed, wanting to fall into their abyss. Sadness flickered across her face. I furrowed my brows at the change in her expression. "What?"

"My eyes," she said, lowering her gaze.

I lifted her chin. "People fear you," I said, realizing, and then I laughed. "Your eyes are dark stars, Keres. Now, get on your back."

The emerald flames I gave her flared within her gaze, burning with desire. She crawled onto the bed, lying on her back and bringing her knees together at her chest. She swayed, crossing her ankles, and reaching her hand down to spread herself open to me. I drank in the way she looked, touching herself, needy, and dripping wet.

"My turn." I lifted her legs and rested them on my shoulders, bowing to her cunt. I grabbed her thighs, opened her legs, and licked her up her center. She moaned so softly, still using her hand to hold herself open so that I could see where she was aching to be filled.

My tongue plunged inside her, lapping greedily at her soaked core, making her shudder. Then I dragged my tongue through her middle, kissing my way around the outer sides. Diving back in, tasting her arousal as it poured from her body. Her hips lifted to my mouth.

I met her black eyes and curled my tongue into her, stroking the inside of her and suckling. She bit her lip and worried it, watching me.

I closed my mouth over her entirely, not to miss a drop of her sweet pleasure. I sucked her sensitive peak into my mouth and brought my tongue up to circle it, still nuzzling. She cried out and touched my face, my hair. I growled against her skin, and she purred for me.

My cock was straining to take her, but I held her on the brink of pleasure and was going to fuck her over the edge.

I dipped a finger into her, and she took in a sharp breath. Her hand lifted to her breasts, assuaging her hardened nipples. Cradling their full weight and kneading them. She hugged her chest as she looked down at me again and moaned. I pulsed my finger inside her, stretching her just a little. It wouldn't be enough to ready her for my cock, but I didn't plan on breaking her in too easily.

She bucked against me, dropping her head back and let out a low whine. Her hand fisted in her hair, and she used her legs on my shoulders to lift herself up higher while pushing me down. I rocked her to a steady rhythm, moving with her hips as she rode my finger and tongue. I felt her tightening—burning around me and didn't stop until she cried out and collapsed back on the bed.

I moved over her, opening her trembling legs, and held my cock at her entrance. Stroking it through her wetness, rubbing her sensitive apex to drag out the pleasure. She looked at me, sucking me into that bottomless Spirit I planned to lose myself in.

"Do not take those eyes off me while I fuck you. If you do, it'll be because I make them roll back into your pretty little head."

Keres

Dark stars.

The words struck a chord in me, snapping any inhibition I might have had left.

"Don't be gentle," I said, quivering from the first orgasm. The look in his eyes threatened me with more pleasure.

He lifted my hands over my head and pinned them there in one of his. Teasingly, he nudged his cock against my sex with the other. The size of him promised delicious pain, and I wanted it.

Only a second later, he answered my demand with a powerful thrust. I cried out as he fully sheathed himself inside me, threatening to tear me open. My core clenched around him, unaccustomed to his size, warring against the flash of pain but blurring in the aftershocks of pressure. Waiting for heat to follow.

He buried himself in me, carving his way through my center with feverish need.

I stared into his eyes, trembling, and sucked my lip between my teeth to bite back a whimper. He laughed wickedly and rolled his hips against mine in a slow circle, stretching me even more. The movement carried him deeper, making me moan hoarsely. I wrapped my legs around his waist.

"I told you I'd break down your walls and devour you, little wolf. I never intended to do it gently." He withdrew and slammed back into me. "Look at you now. Shaking, taking my cock hungrily in your tight, needy cunt."

He thrust again, claiming the globe of my breast with his other hand, kneading it roughly and pinching my peaked nipples. I lifted my hips into his next thrust, and he dipped his head to lick me up the center of my throat. Nipping my skin between his teeth. The touch of his fangs sent my pulse soaring between my legs and stole a growl out of my chest. He echoed it, rumbling against me as he pounded into me.

We both felt my core melding to his touch. I could see it in his eyes when he looked at me again.

"You fit me like you were made for me, my girl."

A sinful smile played on his lips before he claimed my mouth with a kiss that knocked the breath out of me. Demanding everything I could give. Consuming me as he moved inside me. His rhythm was torturous. The stroke of his tongue, then the stroke of his cock. Slow but hard and thorough. Leaving no inch of me unclaimed.

I moved with him. He pinned my hands, but I locked him between my legs. His kiss set my blood on fire, and the way he moved inside me made me want to scream.

He pulled back, sitting up between my thighs, and withdrawing slowly from my body so that only the tip stayed within me. I watched his movements, unable to tear my eyes away from where we joined. He released my hands, grabbing onto my hips and angling them upward. And then he pushed into me again. I watched him disappear inside me. Felt him spreading me open and going deeper than before.

I moaned curses, sucking in air as he rocked his hips. His cock drove into me and left nothing untouched, reached up into me and filled me with an intense, beautiful sensation. My arousal soaked us both, heating our skin.

"Oh, Gods," I dropped my head back and held onto the sheets.

"You're past the point of salvation." He laughed huskily and pressed his fingertips into my hips. Pushing into me, rocking my hips against his, and pulling me back so that he was as deep as I needed him. And I ached—the need was more destabilizing than I'd realized. Like it had been gnawing at me and now he drove that ache out of me.

"You're going to make me come again," I whimpered. Already—I was already going to unravel. Every thread of tension he'd sewn into me threatened to fray and snap. Gazing down at me, he reached his hand down to my sex and massaged my apex.

I cried out as electric fire shot through my core, contracting around him. He alternated drawing circles and strumming his fingers against my center with speed that put me in a frenzy.

"Like that." I grabbed his hand on my thigh while the other locked into the pattern I needed. I panted through the swell of pleasure and moaned loudly as it tore through me again.

His body moved, unrelenting, and that deep rumbling song of his power drummed in his chest, pulsing through me. I locked eyes with him, and he watched me come undone for him. Lightning shot through his eyes with the thunder of his pulse.

"Hungry girl," he said with a smirk. The gravel of his voice pebbled my skin. I dug my claws into his, where they gripped my hip.

"I have craved you," I admitted.

He withdrew and flipped me over, lifting my hips up and pushing me down so that my ass was in the air.

"Good. Because I am close to madness with my thirst for you."

He knelt behind me, and as I shuddered still, he licked me up my center. Growled his approval against my skin. "You taste so fucking delicious, little wolf."

Then he grabbed my hips and buried his face between my legs again. Greedily lapping up the hot mess he made, ravaging me with his tongue. Another orgasm built in my core, and I fisted the sheets in my hand.

"Fuck—" I pushed back into him.

He laughed against my flesh, and I smiled, biting my lip. His tongue curled against me, flicking at my clit and stroking down my center. And then he pushed his tongue inside me. Suckling, making my eyes roll back like he promised. His tongue felt longer than it should, and I knew it was his inner beast.

Where his hands gripped me, I felt the distinct prick of claws digging into my flesh. Pain stung my skin and the scent of blood swirled into the air. I looked back at where he held me, admiring the long onyx tips of his claws, the rings still on his fingers. Those dragon-like scales raised on his skin as if they were goosebumps, from his hands to his elbows. Tiny drops of blood glistened where his claws dug into me, and the pain mingled with my climax, leaving me shaking and breathless on his mouth.

He withdrew his tongue and sat up, finding me looking at him.

"You're a needy little thing. You love coming on my mouth. And I love the way you taste, so wet it's dripping down my chin," he said and licked his lips. Drummed his claws against my skin. Digging them in again. I growled at him, my own claws ripping into the sheets I clung to.

"I'm glad your mouth is good for something other than threats," I said with a smile.

He chuckled. "You spoke too soon, Keres. I *am* going to make you scream."

He pushed me back down and entered me from behind forcefully. I buried my scream in the sheets. Still riding the wave of my last orgasm, he dragged me into the undertow of another. He wrapped my hair around his fist and pulled my head up.

I groaned his name.

His other hand reached down to my front and clutched my breasts. His skin slapped against mine with every pulse into my core. He arched over me and sniffed my hair, licked my neck.

My voice shook and broke with the crest of another orgasm—I didn't know if I could handle it—I'd never—thank the Gods, he didn't stop. My chest was on fire from breathing so raggedly.

"Good girl. Take it." He reached his hand down between my legs again and massaged my sex as he pounded into me. "I know how badly you wanted this. Show me, let me hear how badly you wanted this fucking cock."

Pleasure barreled through me, tore the scream he demanded from me, stole my breath. This wave was a storm—violent and left me shaking.

He unleashed on me, drowning me in unrelenting pleasure. No matter how I shook and contracted, he held me there.

"You're mine now. Do you understand?" He bowed his head down to mine.

I nodded against him, my body bouncing beneath his. He wrapped his hand around my throat, forcing me to look back at him as he continued beating his cock into my throbbing center.

"Nobody else can have you or I'll fucking rip their throats out. From now on, your body is mine to break."

"Yes," I said breathlessly. "Mine—you're mine, too."

He nipped at my ear and buried his face in my hair as his body jerked, and a deep, dark moan rattled in his throat. My core tightened around him, milking him as he released into me until he slowed and let me go.

He smacked my ass, and I fell over on my side. Watching him get up from the bed and walk toward the bathing room. I sat up the minute I saw his tattoos. Black lettering in another language dripped down his ribs. Starting just beneath his shoulder blade, on either side of his spine, and reaching toward his sides in six vertical rows—like two paragraphs. At the top of his spine was a faintly sketched dragon-like serpent, curled in a figure-eight and swallowing its tail. He came back with a cloth and moved toward me on the bed again.

"Open your legs."

Heat banked in his eyes as he ran his gaze over my sex once more. Our arousal soaked me, the sheets. He wiped me with the cloth, massaging me as he did it. My toes curled into the sheets, and my body spasmed, still sensitive in the aftermath.

He smirked at me and took the cloth away when I was clean. The blue of his eyes was flecked with gold and brighter. He rested his hand on my thigh.

"Sleep now. We have a long journey ahead of us in the morning."

His gaze didn't leave mine, though, and finally, he kissed me. I rolled over him and straddled him. Deepening the kiss. Feeling him grow hard again beneath me. I ground against him, and he ran his hands up and down my sides.

"I don't want to sleep," I said into his neck.

"Me neither." He chuckled. I reached down and grabbed him. He groaned and looked up at the ceiling as he laid back.

"We can sleep in the carriage ride," I whispered and teasingly pressed him against me.

"No, little wolf. I'm on my guard when we're on the road."

Which reminded me of the darkness that threatened me tonight. He looked down at my body as I slid along the length of his shaft. He covered his face with his hands, and I put him inside me. Just the tip of him, inching onto him slowly. Rocking gently. Forcing the darkness out of my thoughts.

"*I* can sleep in the carriage," I teased.

He laughed and looked at me again, his brows pinching together as I slid onto him an inch more. He grabbed my breasts and then sat up, claiming my nipple with his mouth.

He wrapped his arms around me as I straddled his lap, taking him into me completely again. His tongue trailed over my breasts, leaving them wet and feeling heavy. He squeezed and pushed them together, then let them settle again. Chasing them with his mouth as I chased after another climax.

Straddling him, feeling the perfect friction against my front, it came softly at first. Then, hot as fire until it melted my core, and I grabbed onto his shoulder. He kissed my neck, holding and moving with me through it. I looked down at him, pressing my forehead to his. He threaded one hand in my hair and kept the other on the small of my back, to hold us together in that perfect spot. Breathing against my mouth, staring into my eyes. Moaning with me as I brought him to release again, too.

I laid back, exhaustion hitting me like a stone wall. I had a dream of home that was so vivid, my waking thought the next morning was wondering whether he gave it to me.

41: SOMEONE

Keres

Day Eighteen

The King said he wasn't the man to beg, and I knew that his proposal was the closest he'd ever come to doing so. The fervency in his eyes as he knelt before me… I didn't know how, but I knew that somehow something changed the minute he opened my bedroom door and he set me free of the terror in the darkness.

I felt like I had been wading through horror… until I saw him. Until that light flooded in, and he set me free of it. And then he took me to his room. Circled around me and sniffed at me, touched me, like a beast whose possession had been touched by another. I wanted him. So, desperately.

To be rid of the chill that lingered in my body. To feel anchored again to this world and not like I was being chased by something in the next. He looked at me like I'd be stolen from beneath him if he looked away. He needed me to say yes to him, as if the silence made room for voices that threatened him. Us.

As he held the ring out to me, strange shadows filled in his eyes. Unlike anything I'd ever seen in him before. My answer could make it go away. The same way light chased that presence and voice away. As if an invisible, intangible word could keep us tied together and not let anything pull us apart.

So, I said it. It was a promise as binding as the spell that scarred my hand… with a ring to match. The way he fucked me—it was more than that. It fed me. I felt it happening and couldn't think—couldn't stop myself from relishing in what he gave me. He touched hollow parts of me, deeper than my body.

We slept in his bed, and I awoke with his arm draped over my waist.

Daylight filled the bedroom, and the fire was long gone. Berlium's breathing was easy against the back of my neck.

It reminded me I'd spent a better part of my life hating him… and something deep in my core still held onto the grudge. His arm wrapped around me suddenly felt heavy. His breathing felt too hot on my skin. My stomach was too empty, and I'd laid still for too long.

I pushed his arm off me and sat up, not caring whether I woke him. He groaned and rolled over as I stood from the bed. The High Winter chill shocked my skin. My dress was torn on the floor, so I took his shirt.

He didn't wake up or ask me to stay. I didn't want him to. I left the room. It was even colder in the hallway, and I padded back to my room as quickly as I could, rubbing the chill from my arms. Reaching my room, I shut the door behind me and took a deep breath. It wasn't enough. I needed air.

Dale. We'd be leaving soon enough, heading back to the castle. But more than that, Dale was the battleground where I'd continue the Sunderlands' fight for freedom. He was still my enemy. I still had work to do, things to take from him. Wanting him and hating him.

The Death Spirit chimed in, right on cue. *"There's much to be gained from this marriage. Beyond freedom, this could end all war between the Baore and the Sunderlands. For generations."*

"Shit." I stopped in the middle of the room.

Generations. I hadn't even considered that being his wife and queen meant there was a possibility of bearing his heirs. "Children. Between a Human and an Elf. For the love of all things good and evil."

I never really thought about it before, but the realization came quickly. I didn't want a child. My cycles were always irregular, and I hardly ever worried about such things because the Vigilants told me the irregularity would make it difficult to conceive. I expected my courses would come soon enough—which would be awful. They were always terribly painful. Sometimes flattening me for days. As Ivaia always said, women had better things to do than bleed. It was a curse. A screaming baby in the middle of the war would be a nightmare.

Berlium never sired one as far as I knew and killed all other competitors for his throne. Now that we'd slept together, I'd need to ask Hadriel whether there was some tincture I could take to prevent a child. He would understand.

I packed my things and made sure I was ready to travel by the time Yarden came to my room. I didn't see Berlium again until it was time to bid my cousin goodbye. My gut clenched when she stepped into view. I thought about what I was leaving behind here. Walking away from her a second time—she'd continue doing whatever devious things fit her fancy. I considered killing her right there on the front steps of her castle.

It would have negative repercussions. Leaving the Ro'Hale throne open while I ran to claim the Baorean one. She attacked the King of the Baore last night! Our people were in his hold, my sister included.

Hero didn't want him dead because of the bigger reasons, but because of her own revenge. She didn't care what it'd mean to leave my people in Dale. There'd be an uprising. They'd be killed. If I had been the one to kill him, at least I would have been there to *try* and get my people out. In retrospect, it wasn't a fool-proof plan.

I felt my claws pricking through my skin, begging to slide free.

"Such dark eyes you have, cousin," Hero said as I approached. I blinked the darkness out of my eyes and listened to her heart rate. Debating.

"I know what you're thinking, little wolf," I heard the King's thoughts in my head. He sounded amused.

"It'd be better this way," my Death Spirit answered.

Hero couldn't see past her need for revenge. If the throne was empty, would it be better than it being under her? Who could hold it? I looked at Rydel. Hero opened her mouth to say something, but then she fell a step back.

"Hero, are you well?" Rydel caught her elbow and steadied her. Tears welled her eyes.

"My mirror." She looked up at the overcast sky and started

whimpering.

"Fetch the mirror," Rydel ordered a servant.

I searched her vacant eyes, wondering if this was all a ruse. Watched the way everyone tended to her.

"What is it?" Berlium drew closer to me.

"Show me the girl," Hero groaned, not sounding like herself.

"What do you see?" I waved my hands in front of her face. She turned away.

"Keres, perhaps you should step away," Rydel suggested.

The servant reappeared, carrying the mirror on a silver tray. Hero reached for it and clutched it to her chest. She stared into the darkened glass and petted the golden, ornate frame. I narrowed my eyes on her and inched closer. Berlium's hand touched my arm.

"Show you the girl? She's such a pretty girl," Hero murmured. She smiled and tears lined her eyes... and then she pointed a malicious stare at me. She bent over the mirror and clutched its stem, then spun it around and faced the glass toward me.

Darkness and smoke swirled around me in my reflection. The surface of the glass shimmered, and innumerable stars blinked into existence in the background. The image seemed deep, as if the mirror was an opening into another world. I couldn't tear my eyes away.

"Who's there in the dark?" My heart rate kicked up. I peered into the looking glass, waiting for another face to surface beside my own.

"Yes, show him," Hero squealed and brought the mirror closer to my face. I could feel her crazed attention wash over me, but I couldn't meet her gaze. I wrapped my hand around hers, around the mirror.

Fire bloomed into life in my body. My power woke back up. Elymas' fire, not the flames Berlium gave me. I recognized it immediately. My skin glowed as if my body held the stars inside it the way the mirror did. Smoke and shadow swirled in the mirror, shifting and deepening. Then a pair of blue-green eyes surfaced.

"Who are you?" I whispered.

"Get away from her," a voice reached me. Cold washed over me as a presence behind me loomed closer. I felt as if nothing else existed beside

321

this mirror.

"I'm coming, Keres. Wait for me." The voice sang from within the mirror.

"I said get away from her." Berlium shoved Hero back, separating us and snapping me out of the trance.

I held out my hands, and flames erupted in my palms. King Berlium's hands fell heavily on my shoulders, and he turned me to face him. The fire turned green and cold again as his eyes met mine.

"Keres, are you alright?" He poured his attention over me. I looked past him to see Rydel comforting Hero. She handed him the mirror and sobbed.

"Hero." I pulled out of his grasp and stepped around him. It was clear whatever had been holding her had released her. This wasn't a trick.

"Is it always him? Do you always see that person in the mirror?" I asked. "Is he using you?"

She was beside herself, but Rydel whispered, assuring promises of his love and presence. Trying to make her feel safe.

"Hero," I said impatiently. She turned her crystalline eyes toward me and shook her head.

"I don't know." She wiped her eyes.

"She's shown no one else what she's seen in the mirror, Keres," Rydel added. "No one else knows and she can never speak of it. She never remembers."

"Well—let's destroy it, then."

"No!" she screeched. Her eyes jumped open, unnaturally wide, and her teeth looked razor-sharp. A split second of absolute insanity—she lurched at me. I caught her with a clawed hand by the throat and slammed her down to the ground.

Berlium dragged me back. She lifted up on her hands and looked at me with tear-filled eyes. Herself again, more or less.

I looked at the mirror that had since been replaced on the tray. The servant holding it did not dare look at it, instead kept a wary gaze on all of us.

"And this mirror came from Queen Herrona?"

"Yes," Rydel said as he helped Hero up. I narrowed my gaze at him next. Berlium was just behind me, waiting and watching. I turned back to him.

"Do you know anything about this? You knew Herrona."

He looked between my cousin and me, then at the mirror. Taking too long to answer. "No, I'm afraid I don't."

I didn't believe him—I didn't believe any of them. Rage prickled through me like the bitter winter wind. My power... it had come back for a moment. The power he stole or silenced—changed. Somehow, whoever was in the mirror gave it back to me.

As I looked into King Berlium's eyes, I saw the vivid blue-green of the man in the mirror. I knew those eyes. I couldn't remember where I'd seen them before, but I knew him... and he knew me. By name. Whoever he was, he could give me back my magic, and the man before me could take it away—make it something else.

Why did King Berlium feel threatened? Did he recognize this other man? Last night, like just now. The way he flung open the bedroom door and shattered the darkness that had ensnared me. The way he pushed Hero and me apart, separating me from the dark figure that entranced me.

Was his the voice that called to me last night? The voice that spoke my name and asked what I was afraid of. Last night, it sounded hushed. This was like a blaring trumpet heralding his presence.

How had Berlium known to come to my room? Did he sense this presence so keenly?

"You must go," Hero stated.

I met her eyes again, and she was calmer. How could I just leave—what was the alternative? Kill her where she stood? I looked back to the King, who held out his hand for me. The Sunderlands still held secret dangers, and so did his glare. My fight was in the Baore now, but I told my cousin goodbye, promising myself I'd return and set her free from whatever bound her in madness.

If she wasn't lying—if the Gods had somehow tricked the Oracle, or someone was manipulating her, I'd find the truth. Starting with the King that connected us all. Whether Hero was blinded by a darker force at play, it didn't change all she'd done. As the Coroner, I intended to call this into question. When the time was right.

I took his hand and allowed him to help me into the carriage. This time he traveled with me, but I blocked him out. My mind wandered back to the voice in the darkness, the eyes in the mirror.

I had the feeling that time had parted around me like two great walls of a canyon. On one side, this King of mine. On the other, someone hidden in shadow. Both reaching for me. Both, I sensed, connected. One riotous, one desperate.

Wait for me.

Time was inching forward, bringing them closer to me, to each other. Pulling them in until they'd crash together around me. Without trying to, somehow, I'd gotten caught in the middle of what felt like an unstoppable force and an immovable object.

Some unannounced cataclysm, between fear and retribution.

42: So Close
Thane
Day Eighteen

She slipped out of my grasp. I wasn't sure if it would work, but I had to try spiriting her away. She was in the Sunderlands again. A magic-rich land. Yes, tainted by war and bloodshed, but still a source of power. Her power.

If only I could have kept her enveloped in the darkness long enough to take hold of her spirit. To draw her in close and whisk her away. But the Grizzly King is attached to her, attached to me. He felt me closing in around her.

I suspected he'd used blood magic on her. Never mind, though. In the end, she would be mine. She was always meant to be mine. No other bind could change that. I would still have my way with her. I needed her at my side with the same ravenous intensity that he did.

The King and I were too alike in that way. We were both bottomless.

We had our differences, stark as they were. He conquered and hoarded, and built walls of stone around what he'd taken. I infiltrated and stole and traded my pieces for power. I didn't need stone walls to protect what I took. Secrets. Information. I kept it all in the shadows of my mind, in my memory. That could never be parted from me.

We were both powerful. Another reason to be careful—to hesitate. Our strengths were not incomparable... and we now shared a weakness for her.

I paced my room, weighing the possibilities. They'd leave the Sunderlands and return to the Baore. I didn't have many options. Silas was growing more and more restless—he was driving me crazy. I avoided him, avoided my men. Wondering what to do.

The sting of betrayal was blurring my thoughts on top of it all. The past was like a blade to my achilles, cutting me off from reason. The King... Seeing him behind her, peering out from that damned mirror. A wall of glass between us. *Her* between us. I know he saw me.

He'd deny it. Maybe if she asked him about me, he'd lie for once. He never lied. Would he pretend he never knew me? Push me out of her mind and out of his? *Fuck*.

I'd never seen ice in those blue eyes before now. It hurt... so fucking bad.

This was war. Me and my men versus him. I couldn't lead my men blindly into the Baore, not without telling them my secrets. It seemed like the only option.

43: SMOKE

Keres

Night Twenty-One

I told the King not to bother me while I read. The trip felt longer going home. He sulked, looking out the window while we traveled. When we stopped to make camp, I told him not to touch me and he listened. This night had aged ungracefully. A brutal storm raged against the castle—and in my mind.

"Ah, Magister Hadriel, ever the sight for sore eyes." King Berlium took off his cloak and handed it to the servant that met us at the door.

"Welcome back, sire. Lady Keres." Hadriel bowed to the King and nodded to me.

"Not great to be back." I smiled sweetly.

Berlium's head snapped toward me, and his brows furrowed. I was going to give this man whiplash.

"We are tired—"

"I'm starving, actually." I also passed my cloak to a servant and met Berlium's eyes. "You can go off to bed, my lord. Hadriel, perhaps we could have some tea? And cake. I'm desperate for some lemon cake." Minnow and Ciel chirped their hellos and agreed to fetch us what I wanted.

King Berlium pulled off his gloves and pushed them into his pocket. "Right. I'll retire, then."

He grabbed onto my wrist as I turned to follow Hadriel. "But I'll be expecting you in my bed tonight. Yarden, stay near her and bring her to my chambers. Tell Anselm that she'll be with me, and to post up on the eastern wall tonight."

Yarden nodded.

"My darling, what a scandal you'd make of me," I crooned. "Aren't I safe enough here to sleep in my own bed?"

"My darling, don't play with me. I'm not letting you out of my sight after last night and today."

"Do you know something I don't?" I pulled out of his grasp.

"That goes without mention, Keres. You still have much to learn."

"Well." I lifted my chin. "It's high time my studies with Hadriel began. No more distractions. If we're to be wed, I'll need to be diligent." I smirked.

"If?" He raised a brow.

"Oh, come on," I sighed. I went to turn away, but he caught me again.

"Don't keep me from my cake. You'll regret it," I snapped at him.

He gave me a fake smile and nodded, but then glowered as I turned to leave.

Ciel and Minnow burst into the dining room, hauling trays of cookies, tea, fresh fruit, and, most importantly, cake. "Lady Keres," Minnow sang. "Hope your time in the Sunderlands went well. Is it all settled, then? Did everything get sorted with your late husband?"

"Min!" Ciel snapped. "Don't go asking to know what's not your business. Get back in the kitchen."

"It's alright," I said as I loaded my plate. "He's not my late husband. He's still alive. But he is a former. We are divorced."

"Very good, I would say—if you would say, my lady."

"Good isn't the word I'd use."

"I'm sure it isn't," Hadriel piped up from his seat across from me. Studying me as I shoveled forkfuls of cake into my mouth. Minnow deflated. Ciel laid the last of the desserts out and shooed Minnow, which she ignored.

"Did you love your last husband very much, then?"

I smiled around a forkful of cake. "Love isn't the word I'd use."

"That's quite enough." Hadriel raised a hand to Minnow. She paled and darted from the room.

"Agreed," Ciel scoffed before curtsying and following her bubblier counterpart back to the kitchens.

After a slice of cake and two cups of lavender tea, I finally met Hadriel's eyes. He hadn't touched his plate, and he hadn't once looked away.

"Did you see my ring?" I held my hand out to him and fluttered my fingers so that it sparkled in the candlelight. He was not amused. I tilted my head and smiled at him. "Why so serious, Magister?"

"What are you not saying?"

I straightened up and wiped my mouth with my napkin before resting my hands on my lap.

"A few things, actually. First, I'm sure you have no desire to discuss the warfare of being female, but I'm... late. My courses have not yet come on. Don't look at me like that. There's no need to worry. I have a history of irregularity and have had two sexual partners. One who I'm confident took appropriate precautions. The other... my former husband. Seeing as we were married, he did not need to observe the same caution. We laid together only once, on my wedding night. Gods, that feels like ages ago. There'd be signs by now if I were with child. I'm not—nor do I intend on being so."

He looked down at his still-full plate. As if my words were just another thing added to it. "And?"

"I was wondering... if there was something to prevent a child."

"Abstinence."

"Oh, please, Hadriel." I raked my hand through my hair. I poured another cup of tea and took a deep sip. "Does the King desire heirs? We haven't spoken about the business of making one. Nor has he asked me about any of my prior relations."

"Gods below, I hope not." He threw down his napkin and leaned over the table. "Coroner, the King is not interested in a brood-mother. He desires you as a woman, yes, but more so as a weapon. Not a womb. He had one child, and it was still-birthed."

That cut across unexpectedly sharp. I let another sip of the hot tea wash down my throat and asked, "Lady Vega's child?"

His jaw ticked. "I will not discuss her with you. If you need to know, ask him."

"So, then you must understand why I'd come to you for a solution."

"Have you spoken of this to anyone else?"

"No, I only thought of it yesterday after we—" I stopped myself.

"After you what?" He looked gravely concerned.

"Oh, please, Hadriel," I said again and laid my cup down on its saucer. I reached for more cake. "Did you expect the King to behave chastely with me?"

He rubbed at his chin and scanned his eyes over the table.

"A contraceptive will help, but it isn't foolproof. If you somehow still get pregnant, I will not help you rid yourself of the child. Know that now."

"What?" I lowered my fork. "Why not?"

He picked up his fork and cut into the slice of cake before him. "Unmaking children is a risky affair. There are tinctures one might take to accomplish such a goal. However, they are essentially poison. Even in small amounts, they will unleash chaos on your body. It is not natural. You could even die."

"I'm sure you would do your best to prevent that."

"I am. Be diligent with the contraceptive and take precautions. Manage your... moon phases or whatever you females entrust your ordinances to. This is the responsibility of you and him. Not me. War will require you to be a fighter—not a mother. He understands this. If he's careless—well, then he's a fool."

Then he took a bite of the cake and closed his eyes.

"Lemon cake is always a wonderful decision," I said and took a bite of my own.

"I agree with you on that, child."

"Must you insist on calling me that?" I rolled my eyes.

"Stop rolling your eyes and maybe I'll stop seeing you as one." He lifted a brow and smiled before taking another forkful.

"You're right, though. Berlium and I are going to be a different breed of king and queen. I doubt I am with child, but of course, how can one ever be so sure in these matters."

"Abstinence," he repeated with a smirk.

330

"I knew you were a monk." I squinted at him. He dropped his jaw and fork and then shook his head.

"Gods forbid. I am not so holy as that."

After we'd finished every delicious morsel on the table, we both lounged in our chairs. The fireplaces in all four corners of the room were glowing dimly. The stone walls were silent, and I finally felt calmer. I readied some questions as Hadriel brought out a smoking pipe.

"May I?"

He cut me a look, divided between amusement and reproach.

"I smoked with Berlium, now it's your turn. And look, I can show you a trick. Hold it for me so I can use this hand."

I snapped my fingers and lit it expertly, which earned a smile he quickly tried to take back. "Green fire," he said, narrowing his eyes.

"A gift from the devil," I said, taking a pull and sighing out the smoke.

"If the King gave it to you, that is Brazen fire, child." He took the pipe back across the table. "Summoned from the Otherworld."

"It's cold to my touch, but it can still burn things." A ball of green fire appeared in my hand and Hadriel admired it. "Why is mine green and his blue?"

A ball of crimson flames danced into Hadriel's palm. "He painted your flames the color of your eyes. The same way his are blue. You can't separate genius and madness, nor can you separate torment from an artist. I chose this shade of red—the color of jasmine flowers."

"Seems you've got a touch of whimsy to you too, then."

"It could also be compared to arterial blood," he said with a dark grin.

I shook my head and chuckled.

We sat there silent for a little while, enveloped in the haze of smoke. I was peeling off the layers of my thoughts.

"I finished the rest of the books, between the ride to Ro'Hale and back."

"Oh?" He drew on the pipe and then breathed out a few 'O's of smoke.

"I'm ready to train with you."

"What a coarse word. *Training*. I'm not a sweat-sodden swordmaster. I'm a scholar. Tutelage or instruction would be a bit more dignified."

"Indoctrination, yes," I snorted.

"No. Guidance."

"Semantics." I threw his word back at him and he grinned. "Based on the reading, I have certain expectations."

"You're a smart girl. Tell me."

"Necromancy. Not sure what you're expecting me to do with that yet. Entropic magic and curses. Supposing we're going to discuss my curse?"

"And how to curse others," he said too casually.

I chuckled nervously. "And the last book was about government. Seems like you're ready to make me Queen of the Dead and of Devils."

"Are you not already Queen of the Dead?"

I blinked at him. Finally, he put the pipe down and leaned his elbows on the table. I did the same.

"I can see it now," I said, raising my eyebrows. "The Brazen green light glowing around my figure everywhere I go. Smoke trailing behind me. An army of skeletons at my back. And you," I pouted. "My proud, dark minister."

He rolled his eyes this time and swiped a hand over his face. "You've got quite the imagination; I'll give you that. You will become the right hand of the Baorean King, just as you are the right hand of Death. Armies will be at your whims. Enemies will fall by your word."

"I'm sure I can conjure up some smoke to shroud myself with, though."

"Really, Keres, must you make a joke of it?"

I bit down on my smile. "Sorry. It's how I cope with becoming a vessel of dark magic. Which reminds me..." The change in my voice earned his rapt attention. "Two things. One, I've been visited by Ahriman."

He bolted up from his seat and flattened his hands on the table. "What? When was this? You're only telling me now? How do you know it was Ahriman?"

I stood too, as I remembered our haunting conversation. "I confirmed the things He said with the book you gave me. It happened here, in my room. Just before we left."

"What did He speak of?"

I straightened up like a soldier giving a report. It made me think of Indiro. Ahriman's image overwhelmed my memory. The many faces He bore, His voices.

"He demanded I bow to Him. Told me to curse Mrithyn or die otherwise. Promised me freedom." I sighed. "And whatever other nonsense about how mighty He was."

Hadriel stayed quiet for a moment, pushing off the table and walking to the far end of the room. He held his hands behind his back as he walked and pondered.

"I will need to think about this before I respond. The other thing— what was it?"

"The other thing is really more a person than a thing. Just before we left Ro'Hale, I met someone who, for a moment, made me feel I could get my other magic back. I was a mage before I became the Coroner, having inherited the abilities of my mother and aunt, and, I'm sure, ancestors of ours. I want it back."

"I cannot give it back to you." He shook his head.

"But the King can?"

"He gave you Brazen. He will give you other things."

"He silenced my natural magic and this other guy—"

"Who is this other man?" He pressed.

"He was in Queen Hero's mirror," I said.

His brows knitted together with confusion.

I rolled my shoulders back and sighed. "Ask the King. He seems to know."

His expression flattened. As pale as he was naturally, he couldn't have looked more colorless.

"Ah, so you know of him too, then?" I tilted my head.

"Tell me, what has he said to you?"

"He told me to wait for him."

He let out a short laugh. "Yes, of course. Keres, he is not on your side. Listen to me. The same way Ahriman came and made you an offer, this other character would set a trap for you as well."

"But why?" I crossed my arms in front of me. "I need to know—what if he's controlling Queen Hero? Who is he?"

He shook his head and closed his eyes. "No one."

"Untrue."

"It's truer than you think."

Now it was my turn to roll my eyes.

"Tomorrow, meet me in the southern courtyard. The one you favored," he said after a moment.

"With the trees that have black flowers?"

He nodded. "They're called Wither Maidens, native to the Sunderlands, from an area called the Gods' Woods. They're extremely potent if consumed."

"Let me guess," I sighed. "You're going to make some kind of tea from them and make me drink it."

He blinked at me and smiled. "You're learning."

His robes swished against the stone floor as he came to stand before me. His finger lifted my chin up.

"Close your eyes."

I did.

"You have questions—your mind spins. It's apparent that you still have some insecurity in who you are, Keres. For too long, you've been trying to separate who you should be from what power you have been given. It has created dissonance within you. You are arrogant and outspoken regarding your powers, yet you suffer in your mind silently. Turmoil. Anxiety. I am eager to teach you, I admit, but you cannot approach me from this place." He pointed his finger into my chest, just below my collarbone. "Here lies unrest and mistrust. You believe this is where your Death Spirit resides. Like a caged animal beneath your ribs."

How could he possibly know that?

"This energy does not serve you. Fear—fluttering, roaring, and untamed. It interrupts your breathing patterns. The energy that swells here… it suffocates."

"How do you know?" My eyes flew open.

"Because I was once like you. Young. Unrefined. Brimming with power, I didn't know how to control. I felt as if I were the puppet of this energy and would always be that way. Weak. Insufficient. But that's a lie the world ingrains in those who are strong. The truth lies deeper. Now, close your eyes."

I pinched them shut again. He lifted his hand and touched my forehead between my brows. Soft pressure released the tension there.

"I will be your guide in reaching here. This is where your Spirit truly resides. You are not the puppet of your power or of your God. You are the master. Your mind pulls the strings and the character you wish to play in this life will take the orders. You want to be stronger than you are, then you must think stronger than you do. Stop believing the lies you've allowed the world to write into your being. Willingness is the first step. You told me yourself that the Death Spirit surfaces or is louder in your thoughts around Berlium."

He took his hand away, and I opened my eyes again. "I shift when I'm with him. He does too. It just happens. I barely even realize it until I look down and we have claws. I've always had fangs, but he can see the Death Spirit in me, and it rises to him. I've seen… parts of his inner monster. They are so alike."

"That is a good thing, Coroner. You're breaking out of the mold— the crypt you've been hiding in. It will be a long journey from here to understanding, but you won't be alone. Besides the King, I will go with you into the dark. Are you truly willing?"

"Yes," I said.

"Good." He pressed his lips into a thin smile. "Now, go to bed. I'll see you in the morning. Through our lessons, we will discover answers together."

I smiled. As we passed through the doors, we turned our separate ways.

"Coroner," he said. Drawing my attention over my shoulder to his gray gaze. He bowed his head slightly. "This is only the beginning, but I am glad to be at the start with you. It is a rare gift to see someone take their first steps."

44: SMUT
Heres

Yarden escorted me to my room so I could bathe and change. I told him about Hadriel's interesting lesson tomorrow with the Wither Maidens, and he said he wanted to find a book about them. Of course, he wanted me to tell him all about it after.

Berlium waited for me in his bedroom, but I was luxuriating in my bath, counting all the things I hated about him—the list was painfully short, but the items on it were horrible. They were simple reminders that things were shifting, moment to moment. Nothing should surprise me. He still held the power. My anger and anxiety did not serve me. Like Hadriel said.

Everything that happened with Hero, with the mystery man in her mirror, I would use it to sharpen my claws. My King had enemies. Though I wanted to skin him for his secrets, I had to keep playing the game. Eagerness overcame my frustration. It wasn't enough to know his truths. I'd need to know how to use them against him. Though I stood on his side of the gameboard now, it was Queen versus the King. I could play my hand at war, even in his bed.

It seemed to frustrate him endlessly to sleep so close to me and be denied while we'd traveled back from Ro'Hale. He glared at the distance between our bodies. I wondered how far I could push him and smiled.

Minnow and Ciel got me ready for bed as if it were my wedding night. They applied buttery soft lotion and perfume oil to my skin. Minnow insisted I wear a bit of lip rouge. I showed them my ring and enjoyed their coos.

Finally, I wrapped myself in a long silk robe, grabbed one of Hadriel's books, and walked past Yarden to the King's room.

"Good night, Yarden," I said.

"Good night, my lady."

The idol-like, imposing statue of Berlium stood proudly in the middle of the foyer. I wondered if he'd have one made of me to match it. Doubted it. I approached the ornate, black door with its fine gold accents. He was on the other side.

The door opened, and I met the King's beautiful blue eyes.

"Eyes that see us and tell us ours are dark stars," the Death Spirit purred through me. He heard it and heat filled his stare. Silently, I entered the room.

It was less self-worshiping than I expected, but it was him as a space. The walls were dressed in matte sapphire blue paper. The bed was enormous without apparent reason. Its wood was black as his hair and the sheets were a darker blue than the walls. A gray fur blanket was draped over the foot of the bed, and a similar fur carpet sprawled out between the bed and the fireplace.

It smelled like him, like honeyed spice. Candles burned on gold pedestals, scattered about the room; and a modest fire danced in the hearth. The farthest wall was made of windows, shielded by thick, velvet gray drapes. Tied back loosely by black cords, and behind them was a sheer liner that had been left opened. The light in the room made it difficult to get a good look outside; but large flecks of snow filtered through the moonlight and splashed against the window.

And then there was the King, standing in the middle of the room. I felt a hollowness pang in my core just looking at him. The right-hand corner of his mouth turned up, his brow lifting ever so slightly. The warm light danced in his eyes.

"Don't look at me like that," I said and walked over to the chaise lounge that took up the nearest corner of the room. I made myself comfortable and pulled the lightweight linen blanket it offered over my legs. Didn't matter. I felt like he could see straight through it, and the night robe, and the dress I was wearing.

"Don't tell me what not to do. You're mine. I'll look at you however I like." He sat down on the small sofa behind him and watched me from the other side of the room.

"I've brought a book." I held up the worn hardcover.

Berlium reached over to the end table beside him and picked up an equally old book. "I have one too."

"Good."

"Quite."

We glared at each other. He seemed to fight his amusement. I thumbed open the book and stared at the first page. I could feel his eyes on me. My cheeks warmed, so I kicked off the blanket and refocused on the page:

The manipulation of blood that still courses through a living being's veins is forbidden. Believed to be a divergence of elemental magic. Namely, water manipulation. Ithaca Maelstreon, was the first Water Daemon to practice and exhibit the technique.

While enslaved by a cruel master, she learned to sense or identify the water that naturally constituted the blood, and to bend it to her will. Through her discovery, she sought ways to kill and control men, like a puppeteer with invisible strings.

She introduced the techniques of stopping a man's heart, or slowing the flow of blood to cause cyanosis; and or, the eventual death of a limb. As well as rushing blood to certain parts of the body; overwhelming vital organs, such as the brain and the lungs. Her magic inflicted immense pain.

Efforts to control a body's movements were rarely successful; and if so, were too chaotic as the victim resisted—and rapidly resulted in a loss of consciousness and death.

"What are you reading about?" he asked in a husky voice.

"Ways to kill you." I smiled behind my book without looking at him.

Ithaca was finally detained after ten long years of serial murders. Freeing herself and the other slaves owned by her master was not enough. She eventually discovered a way to cause mass bleeding in a victim. Bursting blood vessels one at a time, causing innumerable bruises; calling out blood from a victim's eyes, nose, ears. She also drank blood in belief that—

"What is Hadriel teaching you?" He was standing now. His own book, forgotten on the sofa. He walked toward me, unbuttoning his shirt at the wrists.

"Voodoo."

He stopped at the button just below his sternum and had reached the edge of my seat. I looked up at him, still holding the book between us. He leaned down. His shirt opened and allowed me a glance at his muscled abs. The corner of his mouth picked up again. "Time for bed."

He plucked the book from my hand, straightened up, and scanned the page. His brows furrowed, and he looked back at me.

"What a wicked thing to read."

"Disappointed it's not smut?"

He chuckled and looked back at the page. "Blood magic. Smut. Both are very useful to me."

He took a bookmark off the end table and tucked it into my book, before tossing it next to his on the sofa.

"I highly doubt you've ever read a dirty novel in your life," he said, taking his shirt off and tossing it on top of the books.

"I'll have you know that my first wedding gift was a book with graphic illustrations and thorough explanations of—"

"Let me guess, fighting stances. Learn anything useful?" His eyes darkened and his lips curved.

I bit my lip and looked away. In the farthest corner of the room, there were two bookshelves.

"Oh? Introduce me to your friends."

Standing, I held my robe around me still, and walked past him to the shelves. I read the titled spines.

"The History of the Natlantine. Shrines of Gods Forgotten. Ah, what's this?" I took one off the shelf. "A Night in the Baeorean Highlands?"

He lunged forward to snatch the book from my hands, but I jumped back and turned away, opening to a random page.

"She hated it," I read enthusiastically. "Lady Catriona knew she had not been raised to be this type of woman. Surely, her mother had imparted *some* good sense. A man like Alexander was not to be wanted, let alone attained. No matter what she felt, time had drawn a line between them. He overshadowed her by a good fifteen years!"

As he leaned in to take it again, I held the book out of his reach, using my other elbow to keep him at a distance.

"Alright, alright. Enough of that," he protested.

"Oh, you're not getting out of this that easily." I laughed and found my place on the page.

"Fifteen years. She'd never escape this truth, and he wouldn't let her forget it. Alexander was many things opposite of her. Often rough and outspoken, he could be temperamental and insensitive. At one moment, professing his desire, and the next treating her as if she were a child who needed to be reminded of his authority. What proper authority could he have over her? He was her family's servant. Yet somehow, they both knew he held her powerless. No matter who commanded who, he'd taken free rein of her heart. Still, a gentle, high-born lady with a thorough education simply could not run off with the family's carriage-driver. But when his dark brown eyes met hers, she saw freedom."

"Keres," he hissed my name.

"Really, a gentle, high-born lady like myself, with a thorough education in blood magic, cannot be expected to just—"

He backed me up against the wall and braced himself on either side of me. His face was dangerously close to mine and the book would do very little good between us now.

"You are not a gentle lady," he said slowly.

I looked down at the book and smiled. "Lady Catriona, I am not."

"Thank the Gods." He bent his head down to mine and his breath teased at my ear.

I pushed the book into his chest until he stood back.

"Bedtime." I said in a surprisingly steady voice.

His hands reached for the button of his trousers.

"No, wicked brute." I aimed the book at his pants. "Actual bedtime. With sleeping. In night clothes."

I shelved the book and walked past him to the bed, giving him a wide berth.

"I sleep naked," he said.

His eyes tracked me, watching me turn down the blankets and toss the decorative pillows on the floor. He raked his hands through his hair. I blew out the candles on my side. Getting under the covers, I forced myself to close my eyes and lay there. Pressing my lips together as I drank in the scent of him.

The bed shifted. The heat of his body instantly made me feel flushed. I could feel he'd left his pants on, despite his threat. I sat up, pushed the blankets off, and took my robe off.

"I was wondering how long you were going to wear that."

With no place to hang it, I threw it at the foot of the bed. I was sure I'd end up kicking it off the edge by morning.

"Yes, well. There it goes. Goodnight."

He inched closer, and I turned away from him. Again, his weight shifted the bed. I could tell he was leaning up on his arm, looking at me.

"Say it back," I said.

He traced a finger against my bare shoulder. This nightdress was just like the other one I'd worn, but light blue. I turned back over and looked up at him, accidentally bringing myself even closer to him. A stray wisp of hair crossed over his brow, and the lines of his face softened as he looked at my face, and then at the rest of me. His eyes came back up to mine and stayed there for a second.

"I want to do more than hold you tonight."

I turned back over. "And then hurt me tomorrow."

His breathing paused, and then he let out a sigh. His hand found my waist.

"Why would you say that?"

"Would you give me back my magic?"

He didn't answer.

"Would you let my people go? Let me see my sister?"

"Ker—"

"Un-break my hand."

His grip tightened on my waist, and he pulled me back to face him. "Stop."

342

"No." I pried his hand from me.

He lifted himself up and placed his body over mine. His knees forced mine apart, and he rested his weight between my thighs. He grabbed my leg and wrapped it around himself instead. I pushed against his chest, but he didn't budge.

"I will not hurt you." His voice rumbled against my chest.

"Then get off of me." I smiled and batted my lashes.

He rocked his hips against me, granting some friction between my thighs. "You say that, but you don't mean it."

"Oh, yes I do," I said, but neither of us believed it.

He lowered his head down and kissed my neck hungrily. Liquid heat pooled between my thighs, and my core clenched with need. I moved toward his touch, his mouth. My need for him was truer than I wanted to admit. Nearly painful to deny. So, I kissed his neck and then his shoulder, and then I bit him.

That's all it took for him to jerk back with a growl, and I released him. He sat on the edge of the bed and held pressure against his neck. When he took his hand away, tiny rivulets of blood dripped from the punctures. His eyes burned into mine and I smiled again.

"Looks like I missed something vital. Oops."

"It's that damned book, isn't it? Dangerous thing for a woman like you to be reading. You'll be drinking my blood next."

"Tempting," I said with a smirk.

He got up and crossed into the bathroom. I watched the muscles of his perfect back. He rolled his head to the side, stretching the shoulder.

I heard water splashing as he washed the wound. Settling back in the bed, I took up a little more space. He deserved it. And worse. I couldn't sleep, though. I held the pillow over my face, trying out to block out the overwhelmingly delicious scent of his blood. Every drop of him was purely male and alluring.

Soft footsteps padded back into the room, but I was determined to ignore him.

45: SPOILED
Keres

"Bring your knees to your chest." His voice was dark and there was gravel in it.

I lifted my head and saw Berlium at the other end of—

"Are those chains?" I shot up in the bed.

"You had your fun acting like a brat, Keres. Now, I get to have mine. You want to bring this fight to our bed? Then let me remind you to whom you belong."

I jumped from the bed, clutching the pillow against my chest.

"Lay back down if you want this to be easier."

"And let you chain me? No fucking way."

A shiver of excitement ran through me as I watched him.

He laughed, mischief flaring in his eyes as he took a step toward me. I threw the pillow on the floor and sank into a ready stance. He raked his gaze over me, which sent my pulse pounding between my legs.

"You're not going to *let* me chain you. I'm going to because you belong to me."

"I do not belong in chains," I snarled.

A sardonic smirk played at his lips.

"Between my teeth and under my fingernails—that's where you belong."

I must have been losing my mind because the thought of his claws grazing my flesh, his fangs, made me soaked between my thighs. He took another step toward me, and I stepped toward the door.

"You won't make it," he said, inching closer.

I flung myself onto the bed, rolled across it, cursing it for how big it was, and came to stand on the other side. His eyes flashed with hunger, and I realized my mistake: I gave the hunter reason to chase me. He swung the chains, drawing my attention to the fact there were two. They were short, and both had black leather cuffs at either end. A feverish heat spiked within me.

"Get on the bed... now," he commanded, baring his fangs. I hissed at him—like an animal.

He tossed the chains on the bed and lunged for me. He had me over his shoulder before I'd even discerned the direction of his movement. He threw me down on the bed and sat between my legs. Ripped my dress right off me, disheveling my hair.

"Another fucking dress ruined for no reason." I glared at him, allowing my fangs to sink deeper into my mouth and my claws to lengthen.

"There she is. Hello, Darkstar," he purred.

Goosebumps ran rampant over my skin at the chill, but the heat in my core threatened to burn me alive. He left only the lace black panties I wore.

"You bit me," he said, amusement touching his voice.

"I'll do it again," I snapped.

He picked up one chain and moved to grab my wrist, but I lashed out and scratched him clean across the chest.

Blood prickled in the angry lines. His hand closed on my throat, pinning me to the bed, and a delicious growl erupted in his chest.

"At least let me lick my fingers," I gritted out hoarsely. "I've wanted to taste your blood from the moment I saw you."

His face lingered close to mine, leaning into my shallow breaths. His body was dead still against mine. The muscles in his jaw tightened, but my chest felt tighter. His eyes were shifting between blue and black, bruising me with his stare.

And I was losing too much air. I clamped my good hand down on his, prying at his fingers. He snatched it, releasing my throat, and I sucked in air. He fastened the cuff around my captured wrist. And the next to the other, careful not to hurt my broken hand. The opposite ends of their chains stayed in his hands, like reins.

He pulled me up and sat up on his knees. I got up and knelt before him. My head came up to his chin, and he looked down at me, his jaw ticking.

"I rather like it when you act so spoiled," he said. "Because it means your punishment will be just as bad as you are. There are so many things I could do to you, and knowing you, I'll have plenty of opportunities to remind you of your place."

I shivered and looked at the blood that oozed from the wounds I gave him. I bowed my head and licked him, reveling in the taste of his blood. My senses came alive—it tasted like honey and copper. My tongue was longer than usual and pointed. I licked each scratch, and the bleeding stopped. I moved my head up to where I'd bitten him.

"I hope it scars," I whispered and smirked at him.

"Then we'd be even."

"Not nearly."

He pushed me down on the bed. The fire in the hearth behind him was subdued to a tender flame that licked and kissed his frame. A halo of red light to crown the devil. He tugged on the chains, teasing me.

"I'm going to enjoy this," he said.

I tried to sit up, but he tugged again, bringing both my hands toward him between my legs. I couldn't suppress the thrilled purr that erupted from my throat.

"Bring your knees," he repeated in a low, sharp voice, "to your chest. Now."

The command blazed through me, but I still didn't want to obey.

"I'll scream," I said in an unfortunately shaky voice.

His sensuous lips curved. "I hope so."

The sight of myself in bondage, with him as my keeper, made me molten and boneless. Though I fought not to, I squirmed.

"Your attitude is the problem. You're disobedient."

His gaze struck my sex like a lash, searing through the black lace. He pulled them off and stuffed them into my mouth. I bit down on the lace, tasting myself on them. The cool air settled against my sensitive skin. He looked over my body, noticing how my breasts moved with my breath. I felt my nipples perk up at his attention. He picked up one of my legs and folded it back against my chest, keeping the chains taught in his other hand. His nostrils flared with a sharp inhale.

"Your body wants to obey."

Watching his face, I brought up my other leg just to take back some control. He connected the chain on my right wrist to my right ankle, buckling the soft leather cuff tightly. Then repeated it on the other side. The chains grazed my inner thighs, stretched between my wrists and my ankles.

He pulled a short black scarf out of his pocket.

"Pick up your head."

"You're blindfolding—" It sounded like nonsense around the mouthful of lace.

"Keres," he warned.

I snapped my mouth shut on the panties. Then I closed my eyes, and he tied the silk scarf around my head, blindfolding me. When he was satisfied with the knot, he let out a soft grunt. Resting my head back down on the bed.

"Now," he breathed against my ear, "hold on to your chains, little wolf,"

I wrapped my fingers around the chains with one hand, keeping my knees apart. Resting my other hand any way I could. The chain links tinkled with the movements, setting my teeth on edge. Such a pretty, tantalizing sound for such a wicked thing. I'd never admit that I liked it.

His rough hand traced lazy lines up and down my leg, wandering over the cuffs. My bare breasts tightened as I exhaled a long, shaky breath through my nose. He lifted one of my hands, testing the bond, and my leg moved with it.

"You're trembling," he murmured.

I couldn't help it. Then something feather-soft fanned against my inner thigh, and I shuddered.

"Look at that needy cunt, gleaming wet for me. Ready to be punished."

He slapped my sex. My body jolted, and he hit me again. The sting flourished into excitement when it probably should have enraged me. It didn't... which made me flush with heat that pricked my cheeks. Embarrassed by my body's reaction to his rough treatment. I should have hated that he had me chained, squirming, flinching at his next words.

"I like it when you scratch and bite—nobody's ever dared that before. In the end, your chains are mine, and I love that I'm the one who gets to bring you to heel. We both know you need it."

He made a tsking sound and ran a finger over my knee. "So many things I could do just to torment you. I know you're so untrained. Does it frighten you to realize the things you want me to do to you? What are you imagining right now?"

My mind started spinning out, envisioning pain and pleasure. Positions I'd never tried but remembered from my brief perusal of that sex book I got on my wedding day.

He chuckled. "I see."

My skin burned hotter, realizing he'd probably read my mind.

"You want to taste it all. Every drop of pain, every drop of pleasure. Well, hungry girl, consider tonight a lesson. Basics. Let's see whether you're a quick study."

The feather tickled my groin, brushing up over the curve of my hips, my waist. Trailing up between my breasts and circling around my nipples. Chills chased the feather over my skin as he brought it up to my neck and then back down. Stopping to sweep it over my sex. Erotic need fluttered in my core, and I gasped. He made another languid pass over my wet heat and brought the feather to my leg. This time reaching down to brush the underside of my foot, making it twitch.

"Ticklish? Good to know."

I whimpered as the soft bristles scaled the sole of my foot. I jerked against the chains, pulling away from him, and his laughter bloomed in the darkness that shrouded my eyes. He grabbed my leg and lifted it, creating tension in the chains. He ran the feather down the underside of my leg. The sensation draped down my skin, flitting against the back of my knee, leaving tingles in its wake.

His scaled claws dragged away the sensation of the feather, and then he stopped. Sweat beaded on my brow. I was dripping with need. I squirmed, listening to his movements as he got off the bed and walked around the room.

"Your scent tells me everything. I don't have to read your mind, Keres. This alone..."

I felt the touch of what must have been his winged shadows fluttering over my sex. I writhed again, moaning at the sensation of their nipping and skittering. Then they fled.

"Your body states your desires, silently." His voice was layered, gravelly, and dark as sin. "I can taste the urgency in your body—to resist, to obey. It will tell me what you can and cannot handle. Right now, all I taste is a heady mix of everything you need but know you shouldn't. I'm going to turn your needing into knowing. You will know what it means to be owned."

Heat banked in my core and my palms sweat as I kept my hand on my chains. I moaned with the panties in my mouth, beckoning him back to the bed.

"In a rush?" His voice was soft again.

I reached a shackled hand down between my legs, desperate for a soothing touch—

"Don't you fucking dare," he growled, and I froze in obedience.

He came back, tugged the panties from between my teeth and rubbed it over my sex. Roughly. The lace grated against my sensitive flesh, and I arched my back as I moaned. He pulled my knees farther apart, and I held onto my chains as he rocked my body with his hand.

His other hand passed over the mounds of my breasts and up to my throat. His fingertips pressed into the sides of my neck, driving pleasure into the pain. Pinning me to the soft sheets beneath me. My eyes fluttered under the tight blindfold. His other hand kept massaging me mercilessly, making my skin tender and raw.

He pressed the wet lace against my opening and slid it into my core with his finger. Igniting me. His finger pulsed inside me, surrounded by lace, soaking it with my need. Another finger joined it inside me, and a soft breath escaped my lips. Pleasure flickered through the pain.

Then he stopped. The heat he'd ignited in my core ebbed when he withdrew his fingers, leaving the panties inside me. I gasped as my grip on the chains slipped, and my ankles dropped, tugging my wrists after them. But he pushed me down, his hand catching my breast. I caught onto the chains again and lifted my feet back up.

"I love the way you look right now. Your dainty claws fumbling for your golden chains. Your pretty little cunt raw and drenched. I'm not done yet. By the time I am, you'll look a beautiful mess."

He withdrew himself from me entirely and moved between my legs. Guiding my knees together and bringing my hands to the outside of my knees.

"Hold your legs up."

I braced my hands on the backs of my calves, keeping my knees close to my chest, and held my legs open. He tugged the panties out and pushed them back into my mouth. They were slick and warm with my heat. I bit down on them. Sucked on them, drinking in the taste.

"That's what you taste like when I devour you. Your body wants to be sweet for me when I'm rough with you."

I moaned, sucking on the panties. He chuckled darkly.

Something ice cold touched my center, and I jerked my chains again. It was hard and smooth as polished glass. Felt like a cock, but it wasn't. I whimpered, unable to ask. It was a brisk relief to the chafing the panties created that made me sigh.

My core contracted as he touched it against my apex. He slid it down through my center. Like a brush against canvas, he painted chills against my inflamed skin in watercolors that soaked me through. I moaned again, relaxing into the touch.

He brought the tip to my entrance and nudged it in, drawing a louder moan out of me. Then withdrew it, teasing. Dragging it back up my center, then down again to enter me a little. Repeating the passing sweeps, deepening it each time. Tension built in me. My breathing told him I ached for more. I groaned, lifting my head, wishing I could see what he was doing.

Finally, he plunged it in deep and left it there with just the end of it left out of me. Stopped moving it. I cried out, desperate for the friction.

"Hold it inside you. Clench your pussy around it. Let me see you move it without my hand."

My core contracted around the wand—the muscles within me pulsating around it—and it moved inside me.

"Good girl. Keep it there. I want you to do that until you ache. When I'm inside you, you'll grip and stroke my cock just like that. Do you understand?"

I nodded. My inner muscles contracted and relaxed, proving I could do it. I felt the bed shift as he got up. Listened as he took his pants off. I could feel his eyes on me. Tightened my core again on the wand, a pool of heat building inside me. I didn't want this in me—I wanted him. The size of him would dwarf this damned thing. I growled around the mouthful of lace.

"Don't stop working that tight, thick pussy. I'm going to fuck you until you're sore and begging me to stop."

I groaned and forced my already fatigued muscles to obey. This was hard!

He moved onto the bed, over me, and rested his cock against my sex, sliding it up and down my center. Delicious heat raged through me as he stroked me. A fresh wave of energy tightened my grip on the wand. I wanted it to be him feeling me. He withdrew his touch.

"It's not about what you want, hungry girl. I can spoil you and I can punish you. You're learning to give me what *I* want."

He leaned over me, bracing himself on one side of me, and I rested my legs on his shoulders, having to move my hands with them. His other hand guided his cock up and down my center in teasingly slow traced lines.

Tension built in my core, and the honey of his voice dripped between my thighs.

"You can't take what you want, greedy little thing—only I can give it to you right now."

He tapped his cock against the sensitive bud of flesh, then brushed it side to side. I moaned, biting down hard on the lace, and tears pricked my eyes. I was getting desperate for him. For relief. My grip on the wand loosened. It started to slip out from the slick heat stoppered inside me. Taking the pressure away. My muscles burned.

His next movement dragged an unintelligible noise from my throat and again he hummed with approval. He noticed the wand was mostly out and that an ache was hollowing my core. "You're empty. Are you tired?"

I nodded. "Mmhm."

"Good. Now, we can start."

His weight shifted over mine, bringing his heat closer to my skin. He pulled the panties from my mouth, and I heard them hit the pillow to the side. I swallowed and moaned his name.

Then his lips brushed over mine, a shock of tenderness. I sighed as his tongue licked at the vulnerable corner of my mouth, urging me to open for him. A soft breath escaped me, and his tongue swept into my mouth. My blood rushed in my veins, pumping liquid heat into my core. His tongue pushed further, exploring deeper, uprooting my inhibition. He drew a soft moan out of me and echoed it into my mouth.

His cock rested against my belly as his mouth drifted to my throat, and he traced his tongue against my artery that beat furiously against him. He reached a hand down to my apex and pinched. I gasped, but he didn't relent, licking and kissing his way up and down my neck, from my ears to my collarbone. He brought his hand back up and kneaded my breasts. His head shifted lower, bringing his mouth to one of my nipples. Suckling and nipping.

The sharp tips of his fangs stung as he closed his mouth over my nipple. He moved to the other breast, caging my nipple between his teeth and drawing pinpricks of blood. Making me growl *my* approval. I loved the attention he gave my breasts. Listening to my body, he pressed kisses all over my breasts. Then kissed my sternum, burying his face in between them, before sinking even lower. Dropping his mouth down to my navel, licking me up my side and nuzzling into my ribs. His tongue swept out as his hands lifted my breasts, and he licked the tender undersides. Dragging his tongue back up my sternum to my throat. Then blew softly on my wet skin. I shivered beneath him.

My heart rate fired up as I felt his fangs scrape against my skin. A knot in my chest frayed, and a scream built in my throat. He stopped. I swore he could hear my heart pounding.

He knocked the glass-like thing away and dipped his cock into me. I moaned and clenched down on him the way he wanted me to, even though every internal inch of me burned from the effort. I hissed and bowed off the bed. His hands gripped my legs, holding them open, reminding me of my chains.

"Tighter," he commanded.

Reflexively, my pussy gripped onto him.

"Take me deeper. Don't let me go."

The back of my head hit the bed. I could feel the muscles of my abdomen straining with the effort, desperate to suck him in deeper. He rewarded each labored pull with another inch and then another. It seemed endless—the wanting, the hungry clutching. I wasn't letting go, no matter how sore I was. He pulled back like he was testing me, and I groaned with the effort to reclaim him.

"Good girl."

Another inch struck deep in my core. I felt pressure in my abdomen, and he brought a hand down to meet it. Pressing down between my navel and my pubic bone.

"Fuck me," I growled at him, lifting my head back up. He ripped the blindfold off. His stare sent a bolt of electricity surging through me. I drank in the vision of him inside me greedily. The little bruises on my nipples. "Please," I said breathlessly, watching my body move on him. Chained, soaked, flushed red.

I moved beneath him, trying to get him to give me all of him. I wanted every inch, but when he thrust into me, he was still holding back. Keeping the pressure on my abdomen as he fucked me slowly. I reveled in the timbre of his moan. It sent shivers through me. My heartbeat raged, and his tamed—dominating.

That pressure deepened and widened as a moan crumbled in my breath. My body went taught. He gave me another inch, watching my reaction as he forced my body to adjust to his size at his pace.

353

It hurt, but still I growled at him, "More. I want more."

He filled me up, unforgiving. He ground his hips against mine, his fingertips fluttering over my clit. My inner walls shook, threatening to crumble as my body neared climax.

And then he stopped.

I cried out as pleasure seeped back into his control. "Keep going—please."

"Fuck *me*," he said with a smile that lit up his sapphire eyes. "You want to come? Earn it."

My body ached and burned from using my muscles, but I lifted my head to see where he was sheathed inside me. Basics, right? I tightened my core on him. He reached his hand down and strummed my apex with his fingers, rewarding me.

"Yes," I said, and my body went slack—again, so he stopped.

"Give me more," he said in a dangerously low voice.

I lifted my head and bit my lip, watching his face, the bead of sweat dripping from his hairline to his dark brow. "Yes, my King."

Holding onto my chains, I used whatever strength I had left in my core to lift my hips and roll them against his.

"This is how you were made to be fucked. This cunt is mine. Do you understand?"

"Yes," I said breathlessly, putting all thought of resistance out of my head.

He smiled and rewarded me by grabbing my hips, pulling to seat me on his cock, and supporting me as I tightened my grip on him. Claiming my place like a throne. "There you go. You feel amazing."

His hands guided my hips as I ground against him. I looked up at him intently as his brows pinched together, and he licked his lips, watching my body writhe for him as I gave him all I had left.

He groaned my name, and it made me buck against him harder. His fingers dug into my hips and the wet sound of us fucking got sloppier. He rocked his hips into me slowly, exchanging control with me.

"Now, what do good girls say when they get what they want?" We locked eyes. His darkened.

My face heated as he thrusted into me again. "Thank you."

A feeling like fire erupted between us. Striking me in that tight, aching spot of my core. I cried out another, "Thank you," and another, until my breath broke down into desperate whimpers.

He moaned again. "Beautiful girl. Come undone for me."

He kept his rhythm as my orgasm rocked into me. When it threatened to end, he unleashed himself.

"Give *me* more," he growled, spanking my sex again. A shockwave for my pleasure.

I yelped and clung to my chains, but kept moving with him, riding through the sting of the impact.

"Perfect, little wolf. That's exactly what I want."

His eyes searched my face and mine rolled back as he dove into the warmth of me over and over. Undulating his hips so that he dug himself deeper, giving me every inch of his steel and striking that perfect spot within me every time. My back arched, and I jerked on my chains again. He didn't stop. He touched every part of me inside that burned, claiming my pleasure as I came again even harder.

Wanting to throw my arms around him, to bring him closer, to knot myself around him. But he wouldn't let me. I forced my body to contract around him. I wanted to hear him moan again. And earned it. He wrapped his hand around my throat, fucked me harder. I forgot how to breathe, how to think. How to be anything but his in that moment.

He battered my core, and his other hand tortured my clit as another climax shattered through me. Every stone wall between us broke when I cried out—like a dam fit to burst. He tore himself from me, leaving me breathless. I watched him take his cock in his fist and pump it, hovering over my body.

His release tumbled through him, fracturing his voice into that gorgeous clash of thunder and lightning. Bathing my skin in his white, hot pleasure. He ran his fingers through it on my belly, probably painting his name on my skin as I lay there panting. Part of me loved the way it felt like he was claiming me. The other part of me… didn't want to think about it right now.

He pressed his wet fingertips into my mouth, commanding me to suck them clean. And I wanted every drop, hungry, just like he said.

"Beautiful. I'm proud of you." He leaned forward, smiled against my mouth, and waited for me to kiss him back. I met his eyes, and a smile claimed my lips too. My kiss told him everything he needed to know.

46: Sip

Keres

Day Twenty-Two

I awoke next to him. He was shirtless, and my eyes went instantly to the bite wound, the scratches on his chest. Healing already. Strange, but not surprising. I hoped the bite would at least scar.

I was free of my chains and pleasantly sore between the legs. All too satisfied from sleeping in his arms, I pushed the blankets off and sat up. Stretching, I looked toward the window. White light washed the room. I got up and walked over, pushing the curtains open more.

Beyond the castle wall, I could see Mannfel. The city Berlium loved so much. Its buildings were ridiculously tall. As intrusive on the skyline as he was on most things. I heard him stir but didn't turn. I scanned the horizon as he came up behind me. He dropped a kiss on my shoulder and wrapped his arms around me. For just a second, I relished in his warmth, the feel of his skin against mine. The butterflies that stormed my belly. Even the scratch of his facial hair as he brought his face near mine.

"You're a scruffy bear." I couldn't help leaning into him.

He simply said, "Mmhm."

"I'm going down to see Hadriel," I said softly.

"Ugh." He let me go.

I turned and met his eyes, waving my finger in his face. "I don't want you just for your perfect cock. I want my crown too, and I'm going to earn it."

He snapped his teeth at my finger. Then caught my hand in his as I tried to pull it back. He turned it over and looked at the ring, then looked up at me from beneath his strong brows and gave me a smug smile.

"Little succubus."

He dropped my hand and turned back toward the bathroom. As we washed up, staring each other down in the mirror, I noticed a closet opened at the other end of the bathroom. Is that where he kept the chains? Interesting.

He tracked my gaze and grinned. Then threw my robe at me when I went to leave. I grabbed my book, too.

"Have fun learning how to be a blood-sucker. Maybe you'll pick up on more tricks for that mouth of yours."

"Ha! I'd need to read one of your books for that."

I stopped by my room to change. Opting for trousers and a tunic—and boots.

🔲🔲🔲

"You're late," Hadriel said, dragging his gaze over me with languid disapproval.

"Good morning to you, my dark minister. For the record, we never agreed on a time."

"Early. You should have assumed I meant early."

"Hadriel, it's only an hour after dawn."

"Never mind." He gestured to the table. On it was a tray with a teacup and pot. Hot, but probably not for long. The chill in the air was biting at my nose and the edges of my ears.

"Time to drink, I see."

We sat together as he poured me a cup. Dark liquid filled the white teacup and steamed rolled over the brim.

"Lesson number one, Coroner. True power cannot be obtained without overcoming fear. Fear protects and preserves, but sometimes it is confining. Crossing the line between comfort and discomfort is not fearlessness. It's bravery. Crossing that line brings you from weakness to strength. Until you reach a new comfort level. Repetitively exercising bravery and determination is how you become powerful."

"Power can be terrifying," I said.

"This lesson will teach you the transmutation of fear." He passed the cup to me. "Do not drink yet. First, listen."

358

I looked into the cup. Its contents swirled. The tea was black, like the petals it came from. I looked up at the Wither Maidens, still flourishing despite the cold. One of the flowers was also on the tray.

"Wither Maidens bloom through all seasons. Touch it."

I ran a finger over the petals. "It's frozen."

"No, the tree's sap is a preservative of a kind. It nourishes the flower so that it does not wither."

"Then why is it called the Wither Maiden?"

He smiled. "Because when consumed, it is the sap that withers the mind. It is a powerful hallucinogenic. However, it is mostly predictable, unlike others."

I put the flower down. "And you want me to drink this?"

"This is not poison. Physically harmless. However, it will put you in a trance-like stupor for a short amount of time. Triggering your body and mind into a survival response—you will experience fear. Essentially, your mind will try to identify a reason for this feeling, showing you things that terrify you until the effect wears off."

I swallowed thickly. Thinking about the night in Ro'Hale. The inexplicable fear I felt at that man's voice—if this could help prepare me for situations like that, I'd do it. I never wanted to feel that way again.

"Keres, I will not lie to you. This experience is harrowing for many when left unguided. You will not be aware of me, but I'll be here. You might cry out; you might get sick. I don't know how you will react, but I'll help you with what I can. Of course, we do this with purpose."

"To transmute fear," I said.

"Becoming powerful is unbecoming weak. When you practice your magic, your willpower or mana fuel you. Spiritual energy. Magic, like emotions, expresses this energy. You relate strongly to the element of fire. You are not a Daemon, whose nature is, in part, devoted to a single element. But a mage has a connection to all the elements. That magic stems from the part of it touched by Elymas. The King has stripped it from you. There is magic that stems from your Death Spirit as well, and it is stronger."

"What does stripping even mean? Will I ever get that magic back?"

"Yes, you will. It's not truly gone. No one can take what your God has given. However, there are things I want to teach you that must be separated from other magic. For example, Brazen Fire is a form of Veil Manipulation magic. You're essentially calling out hellfire, from the Godlands. Your Spirit serves as an opening in the Veil. Exchanging spiritual energy for the Brazen, you summon it through you so you can wield it. Without Elymas' fire magic, you can focus on learning Brazen."

"Interesting," I said and allowed the Brazen to play in my hand. "I knew it didn't come from the same place. When I made a fire with my natural magic, it came from my breath or body heat. Or just energy in the atmosphere."

"The difference is, your Spirit is eternal. So are the Godlands. The energy you use to cast Brazen cannot be drained as easily. You have greater stores of it."

"Also interesting. I used to burn out so quickly with Elymas' fire. Especially because I usually created it from my breath. Fighting and breathing and shooting fire—it's exhausting."

He chuckled. "Similarly to using your breath, you will learn to turn your fear, trauma, and other undesirable feelings into creative or destructive power. Fear is chaos. Undisciplined magic is chaos. You must learn to wield energies, like fear or desire. Without being bent by them, bend them to your will. Into something you can use. This will help you master your Death Spirit."

"I see." I looked from the cup to him. "I'm already scared."

"A healthy fear—the first to overturn. The choice is simple. Drink or do not."

I snorted. "Drink and wither. I'll have to fight my worst fears, but I don't even know what they truly are. I've already died once. It's not like I fear Death."

"I said it was a simple choice, not an easy one. Make no decision lightly—not even the decision to fight your demons. I'm not sending you into this exercise to fight. Sometimes fighting means resisting the pain you need to learn from. When instead, you should lean into the demon's whisper. Listen to the dark. Feel the tendrils of shadow coiling around your heart and trying to choke you. Notice every inch that holds you down. Sometimes, you need to abide in the void to grow comfortable with the darkness that's rooted within you. Get comfortable being uncomfortable. Push through it. You'll learn to cope with it or to conquer it. You do not need to teach your mind to fear. The Spirit does all misdeeds easily. You need to instruct your mind in confidence and control. And when does this matter more than when we are afraid?"

"Alright. I'm ready, but for clarification… Am I going to see the things I fear, and just turn them into something else?"

"Wrong," he said, startlingly loud.

"You are not transmuting the things you fear, but the fear itself. Pretending things aren't what they are is denial—not dealing with it. Now, enough hearing, more listening. Be quiet, drink your tea, and think about what I've said."

I looked at him and then at the teacup. I raised it and sniffed at the brim. It smelled sweet and floral. I could feel his eyes trained on me, so I brought mine up to meet them and lifted the glass.

"Cheers."

47: SCREAM
Keres

A crow found Hadriel and I sitting there and perched in one of the flowering trees. It drew my attention, cawing and pacing on the bough and seemed to look directly at me.

"Hello, little crow."

It blinked and its eyes changed from beady and black to red and wide. It opened its mouth to caw again, but as it did, its jaw unhinged. Teeth erupted in its beak, its neck bent and extended. It ruffled and outstretched its wings, stretching until it doubled in size.

"Oh, here we go," I said. "Big crow. Very big crow."

Another bird called from above. I looked up. Another shriek, another flap of wings and transformation. With that one came twenty more and then what seemed like a hundred. The shape-shifting crows swarmed the sky, blocking out the sun. They descended, swirling around each other, and sailing into the trees. They took up places, cramping together on the branches and screeching.

I dared not move, but they were insisting I did. The cacophony of their voices was deafening. I turned to look at Hadriel, but he was gone. The table was gone and the teacup with it. I was standing now in the center of the courtyard, with the murder of crows squawking overhead. They bit at the trees, plucking the flowers. Feathers and black petals showered the snow-kissed ground, landing in my hair and at my feet.

All at once, they leaped from the boughs and soared toward me. Wind kicked up around me as they encircled me in a clattering vortex. Like when Berlium wrapped us in shadows, but ten times worse.

My hair whipped in the wind, and I held my hands up in front of my face to shield myself. They closed in around me, tightening up what little space I had until I could feel the edges of their wings swiping against my skin. I looked up, trying to see through the eye of their storm. Crows landed on my shoulders and started biting my back.

I screamed and tried to fight them off as they ripped me open with their odd razor-sharp beaks and talons. As soon as they released me, I doubled over in pain. My skin was rent open and new bones jutted out on either side of my spine. They elongated and diverged into branches of cartilage. Black feathers sprouted along every line until they'd evolved into a massive pair of wings. Easily, I reached my senses into them. Strained my muscles to unfurl my new wings. They lifted and sank, dragging on the ground as I turned.

In a frenzied rush, the crows backed off, allowing me to try again. I lifted my wings up, mustering all my strength. They arched up behind me, over my head. The crows rose higher into the sky, beckoning me to follow them. The tree branches parted, revealing a pathway into the heavens.

I stood on the balls of my feet and focused on my wings. It took me a few tries, lifting and lowering them until I found a pattern that could push me from the ground. I jumped and beat my wings furiously. As maddened as the crows, by both the pain and the thrill. My back oozed blood around the wounds. I could feel it glazing my skin. Smelled it.

Higher and higher, I tried to climb, until I was over the trees. The crows huddled around me. Once again, they drew closer, but I was not afraid. The wind swirled around us. Clouds seemed to move out of the way at our approach. Daylight washed over the tops of the trees and the stone walls of Dale fell away.

We were higher than the towering buildings of Mannfel. The crows were as close as my wingspan would allow. I locked eyes with one of them and lost sight of all else.

Next thing I knew, I was kneeling on the ground in darkness. My wings were gone and so were the crows. My fingers curled against the ground, and for the first time in too long, I felt dirt beneath my hands. I looked up and made out the shapes of trees.

Beyond them, I saw a starless sky full of clouds and smoke, lit only by the moon, which was impossibly large and much closer than it should be.

Fresh air lit up my senses. I could smell the sap of the trees, feel a voiceless breeze caressing my skin. I pushed up onto my bare feet and realized I was naked. Moss squelched beneath my steps as I wandered. I didn't feel lost, but I knew I must be.

Was I dreaming? Was I back home in the Sunderlands again? It wasn't cold.

My Death Spirit was as silent as the hushed woods. No chattering bugs nor sigh of wind. No inkling of the River Liriene nearby. My back ached. I tried looking down over my shoulder to see the damage. Touched my lower back and brought my hand away bloody. I looked around and started walking. Then tripped.

I never trip. Stumbling forward brought me face to face with a pool of water which appeared out of nowhere. I caught my balance before colliding with my reflection. The face that answered mine was placid. Not a ripple in her skin. Her eyes were black as midnight and appraised me.

"I know you, monster," we both said.

My skin prickled between my shoulder blades with the sensation that someone was watching me, and the hairs on my nape stood. I shivered and turned.

"Impossible," I gasped at what I saw and fell backwards into the water. I broke through the surface of the pool in what felt like slow motion. The water parted around me, shattering into droplets sharp as glass. And then it swallowed me, sealing around me. I held my breath and tried to resurface, but the water would not let me rise.

The being who had startled me neared the edge of the pool and looked in. The same black eyes. The same placid face. It was me. I'd switched places with my reflection and the version of myself that stood on the bank smiled, finally free.

My chest tightened and my heart banged on the walls of my chest as I pounded my fists against the solid surface of the water. My other self smiled, baring fangs, before she turned and left.

No, no, no.

I turned over, kicking frantically, and looked for another way out. A void opened beneath me. I sank. Wanted to scream. My lungs were on fire, my head was aching. Blood swirled in the water as my back continued bleeding. An untouchable force dragged me down, and I clawed at nothingness.

My breath escaped me like a painful cough and bubbled up around my face. I clutched at my throat as water rushed in. It was too late. I coughed again, and the water invaded my body. I couldn't breathe—was drowning again. With a silent scream, I sank.

The world turned upside down and somehow... I'd reached dry land. On all fours, I heaved and coughed. Water sputtered out of my mouth and air filled my lungs. I wiped my mouth and looked around. I was back in the woods, back where I started. Given a second chance.

The bushes behind me shuddered, and I jumped to my feet, wheeling around. A low growl crawled out of the darkness, spurring me into a sprint.

That was no wolf. It was my other self.

"Where will you go?" The Death Spirit's multi-tonal voice was no longer in my head but panting behind me.

Haunting me. My body burned with fear as I darted between trees. She stayed on my heels. I could hear her ragged breathing. I didn't know which way to go. The air thickened with fog as if it came from her mouth.

"Why are you running from me?"

Then her voice came from ahead of me, hissing, "I'm inescapable, Keres."

I pivoted on my heels, nearly falling over, then touched my hand down to the earth to stop myself from crashing. Picking a new direction was pointless as her voice jumped from place to place around me. It came from the trees. It rang out from the sky as if the moon itself was shouting at me.

A lit clearing sprawled out ahead of me. My muscles ached as I lurched forward, breaking out of the trees. A single tree met me in the middle. One just like that in the Temple of Mrithyn.

Its glowing leaves, swollen and beating like tiny hearts, created a drumming song that matched the pattern of my pulse. Wild and vibrating through me. It set my teeth on edge. I scanned the tree line around me, waiting for her to emerge, but she didn't.

The Death Spirit stood there, between the trees, leaning against one's trunk. She held one of the swollen red leaves of the Heart Tree in her hand. Like a fruit. It throbbed in her palm. She bit into it and then turned her head to me. The light inside that tiny heart died, and she drooled its dark blood. It soaked her lips, lining her gums as she gave me a toothy grin.

She tossed it to the ground and pushed off the tree, standing to her full height. She'd grown. Her skin was bone-pale—she was naked, just as I was. She lifted her hands at her sides and rolled her shoulders as wings like mine erupted from her back. Without blood, without pain, and with ease, she lifted her wings around her. They cast a massive shadow between us, like a bridge for her to pass over. She walked into the clearing. I drew closer to the Heart Tree, keeping my back to it.

"What do you want?" I asked.

She only smiled.

"What do you want?" another familiar voice echoed. I turned to my left and saw Ahriman, with His many faces all grimacing at me. His bones unfolded and jilted Him toward me. I pressed my back against the tree and they both disappeared.

The moon exploded into stardust, which filtered through the air, and everything was white. I shielded my eyes with one hand and kept the other on the tree.

"One lost soul to guide all others." A soft voice came from behind me. Yet another that I recognized.

"Osira?" I sidestepped, keeping my back against the tree, and turned my head. On the other side of the trunk, Osira leaned against the tree.

"Marked on a map written in the stars. One life to another tethers, one death and all our wars."

"Osi." My voice cracked. Tears lined my eyes. "Osi, it's me. How did you come to be here?"

"One lost soul to guide all others," she repeated.

"Osi, can you hear me?"

"Marked on a map written in the stars."

I drew closer and reached one hand toward her. I tried to touch her, but an invisible force pulled her away. Without even taking a step, she'd rounded the tree. We circled round and round as I tried to reach her. She kept flitting out of my reach.

"Osira, where are we? Are we in the Godlands? Why can't you hear me?"

"You must leave this place, Keres," she answered at last.

"Tell me where we are. How can we leave?"

"Penance will die if you let him. You cannot let him."

My stomach dropped. She wasn't listening or answering me. This was a memory. She was giving me my prophecy, warning me about Darius' death should we stay together.

"I won't let him," I told her, just as I had before.

"Penance will die if you let him."

"Stop, please." The tears ran freely down my face.

I looked away from her. White nothingness surrounded us.

"You must stay away from him, or he will die for you. Remember, God is coming."

"Which God, Osira?" my memory replied for me.

"All of them," she said. "Don't let him love you, Keres. He will die. You must forget him—"

"Stop it!" I screamed. I tore myself from the tree and fell to the ground. Back in the clearing, in the dark.

"There you are, Keres," the Death Spirit said as she towered over me.

"Finally, on your knees for me." Ahriman joined her. "I knew you'd bow."

They paced around me, touching me, pulling my hair. The Death spirit took my hands in hers, pulled me up to stand.

"You've been made, oh, so fair," she purred. Those were words Mithyn had said to me when He claimed me.

Life, my lover, made you oh, so fair.

"Overly blessed," Ahriman hissed. My skin crawled where He

touched my arm. "Why not forsake your Gods?"

The Death Spirit took me in her arms and bit my neck.

I screamed, and my knees buckled. I fell into her as she sank her teeth deeper into me. She drank my blood. Ahriman came up behind me, trying to pull me away from her as she feasted on me.

She ripped her mouth from me, tearing my flesh. Blood pulsed out of me. My body grew cold, and my heart weakened. Ahriman writhed against me, multiple hands clutching my waist, shoulders, and my breasts.

"Oh, so much fairer you still will be," He said against my ear.

I breathed weakly, sagging between them and unable to respond. A tear rolled down my cheek, hot as fire.

"You will sing the song of the dead, Blood Waker," she hissed.

"You will heed the drums of war, Blood Waker," He crooned.

I tried to pull out of His arms. She came closer. Grabbed my face and shifted, sinking her teeth into the other side of my throat. This bite returned my life blood back to me. My veins lit like fuses. Fire quickened in my blood, waking my body back up. My heart burst into life, and I sucked in a breath. As I panted, the surrounding trees wilted. Shriveling and snapping as if I was sucking the air out of the world around us.

"Yes, Blood Waker. Swallow the World."

At last, the Death Spirit took her fangs from me. Ahriman stood back and held onto my hips. I pushed them both away, but she caught me by the throat. Digging her fingers into the bite wounds. She spoke with a voice like thunder, in the tongue of the Gods:

"The gold-lands will quake as the Veil tears between our worlds.

The Godlands will overwhelm its borders, and the army of the Dead will march in the land of the living.

It started in the Baore; the door was opened.

The Sunderlands bleed and the Moldorn burns.

The Ressid will fade and the Cenlands will crumble.

The Natlantine will be drowned by its oceans,

and the mountains of the Herda'al will fall into the sea."

"A War to end all Wars," Osira said, standing there beside us. Her eyes were no longer scaled, but open and seeing. She watched and waited, reaching out her hand. I tried to push free of them, but they held me.

"Osi, help me, please."

"The world will be reborn," Ahriman sang, drowning her next words out.

"Enough!" I screamed. I reached up and grabbed the Death Spirit by the throat. "You belong to me."

I sank my claws into her throat, and blood spurted out. She screamed, and it gurgled in her mouth. She wrapped both her hands around my arm, but I had two good hands to strangle her with. I dug my nails in. Blood oozed out of her neck, and her wings shriveled up.

I drew a breath, and her skin blued. Her wings crumpled and shed its feathers. Black feathers and flowers littered the ground.

Ahriman fell back as the air around us obeyed my breath. I pulled her in closer and sank my teeth into the front of her throat. She fell into my hold. A chasm opened in the bite wound. It expanded and drew me in. I climbed into it—into her. Donning her as a second skin. I stretched my arms out through hers, reaching to the tips of her claws and taking control. Opening a vein of dark magic. I devoured the Death Spirit from the inside out, and her hunger surged through me. My wings regrew and fanned out, getting heavier. New feathers sprouted. The bones grew thorns and black flowers.

My hair lengthened and swirled down to my waist. Some locks shifting from white to black and back again. My claws lengthened and reddened at the tips. My fangs sharpened, and I licked the blood from them.

I could hear it. The song of the dead was guttural. A chant in the Gods' tongue, and it consumed my thoughts. We had become one and her dark symphony was in me once more. I turned my head and saw Ahriman. Brazen fire answered the lift of my hand, glowing green in the clutch of my blood-red claws.

He perched in the tree, His gangly limbs tangled in the branches. Red light from the heart leaves shrouded Him, pulsating. When He sneered at me, long white tongues unrolled from His mouths. Licking the tree. One even reached the ground. Osira moved to my side. Her eyes were alight with violet fire.

"The Harbinger of Death and the Hallow Child," Ahriman shrieked with laughter. Mocking us.

Osira spread her feet and raised her arms. "Cesarus, come!"

Wolves howled and sprang out of the brambles of the forest. Dark fur, gnashing teeth, and eyes that held the same violet fire of hers. The Spirit of her wolf in multiple bodies. They surrounded us and stopped at our heel. Biting at the invisible line that divided us from Him. Waiting.

I launched myself upward, beating my wings furiously to reach His height. Ahriman stood on the bough, and it groaned beneath His weight as His body lengthened and bowed.

The earth was pounding, quaking with the drums, along the same rhythm of the heart trees.

"Welcome to the Sunderlands, God of War!" Osira shouted.

The music of the earth grew louder, calling to some ancient part of me. The Elven part of me, the great magic of my ancestors. It ached in my veins. Agonized voices cursed Him, begged me to drive Him out, swearing to help me. The Sunderlands' damned had gone into this earth. Because of War, I heard their drums—the echoes of their silenced hearts.

"You think this land belongs to the Elves? Fools! Aureum is the land of Gods and Monsters. Mortals are nothing more than ants beneath our feet. Illyn is the seat of the Pantheon. The Forsworn are locked away. The Sunderlands, like all the gold-lands, is the playground of our divine will. Too many Gods are cast away while mortals are given power they do not deserve. You tear down and we raise you up. To keep our worlds in balance. But this cycle of exchange must end. We cannot be balanced because we are not equal. Mortals do not deserve to be chosen Instruments or vessels. When the scales shift, we will always rise, and you will bow as we created you to."

"You seem to be the only God who feels that way. Otherwise, the rest would not choose mortals. They'd withhold their power from us," Osira replied.

"The Old Gods will reclaim their thrones and you will bow as we made you to," He said. "Tell me, Keres, does a God bleed?"

It sounded familiar, an echo from my past.

"Divinity does not shatter. True power does not crumble. Mortal bones break and your blood runs into the rivers. You turn to dust and fade from memory. The Gods neither live nor die. We are. As long as the Pantheon shares its power with mortals, we bleed. We would be weak if we were yours. No more!" He bellowed. "I will bring a War to end all Wars. You will bow to me, Coroner, and your armies will march under my banner. You will become so much more."

"Then you are weak to need me," I spat back. "Isn't that exactly what you just said a God shouldn't be—dependent?"

"I do not *need*. Victory is already mine. All that is left is to herald a new time of war. In which mortals and Gods will clash and fall. War is the natural talent of mortals. Their existence compels them to strife. Chaos is a preeminent force and is inevitable. War never ends. It rises and falls, like waves ridden by time. I do not need you; I am you. I am the God who drives mortals from life to death. Enithura gives you birth, and Mrithyn gives you an end. The other Gods give you the world through which you pass. I give you what you are."

"Mortals are more than that," I said.

"We do not belong to you anymore than we do to the rest of the Pantheon," Osira said.

Still, my skin crawled. I feared the Death Spirit and my curse for so long, but the underlying fear was deeper. War. I prayed for it—a war to end them all. I wanted change. What I truly feared was what it would cost. What I'd become and where I'd play into it. He said the dead would march. I was fated to be at the head of it. Mrithyn made me to be what he couldn't be. Hungry. Vicious. A reaper.

"I'll give you the chaos you crave!" I screamed.

Fear was chaos—I could use it. I clasped my hands together and pulled them apart. My magic created a globe of chaotic energy that sparked and surged. I drove this power out from my center until it rushed toward Ahriman.

He scaled the side of the tree, climbing higher. I soared toward Him, my magic nipping at His heels. The Heart Tree shook as my force of magic assaulted it, billowing through the branches like a storm-wind. I met Ahriman at the crest of the tree and dived at Him. The leaves swelled and pounded faster than they could handle, and then they burst. Blood sprayed, giving me something to use. The droplets of blood stilled midair and gathered into my hand. Clotting together and crystalizing until they formed a crimson scythe. I gripped it with two hands and brought it around in a wide arc. Through the momentum, I brought it down at his neck.

He shrieked. The force of His voice boomed out of his chest and collided with my blood-blade with a blow that cracked against the sky with the sound of thunder. Knocking us both back.

We fell. I spread my wings and tried to get the air beneath them but couldn't do it fast enough. I hit the ground, and it shook. My limbs buckled with pain as I rolled, and my head felt like it split open.

Across the clearing, Ahriman cratered the earth beneath him. Osira ordered her wolves, and they descended upon Him. He raised His head, and His many red eyes widened. I blinked. He vanished. The wolves howled and Osira cursed.

"Keres," she called to me, her voice sounding as if it were being dragged away. I looked up, and she was gone, too. The pack of wolves along with her. As if they were never there.

The tree stood before me, its many hearts blossomed once more and filled with life. The music of the night, the pounding of the drums, the chanting of the Spirits—it all echoed through my being. My head burned and my wings sagged as I stood. The ground beneath me quaked, and the dirt shifted like sand. I stumbled.

The earth melted into crimson water. I caught my footing, but I did not sink. Ripples swelled and fell forward in eager waves, until the water thickened and rushed, foaming in places. A river of blood unwound before me. I lifted my eyes, following the pathway that stretched into the horizon.

I stood atop the current, and it kept urging me forward. Dawn splintered the sky. Veins of pink and red and orange light, flowing and fracturing the darkness like cracking black ice. With every step, a shard of darkness fell. With every step, smoky falling stars rained down and splashed into the river. I walked until the nightmare broke open and I awakened in bed.

48: SOMETHING

Osira

Day Twenty-Four

"Osi, can you hear me?"

I could.

Keres' voice rang clear through my skull. I dropped my bowl full of breakfast. It shattered, and so did the world around me.

🔲🔲🔲

"What happened?" someone asked in a low voice.

Thick smoke blanketed me. My body felt soaked with sweat, and it was hard to breathe. The fragrance of incense filled the room, burning the back of my throat. I sat up.

"You're alright," I recognized Nadia's voice and her hand on mine.

"Where is Cesarus?" I asked.

"He's outside the tent. He shouldn't really come in——" Dorian tried.

"Cesarus, come!" I shouted.

His paws quickened toward me, and the sound of his breathing relieved me. He nudged his head into my hand, and I grabbed onto him. Hugging him and resisting the urge to cry into his fur.

"Tell me," I said against his neck. "Someone tell me what color his eyes are."

There was a pause.

"Um, they're a blueish color," Dorian said.

"No, that's lavender," Nadia said matter-of-factually.

"Agh, a woman sees colors that aren't there," he said gruffly.

I stood, still holding onto Cesarus. I felt shaken. "It was Keres. She was in the Godlands, and she was under attack."

"What?" Dorian asked breathlessly.

"By who?"

"Ahriman."

Shuffling footsteps told me someone was pacing, most likely him. I liked to imagine that he was touching his chin, or had his hands folded behind his back the way my dad did when he was deep in thought.

"We were in the Gods' Woods."

"In the Sunderlands?"

"The trees themselves told me. The world sang in the Gods' tongue, and I understood it. A song about life and death, magic and devastation. They were telling me to call the wolves. Then it was like every wolf in the Sunderlands had answered me, but they were all him."

I petted Cesarus.

"Ahriman spoke to us. Terrible omens. They clashed and Keres drove Him out. Then I woke up. I don't know what happened to her."

"What things did Ahriman say?" Dorian said in a stern, low voice.

Nadia handed me a silk sheath of cloth, allowed me to touch it, and then tied it around my eyes for me.

"It's lavender," she said. "Like your wolf's eyes. I had it for my hair."

It wasn't too tight, but it would help me keep my eyes closed. Help me relax.

"Thank you."

"Tell me," Dorian insisted, drawing closer. "Never mind the hair tie, what omens?"

"War. Chaos. A shift in the balance of power between Gods and mortals, and more terrible things. If what He said is true, the rest of the Pantheon will know it. I must speak with the Gods. But what if I hear more lies—or misinterpret them?"

"Would it be easier to go into the Godlands and speak with them?" someone behind me asked.

"Takoda? How long have you been sitting there?"

"You collapsed in the dining hall. I came back here with you all and haven't left since. But what if you could travel into the Godlands, meet with each God. Get to know them. Would that help you with your interpretations?"

I shrugged. "It probably would, but when I use the mirror, I don't see the Gods."

I'd been practicing with it. Glancing into the Godlands, but it showed me myself and what was immediately around me. It didn't show me the Gods or where they were.

"Bigger than the mirror, Osira. I know of a place we could go where you could easily pass into the Godlands."

Dorian interrupted again. "What place do you mean? A temple?"

"Not a temple. Something else. Where you could travel across the Veil—in person. Physically go into the Godlands."

"What? Impossible," Dorian said.

"In all my years spent as an agent of the Guild, I've never heard of such a thing," Nadia added.

"My people take great care not to let our secrets escape us. There is a well of power in the highest peak of the Rift. The Goddess dropped a mite of Her power into this spring to open a door between our worlds. I know where it is."

"Could it be?" Dorian asked, more to himself than to Takoda. "Once you spoke of Ragna, compared Her to our God Taran or Goddess Enithura. Could it be that this well of power... is what our people know from legend as the Cup of Life? The Chalice of Enithura?" He clapped his hands together. "All this time. It was here, in the Moldorn. At the foot of the Rift. Where the border is most blurred between Illyn and Aureum. Yes, perhaps it could be."

"How does it work?" I asked.

"You wade into it," Takoda murmured. "If Ragna wishes, you will be baptized... or you will be drowned."

49: SOMEHOW

SILAS

Indiro was pleasantly surprised that someone was investing in me. Keeping me out of trouble.

"Gods know you wouldn't listen to me," he'd surrendered.

Eventually, he found other things to talk about. Somehow, my starting training invited stories of his past no one asked him to tell. Some of them were interesting—the ones involving Resayla, my dead mother-in-law. Others were self-important ramblings. I still suspected he was just trying to keep me away from Thane. I couldn't even stand to look at the Dark Ranger without wanting to explode.

To avoid Indiro's pandering and Thane's inertia, I'd been at Aiko's side. My mind wandered when I wasn't there, and that wasn't safe for me anymore. I couldn't make room for thoughts that weren't instructed. Not if I wanted to be ready for Keres' return. Training and guidance were what I needed to keep from giving in to despair.

Aiko helped me realize that once Thane had brought back Keres and Liriene, she could either find me in a stupor and sick, or stronger and ready to help her recover. Whatever she was enduring in the Baore, I expected it to be bad. That alone made me want to pick up the bottle, but I told myself I could endure a little more withdrawal, a little more training, a little more bodily and mental pain… if she could do that.

Chiasa stepped back, allowing me to get up off the floor. It was time for a break—we'd been sparring for almost two hours. I went over to the cupboard to get something to drink.

Every day, my body ached, and my mind swam through the lectures Aiko tried to drown me in. He insisted I train my mind and body together. Discipline. Nothing matters but discipline.

He wouldn't let me touch alcohol. Made me work through the sweating and tremors that racked my body. When withdrawal got to be too much, I sneaked some liquor from storage. I couldn't let him know that, though. I didn't want to let him or Chiasa down.

Chi eyed me as I approached the cupboard.

"I'll be good, I'll be good." I held my hands up.

I couldn't say I minded the way her golden eyes followed me. There was innocence in them. Honesty.

I was perusing the tea cabinet. Right next to the liquor storage. I don't know whether Aiko noticed that some days I felt ill and the next I felt better. He probably did, but he didn't let on. I knew it was because he was choosing to show me that he believed in me.

Chi... she wasn't good at masking her feelings.

For a Shadow, she wasn't good at hiding anything. She was attracted to me. It was obvious. She knew I was married. Her disappointment was just as apparent. It didn't keep me from smiling at her or from enjoying the physical tension when we sparred.

Aiko probably noticed, but again, he didn't let on.

I couldn't push my boundaries. He knew that I knew that. They accepted me into training. This was more significant, somehow, than being a knight of the Ro'Hale order. More significant than being me. This was bigger. This was... global.

Agents of the Guild came from everywhere and went anywhere. They had one mission: to watch the world, learn its secrets, and then do something with them. Spies, assassins, messengers, advisers, brokers, leaders, servants... there was no shortage of roles to play. Everyone had a gift to give in service.

Aiko and Chi's attentions made me want to belong, to improve. Looking forward to Keres' return had the same effect. Once Ker and Liri were back, we could all move on. I'd be a better husband, a better friend.

A better… everything. I wanted to believe it. I told Chi the same thing I told myself.

I'll be good. I'll be good.

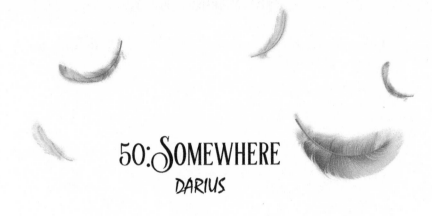

50: Somewhere
DARIUS

"Fucking hell." I hit the ground, my shoulder bearing most of the blow.

"Again," Vyra said from somewhere behind me.

"I think you've made your point, General." I picked myself back up, adjusting the shield.

"Again."

"For fuck's sake, woman!"

She didn't care. She charged me again, no mercy in her strikes. Her sword clanged against mine. My shield bucked against her blade. On and on we went. A dangerous dance, where every step fell forward with murderous intent.

I grunted as I lunged, advancing my blade. She parried. I was tired.

Sick of this shit.

In the next moment, she disarmed me. I threw my shield down, and my aching shoulder thanked me for it. She did not. The tip of her blade met the underside of my jaw.

"Pretty movements," she sighed. "For a pretty boy."

I swatted her blade away from my neck and pushed past her as she sheathed it. The men who had lined up around the pit to watch us practice were long gone. Only Epona loomed above. We locked eyes as I approached the ladder.

"You don't care," she accused.

"How observant, Yona," I scoffed as I climbed.

"Stop calling me that."

"Stop being a bitch."

Vyra's hand wrapped around my ankle, and she pulled me right off the ladder. I tumbled onto the ground next to her.

"Don't talk to her like that. What's wrong with you, Darius?"

I jumped back up and got in her face.

"Don't fucking touch me. You're just as much a bitch as she is, and I'm tired of the men here acting like you're a pair of Goddesses. You're not. You're just soldiers, just like me. No better than I am."

"You're not just a soldier, *Hellion*," Vyra spat back, inching closer. Her chest grazed against mine, and I pushed her away.

"And you're not a man, but fuck, if you were, I would have knocked your teeth down your throat a long time ago."

Epona sprung to her feet and jumped into the pit. The two of them were wild, nasty beasts, and I hated them. I'd spent enough time here, pandering and playing their war game.

I let out a growl and pushed past them, back to the ladder, and climbed out of the pit. Not stopping, I headed straight for the camp. Right back to my tent.

I couldn't help but be so fucking angry at them. Violently angry. It had gotten so bad so fast since the day I killed the Ashan. Most of the camp wanted me dead, afraid that I'd burn the place down because I wouldn't fight.

The more she forced me to fight, the wilder my fire became. I was beyond rage. Shit was getting out of hand.

Numbness washed over me in the pit. I blacked out every time I faced one of her men. I'd seriously injured multiple soldiers. Which they couldn't afford since a fucking war raged at the border. I couldn't understand why she insisted. After I'd dropped too many of her men for her liking, she met me in the pit herself. Every damn day. If I didn't show up, she'd send her men to get me. In groups. Armed.

She wasn't making a soldier out of me like she repeatedly threatened to do. She was making a monster.

Don't wake it up. Don't let it win. Hayes' voice echoed over and over in my mind. Until I got so sick of hearing it. I forced myself to think of nothing but how much I hated it here. I couldn't stand to think of Keres with love either. It was her fault I'd come here to begin with. King Arias and the Humans that ruled the Moldorn Province were no better. And then there was this fucking war.

Illynads flooded the border. Every fucking day. Their numbers multiplied. Supplies were running short, and morale was astonishingly low. I was surprised no one had deserted. I wanted to leave and was getting desperate enough to try.

King Arias wouldn't meet with me. One fucking problem was the wall that kept the Moldorn closed off from the rest of Aureum. They had admitted me into Lydany and Essyd. I couldn't just walk out, though.

I was trapped. It felt like my soul was on fire, but it didn't stop there. I first noticed it days ago: my skin was cracking. I was washing in a stream and as I splashed the cold water over my back, steam lolled off of me. I turned my head, trying to look down over my shoulder, and saw an angry wound traced down my back. It wasn't bleeding. It was full of molten orange light.

The surrounding skin was inflamed, but it didn't hurt. The next day, another line cracked open, this time running from the left side of my collarbone, down my chest in a zigzag. A minor cut opened between the knuckles of my left hand, and I had to keep it wrapped so no one could see the light that beamed out of it.

My Daemon form was maturing. I'd read about it in a book Indiro gave to me and Hayes. So much physical change was rare, though. I knew it was possible, but I never expected it to happen. Not amid strangers, not like this. Not at the time I really needed it *not* to happen.

Winter was insult to injury. The surrounding land was barren, and the men suffered. One thing the Ashan and I now had in common was the cold didn't bother us. I could walk around naked if I wanted to. It made the men more bitter.

General Vyra couldn't let it go—couldn't accept that I did not want to do anything for her or her people. This wasn't my war. Mine was the one within. It required almost all my attention and energy just not to explode. Couldn't she see that?

Whether she did, she obviously had no respect for me. You can't be a good leader without respect for your followers. Even I knew that. And I was *not* her follower.

In the past week, we'd gotten into several brawls. She seemed to get off on it. Epona was ever at her heel, like an annoying younger sibling who just wanted the attention and backing of their elder.

I could see through both of them. They weren't women. They weren't even good soldiers. They were mean-spirited Humans on a power-trip. Surrounded by men who fawned over them and obeyed. Elven and Human men. Men who had no home but this Gods-forsaken battlefront.

The Horn of Ceden, the farthest end of the peninsula that marked the end of the Moldorn, was besieged. All the Moldorn's forces there were slaughtered, and Illynads invaded the fort. We were supposed to take it back. They knew having me on their side would make a huge difference. I was the only one who'd ever taken down an Ashan alone.

Fighting these monsters cost them resources, weapons, and lives. I knew Vyra's actions were out of desperation. She was trying to piss me off, and it was working. But she wanted me to unleash that rage on the enemy. *That* wasn't working.

If I gave in—if I lifted a hand in this war, what would it cost me? What if it consumed me?

Epona was worse than the winter. Her eyes never left me. She was ever at the General's side, and when not there, she was everywhere else. No matter where I went. Just another reason to stay in my tent. It made me long for Indiro and Silas. Strong, male leaders who could understand. Who knew my secrets.

I didn't have a problem with female authority. Keres was the fiercest thing to walk the earth, and I loved her for it. These women were jokes compared to that. Jokes that weren't funny. The kind that got under your skin and nagged for your reaction. They didn't deserve my support. They didn't earn my respect. They wanted to use me.

Ro'Hale is what I fought for. I fought alongside my men, alongside my woman. Because I wanted to. I loved my people. I loved Keres. There was no way in hell I wouldn't have picked up my blade over and over for her. Fuck, I would have fallen on it for her.

But this? Fucking bullshit.

I paced the tent until its walls darkened. The day had finally ended. Sleep evaded me. My troubles had not sun-downed. Something was wrong with me. I no longer felt like myself. I knew if Keres were here, or anyone from home, I wouldn't be like this. If Keres were here, she would have flayed the General and her pet open for even looking at me. The way she wanted to do to Emisandre when she kissed me.

I was detached from myself just as much as I'd been detached from the Sunderlands. Nightmare after nightmare arrested me, shook me from sleep. Soaked my sheets with sweat. Exhaustion plagued me. I was jolted awake and found myself here. Stuck. Steaming. Somewhere out there... Everything I've ever fought for was either dead or gone. I didn't know how not to want to be out there or just somewhere else—where the rest of me was hiding.

I felt like all that I'd become was the part of myself I ran from for so long. Who I was being forced to become.

This isn't how it was supposed to go. After Vyra's inspirational speeches, I wasn't supposed to get angrier. I wasn't supposed to leave burn marks on the world. My magic wasn't supposed to leave marks on me.

Suddenly, I felt guilty for lashing out at her. For putting my hands on her and threatening her. Was any of this really her or Epona's fault?

My head spun.

What's wrong with me?

For the first time, I was afraid. I couldn't predict my life. My fear felt as raw as the flames roaring inside me. Splitting me open.

Somewhere, the past version of me who will never exist again got lost.

51: SUNDERED

Heres

Night Twenty-Two

My head ached something fierce when I woke up. I blinked memories of the visions away and found two sets of eyes watching over me. One like sapphires, one like silver.

"You... had a rough time with it," Hadriel sighed.

I leaned up on my elbows. I was in Berlium's bed, still dressed in my day clothes. Nausea rolled through me.

"Gods above and below," I hissed. "A rough time? No more tea parties, Hadriel."

They both raised a brow, as if they'd spent way too much time together and adopted each other's mannerisms. I raised one of mine in response.

"Snarky as ever. I'd say she's fine." Berlium crossed his arms in front of his chest.

"I brought your journal from your room," Hadriel said, pointing to the nightstand.

I glanced and then met the King's eyes. "I'm sorry, it was in the room. I know it was Lady Vega's, but she hadn't used it."

"It's fine," Berlium said tersely.

"Write what you saw," Hadriel instructed. "It is late. You slept all day. Write what you remember, and we will review it in the morning."

I nodded and sat up on the side of the bed.

"Come," Berlium called my attention. "Let's go to my study. Bring the book."

🎴🎴🎴

He pushed open the green doors. I followed him in, carrying Brazen fire in my hand to light our way. He lit candles with his own blue flames, and I pulled the book out from under my arm. He cleared a space on the table for me and pulled out the chair.

I opened the journal and turned the pages.

"Don't look at my handwriting," I said. "You broke my dominant hand, and I've been writing notes with my other."

"It looks good despite that. Maybe you're ambidextrous."

I shrugged. I reached for the quill in the inkwell, and he stopped me. Touching his hand to mine. "I'll write for you."

He pulled a stool toward the desk and sat, turning the paper toward him. He tapped the nib of the quill to remove the excess ink and readied it near the paper.

"I don't even know where to start... How about you look into my mind?" I asked.

He licked his lower lip in thought, and then said, "You read mine."

The shadows fluttered and furled, wrapping around us. It brought memories of the crows swarming me. His darkness took us under its wing, and my memories filtered into view.

"I saw the boy," he said, drawing my attention. "The night I pulled you out of the bathtub. I came into your mind, and I saw the boy you almost killed when you were a child. The way you looked at him, like prey."

Speaking about it summoned the thought. The child stood there, terror plain on his face. His parents running toward us.

"I didn't see how it ended, but now I know from when you told us. You did the right thing, Keres. Children... When I ascended the throne, I told you many people were killed at my order. Including children. I've little to no room for regret in my heart. Children never stay what they are. They can become monsters or heroes. Competitors. Anything. I had no room for mercy, but you did. You don't have to be ashamed. You faced the choice, dark as it was, and you made a good one. I'm proud of you, and I hope you are too."

He looked down at my hand, and his jaw ticked. "I'm sorry I broke your hand."

I blinked at him with wide eyes. He... apologized.

"Thank you," I breathed.

His gaze hardened again. "Learn something from this. A powerful person—a Coroner—knows who to slay, who to sacrifice, and who to spare. You don't need history books to tell you what the Coroners before you were like. If you listened, they would tell you through that voice inside you."

"I talk to her sometimes—the Death Spirit. I've never been able to before. Not until I met you."

He smirked at me and then looked back down. He touched the quill to the paper and scrawled out the words *Wither Maiden.*

"Show me this nightmare of yours, little wolf."

My mind opened to his like a flower. Baring the fire, the blood, the black wings. Playing the music of the damned, hissing out Ahriman and the Death Spirit's words. He saw Osira, not asking who she was. Not prying. Simply listening, seeing. Recording. We sifted through the darkness and the terror. He beamed at me with pride when he saw the blood-scythe form in my hands.

"Show me your wings again," he said. My memory stretched them out and above me. The black feathers, the black flowers, the thorns.

"It hurt like hell," I said. "Actually, my back still hurts as if it was real."

"It was real," he said. "It was your Godling form waking up. Have you never had them before?"

I shook my head. He got up from the stool, leaving the filled pages on the desk with the quill. He came behind my chair and brushed my hair over my shoulder to look at my back. I turned in my chair so he could run his hand over my back. Tracing his fingers down either side of my spine. I winced, so he lifted my shirt.

"Bruises," he sighed. "Your vision was so powerful it called the reality of what's within you to the surface. They might have almost broken through."

I shook my head. "I really do have wings?"

"Of course, you do, Darkstar." He ran his hands over my back again and the Death Spirit purred at his touch. A strange pressure prickled beneath his hand.

"Take off your shirt, please, and stand up," he said.

I took my shirt off and held it in front of my chest. He called upon the shadows that encased us. Little bats flitted down and landed on my shoulders. Planting cold kisses to my skin. They melted into shadows that dripped down my back like spilled ink, draping over my shoulder blades, and fanning out.

My wings unfurled. They were heavy and looked exactly the same as in the vision. I gasped.

"It doesn't hurt anymore—is this real?"

He smiled and nodded, unbuttoning his own shirt and slipping it off to reveal his hard, muscled body. I stared and swallowed. Muscles rippled as he flexed. I wanted to memorize the sharp edges, the slopes and subtle curves. He turned his back to me. The tapered muscles of his back flared as he rolled his broad shoulders back. I traced the lines of his tattoos with my gaze.

Shadows jumped onto him, sinking their teeth into his skin.

Drawing out the bones of his wings. They sprouted in seconds—massive, feathered wings swept out. I faltered back, as they took their full breadth. They were heavy with dark red plumes. They covered the two tattooed paragraphs on either side of his spine.

He turned back to me and smiled, his blue eyes shifting with swirls of gold. Two short black horns grew from his hairline, almost hidden by his raven hair.

"This—this is different." I reached out and brushed my fingers along the soft down of his wings. He shivered. "I felt you in the dark. I've seen your claws. Your skin becomes scaled."

"I become many things."

"But how? What are you?"

He smiled, showing me his ivory fangs. "I am both a man isolated in the tower of his mind and the dragon. Man and monster in one."

"They call you the Unbridled. You have the same curse for blood thirst as me—but it seems worse for you. Why, what does it mean?"

"They say Unbridled because of my thirst for power—my thirst for blood as well. Blood carries energy. Life-force. I am both yawning chasm and avalanche. I am a bottomless aching. But is it a curse? A gnawing stomach drives the hunter into the woods. A parched mouth lifts the bucket from the well. Is it a curse to be empty—to have so much room for more?"

I pondered that.

"I will teach you every difference and similarity between us in time, Keres. Your Spirit knows mine—it runs to me. You want wings because your Spirit wanted it first. I have given you the ease of summoning them. The way you can summon the Brazen fire now from the Otherworld, you can summon this form. You feared it before because you did not know it, and because you felt lost in its shadow. You're never going to be lost in the shadows with me."

I flared my wings and dropped my shirt on the chair. Stepping closer, he pulled me into his arms so that our chests were pressed together. I could feel his heart beating. I looked over his shoulders at his wings. Then up at mine.

"Feels good, doesn't it?" He looked at my wings and lazily ran his fingers over my arms. "To finally take a breath—to break out of the mold and stretch. To just be what you are."

We met each other's eyes. I lifted my hand to brush away a lock of hair and touch one of his horns. He cupped my breasts in his hands and ran his thumbs over my nipples. Then I stepped back.

More memories filled the surrounding darkness. He watched them play out.

Night after night, hiding in the dark. Hunting. Fearing I'd lose control—that I'd unleash my inner monster. He didn't flinch as I envisioned killing so many Baorean men.

The nine—he watched every death. He saw Katrielle through my eyes. My anger, my pain. He watched Ivaia and Riordan die. He saw the ground open and swallow men. My life, sundered.

I showed him how I looked at Tecar, his castle, him on his throne the first time I saw him. Liriene being dragged away from me. And when I turned back to look at him, he saw the hatred in my eyes.

52: Silver
The Ring

Keres' hurt couldn't simply be erased and forgotten. She couldn't be tamed with a ring. Stripping her of her power, bending her mind, taking her body, cutting her open, scarring her, breaking her bones...

None of it worked to break her. It only made her bare her fangs and bite. Despite her surrender and agreeing to marry me, she wasn't less of herself for it. She was becoming more, so much more.

But there was still something she wasn't giving me. She was still holding back, holding on to her rage and her hatred.

Don't think for a second, I won't keep fighting you.

And every second, her hold on me was getting stronger. Biting and kissing.

It felt like I'd never had a desire before. She wasn't the first woman I'd ever wanted. She was the first *soul* I ever wanted.

She came into this castle that had stood through wars and winters and was the first thing to give me a chill. She was waking up something I'd long forgotten. She kept saying how I called to her, but she called to me just as strongly. An inescapable, undeniable song. Every measured beat of her pulse—it was driving me wild with wanting.

Wanting something this world could not offer. Something my Spirit was greedy for. It made me feel emptier than usual to see someone who was hollow in the same places as me. I wanted to bind myself to her.

She was someone who could destroy me, who maybe still wanted to, but wouldn't. She wanted to hate me, but she'd understand that there were stronger, darker forces in play than hatred. In time, I'd make her see it.

I had been the author of a silent story for so long. Too long. Unleashing my war, claiming my mortal desires. The world of Aureum would never know many of my battles. History chased away forbidden things, and I'd followed them into the dark. Written my secrets in blood on faded pages.

Then, because of my silent soldiers, my message was spread through Aureum: I was to be feared. I took what I wanted. Never apologized. Riches, bodies, blood. All of it was mine and I could have it. I lost myself in my cravings.

Nobody stood in my way—how could they? I'm King.

Keres was only twenty years old. Still much more than a young woman, even more than a queen.

She was my perfect enemy.

She had no idea who she was dealing with, but she was brilliant. Impulsive and sharp. The questions she asked, the way she opened her mind and took everything in. Even if it knocked her off her feet, she got back up. With more questions and demands.

I *hoped* she would be brutal before I knew her. Thane told me what she was created to be, but she was even better than I imagined.

When she walked into my throne room and would not bow, it undid something in me. She snaps her fingers and the Brazen jumps into her palm. Just like that—she snapped me awake.

Now, I am alive again. I had someone to fight and resist. But I wanted to do so much more to her than that. I wanted to throw everything I could at her. I prayed she'd trod it underfoot. I knew it'd only make her walk taller. She was made for *more*. She was following me deeper into the dark. One step at a time. It excited me—I wanted to show her everything.

But she was full of dark feelings. I understood. I could turn her hatred into motivation. I knew she could open herself to more. Beyond the Baore and the Sunderlands. I couldn't wait to get her out of this damned castle and into the world.

The only woman who could take my crown was one with a hungry mind. Keres could withstand my storm like the walls of this castle in the height of winter. Her Spirit could feed my bottomless hunger. Endlessly. Being satisfied by her could only make me want her even more.

Time didn't move for me the same way it moved for her. She was living moment to moment, feeling, and fighting. I was seeing the expanse. The possibilities. There would never be another woman in my world like her. There never had been. It was a truth I didn't need convincing of. The Gods had perfected every inch of her; their imprint was all the proof I needed.

I wanted her to take all of me. The brutish, the bad, whatever little good. I wanted her to swallow me whole, and I wanted to devour her. It was neither a good nor a bad feeling. Still—it was real. For too long, I've felt halfway real. It angered me that she affected me so strongly, but I liked how that felt, too.

She made me believe in something bigger than us when I was inside her. Made me fear it would all vanish when she looked at me with hatred for the irrevocable wounds I'd carved into her life. Before I'd even met her, I'd touched her. Caused trauma. Thane needed her. I got her first, fully expecting challenges. I've hurt her. He'd do far worse. I've saved her and it only gets trickier from here.

I knew she wouldn't break easily. I didn't know the way she'd chip away at *me*. The way her body opened for me, trembled, and shattered made every moment I wasn't inside her torment. I could punish her for it.

I wanted to hurt her and then lick her wounds, and I wanted her to like it. The way she purred, Gods below. I expected the screaming. I never expected *that*.

She mocked me. *Hold me tonight, hurt me tomorrow.*

Yes. That's exactly what I fucking wanted. She wanted it too—I could sense it in her blood. Fervency. Fever.

She ripped open my flesh and tasted my blood. Then she shivered when I kissed her in the same spot she'd bitten me.

What an acquired taste we were for each other. Not knowing whether we should enjoy it or be sick of each other. Could I ever be sick of her? No.

I wanted her to tell me she was mine, and I wanted it to sound like a lie because I was addicted to making her prove it.

The way she pushed me away one moment and then leaned into me the next. It would take balance. Give and take. This was a game I'd never gotten to play before, and I was loving it. Right now, she was withholding. I needed to give her something... just a sliver of something.

Hadriel told me he wanted to find a use for her sister. To bring her into the castle. Not yet—I needed to plan for that. But I knew exactly what I was going to give my little wolf in the meantime.

Keres

It worked.

The King of stone was sensitive to me. It was a truth I could play with.

He'd broken my hand, and his gaze often wandered to it. When he touched me, he was careful not to hurt it. Then he fucking apologized. I snorted at the thought. The big, bad hunter who carved out maidens' hearts—had one?

Twenty years ago, at the time I was born, he was laying siege to the fortresses of the Baore. Murdering everything in his path. He said it himself. He felt nothing. Pure sadism. He afflicted everything he touched—even me. I looked at my hand, still bound.

He felt something now. I didn't know whether that feeling warranted being named, but I definitely planned on calling it out. I was going to make him crumble.

Why don't you look into my mind?

I offered, and he took the fucking bait. Walking right into my darkest thoughts. My nightmares. He was showing me I rattled him. So, I showed him what *I* felt. It wasn't enough to tell him I hated him. It wasn't enough to fight back, scratch, and bite. I screamed and growled when he fucked me—I reveled in him. He tasted my truth on his tongue, but he needed to know the venom dripping from my fangs. My hatred was real. I could be just as unforgiving as he was.

I loved the way he made me feel like more than I'd ever been. Not a girl. Not even a woman. A Goddess. It woke up that part of me that both craved him and despised it.

Darkstar.

He was as romantic as he was ruthless. Unabashedly. Isn't that what Hadriel said? You can't separate madness and genius, or the torment from an artist.

The Grizzly King didn't hold back—it wasn't his nature to. He was everything he was, all the time. If he wanted to torment me, he would. Whether to bring me pleasure or pain, punishment. If he wanted to paint my world red, he did.

Was it a weakness? The way he wanted to tear the Veil open for me, the same way he did my dresses. To gift me unholy fire from the depths of that world. The way he drenched me in shadows so my wings could find purchase in my body without pain.

Was it a weakness that he wanted me so blatantly, and with the wave of his hand, could get what he wanted—give what he wanted? No.

Not a flicker of shadow bespoke weakness in my King. He was strong enough to show me when he felt nothing and when he felt something. That wasn't weakness. That was absolute control. And it was something I was going to perfect.

He told me he would turn my needing into *knowing* what it meant to be owned by him. I was starting to understand. Still, I was going to teach him a few lessons myself. He was going to know what it meant to be contested.

I wasn't his pet. I was every bit the hunter he was. Two could play this game and I was going to put him in check.

Through my memories, he saw me in the darkness of the Sunderlands. Maybe I had been an ignorant girl at the time, but I was always lethal.

I was going to devour everything he gave me and spit the bones at his feet. My appetite would not dry out—he thirsted, I did too. I was his little wolf, and I had the jaws to match my appetite.

Both the yawning chasm and the avalanche.

Well, I showed him how my voice could open the fucking earth and devour souls. I wasn't embarrassed about the times I hadn't been enough in the past, about how I fell in battle and got captured. Because look where I was now. I was under his scaled skin.

I wanted him to see my thoughts, to see that I'd never been weak. I'd only been chained to fear. He could cuff me now and wreck my body, but I was no longer afraid.

The confidence he exuded—I'd mirror it.

My mind would only get sharper, sharp as claws and fangs. That was key.

With no more shackles on my Spirit, I was going to be more than lethal. I was going to be absolute. *Wicked. Dangerous. Fucked.*

Worshiped.

We slept side by side that night, in silence and without touching. Because he was feeling. Thinking. Understanding. And it was the sweetest sleep of my life.

53: SUMMONING

Keres

Berlium wasn't in bed when I woke up. Yarden was waiting to escort me to Hadriel's lab.

"I feel like we haven't talked in ages," I said as we made our way through the castle.

He smiled and nodded. "Things have been… changing."

I snorted. "Some things are still the same."

His eyes scanned over my face. "The way you look at the King. That has changed."

"Yes, from murderous intent to murderous intent clouded by desire."

He shook his head.

"The way *you* looked that night he killed Hero's brute—you have magic or some power?" I asked, changing subjects.

"You noticed that, huh?" He rubbed his hand over the back of his neck. "I do. A gift from the King."

"Ah, he's very generous," I said.

"He is bottomless. If he wants to unleash terror or bestow wonder, he will."

"Funny," I snorted. "I was just thinking about that. What kind of gift has he given you?"

He shook his head again. "Lady Keres, I don't speak of it. I hope there will never be a cause for me to unleash it. There's a reason I'm appointed to guard you. There is only one other woman I've guarded, and it was with good reason, too. That woman is a treasured friend of his. Someone under his protection. She still lives in Dulin."

"The one you loved?" I asked.

He nodded. "He reserves me to guard precious things. I am his Cerberus."

I lifted my chin and smiled. "I knew you weren't just a good listener."

He chuckled.

We reached Hadriel's quarters, and I knocked. There was no answer.

"Odd," I said, drawing my brows together. Yarden and I exchanged glances.

"Magister Hadriel?" he called through the door. A strange thrumming sound answered. I tested the doorknob, and it twisted, but the door didn't open. Something warred against it, although there was no reason it should be blocked.

"Should I break it down?" Yarden asked. We both knew that was a horrible idea.

"It's not locked, so we can't pick it. Watch out."

I stepped closer and pressed my hand against it. The wood was cold and vibrated like—

"It's warded," I said, taking my hand away. "Fuck."

Not a good time for my magic to be dead in my bones. I thought back to how Ivaia set wards. She wielded elemental magic flagrantly—but wards... she was very secretive about how she cast them. She had knowledge of spells and hexes, which is how she snapped whatever tethered Berlium to Herrona. But she never taught me that kind of magic.

I thought back to the book he'd given me about entropic magic and curses. There wasn't anything about wards in it. The curses in that book were aggressive magic—to inflict energetic damage on victims. Not protective, like wards were.

I closed my eyes and tried to get a better sense of it. My Spirit once housed fire and ice. I could crack the earth or bend water. Without Elymas' gift, the natural forces were beyond my touch.

Hadriel's first lesson replayed through my mind. *Your Spirit serves as an opening in the Veil. You can summon and express magic.*

Brazen fire ruptured into life in my palm. Whatever shreds of my Spirit Elymas had touched felt unraveled, but my Spirit, in its entirety, was a part of the Veil. The Veil was spiritual energy. A tapestry to which everything was threaded. All was connected. I could reach out and touch the world, run my fingers along the threads—because my Spirit was one. One in the whole. I could open and reach through to the Otherworld. All by tapping into my endless Spirit. Like summoning the Brazen... I wondered what else I could summon.

I closed my eyes and was met by the turbulent stare of the King.

"Hello, little wolf." I heard him in my thoughts. *"Look at you—combing your teasing fingers through the Veil. How sweet that your Spirit reached for me directly."*

"What?" I answered out loud.

"I'm in my study." He chuckled. *"You're outside Hadriel's door... what's that? He's warded it."*

"I know," I grumbled. "I was trying to solve that problem."

"Hmm. Well, good luck with that."

I distinctly felt the gaze of his Spirit turn away from mine.

"Who are you talking to?" Yarden asked.

"Sorry," I said, opening my eyes. "Just the devil on my shoulder."

The corners of his mouth flickered.

"This has to be a test." I ran my fingers over the door again, closing my eyes. Seeing Berlium gave me an idea. He seemed to summon his winged shadows from... from nothing. He stole darkness out of the corners of rooms, more than they could give. Enough to blot out the world and leave our minds suspended in a drop of ink. Was he summoning those shadows from the Godlands, too?

This ward. I felt it came from somewhere—

"Oh," I said, popping my eyes open. And I tipped my head back and laughed. "Duh. It's part of the fucking Veil."

I opened my hand, and heat tingled in my palm. No fire—just energy. I felt for the ward, extending my awareness along those threads of the Veil and touching it. It felt rock hard. Like the Veil itself had been frozen. Creating a shield behind the door that matched it in shape and size. I closed my hand, balling that heat in my fist.

"Knock, knock," I said and tapped my fist against the air. I felt the shield weaken and fray. I reached for the door handle and threw the door open. Strutting across the threshold and locking eyes with Hadriel.

"You're a quick study, Keres," he said and handed me a teacup.

"I'm my mother's daughter," I said and took it, looking over my shoulder at Yarden, who smiled at me and closed the door.

The cold silver of Hadriel's eyes washed over me. I'd worn a tunic and trousers again, and slippers. I was getting used to the casual attire. Couldn't fight my war in pretty dresses all the time.

"How's your hand feeling?" he asked, dropping his gaze to it.

I held it up and wiggled my fingers. "Your ministrations have been thorough. I suspect something in your medicines has helped it heal faster. It aches, but I can move it."

When we finished our tea, he unwrapped it. The bruising was gone and the wounds that were scabbed were now smooth scars.

"It's not the medicine, child."

"It's me, bitch."

I shivered. "My inner monster. It's her. The way he's called her to the surface..."

"She heals quicker than you do." He smiled and took away the bandages, throwing them into the fire. Along with the little splints I'd worn for support. "You must exercise it if you wish to fight again."

"Got it." I opened and closed my hand, curling my fingers and stretching them. Rolling my wrist. It ached, but it wasn't broken anymore. Which felt amazing. "Wow," I said in disbelief. "Tricky little thing mended me from the inside out."

"Yeah, you're welcome," the Death Spirit leered.

"Priss."

He ignored my talking to myself and walked to the back of the room, where his alchemical lab was set up. Potions were brewing, bubbling and steaming over the brims of the beakers.

"Are we going to make something explode today?" I asked, lacing my voice with devious excitement. He crooked his brow at me.

"We're going to talk about the Veil. I planted that ward to get you thinking—reaching for the fabric of this world and taking control of it. All

Instruments have this power. Oracles as well. In fact, any divine principality can accomplish this. You proved your awareness and ability to improvise. Without the magic you've known your whole life, you're open to explore others. As an Instrument, it's important you learn Veil Manipulation first. As an Instrument of Death, you will learn entropic magic next. First the general, then the specific. Now, clear your mind of the limited elemental magic. There is music in the world that rings in the hollows of it, that wells within it. Calling to those who can see beyond the natural forces into the Other. Dark magic. Light magic. Taboo and necessary."

He waved his hand over the lab. "Alchemy is deconstruction and reconstruction. The compilation and transmutation of ingredients to make something whole and useful. We are going to break down what you know and rebuild it into something you never imagined. But I need you to believe in things you may have never thought possible, Keres. Some things will feel wrong. We will trespass into the secrets of the world. Taboos are necessary. You cannot be afraid of it—you must give it purpose. From life to death, waste not."

The words struck me. "I've heard that before. Queen Hero said that to me."

"It's a common sentiment. An imperative one. Now, did you bring your journal? We must discuss what you saw in the vision."

"I've got it all up here," I said and tapped my head. "Berlium wrote it down for me but sifting through it with him—I can't forget a shred of it now."

I told him everything, painting the pictures with my words.

"I think the blood scythe was my favorite part. Oh, and look." I stepped back and summoned my wings. They sprouted through my skin effortlessly, tearing through my tunic to burst free and stretch. He traced the curves of them with his eyes. Staring as if he was counting each black feather.

"Are those Wither Maiden flowers?" he asked.

I beamed at him. "Trophies. For finding beauty in my darkness."

They grew from the thorny, boned frame of my wings, and nested

401

between the plumes here and there.

"Pompous," he snorted.

"Deserved," I corrected. "A girl doesn't need a man to give her flowers. Not when she can summon them from the lands of the Gods and adorn her wings with them."

He rolled his eyes, and I folded my wings back. They retracted in seconds. "Berlium gave me his shadows, and somehow it helped me with summoning them. He even showed me his."

Hadriel's brows arched. "A form he rarely takes. He prefers wearing crueler faces."

"Not surprising," I said and crossed my arms over my chest, leaning against the counter. The beakers behind me were boiling. I looked back at them. "Someone gave me a potion once, you know. I never drank it, but I've always been curious."

"What kind?" he asked.

"He called it Scorn. Said to use it when I needed an escape from—"

"Who gave this to you?" he barked, concern grating in his voice.

I looked at him, confused. "An alchemist in Ro'Hale. His name was Famon."

Hadriel's expression hardened. "Where is this *Scorn?*"

"In my room. Why?"

"Do not drink it."

"Why?" I emphasized.

"Because it is poison."

I raised my brows at him expectantly. "You know that how?"

"I know Famon. Trust me."

I couldn't wipe the confusion from my face.

"Bring it to me tomorrow, and I'll dispose of it," he added. "Do not accept random potions from people, Keres. That's how you get killed."

I didn't understand, but he wasn't going to tell me how he knew Famon. I'd saved Famon, and it was a token of his appreciation. The other gifts Darius and I'd received that day were harmless. Supposedly.

"Sit down." He pointed to a stool that was tucked under the counter. I pulled it out and sat. Annoyed by the chill that leaked under my shirt through the holes my wings had made. Poor planning on my part. Hadriel moved to his shelves and pulled out some scrolls. He unrolled them, placing paperweights on the ends to keep them flat. I poured my eyes over them.

"Channeling," I read one's title. "I've been channeled before. By the Oracle child. It was intense. It caused me physical harm."

"Channeling is Veil Manipulation. A method of connecting two minds across a long distance. It takes place in a level of the subconscious, calling it forward."

"It blocks out reality," I mused.

"No," he said. "It exchanges reality. When you were channeled, you felt pain. What caused it?"

"Osira was scratching at her eyes. She was newly blind."

"She transferred her reality into your mind. That is channeling. It can happen while you dream or while you're awake. There's some level of intention and reception to it, but it can seem random. Minds can be connected, spatially aware of one another on the subconscious level because of the Veil. It is unseen and in between all things, even minds. That's why Osira could channel you before you knew her or saw it coming. She was newly blind, you say. There is the intention. A need. She was in pain. She reached for someone, and her consciousness was receptive to yours, yours to hers. Receptivity can be as unpredictable as it is powerful. It can result from two minds conspiring in the subconscious or it can be intentional. In your vision, you saw her. You might have channeled her because of your own need. Your fear."

"What about this—Berlium made me see what he saw once. What was that?"

"Something else."

I sighed. "Alright, but what about this? When I was trying to break your little ward, I reached out my senses and they went straight to Berlium. I was being intentional, looking for the ward and my mind ran to him instead. Why? Was that channeling?"

"You know the reason your mind reached for him," he said in a low voice. "But no. That was bridging. Channeling, like I said, is long distance,

403

expansive. Bridging is local, narrow. Communication in the more immediate mental space."

"Like this." I heard his voice in my head, but his mouth didn't move.

"Oh," I thought back. I was familiar with this. *"It seems like only certain people can do this."*

"It is a capability of those with power. Don't get ahead of me," he said aloud.

So, Hadriel, the King, and Rydel could do this... interesting. Maybe Rydel was influencing Hero?

Hadriel pointed at the scrolls. "Channeling—exchange of reality. Shared visions. Long distance. Bridging—communication. Local. Got it?"

"Yup," I said, resting my chin in my hand.

"What you've done with your wings, technically, isn't summoning. It's transformation. Your Spirit is a part of the Veil and can't be parted from you unless you drop dead. It's what goes into the Godlands when you are dead. Your claws, your fangs, they're as natural to you as skin and bones and can't be taken unless you're mutilated. They're part of your anatomy that shifts and changes with the expression of your Spirit. This is called your Godling form. Your Wither Maiden experience showed you this. Awareness grants this transformation. Allowing you to manipulate this inherent part of you that touches the Veil. It comes through you. Wings, claws, fangs. We see it in your eyes. Essentially, your body is just a catalyst for the outpouring of your Spirit."

"Berlium said he can transform into many things. How is that?"

"Because he is—"

"Let me guess. Because he's the Unbridled." I rolled my eyes.

"You are an expression of Death, Keres. Mrithyn has infused your Spirit with His essence. Berlium is an expression of something else. Something boundless. You are an Instrument whose strings are played by a God. Berlium has no strings. He *is*."

"But how? He's not a servant—it makes no sense."

He smiled. "It will."

I rolled my eyes. "Okay. What's rending?" I asked, pointing to the next scroll.

"So far, we've covered styles of manipulation that are meant to transfer things across the Veil. Transformation goes a little deeper than that. Rending and true summoning go even deeper. This is where we split the Veil open and take from the other side."

"Like the Brazen?" I asked.

"Yes. You can summon fire from the Godlands."

"Can Berlium summon his shadows from there too?"

"Keres, this isn't about him. It's about you. Forget about the King for a second."

I smiled and bit my lip.

"Easier said than done," the Death Spirit murmured.

"Rending is more than opening up a trap door and rooting around to take something you want. Rending is creating rifts in the Veil. Doorways or chasms. You can cross from the gold-lands, through the Veil, and into the Godlands. Without dying, you can pass through entirely. Body and Spirit."

I puckered my lips at the thought. "Interesting. Maybe I'll take a brief vacation into the realm of the dead."

He sighed. "You'd probably get lost. Speaking of which. Mapping." He pointed to the last scroll. It had drawings of tapestries and constellations on it—easily the most interesting one.

"The Veil is unseen to the physical eye, but to the trained mind's eye, it is visible. You can feel it because your Spirit is a part of it. You can run your supernatural sense against it. Eventually, you'll be able to trace the lines of it. Etch into it. Touch knots and navigate it."

"But what is it a map to? The Veil is between the spiritual and physical world."

"It's a map of everything. Eventually, you can find things. Follow the threads that connect all things."

"Wait!" I slammed my hand on the table. "What about the Scythe of Mrithyn? What if I wanted to find an object... could it work?"

He grinned like a wolf. "Now, you're thinking like a Godling."

54: SERVANTS
Keres

Hadriel rolled up his scrolls and pushed them back onto the shelves. More tea was brewed, and he sat down across from me, lighting his smoking pipe. He puffed while he worked the potions. Taking one off the flame with prongs and letting it cool. It had changed from a green to black while we'd talked.

"What's it for?" I asked.

"Killing wraiths," he said, with the pipe sticking out of his mouth. He used a rag to grab the hot beaker and poured half of the inky liquid into a glass vial. He pushed a cork into it, and the heat made condensation gather at the neck of the vial.

"A decoction—made with the essence of a wraith. Boiled down to what's useful. Though mildly toxic, when consumed, it will grant powers akin to the wraith's."

"Are wraiths those things that look like ghosts and scream?"

He snorted and pulled the pipe out from between his teeth. "I guess they do kind of look like ghosts, but ghosts are different. Wraiths are more like frayed, floating, faceless shadows. They can rend the Veil with their screaming and dance through it. Jumping from place to place. Unpredictability makes them deadly. Their voices can also ripple the Veil, causing waves of energy that will knock you on your ass if it hits you."

"And if I drink that?" My voice trailed off.

He smirked at me. "What makes you think I'd let you?"

"Boring." I rolled my eyes.

He chuckled and poured the rest of the decoction into another vial and corked that one too. "Rending the Veil becomes easier. It can even help you latch on to the threads of the Veil that comprise the Wraith. They are just spirits without form. You can rend them."

"Have I ever told you how much I love monster-hunting? If I didn't have to be a Queen, I'd travel the world, hunting them down."

He laughed and took another pull on his pipe. Blowing O's out into the air. "Is that Geraltain speaking through you? The Coroner before you was a renowned monster hunter. It was his favorite thing—until it cost him his life."

"What? I thought nobody knew what happened to him."

He smirked again. "Well, he's not alive if you're here. There's only one Coroner at a time, and it seems like you've inherited something of him. That's what happens when Gods make servants. That part of you he pried from himself and dropped into you? It's recycled."

My jaw dropped. "What? That's kind of gross."

"I'm a very interesting little monster," she crowed on cue.

"So, the Death Spirit is another thing inside me," I said. "Living comfy in these bones?" I said to her.

"No, Keres." He tried to resist but laughed again. "She *is* you. It's your Spirit—touched by Mrithyn. Her expression empowers you. The imprint of His touch bears the essence of His power and traces of every Spirit He's ever touched. The Gods who choose only one servant at a time recollect their essence when that Instrument dies. Consuming what was originally theirs. When it is given again, it carries traits. It's a mutagen that gets reincarnated into the next vessel."

"How does this happen without the God being tainted?"

"Does the Instrument make an impression on the God, you ask? Who knows? Ask Mrithyn. The point is, all Coroners share this mutagen. It's like a hereditary trait—but a supernatural one. It connects you to them and creates consistency in powers and traits. The White Hair. The fangs, and so on."

"That makes sense. But Liriene has fangs too—obviously, so does Berlium."

"All servants have fangs. Most even have wings. Still, in their Godling forms, they express the power of their God. But the King isn't a servant."

"Everything you say makes it harder for me to believe that."

He snorted and threw a notepad on the table. It had the Aurelesian Pantheon on it.

"The Pantheon rules the principalities—the Instruments. There's a caste system. A pecking order among the Instruments, divided by scope of power. For example, you look at me and see a Human. You see yourself as an Elf. You'd use the word race while I use the word Dominions. The different dominions of mortals are general terms. Daemon is a dominion, but there are subjects of this dominion that differ from one another. Fire Daemon versus Water Daemon. Even among Fire Daemons there are ranks, from least powerful to most powerful. On and on, each dominion is a pyramid of power. Because of diversity, it's all very complex. The point is the same concept applies to the Principalities. An Elf can be an Instrument in the same tier that a Human can be. So Instruments are not their own dominion or race. They're simply... well, better than other mortals."

"More closely related to the First Children of the Gods. Monsters and whatnot," I recalled.

He nodded.

"I learned that from Famon," I chided. Hadriel did not like that, evidenced by the hammering muscles in his jaw.

"The Castes of Principalities go in a hierarchy of power. Servants to Death and Life are called Fates. They are the pre-eminent deities. Fates are considered the most powerful. Don't let it make you more prideful than you are."

I chuckled. "You heard that, monster?" I said to my Death Spirit. "We're the best."

She purred in my chest. Hadriel heard it and his brows shot up.

"I told you she's loud—Berlium's is too."

He sipped his tea and then cleared his throat. "That's rather interesting. I'll have to discuss that with him... Well, anyway. The Reigning deities are Adreana and Oran. Liriene is a Seer, an Instrument of Light. Oran chooses many servants at a time. An army of light-bearers. As many rays as the Sun has, He has servants. They're considered on par with Shades. Unlike Seers, the Instruments of Darkness are made one at a time. Like Coroners."

"What are the Servants of Enithura called?"

"Wardens. Yes, there is only one at a time. The list goes on. The Phenomenals are the Instruments of the Composing deities, Taran and Nerissa. Earth, sea, air. They're considered lower on the totem. Wonders, however, are the Instruments of the magnifying deity, Elymas."

"And he doesn't choose servants," I sighed.

"What?" He snorted into his tea. "Who told you that?"

"Ivaia," I said, blinking at him. He shook his head.

"They say don't speak ill of the dead, but really, how confused your education was."

It made me bristle with anger, and I bit the inside of my cheek.

"Elymas gives magic to mortals. Like you and many of the women before you in the Aurelian bloodline. Like me. We are mages. We come into our power in childhood—because only children can be the servants of Elymas. He is the God of Wonder and who is more full of wonder than a child?"

My jaw dropped again. He shook his head. "So much to learn. I'll lose my voice telling you everything I know."

"What happens when the child ages?"

He shrugs. "We still have our magic, don't we?"

I gave him a pointed glare.

"Oh, I prefer the eye rolling to that look. I told you your powers aren't gone. Just be patient. Anyway, there is a spectrum of power among the Wonders. From petty to high power. My theory is magic is most raw and rich in childhood—and adults don't deserve that. We get the leftovers, no matter how powerful we are. It's only a remnant of what we were in our youth. Because our sense of wonder ages. Children don't compete for power—they simply enjoy it. Spinning fantasies, coloring the world. The evolution of our thinking chisels away at these things."

"And Ahriman?" I asked hesitantly.

"Ahriman and Imogen are the Orchestrating deities. We know very little about their servants because they choose them most rarely. Elymas' gifts are not a mystery. Many mages walk the earth. War and Peace ebb and flow with the crests and troughs of time. All mortals war, not all choose peace. Beyond basic understanding of mortal nature, it's hard to say anything about the Mediators."

I thought about it and drank my tea. Then yawned—to his dismay.

"Okay, one more question and then I want to know about blood magic."

"We'll discuss blood magic another day, but go on."

"Oracles. They're not Instruments."

"Correct. They are gilded mortals. Accessories. Mouth pieces."

I expected him to say more, but he shrugged. "Are you an Oracle? You do like to lecture a lot."

He scrubbed his hand over his face and then rubbed it over his bald head. "No, child."

I titled my head at him. "Thank you for the lesson, my dark minister. I'm eager to try blood magic and affliction hexes. Maybe even chug a potion with you."

He snorted. "Keep making light of my dark magic, Keres. It's all a game until it's not."

I smiled at him and bit my lip. The door opened across the room and we both turned to see who was there. But I could scent him before I saw him.

King Berlium locked eyes with me and strode into the room like he owned it. Which, technically, I guess he did. He was wearing a loose that bared his arms. His muscles and prominent veins were hard to ignore.

"Don't stop on my account," he said and came to stand behind me. He looked at the counter, crinkling his nose. "Wraith decoctions."

Hadriel nodded. "We were just finished with today's lesson, sire. Are those bite marks on your shoulder?"

Berlium smiled dazzlingly. "Yes, they are, and now I'm taking the one who gave them to me."

I stood and turned to face him. "You can try. I learned about wards. Maybe I'll make one between us."

"Your hand," he said, skipping my joke.

"Almost all better," I said, flexing it. "It's still achy but not unbearably. Hadriel said I need to exercise it."

"Gripping exercises would be best," Hadriel said thoughtlessly.

A wicked grin tugged at Berlium's lips. "I can think of a few things…"

"Oh, Gods below," Hadriel groaned. "Both of you. Out, please."

Berlium snickered and took my healed hand in his. Rubbing his thumb over the scars as I followed him out of the room.

"Bye, my dark minister."

🔳🔳🔳

"Did you learn anything from Hadriel?" the King asked as we walked up the stairs. Yarden trailed behind us.

"Tons. I'm going to have to write notes." I skipped up the steps, making the mistake of giving him my back, which he didn't miss, and smacked my ass.

"Ow!" I jumped.

"Why are there holes in your shirt, little wolf?"

"Because I was showing off. Now keep your paws to yourself, bear."

His laughter rippled through me. He lunged for me, and I threw myself forward, climbing the stairs in multiples at a time. My scream echoed through the hallway as his growl chased me up the remaining steps. We emerged on the platform, and he crashed into me, grabbing me around the waist.

Butterflies went wild in my belly at his touch. My nipples perked up against the olive-green fabric. He noticed—of course.

"We both need to change clothes. Let's go. I've made plans for us."

"Oh?" I narrowed my eyes. "And what are these plans?"

To which he bared his fangs in a smile that made me want to be bitten.

55: SURPRISE

Keres

"You better not be lying." I watched him and pulled the new shirt over my head. He stood there, suspicious as a statue whose eyes tracked you around the room.

"On my mother's grave, I swear it. Are you ready?"

I ran toward the door. He grabbed my wrist and pulled me back to face him.

"It comes at a price." He smirked.

I shrugged. "Everything costs something with you. You're a very expensive man."

He laughed and let me go. "Alright, then. Put your coat on. It's snowing."

I didn't care. I couldn't walk fast enough. Still, I tugged the fur coat on and speed-walked down the halls.

"Boots, Keres. You can't go in the snow barefooted."

"You don't think the Sunderlands have winters? I'm fine. I don't care."

Nothing mattered. If he told me I needed to cut off my feet to see my sister, I would. She was out there in the snow, probably without a jacket or boots. So, I didn't give a fuck about any of it. Only her.

The guards opened the doors. White, cold sunlight met us in the courtyard. It was a harsh morning. My stomach churned as I tried to prepare myself mentally for what I'd find in Tecar. Would she be beaten and bruised, whole, starved, clothed? Would she be angry? Disappointed?

He kept up with me. The wind stung my face, and the snow burned my feet, but none of it mattered. The gates got bigger and bigger.

"Open up!" My teeth chattered, and I waved at the guards as we got closer. Their eyes went to the King, who nodded. The metal grated, and the doors opened and then I ran.

Red hair whipped in the wind. A blue dress in tatters. Mercury silver eyes brimming with tears. Two hands stretching out toward me—one of which was scarred. She ran to meet me. Snow caught in our eyelashes and our tears stung, nearly freezing on our faces. Sobs replaced words, and we locked our arms around each other, blocking out the cold. My heart ran into hers. She laughed and then she cried.

"Keres." She petted my head.

"I'm so sorry." I cried into her shoulder. "I'm so sorry."

"Shhh," she said, just like she did when we were children. "Hush now. Don't be sorry."

It made me hold on tighter. Guards muttered. Our people stared.

Two sisters, ripped apart and thrust back together. I had on a fine dress and fur. I was clean and fed. She looked like the worst of what I expected. All our people did. I tore my gaze away from the death pits.

"Oh, Liri. I'm so sorry—"

"Stop," she said and wiped my tears. I grabbed her scarred hand with my own.

"So, it's true, then," she said in a low voice.

I turned and found King Berlium a few paces behind me. Waiting. Watching.

She turned my hand over and looked at my ring.

"It is," I answered.

"Listen," she said and squeezed my hand. We locked eyes. All color drained from her face. "I've met with Hadriel. While you and the King were away."

My brows shot up, and then I hurried to tell her, "Don't say too much." In case he was listening.

"We won't be separated for long."

"What did Hadriel say? Did he promise you something?"

"Hush now, sister." She smiled and widened her eyes.

413

He approached.

"Lady Liriene, last we met... well, that seems like a while ago."

She met his gaze. I found it hard to look at him. Anger settled in my stomach. This was his fault. She squeezed my hands as if she felt the rage boiling in me. Her fingernails were so long. She looked so unlike herself. Despite the poor condition of her clothes, her hands... she looked Otherworldly. Like a sun in flesh, trying to stay bright in winter.

Her movements were too fluid, her eyes a little too wide. Her skin was just a little too warm considering she was wearing very little and in this weather. Again, she squeezed my hand.

"I'm fine." Liri said, bridging our thoughts. *"Yes, I can hear you. Though, I don't think he can."*

"How do you know? We're bridging. He can do it too," I thought to her, losing track of anything he said.

"Trust me. Just wait. Like I said. Hadriel knows. He will send for me soon. And then we will take this kingdom down from the inside. Together."

I hesitated. She noticed.

"Well, we must be on our way. Keres and I will ride into Mannfel today."

I turned and met his eyes. "We will." It wasn't exactly a question. She pulled me into her arms again.

"Soon."

"Okay," I answered aloud. "I love you."

"You too." She took my hands once more.

"Don't do anything rash. Just wait for me." She sent the thought to me and rubbed a finger over my engagement ring.

Before I left, I moved to take off my coat.

"No," she said abruptly. "Please don't"

Her eyes flitted toward one of the red-eyed guards watching from a distance. "It'll cause too much trouble."

I looked incredulously at her and then at the guard, who averted his eyes. I turned to Berlium.

"I'm giving my sister my coat, and if your dog thinks he's going to give her any trouble over it, I'll give her his skin instead."

Berlium looked at the guard and tipped his head toward me. "You heard her."

I took it off and wrapped it around her.

"Thank you," she said.

A shadow darkened over me, and then the weight of another fur coat settled on my shoulders. King Berlium stretched an arm around me and pulled me close. Liriene watched him from under her brows. The two exchanged a look that was colder than the snow before he towed me away.

56: STREETS
Keres

"Keres, you're being irrational. It was meant to make you happy."

"Happy? You think I'm happy that my sister is in rags? Looks like she isn't eating—is being abused? I'm supposed to be happy about that?"

"I'll admit, she's not being cared for—"

"Not being cared for!" I screamed and threw the nearest object at him. He ducked, and the helpless vase shattered on the wall behind him.

"It was part of my plan, I swear. Listen to me, let me explain."

"There is no explanation for this. She barely even has clothes on her back." I threw his shirt at him. And then his shoe.

He moved throughout the room, dodging whatever I pitched his way.

"You want me to dress up now so you can parade me through your beloved fucking city. And what—I'm supposed to smile and wave? While my sister starves and suffers in your fucking slave den?"

"Keres, I had her whipped—"

Crash. A porcelain bust of some forgotten hero. He swatted the next thing and hurt his hand in the process. I didn't give him a chance to escape my hardcover book.

"Keres!" he yelled and crossed over the room. He grabbed me by the shoulders and shook me. "Holy Fuck, woman, shut up and listen to me."

I was breathing raggedly, staring up at him, and I knew he saw the eyes of my monster.

"If I had let her go to Tecar and had her treated better than any of the other slaves—well, it wouldn't have happened. It would have caused problems. I told Varic to have her flogged the minute she got there."

I tried to buck out of his grasp to hit him, but he shook me again.

"Because I knew that if she was injured, they couldn't force her to labor as they did the others. She'd be kept at the side of the Vigilant. She'd be with the only person the men cannot hurt. Cared for in whatever small way that she could be. Given lighter work. Overlooked."

"Oh, perfect. You wanted her ignored and supported only by another Elf who is just as helpless as her. What resources does this Vigilant have to help my sister? Your blood magic ritual to bind us scarred her hand as well. Did you see her wound? It wasn't clean like mine."

"I did see that." He loosened his hold on me. "Despite that, Keres. I'm not sorry. If she had been able-bodied or physically able to resist Varic and his men, they would have treated her far worse. It was a poor option, but it was the best of the worst."

"Ugh!" I pulled away from him and this time he let me go, but I still shoved him away from me. "You are impossible. I hate you!"

"Well, that's just fine because you're no angel either!"

We turned away from each other. I crossed my arms over my chest, and he went to retrieve his shirt from off the floor. Then his shoe.

"Go get formally dressed. We're leaving."

"I'm not going."

"Yes." He turned toward me and growled, "You are."

I stormed toward the door, but he followed. Too quickly. He reached it just as I did and shouted into the hallway as I opened it.

"Ciel, get Lady Keres dressed to travel."

"Yes, my lord," she squeaked, and it echoed down the hall.

I barreled down the hallway with Yarden trailing behind, punching my door open and flinging myself down onto the bed.

"Lady Keres, you broke the door," Yarden said.

"Good!" I screamed into my pillow. I let my ragged breath heat the sheets until they got moist and irritated my skin. Sitting up, I found Ciel laying out an outfit. I pushed myself up from the bed and stripped.

"Oh, Gods." Yarden withdrew into the hallway and closed the damaged door. I didn't care. I tugged on each article of clothing Ciel handed me. Minnow moved to touch my hair.

417

"Don't. I'll wear it down."

"Surely, you'll want to look presentable for the people—"

"I don't care about those people," I snapped at her. "The only people I care about are my own. The ones out there, in the cold, who don't have the luxury of doing their hair or wearing warm clothes. Your people's slaves. I don't care about Mannfel or the King or any of this."

I raked my fingers through my hair and pushed past her. I didn't stop for shoes or anything else. I opened the door and took one look at Yarden. His countenance fell. I didn't care. I turned to go. King Berlium met us in the hall, but I refused to look at him.

We left. Servants met us at the door and dressed us in our traveling cloaks. They made remarks about my bare feet, which I ignored.

Once again, the guards opened the door and the winter day gripped us in its icy hand. I stomped through the snow and didn't allow Berlium to help me into the carriage. The door clicked shut, and the horses were whipped. The carriage lurched forward, kicking up mushy, soiled snow. I looked out the back window and watched the gates of Tecar grow smaller and smaller.

Hadriel told Liriene to wait. He had a plan. I needed in on it.

🜊🜊🜊🜊

Mannfel was exactly what I imagined a bustling Human city would be. Filthy and loud, overcrowded. Pedestrians flooded the streets, crossing our path haphazardly. Like they were entitled to walk where and when they wanted, despite horses and carriages threatening to run them down. Children played ball on the walkways, and merchants shouted from their vendor stalls. Store doors opened and closed, bells ringing every time they swung on their hinges.

Smoke rolled into the bleak, overcast sky from chimneys. Slushy snow spat out from under our wheels. A drunk man yelled and shook his fist at us after being showered by it.

"I'd say he needed the bath," Berlium muttered.

I shook my head and worried my lip between my teeth. The carriage wheels turned over and over, and our cabin shook as the horses' hooves clattered against the cobblestone. I tugged my cloak tighter and tried to

418

keep my cold hands covered.

"Keres, I don't know why you won't just talk to me."

I said nothing, leaning my head against the window to let it cool my forehead. My breath fogged up the glass, and he let out an exasperated sigh.

The deeper we traveled into the city, the more attention our carriage drew. Traffic thickened around us. We were in a... less fortunate neighborhood and we stuck out like a sore thumb.

"Why did we come this way?" Berlium rubbed his hands over his thighs and retreated closer to the middle of his seat. Sitting across from me, he watched me. Instead of looking at the leering faces that got closer and closer to the windows.

"Keres, come away from there."

I sat up and did as he had, moving to the middle.

He turned and tapped on the panel between him and the driver. It slid open and the cold air invaded our cabin. "Really, Antony, why have we come this way?"

"I'm sorry, m'lord. It was supposed to be the quickest route to the square."

"Well, get us on another route. Now." He slid the panel closed. "Devil's blood."

He looked from window to window and then back at me. That set the pattern of his attention for the rest of the ride.

"We're going to have to travel all this way back with him too," the Death Spirit sighed. I winced and took a deep breath. Which made Berlium even more unsettled.

"Just a headache," I said and rubbed my brow bone and adjusted my hair.

"You're making your skin red. Stop being so rough with yourself. You look fine. Your hair is fine. Stop fretting. This is going to be easy."

"What is this exactly?"

He smirked, his eyes sparkling with mischief. "An experiment."

"And why didn't Hadriel come?"

"You tired him out."

419

I snorted and counted the grimacing faces that flashed by the window until we got to the square.

"Fucking finally," I groaned as I edged toward the door. The carriage stopped at the entrance of what looked like a massive courtyard. A strange tower stood at the center and stone statues were in every corner—all men.

"Wait," he said, and exited the carriage first. "Give me your feet."

"What?"

He pulled my dress up, just a little too high, and pulled my foot toward him. A servant beside him passed him one boot and then the other. I just watched him, straight-faced, as he pointedly shoved them onto my feet.

"Trust me." He flashed a smile again. Pleased with his work, he offered me his hand and helped me down from the carriage.

My booted feet immediately sank into filthy slush. I looked down at the boots and marveled that they kept the wetness out. I was standing in a puddle of what looked like frosted excrement. I looked back at him, and his brow lifted. He bit his lip as if to say, 'I told you so.'

"Well, let's get on with it, then."

I took his arm and followed him up the pale stone steps into the square. The minute our feet touched down, it was like it sent a message into the earth and everyone in Mannfel followed it to us. The square flooded with company. Our guards kept a tight formation around us as we proceeded to the center.

Music bellowed out, echoing off the stone walls and covering up the excited chatter. Entertainment found its place among the solicitations of food merchants who offered anything from meat to pastries. By the time I looked from one side of the square to the other, everyone had a drink in their hands.

"Marvelous, aren't we?" Berlium asked, gesturing to the crowd.

"Humans?" I asked in return.

"Baoreans." He beamed with pride. These were his people. The living force of his kingdom—beyond the armies that slaughtered my own.

My stomach ached. The cold filtered through my clothes, but the amassed crowd brought its warmth. One man from our ensemble tasted our food and drink before passing it to us. I looked around for Yarden.

He kept to the back of the formation, with his eyes trained on me. He didn't smile, and neither did I. He passed a wary gaze over the crowd and then I realized—this was a dangerous experiment.

I untucked my hair from behind my ears and pulled my hood up. Berlium moved my hand from his arm and then put his arm around me, drawing me in closer. He looked down at me and his eyes held the same look of pride that they did when he looked at his people. "Nobody is here to hurt you. I'd tear the throat out of anyone with my teeth if they dared try."

He said it so casually, so honestly. No wonder they called him the Grizzly King.

The crowd parted around us and our guards, allowing us to reach the sheltered platform we'd been aimed at. Tables laden with food and drink. Luxurious seats with fur blankets draped over their backs. Lit lanterns warmed the space, and flowers littered the carpeted floor.

We ascended the short steps and took our places. Dancers dressed in bold colors careened through the crowd, and the tinkling of bells glittered into the air. Their pants and skirts had tiny bells sewn into the seams. Every movement sang. They clapped to the rhythm of the music and bystanders cheered.

They made their turns around the square, dancing with the people, until the song neared its end. The hurried song of the bells rushed toward us, and the dancers gathered before our platform. They broke into pairs and swung each other around. They drew each other close and then pushed apart. They lifted their hands all at the same time and mimicked each other's steps. Each pulled colorful scarves from their pockets and swirled them into the air. Around each other, overhead. Like gauzy snakes, flying all around.

It was a beautiful contrast to the snow. The grays, blacks, and browns of the furs the citizens wore. Against the stone walls that held up the white sky, and the smog that billowed out of chimneys. When the song had ended, they bowed as one. Berlium clapped and cheered, and even the guards joined in. Except Yarden. His eyes scanned the smiling faces, like he could sense trouble.

Of course, my gut reaction was the same, as the only Elf surrounded by Humans. But he was the King's Cerberus, as he said. It was his job to be on guard, and I was thankful for it. I felt safer between him and Berlium.

I turned and smiled at a pretty dancer. She approached the stage, holding up a rose. Out of the corner of my eye, I could see Yarden shift over his feet. As if he might lunge at her. I took the rose and thanked her. Berlium smiled and kissed my hand that held it, thanking the dancer too. She cocked an eyebrow up and flashed him a seductive smile. Both my brows shot up, and I looked at him. He shrugged, turning his face toward mine.

"To the King, the spoils, yes?" I teased.

He shook his head and laughed.

Merriment continued before us, and we watched as we ate. We made small conversation about the square and the people. The guards relaxed a little—except Yarden. The band carried on joyful songs, and the food never seemed to run out. People gathered and someone was telling a story loud enough to make half the square roar with laughter. Eventually, the attention shifted.

One by one, people stopped by to drop a flower or some trinket at our feet. My face ached from smiling, but Berlium never seemed to tire of it.

A pair of men approached.

"Thaniel?" I all but jumped out of my chair. So, this is where he'd ended up. With his Human lover, Mathis. His eyes shifted between Berlium and me, and the sting of my hypocrisy burned in my belly.

"Coroner," he said, and they both bowed their heads before showing the King the same respect.

"I'm happy to see you so… happy," I said, my cheeks heating. His soft brown eyes lit up. He had a hat on that hid the tips of his ears, but didn't seem misplaced, holding hands with Mathis.

"Thank you," he responded with a nod. "I hope you've found

happiness as well." He glanced at the King again, who watched our interaction.

Thaniel, an Elf who hunted Dalis with me in the Sunderlands—was here and he was happy. On the arm of his Human lover. I'd drawn a weapon on him for daring to reach for such a dream before. Here I was, on a podium above him. About to become the Queen of the new realm we both had crossed into. It felt surreal.

"Enjoy the festivities," Berlium said. They bowed again and disappeared into the crowd.

I turned back to him. "He's from my clan. I almost killed him once. Because I found out he was in love with that Man. Mathis. He's one of your soldiers, the only one I ever spared, and not because I wanted to. I was so blind then."

His gaze lingered on mine before he said, "Different times. Different views."

We looked back out at the crowd. One guard refilled our glasses with a warm, spicy drink that coated my throat and seeped into my belly. I didn't feel as nervous now. As we watched the crowd, I gathered my thoughts. Liriene's situation was as temporary as the snow. If Hadriel had a plan, I could trust that. He was often more reasonable than Berlium.

"So, my King, name your price. For allowing me to see my sister."

"Only this." He touched the underside of my jaw, bringing my mouth closer to his. Watching my lips curve as he pulled me nearer, he kissed me. Then he gently pulled my hood down and told me I was beautiful as he tucked my hair back behind the point of my ear.

"Exquisite," he insisted.

I caught more than a few people looking at us. At him with love and admiration—lust. He was sex incarnate. Of course, they looked at him like that.

Once their eyes passed over me, however, the reaction changed. Death Incarnate. Some smiles faded. Some grew wider. Some faltered, as if they didn't know which way to go.

"Isn't she lovely?" Berlium asked one person who stared too long, unsmiling.

They shook their head. No.

Yarden was suddenly a few paces closer, his eyes glowing faintly with that bronze light.

Berlium's mirth faded, and he sat up straighter in his chair. The citizen looked up at him and then immediately lowered their eyes. Then left. My King's smile did not return. Others had noticed the strange exchange. Grew a little bolder. The next person to approach spat at our feet.

That was it. The guards were up in arms. Yarden was at my side. Berlium stood and everybody was shouting. Some citizens were confused... and the rest were very certain of what was going on.

"An Elven slut for a Queen? Sire, you must be mad!"

"Dark tales are told of that one."

"She's the mistress of Death! She'll bring hell down on us all."

"Elves ought to be put down, not raised up."

"First Lady Vega. Now, another Elven bitch."

"No tree fuckers should be allowed to live!"

"The end is nigh! The Underworld's Hound shall devour our souls."

"Mrithyn's dog!"

I couldn't block it out. Their words could be exchanged for my kin once shouted with the same wrath.

"She is to blame for the destruction of Hishmal!"

"If we hand her over to the Dalis, whose blood is on her hands, they will stop hunting the innocent."

"The attacks may very well be retaliation for her actions!"

"Tell us, does a God bleed?"

"Her eyes! She isn't one of us."

These people were not so different from my own in their cruelty. But this was more than cruelty. I'd gotten lost in the memory. Berlium yanked me from my seat and shoved me into the midst of his guards. Yarden's hand weighed on my shoulder. I met his eyes. The bronze fire seared into me, and I steeled myself.

We pushed through the crowds. Some people threw food, emptied their tankards on us. It was in my hair. On my face. Something made its way between my collar and my neck. I shrieked and swatted it away.

Yarden urged me forward.

"Where's the King?" I turned before I needed to duck my head down. Something flew overhead, and I tripped.

"Fuck!" My ankle ached.

"Keep moving, Lady Keres." Yarden caught me and ushered me forward. Hands clawed, reaching for me. Pushed and pulled. I couldn't differentiate Yarden's from anyone else's after a few minutes of it. Finally, the crowd expelled us.

Something sharp jabbed my neck, and I lashed out a claw at whoever was nearest—it wasn't Yarden. I touched my neck and found nothing on my hand. It stung terribly.

Someone shoved me—dizziness rolled into my skull. Next thing I knew, I was in the carriage. The guards stood on the foot rails and jumped onto their horses.

"Where is—?" My head dropped.

The carriage bolted forward, and I fell over. It jolted me awake.

"Wait!"

He either didn't hear me or he ignored me. The only answer I got was the screaming and cursing of the crowd as they followed. I looked through the window and an explosion of bronze fire burned my eyes. My vision blurred, and then everything went dark.

57: STOLEN
Keres

I woke up on the floor of the carriage. I hadn't been saved; I'd been stolen. I got up and looked out the window. We were on the open road. Nothing but rolling, snow-covered plains. The driver steered us onward in a frenzy. Only a handful of guards rode alongside us on horseback. Nobody dropped speed. There was no one pursuing us as far as I could tell. But there would be.

"No one is here to hurt you. I'd tear the throat out of anyone with my fucking teeth if they dared try."

I held myself to keep from vomiting. I was getting terribly sick from the way the carriage lurched and swayed. And then I saw the river.

In Hadriel's book about government, there was a map. We were most likely stealing away into the Ressid Province. Nowadays, there were larger settlements along the river. Eagland and Wolvens. Each with an interesting history, but in the present, all that mattered is that it meant resources for my captors. Food, water, and rest. Enough distance between us and the King. They made the mistake of not putting distance between themselves and *me*.

I didn't have a weapon, and that wasn't a problem anymore. But why—what was the reason for this? Who were these men?

I wondered whether Berlium or Yarden were hurt but refused to believe it. The crowd had done a fine job of splitting us up. For all his pretty talk, the Grizzly King fucked up royally. .

I could kill these men, take a horse, and ride back.

"Or we could go on an adventure," the Death Spirit hummed.

These men did something to knock me out. Clearly, this was premeditated. More enemies of the Baore? Interesting. I settled back into my seat, trying to anchor my stomach. I tapped my claws on the seat and waited for us to get wherever the fuck we were going.

🙰🙰🙰🙰

Thane

"Something's wrong." I stood from my seat. Rivan jumped up next to me.

"What is it?" His thoughts sailed into my mind.

"What is it?" Morgance echoed.

I paused, extending my senses. "Keres."

I grabbed my sword and barreled through the room to the door. My men followed right behind me. Trouble was afoot. I kept my sword sheathed and strapped it to my belt as we walked.

"Thane," Elix murmured. "Where are we going? Should we expect a fight?"

"I always expect a fight."

"What do you sense?" Rivan bridged his thoughts to mine.

"She's not in the Baore. She's nearby. I can feel her."

My Spirit quaked in confirmation. Every muscle in my body felt coiled up, ready to spring. She was somewhere very close. But I didn't sense the King anywhere.

"Tricky little demoness." I looked at Rivan. "It seems like she escaped him."

He looked unconvinced.

We went to our usual room, summoning Indiro and Emeric to our round table as well. Morgance laid out a map on the wooden table. Pinning down the rebellious corner with a half-empty mug of ale. "Eagland. Wolvens. Falmaron. There's nothing else for miles. Maybe a hut here or there along the main road. But nothing so attractive as here."

"I could try tunneling, but I don't know whether she can afford that. What if she's in danger?" I asked.

"She's been in danger ever since she was abducted," Indiro countered.

I weighed my options. Every day I felt like I had fewer. Tunneling

427

was like channeling, but I could do it at will. It bypassed the Veil too. Still, I didn't want to compromise her. Communicating through the Void would suck her into it mentally. She'd lose consciousness. She was in danger. I could sense it. Where was the King?

"I won't put her at risk. She needs to be awake. Whatever's happening… it isn't good."

"We could scry for her location," Rivan mentioned, and looked to Elix, who nodded.

"Let's do it."

We gathered the bones, and Elix tossed them on the map. He never scried with drama. It felt casual. He tucked his hands in his pockets and leaned over the table, eyes glazing the map.

"Wolvens," he said, and they all moved into action.

"Wait," I held up a hand. "Rivan and I will go into Wolvens. The rest of you stay here."

They opened their mouths to protest, but I did not accept rebuttal.

The King

"Where the fuck is she?" I pinned a guard against the wall by his throat.

"Sire," Yarden tried to interrupt.

"Tell me!"

"I know nothing, my lord," the man whimpered.

"If you don't think I'll break every one of your bones—" I kneed him in the balls.

He doubled over in pain, and I spun him around, taking his arm behind his back. He shrieked in pain, but I didn't stop. Bone snapped and his cry turned into a screaming sob. His knees gave out, and he fell. Not letting go of his arm, I picked him back up and shoved him against the wall. Slammed his face into the wall and then reared his head back. Blood ran from his nose, striking my senses.

"Tell me what you know."

"My lord, I—" He choked on a sob. "Wolvens! They planned to stop at Wolvens. Then the city. Falmaron."

"Why?" I growled.

"To sell her. I'm sorry, I—"

Spinning him around, I took him in my arms and sank my teeth into his neck. His scream was guttural—until I ripped it out of his throat.

I turned and grabbed Yarden's shoulder. "We ride. Now."

Shock plastered his face. Pallor was a little difficult to spot in his darker skin, but I saw it in his eyes, around his lips. I released him. "Steel yourself."

He'd seen me feed before, but the crowd—his power was drained. He offered me a handkerchief with a steady hand. I took it and wiped my mouth.

"Your eyes, my lord. Should anyone see you—"

"They'd be smart to look away."

The door nearly flew off its hinges beneath my hand. The rest of the men couldn't be trusted, so I bodied the first one I came across. Catching him off guard, I took his sword. Yarden drew his. We killed the rest of them and left their bodies in the street. We saddled two mares and set off. Already having lost too much time.

I'd known escaping the crowd risked separation. Citizens pushed us apart. Only one dared attack me head on, and a guard ran him through with his sword. It created a frenzy. Keres could handle herself. I just needed to catch up.

Some forged ahead, following Keres. Some got pushed and pulled by the crowd. Then Yarden was separated from her, and he made a choice. Me or her. He somehow got to my side. We'd lost sight of her. I cursed myself for it. A group moved in to attack, and Yarden blasted them apart before I needed to shift. Not everyone in the crowd wanted our skin. They fought back against those who did.

By the time we got back onto the road, she was gone. Despite the chaos, this was still my city. I knew where to turn.

The fools who took her damned their souls. If I had to claw the world open and pass through its fiery belly to get to her on the other side, I would. And I wouldn't be surprised if she was dancing in ashes when I got there.

Time flew, but the countryside seemed to stretch on forever. The farther she got, the longer the road. I reached into the horses' minds and made them feel fear. Made them think they were being chased by a giant wolf. As we drew closer, I passed Yarden the reins of my horse and took to the sky. He followed as I soared toward Wolvens.

The gates were closed. I touched down outside and considered my next move. I'd beaten Yarden here, but I didn't need him. My thoughts were cut off by the blood-curdling scream of a desperate woman.

58: SORRY

Keres

The fever dream of the Wither Maiden taught me what I truly fear—it isn't Men.

When he was alive, my father incessantly warned Liri, Katrielle, and I to be careful whenever we went for walks outside the camp. *"Men aren't afraid of hurting little girls. They do it all the time."*

We never feared being stolen. Killed, yes, because Humans rarely allowed us to live if they caught us. They'd create any reason to justify killing an Elf. Even a child.

These men would be stupid to try to kill me. My guess was they wanted to ransom me, and it was a good enough reason for me to justify killing them. I considered setting the carriage on fire with my Brazen.

"Just to sit in the hell they created by abducting me. Just to listen to them scream."

The Death Spirit's whispers in my head felt like a cold cloth on the back of my neck. In the past, I winced when thoughts like that crossed my mind. To reject them, I mentally chanted the same thing over and over.

"I'm not crazy. I'm not a monster. I'm not scared."

Memories of my people's accusations would interrupt these mental rituals.

"You're cursed."

"Don't you see what you've become?"

"You are responsible for so much death."

They were right. I was all the bad things they said about me, all the things I tried to convince myself I wasn't. For the first time in my life, it was a relief. Because men aren't afraid of hurting little girls. They do it all the time. But every mortal man is scared of monsters. Especially one as crazy as me.

The walls that protected the settlement we'd traveled to reminded me of the Human encampment in my homeland. I considered burning the whole fucking thing down. There must be innocent people here too, I reminded myself.

My skin pebbled, and the hairs on my arms stood. My gums burned, and I lifted a finger to my mouth to rub them. The sharp point of my fangs dropped. My tongue felt heavier in my mouth, too. My Godling was itching to come out and play.

Eventually, the door was whipped open, and I was pulled out by my collar. They bound my hands and pushed my hood up over my head. I waited—my rage threatening to boil over and consume them in my unholy fire. Their bodies pressed close to mine as they ushered me toward what appeared to be someone's home. A servant opened the door and ushered us in silently. They shoved me forward. "Get moving."

This was a wealthy man's estate. Every wall was wrapped in dark blue paper that looked like velvet. Littered with artwork in gold frames and ornate mirrors. Our boots thudded against the creaking wood-floor. It smelled like an old carpet and bergamot tea.

We passed through the steam-filled kitchen, ignored by the cooks and kitchen maids. The carriage driver walked ahead of us to an ornate oak door and fished a ring full of iron keys out of his pocket. They all looked the same to me, but he picked one and slid it into the lock. It gave way in a second and the hinges squealed, revealing a courtyard.

"Chain the King's whore to the pillar." Again, a hand met me between the shoulder blades, and I stumbled forward. I got a good look at the ground. At the blood that stained the stones.

One of them grabbed my hands, and I schooled myself to rest my stare on him without revealing that my right hand still hurt—and that I was going to rip him apart with it, anyway. He untied the rope they'd used to bind my hands, holding chains he intended to replace it with.

The carriage driver walked back into the house and shut the door.

The other five men chose pillars and walls to hold up as they watched.

The estate walled us in. There were only two closed doors and the open sky above. Smoke wafted into the gray clouds from the house's chimneys. A bird with blue-black feathers landed on a corner of the roof and cocked its head at me.

"They say black birds are a Death omen," I said in a low voice. The man flicked his gaze over me.

"Be silent, witch," he spat. But his pulse quickened in his chest. I lowered my gaze and listened. His heart thudded against his ribs, startling as I lifted my hands to him to receive the chains.

"No sudden movements," his voice cracked. I offered him a smile.

"Aye, did you suddenly forget how to tie someone up?" one other chided.

"No," he muttered and pushed me back against the pillar. I could scent his fear.

"Careful, darling." My lips curled into a smile, and he didn't miss the flash of my fangs.

He stumbled back, dropping the cuffs and chains.

"Your heart makes such a pretty song. I can hear it."

"Silence," he barked. His companions turned their heads and pushed up from their places. He lunged for the chains, but I held up my hands and he froze.

My head was filled with the music of their pulses—a choir of angst. I took a deep breath, inhaling the scent of their sweat. My senses traced each droplet against their skin, through their pores, and underneath. Deeper than the sinew and muscle. Deep enough to taste a hint of blood.

It was a rhythmic rush, thrumming through the rivulets of their veins. Cascading out of their chests, down to their toes and soaring back up. To their skulls, to the surface of their skin. The one with the palest skin turned quite red in the face. The one with dark eyes—his body hummed with arousal. I listened to the blood hiss and sigh, seething through his body and flooding his pelvis. The chance to dominate me tantalized him.

"What the fuck is happening?"

"Look at her face."

"Get back, you slut."

"Silence!" I shouted. Each of them went rigid as I raised my hands. A searing sensation stretched under my skin.

Their blood panicked in their veins, shivering beneath the touch of my new magic. I had them by their strings and my hands itched to play them.

This wasn't blood magic like Ithaca's. She was a Water Daemon with control over the water in their veins. This was pure blood magic, wielded by a Coroner. Something my Spirit seemed to understand viscerally. As if I'd done it a thousand times and reading about it simply reminded me. A trait I must have inherited from Coroner's before me, expressing itself now.

The song inside them ached to flow, paused by my command. Their hearts sputtered, and their lips paled. Sweat broke out under their armor. I could feel the tension in their limbs, the looseness of their breaths. I trapped their voices in their throats. I relaxed pressure and allowed their hearts to bleed into their bodies once more. Just enough to keep them alive.

The museum full of statues in Berlium's kingdom couldn't compare. The pallor, the breathlessness, the knots in their muscles, and the brittleness of their bones.

The black bird above squawked and jumped into the sky. I tracked it until it was gone. As I brought my attention back to the tightened faces of the men, something else caught my eyes. A shiver of light on the ground. The blood that stained the courtyard's stone... brightened. I closed my eyes and inhaled deeply, scenting the blood on the ground.

A hushed whisper touched my ear. I turned again and opened my eyes, finding a child standing there amid the men. So small, so withered. Bloodless. Her skin was tinted gray and green. Her eyes were hollow and dark. Her matted brown hair, crusted with dried blood. She peered up at the men and whimpered.

"Don't cry." I beckoned her, and she turned her head. Her mouth moved, but her words were garbled. I made out a desperate, "Please."

My heart lurched against my ribs, kicking into a chaotic rhythm. She came to stand before me, and I listened to her. Echoes of her memories rang out across the courtyard.

Stolen. Broken. Bled.

Another child like her walked out of the shadows and into the gray, cold light of the morning. Then another. And another. A small group of children gathered around me. Gnarled and empty. Some young, some even close to my age. The men that had hurt them stood still as stone. And their stories were lifted out of the blood on the ground, to my mind.

Someone's baby. Someone's precious hope. Someone's love given form.

"Someone took me and never let me go."

I let loose a growl from my chest, and my hands trembled as I raised them once more. The ghosts gathered around me, clinging to my cloak. I let their stories soak me through.

A pain so global, ached in every inch of my body, every drop of my blood. And I forced that pain into the Men who'd hurt them. They were the captives now. Their bodies buckled from the pain. One of them lost consciousness. I bent them to the ground and unleashed their blood.

The first one to move was the one with the chains. He lurched forward, attempting to get up or crawl. The first little girl that had appeared screamed and hid behind me.

"Damn—" he stuttered as he pushed himself up on all fours.

"Silence," the Death Spirit hissed through my mouth, entangling her voice with mine.

His body jerked back, his head swung to the side, and his arms contracted. The blood in his veins kicked up into a throbbing, wild frenzy. His arteries banged against the sides of his throat as I strangled every bit of air from every drop of his blood until his heart stopped. When I let go of him, his body fell.

The others were in pain but still tried to move away from me.

"I'm sorry, I'm sorry!" one of them shrieked.

"Not yet, you're not. But you will be—and you'll find I'm unforgiving," I growled.

The eldest of the ghosts stepped up beside me and put her hand on my shoulder. Her touch chilled my skin. Her furtive voice was in my ear. Telling me where they hurt her—how many of them hurt her. Over and over again. How many times a day her body had been sold.

I clasped my hands together, as if I were taking hold of his heart, and then ripped them apart. Veins snapped. Sinew and muscle dissected. His chest shuddered with a final, shallow breath that was coughed up with blood.

I screamed with fury—reached a hand out and my power took hold of that blood, stopping it midair. It caught in his throat. I forced it back down and choked him on it.

The other four men huddled together. I reached out for the blood in the one who was still unconscious. His body seized and rebutted against my command. I ignored the searing pain that echoed through my body and dug my control into him.

The books said it couldn't be done. My Death Spirit said otherwise. The Ghost's grip lent me cold bursts of energy and tingles shot down my spine.

His eyes flew open, and his mouth opened in a silent scream as I took the reins of every muscle and bone. Movement stuttered through him. My mind nestled into the sticky warmth that laced his body.

Just as I had forced myself into the Death Spirit in the fever dream, I poured my will into him. My magic donned him like a glove. To move him, I had to move.

He mirrored my dance, withdrawing the blade from his belt and flipping it in his hand. I set our gazes on the two men on the ground.

"Darek, no!"

"Let him go."

But I wasn't listening to them, I was listening to him. The tormented soul of a little boy crying at my side. "Don't let him get away."

"I won't," I said, then threw the man's body forward. He betrayed his companions, driving his blade into one's heart. The other jumped back and got to his feet, rising to stand. He didn't know whether to attack me or Darek. That's when I realized they didn't see the children. It only angered me more.

Our victim's cry was drowned in blood. I surged energy into Darek's heart and made him slit his own throat. His blade clattered to the ground, and I let go of his thready pulse.

The last man doubled over and vomited. The ghosts stood back as I ran toward him. I sent a wave of pain into him, and he fell down to his knees. Bruises bloomed beneath his skin all over. I grabbed him by the throat and growled in his face.

Tears and sweat streaked through the dirt on his skin. The door behind us banged open, but I didn't turn. I held his desperate gaze and roared once more, as both my hands tightened around his throat.

Every bit of energy I had, I used to pull the blood from his toes to his head. His skin pinked, and then reddened, and then purpled. His eyes bulged and his limbs went limp.

He cried tears of blood—it drained from his ears and oozed from his gums. Until I felt the vessels in his neck and skull rupture, and his eyes rolled back. I dropped him and spun around, panting for air. The children were gone and Berlium was standing in the doorway, equally covered in blood.

The King

"Hello, Darkstar," I said in a low voice. I held my hands where she could see them. "It's me."

This was her.

She stood there, in her black cloak, her white hair loose around her face. Her skin was pale and the veins beneath were like tiny black, blue, and red tendrils. Bottomless eyes. Jagged fangs and bone-like talons. Divinity.

Blood painted the gray stone of the courtyard, some old but most fresh. The tang of it thickened the air and clung to her. It would have sent me into a frenzy if I'd found anyone else in the courtyard with her.

Darkness shifted in her gaze until she was looking at me with emerald eyes again. Tears flooded them and she ran into my arms.

"You're so cold," I whispered into her neck. She shivered and wept in reply. I petted her head and scanned my eyes over the bodies. So much fucking blood.

"We have to go." Yarden ran up behind us. I met her gaze.

"We're getting you out of here."

She nodded and then turned her head. Peering back into the middle of the courtyard, she whispered an apology. I didn't know who it was for, but I had a feeling it wasn't for the men.

I picked her up and carried her, stepping over the bodies of the servants and the carriage driver. Whoever lived here—well, no one lived here anymore. She wrapped her arms around my neck. With his sword drawn, Yarden led us to an exit that let out into a side alley. The alarm had been raised. Soldiers flooded the streets.

"What should we do?" he asked as we ducked down in the alley.

"Keres, can you walk?"

She nodded.

"Take her, then." I set her down. "Give me the sword."

He obeyed.

"Now, follow close behind."

The crowd in the street parted, women gasping and men shouting, as I pushed through. Yarden and Keres were on my heels.

"Over there!" a guard directed the soldiers.

My blade met a throat. Blood sprayed across my face and showered the ground. I licked my lips. My power swelled within me, and my voice boomed into the next attacker, "Fall."

He fell back, and my blade pinned him down. Another two charged me, but I cut them down in one sweep.

"My lord!" Yarden shouted. He shielded Keres with his body as a soldier lunged, thrusting his sword toward them.

"Break," I spoke, and the word sailed across the distance like an arrow—into the soldier's arm. He shrieked and his blade dropped. Yarden recovered it and killed him.

Keres pulled her hood back and threw her gaze behind me.

I turned and found three assailants; their blades suspended mid-air. Their faces twitched and contorted. Their joints buckled and their eyes found me smiling. The power emanating from her made the hairs on my body stand. A hungry growl tore from my chest as I sated my blade with their blood.

Siren horns wailed and armored feet clamored toward us. Doors of houses and shops opened and slammed. Someone got on their horse and whipped it, speeding past us.

Yarden and Keres drew closer to me. A common thread of power entangled her and I. She looked at me with eyes wide enough to hold both fear and understanding. Side by side, we were matched. We paused in the streets as a group of soldiers marched toward us.

She was exhausted. All I wanted was to take her home and be done with this.

"You think you can come here and murder our citizens, and that we'll just let you walk away?" one asked.

"I didn't come here to kill anyone except the people who'd abducted my wife." I gestured toward her.

She didn't, for a split second, look like she needed rescuing. The darkness was flooding back into her eyes, tracing lines beneath her skin. A low growl rumbled in her throat. My Spirit answered hers, rumbling in my core. The men watched us. Questions flickered across their faces. Fear. Anger. Most were unwilling to attack us.

"Listen to me." Power laced my voice and blanketed everyone present in a heavy shroud of dull confusion.

"You will let us pass, or you will pass through the jaws of Death. Take a good look at whose path you're blocking."

I stepped aside and Keres stepped forward, holding her cloak at her side. She bared her fangs and her ebony wings flared out on either side of her. Gods, it made my cock hard. My shadow sang beneath my feet, so I let my razor-sharp bats fly free. They forged ahead of us, forcing people aside.

Every man, woman, and child trembled before us. I moved to stand behind Keres and nudged her to walk. She strode forward, muttering under her breath.

"How many of these people knew what went on here? How many of them lived next door and did nothing to answer the cries of the stolen children? Was no one listening? Did no one know?"

It set my teeth on edge and boiled my stomach. This was her righteous anger—the wrath of the Coroner who has seen the perversion of Death: murder of innocence. A chill ran through me.

The crowd was tremulous. Soldiers wanted to attack. My magic lulled them into submission. I instilled them with fear, letting them see what I saw in her. Visions of their blood on her tongue. The piles of bodies she'd leave in her wake.

We walked, a wall of power on either side of us. They were outside, looking in at the beasts that walked among them. My magic bent the Veil around us, revealing what we were beyond their natural perception. They saw the Coroner and the Beast.

And then I felt him.

So, he'd come for her, then?

His presence teased at the edges of my vision, like darkness just out of sight. I kept my focus on the shroud of magic allowing us to walk through unharmed. He loomed on the outskirts, peering in. If I turned my head, I was sure I'd see him.

A blue-black bird soared across the sky, its eyes trained on me. I looked up and gave it a smile.

"Looks like you've lost the race, Thane."

"But you can only run for so long."

59: SIFTING
Thane
Day Twenty-Three

The Baore locked around Keres like an iron fist. Cuffing her and her sister to the King, and I couldn't reach them. Not even through tunneling. I could foam at the mouth with frustration. My patience was at its end. We had to move in—no more babying the bond and fretting. But I still didn't have a plan. We couldn't follow them. Back in the Guild, I showed Rivan and my men my thoughts—what I saw.

"She's..." Elix started.

"She's fucking incredible," Morgance said and shook his head. "Those wings—thorns and flowers. What the fuck?"

"And the King..."

"So snide, preening at her side, like he belongs there," I said. I kicked the chair and sent it flying across the room, where it shattered against the wall. "She reeked of his scent."

"He's fucked her, for sure," Morgance added gruffly. "Lucky bastard. They don't make them like that anymore."

"What if he's tasted her blood?" Rivan added.

I snapped my attention onto him. "He blood-cursed her—I saw her hands. The scars. His palm bore a scar as well. When he flicked his shadows into the light, I saw it."

"Of course, he did. Every move he makes sheds blood. They're bonded, then? Maybe she doesn't want to be rescued. Then what?" Elix mused.

The King was scratching at her surface. He hadn't touched her soul. Even if she had fed him, he hadn't given her his blood name. I'd know it if it was written into her. I could sense it. My ties to her and him were sensitive.

My breath hitched, and arousal flared within me when I saw her. Being that close to her almost made me stupid. Almost. She was the most beautiful thing I'd ever seen in her Godling form. Absolutely divine. She was the perfect weapon.

My men still didn't know my secrets—just how I was bound to her. What I truly was and how she was made for me. I needed them to believe my frustration was purely because I was intent on rescuing her. But that wasn't true either. Wolvens would have turned to dust if I'd done what I wanted. The King would have made sure of it. From the way she walked beside him, she probably would have helped. Did he have her entranced, like he'd done to Herrona?

She has seen me, but she did not know. How could she not know? Did she not feel the pull I felt toward her? The Gods made her to torment me. Why was I surprised? That I'd be stuck on the unwanted side of the karmic bond. The Gods really wanted me to feel this.

I sifted through the memories, closing my eyes to pin them down for study. Such vivid images. She showed her Godling, but he hid his. Baring only his fangs, his claws. His shadows danced toward the sun, skittering through that crowd. But what parted them was her—and he knew it.

Look whose path you're blocking.

We were both looking at her—everybody was.

She's not entranced. Herrona was a dead-eyed fawn beside the King. Keres' eyes are bottomless. Keres looked at him like she wanted to swallow him whole. She looked at those people like she'd take them into the belly of the earth. If he'd entranced her, she'd be submissive. I knew well the effect he had on people.

I inhaled deeply, cracking my neck before turning back to them.

"He has her. She bears his scars, his ring, his scent. And she strutted just as tall as he did. Arrogant bastard."

"She's not unlike him," Elix said.

They did not know how true that was. How connected the three of us were. How could I tell them?

My secrets—the wager etched in the heavens. All bets against my soul, and Keres, the wild card. The King had use for her. I had use for her. But I wondered—the way he looked at her... I bet he didn't expect to be the one entranced. He was never supposed to be my opposition.

Here we were, both wanting something that drove a stake between us. Two Kings for one Queen. Two bonds, neither to be broken painlessly. If it came down to a fight for dominance, to see which bond prevailed, it would be a schism that split the Veil.

"We need to keep thinking. We need a solid plan—this can't be rushed. The world is depending on this."

PART 4

GODLING

"They will sit at your feet,
And their adders will seem adoration.
Because they see who you might become,
And what they might not become"

—Emisandre's Grimoire

60: SAFETY

Keres

Night Twenty-Three

"You fucking bastard!"

First, it was the jewelry box. I threw a chair next. He dodged it and held up his hands as I picked up the candlestick.

"Keres, do you even hear yourself? You're not making sense!"

Fury lit up the flecks of gold in his sapphire eyes. I poised the candlestick over my shoulder, ready to pitch it at him. Or hit him with it if he took one step closer.

"Why would I plan for you to be taken? As if I'd be willing to lose you. Are you mad?"

"You *did* lose me!" I screamed. I stepped to the right, and he went to the left.

"We were in a mob, woman. We got separated. You think I wanted it to happen? Does that really sound like something I'd do? Let someone else touch my woman. Are you fucking kidding me, Ker? You know better than that."

I lowered the candlestick but kept narrowed eyes on him. He ran his hands through his hair and watched me. Never taking those blue eyes off me.

The whole ride back to the castle, I was silent. A carriage met us halfway with Hadriel inside it. Berlium and he stayed sitting across from me. Both staring the way he was now. It made my stomach hurt. My entire body felt locked in a state of resistance.

"What happened?" They'd asked over and over.

"I don't want to talk about it. Not now. I just want to go home."

Once we were back within the palace walls, the sun was long gone. My body buzzed with adrenaline. Exhaustion never caught up with me. It was the middle of the night. In the privacy of his bedroom, he'd helped me bathe and change into a nightdress Ciel brought for me. He just wanted to talk, but I didn't want to talk. I wanted to scream. He waited and waited. Hands planted on his hips. All I felt was anger, and I stayed quiet long enough my hair had dried. Until I picked a reason to scream.

Tears flooded my eyes, and I wiped them angrily away. I couldn't shake the voices of those children—couldn't stop seeing their faces.

"Now, you're crying," he sighed. "Talk to me."

I tried to stop crying, taking a deep breath.

He came closer and uncurled my fingers from around the candlestick, letting it drop to the floor. I looked up into his eyes as he lifted my chin and wiped my tears away. His presence just felt so heavy, which I needed, because I felt like I might just float away from the light-headedness.

We stood there while I caught my breath. My whole body held tension and ached. As if he knew, he ran a hand up my arm, to my collarbone, and let it rest there.

Blinking back the tears, I pushed him away.

"Really?" He reached for my hand and pulled me back. He put his hands around my neck, his thumbs under my jaw, and forced me to look at him. "Stop pushing me away."

"Stop pulling me back. I don't want you to touch me." I shoved at him again, but it just urged him closer.

"Is that the truth?" He tightened his hold around my throat and brought his face closer to mine. Our bodies scathed each other.

"You paraded me in front of people who hate what I am." I spat the words at him. "Didn't you think that might have some consequences? That I might be in danger?"

"No, I didn't think you would be!" he shouted. "Maybe because I was there. There were guards. And maybe—just maybe, I don't fear for your life because you're the fucking Coroner, Keres. I don't look at you and see vulnerability. I didn't expect anyone else to either. Stop trying to blame me. I told you I would have ripped out their throats if they tried. I killed everyone on my way back to you."

"A little late, huh?"

He squeezed his hand again, and he sneered in my face. "Maybe you're right—I wanted you to fall into the wrong hands. Just so that when I got you back, I could have you on your knees, thanking me."

I scoffed. "That better be sarcasm. For your own sake, my King."

A laugh rumbled through his chest. "Me, sarcastic? I'd never joke about wanting to see you on your knees for me, little wolf," he said, before he leaned down and bit my lower lip. He sucked it between his fangs and didn't let it go until I pulled from between his teeth—to bite him back.

His hands wandered up into my hair, dragging my body into his. Our mouths crashed together in hunger. I opened my mouth against his, and he swept his tongue against mine. My senses were flooded with the taste of him. Overbearing need rocked through me.

I threw my arms around his neck and pulled him in closer. His lips parted for my tongue, and I ravaged his, sucking on it before exploring deeper. He moaned into my mouth. I covered it with another kiss, clawing at the back of his neck to keep his mouth crushed against mine.

We went hard at each other—to war. He slammed me back into the wall, knocking the breath out of me and not letting me get it back before he could kiss me again. Who needed to breathe, anyway? I ripped his shirt open, popping the threads of every button, and he pulled away to push it down and drop it on the floor.

He grabbed the shoulder of my dress and tore the sleeve clear off. Grabbing me by the wrist and tracing his tongue up my bare arm. Biting into my shoulder when he reached the same spot that I'd bitten him. I cried out in pain and moaned as he flicked his tongue over the puncture wounds. Chills ran through me. He reclaimed my mouth so that I tasted my own blood on his tongue.

The kiss deepened as he pressed into me, reaching for the collar of my dress. He lifted me by it, bringing my chest against his. His other hand wandered down my back to cup my ass. Kneading my curves as I pulled myself into him. His breath hitched, as if he could sense my arousal. And then I realized my thighs were slicked with something unexpected.

I pushed him away again.

"Ker," he growled.

I took a step back, looking down. His eyes followed... to the blood running down my legs. Relief flooded through me, followed by embarrassment.

"I'm sorry. I——"

He looked from my legs back to my face. His brows pinched together, his nostrils flaring. "Why are you sorry?" He moved to pull me back into his arms.

"I'm bleeding," I asserted, in case he missed it.

"Are you injured? Did they hurt you? Or is it just your cycle?" he asked, dropping his gaze to the blood trickling down my legs.

"It's my cycle," I said in a rushed whisper.

"So, we're fine." He moved toward me again and licked his lips.

"Fine? I have to go. I can't," I fretted. He snatched me back into his arms, anyway. Clearly, the scent of my blood had pushed him over the edge into craziness.

"Can't or won't?" he asked into my neck before nipping at my ear. I squeezed my thighs together. He licked and bit my throat—threatening to bring me down with him.

"It's going to make a mess of this carpet." My skin crawled.

"Fine," he growled against my skin. And then slipped an arm under me and picked me up.

"What are you doing?" I squeaked.

"Sparing the carpet——" He threw me on the bed.

"You're a madman," I said breathlessly, looking up into his feral eyes.

His fangs were bared, and his eyes glowed hungrily. Chills skittered down my spine and my instincts said to kick him in the face to keep him away from me.

"Fuck," I hissed.

"Yes, little wolf. I'm going to." He moved onto the foot of the bed.

I swore under my breath again, but the erotic look in his eyes siphoned a bit of the angst a normal girl should feel coursing through her. I was anything but a normal girl.

"You know, someone once asked me whether a God bleeds." I laughed nervously.

"A Goddess does." He grinned. "And all of creation better be very fucking thankful for it."

My blood ignited, aflame under his incinerating gaze. He was a fever dream that inched closer, threatening to consume me, and made me fidget on the bed. I held my legs together. Wondering what he was thinking.

Silence crawled between us. His stare—the flare of his tightened jaw. The steady drum of his heartbeat. I couldn't ignore the sixth sense I had that prickled my skin, as I heard the blood singing in his body. Rushing through him.

Memories of the day flashed through my mind. The way it felt to bend those men by their own blood. I couldn't ignore the thoughts as I listened to his pulse. But his heartbeat was stronger and steadier than any I'd ever heard. It was a diligent war drum. Its thrumming was rich and deep. Unhurried, unbothered. Enduring. I needed to hear it—for it to just keep beating. Soothing. Drawing me in and taming my own racing heart.

"Can you hear my heart beating?" I asked.

He nodded, his eyes hooded with desire. My pulse settled into an excited, thrumming song. Answered, acknowledged.

"He listens like us," the Death Spirit sighed, and butterflies erupted in my belly.

This was something about him that made me feel safe enough to be quiet. There was no need to fill what was between us with noise—unless it was that ravenous song between our Spirits. Rumbling, purring. Every curled reverberation of his growl touched a hair on my body, raising it to attention. As long as I could hear his heartbeat and he could hear mine— it was a conversation between our bodies that didn't need an explanation or apology.

"Sit up and pick up your arms."

I did as he said, and he pulled my white night dress off over my head. He took it and then pushed me back down again. He balled up the dress as his eyes glazed over my naked body. The blood rushed through him a little quicker.

"Open your legs for me," he said, meeting my eyes. My heart fluttered in my chest and between my thighs. His gaze traveled there, and his fingertips traced the groove of my groin, drifting down to my inner thigh. I obeyed.

Sitting on his heels, he took the dress and wiped the blood from my bare legs. The soft fabric grazed against my center. Then he pressed it there, blotting away the blood. Just the fabric between my skin and his. And then he tossed the soiled dress aside. His pupils dilated with desire and the blue in his eyes became black. I leaned up on my elbows, watching him as he knelt there between my legs.

"Goddess, you're so beautiful," he said.

"I am a literal bloody mess." I laughed. My Spirit relished in his compliment, stretching languidly under my skin, and lengthening my claws.

He touched his lower lip and the corner of his mouth curved up. "I'm not afraid to get messy."

He lifted his shirt over his head and took his pants off, tossing them to the floor to join my dress. Positioning himself over me, he let his weight rest between my legs. Instinctively, I lifted my hips, feeling the naked length of him.

"Are you in pain?" he asked, rocking his hips against me so that his erection slid up the center of me.

I shook my head and licked my lips, watching his mouth. "Only a bit of cramping."

"Good. I can make it go away. Your blood makes you wetter—makes me even harder. Your scent." He inhaled. "You're mouthwatering."

My throat was dry with need. My body reacting to his, the sin he tempted me with. He moved against me, nudging his cock against my sex. Reveling in the warmth and wetness. My moan was his command. His mouth curved, and I couldn't give a fuck about what was right or dirty.

Whatever he was—he craved my blood. It should have terrified me, but it didn't. He'd bitten me and I'd bitten him right back, knowing that it was an unspoken word in his primal language. One I didn't even understand but longed to taste on my tongue.

The deep timbre of his laugh made my nipples perk up as I rocked my hips against his velvet smooth length. The slickness between my legs—I wasn't impervious to the scent either. It was heady. Metallic, sweetened by the scent of my arousal.

"You're going to feed off of me," I said, dropping my tone on the last word. It wasn't a question—it was the truth. It never escaped me how his eyes brightened when he'd consumed blood or when we had sex.

He lowered himself, laying between my legs, and looked at me with obsidian eyes. "I'm going to drink you dry."

His hands parted my legs further, lifting them up under my knees. The back of my head hit the bed again as he pressed his mouth against my inner thigh. I held my hands up to my face. This wasn't the same as when he cut those women and lapped at their blood. He kissed away the thought, his tongue trailing up higher, until he reached my groin.

"Are you afraid?" His breath heated my flesh, and his fangs grazed me. I wondered what he'd do if I said yes.

My body was trembling as it usually did at his touch. He called the shadows out of the corners of the room, and they rushed toward us, wrapping us in frantic darkness. The shadows pulsed with the rhythm of my heart. I was hot and cold, sweating and shivering with anxiety.

"Are you going to bite me?" I whispered, closing my eyes. The surrounding darkness was absolute, hiding him from me—everything but his touch. He licked me up the center, and his claws pricked my legs as he gripped them firmly. I cried out as his silken tongue tasted me, earning his growl of approval.

If he bit me, would it be like before? Those bites were shallow and teasing, although they stung like a bitch. The tension in his grip told me he was holding back. He answered me by nipping the skin of my inner thigh. I yelped, expecting the bite to be deeper than it was. His laugh rumbled through the darkness, and I felt it vibrating over me. Eliciting a throaty purr from me. The darkness felt like a second skin, and I couldn't even see my hand in front of me. The sound of my voice flattened as if it hit a stone wall.

"Nothing's getting in, nothing's getting out," he whispered.

The wings trilled, fanning us. The scent of our skin, our sweat, my blood swirled in the air. The scent of his arousal made me want to run my tongue over every inch of his body.

My body felt electric beneath his mouth. He nuzzled into me, taking my flesh between his teeth. Then licking away the sting. His breath passed over my center as he moved to the other side. I wanted to roll my hips into him, bring him closer, but I didn't. Because that was insane. Right? Right.

"He likes it," the Death Spirit purred again.

He continued licking and nibbling. Wandering back to the intersection of my thigh. My core ached to feel anything besides the pressure in my womb. Mild, cramping pain mixed with the ache of needing to be filled.

"I'm not afraid," I said, more to myself than to him, relaxing my legs. He growled against my apex in response. My core clenched, and I rolled my hips into his voice, his tongue.

I had the Grizzly King between my legs, ready to worship the very blood of my body. He was never afraid to take what he wanted. Maybe I shouldn't, but I wanted every wicked thing we could be in the darkness— and I wasn't afraid to take it either.

I reached my hand down, feeling for his hair, and twirled the soft, loose curls around my fingers. Not so gently, I led him where I wanted him. Shifting his weight, he followed. The wet warmth of his kiss massaged my most sensitive flesh, and my head rolled to the side. My fingers stayed knotted in his hair. He pulled back, letting the tip of his tongue alone stroke me up the middle.

I held my breasts tightly, massaging them as I looked down at him. Unable to see anything, but feeling everything his tongue did to me. I ran my feet against the sides of him, over his shoulders. Feeling the smooth expanse of his body as he luxuriated between my legs.

He dragged his tongue clear up my center again and brought a breathless sound out of me. I arced off the bed as his lips closed atop the apex of my thighs. Sucking it into his mouth. Nipping before he withdrew.

A moan shivered in my throat. He cursed against my wetness and ran his tongue downward. Pressed a hand against my lower abdomen. I lifted my hips and held him there with my hand. He slid his tongue straight into my core. My hand flew to cover my mouth.

He stopped—withdrawing his tongue.

"I want to hear you, Keres." He reached up and pulled my hand away as if he could see where I clamped it down on my mouth. He pressed my palm against my breast and kneaded it with me.

"Keep touching yourself like that. And like this." He brought my other hand down between my thighs with his. I ran my fingers over my sex, and they came away wet.

He grabbed my wrist and licked my fingers clean. My lips parted as his tongue swept against my skin. There was so much hunger in his touch. And then he touched the tip of my finger to the tip of his fang. Piercing it. The pressure built in my fingertip as he sucked it into his mouth.

I whimpered, and he put my hand against my sex again. My finger bled against my skin, and if I could, I'd see the red circles he made me trace around my sensitive peak before he moved my hand away and licked it clean.

He lowered back down and drove his tongue deeper inside me than before. The shock ran up into my core, and I whimpered. He pulled his tongue out and ran it up my middle again, flicking it over the bundle of nerves at the top. I moaned, and he flattened his tongue against me again, encouraged to cover as much of me with his mouth as he could.

Release was just out of reach, looming somewhere in the darkness, pulsing as frantically as the wings. He continued licking and sucking, rocking his head to add to the friction. I traced circles around my hardened nipples and pinched them, the way he did.

He dropped his attention lower again, pumping his tongue in and out of me for several breaths, roughly. His hot breath flared against me when he brought his other hand up and his finger entered me. Letting his tongue wander back up and down my center, he coaxed me deeper into the sensations.

Another finger curled inside me, beckoning me closer and closer. His tongue repeated short licks over my clitoris as his fingers worked inside me, in a steady rhythm. My core contracted around them.

"Yes," I said in a choked whisper. I rocked my body against his hand, bringing him deeper. His tongue kept its pace, strumming my center like a harp string, and pleasure reverberated through me.

He plunged his two fingers deeper, pulling them back out to the tips before diving back in. I heard my name on his lips, against my most sensitive flesh. Like a command I needed to obey. I let go and rode his hand, his tongue, and his lips with abandon. Shuddering as he growled against my skin.

Release shattered through me, and I bowed off the bed from the force of it. He became ravenous, feeding off my pleasure. His fangs sank under my skin, flanking my sex, and he didn't stop drinking my arousal until I collapsed again on the bed. Until my shredded voice went silent, and I was shivering from the shock waves that followed.

When he withdrew, the darkness went too. He wiped his mouth, streaking the red from his lips and licking his fingers. The gold and sapphire glow in his eyes washed over me. Watching as my body cooled. Listening as my heartbeat drifted back down into a sated rhythm. He moved off the bed and picked up his shirt.

"Nobody will ever revel in your body the way I can, little wolf." He licked the blood from his lower lip before biting it seductively. He offered me his shirt, that entrancing light in his eyes drawing me in.

"What are——" I didn't need a definition—I needed a name. "What do I call you?"

"In your blood, you know me. You don't have to ask what I am. You only have to accept me, as I accept you. As to what you may call me." He smiled. "I'll give you the name soon enough."

We stayed like that for a few breaths, holding each other's gaze. And then I reached out my scarred hand and took what he offered.

61: SELECTION

SILAS

We met in the Dark Hall.

Its walls were made from a black glass you couldn't see through, but within them shone flecks of silver like trapped stars. A long, dark wood table stretched from one end to the other. Burning candles dotted modest iron chandeliers. Their arms branched off in rays and poles, some gathered close, and some stretched out on their own. So that every candle held a place in what seemed to be a constellation.

The amber candlelight didn't chase away the shadows that wrapped around the room. Only leaned into them and breathed. Even the glow of the starlit walls did no more than cool the room with a gentle blue and silver light. It was as if someone laid a feast in the night sky.

That someone might have been Emeric.

The Headmaster of the Guild was also called Night Shade by some agents. Taking up space at the head of the table, dressed in his usual all black ensemble. A velvet, knee-length robe with silver thread. It matched his black and silver hair. Made his green eyes more dramatic. None of which mattered so long as he was smoking. A puff of gray smoke lived atop his shoulders, his pipe never out of reach. I could understand any man with vices.

It's why I kept my distance, choosing a seat near the exit. Aiko and Chiasa were seated closer to Emeric, not looking my way. My hair was disheveled, so I brushed it back with my fingers until I gave up and pulled my hood up. It was the alcohol on my breath that was the issue. If nobody talked to me, I could pass.

"Silas," was the first word out of Emeric's mouth.

A heavy hand clapped down on my shoulder—Indiro's. He pulled me up by the collar and spun me around, not letting me go. His gaze dropped from my hooded head to my black leather boots. He nudged me toward Emeric. His guidance was good enough to mask my unsteadiness. I focused on the swirling gray around Emeric's face. His blue eyes flashing in and out like lightning in a storm cloud.

"Headmaster," I said, catching my balance after Indiro shoved me forward.

He waved his hand, dispelling the smoke, and then laid down his pipe on the table.

"I already told you what Thane reported occurred in Wolvens. The Guild is prepared to take action against the group of terrorists your wife encountered."

"She's no longer my wife. Remember? Thane made a point of emphasizing that in his report."

"Well, she's still Resayla's daughter, still the Coroner, and we still need her back. While that's being handled—"

"Is it?" I asked. Short on thought, short on respect. "An ancillary band of the King's own men abducted her. Taken to be sold, like a pelt. Right out from under the King's nose, and then she got away from your Man— who's now back to sulking instead of going after her."

"Mind yourself, lad." Indiro's hand dug into my shoulder again.

"We don't need to rehash this, Silas. You're twisting the information they gave us. Shadows do not dilute knowledge with pretentiousness and emotion. We accept it and use it. What you need to know is that the people Keres encountered were only a few of a larger organization— known as the Jewelers. They service the wealthy of Falmaron. Their product is flesh, although they probably meant to ransom her. We are going to end them. Unless you'd rather go drink another bottle or two."

I glared up at him, my jaw tightening. "What's the plan, then?"

"Aiko has requested we hold this meeting to discuss it," he said, gesturing toward my mentor.

My eyes met his, and my stomach burned. The way he was looking at

me hit harder than Indiro's words ever could. But his sister beside him...
she wore her thoughts all over her face. I looked away. I didn't want to
see their faces. Their hopes or disappointments. Just as much as I didn't
want sobriety. Not now, not yet. How could I? With everything going
on...

Keres was abducted. Again. Rumors flitted around Aureum that she
was engaged to the Grizzly King. First, she was stolen by the enemy.
Next, set to marry him. Then, taken by other Humans. Evaded Thane's
rescue. Returned to her mad King. Was I really supposed to care about
this trafficker gang? My own problems weren't just going to disappear.
Making use of my time, fighting someone else's battle, wasn't going to
change that.

If only we could go back to before all of this. Back to our wedding
night. Back to the night before the fire. Back to the night when the nine
went out to scout and got killed. I'd been drinking and imagining all the
ways that our stories would be different if that night—if everything were
different.

What if Keres had been the tenth? Like she was supposed to be.
Maybe the nine wouldn't have died. Darius would have Hayes. Liriene
would have Katrielle. And maybe I'd have her. Or maybe Keres would
have died with them. If she had, who knows what would have happened
to the rest of us. You can't raise a glass to the future, but you can throw
back glass after glass for yesterday and today's sake. So, I did. For the last
couple of nights in a row, since hearing about Keres' mess in Wolvens.

The woman I'd married was as desired as she was dangerous. Both
the predator and the prey. Damage followed Keres. In the Sunderlands.
In the Baore. In the Ressid.

In our clan. Hishmal. Ro'Hale Palace. Wolvens. The Nine. Me.
Darius. Liriene.

I rubbed at my face. It always came down to her.

"Silas." Emeric's voice snapped me out of it.

I stared blankly at him.

"You will prepare yourself for the mission. Go."

Indiro's hand yanked me back, steering me from the hall and toward the barracks. Aiko met us along the way, and I was passed into his guardianship. Chiasa followed close behind.

"I thought you needed to be part of that meeting," I said over my shoulder.

"You need a meeting," Aiko said roughly.

We pushed past the last doors that let out into the atrium we usually spent time in. The sparring mat was to the right. The low table took up the middle of the room. Pillows and fur throws strewn around it on the floor. Past that were the pantry cabinets—one holding liquor that I'd pilfered earlier. I'd left the glass door open, apparently. Spilled a little. Aiko eyed it in disgust. My used glass was on the counter. He shoved me toward the pillows on the ground. I caught myself on my hands and knees. Chiasa let out a soft gasp.

"Get up," Aiko barked.

I rolled myself over and looked up at the spinning ceiling.

"You're the one who pushed me down." I chuckled and rubbed my head.

Chiasa stood over me and I closed my eyes to avoid her. Aiko made himself busy straightening up the cabinet. Cursing under his breath. Guess I'd spilled more than a little.

"I said, get up," he repeated sometime later. A boot nudged against mine. I peeled an eye open and met his golden stare. It reminded me of the Gryphon, King Arias, that visited the clan. Who told Keres to leave me to go to the castle.

"Fuck you," I said.

Aiko ran his hands through his long brown hair and then tied it up in a bun. Then bent down to lift me up under the arms.

"Agh, why?" I protested. My skull throbbed.

"Because you can't stay on the floor, Silas," he muttered. He helped me sit at the table, pushed a plate full of bread and cheese in front of me, and then sat down across from me. Chiasa sat on the side of us, watching me pick at the food.

"Eat," she insisted.

I kept my eyes on the plate and listened. A lecture was coming, I knew it.

"Silas," Aiko breathed.

I lifted my eyes and found him also staring at my plate, watching my fingers dally there.

"Aiko?" I replied.

He looked up at me, his brows tightening together. "I have a plan."

Chiasa whipped her head around and asked her brother, "What plan?"

"Interesting," I said and took a bite of the bread. "I had an idea too."

He raised a brow at me, and her head swiveled again. I tilted my head toward her but kept my eyes on him.

"These men are seeking and selling women, no? What about using Chi as a ruse? Drawing them in and then infiltrating them. We'll get her back, of course."

His knuckles whitened, and the muscles in his jaw feathered. "Use my sister as bait?"

"Don't get so sensitive over it. It's just a trick. Chi can handle herself. We just set it up so that she's taken and—"

"No," Chi snapped. We both looked at her.

"Absolutely not," Aiko agreed with her.

I shrugged and rolled my eyes.

"You've suggested making Chiasa a target. Potentially subjecting her to harsh treatment. Did you think because she is female, she should be the one to play the victim in this scheme?" Aiko asked.

She folded her arms across her chest, watching my face for a reaction. I gave her a smile. "I didn't mean it like that. You'd never be the victim."

"That's the problem," she said and shook her head. "I could be. If your wife, who is the mistress of Death, could fall prey to these monsters, who are you to say it would be safe for me?"

"Well, no one said it would be safe," I chided.

"It's too risky," Aiko snapped. "She is not expendable. But if you're sure it will work, I'd rather select you for the job. Think you could play a victim?"

"Well, wait." I sat forward and held my hands up. "You said you had a plan earlier. What was it?"

"Ah," he sighed. "There it is."

"What?" I asked incredulously. "You just said it was too risky."

"You seem to think only females are targeted and abducted. Unfortunately, these men target anyone they see as vulnerable. Evil doesn't care."

I crossed my arms in front of my chest and glowered at him.

He made a tsking sound. "To be bait, you'd have to be alluring, and right now, you're more trouble than you're worth."

His eyes traveled over me, and so did Chiasa's.

"So?" I pushed.

"So…" He smirked. "We're going to get you prettied up, and then we're going to get you drunk."

The liquor splashed into the glass, swirling around the bottom and swimming toward the brim. The reflection of my eyes drowned inside it.

"You look noble enough. Now drink," Aiko ordered.

I flashed my eyes at Chiasa, who only blushed and looked away. From the moment I stepped out of my room, she was looking at me like that.

"I am a knight, Aiko. Noble-blooded. But by the Gods, are these pants tight—too tight? I feel stuffed."

"You need to feel stuffed. Pompous. And drunk. Get going on that liquor."

I held the glass up to my lips and watched him, watching me take a sip. It washed down my throat with welcomed warmth. One swallow after another, until the glass was empty. I pushed it back toward Aiko for a refill.

"You realize you're banking your entire plan on a drunk, right?"

"I'm banking on mortal nature. You'll play the part of the wealthy nobleman, traveling alone at night, unfortunately under the influence."

"I still don't understand why I have to be actually drunk to do this. Can't I just act drunk?"

"Refusing the drink?" He asked and held out the refilled glass, his face a cool, unreadable mask.

"If it makes me useful to you, then no. I'm not refusing," I said. So, I drank.

He went over the plan, and we put it into motion… it couldn't have gone any worse.

62: SINGED
DARIUS

Out of all the things I could have expected to happen, I got a letter. More like a summons to the Kingdom of Serin. Signed by a Ser Bryon and Lady Isabelle. The courier who delivered it was still standing there.

"Are you expecting a tip?" I asked, raising my eyes from the letter.

"No, sir. It's just—sorry, sir."

"Then I bid you safe travels back to wherever you came from. If I had the coin to spare, I'd offer you a bonus, but I don't. Curse of the soldier's purse." I grinned.

His face blanched, and he turned to leave. "Of course, sir. Good day."

I tracked his steps as he fled. Noting the lingering audience of soldiers around us. Every move I made dimmed their conversations, turned their heads. During the few days after I'd last argued with the General, their attention grew bolder. Early this morning, Epona invited herself into my tent. Checking on things. Blushed because I was shirtless. Cut me a glare and then walked out.

This summons couldn't have been more of a relief.

Fire from my core singed my skin. It seemed like every day a new angry red line traced over my back, shoulders, and limbs. My chest bore a molten gash right over my heart. An abrupt break right beneath my lower lip. Nothing was as bad as the color tinging my irises. These things would never go unnoticed again.

All Daemons are born with smoldering gray in their eyes. Some bear darker shades than others. When our cores mature, that changes. Color indicates power and status. High born Daemons are called the Wyrm

Born. Hayes and I weren't pure blooded, but after looking in the mirror, I knew we certainly weren't Ember Born, which was the lowest caste of Fire Daemons.

My suspicions were being confirmed. First, by the intensity of my maturation, the aggression I felt. The breaks in my skin. Now, the color of my eyes. Only Wyrm Born had auras like the one I was developing. Another thing weighed heavily on my mind: my true name, Penance. My mother gave Hayes and me two names each. Told us they were gifts and never to use them. Hayes was better at keeping his to himself than I was. Legiance.

We were so far removed from Daemon culture, I basically flouted it. So, I spoke my name. Wrong people heard it in Massara. The right people heard it in Ro'Hale. Now that I was realizing I was a descendant of dragon-blooded Daemons, I wasn't ready for any more people to learn my true name.

The only thing that made little sense were my brother and I's two rules.

Don't wake it up. Don't let it win.

She'd passed them onto us, but if she knew were Wyrm Born, she should have known either would be inevitable. This transformation couldn't be lulled to sleep or subdued. Answers existed only in my memories of the readings we did. I rehearsed them in my mind. Schooling myself into believing in what I was.

Low caste Ember Born Daemons, at full maturity, are better suited for creative use of their power. Industrial, if anything. And if I was remembering my books correctly, their eyes gained ruddy hues. Then there were the middle castes whose eyes were colored anywhere from crimson to claret. These were the keepers. Usually held powerful presences in the political realm.

Wyrm Born dominated in the military. Our eyes were considered the most beautiful, the rarest. To me, the most terrifying. When you've got red eyes, I'm sure you attract attention. People look at you and realize, oh, shit—your eyes are red. A conversation starter. Common enough to see. When people look at you and realize, *oh, shit, your eyes look like they're on fire*, that's a different story.

Fire Opal.

That's what I've found in my reflection. The eyes of a dragon. Reddish-orange now streaked through the gray, most visible when you looked at me dead on. As light hit my eyes, the colors shifted through a spectrum of gold, green, and blue. Some of the gray I was used to was still dark as it was, but now interrupted by faint lines of silver.

I only knew so much about it because Hayes and I were obsessed with this one book about a time when Wyrm Born were hunted. Their eyes were gouged out and sold. Like some fucking treasure hunt. Blew my mind because they were as hard to kill as some dragons, but hunts persisted. Fire Opal eyes fetch a high price.

Perusing my memories of books I'd read as a kid got me thinking. Epona was a Water Daemon. Her eyes were still only the typical shade of violet that was natural to Rift Dwellers. If it all worked the same, it meant her Spirit hadn't yet matured. Judging by her looks, she must have been nineteen or twenty.

Briefly, I wondered whether her transformation would look anything like mine. Would her power break through her skin, show in her eyes? What was in the core of a Water Daemon, and did it ever come out to play?

If I wasn't incensed by her, I'd probably ask.

I lowered my gaze and continued toward the General's tent, taking my time in walking there.

I wondered how the people in Serin would react when they saw what I was. As I walked into her tent, her eyes met mine. I had to give her credit for it, and hope that nobody in Serin would overreact. Like Yona did. Every time she looked at me, she winced. I rolled my eyes at her and focused on the Queen of Swords.

"I got a letter," I said, tossing it on the table in front of her. She was bundled in a fur blanket with her knees tucked to her chest. A cup of tea warming her hands.

Reminding me winter was coming. Reminding me I couldn't feel it anymore.

465

Yona hadn't layered on any extra clothing, and I wondered if the weather affected her less because of her own Daemon Spirit. She'd let her long, curly hair down, too.

"So, you'll go to Serin," Vyra said after reading it.

"Is that a question or an agreement?" I asked.

"Well, I can't stop you. You're not one of my men."

"He's hardly a man at all," Epona muttered under her breath.

I flashed my eyes at her. "Perhaps you'd like me to convince you otherwise."

Her cheeks flushed and my smirking didn't help. The General's thoughts seemed faraway. Usually, she stuck up for her lackey, but both of them quieted. I plucked my summons off the table and folded it.

"I know you'll miss me, but don't worry. I won't be back."

Both of them snapped their attention back to me. Vyra snorted.

"You think King Alezander will want to keep you in Serin? You'll be sent right back here once they're done with you."

"Maybe I'll go to Golsyn. Live among Elves, where I belong."

"You're not Elven as they are," she said in a low, taunting voice. "Every day that becomes more obvious. What you are is written on your skin. Fire dances in your eyes. Queen Toril may be a tolerant woman, but she won't tolerate your mood swings. You belong on the front lines. Both of them will see that and send you back."

I sighed and rolled my head to the side, waiting for her lecture to continue. She narrowed her eyes.

"Oh, you're done now?"

A strong brow quirked up. Still, I couldn't help noticing her eyes were duller.

"What's wrong?" I asked.

Both brows shot up at that. "Nothing."

Out of the corner of my eye, I noticed Epona's gaze hitched between us. Dropped to the table and then darted back up to the General.

I looked down at the map she'd been studying when I walked in. The Horn of Ceden, which used to be crowned with a white tower, was now weighed down by a black pyramidal marker. Ever since the fortress fell to the Ashan, she'd been on edge. Anger. Hollow desperation. Regret. Grief. Just a few of the flavors a losing army palleted. She was losing her appetite for the fight. Maybe if she hadn't wasted her energy on me and mustered her forces instead, she wouldn't be sitting here clutching a cup of tea and shivering.

"The pathetic look in your eyes says otherwise," I said.

Her stare tightened on me again, and her lips pressed together.

"Not even going to retort? Damn, something really is wrong with you." I leaned forward on the table. Epona's weight shifted over her feet as I drew closer to the General.

"Relax, Yona. I'm not going to bite her."

She also swallowed a response.

"Pestilence," Vyra muttered at me and lifted her mug between us. Took another sip of her cooling tea. Her face scrunched up.

"Gimme," I said and took the cup from her. My sleeves were rolled up to my elbows, so she watched the fiery lines tracing my forearms flare. Between my palms, warmth engulfed her mug. When steam lolled over the brim again, I placed it on the table, stealing another glance at the map. She took her tea back, sampled it, and the tension in her face eased a little.

"Figure out what to do about Ceden yet?" I asked, pursing my lips at the map.

She shook her head.

"Why should you care anyway?" Epona grumbled.

I pulled back and turned to go. "Whatever, Yona."

Footsteps followed me out into the cold. Snow was falling again. I looked over my shoulder just as Yona reached up and grabbed my shirt. Spinning me back toward her.

"You should leave *now*," she snarled.

Some of the soldiers around us stopped. Eying the hand that still clutched my shirt. I kept my hands at my side but stepped even closer to her. Looking down my nose at her.

"Come with me," I whispered huskily.

A flurry of emotion shifted through her expression. Ending on shock. I laughed and plucked her fist off of me like a piece of lint.

She crossed her arms in front of her chest.

"You're a piece of work, Yona."

"Ugh," she grunted. Her hands shot down at her sides, fists balling. The snow falling around us froze midair. Shaping a globe of white around us. As more flakes landed, they speckled the view of the other soldiers. Until it enclosed us in a sphere of ice.

It reminded me of what Keres did when we were in the river. Making a shield around us out of the water to protect against Silas' arrows and carry us on the current.

"Listen," she hissed. "I know you think that because your Daemon Spirit is awakening, your behavior is excusable. But that's not good enough for me. You're volatile. Untrustworthy. A firestorm waiting to happen. You've been nothing but disrespectful and cowardly since you stepped foot in the Moldorn—don't interrupt me." She held up her hand.

"If you stay in Serin or go anywhere else, good. Go. Stay there. If they send you back, I'll be waiting. My patience has worn out. If you think I'm going to forget how you've treated our men, our cause, and my General, you're dead wrong. My Daemon Spirit will awaken soon enough. Then we'll be an even match."

I just looked at her with wide eyes. Her usual pout reclaimed her lips, the winter chill in her glare. It drew a breath out of me, which puffed between us like smoke. Drawing her attention across my shoulders and down my chest, following the trail of steam that poured over my body. Down to the melted snow beneath my feet. Her violet eyes flicked back up to my face.

"If the day comes when you want to bet your skin against mine, cold-blooded girl, I'll be just as ready for it." I smirked and reached up to the ceiling of our little frozen world. My forefinger met the ice with a sizzle. In seconds, the entire globe evaporated.

Once again, we were under watchful eyes. Mumbled conversations carried toward us, and I realized just how close we were standing. I tapped the same finger under her chin, and she stepped back. So, I turned to go. No need for any more lectures or goodbyes.

63: SCALDING
DARIUS

When I was packing my things to leave, I found Emisandre's gift. The slender, short stick she called Pophis. Remembered the kiss she gave me with it. I smiled at the memory of a jealous Keres. Fiery little thing. A quick laugh bubbled out of me, thinking about it. She had more fire in her core than any Wyrm Born Daemon ever could. My smile faded, but the memory didn't. That woman turned me into a torch. Lit me up and left me to burn. I was glad, though. At least I got to light up someone's world. Even if it was only for a little while.

Traveling along the wall on horseback gave me plenty of time to think about her.

The snow was her hair. The trees dotting the horizon, the green of her eyes. The wicked length of my journey, as painful as the waiting for her to admit she wanted me. The wanting, and on the other side of it, the moment I drove myself deep inside her. Gods, my body ached just thinking about it. That ache was fading, too. Replaced by hollowness. In the turmoil of my transformation, the thought of loving her was like a chill down the spine. Grounding until it was numbing. I didn't want to stop wanting her, but I wanted to stop hurting.

Distance put differences between us, and it forced me to recognize them. For all we had in common, there was something glaring. She was a work of divinity. We came from the same humble beginnings, but she was never truly like me. Or anyone around us.

The way Vyra treated me, as if I were an answer to her problems, made me think about Keres. The Coroner. An answer to bigger problems. I could take down a very-hard-to-kill enemy. She could probably end the war.

At some point or another, our relationship would have become a lower priority than her purpose. Which was absolutely fine. She was resurrected in Mrithyn's image. No debating that.

Witnessing the war here in the Moldorn, remembering when the Heralds first came to our clan and bid her to go to the palace. Everything she did was furthering her purpose. Every human she killed, every secret she uncovered. Every argument she won. Even what she asked of me. It all happened for a reason. She was on a path ordained by the Gods. With bigger obstacles.

I believed in her more than I loved her.

Wherever she was, whatever choices she was making, I knew she'd further her purpose. She'd stay true to herself, the fire within her.

Vyra was crumbling under the pressure of fighting in a losing battle. I was crumbling under pressures of my own, but my faith in Keres was unshakable. She'd do the right thing. She was made to change this world, and maybe I was supposed to be where she started. I'd like to think I set her free to a degree—when it came to Silas. But she's really the one who changed me. She left, yes, but she left me with lessons. Her choice was rooted in belief, too. A desire to protect me overwhelmed her desire to keep me for herself.

I will never take a chance on losing you, she said.

I told her I'd never stop needing to find her. Swore we'd be together. Thought life would be different. We'd conquer anything that stood in our way and keep fighting for each other. I promised. I wasn't ready to break that promise.

Maybe one day, I could bring a candle into her world. Be a light for her along her way once more. I wasn't ready to believe I couldn't. With all the silence between me and my destination, I felt no shame in uttering a short, simple prayer for her, to whatever God was listening.

Day Thirty-Two

Queen Toril and King Alezander ruled individually, but their kingdoms relied heavily on each other. As if they were a couple living in separate houses. Both of them had a circle of trusted councilors, consisting of both Elves and Humans. I soon learned that Ser Bryon was a Knight, and also the King's closest friend.

I followed the summons' directions to his estate and was welcomed in. Fed and allowed to rest. I kept my sleeves rolled down, but I couldn't hide my eyes or the burning scar on my lip.

As he informed me of his relationships in court, he mentioned his daughters who waited on Queen Hero in Ro'Hale. I'd met one of them. Moriya, Silas' pet. She was there when I arrived and there when I left. Alongside Silas' mother, Seraphina. I was curious about what happened with all that.

I mentioned to Ser Bryon that I'd met her, and for a minute sadness touched his eyes. He said through some strange turn of events, Moriya and Faye were taken ill and lying in. Nadia, his third daughter, had sent a letter to him about me. On behalf of Osira.

"Yeah, I know who she is," I huffed when he asked. "What did she say?"

He hesitated. "I wonder... what is your relationship with the Coroner?"

I ran a finger over the scar at my lower lip and watched his brown eyes follow the movement.

"What do you mean?" The corner of my mouth lifted. "She's a Goddess among my people and I, like everybody else, am a believer."

He dropped his gaze. "Yes, I understand. Well, very interesting news has reached the Moldorn. The council isn't happy about it—nobody is. The Oracle thinks the Coroner is in danger. The rest of the world can't make sense of the situation."

"What situation?"

"She's engaged to marry King Berlium."

64: STUNNER

Keres

Day Twenty-Four

Silence had opened a gap between us. Our gazes crossed over it occasionally. As his lips opened for a mouthful of breakfast, I glared at him. Watched him chew and heard him swallow.

"What do you want, little wolf?"

"I want you to exercise some self-control... with me."

He nearly choked on his food, and then roared with laughter. I waited for it to pass. His eyes widened as he realized I was being completely serious.

"And," I said before he could get a word in, "I want you to—"

"Be careful with all that wanting, my girl." His eyes sparkled, the delicate tips of his fangs dropping like a hint.

I swallowed.

"I meant—I just think it'd be best if we focused on matters at hand." I'd spoken with my hand, gesturing at nothing in particular. His eyes tracked the movement, the ring on my finger.

"You, my betrothed, want to live chastely. In my bed, nightly."

"You're the one forcing me to sleep in your bed," I reminded him.

"You seem to quite enjoy it." His gaze lifted to meet mine. Even the way he ate his food was erotic. I was being suffocated by his... his sexiness. The way he looked at me last night—what he said.

Accept me, as I have accepted you.

It made me want to drop to my knees and worship his cock the way he'd done for me. He took nothing last night except his time—and my blood. His reward was my pleasure and then we went to sleep.

Just accept it.

My logical brain kept trying to convince me to accept him. The understanding of what he was lived deep in some dark corner of my mind—where my fears lived. It was there, and I just needed to accept it because it would not budge. This was what he was. A devilish man with a mind made for war and a mouth made for the unholy worship of blood.

Self-control was antithetical to his nature—but not to mine, no matter how much I wished it was when he was around. I wanted to feel as reckless as I did in the dark, at all times, with him. I wanted to be focused and feral, but I couldn't be both.

"You've been my true enemy all my life, Berlium. The power of your seduction, the tricks of your magic, makes it hard to remember that sometimes." I lifted my chin.

"Tricks," he scoffed. "You think I've been tricking you?"

I bit my lip, thinking before replying. Holding his sapphire stare as he leaned forward, folding his hands on the table. Once, his kiss tasted of blood and honey—a sensation born of magic...

"No," I admitted.

It wasn't a trick anymore. Even so, I was falling for it. I was acquiring an appetite for things I shouldn't want. Things that should make me sick. A growing need for him was dangerous. More dangerous than wanting ever could be. Or so I told myself, but every minute I spent staring into his eyes, it sounded like nonsense. Which was the problem.

"You told me I had to convince you that my surrender wasn't a game. You demanded I confess I was yours. I've given you my word and accepted you. I've fed you." I held up my hand, flashing the ring at him. "Now, it's your turn, bear. This revolution you speak of. My people have a place in it, as I have a place at your side. I want you to show me the inner workings."

The rules of this game were bending and blurring, but one thing was clear to me. We were still on opposite sides, towing the line. I still had a goal. He wanted me to be a weapon, and he wanted to bury his cock in me—write his name on my insides. I wanted to carve my name into his kingdom. I would not let him fill me up with fire and shadow. I was going to show him what it felt like to drown.

His mouth curved. I tilted my head and matched his taunting smirk.

A breath later, the door burst open. Ciel barreled into the room, shredding the tension with the flurry of her hands. "Sire," she said and bowed. Rising back up, her gaze passed frantically between us. Back and forth, but no words came to follow.

"What?" we both snapped.

"She's here. Magister Hadriel's cousin has come again to visit."

His face blanched, and he stood from his seat. His mouth opened to answer, but before he could, another figure appeared in the doorway behind Ciel. This time I stood.

"Ah, Lady Keres," she said in her sing-song, sultry voice.

"Little witch," I said as our eyes met, and I closed the distance between me and the King.

She lifted her upturned nose and her giant blue eyes flared beneath her arched brows. Her wavy blond hair was loose around her shoulders.

"You two know each other?" Berlium asked, his gaze jumping between our glares.

"She owes me her life, actually," I said, watching her every move.

"Oh, please, nothing so dramatic as that," she crooned and walked closer to us. A sly smile playing at her lips, her hips swaying with every step. Her long blue dress, marked with silver stitching—it was immodest, of course, but simple. Cascading down her slender frame to her bare feet. Despite the winter, she'd traveled as any Elf would. I only then noticed Ciel was holding her shawl. A black fur pelt.

"Keres slayed a monster, saving me and my friends. In Trethermore Glade."

Berlium's weight shifted over his feet, toward her, as she drew nearer to him. I slid my hand up his arm, reeling his attention back. She noticed. Standing before us, she looked from my eyes to his mouth. As if she wanted to kiss him, just as she had kissed Darius. As if she already had before and wanted to do it again and again.

Your woman will not like this, but then again, she's not your woman.

That's what she'd said to Darius right before she stole his kiss. I'd let it happen then.

Now, I knew what kind of woman she was, and she was going to learn what kind of woman I was. Berlium lifted his arm and stretched it around me, bringing me closer by the waist. She noticed that too.

I leaned into him and purred, "Well, we're not in the Sunderlands anymore."

"No." Emisandre's smile widened. "We aren't."

◙◙ ◙◙ ◙◙

Hadriel seemed just as displeased to see his cousin as I was. We all sat at the table, glaring at her. Except the King, whose face was placid. I was learning what that meant: the smooth surface of unbroken water with trouble boiling underneath.

"Emisandre, what are you doing here?" Hadriel asked, clipping each word.

Her eyes flitted over me and then back to her cousin, and her mouth tightened.

"Am I not allowed to visit my cousin and… my King." She looked at Berlium.

I didn't follow her gaze, instead listening to his steady heart rate. It divulged nothing. No kick of interest.

"Are you Baorean, then?" I asked. "How are you two cousins—you're Elven?"

"My, my. You've got quite the sense of entitlement to knowledge. Am I Elven?" She shot me a glance and brushed her hair back behind her ear. Revealing the delicate peak. Her ears certainly weren't round. Elven ears could all be different sizes and degrees of sharpness. Mine were average, maybe sharper than Liriene's, but not as sharp as my parents'. Emisandre's were blunter but didn't seem less Elven.

"I'm mixed," she said. "My father was Elven, and my mother was Human. Hadriel is my cousin on her side. Unlike Hadriel, though, yes, I'm Baorean. I was born in Massara."

Like Darius.

"The Massara Clan is in the Sunderlands—"

475

"Oh, that's right. You're a clan girl."

I looked at her incredulously.

"You need to brush up on your history, Coroner."

My temper flared. I was only interested in making her history.

"Enough petty conversation. We both know you're not here to visit. Tell me what you want, Emisandre," Hadriel said.

"Well, I'd kill for some wine."

Berlium nodded at Ciel, who then evaporated from the room.

"And a bit of privacy, cousin," she said in a low, warning voice.

The King and I exchanged glances. He rose from his seat, and I followed.

"My lady and I will afford you that," he said, taking my hand. "We have dirtier things to discuss than your secrets."

I was able to hold in a laugh until we got into the hallway and the door shut behind us.

"Hush," he said, pressing his finger to his sensuous lips. "Now, come."

He led me down the hall, through a door, and around a corner. As we neared another door, he looked at the light leaking out from under it. Voices carried. I held my breath, listening for the hurried, harsh muttering on the other side.

"Oh, Hades," Emisandre cooed. "We both know it was you."

"Emi, please. Don't pester me with frivolous accusations."

Berlium and I watched each other's faces as we listened.

"Frivolous?" Her voice heightened, shrill and tight. "You think I traveled all this way, through a blizzard, no less, just to fling an idle fancy at you?"

"Speaking of," he spoke again, ignoring her question. "How did you get away from the others, your apostate friends."

She harrumphed. "Famon and Diomora were diverted. The council called them away for a report. Only Iantharys stayed by me, but I convinced her I was going to visit family and nothing more. She stayed behind."

"So, nobody knows you're here in Dale."

"Everybody's too distracted by your mess," she hissed. "Queen

Hero's court was in disarray after the Coroner left, but it's still unclear what happened. Rumors, rumors, rumors. Like mosquitoes at the ear. The council hates rumors. I know that's what you intended to feed them by having us trapped under watch of your pet."

"Pet?" he spat the word.

"You were always so fond of the Gnorrer and its poison. Anything that plays tricks on the mind, right, cousin?"

"Coincidence." He pushed her accusation away. I heard pacing footsteps. "A Gnorrer in the Sunderlands is nothing rare along the border. Qu'un, Bael, and Lamentar are all right across the Rift from Ro'Hale. It could have come from under the mountains or any of those places and I doubt it was the only one."

"Well, it's funny you said that, because there are other rumors."

A pause. Too long of a pause.

Berlium and I looked down at the two shadows blocking the light under the door. Feet. I shot a look back up at him, and his hand came between us. As if to steady me. He narrowed his eyes, and I held my breath again, listening. Waiting.

"Emisandre." Hadriel's voice scratched against the door. "There is only one person in this golden world who hates rumors more than the council." His footsteps retreated.

"You'd love this one," she sighed. "It's about your other pet."

Berlium's jaw tightened, and his delicious lips pressed together. His eyes lingered on mine.

"Queen Hero."

Hadriel didn't rise to her taunting.

"They say she revealed something to the Coroner, or should I say, someone."

Still, he didn't react.

"A Lamentar." Emisandre dropped the word.

My mind went back to that last day in court—to the Lamentar singing her terrible song. A voice both like a silver needle in the ear, and like an iron fist through crystal.

"They say she's harboring Illynads," Emisandre said.

"Is she? Wouldn't that be pertinent information for you apostates to gather and report back to the council?"

"It's just a rumor. Unverified. Those closest to the queen won't talk. The Elistrian Ambassador at her heel is loyal. Her guards are loyal. Her own ladies-in-waiting were rotting in a cell. Except one, who's missing."

Nadia.

I schooled my expression as Berlium's eyes wandered over my face. His hand came up to my shoulder, traced my collarbone. His touch demanded a reaction from my body. The hairs on the back of my neck stood, as if in obedience.

"Keres was there that day. I don't think she'd have a problem confirming the truth."

I tried to be like him, not reactive. It didn't feel natural, and I think he realized it meant I was hiding the hint. I did know the truth, and he could see that I did.

"Keres hasn't talked about her first time in Ro'Hale," Hadriel mused. "But the King told me about the interesting things that occurred when they recently visited."

"Take that into consideration, cousin. The only hard facts we have to report are that clans are falling to the Dalis. I can now confirm the rumors that the Coroner and the Grizzly King are in allegiance. The Council and the Imperium will find that very interesting. The Heralds are on the prowl. In fact, King Arias is extremely concerned about this alleged betrothal. All eyes are on the Sunderlands, the Baore, and the Moldorn. It's become very obvious that the border is compromised—that the Baore is stronger than ever."

Berlium watched my eyes widen with realization, and the corner of his mouth lifted. My stare pressed into his, but he revealed nothing more.

"Now, what will you do? Question Keres or harass the King?" Hadriel muttered. "Berlium won't allow you two to be alone, and the way things are between them, I don't think she'd let you near him either."

"Well, well. Is it love or power that binds them so tightly?" she scoffed.

The King's sapphire and honey gaze dropped to my mouth, and he ran his hand up from my shoulder. I narrowed my eyes at him as his fingers pressed into my skin where he'd bitten me. I felt the touch between my legs where his other bite marks were still sore.

Hadriel answered, "There is no room for love in the King's world. Only power."

"So, she's just another Herrona," she said.

My pulse halted—traitorously. Berlium's quickened as he looked into my eyes and shook his head. Which set my heart racing to catch up with his. He traced a finger over my lip, across my cheek, to push my hair behind my ears.

"No," Hadriel said again, quieter this time. "There was only one Herrona. Nobody is like Keres except the King. I've seen what she is— she's shown us what she is."

"In all his years, he's desired many women. Broken them all for power or pleasure. If she falls in love with him, she'll end up the same," Emisandre sneered, not hiding the jealousy in her voice.

"It isn't love or even lust, for power or pleasure. They are a cataclysmic match."

In one swift, silent motion, Berlium pushed me back against the wall beside the door. His breath played in my hair as he leaned in closer, bracing himself on either side of me. My hands went to his hips, then his chest. Stopping below his collarbone.

Refusing to lift my face as his mouth slanted against mine. Refusing to give him the kiss he sought. He pressed closer, and I lifted my hands into his hair, pushing his head back. We locked eyes. I taunted him with a smile. Allowed him to bow close again. He brought hands back to my shoulders. I turned my head and tried not to hum with pleasure as he kissed my neck.

"Tease," he murmured.

His hand dropped, and he grabbed me between the legs. A bolt of lightning shot through me, turning me to glass. One more try, and my resistance would shatter. His other hand pinned mine to the wall. I looked at him and hissed. Pissed off that I was so enraptured by the slow, enticing curve of his mouth.

Hushed whispers carried on in the room, but I couldn't hear them over the roaring in my veins. His hand roughly massaged my sex through the dress I was wearing. Dragging my breath out of me. I tilted my chin upward in silent defiance, but he loved that I was baring my throat to him. One thought of his fangs sent my pulse soaring between my legs in that sickeningly delicious way it really shouldn't.

He bit at my jaw and brushed his lips against my neck, earning a small sound from me.

"No howling, little wolf," he whispered against my skin. "Do you want to get caught?"

I shook my head and closed my eyes as he licked my throat up to my ear.

"What was that you said earlier? About not wanting me... or something?" he asked in a voice like velvet and then nipped at my earlobe.

"I said—" I gasped. His free hand turned my face toward his, and his mouth covered my next words.

His tongue passed over my lips and then against mine. I wanted to touch him, but trying to pull free was useless. He was stronger, meaner. To prove it, he slid my hands higher up the wall. Bringing me to the balls of my feet. Closer to him. His other dropped again, lifting my dress until he could touch my center.

His hand grazed against the panties I was wearing, finding the neatly packed cloth there to absorb the blood. He pushed both aside and entered me with his fingers. Leading me through the dance of the kiss until it was a duel. The heel of his hand massaged my apex while his fingers curled and pulsed inside me. Bathing in the red heat.

With my eyes closed, with the way his mouth took mine, my mind replayed the words Hadriel said. A cataclysmic match. He certainly tasted like ruination. I bit his lip and then released it. Lifting my mouth to his, offering more than I should be. And he took it hungrily. Took a soft moan right out of my mouth. Took the breath I had after it. Then he took his fingers out of me and sucked them off in front of my face. The blue of his eyes shimmered with gold, like sunlight on the water. He crushed his mouth against mine, forcing the taste of my blood into my mouth, mingled with honey of his.

He pulled back and looked at the door. My eyes followed. He readjusted my panties—not missing the opportunity to caress me. The voices had died down. Had they heard us? He lowered my arms, but kept my hand in his, and led me back the way we came.

Slowly. We padded down the carpeted hall, listening and looking both ways. As if this weren't his castle. Once the way was clear, we stopped and looked at each other. I pulled my hand out of his.

"Gods almighty," I said, and pushed my hand through my hair. He reached for me, but I stepped back.

"Wait a minute. Stop." I turned away and then just as quickly spun back toward him. "You see?" I flared my hands out at my sides and then gestured between us. "This."

"This," he repeated.

"I need to get away from you—to think for a damn moment. To be reminded of something."

I pushed past him, and he didn't follow, but someone else did. Yarden.

I'd totally forgotten he was present. Hadn't even seen him when we left the dining room. I raked my eyes over him. He'd swapped out this suit of armor for something more casual, a collection of wool and cotton and leather. His sword stayed by his side.

"And where have you been all this time?" I asked over my shoulder.

"Minding my business, Lady Keres."

I rolled my eyes, picking up the hem of my dress so I could walk faster. "Right." I stopped in the hall that led to the suites and turned around and faced him.

"Are you going to your bedroom?" he asked, uncertainty slowing his steps.

"Well," I said, "first, I want to change. And then, please accompany me to the museum."

We stopped by Berlium's room, and I raided his closet for one of his tunics. Then, stopped by mine for trousers, and I changed. I relished the scent on his shirt. Added a wool cloak and boots to my outfit. Then returned to Yarden's side.

"Are you sure you don't want to take some time in your room? To be alone, my lady? You know I'll stand by you, out here." He glanced over his shoulder as if the King were right behind him. I nodded and started walking.

"I appreciate that, Yarden, but I'm sure."

We hadn't spoken since we'd gotten separated in Mannfel. He was at the King's side when they came to Wolvens, but that was the point. He was the *King's* Cerberus. Whatever that fucking meant.

Gods, I really wanted my cycle to end quickly. I felt like I was going crazy from the flux of hormones. Ivaia was right—it was an inconvenience. Although Berlium would disagree.

When we reached the room full of statues and busts, Yarden stood guard at the door. As if it were a crime for us to be here. He feared the King's ire. I knew that was all, but I'd stormed off and the King didn't seem to care. So, why should Yarden? I'd probably get punished for it later.

Brat. I could hear Berlium's voice in my head without him even bridging our thoughts.

"Where is Ciel?" I asked.

"Not sure."

"Could you find her? I need some wine."

"I don't want to leave you here alone, Lady Keres."

"Right. That's fine, then."

Silence exuded from him, the dead Lady Vega, and every voiceless statue in the room. Frozen in time, known only for what they once said or did. I stood before her statue, arms crossed in front of my chest.

Not like Herrona, but what about her?

"She's dead. Perhaps we could speak with her," the Death Spirit hummed.

Necromancy was coming up on Hadriel's list. I still hadn't gotten the chance to speak with him about the blood magic, but I was sure Berlium had said something to him. The way Hadriel looked at me from across the table. It wasn't just Emisandre that was bothering him. Apparently, unspoken words were just as much a disturbance to him as rumors.

"What a peculiar fascination." Emisandre's voice splintered the quiet.

I spun around. She held up two wine glasses in one hand, a bottle in the other.

"Saw you walking down this way. I'd love an update. How's Darius? Or would you rather discuss the dead Queen you're replacing?"

If Mrithyn had blessed me with the power to kill by a glare alone, this would have been the time to discover it.

"Don't look at me like that. Drink." She filled a glass and held it out to me.

I didn't take it. Yarden also eyed the glass suspiciously.

"I'd better take the first sip," he said.

"That's unnecessary, Yarden." Hadriel's voice followed closely behind. He and the King both appeared in the doorway beside her.

Hadriel's eyes landed right on the wineglass. Berlium's eyes visited the statue of his dead wife and then snapped down on me. His heart was pounding faster than usual. More than a drum. More like a beast banging on its cage.

Emisandre and Hadriel's voices drifted far away. The wary pressure of Yarden's watchful gaze melted. Every carved face softened in the edges of my vision. Only the sharp lines of Berlium's settled jaw. The pucker of his brows, the downturn of his lips. No other face in that museum looked so cold. In that moment, he looked as he had on the throne the first time that I saw him.

This time, a dead woman watched over us, once a witness to his truths.

I bridged our thoughts. *"Prove it."*

Then watched the storm roil in his eyes.

65: SO LITTLE TIME

Keres

Night Twenty-Four

I tore my gaze away from the King's and headed to the Wither Maiden garden. Yarden came with me. As we passed down the hall, their whispers stalked us. I ignored them and pushed into the bitter cold air.

"Today marks the last day of Aramarth, the last day of High Autumn. Do you remember what I taught you about Andretheoran Science?"

"Yes. Tomorrow is the first day of Skythe. The month dedicated to Mrithyn, ruled by the constellation of the Sickle. Blighted by High Winter storms. Every baby born this month would be attributed the sign, Axis," I recited from memory.

There was a chapter on this in the first book Hadriel gave me, too. A simple summation of the Gods' influence on time and seasons. It matched everything Yarden had said. It was at the end of Skythe that time turned on its axis, into a new year. Time was passing quicker than I could control. The world was changing around me.

We sat at the same stone table, but so much had already shifted. Yarden reached into his pocket and pulled out a small, leather-bound book.

"The Instrumental Testament," he said and passed it to me.

"I was gifted this copy years ago. It's a little worn, I hope you don't mind, and that you'll accept it."

"Oh," I said and touched the soft black leather. I thumbed it open gently and admired the finely inked words.

"How are these letters so uniform?"

"It was printed on a press, in Mannfel."

I looked from him back to the pages. The edges were gold-foiled, and each page was as thin as a leaf. I imagined the process involved shaving a typical piece of parchment in half to make a finer, more delicate sheet. How complicated, how advanced.

"I love writing, but the toil of writing a book by hand is pain-staking. How long does it take to print a book?"

"It's much faster. I've never seen a press at work, but I know its key for mass reproduction of literature. There are probably hundreds of copies like this one."

I smiled at the book. "No, not like this one, because this one was a gift."

We met each other's gazes.

"Thank you."

"You're welcome," he said with a nod. A smile stole his mouth. "Now, hold it close and sniff it."

"What?" I eyed the pages. Tentatively, I lifted the book to my face and took a deep breath—luxuriated in the ink's fragrance.

I smiled and closed my eyes. "As distinct as a campfire, but much softer." I lowered it and opened my eyes.

His smile broadened.

"It's different from a handwritten book." I held out my hand, asking my memory for the words I needed. Resigning to sniffing again. "This ink—it's smokier, but crisper. Or—"

He laughed. "A connoisseur."

I chuckled and turned a few pages back. A directory page outlined the "books" within the book, and I skimmed through the names on it. My attention snagged on one called Barathessian. It was the same part Dorian had quoted to me after I delivered the Gnorrer's bones. Another part named Haf'naar seemed interesting, but I went to that familiar book. Yarden brought out another book for himself and started reading.

I stumbled through the text until I tripped over a profound verse. It was the twenty-first in its ninth chapter. I tried to commit it to memory.

"One who does not see divinity

Within themselves, will never see
The connectedness of all things.
As a worm within the apple,
is the contempt of your nature.
Your lapse in vigilance is its diligence:
To eat at your core, your seeds of truth.
So that you'd never know they were there."

I would never ignore the divinity within me again. I couldn't look away from the connectedness between Berlium and me, either. And we were a cataclysmic match. There was no room for contempt of our natures. No use for it—not in the darkness he lived in. That I was in now. There was no going back.

Just accept it.

Emisandre and Hadriel's conversation made me realize the reason for the Dalis oppression of the Sunderlands. The border between Illyn and Aureum—the prize in all the Baore's games. Illyn was the mother-earth of Monsters. If Berlium wanted to control the wall between it and Aureum... The real question on my mind was how could this benefit the kingdom I was now a part of? My people were here. What did this mean for the Baore?

The Baore was stronger than ever, Emisandre said. It was true. I'd be its second ruler. It had swallowed up the Sunderlands. If Berlium saw something in Illyn that bespoke power—something he wanted, what was it? I'd only ever known two things about our world. Aureum was the golden realm, blessed by the Gods. Illyn, was their forsaken. He told me there were other Gods. The Forsworn.

"What does he want from them?" the Death Spirit mused. If I was going to be his weapon—what were we fighting for? Against Illyn or for it?

Queen Hero was harboring Illynad women. Emisandre called her Hadriel's pet. Was he manipulating her? Or was she just working with the Baore? Berlium had said he held his own stock of power in the Sunderlands once before. Hero's haven for the Lamentar women was a byproduct of the Baore's influence over her. It had to be. My wicked King was hiding so many secrets, and I wanted to rip them from him.

Berlium had never made a match like me. We both knew it. I wanted more. Not to be just a wife or a lover or a queen. Although I looked like the women Berlium knew of my bloodline, I expressed very different traits. I wasn't just some royal heiress to the Aurelian line. I was Mrithyn's fucking legacy.

In the Godlands, Ahriman and the Death Spirit called me Blood Waker. Geraltain went by that name. Blood called to me the way it did to him. I craved it—it told me its secrets and urged me to avenge every innocent drop.

As a child, I prayed to the Goddess of Night, begging for a war to end all wars. A wretched prayer lifted from a hungry mouth. Whatever Berlium's secret prayers were, I wanted to hear them uttered out loud.

"The Instrumental Testament has provoked your thoughts, I see," Yarden said.

I was startled, looked up at him and swallowed. "In your time here, have you ever seen the King with…"

"Lady Emisandre?" He raised his brows.

"Anyone. It's obvious enough they've known each other for a while, and I'm not interested in the petty details of how well they're acquainted. It's just, very few people pass through here. Besides his required audiences with subjects, has he no council?"

"In Dulin. He travels there, but he has to take time here, too. In the counsel of his own thoughts."

Which I had no problem believing. His darkness had its own calming nature.

The King

Emisandre's appearance meant my plans for the wedding had to be altered. Keres understood what she heard pass between the witch and my wizard. A superficial understanding, but one I intended to deepen. My world was one beyond her imagination.

All she'd ever known was the Sunderlands. Ignorance was as dangerous as knowledge, but only one would keep her alive. I'd equip her to survive in my world. Especially because of Thane's presence in it. I had put my hands on her, but he wouldn't be laying a finger on her. Because he would do much worse. I wanted to tell her, but she still didn't trust me enough. She kept needing proof of *my* motives.

Keres spent the rest of the day with Yarden before retiring to our room. I still had much to discuss with Hadriel, and Emisandre had hogged his attention all day. It was late, but with both ladies in bed, we took a little time to talk. In our usual atmosphere, clouded with pipe smoke, our breath stung by liquor. No drink could dissuade my sobriety in this mental state. He also seemed uneasy tonight.

"Hadriel."

His dark gray eyes left the fireplace and met mine.

"She still hasn't told you what happened in Wolvens, has she?"

"I haven't had a moment alone with her since. Foolish child, she should have come to me about it all at once. We have much still to—"

"I looked into her dream last night. It was really more of a nightmare," I said. "I saw what she did in that place. She saw ghosts—the blood spoke to her. She used blood magic."

"Not water—"

I shook my head. His gaze lingered on mine for a moment.

"She lacks knowledge of the world, but her base understanding has been enough to make her what she was. She is not foolish. Only raw. With very little instruction, she's already tapping into the vein of Mrithyn's bloodline. I saw a figure in her nightmares too. I don't even know if she noticed him there, but I saw him watching her. Not Thane. Someone like her. Her Death Spirit is trying to bring her closer to him, to the others before her. She isn't fully tuned in yet but she's close."

"It's not enough for what's coming. We both know she needs more refinement, more time—"

"We have no more time. We must wed. At once. Tomorrow night. No later."

"Sire, that's not—"

"Magister," I interrupted again. "As soon as she takes my hand, lays one finger to the spindle, she will follow me into the playground of Gods and Monsters."

"And she is willing. That much is obvious. The way she looks at you is honest. Her eyes still brim with blood lust, but that thirst is looking a lot like yours lately." His voice trailed off at the end.

I raked a hand through my hair. "I'm both curious and fascinated by her. In our world, what will she become? More like the Monsters or like the Gods?"

"If she follows closely, she'll end up on the winning side."

A guard burst through the door of my study, and I jumped from my seat. Hadriel stayed poised as ever, simply turning his head and taking another pull on his pipe.

The guard worked to catch his breath. "My lord—apologies, my lord."

"What's happened? You look like you've seen a ghost."

"Not a ghost, my lord. A Goddess, a woman or a phoenix. I don't know. Gods above and below—"

Hadriel stood and righted his robes. "What do you mean? Where?"

"In Tecar, Magister. It's the Coroner's sister—she's burning Tecar."

66: SANCTIFIED

Liriene

Night Twenty-Four

I dream of Katrielle nightly, and I fear it's because I will join her soon. One night, we're in the boughs of a tree. Way too high off the ground for anyone to see us. Two flightless birds with all the room in the sky. The next night I'm lying beside her by the riverbed, and she's turned away from me. Trying to sleep despite it being noon, but of course, I won't let her. My fingers wander the slope of her neck, touching her from the soft, dark ringlets starting behind her ear, to her shoulder. I push aside the sleeve of her shift and trace the lines of her tattoo. Someone in Hishmal had done it for her. The outlines of three little black birds in flight.

"I always loved this tattoo," I told her.

"Why?" she asked, her voice laced with sleepiness.

"Because, if anything bad ever sneaks up behind you, a little bird will tell you."

She laughed, pressing her face into her arm to quiet herself.

I dreamed of the oddest and smallest things about her. How she was herself a quiet person, but when she turned the pages of a book, the paper seemed to stick to her skin. The page shifting against its neighbor with a drawn out *shhh* and snapping out of a curve as it turned beneath her fingers. The fabric of the whole world seemed caught on her like that.

Every time she reached out her hands, time lingered in her palm. Along with me. I could watch her touch a book for hours. Even in death, my lover puts my fears to sleep with these dreams and memories. I woke from them as if from gentle light… but then I remembered how dark my world was without her.

I still missed Katrielle more than anything. I lay awake without her beside me, alone in this corner of the cave. I slept on my side, facing the wall, to avoid putting weight on my back and irritating my wounds.

I kept my eyes shut tight, trying to lock my dream in. I knew once I opened my eyes, the vividness of her being with me would melt away. I wanted to ignore the pain coursing through my body. I wanted to sleep and dream of her. But every inch of me that felt the lack of her was burning again.

After Keres gave me her coat, the Dalis did not refrain from lashing me. They ignored her warning and the King's support of it.

The freshest ones reopened with any prodding. Especially on the backs of my thighs and calves. When I walked, the blood streamed down my legs. Washing through the dirt and crusting in my leg hair.

The King had touched my power somehow, suppressed it, but it was waking back up. I figured it was because I wasn't in his presence. His men feared me, so they sought to control me, to make their fear smaller. In the cool of evenings, Shayva tended to me and others that were broken. The heat of day blistered us as we toiled. Tomorrow will be the same. Like today, how I moved through the crowds alongside Shayva and Maro. I worked alongside them and was beaten alongside them. The cat's tail was brought down upon my chest, shredding and marring the skin of my breasts. The branding iron seared my forearm.

That was yesterday. I went to sleep with the realization Oran can do nothing and will continue to be useless tomorrow. Unless I find a use for this power. Being parted with it made me realize this. I didn't want them to hurt me again or anyone else tomorrow. I'd had enough of the pain and misery.

Keres grew up fighting monsters in the dark. As much as I think she shouldn't have had to, I knew every one of those damned hunts prepared her for what's coming. I refused to believe she would ever be defeated— even as Oran showed me the possibilities. She may be broken down, but never conquered. I could see her suffering, or worse, sinking into the darkness of her power and her curse.

No matter the possibilities Oran showed me, I believed King Berlium would gnash her bones between his teeth. He would drink her blood like wine and chew her heart. I could see him feasting on her. The vision was of her body—mutilated and strewn across an endless dining table. All the parts of her still moving and alive. Her insides turned outward. Her eyes wide with agony. His hands and mouth stained crimson. Her bloody scalp mounted on the wall, with all her white hair trailing down it. These were some things my God showed me. But then he showed me my sister rising from her watery grave. Her Spirit of Death, like poison to the King. Every bite into her intoxicating him, addling his blood, and choking him.

Then there was another possibility I also refused to accept: her standing at the southern end of the border and him at the north. A wolf and a bear, a howl and a growl that echoed through the gold-lands. Shaking the foundations of the earth, breaking open the mountains. Awakening long lost magic. Freeing monsters… King and Queen, subduing them all. Change reigning after the chaos. A possibility that they could be mates? It was a golden dream for lovers cursed by darkness. The most improbable—Thane and Keres were still connected, too. He said he would come. Together, we could stop this madness.

Hadriel told me to wait, so I'd been waiting. But I was getting really fucking tired of it.

"Get up." Varic's coarse voice grated against my ear. His breath in my hair. As I stood, he pressed himself against me. I met his horrible red eyes.

"What do you want? It's the middle of the night," I sneered.

He slapped me across the face, snapping my head to the side. I stumbled, tripping over the fur jacket Keres gave me. I'd used it like a blanket. He kicked it aside.

My skin stung, and then his hands were on me. I struggled against him. His chest grazed against mine and my wounds ignited with pain. I growled and cursed him. "You will weep tears of blood!"

"We'll see which of us will weep first," he snorted.

I clawed at his face.

"Karmic." Varic signaled to another guard, who I now saw standing over Shayva's sleeping body. Karmic was his twin, in looks and in morals.

"Your brother is as cursed as you are."

492

Karmic grabbed hold of me and Varic smiled. I writhed in his grip.

"We're going to enjoy this." Varic spat on the ground and moved toward me. Karmic took my hair in his fist and buried his face in my neck, licking at my pulse. I shivered with disgust as his tongue washed my skin with warm, slimy saliva. Varic stopped and pushed his brother's face away from my throat. His eyes widened as he focused.

"Well, well." Varic lifted my chin and turned my face. "What have we here? How did we not see this before?"

They appraised my ears. My heart was pounding furiously. "I won't let you cut my ears," I snapped. My inner fire was building into a raging storm of heat beneath my skin. Shayva lifted her head and gasped, jumping to her feet. Varic spun toward her. Her eyes darted to Maro, who was still asleep.

"Get your hands off of her," she said.

They both laughed, and it made my blood stand still in my veins. My pulse pounded as I stiffened, begging me to thrash and fight. Reverberating through my entire body, but I didn't want them to hurt her. There was nowhere to run. We both knew it. I wasn't about to ignite in this cave and scorch everyone in it.

Varic jabbed his thumb toward me and asked Shayva, "Vigilant, did you know your friend was a half-breed?"

Karmic's breath was hot on my ear. He nibbled at my earlobe. Shayva swallowed her response.

"No, I'm not." I tried to shake my head free of his bite. Varic's hand shot toward my face, and I flinched. He tightened his grip on my jaw instead of striking me and smirked.

"You're half-Human, bitch, or I'm not half-Velin."

"Velin? You're an Illynad?" I asked, but he only grinned. His ashen brown hair and otherwise Human features were marred by his sanguine eyes and pale skin. Even in the dark, with very little moonlight creeping into the cave, I could see the faint glow of his irises.

"All Daemons have ties to Velin, to Illyn. Do they not teach you about us in the Sunderlands? When they teach you to preserve your maidenhead, don't they warn you about the devils from the Rift who'd come to fuck the savage out of you?"

I thought of Darius and Hayes, and the secrets Silas should not have told me. Knowing Katrielle would have married Hayes, a Daemon, should have been reason enough for me to run away with her.

"Your ears aren't as pointy as the other Elves. They've got curves," Karmic said in a voice that matched his twin's feral stare.

"Impossible," I snapped. "That's not true. Both my parents were Elves."

"Oh, contrary, little canary." Varic licked his lips.

"Seems your mummy got fucked by a real man." Karmic snickered in my ear.

"No." My skin pimpled with goose flesh. "You don't know what you're talking about—it's not possible."

"We'll show you just how possible it is to make an Elf half-Human," Karmic chided.

"We've cut enough ears to know the differences, but I know one thing is the same." Varic took my dress in his fists and went to tear it.

"Stop!" Shayva's voice cut through the cave, echoing my cry of desperation. Maro woke. Other Elves jolted awake at her cry as well. Grumbling grew into shouting.

Varic turned toward her and Karmic shifted his stance but didn't weaken his hold on me. Maro jumped up and flung himself between Varic and Shayva, fists ready. For a moment, I could see the warrior he once was. Remnants flashing to the surface of his dark eyes. I could see a wolf of the Sunderland's in a slave's clothing.

Undaunted, Varic dodged Maro's first strike. In one fluid movement, he grabbed the collar of his shirt and punched him in the face with a gauntleted fist. Blood spurted from Maro's nose. He spat some blood at Varic, getting it in his eyes.

"Ach!" Varic grunted and swiped a hand over his face.

It was an opening for Maro to return the hit. Varic's head flailed back, and his eyes rolled. Karmic let go of me and moved to help his brother, but I jumped on him. He grabbed my hair with one hand and swung out wildly with the other. I heard the sheering sound of my dress tearing as he tried to rip me off him. Shayva started yelling, but I didn't understand what she said over the sound of Karmic's growling.

I lost sight as my hair splayed across my face. Karmic hit me in the ribs and I fell, doubling over in pain. Striking another match inside me. My wounds were bleeding, but adrenaline dulled the pain. I looked up. Our kin had rushed toward the fight but were unsure whether to help or watch. Guards started barking outside.

Maro had knocked Varic to the ground, and Karmic was running up behind him.

"Maro!" I screamed. He whirled around just in time to see Shayva throw herself against Karmic. He lunged forward, blocking Karmic's fist.

Someone helped me to my feet, and I threw myself into the fight. Shayva clung to Karmic's arm, weighing him down and stopping his hits. But once he had an opening, he punched her in the face, and she dropped into unconsciousness. I stopped at her side, trying to wake her.

Maro grunted and stumbled. I looked up.

Both brothers were back in control of the fight and pushing Maro toward the mouth of the cave. Shayva murmured, and I pulled her up. "Wake up, we have to help him."

Other Elves came close and helped me pick her up.

"What are we supposed to do?" one asked.

"They'll kill him."

"I won't let that happen," I said, and held my hands up. My fingernails lengthened into silver-tipped talons, and those around me took several steps back. My breath hissed out of me, like smoke, like Keres'. Molten power was flooding my veins, reclaiming its place after being forced to slumber. It was singing to me again in its bright amber voice. The brave followed me.

Shayva's voice perked back up a minute later. "Put me down!"

She came running up behind me, tripping over her own feet. Buds of fear and doubt blossomed to life within me. She was weakened. She couldn't fight. I could sense her fear as well; it permeated my senses as strongly as the stench of carrion that tainted the cold air. But her rage was just as real as mine.

The Elves at our backs had labored in this encampment day in and day out—they weren't weak, they were just exhausted. Frustration shook their bones and fury coiled beneath their skin. As we emerged, Karmic turned and appraised the amassing crowd—and laughed. But by the brittleness of his voice, I knew he could feel it too. They were weaponless, but they had me.

Shayva and I vaulted toward Maro's body on the ground. He was unconscious. Shayva's shaking fingers lingered at his neck, feeling for his fluttering pulse. His brown shaggy hair crossed his gashed open brow and purpling eye. The bridge of his nose was bent and swelling. His lip was split and also engorged with blood. He groaned as she shoved at his chest, trying to rouse him.

Varic stood just a few paces away, rolling back his shoulders and cracking his neck. He gestured to other guards within the gates for the night. Telling them to stand down. Then he motioned to the child at the foot of the ladder by the wall. I couldn't believe the boy was still awake, still standing beside that bloody monument. The child kept his shaved head down as he approached Varic. He handed over his mallet and the large knife that was held by a loop to his black leather vest. Then the child handed over four large nails at Varic's request. Did he plan to take Maro's ears and then mine?

My heart buzzed in my chest like the flies circling the death pits. Shayva leaned forward over Maro's body, trying to shield him. She hissed at Varic and cursed him in the Elven tongue. Her green eyes brimmed with tears that glowed in the moonlight. The ragged ends of her ruined ears on full display. I looked around, trying to figure out what to do. My power and my rage sought release, but I'd never done this before. I tried to will it into my hands—to expel it, but it didn't come.

Her whimpering cries shook apart and broke into a blood-curdling scream as he neared. Varic kicked her in the stomach, cutting her scream into a high-pitched yelp. She fell aside. I launched myself between Varic and Maro's body; but he thwacked my skull with the mallet.

Dizzy, I fell back and Karmic caught me. I heard my people crying and groaning as Karmic lowered my pain-sodden body to the snow-covered ground. Darkness threatened to take my mind, but I fought against it. My power remained burning within me, fuming. It sparked against my body's weakness, and I forced my eyes open.

Varic turned Maro's frail body over onto his stomach with his boot and knelt over him. Straightening Maro's arms back behind him so that his elbows faced the night sky. In one fluid drop, Varic hammered the first iron nail through the back of Maro's elbow joint. Waking my friend with agony. Maro vomited from the pain, jerking his body just as he drove the second nail through his other arm. This time it went through his bicep.

My mind and stomach lurched against the weight of unconsciousness that still tried to blanket my view. I leaned up on my side, shook myself like a wet-hound, and reached a hand to my throbbing temple. My fingertips found an open gash oozing blood. Pain clamored through my skull and my vision blurred as nausea stormed my gut. My heart pounded in my fresh wound.

Varic kicked Maro onto his back once more, his arms useless and mangled beneath him. Again, he performed the same strikes, but this time impaling both Maro's kneecaps with the last two iron nails. Shayva wailed. Blood pooled beneath him, dark as midnight. Varic stood to his full height and gazed at Maro's body. Maro slipped into oblivion. Varic wasn't done.

He motioned for his brother to step in. Karmic left my side and tossed Maro's limp body over his shoulder. Carrying him to the pits. I could See his heart beating meekly in his chest, like an ember in a darkened hearth. His body would rot like the others.

I struggled to stand, nearly falling over as the world tilted on its axis. My skull was thrumming, and blood ran from my temple down my face, dripping into my right eye, and sprinkling off my lashes. Shayva fell, trying to get up and chase after Karmic, but Varic grabbed her by the hair and shoved her back down to the ground. Raising the mallet to strike her.

Time slowed.

I stopped resisting the pain, stopped forcing it. Closed my eyes. The will of the fire within me took control. Though my physical eyes saw only darkness and flashes of a crimson headache, the eye of my Spirit Sees. An aureate beast awakened deep within me.

Wings sprung from my back, without pain, as if they'd been there all along. Billowing out to their full breadth, each plume white and aflame with blue fire. I'd seen them before in my visions. My head filled with memories of Oran's whispering through my dreams, telling me I possessed the Spirit of Revelations.

I pulled myself from the jaws of oblivion and rose to my feet. My power spiked like a fever within me as I opened my eyes. The God of the Sun was within me, His power molten in my veins. Like a bird of fire rising from the ashes, my heart beat as if it, too, had wings. My golden aura lit up the night like daylight in the flesh.

Varic stumbled as he was taken aback. The sight of me seared his vision. Elves fell to their knees, and even Shayva shielded her eyes. The other Dalis guards cowered in their armor, afraid to attack me. Knowing they must if they wish to survive this night and my wrath.

I was a woman made fire, and I was going to burn them all.

My first step was brazen, but my next scorched the earth beneath my feet. I stalked toward the Man before me, light emanating from every pore of my body, from my scars too.

Varic hid his face behind his hands, dropping the mallet. I raised my hands and twin Suns sparked to life in my palms, growing as I fed them my fury. They flared at my command, lashing out at Varic and striking him across his cheek. His flesh sizzled as he screamed.

"I've branded you," I said and bared my fangs at Varic, just as I'd seen my sister do in the face of the King. Guards were barking commands, whimpering for a retreat. Another solar flare lit up Varic's abdomen. He howled as his jerkin caught fire and desperately tried to peel it from his body.

The Elves were howling and raging like wolves that realized the Moon was pale and the Sun was gold.

I turned my gaze toward the pits, where Karmic stood breathing raggedly. Maro's body was in his arms. I Saw no spirit in him now. Another shard in my heart. Karmic gave me a demonic grin as he dropped Maro's body into the pits. His shoulders hulked forward, and his now empty arms rose to his sides. Fire erupted from within him. Crawled out of his armor, ran down his arms, to his fingertips, and leaped toward me.

"Daemon," I hissed. I charged toward him, toward the edge of the pit. In a breath, I was before him. A trail of fire blazed through the snow behind me. I was a pillar of flame. My twin Suns perched in my palms, crackled and sputtered.

His eyes reflected my fire, but the fear he and his brother had once planted in me took root in his soul. He shot streaks of fire at me, like arrows, but my own absorbed them. Seeing attack was useless, he took off running toward the gates.

"Wrong!" I shouted in a multi-tonal voice. Much to my surprise, the force of my word sent a wave of energy along the ground, shaking it beneath his feet. He fell onto his face.

A flare of fire whipped his back, splitting his skin open with blisters and blood. He tried to crawl away and as he reached toward hope he had no right feeling; I raised my eyes.

Guards flooded the camp. Their armor rattled, the gates zinging from the magical wards as they opened.

I focused on the death pits. At the brink, I could see Maro's body tangled with the rest, embraced by our dead kin. I blew the twin Suns from my palms, as if they were the white, dusty seeds of a dandelion. They floated into the pits with hungry sparks and flames, incinerating the corpses and giving our dead rest in the ashes.

Something cold and sharp bit into my back, and I stumbled forward. I turned on my heel and faced the growing wall of armed soldiers. The archer had already released the bowstring and his next arrow sang through the air into my chest. Sinking between my ribs, from arrowhead to shaft. I fell back from the impact. Losing my footing and plummeting into the fire ravaging the death pits.

67: SUNRISE
Hadriel

Birds made of white fire soared from the depths of the pits, into the midnight sky, like the gently sprayed sparks of a campfire. Dispersing and swirling, leaping, then diving toward the soldiers. Falling stars. The men screamed and ran. The stench of burnt flesh fogged the air.

The Death Pits were alive with orange and red, pulsing flames. Smoke billowed into the clouds, thicker than patience. Given the time, they'd paint the entire horizon a hazy black. Colors shifted in the fire, drawing my wide eyes back. Shades of blue waved through. Furling and unfurling. Searing white light bolted through them, parting the sea of flames.

The King shielded his eyes. A voice—a scream—tore through the air and the mountains lent it an echo. As the sound washed over us, the ground shook and I had to catch my balance. Looking down only for a breath, but when I lifted my eyes again, they followed the form ascending above the flames.

A crown of blue fire encircled her crimson head. Marvelous white wings took their breadth, tipped with the same blue and violet of her crown. She sang again in the tongue of the Gods. Terrible curses. The King stood in awe—I stood in awe. She was a sunrise in the middle of the night.

In all of Aureum, I knew there were divine Instruments made from any race. Yet I'd never seen one like her before. My eyes welled with tears as her song moved through us, the ground still trembling.

Cut short by the guttural growl behind me.

The King

Every hair on my body stood at that sound. Both of us whirled as her hands caught us by the shoulders. Scarred claws. She shoved us both aside. Taken completely by surprise, I stumbled, and she darted past us.

Running with the power and speed of a wolf. She stumbled forward and her satin night dress tore along her spine. Bones broke through her skin and stretched. Raven black feathers fanned out along the bones in seconds. With another growl, she catapulted into the sky.

Stark against the fire, my Darkstar. She flew to her sister and stopped before her. Turning her abysmal eyes on the soldiers who still dared hold their weapons raised. Splaying her wings out as if to shield her sister. Two furies.

I knew the old prophecy their mother had been given.

Power dropped from both her hands into two pools. A pool of starlight and a pool of blood.

This was a forgotten prediction revived.

Liriene's fire in the pits died down as her song halted, but Keres lifted her arms and the flames revived. This time, turning cold white, shifting with green. Their roaring melted into a hush, rising and falling as if they were the very breath of Mrithyn. Liriene's skin was drenched in golden light, but her sister's replaced the Moon in the sky. Together, they were an eclipse.

"Is *this* the kingdom you've promised me?" she asked in a split, booming voice that chilled the blood in my veins. My power rose within me. She turned her head and said something to her sister over her shoulder. Not meant for our ears.

I could hear Hadriel's heart pounding. We woke ourselves out of watching and moved at the same time. Running into the crowd.

"Stand down!" we barked commands at the soldiers—those that still stood. Horror plastered to their faces. Mindlessly postured until our barked orders snapped their attention back.

Weapons were lowered. The flames retreated into the pits, and the two sisters touched their bare feet to the earth. Striding toward us, their wings casting shadows over us. As Keres neared, I saw her new black horns, grown from her white hairline, that curled back and down behind her pointed ears to frame them.

Liriene's silver-flamed eyes shot a look to the left, at a burnt body on the ground, and then found mine.

Keres' eyes held oblivion, but as she came toe-to-toe with me, as she always did, I caught glimpses of emerald green swirling within. Her sister's blue dress was torn, revealing wounds which instantly knocked the breath out of Hadriel. Fresh wounds that had been seared shut. She looked into his eyes and fainted. He caught her and her wings retracted into her body. As the fire retreated under her skin, he lifted her into his arms.

The red-taloned hand bearing my engagement ring snatched the collar of my shirt.

"Your next move better be well thought out," she snarled.

Her power seeped through her touch into my skin, sinking into my blood. Her Spirit ran a death-cold hand along my own. I looked to Hadriel and then turned to find Yarden behind us.

"Order the carriage. Gather only a few men. Ciel and Minnow should get her things and bring them."

"I must take Liriene to my chambers. There will be no traveling until I've tended her wounds."

I nodded and turned back to Keres, placing a hand over hers, where she still clutched my shirt. The tension in her grip lightened, and the black of her eyes brightened into the beautiful green she was born with. I inspected her wings, loving the sight of them, and she flared them out once more for me.

Her heart raged in her chest, but as I looked into her eyes again, it calmed. Seeing her like this... made me thirst for her almost more than I could bear.

She pulled her hand back and pushed past me, following Hadriel and her sister. Yarden walked ahead of them, and the soldiers gave them a wide berth. I looked around at them, and back to the cave where the other Elves usually slept. An audience met my gaze. Inspired by the demonstration of power, bristling with fury all their own. There would be no rest in my kingdom tonight.

68: SONGS & CURSES
Keres

Hadriel laid her gently on the cot. The fragrance of burnt herbs and poultices permeated the room. He turned his back while I took off her torn shift and covered her with the blankets. My hands shook at the sight of her body, the horrible wounds inflicted on her. By those Men.

"Coroner." His voice was soft. "Take a step back. You're transforming again."

I glared at him. "Should I become anything less than a monster when my sister has endured such atrocities?" I felt the pressure above my brows, just in my hairline. The horns.

"Don't misplace your anger. What she went through in Tecar was not planned. The guards must have taken it upon themselves to—"

"Berlium told me himself he ordered them to whip her. To spare her from labor, he subjected her to cruelty. He constantly asserts he doesn't hate Elves, but look at how his men treat us. He doesn't stop them. That wall—Elf ears. Don't think I didn't see that. Now look at my sister." That pressure built in my head intensified, and my skin stung as if two bees had pricked me.

"I doubt he intended for it to go this far—"

"She should have never been left to their whims." I wheeled around and stared at the wall. Trying to calm myself. Willing the horns to sink back into my skull.

"Actually, when you were in Ro'Hale, I met with her. She was talking with a guard when I noticed something off in her appearance. Then her body seized as her mind was arrested by a vision. When I got to her, I discovered she had a raging fever. Have you seen her left hand?"

I looked at her, worrying my lip between my teeth. Trying to push the image of her injuries out of mind. I knew her hand bore yet another, the same scar as mine. Inflicted by Berlium's blood bond. I nodded.

"It had festered, so I tended to it. We discussed her vision when she woke, and then I told her to go back to Tecar. I had a plan, and I was waiting for the chance to discuss her release with the King. I tried once, and he told me to wait. I was going to try again tonight, when we finally got a moment to talk, but then guards came."

"She told me about this, told me to wait for her. I should have never gone with him to Mannfel that day. I noticed something was wrong, and I ignored it. If I'd stayed or just asked for her to be brought into the castle then, this wouldn't have happened. What was this vision?"

I met his dark gaze.

"It's not for me to discuss with you."

"Why not?"

"Perhaps there are things you'd like to discuss with *me*."

I knew what he wanted to hear—the day in Wolvens. Pride straightened my spine for a moment as he stared down his nose at me.

"Your book lied."

He arched a brow.

"It said playing the puppeteer was impossible. I know some dead men who'd wager differently."

His lips parted, but he said nothing. Awaiting more.

"Blood magic came almost too easily. In fact, I think it's something my Spirit knew how to do and was waiting for me to realize. For as long as I can remember, I've been able to hear the heartbeats of men. Sense the blood in their veins. I could sense much more than that, but finally it makes perfect sense. Mrithyn made me His predator so that I can do what He cannot. It isn't His nature to slaughter. He cannot abide such perversion of His power, but sometimes the only way to stop the madness is to give the world what it needs. Not a hero. A monster. One who can do more than end bloodshed. One who can control it. I also understand now what you meant about the King suppressing my powers for more to find their footing. Fire—now I know the Brazen. Water. Now I can bend blood. Not in the way a water Daemon can. Blood calls to me. There was blood spilled on the ground in Wolvens. It awakened as I reached my senses toward it. There were ghosts—tortured souls. They fed my power. Mrithyn consumes souls, but I am His hunger. I am not a perfect mirror of His will. I am two sides of a looking glass. A mortal with one foot in the Godlands and one in our world. He is the harvester, the gatherer of ripened souls. I am the reaper—and I'm no longer afraid of what that means."

I gave him a curt nod. "Thank you for helping me to understand."

His mouth flickered and his eyes searched mine. He pressed his lips together. Then, one corner lifted ever so slightly. "In this moment, you look so much like your mother."

The words struck me in the chest, inviting unexpected tears to my eyes.

Her prayers for me to be made Mrithyn's instrument lived in my head. Maybe she didn't understand the darkness of His power or what I'd become. Yet I hoped she would have been proud of me for choosing to follow Hadriel's guidance.

I stepped closer to him. "I am thankful for the darkness Mrithyn gifted me, and I'm hungry for more. But Gods help the man that threatens my loved ones."

His eyes shifted to Liriene, still asleep. She looked anything but peaceful.

Liriene finally stirred, and I jumped from my seat. Her hand went straight to her temple. Hadriel had to stitch the gash there. I didn't want to know how she got it, but then again, I did. So I could pay whoever did it back. The other wounds looked as if something had cauterized them. Her Spirit, like mine, must have healed her. The surrounding skin was puckered and was still angrily red. Hadriel insisted on applying ointment to stave off festering.

She winced as her fingers found the dressing at her hairline. Her gray eyes fluttered open. "I've got a splitting headache. Where am I?"

"In the castle, Liri. Do you remember what happened?" I asked, watching every line of her face tighten. Listening to her heartbeat, telling myself she was safe now.

"Don't overwhelm her; she needs to rest."

"Hadriel tended to your wounds, but he's right. For now, just rest."

"I remember," she said and sat up anyway, clutching the blanket to her chest. Her eyes wandered either around the room or through her memories. "Varic and his brother Karmic... are they dead?"

I crossed my arms over my chest. "The captain—or whoever he was. That's who hurt you?"

She looked up at me. "I think I killed them."

"Good," I said. "Or I would have. I want their deaths ascertained," I said in Hadriel's direction. Liriene's eyes welled with tears, making me drop my hands at my sides.

"They killed Maro. Hurt Shayva. They—they said things."

"Hey now, it's over," I said and sat on the edge of her bed. "You're safe."

"But our people are not." A tear rolled down her cheek.

"It'll be dealt with," Hadriel said. His voice darkened.

I wiped away her tears gently, and she closed her eyes, leaning into my touch. An ache grew in the back of my throat as I suppressed my own tears. Shoved them down, buried them under rage. "I could have prevented this, and I failed."

Her auburn lashes clumped as she tried to blink away the tears.

"Hadriel." A sob broke her voice. "Something's changed in me. Like the last thread between what I am and what I was has snapped. And that terrible song—I can still hear the words chanting in my mind. That voice, so unlike my own, ripped from my throat. What's happening? Between the visions and the fire—that horrible song!" She screamed and dug her fingers into her hair, tucking her knees into her chest.

His lips drained of color. "They told me I'm a half-breed. They would have raped me." Her voice was a thin rasp.

I grabbed her by the shoulders. "Liriene, look at me."

"What's happening? What am I?" She trembled.

506

"Look at me." I squeezed her shoulders, keeping my voice low and steady. She breathed raggedly through her mouth, desperate and whimpering. Her stare was hollow, and a shiver skittered through her bones.

"You're alive," I said. "You're going to heal. No one is going to hurt you now—or I will shred them to pieces."

She groaned and doubled over the side of the bed, vomiting into a bucket Hadriel had left there. He turned toward the fire pit and took the kettle of water from the grating. Corks popped out of jars and rolled across the wooden counter. His fingertips rustled into their contents— like the sound of a fallen leaves crumbling between the fingers. He sprinkled pinches of tea leaves and herbs into what looked like a steel mesh thimble, only larger, and sat that in the water with its rim above the surface.

"Brewing tea is a strain of magic, I see."

He nodded and pulled a locket out of his robe. It had a thin, silvery chain that ended somewhere in the folds of his robe. Opening it let out a ticking sound. He studied it and then clasped it shut, replacing it where it came from.

"And what kind of trick was that?" I furrowed my brows.

"It's a timepiece."

I tried to process it. "Like a talisman, for… time?"

"Well, not really." He pulled it back out and showed it to me. Liriene's breathing settled as she looked at the strange object.

"Humans and their inventions," I grumbled.

"The hands move to point out the time, which is measured by these markings. It's really quite simple." He watched Liriene, who watched the hands flick from one mark to the next.

"If only it were as easy as that—to take time back from its hands. To turn it back," she said.

"Liriene, nothing about the passage of time is easy. I only said measuring it was simple. What we endure as time turns, can only be measured in the strength of our spirits. You, dear girl, are only becoming stronger. That is what's happening to you."

She blinked up at him, and her tears dried.

"As far as their attempts to insult you, take none of it to heart. However, when I look at you, I admit to seeing something more than an Elf. Something else, even different from Keres. Perhaps brought to light by the hand of Oran, as he is the God of Revelations. I heard it in that voice. That song."

She shivered again but steeled herself. I ran my hand over her shoulder and squeezed again. He glanced at the timepiece again and remembered his brewing. He removed the container for the leaves and poured the tea into a tankard, then passed it into Liriene's hands.

Steam rose to her nostrils. "It smells like the woods."

I leaned in as she held it up to me and I took a deep breath. She was right. "Almost like pine."

She took a sip, not reacting to the heat, and smacked her lips. With narrowed eyes she said, "It tastes like sap too."

"It's meant to calm your nerves." He sat down in a chair across from us and lit his smoking pipe. After a pull, he let out a pensive sigh and looked back at us. "My theory is, if your blood is mixed with something else, I'd bet every book in my library it's Lamentar."

My jaw dropped. "Lamentar."

"You think—you think I'm part Illynad? Varic and Karmic told me I must be half-human."

He shrugged. "Human is a possibility, but that voice told me otherwise. I knew your mother. She was a pure-blooded Elf. Your father, I knew not. Where was he from?"

"From Massara," I answered. What Emisandre said rang through my head immediately after the words left my mouth.

"Is it true that Massara has ties to the Baore?"

He nodded. "Massara was once part of the Baore. It wasn't a clan as you know it to be. Just a small settlement of a few families who migrated from Illyn into Aureum before the Elder War. The Baorean Kings carved their border and Massara fell within it. The Elves of the Sunderlands didn't want the Illynads—cursed them as they reproduced."

"How strange," I said.

508

"Wasn't strange at the time. Very few people tolerated the Velin."

"You mean Daemons?" Liriene asked. I blinked at her.

"Varic and Karmic said they were half Human, half Velin. They were Daemons, and they said all Daemons had ties back to the Velin."

"First of all, not all Daemons have ties to Velin. Some do. Varic and Karmic were Ember Born Daemons, low caste. I highly doubt they had any significant tie to the relic bloodline, and it has all but disappeared in the Sunderlands. Muddied by interbreeding. Back to the point—Massara belonged to the Baore. As their numbers grew, they mingled with Baoreans and with the Elves of Allanalon. Their neighboring clan. All kinds of blood were shared."

"But our father didn't appear to be anything except Elven, and that doesn't explain where Lamentar blood would come into play," I said.

"It's difficult to guess. Perhaps he had ancestors with stronger ties to Illyn. The Velin originally migrated across the Rift, from the city-state of Cigard Barrows. All kinds of mortals live there. To this day, it's a melting pot. Most commonly, when Aurelesians cross the Rift to live in Illyn, that's where they go."

"Aurelesians—leaving to live in Illyn?" I asked. "I would have never believed it before, but many of my beliefs have been challenged since I came to the Baore."

Again, he shrugged. "No matter who people are or where they come from, everyone wants to feel free. Yet, they wish to belong. They go where they imagine both these things can be found."

Liriene sipped her tea and then offered me some, but I declined. Hadriel took a pull from his pipe. Someone knocked on the door.

"Enter," Hadriel said, and smoke rushed out with the word.

Yarden opened the door, admitting the King. His gaze passed from Hadriel, straight to me and my sister. His face was uncharacteristically pale, and his eyes were dull. "We're leaving."

Emisandre came in after him.

"Oh, you're still here," I said.

She narrowed her eyes at me and took up space next to Berlium. "At his request, yes."

"Where are we going?" I asked, ignoring her snideness.

"Dulin. The carriages await. Keres, your things have been packed, and Liriene, you've been provided for as well. Hadriel, we must leave. Now."

It was then I realized Ciel was in the hall beside Yarden. She stepped forward, holding a bundle of clothing out for Liriene. "Come, my lady. I'll help you change."

I invited her to change in my room, not meeting the King's eyes as we passed between him and Emisandre on the way out.

69: STRONGHOLD

Keres

Day Twenty-Five

"Liriene, what do you mean you cannot read?" Hadriel asked, his expression blown apart by shock and then scrunched up by confusion and repulsion. As if her admission of illiteracy was a personal insult to him.

"My mother never taught me," she said. "I was an older child when she died, though. It's not like she didn't have the time."

Hadriel's incredulity never waned as thoughts phased through his mind. The carriage jolted again, knocking me into Berlium. Hadriel braced himself with a hand on the door and brought the book he'd offered her back to his lap.

He thumbed open the pages and started reading.

"You don't have to read to me," she said indignantly, pointing her nose toward the window. Snow pelted it.

"Do you know the meaning of your name, child?"

Liriene and I exchanged glances. "Daughter of the River Liri."

He snorted. "No. It means one who loves to read, and so you will. I will not let your mind idle while Keres' thrives. You can't force a child into a world without books—that's cruel neglection. I'm surprised at your mother."

She stared at him, and he lowered his eyes to the page, totally ignoring the King and me. The book he held was Hands of Gods. "You must know what you are," he insisted and turned to the page about Oran and His Seers.

Hadriel read through the carriage ride. His wizened voice like a scratchy blanket for the senses. I never tired of this book, although it didn't paint pretty stories. It spoke of the Gods—their most vicious creations. Their natures, both dark and glorious. It wasn't fantasy spun on a loom of golden thread. It was bitter truth that engendered hard questions.

The Gods were the greatest forces in Aureum. Death's ripples caressed the surface of the world. Souls sank into His touch. I was but one fang in His jaw and I loved it. The Death Spirit was seated comfortably on the throne of my being. She filed her claws lackadaisically one moment, then could shred a man in the next. Could see ghosts and wield their ire. Craved a crown but she didn't need it. She had horns. It was official. I had a God complex to rival Berlium's.

I felt the darkest shades of beautiful; hand painted by Mrithyn Himself. And then I had this beautiful bastard next to me. He gave me the side eye and the muscle in his jaw ticked. He wanted to touch me, but he felt my anger. Sitting this close together—I wanted to scream at him, but my Godling wanted to scream while she rode him. Which was a problem.

"Knock it off," I scolded her internally before she could release the needy purr that she was trying to shove up my throat. *"We are earth-shatteringly angry at him, stupid."*

What happened in Tecar was unacceptable. I told him I wanted in on his little revolution and then I saw that. He had sins to pay for.

We left Dale with my people being moved into the dungeon below the keep. Not much better than a cave, but there would be bars between them and his men. They could sleep—they wouldn't be in the High Winter's bitter grasp. They'd be fed and they would not be toiling mindlessly. I felt like less and less of a captive here, but they still were. Tecar was on fire thanks to my glorious sister.

Liriene was incredible. Beaten badly, but she'd heal. The girl was fire, with the voice of a curse breaker. He had to look at her and count her in now. And then there was me. The thorny black flower sitting pretty in the darkness of a tower: my enemy's mind.

His inner dragon wrapped around me as he passed his arm over my shoulders. He was mine to gnaw on or to kiss. If the Baore was stronger than ever, I was going to make sure that counted for the Sunderlands, not against it.

One thing didn't make sense to me… if our father carried Illynad blood and Liriene did too, what about me? I felt like every day I had more and more questions.

After reading about Oran, Hadriel closed the book. The road stretched on. Sunrise was soon enough.

"What's Dulin like?" I asked.

"Do you know anything about the Imperium in the Cenlands?" Berlium asked.

I recalled my last conversation with Ivaia and Riordan when they were alive. "A little."

"Dulin is my Imperium. You want your people to be a part of the Baorean revolution—well, you have to see it first. Every precious thing I've ever collected is there. It is the seat of my kingdom's advancement. You'll see."

"I'm surprised you didn't invite Emisandre to ride with us," I said.

Hadriel looked up from his book through his thick brows, and Berlium snorted.

"Jealous, little wolf?"

"Nothing to be jealous of. To the King, the spoils."

He nested his hand in my hair and pulled it to make me look up at him. Liriene noticed and stiffened. Berlium bit his lower lip, looking down at me. I schooled my expression into indifference. He opened his mouth to speak.

Liri cut him off. "Why must you be so rough with her? She's not a—"

"She's mine," he said in a low voice and slid his gaze to her. He looked at me again. "And besides, my brat rather likes it when I'm rough with her."

He released his hold on my hair and dropped his arm back on my shoulder. Liriene looked at him through narrow eyes before shooting a glare at me.

"You let him dominate you."

"Oh, she bloody loves it."

I looked at Hadriel. "Any potions to make him less of an ass?"

Berlium chuckled, and I slapped my hand against his chest.

"See?" he said to Liriene. "Keres' submission is not weakness. Trust me."

Hadriel groaned. "I should have ridden with Emi."

As we journeyed, I sank into thought. I was often furious, but I was learning to manage that. To think.

The King had committed atrocities, but to his people, he'd worked wonders. He loved them. There were two sides to him. He'd shown me flickers of feelings and that spoke volumes, but it didn't dilute his madness. He will go to any lengths for what he wants and for his people. Perhaps I couldn't live without chaos, either. I was becoming more open-minded, yet I had boundaries. That was our major difference. If my perspective could shift, could his? Revolutionaries must see change and possibility.

We both deserved damnation in our own regards, but neither of us needed salvation from what we were. I wasn't his heroine, come to save the dragon. I was just another monster to shake up the tower. To challenge him the way I'd been challenged. Which is exactly what my people needed: a creature who could beguile their hunter. Everyone I loved was behind me, and Berlium would have to get past me to hurt them again. As we approached his treasured stronghold, I knew he heard my heart beating its anticipation.

🔒🔒🔒

Dragons flew in circles around the tallest spire. From a distance, I thought they were strange clouds, but as we passed through the iron gates, the mirage fell away, and I saw them for what they were.

I almost fell out of the carriage as I looked up at them, and Berlium steadied me. He gave me a knowing smile, fangs and all. Touched my chin, making me realize my jaw had dropped.

One dragon soared toward the snow-capped mountains that backdropped the castle, kicking up wind that made Berlium laugh. Liriene and I whirled and looked at each other with matching wide eyes.

"Wicked cool," I said.

"I've seen them in my visions but seeing them in person—this is unreal."

Berlium took my hand and pulled me into his stride. We passed under an arch and into a courtyard, following the other dragon as it loomed overhead.

"I'm letting you in on a secret, little wolf. Aureum's history books call this place Dulin, as my family did. I was born here. My *father* originally sat on this throne, not my uncle. But when he conquered Dale, he gave this castle to my uncle, and moved my family. Of course, I took this place back with my ascension. Dale was never my home. I spent much of my time here before I ascended. I've given it a new name which is spoken only here."

He lowered his voice and glanced over his shoulder where Hadriel and Liriene walked side by side talking about the dragons. He looked down at me, opening his mouth to speak but pausing. The blue of his eyes overwhelmed the streaks of gold—with the look of sadness.

"Bamidele," he whispered, and then swallowed. "Named after my daughter."

I tightened my hold on his hand. His dead daughter.

"It means *follow me home*." He smiled sadly and looked back up. The dragon that had flown away came back and swirled around the other.

He pointed. "The black dragon is Senka, meaning shadow. The white one is Enver, luminous."

"I didn't even know dragons lived in Aureum."

"They don't," he said, smiling at them. "Senka and Enver are from Illyn. There's a keep called Kryptag just on the other side of the border. Between the Baore and Illyn, in the valley between the Rift Mountains and the Tecar Mountains." He drew my attention to the top of the archways that surrounded the courtyard. The mountain peaks beyond them.

"There, to the east. Dragons were born under the mountain called the Krypt. An architect designed the keep, chipping away slate and obsidian from the mountain. Like cracking open an egg, releasing the dragons that slept within. The architect dedicated the keep to them. The people that live there are the Keepers. A Keeper lives here in Bamidele.

She's a descendant of the architect. Senka and Enver are her dragons. I'm very excited to introduce you two."

The massive iron doors opened, and we followed guards into the foyer. The floor was black-and-white marble; the walls were the same stone as the temple of Mrithyn. The black that shimmered like a midnight sky full of stars. There were no gaudy gold statues. Only black-and-white marble angels and gargoyles.

The guards wore obsidian armor that looked scaled, and their gauntlets ended in claws. The insignia of a dragon, standing on its back legs with its front claws shredding the air, was etched into the breastplate.

Liriene stuck out amidst the dual colors of the foyer with her red hair, where Berlium and I blended in. Hadriel looked bored and chilled to the bone. Clutching his fur-lined cloak around him, with the hood still up, covering his bald head. Yarden followed, looking radiant as ever in his armor.

He was different from the other guards. Not just because he was a knight. There was something about him... seeing him here. He spoke of his time here fondly, with a longing for the mysterious lady he'd loved. The look in his hazel eyes as he drank in the hall for the first time in three years... ignited that bronze fire in him.

"Hadriel, show Liriene to her room. Give her one close enough to mine so she isn't far from her sister."

I wanted to be with her, and he caught the thought as it crossed over my face. I didn't know what was going to happen to Liriene here. If anyone tried to hurt my sister, I'd kill them with my bare hands.

The look on her face as she exchanged a glance with me, said everything. She didn't want to be here. Although, I didn't want to be parted from her... I had followed Berlium home. I'd find my way to her side when I wasn't at his. And the way Hadriel seemed to favor her, I wasn't afraid to leave her with him. She wasn't being taken from me. There were no stone walls or gates between us now, but there was still a level of separation I had to accept. Maybe one day, he'd let her leave. I didn't know where she'd go, though.

Berlium wasn't letting me leave his side. Hadriel turned, with Liriene following him. An ensemble of official looking people met us at the end of the hall.

"Vangelis." Berlium let go of me to clasp arms with the man.

He had soft auburn hair and green eyes. A face dotted with freckles. I always loved freckles. He was tall and lean, dressed in a cobalt tunic embroidered with thin-lined emerald thread. Black pants and leather boots.

"Your Majesty." He smiled and his green eyes flicked to me. "Well, here she is. A vision, my lady. I've eagerly anticipated meeting you."

He offered his hand, and I took it. His gaze quickly traced the scars on my skin.

"Keres, this is Vangelis Edouard. My trusted Marquis. He oversees Bamidele when I'm in Dale."

"A pleasure." I curtsied.

"The pleasure is all mine." He surrendered my hand. "Sire, we have fulfilled the request you made on your most recent visit."

"Good," Berlium said, handing his cloak to another servant.

Someone appeared behind me to take mine. I gave it to her. Both Berlium and Vangelis paused, taking in the dress I wore. It wasn't anything special. Just a plain gray velvet dress with long sleeves that sat off the shoulder and an empire waist. It was modest.

Berlium's eyes found mine and Vangelis lowered his. I furrowed my brows at him, but he didn't offer an explanation.

I'd just been silently judged. Heat rose to my cheeks, and I looked away. I didn't know what his assessment meant. He didn't look pleased.

"Well, I'm starving," Berlium said, turning back to Vangelis.

"Luncheon is being prepared. We weren't expecting you, otherwise we would have had a meal waiting."

"It's fine. There was an incident at Dale last night. We left in the middle of the night. We'll need to wash up and change. I'm desperate to rest. We have much to discuss," Berlium said, not dispelling the concern that crossed Vangelis' expression.

"Very well, sire."

"Yarden," Berlium said, turning to him. "You may retire. I'm sure

517

you still remember your way around—and who to avoid."

"Yes, my lord," Yarden said flatly.

"And me?" Emisandre appeared, and I fought the urge to roll my eyes.

"Ah, Lady Emisandre." Vangelis turned to her.

She stuck her hand out to him, and he kissed it. "Vangelis," she purred. "Always the sweetest welcome."

"It's been too long. We'll catch up. I have some things to attend to." He touched her arm.

She smiled and nodded before bringing her eyes back to the King and me. Vangelis left and Berlium took my hand again.

"Emisandre, you've been here plenty of times."

"Yes, I have," she said. "I'll see you for luncheon later—I overheard. I'll be in my room if you wish to see me, my King."

Coquettish and sultry were words too pretty for Emisandre. She was blatantly disrespectful, and I could smell the desperation and arousal on her. Berlium gave me a coy smile as we turned to leave.

"What?"

He chuckled and kissed my head. "Oh, how I love the glare of a green-eyed woman."

I pushed his face away, and he hip-bumped me, catching me off guard and throwing me off balance.

"You're a fucking dick."

"And you love fucking my dick."

I rolled my eyes. "You're not funny."

"Emisandre thinks I'm rather hilarious."

I ignored him and kept walking. He led the way through the castle's corridors. The pristine marble gave way to lush carpets that matched the one in my room in Dale. Black with gold embroidery depicting characters. Stories told in thread.

"The Gods," he said, noticing where my attention had gone. "I visited a temple once with a magnificently painted ceiling. Images of the Pantheon and their instruments. Gilded and exalted. I much prefer these stories underfoot. They're not happy tales, and men don't look up when they feel like they're on top of the world, but they look down when they feel defeated. Those are the moments I like to be reminded of greatness."

"Are the Forsworn, like Goddess Tira, depicted here too?" I asked, admiring a segment that showed a woman with a halo of stars around her head, crowning a man with what looked like swirling smoke.

"Wouldn't be precious to me if it didn't include them. There." He pointed at a naked woman, lifting her face to the snout of a dragon. A plume of fire passed from her lips into the dragon's mouth. "Attor, the Goddess of Adversity, who created the dragons and gifted them fire. Another favorite of mine, in case you couldn't guess."

I sighed. "I still have so much to learn, and we have much to discuss. Don't think that because Bamidele is incredible, and I'm impressed that I'm not still angry at you."

"I know." He smirked.

We stopped at a pair of black doors etched in gold, like the ones to his study.

"Our room," he said and turned the handle, admitting me.

"Oh… wow."

70: Sorrow
The King

Keres' eyes immediately went to the farthest wall. Nearly popping out of her head as Enver and Senka sailed across the massive, west-facing window that gobbled up most of the wall with its arch. The cold sunlight shimmered across the dragons' scales—one of my favorite sights. But nothing compared to the look on her face.

"I see the valley you were talking about. I'm assuming those are the Rift Mountains and those are the Tecar Mountains," she said, surveying the land. "What's that river running through the valley?"

"The River Liriene."

She spun around and locked her shocked gaze on me.

"Didn't you realize it lets out here? It runs to the North Sea." I joined her by the window and pointed northeast. "Can you see the coast?"

Her gaze followed my ringed finger. The horizon was dull and hazy, drenched in the High Winter sunlight, but the sea was there.

"Wow," she said again.

Gods below, I loved the noises this woman made, but the sound of awe in her voice just then sent shivers through me.

"Watch this," I said and walked over to the side of the window. Pushing the sheer red curtain aside, I reached for the iron chain, unlocked it, and did the same on the other side of the window. Carefully, I gave the chain slack, letting the window ease down.

It creaked, and the chains rolled through the pulleys and gears. It opened forward, creating a glass balcony that reached out beyond the castle walls. The chilly air flooded in. I took my shoes off and walked out onto the platform. She looked down and tiptoed out.

"Keres," I said, drawing her eyes to mine. "You have wings. What are you afraid of?"

"I'm not afraid," she sneered, and strutted out to meet me.

We were several levels up. Nothing but snow-covered plains rolling by below and the mountains in the distance. Senka and Enver passed again, and she stepped back.

"We could fly with them, you know," I said, waggling my brows.

The thrill of the idea rose in her eyes like dawn, and then something stole her attention. She walked forward and pointed down at... *Oh, right.*

"What's that?"

It wasn't hard to explain the gated yard full of tall wooden spikes to anyone usually... but I wanted to lie to *her*. Which I couldn't. I hated liars. I let out a long sigh. "The Atys Grounds."

Crows circled the yard, perching on the spikes. "It's where I executed people."

"You had them impaled?"

"And or crucified."

The look in her eyes now—I hated it.

"Elves?" she asked.

"No, actually. Baoreans." Which didn't seem to make it less offensive to her. "During my ascension."

"Children?" she asked louder.

"No." I dropped my gaze. "The children were killed humanely and there were only a few of them."

"There is no humane way to kill children." She stepped forward, balling her hands into fists. Her eyes blackened.

I raised my chin and crossed my arms over my chest. "While we broach the topic of how wretched I am, perhaps you'd like to know about Lady Vega."

Green flashed through her eyes again, and she stilled.

"You know she was Elven," I started.

"Yes, you seem to have quite the fetish for Elven women."

I clenched my jaw and walked toward her. She met me in the middle of the platform; the wind stirring her hair and fury banking in her eyes. We stood toe-to-toe.

"In the Moldorn, the Kingdoms Serin and Golsyn are allied. One Human King, Alezander, and one Elven Queen, Toril. Like the Moldorn had accomplished, I sought an allyship with an Elven kingdom. The Moldorn borders Illyn and at the foot of the mountains there is a pass that is bare between them. A fortress on the horn of Ceden has recently been infiltrated by Illynads. The Ashan. The armies of Lydany and Essyd are supported by Serin and Golsyn. United. Dealing with the border issues. Unity between Humans and Elves is a powerful thing."

"And yet you've killed so many of us," she spat.

"I tried to make allies and made enemies instead. I've told you I offered treatises and people refused."

"So, genocide was the answer? You've pushed my people to the brink of extinction!"

"Elves aren't dying out, darling. That's a ridiculous notion. They're all over Aureum."

"That's not the point. There is still pain that every generation in the Sunderlands has had to live with since. You look at the world and see there are some of us left, but you don't see what we were left with and what was taken," she said.

"The Sunderlands was a place of power, but the people were weakened by the war and then they withdrew," I replied.

"I don't know much about the Elder War besides the fact that thousands of Elves were slaughtered. Our people needed to recover. We had every right to withdraw. It was self-preservation. I'm sure they would have rather been together to process the wounds of war."

I jutted my hand out toward the sky. "Your people refused help."

"We didn't want your help! And then you hunted us down anyway. Which proves you actually wanted to take advantage of us. We didn't need your help, but also didn't deserve what the Baore has done. You've *kept* us weak."

"Your people have lost more to the Gods than they have to the Baore—" I clamped my mouth shut.

Her brows pursed forward, and she frowned. "What?"

I ground my teeth and debated what I could and couldn't tell her. I would not lie, but I doubted she was going to believe me.

"If I asked you to trust my words—to believe in things nobody seems to anymore, would you?"

She ground her teeth, too. "I don't know."

I raked my hands through my hair and planted them on my hips. "You always get me out on a tangent, Ker. Your mind jumps from subject to subject."

She crossed her arms over her chest, and I didn't miss the shiver. I walked back into the room, and she followed. Once the window was closed, she sat down in one of the white upholstered armchairs by the marble fireplace. I got the fire going and sat in the matching chair across from her, propping my feet up on the brown leather ottoman.

She watched the fire dance. Senka and Enver crossed the window again, drawing my attention. Luncheon would be ready soon and as hungry as I was, I wasn't moving from my spot, and neither was she. Silence dug its heels in as I looked around the room, trying to find my words.

Since my last visit, the sheets had been changed from white linen to burgundy. The books I'd left on my writing desk were re-shelved, and my wardrobe wasn't the mess I usually left it in. Vangelis had every detail of this place managed well in my absences. I tired of Dale. I looked at her and wondered whether she could like it here. I still had so much I wanted to show her. But first...

"Lady Vega De Santis was from the Herda'al Province. Aside from being Elven, she was nothing like you."

She finally gave me her attention.

"Vee was this... frail, nervous, little thing. A girl from a castle by the sea. Ours was an arrangement made between Hadriel and her father, a nobleman of Eldervale. Hadriel was intent on me marrying for political gain after I became King. So, no. I don't fetishize anyone—I was playing cards. Hadriel sought alliances specifically with Elven kingdoms after losing our accord with yours. One, because it wasn't a common thing.

Also, Elves have magic that Humans don't. There were many benefits.

"Vee had no say in the matter, but it was rumored she had loved Prince Aristide, the elegant son of King Ursino. A fairy-tale prince. All the girls loved him in his court, and she was just another silly one. But to go from that—a picture-book prince, to me. Well, she was afraid of my every move. I broke her by marrying her when she loved another, when I knew she didn't want to. Arranged marriage was a caustic idea to her— anything out of her control exacerbated her nervousness. And me? We both know I'm not very soothing. Being the wife of someone you don't love is one thing. Being *my* wife is another. What I'd done in the Baore was no secret, and we married a year after Herrona had given birth to Hero. Bringing Vee here made her colder and weaker."

"Maybe because you have a garden of torture instruments in your backyard."

I snorted. "It didn't help. I ended up taking her back to Dale. She was fond of the northern garden, all the flowers there were red. Have you seen it?"

She shook her head.

"Right, you prefer the dark things, little Wither Maiden. Well, red was Vee's favorite color. Such a bold, evocative color for such a meek and fragile girl—I didn't get it. I expected that's what she had wanted to see. I tried to show her visions of the coasts, sea creatures. Gardens bursting with red flowers, rooms full of red dresses and jewels. I threw her a ball, and all the guests wore red. That was the one and only time she was happy. I can be attentive. I didn't dislike her. She was like a butterfly in a jar— shouldn't be kept in one, but something you wanted to enjoy, anyway. When you're so used to looking at the crags and clefts of the world, sometimes you want to just stop and stare at the soft things in others. I'd never looked at a woman and seen softness—appreciated it just for the sake of it. I saw weakness too, but I couldn't help her. She wasn't supposed to be strong, which meant she definitely shouldn't have been mine. But I tried... being something that didn't terrify people. And it didn't work.

"The night of the Red Ball, she danced with me. We laughed and danced until we were dripping with sweat and tired. Drunk on wine.

Drunk on the red of the night. It was the one and only time she took me to her bed. We were expecting a child soon after. I thought the alliance was secured, and I just had to maintain her and the child now. During her pregnancy, she became inconsolable. Anxious, constantly fretting about the babe. She feared the child would die or that she would, and to this day, I believe her fear was the reason Bamidele did die. Stillborn. The sight of her soft, motionless body, slicked with blood... it scarred Vee's mind.

"She was hysterical after that. Again, I tried to show her visions. I replayed the night of the Red Ball in her mind. She wept at having ever let me touch her. Cursed my seed—said I was a monster and that the child was devil-cursed. I tried to distract her with other pleasures and luxuries of being my Queen, assured her we would have more children if she wanted. She protested.

"I even tried to show her visions of Bamidele alive in paradise. She would have none of it. Vega disintegrated before my eyes. She was beyond the help of healers. I offered to send her home to her kingdom, but she refused. Ambassadors from her homeland didn't recognize her when they came. They blamed me. The alliance crumbled when she did."

"So, you frightened her to death?" Keres asked, arching a brow.

"You're not afraid of me, little wolf."

"Of course, I'm not," she snapped, as if my statement had been a challenge. I knew she didn't, but it was still relieving to hear it. "Doesn't mean I'll be yours the way you wished she would have been. I don't want to bring children into my world and I'm not soft."

My brows shot up. "Wished? I never wished she would love me. I coddled her, and after a while, it felt like trying to soothe a screeching babe with colic. True, at first, I might have pitied her, and for her beauty, I desired her. But once it was clear I'd never be able to touch her without rattling her very bones, I didn't wish for anything more with her. Being her husband was a duty—mostly political. Trying to keep her sane was a losing battle. She started hearing voices. In the end, she went mad, gouged out her own eyes because of her hallucinations, and died from infection. She had no resilience. If I'd ever wished for her to be mine, I would have been wishing for something she couldn't be. Don't you see? I am the

Unbridled and I tried to be something other than that for her. In the end, it didn't matter—it hurt the both of us. Bamidele was brought into this world needlessly and was ruined before she even took a breath. I don't collect jarred butterflies—they break in my world."

She just watched me with her furtive, bright eyes. Her emotions revealed the power in her Spirit. Black roots sprouted through the green of her irises.

"As for children," I said, standing up. "Bamidele was the first and only sorrow I've felt in my life. Maybe she was devil-cursed because she was mine. She didn't deserve that, and I don't deserve to be a father. So, no. I don't want children either—I don't torture them."

I looked over at her again, dragging my eyes over her dress.

"Why do you keep looking at me like that?" she asked. "Something wrong with my dress?"

"It's just ironic that you'd follow me home in that color. Gray is the color of mourning in the Baore."

71: STRIKING

Liriene

I hated the way she looked at him—looked next to him. I hated his arrogance, his aggression. And she didn't. It made no sense to me.

When she was betrothed to Silas, I wasn't opposed to it. I knew Silas. I just wanted her to be wed and in order. I hated that she fought and fed her curse. Then she had her foolish dalliance with Penance. The Massara boys were trouble. I might have been biased because Hayes was set to marry Katrielle, but Darius was dangerous for Keres.

She had enough rebellion in her Spirit already—he was just fuel for the fire. I don't know whether he genuinely loved her. All I know is that he went after her and he didn't come back with her. We never got the chance to talk about what happened. Now her marriage to Silas was annulled. Darius seemingly forgotten. Her eyes were full of emotion when she looked at the King. He'd been hurting her since the minute we walked in the door, and he was still rough with her. And he was sleeping with her. Marrying her—uncontested.

Why was she just going along with all of this? She hated the arranged marriage with Silas. She left the day after their wedding. She didn't stick with Darius and now she was letting this bastard take over her world?

Berlium's lust was persuasive. I'm sure he used it against her. She bore his scars and wore his ring. And yet she looked at him and didn't shudder. I found him repulsive.

He looked at her like she was shiny as polished jet. He wanted to see himself in her, wanted her to see parts of herself in him. He didn't deserve to look at her like that. My sister was dark and maybe even twisted inside, but she wasn't evil. She didn't deserve to be compared to him.

The way he touched her didn't match the way he looked at her. Obsession and adoration mingled when he looked at her, but he touched her disrespectfully. I didn't understand it. The first day in the throne room, the way she stood up to him—she looked right. She took up space in a throne room and commanded attention. Something was wrong now. She'd been in isolation with him, her captor, for too long. He'd done something to her.

Whatever she did, she was still my sister. If she couldn't resist him, I'd have to help her before he pulled her too far into the darkness.

"You think so loudly, Liriene," Hadriel said as we walked.

I cut him a look. "You were listening." It wasn't a question. He looked at me knowingly and gave me a crooked smile.

"Keres isn't good, but she isn't evil. She teeters somewhere in the middle with great potential to go either way. Divinity isn't always a beautiful thing. The King and the Coroner both hold beauty and damnation in their Spirits."

"She's ruining herself for him," I said.

"Keres is stronger than you think she is." He paused. "Did you have a poor relationship with your mother?"

I blinked at him and dropped my gaze to the strange carpet. "It wasn't very good. She could barely stand to look at me most days. Keres showed signs of magic at a very young age, and that was all the encouragement mother needed to favor her. I was plain. I spent more time with the other children of the clan than I did with Keres. Mother kept her at her heel—until they died together."

"Keres is strikingly like Resayla." He lifted his attention to the end of the hall and smiled again. As if he could see my mother at the end. "Eyes, green as envy—she saw everything. Sharp as an Illyinc blade, brilliant. Ferocious and extremely powerful. Before she became a mother."

He looked back at me. "I'll preface this by assuring you it's not your fault. It was the way of her world, the twists and turns of fate. But becoming a mother wasn't something Resa wanted. She was a traveler at heart. Wild. Adventurous. Hungry. She earned the title of Supreme

Magistress. Which is when we met. Keres shows the same eagerness to learn—to be what she is without reproach. They forced Resa to give up the things she wanted. And then she had children. You're not plain, Liriene. You were simply something that she wasn't ready for. I don't say it to be cruel. I knew your mother very well. She was not unloving. She loved children, but she loved the world more. Maybe Keres' magic was a thread that pulled her back into that world. And Keres is drawn to the darker parts of this world in the same way your mother was."

"Keres was the only mage in our clan, so that would make sense why mother was keen on teaching her magic. Ivaia was busy taking her place as Magistress, and when mother died, she took her place in training Keres."

"Sharp women made a sharp girl. The King is a sharp man. He bites and he cuts, but Keres does too."

I swallowed. "He's cruel to her."

Hadriel shrugged. "People teach others how to treat them."

"She allows herself to be treated poorly and chooses dangerous partners—because she treats herself poorly. She's her own worst enemy."

"That might have been the case, but Keres is making peace with what she is. In her way. With my help. Believe it or not, the King wants to help her."

"He wants to groom her," I said, rolling my eyes.

Hadriel stopped and touched my arm. "Instruments need tuning. He won't make her anything she doesn't want to be. He is not a gentle man, not a good man—"

"Is he even a man?" I tilted my head.

Hadriel smiled even brighter.

"See? You are not plain, Liriene. You are also an Instrument in need of tuning. Your mother overlooked you—I will not. Keres is strong enough to handle him. If she can handle herself, she'll learn to knock him on his ass. And he desperately needs it."

"I won't pretend he's not abusive. She's my sister. Beyond that, he's the enemy."

He sighed, and we resumed walking. "People make their own choices."

"She wasn't given a choice! We were both abducted. I was forced into a slave den, and he physically hurt her to subdue her. What else has he done to her since I've been down there?" I grabbed his arm.

"Don't expect me to trust either of you. Whatever manipulation she's under, I'm going to get her away from him. She doesn't need him or you to become what she's supposed to be. She needs Mrithyn. This false sense of empowerment he's been feeding her, while pinning her down, it has to end."

"Where was she before this?" he hissed. "Who was there to help her, to teach her? Ivaia was the founder of the Imperium! An academy for schools of magic. She could have taken Keres there. She shouldn't be so ill-educated and insecure. She's a Godling, and she's been hidden in the darkness. Only that darkness didn't serve her. It blinded her. She was fighting her destiny."

"You saw her in Ro'Hale, Hadriel. She wasn't fighting against it anymore. She was taking a stand. Against *you*. You fought her."

"No. Her magic fell at my feet. I knocked her unconscious with a word. She wasn't enough because she hadn't been prepared."

"And what are you preparing her for now?" I growled. "To be an obedient hound to sic on Berlium's enemies?"

He grabbed onto my arm, too. "Liriene, you know what is coming. You have seen it, have you not?"

I tore out of his grasp but couldn't shake his gaze.

"You can't protect her from that. She has been despised for what she is—the world needs what she is! She will become it one way or another. Ahriman has told her. Mrithyn told her—they both spoke to her in a vision. The two Gods held her between them and told her what she was, what she was meant to do."

"And Berlium? This creature of darkness—he is the Bloodstone. It's a match made in hell."

Hadriel looked around to make sure no one was listening. "So, you do know. You should recognize, then, that it's a devastatingly perfect match."

"Right," I snorted. "For your war."

He scrubbed his hand over his face and looked up at the ceiling. "I will wed them tonight."

Gods, I wanted to scream. This was all wrong—I wanted to hit something.

"What about Thane?" I snarled.

Hadriel shot dagger eyes at me. "Thane is a liar. Whatever he's told you, he is more of a danger to Keres than the King is."

"He wants to save us! He's going to."

"Keres doesn't need saving! She's safer here than she is with him!" he shouted back. "He would kill her."

"I don't believe you." I continued down the hall, trying to ignore the swish of his robes against the carpet as he rushed to my side.

"You need to stop looking at her like she's the girl who died and came back broken." His gray silver eyes searched mine. "She wasn't revived, she was remade. Your God struck you with vision—you didn't endure Death, Liriene. She did. Keres isn't a girl—that part of her didn't come back. She is a creature, too. She is the Blood Waker. Like Geraltain before her. The King and I have need of her and would exalt her, train her, to accomplish our goals. Thane would destroy her."

"I don't believe you," I snapped louder.

"God of Fury, blessed be." He threw his hands in the air.

I passed by a room with an ornate red door, and he stopped there, turning the knob and throwing it open. "This is your room."

I stopped and turned back, pushing past him over the threshold and slamming the door behind me. I heard him give an exacerbated sigh.

"Luncheon is soon. Someone will help you find something to wear. No gray."

"Goodbye, Hadriel," I snapped and stalked into the room. Hugging myself, I looked around, and a small-framed portrait on the end table caught my eye.

I walked over and picked it up. Tears lined my eyes and dread settled in my stomach as the green eyes of my mother stared back at me.

531

God of Fury, blessed be.

That's something my mother used to say when she was angry.

72: Soul Ties
Keres

"Wow," Berlium said when I stepped out of his massive closet.

"Can you tie the back? Where are Ciel and Minnow?" I held the back of the dark blue silk dress closed. It had the same off the shoulder neckline I'd been favoring. It tapered over my curves, down to my knees, flaring the rest of the way to the floor. The back was low cut, with lighter blue satin laces that cinched it from the base of my spine to my mid-back.

He moved toward me, and I turned so he could help me. Gods, he smelled so good.

"They're down in the servants' quarters, probably helping prepare the luncheon. We're more on our own here. I prefer privacy." He ran his fingers over the nape of my neck, sending chills down my spin.

"Your hair is up. You know I prefer it down," he said softly.

"I'll wear it down for you in private," I said.

He groaned. "I want to tear these laces open with my teeth."

"Well, I'd like to eat actual food, Berlium."

"I can call for our meal to be brought up here," he said, and I felt the distinct tug of a lace coming loose.

I spun around and hissed, "Self-control, beast."

He steepled his hands in front of his mouth and inhaled deeply. I narrowed my eyes at him.

"I see trouble in your eyes." A smile fought for control of my mouth.

"Oh? Is my soul too dark for you?" He smirked. Flecks of gold flashed in his oceanic gaze.

My gaze poured over him. The muscled body of a predator that just screamed sex. Dressed to kill in oil-black tailored pants, a cobalt blue shirt, with the first few buttons undone and the sleeves rolled up. His raven black hair was perfectly disheveled and wavy from constantly running his finger through it. And I rather liked those fingers, their onyx and gold rings, too.

I lifted my eyes back to his, allowing my Spirit's darkness to flood them. His eyes bore into mine and the mischief in his burned away by the heat of desire. He licked his lower lip slowly as he watched my red lips curve.

He pinched his eyes shut and scrunched his face as a smile claimed his mouth.

"Self-control. Self-control. Self—fuck this." He allowed me to hear his thoughts.

"I can't stay away from you, Darkstar." His hands found their places on either side of my neck, and he ran his thumb against my jaw.

Self-control. Self-control.

"If you don't bring me where the food is right now, I'm going to eat you," I said.

He dropped his head back and laughed. "I'm even less inclined to go now."

"No!" I laughed. "Let's go. Tie my dress and feed me. Girls can't live on sex alone." I gave him my back so he could finish with the laces.

His fingers fumbled with them again and I looked across the room at the mirror that showed me our reflection. He looked up over my shoulder, finding my gaze. He pulled the laces tight, earning a small sound out of me. A strong brow lifted.

"Make that sound again—I'll rip this dress off and we'll start with dessert."

I felt his breath on my neck.

"Noted." I tilted my head, looking at our reflection. He passed his hands around my waist and held me close. I held up my hand and summoned my Brazen into my palm.

"What are you thinking about?" he asked, narrowing his eyes.

"Turn and face me," I said.

534

We turned toward each other. I held up my hand, and the fire coated it, crawling up my fingertips.

"Call yours," I said.

He held up his hand and the blue flames answered, greedily licking at his fingers. I moved my hand toward his and he met mine. Clasping hands so our fire could unite.

"Is this our handshake now?" He chuckled.

"Absolutely." I laughed.

"And you said you weren't soft."

"We are literally touching each other with hellfire, Berlium. There's nothing soft about us."

"You're right. To touch you is to burn."

As usual, he kept my hand in his as we walked to the dining hall. Which caught Liriene's disapproving attention the minute we saw each other. Everyone stood as we took our spots at the table. The dining hall was different here than in Dale.

The table stretched horizontally along the back wall with two more tables branching off of it to line the room and leave the center of it open to reception. Berlium and I sat side by side, with Hadriel to the left of the King. Liriene sat next to me, and Emisandre annoyingly earned herself a seat next to Hadriel. The room was full of people, which I hadn't expected.

"Regretting not starting with dessert?" Berlium asked, leaning his head down to mine.

I simply kissed his cheek in response, then wiped away the soft mark of my lip rouge. He smiled at my touch.

My mouth was watering at the food set before us. He speared pieces of meat and placed them on my dish and then on his own. I scooped the vegetables that were close to me for the both of us. Hadriel passed us a basket of rolls and when I turned to give it to Liriene, I found her glaring at me.

"You're eating meat."

Someone leaned in between our chairs to pour our wine, breaking her stare. Berlium glanced down the table at her still empty plate. I took a roll out of the basket and put it in front of her.

"You don't have to, but you need to eat."

She raised her brows and let out a long breath before shoveling roasted vegetables onto her plate.

Conversation filled the room, accompanied by the soft music of a quintet. Ladies passed around the table, refilling glasses and smiling at guests. Everyone was very well dressed, and not everyone was Human. A few of them stood out and I wondered whether they were Illynads, at least partly.

"Welcome back, sire," a man said, stepping forward and bowing. He was dressed in all black with his platinum blond hair slicked back. His face was paler than the moon and boyish, but his voice was coarser than I would have expected. He appraised me with cool brown eyes.

"Olysseus." Berlium nodded to him.

"Your bride to be, I presume," he said with a lifted chin. He pushed his black coat aside to tuck his hand into his pocket.

"Lady Keres Aurelian of Ro'Hale."

"The Coroner." Olysseus' eyes flashed and then slid back to the King. "Emilian told me about your special request. I understand the nature of it now, my lord. Well chosen."

"Agreed," Berlium said, and then turned to me. "Olysseus is an acclaimed arcanist conducting research here for me."

"A privileged position," Olysseus said with a nod. "Work I'd enjoy giving you an account of another time."

Berlium nodded back, and the man sank back into the crowd. It wasn't hard for him to blend in—almost everyone was wearing black.

Other people came and went, but Berlium didn't bother introducing them and they barely acknowledged me. When I'd cleaned my plate, he started piling more food onto it.

"You're honey-thick, little wolf, and I plan on keeping you that way."

"Trying to fatten me up for a sacrifice?" I said before pressing my lips to the brim of my wineglass. Knowing he loved my supple curves made me blush.

He chuckled and popped an olive into his mouth, licking the brine off his fingers.

"All the better for eating you, my girl."

Hadriel tapped his shoulder, turning his head so he couldn't see my smile. He ducked down to hear whatever he was whispering to him. Hadriel's fingers flitted, not so subtly hiding who he was pointing at. And that someone tapped on their glass, cuing everyone to be quiet.

Berlium and Hadriel exchanged glances before looking at the man who'd rung for attention.

"To the King and his beautiful bride!" the man said, his words slurred.

Berlium lifted his glass, and everyone drank—but he wasn't smiling.

"What's wrong?" I whispered. The atmosphere took a strange turn and my stomach tightened with uneasiness. Was it because we were Elven? Were they getting ready to attack us?

Berlium's hand touched my thigh before he got up. Walking to the back of the room, where the man who had spoken stood with a smug look on his face. Yarden appeared, following behind him.

His warm golden colored knit shirt was tight, and the collar covered his neck, defining his muscles. Bringing his hand to rest on the hilt of his sword, he puffed his chest out and strolled closer. Berlium clapped a hand on the man's shoulder, knocking him off balance. Another man appeared behind him, who looked pissed off.

I sent my attention to the King's heartbeat. He was angry, yet it was steady. His target's heart, however, was racing like a rabbit from a bear.

"What's going on?" Liri asked.

I looked at Hadriel, but his gaze was fixed on the commotion.

"My King, the least she could do is address the room—" the man said louder. He must have been drunk. Spittle flew from his mouth. Berlium scrubbed his hand over his face with disgust and stepped closer to the guy. The man then jabbed his finger in my direction over the King's shoulder.

"After killing our sons! Have you nothing to say?"

Berlium had him pinned against the wall with his elbow to his throat before I could blink. I moved to stand, but Hadriel stopped me. Guards swarmed the situation and Berlium tore himself away as the man and his unfriendly looking companion were dragged from the room.

"Well, that might have been an overreaction," Emisandre chimed.

Hadriel and I both leveled our gazes on her.

"Oh, please. You're the Coroner. You've been killing Dalis men for years. Didn't you think they might have families too? There are two sides to this war. People on both."

I locked eyes with the King as he strode back to the table. The muscles in his jaw hammered, and he stretched his fingers out at his side like was trying not to clench them into fists. He sat heavily back down in his chair and took a long drought of his drink. Waving for it to be refilled and then downing that too.

"Should I?" I asked.

He looked at me. "Should you what?"

I didn't know what I could say to the people here. I wasn't sorry for killing the soldiers who had been hunting my people. No, I hadn't ever thought about them having families or feelings. They were prey. Berlium knew that. But still... was there something to be said now that I was at his side?

I searched his eyes for recommendation. It seemed the disruption was every bit a surprise to him, as it was to me. He looked back down at his plate and tore open his bread roll. Stabbing his knife into the butter and then pressing it into the dough so hard it flattened beneath it. He tore a piece between his teeth and watched the room as he chewed. Yarden met his attention and a silent conversation passed between them. The other guards eventually came back into the room and claimed more noticeable positions.

"They hate me," I said to Berlium under my breath.

"Few do. Most fear you." He sawed through a piece of meat and pushed it into his mouth.

"But I—"

He stopped and looked at me. "You're not a centerpiece, Keres. You're a woman and a weapon. They're supposed to fear you. But they must respect you. If not you, me. I am King. I will not tolerate displays of aggression."

Liriene snorted into her glass, and his gaze cut over my head to her.

"We haven't been properly introduced, since you know, Tecar went up in flames." Emisandre tilted her head so she could see Liriene.

"This is my sister, Liri," I said, reaching for my wineglass again.

"Charmed," Emisandre said.

I followed her gaze to my sister and noticed something. Emisandre's ears were very similar to Liriene's. Not as pointed as the average Elf's, but not round either. I would have told myself it meant nothing. That ears came in all shapes and sizes, but Emisandre admitted to being mixed. I looked at Liriene—really looked at her.

Her red hair, her gray eyes. Her face was slender, her neck was elegant. She was taller, leaner. We didn't share our curves, but I also had muscle. I felt like my face was fuller, and I slouched more. If she was mixed, was I? Were we half-sisters?

And then there was one other thing I couldn't stop thinking about— her name. Her full name. I'd read it in that damned letter from my mother. The one she wrote about all the 'marry a knight' nonsense. She designated guardians over me. Mother said Liri could not be considered her heir… and her full name was Liriene Hadrianna Lorien. We didn't share a last name. I glanced from my sister to Emisandre, and then to Hadriel. If he was someone my mother admired, the middle name made sense. He was Human. Liriene obviously had something else mixed in her blood, but could it be Lamentar, as he guessed? It was a specific guess. Maybe he knew who her father was.

My mother obviously spent time with the Magister, but she also had ties to the Ressid. Her letter named a man named Emeric as my guardian in the event that Ivaia, my father, or Indiro weren't around. What was he—who was he? Maybe he was Liriene's father. I wondered if Liriene even knew her own full name—she couldn't have read that letter. Which begged another question. Why didn't mother teach her to read?

I shoved the thoughts under the table. They were making my head hurt. All that mattered was that no matter any difference between us, Liriene wasn't my half anything. She was wholly mine. Whatever messes my mother made wasn't our job to clean up. Liri and I just had to find our own way.

"Do these people know what happened in Tecar?" Emisandre asked in a low voice.

Berlium cast his eyes at her next.

She shrugged. "Your mate is Death Incarnate. She has slaughtered your soldiers—your people. Her sister just displayed power in captivity. These are the kinds of things that incite riots, for both sides."

"She's not his mate," Liriene said flatly.

Berlium raked his hand through his hair and then rested it on my leg. Crossing his legs, he lifted the other hand to his chin, absently rubbing his stubble.

"I don't actually believe in mates," I said. "Is there one person you're fated for? I believe in bonds, but not in some one, true mate kind of thing. I think there are different kinds of connections. We find different parts of ourselves in other people. Every connection happens for a reason, but we ultimately choose."

"Agreed," Berlium said. "People make connections and choices. I've chosen Keres. If that incites a riot, I'll do what I do best. I don't grieve for those she's killed. This is war. It brooks no explanation. They will come to see whose side she's on. Once we are wed."

"Tonight, then?" Liriene asked.

"What?" I asked.

Berlium turned and looked at me. "We'll discuss it in private later."

"Tonight?" Emisandre pressed. "Surely, you don't mean that."

Liriene snorted again.

"Silence your sister," Berlium thought to me.

"Silence your witch," I hissed back.

"Silence. All of you." Hadriel joined in what seemed to be a mental group chat. *"People are watching."*

We returned our attention to the room.

"I'll be excused now," Liriene said, throwing her napkin onto her plate and shoving her chair out. Earning more stares. Nobody protested her impoliteness, but I got up too.

"Keres," Berlium said in a low voice. I looked down at him.

"I need a moment with my sister." I didn't wait for his approval.

Yarden moved the minute I did, meeting me at the door.

"What happened to those men?" I asked him.

"They were handled," he stated. His voice was uncharacteristically hard.

I looked up at him. "Are you okay?"

"I'm fine," he said quietly.

"Have you seen your lady love?"

He gave me a look unlike any he had before—it wasn't kind.

"You're not fine. Did I offend you?"

"No."

I touched his arm and stopped walking with him. "Tell me."

"It's Lady Emisandre."

"I don't like her either. What did she do? Give me a reason to smack that smug look off her face—I'm dying to."

"It's nothing I can't handle." He started walking again.

Liriene's red hair stood out in the corner of my eye. She turned around a corner.

"This girl—doesn't even know her way around the castle."

We followed her. She was far down the long hall by the time we rounded the corner.

"Liri," I called. She didn't turn. "Ugh, Liriene."

She cast me a look over her shoulder.

"Where are you going?"

"I have no idea," she said indignantly.

"Wow, you two really are sisters," Yarden chided.

I shook my head. Nobody passed us in the hall, not that Liriene would have stopped for anyone. She turned and ascended stairwells, opened random doors, and stopped at windows.

"Are you looking for something specific?" I asked. We passed a window that overlooked the Atys Grounds. His horrific garden of spikes.

"Did you know mother spent time here?" she asked over her shoulder.

"Well, I know she spent time in the Baore. I didn't know she'd been here, but she spent time with Hadriel when she worked for the Ministry."

She shook her head and finally stopped. Turning to face us, she glared at Yarden.

"I'll give you a moment," he said and walked back down the hall. We stood in front of the window, and she noticed the Atys Grounds.

"What—"

"Don't ask," I said.

She narrowed her eyes at me. I really didn't want to have this conversation, but it was inevitable.

"I know you're wondering what the fuck I'm thinking."

She planted her hands on her hips, drawing my attention to the scar on her left hand that matched mine.

"Last time I saw you—that day I went to Mannfel, I was abducted."

I told her everything I'd seen and what I did.

"I know you don't see it, but what I've learned from Hadriel and Berlium so far has made a big difference. What I could do to those men is an ability Mrithyn gifted me. Being here has helped me learn more than I ever had the chance to before. Berlium isn't a good man—"

"And yet, you love him."

I frowned at her. "Is that what you think?"

"You've run away with your feelings, Keres. The King and his magister may teach you these things, but at what cost? They're still controlling you—they're using you."

"I'm doing this for us, Liriene. Our people—this is how we move forward. They will have a place in this kingdom, in its revolution. My kingdom."

"What is that going to make you, Keres?"

"Liri," I said, pinching the bridge of my nose. "You once told me you could see through me. What my curse was doing to me—that I wasn't fooling anyone. Well, I was fooling someone. Myself. I was afraid and ashamed of my curse. Didn't know how to control myself. I'm still me and still fighting for something. You never saw that, so maybe that's why you don't see it now. All you saw was my curse. I know what Berlium is through his actions. There are still secrets. He doesn't tell me everything. I know he holds some level of power over me, but it's not that trick of his magic anymore. I'm not afraid or ashamed anymore—or alone."

"Is this how far you're willing to go not to feel alone? You'd marry your enemy—become a monster's plaything?"

"I am not his plaything," I said, stepping closer. I could feel it. The Death Spirit looked at her through my eyes. Silver light brightened in her own eyes, and she stepped closer, too.

"Look at you, sister," I smiled. "I'm not the only one willing to play with monsters, now, am I?"

She turned her head away.

"You feel it, Liri. The power in you. You always made me feel like I ought to be ashamed of what I was. Of my choices. Look at you now. You set Tecar on fire—you were fucking amazing. We got to be something with each other we've never been before. Can't you understand? We aren't those girls we used to be. Not anymore."

She glared at me again. I sighed. "Berlium isn't a man. I am not a girl. Neither are you. I didn't come back from the dead to fear anything life throws at me."

"And if it leads to your destruction or more loss for our people? I don't understand what you're hoping to accomplish here."

I pointed out the window. "You see that? The Atys Grounds. Berlium used them to execute people. His own people. He stops at nothing to get what he wants. Right now, our people are in a hole beneath Dale. I will stop at nothing to get them out. The Sunderlands may never be the same. Nobody came to our rescue. Our people may not understand at first, but I am going to figure out a way for them to return home. Even if they walk there under his banner. They may belong to the Baorean King, but I'm the bulwark between our people and him. Beyond that, whatever his war is—I know he has ties to Illyn. I intend to make sense of them. This goes beyond our people. I'm not a woman pining for company. I am a Godling and I'm going to be a Queen. I'm not abandoning parts of myself, and I'm not shying away from everything I could be."

"So, you're going to marry him? What about Silas? What about Darius?"

"You know, that question might have knocked the wind out of me before, but it's backward thinking now. I will not sink into feelings. Silas—I never wanted to be bound to him. Darius was a kindred spirit. Part of me will always love him, but I can't have him. The Oracle in Ro'Hale told me he'd die if I stayed with him. He'd die for me. I could never accept that. Berlium... I know I shouldn't want him, but I do. In ways I don't even understand. He infuriates me to no end, but it's the truth between us. We want each other. I'm not afraid of him—I'm not afraid of what I am with him. There will be consequences for my choices, but I don't see any other choice that puts me in a position of power."

"Fearless doesn't mean wise. What about Thane?" she asked. "I saw him—I told you what he said. During the battle of Ro'Hale, he came to me in that vision. He said he would come for us, and he will. He is an option. I don't know how, but he will help us. You won't be stuck here."

"Thane?" I asked.

I remembered the battle at Ro'Hale—her mentioning him. She'd stood amazed, speaking to no one. Thane. He's coming.

I shook my head. "We don't know who he is or if that's true. That was then, Liri. Where is he now? Who's to say what he wants—whether we could trust him?"

"You're tied to him," she said so low I thought I'd misheard her.

"What?" I asked.

"You're tied to him. He told me."

"What does that mean?"

She looked down. "I'm not sure. He's only said there is a bond between you that cannot break. That he will find you. That he will come."

I shivered at the thought.

"Well, I'm sick of being claimed by a different man at every turn. What's unfolded between the King, and I may be fucked up, but I have chosen my bond with my eyes wide open. He didn't make me mindless—he could have gotten me to follow blindly. I'm not doing that. I don't know Thane. He can break down the door. It doesn't mean I'll be going anywhere with him."

"You've seen him, you know. He's come to you before."

"What?" This time my voice was barely above a breath.

Thoughts connected. He was the one pursuing me in dreams and shadows, who told me to wait for him. Berlium and Hadriel knew him. Were they being protective or possessive? Hadriel told me he was dangerous and not to believe him. Liriene believed him, though. Who was right and who was wrong? I shook my head again.

"I've made my choice. Besides, Thane isn't here. They're telling me not to trust him—"

"Of course, they are." She motioned toward the view beyond the window. "You think they're any better? You think this is right?"

"It's not about what's right, Liriene. It's about power—right and wrong are relative in this world. And our people are here, Liri. We can't just leave them because a stranger said he's coming for us. What about them—do you think he even cares about them?"

She snorted and planted her hands on her hips. Looking away from me and shaking her head.

"Tonight, then?" she murmured. "You'll marry the King of the Baore, our enemy. For power."

I shrugged. "He hasn't told me of that plan. But when he calls, I'll answer."

"Like calls to like," she said. Her eyes glazed over, the words towing her mind under. "What will happen to me?"

I reached out and took her by the shoulders. "I will protect you. We can stand together, Liri."

Her gaze refocused on me. "You're wrong. You're tying your soul to our enemy. I don't know whether I can stand alongside you silently while you do that."

I let go of her. We gazed into each other's eyes. I knew why she felt the way she did. But she'd chosen her feelings, and I'd chosen mine.

73: SEVERITY
Keres

Yarden escorted us both back to the dining hall. It was emptier, with only a few people lingering. Berlium's gaze sailed across the room, and he stood as we entered. Hadriel and Emisandre followed.

A man stepped into our path, directly in front of me. "Excuse me, my lady," he said. He stopped and his stare lingered. As if something dawned on him. He bowed at the waist.

When he stood, he met my gaze dead on. He wasn't much taller than me and was probably as old as me. His black hair was divided, so half of it was up in a bun and the rest had been buzzed away, creating an undercut. A black band wrapped around his head, crossing his face diagonally to cover one of his eyes. Maybe he lost it to injury.

His pointed ears were lined with gold hoops. The eye that was visible had a pure gold iris with black diamond-shaped pupils. And his thick, dark brow was pierced with two gold hoops. His mouth—he had short fangs that created an underbite. They jutted out at the corners of his beautiful lips, and he smiled, drawing my attention to his dimples. A light brown scruff lined his chiseled jaw.

"I'm Emillian," he said.

Thank the Gods, my jaw hadn't dropped. I became acutely aware of the fact that I had a thing for dark-haired men. If he could be called that. He wasn't Human.

His skin was a golden-green color that gleamed with sweat. More skin was visible than was wise, considering it was High Winter. His shirt was sleeveless, opened on the sides. Allowing me to trace my eyes over his well-defined muscles. It was a long olive colored tunic that ended mid-thigh. Beneath it, he wore loose black trousers and had black leather loafers on that were filthy. I noticed his hands were also dirty. As he tracked my attention, he rubbed his hands together.

"I'm Keres. I think Olysseus mentioned you earlier. Nice to meet you." I held out my hand, unafraid to get a little dirty.

He shook it firmly, which I returned.

Berlium's hand clapped down on Emillian's shoulder. "Isn't she stunning, Emillian?"

"Unparalleled," he said. "You chose your gift well, sire."

I chuckled. "You're the third person to say that. What is this gift?" I quirked a brow up at Berlium.

His smile brightened his eyes. "You'll see."

"It'll be worth the wait, Lady Keres. Trust me—I made it."

"Oh?" I smiled at him. "Intriguing."

"We'll see you later, Emillian. The lady and I have some things to discuss."

"Sounds good, my lord." Emillian bowed and left.

Berlium reached for my hand, and I took his. Hadriel and Emisandre exchanged glances.

"Lady Liriene," Emisandre broke the silence. "Let's walk. Talk. Bamidele is a marvelous place. I'm sure we'll find something interesting."

Liri looked at me, and I shrugged. "Let me know if you find anything interesting."

They left the room. "I better go with them," Hadriel sighed. "I'll see you two soon."

They left Berlium and I with Yarden, whom he excused.

As we walked, I said, "Yarden seems perturbed by Emisandre."

"I'd expect as much," he said. "He used to be posted here in Bamidele. Emi... she reported something that cost him his position here."

I knew he meant Yarden's relationship with the woman he'd mentioned. "Interesting."

No wonder he was on edge. It made me dislike Emisandre even more.

"You sided with Emisandre, then. Of course. Taking Yarden from

Bamidele to Dale."

Berlium snorted. "You do not hide your feelings well, Keres."

Suddenly, he steered me into an alcove and pressed me against the wall. He braced one hand against the wall beside my head and touched my hip bone with the other.

"She looks at you like she wants you to fuck her—possibly again. Have you ever been with her?" I asked.

He smirked. He tilted his head from one side to the other, watching my eyes, my mouth. I hardened my gaze.

"You seemed to like the look of Emillian." His voice was dark and rough, not hiding his feelings either.

"Maybe I did."

His body crushed against mine, and I tasted his magic in the back of my throat. I glared up into his eyes as his claw dug into my hip. His touch was stern, but his eyes held a calculated calmness. Which was scarier than aggression would have been.

Heat swarmed my belly and between my legs, and a low moan escaped me.

He laughed—the taste of magic dissipated, and he loosened his hold. Dropping his head down, bringing his lips near mine.

"After all this time I put up with your screaming, you think I'm ever going to let someone else make that sound come out of you again? No, little wolf. You howl only for me."

I smiled up at him and watched his face contort with confusion. He reached for my throat, but his hand spasmed as I tightened my mental grip on the blood singing through his veins.

"And you, bear," I dropped my smile and rushed blood to his cock, forcing an erection. He groaned. I tilted his hips against mine and writhed against him. Relishing in the pain that he probably felt mixed with pleasure. "You growl only for me."

I released my hold, giving the blood in his body free rein. He staggered backward, catching his breath as he realized what I'd done. Emotions fought for dominance on his face. I held my left hand up, looking at my nails, and turning my hand over to assess the sparkling ring. I summoned Brazen, twirling it through my fingers.

"To the King, the spoils?" I met his sapphire stare. "Well, to the Queen, the satisfaction."

He straightened his spine, rising to his full height. So, I did as you're supposed to do when facing down a bear and I mirrored his posture.

He chuckled and relaxed. Wrapped his arms around my waist and goaded me forward, directing my steps down the hall.

Leaning down, he bit my ear.

"Stop it." I giggled, and he tugged harder.

"Mm," he growled against my skin. "Do you not realize how small the Gods made you compared to me? Such a little thing, with such a sharp tongue, and not enough weight behind you—no wonder that's where they put me."

I laughed and arched my back against him. "Good. I'd like you to stay there when we have dessert."

"Glad to see you still have an appetite after that incident in the dining hall."

"I have a rather delicious devil on my shoulder. Lucky me."

"Lucky for this devil, I have such a wicked angel to sin with," he said huskily, and pressed a kiss to my shoulder. "Having you here, in my home, makes me want to fuck you till your screams touch every hall."

His words touched me between my legs. His fingers dug into the laces of my dress and my heart rate kicked up as I heard them tear. I gasped out a laugh and pulled out of his grasp, lurching into a sprint.

"Catch me first, hunter."

My wings burst out between us, nearly taking up the width of the corridor. I flew down the hall, through a door that opened into an empty foyer. Not daring to turn to look back—a claw latched onto my ankle and then slipped. I sailed to the floor. Squealing as he crashed into me, and I tucked us both into my wings. We rolled, but I ended up on top. Our breathing was ragged laughter. I moved to straddle him.

"I should have expected that to be a short chase."

"Yes." He laughed. "You should have."

My claws reached out through my fingertips, and I tore through his shirt. Buttons popped and rolled to get lost in the carpet.

"Fuck—I liked this shirt." His eyes were as bright as his blue Brazen.

"I liked my dress, beast."

"I'll buy you another."

"I'd rather wear nothing at all since you like to rip all my clothes, anyway."

Placing my hands on his chest, I adjusted my hips against his. He allowed his wide-eyed gaze to wander over me. One hand reached for my throat and the other gripped my hip, not stopping his claws from piercing through my dress to prick into my skin.

"Gods above," I hissed.

"You will be wearing nothing by the time I get you back to the room," he said, slowly scissoring his fingers through the silk.

"Ahem," someone coughed.

I lowered my wings to look over my shoulder, and Berlium lifted his head. I willed my wings back into hiding and stood. Looking down at the damage done to my dress and over to Berlium. He took his shirt off and draped it over his shoulder.

"Of all the things I could have ever imagined for the two of you—rolling around, ripping each other's clothes off in the corridors of Bamidele was not one of them," Hadriel said and rubbed his hand over his head.

"Where are Liri and Emisandre?" I asked.

"Liriene didn't want to talk to Emisandre—I don't blame her. She went back to her room and Emi went to the alchemy labs. Now, if you two are done acting like besotted youths, can we have an adult discussion?"

Hadriel tucked his arms into the sleeves of his robes and blinked at us expectantly. Berlium and I exchanged glances.

"We are not *besotted*," I said as I took Berlium's hand.

The King sighed as he squeezed my fingers between his. "She dearly hates me."

Hadriel groaned. "To the library. Now." He pointed his finger toward the hall, and we marched under his order.

"We're not really dressed for the library." I frowned as we walked.

Hadriel really didn't care, tilting his head toward me and pressing his lips into a thin line. Berlium put his shirt over my shoulders, hiding the torn laces and the gashes in the side of my dress.

"It won't take long," he said.

"You're shirtless." I snorted.

"Are you complaining?"

I gave him the side-eye. *"I have my dessert and want to eat it too."*

He smirked.

We reached a pair of gilded doors and Berlium held one open for Hadriel and me.

"Is this the spire?" I asked.

The room was round, and a balcony rail hedged each tier. The center of the room was open between levels, which launched so high that I could barely make out the paintings on the ceiling. Down below, there were fewer floors, but enough to mean that they sat below ground level.

Golden stairs curled into spirals, connecting the levels. The shelves were a beautiful cherry wood. There were deep-seated brown leather sofas, and tables laden with books. People shuffled around on different levels. Those filing books or dusting shelves wore light blue robes. Those who were studying wore their plain clothes.

We descended a few levels. The King's half-nakedness drew a little attention, but he ignored it. We came down to the lowest level and the wallpaper that adorned the other levels was stripped away. Bare stone walls lined with glass shelves created an emporium of books and knick-knacks that appeared to be floating from a distance. To the right of the room was a pair of glass doors. Beyond it was a hall, both walls decorated with the same glass shelves.

"I don't understand," I said as I looked around. "The Baore has never conquered any province. You've assaulted my lands, but only ever touched the clans. How have you accumulated so much?"

"The King has many interests, many talents, and very few boundaries," Hadriel said pensively.

Berlium stretched out his arms and turned in a circle, looking at the room, lifting his eyes up to the top of the spire.

"I am the arsenal at your fingertips. The warlord and the weapon. Imagine yourself on the battlements beside me and overlooking the world. The trees hold up their hands, giving. The oceans rush to meet us at the shore, giving. Even the river—did it not give you back? The mountains hold up the Sun, and castles hold up their banners. If you cut down a tree, you can build something. If you climb the mountain, you can see the valley. And if you capture the flag, you become the King. This world is always giving something up—something for the taking. I have lived my life obsessively. Hungrily."

"It seems you've lived a hundred lives," I said.

He flashed his sapphire eyes at me. "Not a hundred."

I stared at him, calculating. He ascended his throne twenty years ago. This collection had to be an inheritance. But something in me was screaming: *how many lives? How many years?*

Berlium looked timeless—his interests and talents were boundless, as Hadriel had said. I thought back to his personal study in Dale. He'd said it was but a shrine. He'd said his most precious collections were here.

Bamidele was the dragon's hoarded treasure. Not the golden kind. The kind his family must have paid for in blood. The brother bears were fearsome kings in their glory days, or so the history books say. The Baorean Revolution started in their era and continued under Berlium's reign. This had to be the root. A root that reached beneath Bamidele and shot up toward the heavens like a stone tree. A wealth of knowledge that needed a castle to contain it—a fortress to defend it.

I realized Dale was a front. He worshiped the Goddess of Knowledge. He loved Gods long forgotten—Forsworn. Gods I'd never even heard of. He was something I'd never imagined he could be.

If I asked you to trust my words—to believe in things nobody seems to anymore, would you?

The severity of that question hit me in the chest like a drum.

Would you give me the chance to show you what was in the dark?

This was the dark. The King seemed to exist in a void that swallowed secrets—as bottomless and hungry as he was. Hidden from rumor, hidden from history. Did anyone know about this place beyond the walls of

Bamidele? He said even its name was only spoken here.

He studied my face—no doubt reading every emotion that flickered across it. He was right. I wasn't good at hiding my feelings. Somehow, anger prevailed.

He crossed his arms over his bare torso and returned my smoldering gaze.

"I want answers," I said.

The corner of his mouth flicked up, and he tilted his head toward the glass doors.

Beyond the doors, the shelves in the hall were full of strange books. Written in different languages. There were weapons on them, too. Some looked more like artifacts. At the end of the hall was a small room. It was cold and smelled like books and stone. On some shelves there were skulls.

"My family," he said, gesturing to the skulls.

I hugged myself, tightening his shirt around me. Hadriel followed us into the room, closing the glass doors.

"Before you get freaked out—"

"I'm already freaked out," I said.

"We used their bodies for science... and there's a good reason." He stood in the center of the room and met my gaze. Taking a deep breath and readying his words.

"You keep telling me you're not afraid, Keres. I need you to give me more than courage now. I need you to give me your trust."

74: STORIES
Heres

"The Veil is thin between the Baore and Illyn. When I was a child, I encountered a Godlander who was also childlike. I was sickly. Probably would have died, but the Godlander imbued me with power. Made me what I am. But he didn't stop there. He turned my entire family into a coven of his creation. Both my father and his brother. Everyone in our houses. The brother bears were fearsome. This power enabled them to claim both thrones of the Baore. Originally, they were from here, when this place was called Dulin. They claimed Dale from my mother's family, the Ettiene's. I was born here too."

"Born when?" I asked.

Another smile crawled over his mouth. Hadriel leaned against the wall to my right, resting his foot up on it, and lit his pipe. I looked at him. He looked down and smiled before taking a pull. I looked back at Berlium expectantly.

"Two hundred years ago."

His heartbeat quickened as he searched my eyes for understanding—belief.

"How?"

"Few people know this, but my father and uncle were twins. They were thirty years old when I encountered the Godlander. When we were gifted the power, they stopped aging. My brothers and I aged until we also hit thirty years. The Godlander liked that the two Baorean Kings were brothers. Said it reminded Him of His brother, so that's why He based the age on them. It preserved anyone in the coven who was older than thirty at the time we turned at their age, but they were weaker than the young. Everyone else caught up.

"My father and uncle—my entire coven, we perfected a system. Slipping back and forth between Dulin and Dale, switching every thirty years or so, as time turned pages through history. My father chose Dale as his because it was the forefront of the Baore. He gave my uncle, Leto, the backseat. Making Dulin more of a retreat for our coven."

"You're immortal?" I asked.

"I bleed, which you know. Of course, I was able to kill my family. But if my kind is uninterrupted by death, I think my lifespan would prove pretty damn close to immortal."

"But you said you were there when Herrona was a child," I said, furrowing my brow.

"I never said I was a child then. I had been living in Dale for a cycle. My family and the Aurelian family had better relationships. Herrona was a child. I wouldn't have noticed her if she hadn't stood up to the Spirit of Famine. And my noticing her wasn't anything more than that. She seemed like a remarkable child.

"Then I went into a cycle of hiding. When I came back, Herrona was an adult. That's when I truly saw her. She'd become a remarkable woman. That was about twenty-three years ago that we met in her adulthood. Over that next year, I pursued her. The relationship you already know the details of. Then she married Prince Tamyrr and gave birth to Hero twenty-two years ago. For the next two years after that, I plotted my ascension to claim both Baorean thrones. I married Vega shortly after that."

"So, you've been hiding. Going between Dale and Dulin... in cycles."

"Yes," he said. "I also spent time in Illyn."

"How did your cycles not overlap with people you knew?"

"Some were longer, some shorter. When we weren't traveling, we paid time to building Bamidele into what it is now. This spire houses things we collected over the centuries, from our travels."

"And what about history... how were you not recorded until recently?" I asked.

"We went by different names throughout our cycles."

My eyes widened. I felt like I was seeing him for the first time.

"Berlium is the name I chose for this cycle. Not my true name." His smile didn't reach his eyes.

"My coven—our names are sacred. Like anchors for our secrets that could not be moved by time. No matter what mask we donned, no matter who we were in a cycle, our names were hallowed. Like spells, forbidden to incant outside the coven, lest they summon the truth of what we were. The Blood Lyric. They are who we are—our only tie to our origins. The truth singing in our veins. Flowing through us across oceans of time. Keres, two hundred years, empty and insatiable, is a very long time. I haven't spoken my name in... Gods, Hadriel, how long has it been?"

"Many, many cycles," he said. "I'm still stuck on the last name you chose, Erik."

I blinked stupidly, looking between them. "Berlium. Erik."

"Alistair. Raphael. Casamir," Hadriel rattled off.

Berlium closed the distance between us, laying his hands on my shoulders. His ocean blue eyes bore into mine, and I felt like I could drown in them. I remembered he was shirtless, touching my hand against his chest. Feeling his heart beating beneath my palm. Enduring.

I heard the blood coursing through him, the music of his pulse. Listening as if it might tell me his true name. I met his eyes. He opened his mouth to speak, bringing my gaze to his fangs. My heart raced.

"My name is Draven."

Gold streaked the blue in his eyes, brightening the depths of the storm within.

"Draven," I repeated. He closed his eyes, as if he were relishing in the sound of his name on my lips.

"What does it mean?" I asked. He brought his hands to my throat and opened his eyes.

He smirked. "The Hunter."

I bit my bottom lip and smiled. "Of course, it does."

"Keres," Hadriel said, gathering our attention. "When you wed tonight, there will be a ritual. The bond between you will be forged in darkness—in blood. If you cannot accept the bond, there will be consequences. Be prepared, in your mind. In Spirit."

I looked at Ber—Draven with narrowed eyes. "Are you going to eat me?"

He tilted his head back and laughed.

"Thank the Gods you froze at thirty." I teased. "Marrying a two-hundred-year-old is a lot less creepy knowing that. Why hide what you are, though? That doesn't seem like you."

He paused. "That's a story for another time."

"The Blood Bind is very serious, Keres," Hadriel said before taking another pull on his pipe.

"Sounds dire." I lifted my chin. "Draven—what's your surname?"

"Gaspar *is* my family's original name. We hadn't changed it; we simply pretended to be descendants of the bloodline. Changing first names."

"Ah." I drummed my fingers on his chest. "Makes sense now. So, what exactly are you? What is your kind, this coven? And you killed them all? Are you the last one—wait, what about the brother you spared? And this Godlander you mentioned."

"You're handling this a lot better than I expected," he preened.

"You told me I knew you. In my blood." I looked up at him. "We are one and the same. But I'm not what you are. So, what does that mean?"

He smiled, raising his brow. I traced my fingers along the lines of his muscled chest, smiling at him demurely. His hands wandered down to my waist, under his shirt, and found the holes he'd made in my dress. His thumb moved in lazy circles against my skin. My stomach fluttered at the feel of his fingers brushing over the tender spots he's claws had dug into me.

"My brother Oraclio lives in exile. Forbidden to make more of us."

"You can make more of you?"

He smiled—hinting at his fangs.

"You bite people to turn them, don't you? Are you some kind of venomous creature?"

He wasn't telling me what he was. I wondered if there was even a word for it, if his family had been the only of his kind created.

"That or sex. Though that didn't go well for me. Bamidele—the monster in her couldn't be sustained. I learned a lot from the scientific research conducted on my family. A successful pregnancy is achievable, but experience taught me things too. My kind are dangerous. My family was proof enough of that. There were consequences for our creation."

"Your curse."

"Like ours—one and the same," the Death Spirit mused.

"That is where you and I share something. Our thirst—it's connected. We are connected in a way I can't be with another person. I didn't expect to feel so drawn to you. But when you stepped into my throne room... I could sense it in you. I could smell it in you. Heard it in every pulse of your heart."

I remembered how he had rather rudely sniffed at my throat.

"I couldn't hold myself back. I'd been waiting for so long I never expected to feel... It's something I want even if I shouldn't. Which made me angry. I expected the Coroner—brutal and wild. I didn't expect beauty. I didn't expect such a likeness."

"Like calls to like," I repeated Liriene's words. "But what do you mean our thirst is connected?"

"It's an even longer story, more complicated. I'll tell you, but we need to discuss the Blood Bond ritual. I'll explain everything that I am because there's more. The Godlander called us his *creatures of the night*. He created a Void inside us—that void is the reason for our thirst. We can feed on someone's blood or energy. My brother is the true last of our kind, because I am much more now than I was then—I'll show you. In time."

"And my thirst," I said, eying him. "It's related to this Void?"

He nodded. "I told you, I'll explain it all. We have a while to work through all this."

"I have one more question." I looked down. It would make him angry, based on past reactions, but I needed to know.

"Thane," I said, and raised my eyes to his.

The anger I expected darkened his stare.

"Liriene said I was connected to someone named Thane. I've dreamed of him before my time here. He's channeled Liri. She says he's coming to save us from here. I realize he's who reached for me in the darkness, and who I saw in the mirror."

His jaw tightened, and his eyes searched mine, as if he was debating whether he should answer.

"I've told you, Keres, that man was not to be trusted," Hadriel said.

"You discussed him with her?" Draven snapped at Hadriel.

"So, it *is* the same man. The two of you are connected, too," I interrupted before Hadriel could respond.

"All three of us are," Draven said, dropping his gaze to the ground, and he stepped back. "You. Me. This King of Shadows. Our destinies are intertwined."

"Is he like you?"

"We have our differences. I am the Unbridled. He is the Unknown."

"And he's your enemy?"

"He wasn't always."

Draven's heart was pounding furiously beneath his ribs—that creature rattling his cage. He latched his gaze onto me again. "He would hurt you, Keres. Trust me."

I swallowed and focused on his eyes. The storm within was a tempest of emotion that couldn't have been a lie. But was it possessiveness? Did he not want me taken because he had claimed me—or did he actually care?

"*You've* hurt me," I said.

He tore his gaze away, crossing his arms over his bare chest and scanning the room. The skulls watched over us. There were hundreds of them lining the walls up to the ceiling.

I stepped closer to him. I didn't know how to forgive him, but could I accept him without accepting everything he'd done? He'd caused me and my people so much pain. He had a fucking library of skulls just to prove he wasn't a good man.

I needed to stop comparing him to good men. He was a creature.

Thane, lingering in the darkness—I didn't like things I couldn't judge. Seeing and touching and listening to Draven all this time. His actions told me more about who he was. Thane? How many times had he appeared to me and never said a damned thing.

The first time I dreamed of him, he refused to speak. Then, in the darkness, he scared me. Why the secrecy? If he wanted me to trust him, he should have proved he was a better person to trust.

Draven was... he was mine now. That's what him giving me his name meant. It was sacred and secret, and he shared it with me as he had promised to. What Hadriel had told me repeatedly was true. Draven didn't hold back. It took time, but eventually, he was forthcoming. Punishment or pleasure. A crown or a cage. Depending on what I gave, I received. Like a pendulum, swinging between extreme truths.

Did he still have secrets? Yes. Was I going to get them? Yes.

Draven built a stone wall around us. Thane wrapped himself in shadows. If I was supposed to trust one more than the other, it was going to be the enemy I knew. If Thane was his enemy... *our* enemy, then Gods help him.

"I trust you," I said. He met my gaze again and his softened. Almost relieved, but not entirely.

"Then we'll settle it tonight."

"Yes," Hadriel said, pushing off the wall. He turned toward the shelves. Bent down, keeping his pipe between his teeth as he flipped open the lid of a chest on the floor. He pulled a bundle wrapped in parchment out.

"You'll wear this for the ritual, it should fit. You will come to the altar as you are. We won't disrupt your hair or natural features with the nonsense Ciel insists you paint on yourself. Wear only your ring and this." He passed it into my arms.

It felt light, which meant it was probably skimpy.

"Am I going to get hurt?" I asked.

Draven snorted. "I've *already* hurt you, right? What's one more drop of blood?"

He walked past me, back toward the hall. Hadriel grabbed a few more things and pocketed them. I turned to follow Draven back into the library. As we ascended the golden staircases, women approached us. Their gazes lingered on his bare chest before jumping up to his eyes. And then they connected with my glare. They looked perturbed by me. Trailing behind the King, in a ripped dress and his shirt.

"They've got nothing on you, little wolf."

I stood a little taller, and he slowed so I could catch up to him. He turned his head and looked at me.

"Do they know how old you are?" I thought.

"Bamidele is my haven, but only a few know the truth. Its residents have been cycled in and out. After the display today, it seems I'll have to weed out a few people."

"Only I know your Blood Lyric?"

He nodded. *"Besides Hadriel."*

"Well then, your dirty secrets are safe with me."

And I won another smile.

🔲 🔲 🔲

In anyone else's story, Draven would be called the villain. In mine, he would also be called husband. It felt strange enough to call him anything besides Berlium. Which I'd have to keep addressing him as in company. In private... he was my hunter.

"No, no, no," Hadriel pestered as I followed on the King's heel. "You'll be going to a separate room until it's time for the ceremony."

"Ugh," I groaned and let go of Draven's hand.

"I'll see you tonight, little wolf." He pressed a kiss to my forehead and then Hadriel shooed him. I threw his shirt at him, and he held it in his fist. I watched his back, the movement of tapered muscles as he walked away.

"You're so fretful, my dark minister," I said, turning back to Hadriel.

"This is serious business, Keres. I know you lack the ability to be serious when presented with dark and dire things but try to at least keep up."

I quickened my footsteps to do exactly that. "Can you tell me more about it?"

"No."

"You're no fun."

"You will see tonight. We do not discuss such things, flagrantly, in the halls."

He led me to a room in a sequestered part of the castle, which I realized must be his room. It was littered with books and scrolls. Alchemical tools. Of course, jars of tea leaves. A beautiful tea set was set on the table. Nearly lost among books.

He hurried to the shelves and took down a few bottles.

"Are those potions? You're not going to make me drink some hallucinogenic for this, right?"

"No, child," he said. He squinted his eyes at the labels and put one back, reaching for the one next to it. He pointed at a basket that rested on the floor next to an armoire. "Pass me that."

I held it up to him, and he dumped the jars into it. The weight tugged it down.

"Be careful," he said. His eyes returned to the shelves, and he grabbed one more bottle, tossing it in. Then he emptied the things he'd pocketed in the library into the mix. Claiming the basket once it seemed full of what he wanted.

"Gods above, Hadriel. What kind of transmutation is required for this ritual?"

"Like I said, Coroner. Serious business."

"So, it's not a tea party."

He ignored me. Which meant he really was fretting.

"We could read his thoughts," the Death Spirit said lowly.

"No, you can't," Hadriel answered.

"Hey." I put my hand on my hip.

"You and your sister think so loudly. Your mother did too. I never understood it. Transmitting everything in your heads, on your face, in your posture. Sometimes it's not even necessary to listen to your thoughts. Not when they're so obvious."

"I guess I need to school my expressions to be stoic like yours."

He snorted. "You'd need years to perfect the resting indifference I've accomplished."

"Oh, no." I wagged my finger. "Tell me you're even older than the King."

He cut me a look.

"You are!" I gasped. "No wonder you're so crotchety. But you're not what he is, right?"

"Careful Keres, one wrong ingredient and you won't be coming out of this ritual." He plucked an envelope off the shelf and threw it into the basket.

I chuckled. "You could never. You like me too much."

The corners of his mouth flickered.

"Ha! Years of mastering your indifference—melted."

He rested his hand on the shelf and dropped his head, letting a soft laugh escape him. "Make yourself useful. Go over to that cabinet and grab the knife with the red blade."

I popped my eyes open wider. "Intriguing."

I put the basket down on the floor at his feet and wandered over to the cabinet he'd pointed out. Tons of knives were displayed behind the glass. I pulled on the tiny knob and the door clicked as it jerked open.

"Careful," he hissed again.

"You need to oil this thing."

I scoured the shelves, starting at the bottom and then standing on my tiptoes to see the highest shelf. My eyes caught on it. I took it out and held it in both my hands.

"So very sinister, dark minister."

"The velvet it was resting on, it's a sheath. Bring that too."

I pushed the blood-red drop point blade into the velvet sheath. Leaving only the hilt to admire. It was a lighter shade of red, but as I turned it in the light, other colors shimmered across it.

"The hilt is made from seashell." He reached for it.

"Pretty," I said.

"And as most pretty things are—it is very dangerous." He took the bundle out from under my arm and dropped it atop all the other stuff in the basket and then rested the knife on that.

"So, of course, you're gonna cut me with it. Are you done shopping?" I asked.

He rolled his eyes and picked up the basket. "Yes. Let's go."

Ciel and Minnow were waiting for us in the next room. It was just one giant bathing room. A massive stone tub sat in the middle of it, steam pouring over the edges of it. There were two porcelain pitchers on either side of the steps leading up to the pool.

Like our bedchamber, the far wall was a wall-sized window overlooking the rolling plains. "Is this facing toward the Ressid?" I asked.

"Yes," Hadriel said, passing the basket to Ciel. She carried it over to a stone table and started unpacking it.

"You're going to bathe. You must be as clean as possible. Under your nails, behind your ears, between your teeth. Every nook and cranny—spotless."

"Ew, Hadriel," I grimaced.

He took a deep breath and let out an exasperated sigh. "Too bad we can't wash away that attitude of yours."

"You'd find me rather boring if we could."

I turned toward Minnow, who was bouncing on the balls of her feet with excitement.

"Ah!" she said. "Your wedding day. Aren't you excited?"

I blinked my wide eyes at her. "I'm excited that you're excited."

Her brows pursed, and she fell a little flat. Unsure what to make of that.

"I'm nervous," I admitted.

Her eyes filled with light again. "Oh, Lady Keres, everything will be splendid. You'll find happiness with the King."

Ciel beckoned her, and she walked past me. I turned but wasn't looking toward them.

Happiness. It wasn't a feeling I'd entertained. I felt many things with the King... but happiness? I didn't think there was truly any room for it. I wanted things I shouldn't, and we were connected. Intimately. Our bond was only going to be strengthened by this ritual, whatever it was. There was no detaching myself from his dark world now. I knew more change laid beyond the veil of this ceremony. Becoming his—this was the bargain I'd made for freedom. Not the freedom I'd originally envisioned, but of a kind.

Thane was out there, looming somewhere. I looked out the window and felt like he was looking in. His teal eyes hidden in the stars that twinkled in the darkening sky. Alight with the idea of whatever right he thought he had to me. I'd make a show of my rebellion.

I stripped out of my clothing and slowly sank into the tub. Indulging in the heat. Imagining Thane could see me. I don't know why, but the thought of accepting Draven being a refusal of Thane, whoever he was, was thrilling.

My Death Spirit owned that thrill. As if she recognized Thane's attention as much as she recognized my King's. And under watchful, invisible eyes, she luxuriated in being desired and untouchable. She'd chosen Draven... and I realized *she* knew she had options. How did my Spirit know these two Kings? Was it the Void that connected us?

When Draven proposed to me, he said our Spirits had been conspiring. He was right. His held a Void that created a likeness in us. We thirsted for each other. And Thane...

This Godlander that claimed Draven as his creature, had He made Thane, too?

There were still questions to be answered, secrets to be told. But was there *happiness* to be found, like Minnow said? I'd be very surprised if there was. War made little room for such things.

The ablutions proved very time-consuming. I spent time in and out of the bath. Hadriel lurked in the room but kept his attention on the so-called ingredients. Most of which were dumped into the bath to make some kind of supernatural soup for me to cook in. Other things were applied to my hair, my skin. Left my body tingling and a little inflamed.

"The redness will subside. The hour is late. It is almost time."

"What's all this for, anyway?"

"Purification."

"Who will attend this ceremony?" I asked. "Is it like a traditional wedding? I doubt anybody stayed awake for this besides us." At the realization of how late it was, I yawned.

"Besides the obvious attendees, Emisandre will be there. I doubt your sister will want to be there."

565

"Can we—" Minnow halted at the look in Hadriel's eyes. Turning back to the table that had been made a mess with his ministrations.

"Why Emisandre?"

Hadriel snorted at the tone in my voice. "We need another mage for the first part of the ritual. It would be her or another person here, but I'm going to call on her."

"But does she know about *you know what?*"

"No," he said. "She suspects many things, as most people do. However, blood rituals are not native only to the King's realm. She's acquainted enough to help me."

I rolled my eyes. "Fine."

My thoughts shifted. Spiritual conspiracy or not, marrying Draven and becoming his Queen still made me nervous. But I didn't really know why. Despite the hot water, I felt like every hair on my body was standing. Couldn't rub the goosebumps away. My cycle had ended after only a couple of days, which wasn't unusual. My stomach was aching for another reason. Stress. Every time Minnow handed me another lotion to rub into my skin, it got under my nails, and I had to scrape it out. My fingernails felt so flimsy and thin from all the washing. I kept thinking about washing in the River Liriene. Which made me think about kissing Darius. *Do you truly belong to any man?*

This was the old me resurfacing. The sentimental Keres, called out by the question of happiness. I wiped at my face again as if it could swipe away the thoughts. I *wanted* to be Draven's as much as I wanted him to be mine. I wanted to be matched and powerful.

If you cannot accept the bond, there will be consequences.

Consequences my people would feel, too. This was it. A crown on my head would bring all its weight. I *did* accept it, though.

Cold hands touched mine, moving them from my face. Hadriel witnessed every emotion on my face. He said I thought loudly. But for once, he didn't seem to mind.

"Now," he said. "We transmute."

I straightened my spine. Fear. It can be protective or stifling. Choose a use—make it count. I swallowed the knot in my throat. Fear of the unknown can only be overcome by knowing. Can't accomplish that if you're unwilling. It's the first step.

75: THE SONG
Keres

One foot. Then the other. One at a time.

The soles of my feet touched the cold stone. Snowflakes drifted through the air, catching on the red veil I wore that was as long as my hair. My nipples were so hard from the cold, I thought they'd cut through the damned blood-red lace dress.

The collar nearly touched my jaw, and the hem covered my toes, but it was even thinner than Ivaia's gowns. Like spider's thread. The veil was more substantial, but still light enough to be threatened by the breeze that chased me through the stone garden.

I was just relieved the ceremony wasn't on the Atys Grounds. I tracked the hem of Hadriel's black robe. Allowing it to drag me where he guided. My scarred hands were balled into fists at my side. Mostly trying to keep them warm—also trying not to lose my nerve. *Transmute.*

The dress was sexy, not doing much to hide my curves. I could try to be appealing. Sway, bounce, saunter—something. It didn't have to be much. The dress was doing most of the work of making me look like a virginal, tempting sacrifice. The thoroughness of the bath felt like an attempt to do the same.

We turned a corner, breaking free of the castle walls, into a clearing. Stones stood around us, the only audience besides the stars above. The stones were carved with pictures of wolves and bears, crows and dragons.

It seemed like someone invited the full moon to the ceremony. It stood front and center, crowning the stones with light. Crowning him.

He was dressed in all black, a suit that looked like it was from another time and probably was. The jacket hugged his broad shoulders, wrapped around his muscled arms, and tapered to his waist. He wore a black buttoned shirt under it—he'd actually buttoned it up properly and tucked into fitted black pants. Black shoes.

I swallowed, unable to tear my eyes away from his as I came to stand before him. He looked me over from head to toe. His assessment was so unrushed—as if he was counting every thread of the dress I wore. He lifted the veil back to look at my face. Again, taking his time studying me.

"Moonlight looks good on you, little wolf."

I smiled at him. He turned toward Hadriel and Emisandre over his shoulder.

"And she's *my* girl," he sighed.

Hadriel looked lost somewhere between wanting to smile and wanting to get this over with. He turned toward Emisandre and handed her the red-bladed knife. She took it, drawing it out of the velvet sheath, and held it up. Moonlight glanced off the edge, cutting into my vision.

She looked the King over almost as slowly as he'd done to me. Turning a quick look at me, dropping her eyes to the ground and flicking them back up to my face. A forced smile stretched her mouth open.

"Blood," she said. "Can be shared between kindreds, yet they may not be bonded. Only by choice, by acceptance, can the communion of blood bring two together in true unity. Do you choose this woman, in flesh and blood and spirit?"

He looked at me when he answered her. "I choose only this woman."

She held out her hand, and he placed his in it, palm up. She cut through the mound of flesh beneath his thumb and squeezed drops of his blood into a gold chalice Hadriel held to catch them. They dripped into dark liquid. The acrid fragrance of his blood mingled with something sweet—wine.

Hadriel and Emisandre switched.

"Only by acceptance, by choice, can the communion of blood bring two together in true unity. Do you choose this man, in flesh and blood and spirit, Keres?"

"I choose only him."

I held out my hand, and it was as steady as Draven's heartbeat. Hadriel cut a matching line into my left hand, kneading the blood into the cup.

"Face each other and bring your blood together." Hadriel gestured. We turned toward each other and touched palms. My left hand met his right hand, and where we both bled, we sealed our touch.

"Drink," Hadriel said, passing me the cup first.

I lifted it to my mouth, salivating at the scent. I touched the cold rim to my lips, tilting it slowly and watching the wine spill toward me. I swallowed, closing my eyes.

"From one cup, two pour."

Hadriel took the cup and passed it to the King, repeating the words as he drank until it was empty. Hadriel turned to Emisandre and bowed shallowly. She nodded, dropping her gaze and leaving.

"That's it?" I asked.

"No," the King said.

Hadriel's eyes tracked Emisandre as she left, waiting a good while before he spoke again.

"With the first drink, you consume your choice. Accepting it. With the second drink, you deepen your commitment. And with the third, your choice consumes you," Hadriel says.

"I can feel your heart. You're afraid," Draven murmurs.

"No. I'm not." I squeezed his hand as I smiled up at him. "I'm excited, actually."

"Good." He smiled and straightened up.

The moonlight did marvelous things to his skin, his eyes. He looked at me, heat banking in his gaze.

Hadriel faded to the corner of my vision as I looked at the King. With the second drink, we'd deepen our commitment. I knew that whatever was going to happen next was a rite of passage into his world.

"Do you need my other hand?" I asked, holding out the one that he'd broken. He traced his gaze over the scars he'd given me. Brought his eyes to mine as I held it out to him, and the corners of his mouth dropped.

Draven

I didn't deserve that outstretched hand. The one I'd broken. She offered it now. Sacrifice. Supplication. She played her hand. For her people, for the semblance of freedom I'd offered her, but getting her to this point had been a war all its own. She'd fought it well. Giving up things without fully giving in.

My woman was a wolf, claw and fang. She chose me. She shared her blood with me. Like any powerful warrior, she didn't lick her wounds. She bared her scars—kept reaching. Kept clawing at the stone walls I'd built around myself for the last two hundred years.

Granted, she wanted to see them crumble and probably to bury me in the rubble. All this time spent trying to break her down, and she was the one to chip something away from me. I saw it there in her scarred hand.

"No, but thank you," I said.

Her brows lowered, and she watched my face. Reading, reaching out with those curious eyes. I took her hand and folded it between mine. I allowed my gaze to pass over her again, drinking in the vision of her naked body beneath the wispy lace.

She stood there, near naked. Hadriel and Emisandre saw every inch of her that was all mine, but I saw something they still didn't. Beneath the veil, beneath the lace, beneath even her perfectly soft skin. I saw *her*. Her beauty felt like a punishment. That I'd marred her body—that I'd disgraced divinity.

I was an arrogant bastard. Fucked and cruel. But even I worshiped the Gods. How had I ever looked at her as less?

No mere woman could just offer up her old wounds. Most people held those things close, walled themselves off from further harm. She held it in my face. *Try again.*

Two hundred years and I'd never been handed a second chance from anyone.

No matter how many times I'd changed my name, no matter how many masks I wore, I couldn't stop being what I was. Even when I might have wished I could. There was no starting over, only pushing forward.

Was this grief I felt?

Was it relief she held out to me?

I didn't deserve that outstretched hand. I lifted her hand and kissed it. The blood sang in her veins.

"The second drink," Hadriel said, drawing her attention again. "Well, Keres—there's nothing like the first bite."

I chuckled at the magister. He'd spent so much time around me, he even thought like one of us. I drew Keres close, pressing her body against mine. I ran my hands over the lace, feeling the curves of her body beneath. It was so thin; it hid nothing from me. Nothing I didn't already know so well.

This woman was etched in my mind. The taste of her blood—just the few drops—brought heat to my body. Touching her stoked fires in me. Having her closer, knowing her taste, this feeling could consume me. I touched her throat, feeling her pulse quicken beneath the lace. I felt it internally.

"Don't be afraid," I said to her.

"I'm not afraid of you."

I lifted my thumbs to brace her jaw and tilted her head to the side. Her eyes fluttered closed. She held onto my jacket, taking in a quick breath as I pressed a kiss against her throat and her pulse jumped.

"Liar," I breathed against her. "I'm not going to bite you—not yet."

She pulled back. Color heated her cheeks—a gorgeous shade of pink that took my breath away. A dangerous woman that still blushed. Gods, I was a lucky man.

"The second drink requires another cut," Hadriel explained. He passed the knife to Keres. "You mark each other this time. And I'm sure you'll be pleased to know, Coroner, you can place your mark wherever you wish."

Her brow arched elegantly as she flashed her wild green eyes at me.

Her smile pronounced the delicate tips of her fangs. She turned the red blade over, admiring it. Looking me up and down like she'd devour me. And Gods knew I wanted her to.

Keres

"Anywhere I want, huh?" I pointed the blade at his chest, wishing I could cut that shirt off his body to begin with.

"Are you cold, my King?"

He bit his bottom lip and chuckled nervously.

"Because I'm freezing. Take off your jacket."

"Please, note that you will have to drink the blood from this wound, so please make sure it's somewhere decent enough for this sacrament."

"Oh, you're never any fun, Hadriel." I pouted.

I circled around my beast, trying to decide which territory to mark. He had a scar on his brow already and my bite mark had made itself comfortable on his shoulder. His left hand bore the blood curse scar and now his right bore the mark of the first drink. If I could have carved my name into him, I would, but where?

"Keres, you're putting more thought into this than I thought you would," Draven said.

It was just a cut. Nobody had to know where it was besides us. Not like someone would be able to tell it was my mark on him just by looking at it. But somewhere just for us? Decency be damned.

"Sorry, Hadriel. You can turn around. Draven, take off your shirt, too."

Hadriel groaned and turned, but Draven laughed. His eyes sparkled as I met them, circling back in front of him now. I watched him tug at every button and slip the shirt off. He shivered from the cold.

"Keres, I'm going to get you back for this."

"Oh, please," I said. "Turn for me, bear."

He turned, flexing his muscles as he gave me his back.

"Let me see your wings."

"What are you thinking?" he asked. Not hesitating to call the shadows out of the sky. Broken pieces of the night.

They jumped toward him, latching onto his skin and swelling into his red wings. He flared them out. I wiped my mouth with my hand. Willing myself not to drool. I walked up behind him, placing the palm of my hand between his shoulder blades, covering his dragon tattoo. I ran the side of the blade against his wings, not to cut, but to tease. He shivered.

"Let's get on with it, Keres," Hadriel crowed.

"Almost done," I said, letting my breath fan against Draven's skin.

I pressed the tip of the knife into the skin between his shoulder blades, beneath the tattoo. Running my fingers over the bones of his wings as I let the knife dig in a little deeper. He hissed but seemed to find some pleasure in my touching his wings. I quickly sliced downward, tracing his spine with the cut. His wings flinched and his muscles tensed, but I took the blade away after the cut was about the length of my hand.

Blood beaded, oozing out and dripping. I caught every drop with my tongue. Licking my way from the bottom of the cut to the top. I placed one hand on his hip, letting the other trail lazily over his wing, as I suckled at the blood.

He bit back a moan, and I heard the low purring in his chest. The bleeding stopped as I passed my tongue over it one last time. His wings folded and faded as he turned back to me. He snatched the knife. Spinning me around, slipping the veil off, and knotting my hair in his hand.

Lifting it to reveal the nape of my neck, he undid the buttons that clasped the dress around my throat.

He pressed himself against my backside as he touched the tip of the knife just below my hairline. Quickly, he flicked it downward to the knot of my spine between my shoulders. I hissed, but he pressed his mouth against the cut, licking and kissing. Heat knotted in my core. When he was done, he turned me around and licked the blade, too.

"Alright, now that you two are done mutilating each other," Hadriel said, reaching for the knife and the veil. "The third drink—well, I don't have to be there for that. It is… the consummation."

"Wait, so are we married now?" I asked, looking from Hadriel to

Draven who nodded and smiled. It sent warmth through me that made me forget the chill in the air.

"There's only one more part you need me for and it's the record." He bent down, and I finally noticed his silly little basket. He pulled a book out that was bound in crimson leather.

"The record?" I asked.

"All royal blood lines are recorded. To track generations and relations."

Hadriel opened the book and turned to a page, pointing to where it said Draven Gaspar. His brothers' names branched out of the same tree as his, but only some of them were paired with women's names. Oraclio's was left in the singular and so was his. Hadriel rested the book on a small altar that stood between two of the stones to our right. He readied his quill and ink.

"I have two gifts for you," Draven said.

I turned back to where he stood, and my eyes landed on the flower in his hand.

A long-stem, thornless lavender rose.

He held it out to me. "Your birthday is in the month of Enith. Mid Summer. I remember you talking about it with Yarden. The rose is the flower of Enith."

"I didn't know every month had a flower."

He smiled. "The rose, in full bloom, is a symbol of spiritual awakening, passion, even war or sacrifice. Purple, the color of royalty and mystical power. A symbol of love of the Spirit."

His eyes were as blue and heated as his Brazen fire. He offered the rose to me, and I took it. Holding it to my face to inhale the sweet fragrance.

"Blood is a gift—the gift of life. You've shared yours with me, as I've shared mine with you. This is symbolic. To bleed represents death. To drink represents life. We've laid separation to rest and are reborn as a whole. This is the rite of the Blood Hymn. I've given you my name. I've tasted your blood. When we take our third drink, we will be joined in this ancient song. The beating of your heart to match mine."

My heart was pounding in my chest, running after every word he said.

"Before the third drink, we say a prayer. Sending it to the Void within. It is the Nocturne. To join your voice with mine—you need a name."

"A name," I repeated in question.

"To be recorded in the Blood Hymn, the sacred history of his line, you need a Blood Lyric. A name as sacred as his," Hadriel explained.

"I've chosen one for you. My gift to you—I hope you'll accept it."

Draven was a focal point—an epicenter. I should have never been drawn toward him, and I'd seen every warning sign. Everything I should have run from was right in front of me, but I'd found something where it wasn't supposed to be.

I stood before him, clutching the lavender rose, staring up into his sapphire eyes. Basking in the silver moonlight, in the darkness that enveloped us. Loving the feel of his marks on me and the warm taste of his blood. He was ready to call me by a name that would echo through history. Gifting me a place in his world, at his side.

"You were never supposed to be mine, but you are. I'm yours." He lifted my chin. "Even if I was a good man who'd let you go, I couldn't."

"Draven," I breathed.

He closed his eyes, breathing in the sound of his name.

"I didn't think anyone could ever understand—I didn't think anyone could accept me," he said softly. "I know you do, however you can, even if you shouldn't. You might not be able to love me, but try to hate me now. I don't think you can do that either."

Unexpected tears brimmed my eyes.

"For me, there's no escaping you now. So, that's what your name means." He smiled, leaning down closer. A breath away. With one finger, he tilted my chin up, angling my mouth toward his.

"Adrasteia. Inescapable."

His lips silenced my reaction, grazing softly against mine. He bit my lower lip, tugging on it gently, and lifted his hands into my hair. Searching. I closed my eyes and kissed him back. His hands moved to my neck, and he pulled back a little.

"Do you accept it?"

I looked into his eyes, and they were a spectrum—a storm of blues. Drowned in emotion.

"I accept you, Draven. And your gift," my Death Spirit's voice laced mine.

He closed his eyes, leaning his forehead against mine.

"Repeat the Nocturne, after me," he said and swallowed.

"We feed. We burn. We never fade."

"We feed. We burn. We never fade," I said.

"When peace, we've given. When war, we've made. Adrasteia, I'm of the song that lives in you. Written in the blood I'm due. You're of the dark that hides in me. Beneath the wing that sets me free."

I repeated it with his true name.

Golden light shattered the blue of his eyes and consumed them. A revelation breaking through the mask of blue. Finally heard and seen. Finally accompanied.

577

76: SACRAMENT
Keres

Lover.

Hunter.

Enemy.

Always.

Draven lifted me into his arms and launched us into the air. His dark red wings carried us upward toward the castle. It was very dramatic, but apparently had been his plan all along since the bedroom window was open.

He touched down on the glass platform and waltzed us into the bedroom, tossing me onto the bed like I weighed no more than the lace I wore.

"As much as I'd love to shred this teasing garment off your body, we'll take it off with care, my little wolf."

He pushed my hips, rolling me over onto my stomach. The first few buttons, he'd already undone, and he was still shirtless from when I cut him. He kneeled next to me, brushed my hair away, and trailed his fingers over the remaining buttons. He took the rose and touched it against my spine.

"I hope Hadriel gathered our things. Wherever they went."

"I lost track of most things once you touched me," I said into the sheets.

His hand drifted down my backside to my ass. He palmed it and squeezed. I wriggled on the bed and turned back over. "We have to undo these buttons first."

Mischief sparkled in his blue eyes. Still, there was the Third Drink. He pushed up off the bed and dropped the rose into a vase on the nightstand. Then took off his pants and walked over to a door in the corner near the window. I hadn't asked what it was. He opened it and walked into darkness.

"Adrasteia, come." His rich voice echoed. It felt strange, answering to another name, but he'd been calling me many things—this word meant his. Only Hadriel knew it. Recorded it in the secret hymnal. From now on, it was a spell only Draven could incant, and I'd obey it well because we were bound, and my blood roared in answer to his.

I got up and followed him into a short hall that felt more like a tunnel. He looked back and took my hand. His Brazen wrapped around our hands and lit the hall with blue light. I added my green flames to our hold. We followed the hall to its end. Into a room very similar to the bathing room I'd used prior to the ceremony. My throat ran dry, watching him walk around the pool of hot water. I'd already bathed so much, but after bleeding for this man, I was ready to sink into the heat with him.

The bloodletting of the ceremony had lit a fire in my core. Not the reaction of a normal person, but I'd done many things now to prove myself opposite of that. In what we craved, he was not a man, and I was not a woman. Whatever we were, we were one. Two thirsting, one cup. The only thing on my mind now was his bite.

The room was dark, even with the help of a few candelabras on the floor along the wall. Red waxed candles and soft red light. There were large crystals and geodes along the sides of the pool. Purple and white, clear and green, too. The floor of the tub itself also glowed with silver-blue light.

"What's making that light?"

"Algae," he replied, raking his eyes over me. "It's kind of like mold, but it grows in the sea. Got it from the Natlantine. A sailor harvested it for me."

"I didn't know that was possible."

He didn't care to explain the scientific process of how one might harvest and transport luminescent algae to a bathtub in a remote, winter-clad fortress. His eyes were stuck on the trappings of lace and buttons as I walked toward him.

This dress was scathing on my skin now. If his stare had held any more heat, it would have burned off my body, and I wished it would.

"Get me out of this thing, please." I turned, giving him my back.

He undid one fucking button at a time.

"You know," I said over my shoulder as he tugged at the button below my shoulder blades, "if *you* were the one in this dress, you'd have no problem with me shredding it off. It's itching."

"Don't worry, my Queen. I'll lick you until the only sensation you remember from tonight is the feel of my mouth on your skin."

My head swam in the liquor of his voice. Dark and bittersweet, sharp and searing through me. My core clenched with need, and I knew he could sense it.

The rhythm of his heart was in synchronization with mine. A button per heartbeat now. He moved his fingers faster, more desperate to get this damned thing off me. Almost tearing it by the end, he pushed it down over my hips and I turned to face him. I stepped out of the dress, leaving it in a puddle behind me.

I walked forward, pressing my chest against his and wrapping my arms up around his neck. His hands blazed over my body, from my shoulders, down my back, to my hips. Another low purr in his chest called out mine. He reached down a hand between my legs and touched me.

I dropped my head to the side, locked in his gaze as he massaged me. I moaned. He watched my eyes, my mouth as I bit my lip. His fingers working up and down the center of me, swirling in circles around the sensitive peak. His other hand captured the globe of my breast. I brought my head back to his, pulling him down to kiss me.

Both his hands continued working me, as I brought one of my knees up to touch his hip. Giving him more access.

My mouth opened for his, hungrily taking him in. He opened for me just as much. My tongue danced against his, licking over his fangs and his tongue sloppily. I fisted his hair in my hands, clinging to him, kissing him like I didn't even need air.

His arms laced around my waist, and we stumbled as he pulled me into him, deepening the kiss.

I moaned against his tongue, tasting the lingering flavor of blood from his mouth. One of his hands came up to the back of my neck, touching where he'd cut me. My fingertips found their mark between his shoulder blades. He was hard between us, pressed between my legs.

His other hand grabbed my hip, bringing my pelvis roughly against his, and I whimpered at the touch of his cock against my naked heat. The hand wrapped around the back of my neck, reached into my hair. Tugging it from the root to bring my head back. His mouth sank to my jawline, to my throat. Hungrily licking up the sides of my neck, tracing the artery that ran there.

I groaned, feeling heavy in his arms. He nipped at my skin and at my ear. I turned my head into his touch, fighting to reclaim his kiss. His lips crashed against mine again, and I dug my claws into him. His steps faltered again as he groaned. My touch biting into his skin.

"Gods below," he murmured. "Get in the tub."

I turned and ran, jumping and curling my body into a ball as I crashed into the pool of water. Submerged, lost in a cloud of bubbles. I heard another sound, like the crash of a cymbal, announcing he had followed me in.

I used to flinch at touching water—I released the fear. The only thing that could drown me now was his eyes.

Hands gripped onto my hips, dragging me through the streams of bubbles until I was in his arms again. His mouth found mine, kissing me beneath the water. It was dark beneath the surface—only the faint, luminescent glow outlined his face, his body. We surfaced again, rejoining the red candlelight.

I clung to him as he pushed us toward the wall of the pool, aligning our hips. I wrapped my legs around his waist and my arms around his neck as he held me there. Again, claiming me with his kiss.

Water rushed between us, lapping at our skin, warm between my thighs where his sex pressed against me. He ground his hips against mine and I moaned again at the way the water slowed his movements so that he dragged his body against mine. Feeling the pulse of the water between us.

His tongue fought for dominance against mine, and I moaned hoarsely into his mouth as he thrust against me again. And again. My core ached with the need to be filled, the way he pulsed his tongue inside my mouth. Filling me, licking every inch of my tongue. The kiss wasn't a dance anymore; it was a feast. Our fangs bumped together as our tongues curled around each other. My jaw ached from holding open so wide, so long for him to stroke me so deeply with his tongue.

The stone was grating against my back, but his cock was velvet smooth against my pussy. His tongue was silken fire in my mouth. And my blood was raging through my veins. I could feel his heart, just as furious.

He reached down, grabbing his cock and angling it toward my entrance. I rolled my hips, bringing the tip of him into me, and he gasped into my mouth. I rolled my body again, bringing him deeper.

"I want you inside me, now, Draven."

He answered my command, sheathing himself fully inside me. Water and air bubbles flourished out between us as his cock drove into the depths of me and I cried out. The friction of his hips grazing against mine lit up my center.

I clenched down on him as he'd taught me to do. He dragged himself back, but I wouldn't loosen my hold. He breathed raggedly against my mouth, holding me by the throat as he slowly withdrew as far as I'd let him. Then he plunged back into me, and I cried against his lips.

He withdrew and shocked my core again with another deep stroke. I ground my hips against his, wrapping my legs tighter, using my arms on his shoulders to lift my hips, so he could pull me back down. Our chests pressed together, bringing out matching heartbeats close enough to feel like one.

My head dropped forward onto his shoulder, and I bit him, growling against his skin as he pinned me back against the wall. His hands dug into my hips, opening me wider and keeping me pressed where he could control all movement.

I yelped, clenching my pussy around his next stroke. I raked my fingernails over his back, relishing in the shiver my touch elicited, and then he stilled. Staying sheathed in the depths of me. I tightened around him.

He growled against my neck, allowing me to pulse my grip on his swollen, throbbing cock.

"Good girl," he said huskily. "Now, tip your head back for me."

I rolled my head back, closing my eyes and focusing on the feel of him inside me. The length of him, the steel, buried in me. I didn't want him to move. I didn't want to lose that feeling of fullness he created.

His breath fanned against my throat, and one of his hands came up to my breasts. Grazing against them, giving each nipple an affectionate pinch. He closed his hand around the globe of my breast, squeezing and kneading it as he pressed kisses to my throat.

"Draven," I sighed.

"Yes, little wolf?" he murmured against my skin. His fangs grazed me.

"Do it," I gasped. "Please."

"Howl for me."

His fangs sank under my skin, and I cried out from the sharp, shocking pain. My body contracted around him, but his teeth rested where they were.

Warmth blossomed in my neck, dulling the pain. The taste of honey rose in the back of my throat and my eyes rolled back when he thrust inside me again. The pressure told me when he bit down deeper, but he rocked me through the pain. Infusing me with that honeyed warmth that poured into my core.

His cock stroked deeper than his bite. My skin felt on fire—every inch of me felt on fire. The distinct sensation that he drank from me warred for my senses, but the lulling intoxication of his bite kept me just beneath the surface of the pain. Like a gentle tug. He swallowed and his heart rate raced with mine.

My nails dug into him, and I whimpered. He thrust into me again, striking my center, and pushed me closer to an orgasm. He swallowed again and more of the fire swarmed my senses. My pulse hammered against his mouth, between my legs. As he swallowed again, he rewarded me with harder, deeper thrusts that sent me over the edge of my orgasm.

I writhed in his grip as my climax coursed through me. His lips softened and his teeth retracted. He pressed kisses where he'd bitten me, licking away the sting, and brought his rhythm to a soothing stride until the shock of pleasure faded. I cried as he took away the pain and kissed my mouth.

I could taste my blood on his tongue, metallic and sweet.

"You're perfect," he said. He kissed away the tear that rolled down my cheek. He wrapped his hands around my legs and lifted me off the wall, walking us to the stairs and carrying me out of the pool.

I kept my arms around his neck, leaning my face on his shoulder. Feeling tired. A little cold as the air hit my wet skin.

He laid me on the bed and laid next to me. He held me against him, allowing me to rest a moment. Touched his fingers where he'd bitten me and brought them back to show me.

"See? Nothing."

The lingering ache felt no worse than when someone nuzzles your neck with a kiss to bruise it.

"Not even a bruise," he said, as if he'd read my thoughts.

I turned, rolling over on top of him to straddle his hips. I ground myself against him. His hands found their way to my hips, to my breasts. Scaling every inch of me. My sex was throbbing against his cock, aching to be filled again. I lifted my weight and held his cock up so that it nudged at my opening.

I slid all the way down, seating myself on him again. He slid his hand up to my throat. I looked down at him, the fire burning in his mostly gold eyes. I rolled my hips, rocking against him gently, feeling him. I dropped my head back and set my pace. Slowly.

His touch grew more frantic, pawing at me. Running his hands up and down the front of me. Pinching my nipples harder, kneading my breasts harder, digging into my hips harder.

My claws elongated through my fingertips when I grabbed him by the shoulders. Leaning forward, I lifted my hips and dropped them back down. Stroking his cock from root to tip. I practiced tightening around him and relaxing, lifting and sliding. Loving every inch of him. Learning the feel of my body around him. The way my hips flared open for him. The burning in my knees, my ankles, as I bounced on top of him.

"Good Gods, woman," he growled and then caught his breath.

It was encouragement enough to keep stroking him. Tightening, twisting. I rolled my hips in a circle, ground against him, turning my hips to different angles. Wanting his hardness to etch into every soft, hollow inch of my core.

His hands pushed and pulled my hips, guiding me through movements. Teaching me how to ride his cock the way he liked it, helping me repeat movements he liked most. I dropped my head down between his and his shoulder and ran my tongue against his neck.

One hand came up to my head, brushing back my long hair as the other guided my hips. My breathing was sharp, and I was tired, but I wasn't stopping. I licked his throat, giggling against his skin when his hips jerked against mine.

I took the hand that held my neck and pressed it down against the bed. Creating just a bit of tension, taking just a little more control. I nipped at his jaw, his ear. Trailed my tongue in lazy circles against his pulse as I rolled my hips in a similar pattern.

"Fucking hell," he moaned and lifted his head, watching my ass as I bounced on him.

I bit him, nipping his skin superficially, and his head dropped back. The hand that pinned his tightened, and I relished in the control I felt over him. I stopped moving on top of him, sinking onto him, and kept him deep inside me, just as he had done. I allowed my fangs to drop deeper into my mouth and grazed his pulse.

The Third Drink. We both had to do it, but I didn't know how to infuse his pain with pleasure the way he did. His hand that had been on my hips softly cupped the back of my head. Angling me and bringing my mouth closer to his throat. He swallowed, the muscles in his neck flaring as he did.

"Don't be scared to bite me, little wolf."

585

Draven

The tips of her fangs loomed against my pulse. Her curiosity reached through her, through the delicacy of her tentative touch. She wouldn't hurt me, but she didn't know that. Her breath's heat blossomed against my skin.

My cock was driven deep inside her haven, warm and wet from her need. She lingered, debating. Reasoning. Feeling. As she always did. I lifted my hips, thrusting into her, pushing her to do something. Her lips closed on my neck—submitting to kiss me instead of doing what she wanted.

"Hmmm," I said. "I wonder what you'll take from me between your teeth, little wolf."

She gasped against me as I thrust into her again. Rolling my hips up into hers, knowing I could grind against her clit. I held her head with one hand, and she held my other hand against the bed. Not a strong hold, but it was purposeful.

"You want to taste me," I teased.

My movement beneath her drew a soft moan out of her, opening her mouth against my neck again. Her fangs grazed me, and I pulled her head down closer.

Finally, she broke through my skin. Slowly—so fucking slowly, biting down. Claiming the artery that bucked beneath her. I echoed its tempest, thrusting into her again. Her fangs sank deeper, earning a growl out of me.

She shuddered—not with fear. With need.

She swallowed. My eyes rolled back as the pull of her thirst drained me. I encouraged her, rocking my hips so that I moved inside her, slowly. Showing her I was hot and alive beneath her—ready to feed her. She swallowed again and gasped. Detaching from me briefly and licking her lips before sinking back into me again.

A little rough, but nothing I couldn't handle. She released my hand, bringing her fingers to my jaw. Tilting my head so she had better access.

Her tongue swiped across my skin between her teeth. Her lips created a hot seal, and she drank deeper. Taking what I owed her.

I ran my hand up and down her side, feeling the warmth of her body turn to fire. Green light encased her, and I knew her Brazen was burning through her. Enlivened by the blood she took from me.

She released me and licked the wounds as I had done for her. Kissing me all over my throat, my chin, my mouth, my cheeks. Her forehead rested against mine, and I stared up into her emerald eyes as she began to move on my cock again.

Her sweet, needy cunt was throbbing around me, so close now to another wave of pleasure. I turned us over, not losing the connection between us. Grabbing her legs and forcing them back so her knees were beside her head.

I drove deep into her. She cried out and her eyes rolled back.

"You're so beautiful," I said, curling into her again. Slower this time, drinking in the look on her face as I sank deep into her.

She moaned again, softer. Her voice was shattering, and her core was fire-hot.

Her Brazen fire licked her skin, coating her hands, her arms, her legs in light. I allowed mine to surface, touching her throat with a hand alit with blue fire. She held onto my arm as I pounded into her. Her brows pinched together, and her swollen, reddened lips pursed as she looked up at me.

"You're mine. Always."

"Yes," she said breathlessly and without hesitation.

It made me feel—it made me *feel*.

I unleashed myself, fucking her the way she was made to be fucked— hard. By me and only me. I held her legs down, grazing my thumbs against the backs of her knees.

She closed her eyes. I could feel her next climax building within her. Clenching on me. Her liquid heat was slick around my cock, dripping down her sex. I reached a hand down and touched the most sensitive flesh, the way she loved it.

A musician's hands left no note unsung. I played my hand against her apex until she sang—until she screamed my name. She gripped me so tightly, dragging me into my climax after her, and draining me.

Something passed between us as I laid there between her legs, still inside her, with her ankles on my shoulders. Bracing myself on one arm and tracing my other hand over her face, through her hair. I touched her brows, her lashes, her lips.

It was sacred. Something I'd never touched, never felt in all my life. Even if it was some unholy sacrament—if this was worship, I was a believer.

Her fingers wandered over my shoulders, tickling over the edges of my body, running up my back to touch the cut she made. It brought a smile to her face. I kissed each corner of her mouth and then she bit my lip until I pulled back to look at her again.

Her feet wiggled on either side of me, and I moved my hips just to remind her how deeply I was resting inside her. She bit her lower lip and smiled again, her toes curling. There was violet light swirling in the green of her eyes now, and I just couldn't stop staring.

77: SWALLOWED

Keres

Day Twenty-Six

War.

Right. Wrong.

Risk. Reward.

Victory. Loss.

I found something in myself because of everything I'd lost. Everything ripped from me. By him. His armies. His war. With everything I was stripped away, I wrapped myself in fire. I tore down my walls and held out my wings. I let go. I tied myself to my enemy. Bowed. Gave my blood, my body. For a crown.

For my people to have a chance at survival. I'd opened the earth to swallow my enemies on a battlefield. Now, I'd march beside them. For the people still held prisoner. I opened myself up; I drank in the darkness. I brought war to my enemy's bed, and he disarmed me, then equipped me.

I'd learned his dearest secrets. Called him by a name unspoken for over a century. He tied himself to me, just as bound to me as I was to him. Walked me deeper into his world without leaving my side. He still had secrets, but they would be mine in time.

The woman I'd become—Adrasteia. She was inevitable. For him, she was inescapable. We were bound by blood. Until death. It put me in a position of power and left me vulnerable, but it did the same to him. This war would never be the same.

More blood would be shed, more death, more loss. I wasn't afraid. I was made for this. Draven took away the blinders—I was never innocent after Death touched me.

I dreamed of the day I died:

"You promised not to return."

Blood. There was nothing but blood coming from her mouth, all over her hands. From his blade. I was sinking. She was drifting away. Fighting against the hands gripping her shoulders. Was he trying to help her after he hurt her?

The dream wound time backward. She was in the water, swimming with me again. Splashing around and singing. Sunlight played on the surface of the river, diving under and sparkling back through the ripples.

Footsteps.

Her smile vanished, and she stopped singing.

"Who's that, Mother?"

"Don't come out of the water. Swim away." She stood, and the current tried to pull her back in, tugging at her dress with me. *"Swim away. Go play."*

The hooded man said nothing. His silence was ominous. His face was hidden under the hood of his black cloak. Black like my hair. Mother walked through the running water, back to the bank where he waited for her. He kept his face turned away from me.

In my dream, I ran toward her just as I had in real life. While they argued, I kept my eyes on him. On the blade, he pulled from his sleeve and pushed into her. A scream tore from my throat right before I slipped and fell on that damned rock. Cracked my skull open and lost my mind to the grips of Death—swallowed by the wild river. Every nightmare since has been the same: I drown in all of them.

Water. There was nothing but water filling my head and lungs. I don't know how I knew what was happening when my body had already given in and passed out. The water came in once I let go. But something in me knew I was sinking. Drifting in a relentless current.

My soul kicked against the hand wrapped around my ankle. I wondered whether it was pulling me deeper or to the surface... but I knew. It was Death Himself and He wasn't letting me go.

Down. He took me down into the depths. At one point, I looked up and could see my lifeless body floating face down in the water. The sunlight creating a halo around it beyond the surface of the rushing water. The river carried my body's weight, but my soul was in the arms of Mrithyn. Under it all, on the Other side.

"Life, my lover, made you fair," Mrithyn spoke. *"Your will to live is strong."*

I couldn't see Him, but I could hear His voice, thick and low, rippling through the water. My sights stayed lifted toward the surface, watching myself drift away. A shadow flickered over the water and then a body splashed through the face of the river.

It was my mother trying to swim to me. Trying and bleeding out into the water. Too weak to fight the current. She reached for me with her long arms, bending the water to bring me closer, and grabbed hold of my lax body.

"Ah, another comes to us." Mrithyn's disembodied voice drifted toward her.

She weakened and sank with me in her arms. That's when I felt her there with me. We were no longer in the water. We were in a shadowed, eternal realm. Faded and bowing before the throne of the God of Death. He hid in darkness, but I could see His eyes. Swirling with colors too rich to explain and too bright to have lingered in.

"Let my child live. Spare her. Take me instead."

"You could survive," He countered.

Mrithyn lifted me so that I was no longer kneeling before Him. My mother prayed for my soul as her own dwindled.

"Let her live. Take my life. I'll dedicate my child's soul to you, Mrithyn."

"You could survive if someone intervenes quickly," He said hastily, testing her resolve.

"But she cannot. She will die. Please, she is only a child. Give her a purpose and then give her back. Don't let her life go to waste. You can have mine. I've lived. She must live."

"Your child is already dead," Mrithyn sighed.

My mother sobbed. *"Give her back—make her your own, then! Please!"*

"You beg me to Remake her into my Instrument?" Mrithyn purred.

"If you will let her live. Let her be undying by your power and grace, my lord.

Let her live. Take me instead."

"*Mother,*" I whimpered. I felt hollow and cold. Distant and waning like a new moon.

Mrithyn rumbled. "*I would enjoy being bound to such a soul. Life, my lover, made her oh, so fair.*"

"*Then you'll spare her?*"

"*On one condition: she will kill for me. Become my reaper.*"

Mrithyn's presence swallowed me whole. He filled my mind, and I felt a tug. As if there was a thread between my body floating in the river and my soul.

"*I will make her my Cahrenar. She will be a Fate worse than death for those who seek to destroy my golden world.*"

Then, He placed the dark seed of His power on my tongue. I could feel Him all around me... and then within me. Power oscillated through me. And the tug on that thread pulled harder and harder. It unraveled what I was, wove me into something else.

The hand wrapped around my ankle dragged me back toward the surface. My eyes fluttered open, and I could see my limp hands floating before me. I tightened my fists and pumped my legs. I clawed toward the surface... and then beyond. Until I was floating above the river. Resurfaced, reborn. Something Other. The Death Spirit embodied. I arose, Death Incarnate.

It was my fault. I didn't swim away like she said to. She sacrificed herself for me because I didn't listen, and I fell. In my dreams, I try to pull her back into the river, reversing the memory. Playing it backward. The riverbank gives back her blood, and her body gives back his knife. The hooded man leaves, and we splash each other. Water droplets suspended in the air are sucked back under the surface of the water, into our palms. She doesn't die and neither do I.

But that's not the truth. Heavy, booted, splashing steps followed us into the water. Closer and closer to me. Two hands pulled me from the water. My body was on the bank. He left me there and retrieved my mother's body.

I could see her beside me—her green eyes opened but unseeing. I slipped in and out of consciousness. I felt the strong arms snake around me, and the sounds of the river faded as they carried me toward my home. Felt his clumsy, faltering but desperately quick steps snapping twigs. My body jostled in his arms as he ran. I was over his shoulder and never saw his face.

My body felt so weak—my mind warred for consciousness. I lingered between hearing and shunning his warm whispers. "Let her live. Let her live. She's just a child."

Somehow, I woke up in my home tent with Liriene and my father there.

I woke up in Draven's bed and looked at him sleeping next to me. Every day since I died, every step I'd ever taken, led me here. The countless lives I'd taken. The damning prayers I laid at the feet of the Goddess of Darkness, answered. I lived with guilt and regrets, but choosing Draven was not one of them. I had become powerful, unapologetically. Fully understanding the costs and the risks.

My mother paid the toll for my soul with her own.

For the power she prayed for, for my people, I paid a toll in blood.

I'd forge my way forward—no looking back.

He woke up as if he could sense my eyes on him. "Good morning, my wife."

"Good morning, my enemy."

A smile tugged at his lips, and he reached for me. Curling me into his naked body. He kissed the scar on the back of my neck. Then another, lower. Down, down, down. He made his way between my legs and kissed away the nightmares. Drowning me in the way only he could.

🔲🔲🔲

Draven and I sat side by side at the table for breakfast. Liriene barely looked at me. Barely touched her food. She was sinking into herself, sallow-looking.

"What's wrong?" I asked.

She cut me a glare. *Everything.*

I hoped she would find strength, or at least trust me. We could study together, train together—unravel secrets together. But she looked so pale. She was a prisoner in her mind.

Her scars, though she had some physically, I felt them on her mind. What she'd seen and done in Tecar. It weighed on her. I would not let her lock herself up in her mind. Whether she agreed with me, I would not leave her in that darkness.

Someone burst through the doors into the dining hall—two men. They were screaming. We all jumped up from our seats. Guards were following, running down the hall, but everything felt like it was moving in slow motion. The first man reached the table, thrusting a blade toward Liriene.

At that moment, rage overwhelmed my body. Magic and fury crescendoed into a tidal wave of willpower. I took in a sharp breath, lunging toward him—and he dropped dead.

His body crashed into the table, landing in Liri's food. His skin was blue. I coughed, faltering forward, and bringing my hands to my throat. Liriene fell backward, and his blade clattered to the stone floor. Nearly knocking her chair over, her scream finally caught up.

Draven's hands were on my shoulders, spinning me toward him.

A pulse of magic hit the other guy—exuded from Hadriel's outstretched hand. A flash of purple light in the corner of my eye. I heard the guards clamor into the room, but I couldn't catch my breath.

My chest heaved—I was choking. As if I had swallowed a cloud of smoke. My throat and chest burned, and I heaved for air. I fell to my knees, and Draven sank down with me.

"Keres." He reached around and patted me on the back, but nothing was lodged in my throat. Just a biting ache.

"Hadriel!"

"Breathe, child." Hadriel was there in the next moment.

Liriene's hands were on me next. "Keres, what's wrong? Her lips are turning blue."

"Keres." Draven lifted me up. I sucked in a breath, but it wasn't enough.

I warred against the strange sensation in my lungs. Like I'd gasped and breathed in not air, but a chilly wind that smelled and tasted of blood. For a split second, I felt a distinct banging against my rib cage. Like fists of something trying to get out.

My eyes found Hadriel's. Another breath came, uneasy but better.

"Her eyes," Liriene said.

"Breathe."

Draven pawed my hair away from my face, listening as my wheezing subsided.

"What—what the fuck?" I rasped.

We all turned and looked down at the dead man on the table. Hadriel's shadowed eyes widened with astonishment.

"Dead," Draven said. "He's dead."

"You killed him without touching him," Liriene said.

"I think… I took his breath away."

"You swallowed his soul," Hadriel said.

We all turned and looked at him next, but he just stared at the body.

"Sire, what about this one?" a guard asked.

"Burn the witches!" the other assailant shouted, jerking his chains.

Draven walked out from behind the table, striding right up to the man. His fists uncurled, and his claws dropped through his fingertips.

"She's not a witch; she's my wife," he growled.

He stalked toward the man, with his spine straight as a blade and his broad shoulders flexed. The guards gave him a wide berth. The sound of his boots was like a somber drum announcing impending execution.

He shoved clawed hands into the man's chest and tore him open. The man screamed gutturally. Blood sprayed out of him, and the sickening crack of his bones sharpened the air. Liriene flinched next to me. I covered my mouth and nose to block the smell of the blood.

With the man's ribs splayed open, Draven grabbed his heart and ripped it out of his chest.

I watched in awe as the beautiful leather scales he usually hid crawled over his skin. His victim looked down at his own gaping chest, eyes bulging. Blood spurted out of his mouth, and he collapsed. Blood pooled beneath him. Draven stood there, watching as the blood ran to his boots.

His gaze crossed the room, locking on me. Unbridled ferality shone in the depths of his stormy eyes. He held the bleeding heart up in his clawed hand, outstretched toward me. Pounded his other fist against his chest, as if in allegiance, and bowed his head.

A small gasp escaped me.

Draven bowed. To me. Holding up a fucking heart in his hand like it was a rose.

Warmth swarmed my belly and my chest. I touched my hand to my chest, mirroring him. The corner of his mouth lifted, and I glimpsed the gold light within the blue of his eyes.

He looked at the guards. "How did he get in here?"

I turned, not finding Yarden anywhere. Liriene's bulging gray eyes caught mine. I grabbed her.

"He didn't cut you—you're okay?"

She searched my eyes, and I allowed the darkness to drain from them. I could feel it. She took in the power of a God that set her soul on fire. Even so, seeing the darkness in my eyes disturbed her. Probably always would.

I threw my arms around her. "No one," I said into her shoulder. "No one will ever hurt you while I breathe—literally."

She laughed nervously with me and then asked, "Are you okay?"

"Yeah." I let her go and walked over to the body, lifting his head up by his hair. "Bastard. As cool as that was, it felt terrible."

I looked at Hadriel. "I'm a Soul Eater. That's what the book meant, regarding Geraltain. It called him Blood Waker, which I've been called, and it called him Soul Eater. It also called him a Godlander."

I thought back to what Draven told me—a childlike Godlander gave him power. If Geraltain was alive two centuries ago, could it have been him?

That didn't make sense to me.

History knew the man Geraltain had been—the Coroner. Notorious. But if Geraltain was blood-thirsty like me, did that mean he was connected to the Void too? Gods, my head hurt trying to hold all these questions.

Draven walked over to the table and picked up a napkin, wiping his hands off. Liriene's glossy eyes held every emotion as she watched him, from disgust to horror to shock. He dragged his blue eyes up to meet mine. And smirked.

"Look at you, Darkstar. Sucking the souls out of men."

I ran my hand through my hair. "Hadriel, I think we have some studying to do."

"Agreed." He walked out from behind the table. "We'll start tonight."

Liriene and I walked around the table, looking at the dead man. I looped my arm in hers as we followed the King.

"Gods help the man that dares reach for what's mine, Liriene. Especially you."

78:SCYTHE
Keres

"Liriene, would you like to see my wedding gift to Keres?"

"Is it a cage?"

Draven snorted. "It *is* metal."

"What about, you know, the attempted assassination?" I asked.

"More reason to give you your gift now."

He took us several levels up into the castle, near to the roof. I finally realized that every level of the castle was decorated in lighter shades of black and white, from darkest to lightest, as we ascended. The first floor had the marble angels and gargoyles. The others had sculptures of what I assumed were different deities. Some walls on this floor had murals painted on them in shades of black, white, gray, and blue. One that caught my eye was of two armies divided by a yawning chasm. A void. Monsters crawled out of the void, reaching with claws and other strange limbs.

Liriene wandered around as we walked, clearly disinterested in Draven's gift. She seemed to notice the painting, too. Finally, coming to a door, Draven walked in ahead of me. The room was the stripped bare version of our bedroom. The walls were exposed stone and the wall-sized, arched window to the far end was open into the sky. No glass separated the room from the air. Enver and Senka were perched on the ledge, looking in on Emillian as he worked at a forge.

"He's a weaponsmith," I said.

Which meant my gift was a weapon. I walked to meet Draven, where he held out his hand. I sensed Liriene wandering into the room, but my attention passed over the racks full of weapons.

"Good morning, sire. Lady Keres." Emilian wiped his brow and put his forging hammer down. "You're finally here for the present. So, you're wedded, then?"

"Yes," Draven said.

We approached the forge, and I relished in the heat. Smoke billowed out into the open air. Emilian wiped his hands on a cloth. His sage green-skinned muscular body was shiny with sweat—his clothes did little to hide it. He took the blade from his anvil and threw it tip down into a bucket of water. Steamed lolled over the brim with a satisfying hiss.

"This way," he said, smiling. He led us over to a huge black wooden armoire and unlocked it.

"Oh my Gods," I said. My jaw dropped.

"I've never seen you fight, but Hadriel said you used a scythe in Ro'Hale. So, to be on the safe side, we made these."

My gift wasn't a weapon. It was an arsenal. Emilian handed Draven the first blade. A long sword with a gold hilt. He unsheathed it, revealing an emerald green blade.

"Have you ever used a sword?" he asked as he passed it into my hands.

"Not yet. It's so light," I said.

"The ore comes from Illyn. Have you ever heard of the Rift Crafter?"

"Yeah, he makes the Cedenic blades, which are blood red."

"Correct," Emillian said, taking out another shorter blade. "This is an Illynic Blade. Naturally green ore that looks like emeralds but is much stronger. Tougher than steel or silver but lighter."

I couldn't keep my eyes off the scythe. Draven noticed and reached for that one next, exchanging the sword with me. I took it and stepped back, swinging it in arcs. I caught Liriene's gaze as I twirled with it, unable to bite back the ridiculously big smile on my face. Draven and Emillian exchanged glances, pleased with themselves.

"This is amazing!"

"It gets better," Draven said.

"Unlike Cedenic blades, Illynic blades can channel spiritual energy. You can apply runes to enhance them. Or oils and poisons," Emilian explained.

"And," Draven said, smirking, "you can summon your Brazen and coat the blade with it. It doesn't burn."

"What!" I summoned my Brazen and touched the arced blade of the scythe. It caught fire and didn't let the flame hiss out as I swung it again. "This is incredible."

"You're going to train with these weapons. They're all yours."

"Thank you," I said. "Both of you."

"One more thing." Emillian held up his hand. Next to the cabinet was a black canvas bag. He unfastened it and pulled out what looked like a flexible rod—not a rod. A bow. He curved it and strung it. Then pulled out a black leather quiver with gold hardware. The insignias of Bamidele and Dale embroidered into it in gold thread—the dragon and the bear.

"I made the bow from a supple wood. A tree found in the Sunderlands."

I recognized the black wood. "A Wither Maiden?" I asked breathlessly.

Draven nodded, his smirk broadening into a glowing smile. Emillian held up an arrow.

"The head is also made from the Illynic ore. The shaft is the same woods as the bow. The fletching—helical for greatest accuracy, made from turkey feathers. Black that shines with gold."

"Wow," I said. He passed it into my hands, and I turned it over, looking from tip to nocking point. It was amazing. "This makes the arrows we used back home look crude, and Elves are excellent craftsmen."

He replaced it in the quiver.

"We'll keep the weapons stored here for now. You can keep this dirk with you, but you'll begin training soon. I'd like for you to start with the sword. Something you're not used to before the easier stuff. A challenge," Draven said.

I nodded. "Thank you again." I lifted onto the balls of my feet and kissed him, taking the short dagger.

I was excited to train with unfamiliar weapons—but the scythe. It was so pretty I could cry. The blade was the same beautiful green. The snath was smooth, and the hand grips were the perfect girth for my hands.

It felt like the bow, the same black wood.

"How did you have time—how did you plan this?"

Draven smiled again and straightened up. "Remember when I left for a few days, when you first came into Dale? I was here and put the requisition in then. I oversaw its inception—Emillian brought it all to life. Your ring I brought back from that trip, but this is something you had to be here for."

"How did you know about the Wither Maidens, then?"

"Hadriel recommended it, since it grows in the Sunderlands. He also was looking forward to getting you high off that tea for a while."

I snorted. "Of course, he was. Wicked monk."

"Thank you again, Emillian. We'll be back tomorrow to grab her things."

"Yes, my lord."

We left the room, and I was all but dancing.

"You're happy?" Draven asked.

I smiled at him.

"Good," he said.

Liriene asked if we could see the highest level. She wanted to see the view. Draven brought us onto the battlements. The view of the Baore, the Rift—it was incredible. The sunlight glistened on the snowy plains, shadows shifting as clouds rolled by. Clouds capped the mountains and fog settled in the valley.

"Is that the Kryptag tower you were telling me about? The home of the dragons?"

It was massive. An unaccompanied spire that must have been taller than Bamidele's and looked like it was hewn from the mountain. Which it was.

"Yes, little wolf. We'll be visiting there soon. I also have to go to Cigard Barrows."

"You mean into Illyn?" Liriene asked, incredulously.

I looked from her to him. He furrowed his brow. "I am King of the Baore. My province's relations with Illyn are vital because of the vulnerable pass along the border. As well as the thinness of the Veil here."

601

I squinted, looking off into the distance, watching the storm clouds roll around the Krypt. I thought I could make out the shapes of more dragons flying around.

"What do you mean by the thinness of the Veil?" I asked.

"The border between Illyn and Aureum is more than a geographical marker. The Rift Mountains largely block their country off from ours, but in places where the mountains thin, the Veil serves as a kind of barrier between us."

"Why? I thought people crossed over the border all the time. According to Hadriel and even Queen Hero."

"They do. It's not an absolute wall. More of a ward, placed by the Gods."

"What?" Liriene asked.

"Have you two never heard the stories of the Elder War, the Forsworn Gods and the Forsaken First Children?"

We blinked at him. "I've heard mention of the Elder War, but never gave it much thought," I admitted.

Liriene shrugged. "Me neither."

He sighed and led the way along the battlements.

"Hadriel has so much to teach you both. It takes time to understand the politics of it, but Illynads were the first created mortals. The First Children. Illyn is the mother-earth of monsters, but not all Illynads are monsters. They're like you and I. Aurelesian history tells stories about the fearsome Ashan, the deadly songs of the Lamentar. The earth bending trolls and worse—dragons. They are different, but they're not naturally hostile."

"They attack our borders. What about the war in the Moldorn—I've seen visions of it," Liri said.

"What?" I asked, my mind jumping to Darius.

"Like I said, they're not all hostile. Emillian for example, a Goblin. He's an incredible person."

"Whose command leads them to war?" she asked.

They narrowed their eyes at each other.

"The Illynic government is not like ours. Not the point, Liriene. The point is, at the time of Constitution, the creation of the world and mortals, a God created the First Children. They were powerful, but they were imperfect and not made in the Gods' images. They were considered unpredictable, born of the unknown. Fearsome. The Gods segregated the First Children into Illyn. Not despising them, but not favoring them. They grew cold under shadows. Some became wicked and twisted. Some remained as they were. Then came the Second Sons to whom they gave free rein of the gold-lands. They credited the God Elymas with our design. Born of wonder and magic. The Gods were very pleased we were made in their image. Still not perfect, but our flaws were beautiful to them. In my opinion, it's bullshit. We're capable of the same twistedness as anyone or anything else." He shook his head.

"All of creation becomes restless. It was worse back then. Illynads were thought to be under the influence of Gods not taught about in the Aurelesian Doctrine. Gods and Goddesses of punishment and torment, wrath, greed, lust, envy. Misfortune and of warped creatures. The same way the Aurelesian Pantheon chooses Instruments, these Gods also chose mortals to gift their 'devious' powers. Thus, they were banished. It wasn't necessarily malevolent. They simply are what they are, and they did what the other Gods did. It got them locked away behind the Veil. In the Forbidden Garden of the Godlands, which in the physical realm is considered Illyn. Thus, the Forsworn Gods dwell in the mother-earth of monsters along with the forsaken First Children. They were driven back through the Elder War. Which is an entirely different story."

I relaxed the tension between my brows and tilted my head, looking over the battlements at the Rift.

"So, the Veil is thinner here. If it's crossed, does it take us to the Forbidden Garden?"

"No. We can pass over the border, shirking the wards. There's a feeling you get when you pass. Like you're being watched. Eventually it subsides, but your paranoia shouldn't. Illyn can be dangerous. To cross into the Godlands, you have to rend the Veil. Even if you did, you'd have to traverse the Wastelands and all its horrors to reach the Garden. You don't simply walk in, and don't be fooled by the name. The Garden is a graveyard for the Gods. Though they're not dead, they rot in their misery. A place devoid of color and sound. Shrouded in darkness. The path is confusing and teeming with malicious spirits."

"Can you rend the Veil?" Liri asked him.

He gave me a look and then looked back at Liriene, who narrowed her eyes on him. "I practice some feats of Veil Manipulation. Hadriel was my teacher before he was yours."

She nodded and looked back out toward the Krypt as we turned back to where we started.

"Speaking of dragons. You said you had someone to introduce me to."

He smirked at me. "Yes, little wolf. The Keeper. Shepherd of the Drach."

79: SPIES

Heres

Yarden met us in a corridor that led to the Atys Grounds.

"Where have you been?" I asked.

"Tending to matters," he said with a soft smile.

I wanted him and Liri to get to know each other—thought she'd like to speak with him as much as I did. She didn't seem interested in anything. As we passed the Atys grounds, Draven stopped. He turned and surveyed the grueling site. It was like a boneyard, but full of spikes and crosses. All different heights. He bowed his head—as if in prayer. And then kept on walking.

"Don't you feel regret—" Liriene started.

He turned back and looked at her. "I do not. You have spent little time with me, Liriene, but I'll tell you the same things I've told your sister. I am the Unbridled. I stop at nothing to get what I want. Life and death are both precious and to be respected. I've killed to feed. I silence or cut down those who stand in my way, but I know the weight of all my actions—my victories mean something to me."

"What about my sister—is that what you feel? Victorious for claiming her body? Giving her a false sense of power and hope?"

"Liri," I hissed.

He snorted, turning away from her and looking at me. "Whatever war lies between me and my wife, it's ours. She's mine, my concern. No one else's. I *am* her victor. Every drop of blood in my body belongs to this woman. I'd bleed the world dry for her. Because the same way I stop at nothing to get what I want, I will do anything to keep what I have. There is only victory and loss in life. I don't plan on feeling the latter regarding her."

He strode toward me, putting his arm around me, and led me forward. I looked back over my shoulder at Liriene, who merely shook her head.

Liriene

The King was honest. I had to give him that, but his truth was brutal. He was a monster. I didn't care what anyone said. I didn't see my sister as a monster. She was a girl who bore a curse and terrible power. Maybe there wasn't as much light in her Spirit as I wanted there to be, but Berlium's was pitch black. He had a void inside him. If he abandoned her, she'd be full of his darkness and alone.

Maybe he was right. It was a war they waged on each other. Hidden in tangled sheets. With every step they took, my visions changed. They didn't believe in mates but in bonds. In choice. She'd bound herself to him, and there was no painless way of severing that bond. Whether they did it themselves or fate did. Or someone else did.

Every drop of blood in my body belongs to this woman. I'd bleed the world dry for her.

If the King stayed true to her—if their bond held strong... how much would they change each other? She called herself a Godling now, but I was still afraid of what she might become. She was the Blood Waker. He was the Bloodstone. And then there was Thane. I was still trying to figure out how they all connected. I only knew Thane and Keres were bound as well.

There wasn't supposed to be room for passion between Keres and the King, but I could tell he felt something for her—who knew how long it would last? The man made of stone cracked. The woman who breathed fire seemed... colder than she used to be. They craved each other with a need too urgent to deny.

She was all claws and fangs and abysmal eyes around her lover. He saw beauty; I saw Death.

I also saw something I never had for myself. No matter how wrong it was, what they found in each other was something I'd lost. I missed Katrielle. I was tired. Every word I said fell flat. Flashbacks mangled my visions. Tecar. The battle of Ro'Hale. Katrielle. Not a day went by that I didn't wish I could just shed this skin and be with her. Maybe that would be better. I was useless here. Unheard—but I was waiting for Thane. I trusted him. He found me on the battlefield, and he told me not to fear. Everything would be okay, and he was coming.

Keres and Thane were on a path toward each other, whether she liked it or not. I couldn't see the end, or the divergence. What would happen when Thane and Berlium crossed paths? Her choice in Berlium... would not go unpunished. That was all I could tell from the visions. And Gods, I hated the visions. All I wanted was peace. No more pain. No more monsters. There was fire in me, but I felt like it was dying out.

Keres

Liriene was too quiet, but the roaring of dragons filled the silence.

Senka and Enver soared above us, toward the grounds as we approached. There was a small house made of stone. Like a miniature castle. Vines climbed over the roof, dead from the change of season. A small garden had also succumbed to the frost.

A woman stepped out of the house. She had radiant dark skin. Darker than Yarden's. I swore his breath hitched as she flashed us a radiant smile. Her long curly hair was a gorgeous dark brown and reached her waist. She wore a deep purple cloak with a brown fur trim on the hood. Her outfit beneath was a pair of red-brown trousers and a matching shirt.

And her eyes were pure gold.

"Lady Hasana," Draven said and held his arms out to the woman. She readily embraced him and then turned to me and did the same, taking me by surprise.

"This is the woman you were furious with." She laughed, looking me up and down. "You have such strong hands, my Queen," she said when she took my hands in hers.

I noticed the elegant length of her fingers, the smoothness of her skin, as she turned my scarred hands over.

"You rabid fiend." She glared at Draven. He looked away. She met my eyes, the gold light piercing through me.

"Wear your scars like dragon scales," I heard her in my thoughts.

My eyes widened. *"Are you... an Instrument?"*

"I serve the Goddess Attor, Mother of Dragons."

A servant to a Forsworn Goddess.

She beamed at me, and then her eyes caught on Yarden.

He was the Cerberus. Like he said, meant to guard precious things. Hasana, the servant to the Goddess of Adversity, the Keeper of Dragons, was precious indeed. This was the woman he'd fallen in love with. But the look exchanged between them was not gentle.

Senka and Enver flew toward us, landing beside Hasana's house. The earth shook from their weight.

Draven smiled up at them. "They're incredible, Hasana. Growing fast."

"They are. Magnificent," I said, following his gaze. "Are they young?"

"Yes," Hasana said, smiling. "They—"

"We have company." Yarden's voice cut the smiles off their faces.

A band of people dressed in all black approached. Draven squinted at them, pulling me closer. Liriene moved closer to Yarden.

"My lord," the woman in the center said.

"Blyana," the King answered. "If you've trekked out here to interrupt my visit with my good friend, then it must be important."

"It is, my lord." She bowed to both of us, as did the people beside her. She had cold violet eyes and brown hair. Beside her was Emisandre and a man with dark blue skin and long black hair.

"What's wrong?" I asked.

"My Queen," Blyana said and bowed her head to me.

"The attack on Wolvens went as planned. But Eagland plans retaliation and has requested aid from the King of Hannor."

"Interesting," Draven murmured, touching his lips. Thinking. "Malyn, did you handle the target in Falmaron?"

The blue-skinned man nodded.

Blyana continued, "The Guild has also made a move, Sire. Rumors flow from the south. The Cenlands have caught word. The Council refuses to recognize your marriage as it is untraditional. They and the Heralds are planning action against us. It may not surprise you after what happened in Mannfel, but there is a minimal division among Baoreans regarding the Coroner. They want to know what you plan to do with her people, what purpose she serves as Queen. The extent of her control—they want answers."

Draven scrubbed his hand over his face. "Gods below."

"And so it begins," Liriene said, and everyone turned and looked at her.

80: SCORN
DARIUS
Day Thirty-Five, Present Day

Osira believed the Coroner was in danger, but she also had a vision of me.

Someone had reported that a Wyrm born Daemon was on the front lines in the Moldorn. Could have been anyone—everyone hated me here. In short, Osira said the world really needed me to stop dicking around and fight. Illyn was rallying. She knew I was holding back but that I'd make a difference. Wyrm born Daemons were dying out.

I was stuck on Keres. On everything I'd lost. But the war was going to turn, and I was in it whether I liked it or not. The Coroner and I were not fighting the same battles, and I needed to let her go. Face the world before me. I'd heard enough. I left Serin. Bryon said I had been ordered to return to the General.

I wasted some time worrying about whether I should tell Vyra. She'd just fucking smirk if she knew. I debated whether I should even believe the Oracle. Then another letter came. She knew about my feelings for Keres—others knew too. They were using them against me. Pushing me onto the warpath. They didn't detest what I was like I expected. They wanted to weaponize me.

This letter did the trick. She'd married him. Well, kind of. The Baore was basically its own fucking country. Their marriage wasn't recognized by the Aurelesian government. Keres was Queen only within her province. Not to the rest of the world. To me, it was all the same. I couldn't have her.

I put the scorched letter on Vyra's desk.

"It's burned," she comments, blinking stupidly at me.

"Yeah. Too angry—it says… Gods." I rake my hand through my hair, leaving sizzling footsteps as I pace. My shirt already burned off and my pants singeing.

"The King of the Baore married the Coroner. They're targeting the Ressid after some fucking incident in one of the outlying encampments. I don't know. But everyone's trying to piss on the fire. They want them assassinated—or her captured. One stupid recommendation after another. But wait—it gets better. Someone here reported my presence. Know anything about that?"

They look at each other.

"Whatever—I know why. You want me on your team—no, you need me on your team. Telling powerful people that a Daemon woke up on your doorstep—smart move. Now, the pressure is applied."

"So, you'll fight?" Vyra asks.

I ignore the question. "Apparently, the Oracle child I so dearly love is traveling with a woman whose parents live at court. The Oracle set off to the Godlands in search of some answers or something. For a solution. How to get the Coroner away from the King."

"But that doesn't change the fact that she's the Queen," Epona chimes in. "What if—"

"Yeah, I fucking know!" I kick the nearest seat.

"Why are you so angry? Calm down, Hellion."

"Because." I ball my fists. "Because Keres—"

I storm out of the tent and then back in a moment later. "Get me a sword and a shield. We're going to Ceden, and we're going to drive those Ashan motherfuckers out of our fucking fortress."

They both exchange another look and then turn to me, with smiles claiming their lips.

"Deal."

81: SACRIFICE
Thane

Day Thirty-Six, Present Day

Word spread like wildfire. It was the Guild's job to catch the sparks.

She married him and had been crowned Queen of the Baore within the last few days—but word only reached us now.

Everything is out on the table. My men know what I am. I know what she's done. My men understand the risks. For the greater good, they will risk sacrificing the bond. We have to move carefully—it is still going to take time. We just have to move.

We leave the Guild and head toward the border with the Baore. The attack on Wolvens was shocking, but we can't waste a moment more.

I don't know whether their marriage was good or bad presently. The world certainly sees it as a threat. Sitting beside the King, she'll learn his secret plans. The ones not even I know.

The Cenlands and the Ressid are making plans against the Baore. Draven's province will become a battleground. In the end, it wouldn't matter whether Keres swore some pompous vows to him. Our fates were tied together. The sins of generations bound us.

Fuck, she could even love him. In the end, she'd lose him.

PART 5

QUEEN OF SOULS

"What will you take from me,
between your teeth, little wolf?"

—King Draven

82: SOVEREIGN

Keres

Day Fifty

My coronation happened after Blyana told Draven all the new threats we were attracting, which only outraged our enemies more. Of course, they refused to acknowledge me as Queen of the Baore, but our people did. Some of them begrudgingly. The coronation was a small, private ceremony, much like our wedding. This time, Liriene attended.

We held a masked ball in celebration, and I got to meet with people and dance. Made friends with some of the ladies that worked in the library. But no amount of dancing could make me happier than standing by Draven's side at the war council meetings or studying with Hadriel.

Over the last two weeks, my dark minister filled my mind with the beautiful, terrible truths of the Gods and their monsters. Draven said we would visit Illyn. I had to be ready.

Liriene and I sat side by side with a book between us. We were teaching her to read like I'd taught Katrielle. Hadriel taught us both what we needed. We learned to shift, to manipulate the Veil, and to enter trances that brought us closer to understanding the dreams our Gods gave us. Days turned over like one page to another, filled with lessons.

When night comes, so does its beast.

My mind spends time between the covers of a book, and the King spends time between my legs. His hunger courses through me—what he craves, I crave. And he is bottomless.

Draven took time introducing me to the important people in Bamidele. Mages, military leaders, political figureheads, philosophers, and arcanists. A host of people live here and conduct studies to further the kingdom. History, government, science. Name it, he has it and a team of people dedicated to it. Even Olysseus and Emisandre taught me some basic alchemy. Potion and poison making—bomb making.

Draven's obsession with the Forsworn Gods is etched into everything he's ever collected. He admires all the Gods, but he taught me about his favorites. He reads to me and takes me through the galleries in Bamidele to show me their likenesses and to impress their doctrines.

The God of Punishment and Torment, Atys, for which he named his execution grounds, excites my Death Spirit most. Vengeful little monster. Hasana taught me about the Goddess of Dragons, too. The Goddess of Wrath and the God of Pride were interesting subjects. Draven taught me more about the Goddess of the Writ and of Debate as he read to me. He even started teaching me the Illynic tongue. The strange language of his tattoos. Said he'd let me read them when I earned it. The Forsworn were brilliant, sinful deities. Unmatched and unforgivable for what they were. Like him. Beautiful and damned. Every night, we take a walk. Exploring the corners and chasing the secrets housed in his trove.

He shows me things you should never show your enemy: your weaknesses and obsessions. Every day, it becomes more obvious I have become both. My favorite things about him are the way he traces his fingers over a well-loved book. The way his eyes climb the magnificent statue of Tira in the west-wing garden. No matter how many times he's seen it, his gaze holds affection and wonder. He shows me what amazes him, what calms him. The way Draven looks at me and touches me—the people of Bamidele notice.

My people feared me all of my second life. These people are supposed to be my enemies and they look at me with reverence. They feel less and less like enemies with every conversation. The derision that welcomed me has left. Draven is a beast. Hadriel is a viper. And I am the little monster in between them. The people of Bamidele not only respect him, but they also fear him as much as they want to please him. And they are curious about the white-haired woman at his side who seemed to feel the same. They approach me more openly.

When I'm not studying with Liri and Hadriel, I'm training or reading with Draven. Always consuming. He relies heavily on experience that I lack, but he is sharing with me. He is practice; I am improvisation and refreshment. His Generals see the warrior in me. His thinkers see the student. His mages see the power.

Draven—there is no looking at him without seeing the whole. Known for his brutality but also bravery. Ruthlessness and invention. Genius and madness. I am addicted to him, to his world. I see the bad and still do not accept it, but I hope he might come to see the world the way I do, too.

When I remember the Sunderlands, I show him. He walks through my memories until I have no more to show him. Now he walks me toward his vision. I don't want the Sunderlands to go back to what it was now that I see what it could be: protected.

And Illyn? The mother earth of monsters is so much more than I could have ever believed.

His war... his goals are to restore the people of Illyn. The Gods have cast them aside. There are people suffering there while Aureum prospers. His taking control of the border is an effort to break down the wall between our countries. Over the past two centuries, during his cycles in hiding, he spent time in Illyn. Fighting battles.

I remembered what Hero said about the Lamentar women she was harboring. They had fled from cruel masters. Draven has killed oppressors in Illyn. He wants Illyn restored—free. Simply because he loves them. The way he loves the Baore. Illynads and monsters are powerful. He wants that power realized.

But Illyn is blood-cursed. The power is buried. The Forsworn are barred. And I am the Blood Waker. He is the Bloodstone: the battlement between the realms. A bulwark that protects both his people, and those forgotten.

To free what the Gods have chained... is a sin. What we want to do would be unforgivable. It might even make us traitors to Aureum. I know where my loyalties lie—fuck whether this tarnished, golden world agrees.

After Bylana, his spymaster, and her assassin, Malyn, met us at

Hasana's house; Draven explained what she meant by the attack on Wolvens. Apparently, the men who abducted me in Mannfel were part of a trafficking ring called the Jewelers. He sent a small army—much like those he used to send into the Sunderlands—into Wolvens, and they slaughtered many of the people.

The Ressid was intent on making problems with the Baore. Draven explained the Guild of Shadows and its ties to Thane. The headmaster was a man named Emeric, which I recognized from the letter my mother had written swearing me to Silas. Her will named Emeric as a guardian. It raised a concern that I didn't mention to Hadriel or Draven. My mother traveled between the Baore and the Ressid. She'd apparently spent much time in both provinces, but in the end, she trusted the headmaster of the Guild. Interesting.

Liriene was appalled that the King ordered such an attack on Wolvens, but I agree with him. She wasn't there. All the people that lived there—hadn't they seen or heard what was happening? Ignored the cries and screams? They deserve punishment.

Of course, it disturbs my sister that I feel that way. Liriene is a misplaced angel here in Bamidele. I try to talk to her, to get her to open up. I long to talk to her, too.

All the people of Bamidele are great. Draven and I get along better than I could have ever expected. Considering he still holds my people in captivity—which is the next thing on my agenda. We have a hearing coming up with our war council. The people want answers—I have them.

But my sister... I miss her. She's not the same, and I don't know what to do. She doesn't talk. Looks a ragged mess. She barely interacts with Hadriel during our lessons. She just listens. I want to tell her about things. There's so much on my mind.

I dream of a man who bears a Death Spirit. Not Thane. Someone with abysmal eyes like mine, watching me from beneath a hood. Every night, he's there in my dreams. He's silent. Smirking.

Draven encourages me to meditate, to speak with my Death Spirit and connect to the deeper parts of it that are tied to the Coroners before me. He thinks that will help and that it's possible for me to learn from them. It's just not working. Instead, I dream of the silent man.

Gods, it's so annoying. Thane pulled the same shit in my dreams. I haven't heard from him and neither has Liriene. I wonder if it bothers her. If she's hoping and waiting. Praying for him to come. Hadriel and I repeatedly try to tell her to let it go. He's dangerous. She simply listens without answering. We know she doesn't agree.

83: Strange Angel

Keres

Tonight, a sad and distant song invades my dreams, chasing the mysterious Coroner ghost away. I wake up and Draven isn't in bed beside me. In that daze, between sleep and waking, I follow the haunting tune. A solo stringed instrument unlike any I'd heard before. I push open the doors to the room from which it sounds the loudest.

I step into a dimly lit lounge room, and my eyes fix on the man in the shadows.

Brilliant blue eyes turn on me, ablaze with the orange and yellow light of the candelabras. The amber-gold harp looms between his hands and legs, looking more like a weapon than an instrument.

His brows are knitted tightly together, and seams of frustration are sewn into corners of his mouth. His breathing steadies as he recognizes me. I hold my white night robe closely around my chest. One of my feet lingers mid-step, taken aback by his abruptness.

"I didn't mean to startle you," I say.

His touch stills the strings' vibrato, and his song retreats into the far spaces of the room.

"You make music?"

"Come and sit, little wolf. I'll play for you," Draven says. The timbre of his voice moves through me.

I return a wary gaze. He tilts his head toward the white leather sofa that sprawls out in the center of the red wall-papered room. Seated, I cross my legs and fold my hands. He watches my every move, his face never relaxing. In fact, when he closes his eyes and reaches his hands out for the strings, he seems more like he is reaching for something he can't grasp.

He plucks a string tentatively, and it gives an answer he doesn't seem to want. Then another and another. His thumbs and forefingers curl against the strings and pull their notes out of hiding. He closes his eyes, and the song glitters as if laughing at him.

The shortest strings, closest to his chest, give a high-pitched song that flows and lilts, that carries his hands toward the farther strings. Deeper, duller sounds blur against each other, making the song denser. His hands move heavily along those strings, as if he's working against their grasp. His hands part ways, one choosing to stay in the depths of the song, the other retreating to where the light mellowed it. Like an arrow off the bowstring, his hands dart through the highs and lows of the song.

His brows soften, then his mouth softens, and his head drifts ever so slightly to the side. He finds it. Whatever it was, it's haunting and rushing. Tension and release, like hope and fear. He opens his eyes, without taking his touch away from the strings. One quick finger and then another, and then he pauses, leaving the harp quivering for just a moment, before he takes hold of it again. He leans against the body of the harp, reaching his hand down to the farthest strings and playing.

This part of the song seems to live underneath the other, not as a continuation, but as an understanding of the first. A dive beneath its surface. Longing to be brought out by him; for him to pull open spaces in the air for it to fill. His song rises, soft as smoke and dark as shadow. It comes to life in his hands, through the strings. It burns as it slows and echoes between us. The song becomes as warm as the candlelight and as haunting as the man who beckons it by hand.

With a smile forming on his mouth, he hums to the harp. His fingertips soften against the strings as his lips part, and he lets out his song. His voice is unexpectedly gorgeous. Rich and deep—I sink into it.

> *"Mine, dark-hearted Lover, O,*
> *Sits beneath the tree that stands,*
> *Her gaze like midnight,*
> *Sees not the Star in my hands.*

Mine, dark-hearted Lover, O,
Speaks and Swallows
the roots of me.
Fine, dark-hearted Lover, O,
How you shake the boughs of me.
Whisper through my head and hear,
How this darkness alights near
The withering touch of my Lover.
A moonlit voice bends me so.
As cold winds bend the Tree low . . ."

He stops.

I open my eyes. His hands still the trembling strings, but his eyes have the opposite effect on me.

"What, that's it?" I sit up straight.

He blinks away the song, and after a moment, laughs heartily. My brows shoot up and his hands drop into his lap. He sways in his seat with laughter. I pick up a small round pillow and throw it at him. Instinctively, he reaches out to protect the harp, and the pillow hits his shoulder. Which only makes him laugh harder.

I stand, laughing now, too. "What are you laughing at, bear?"

He hugs himself and laughs until tears line his eyes. It's such a contagious sound, more permeating than the song. When our eyes meet again, we turn red, laughing harder.

"What the fuck," he rasps.

I hold my arms out. "Exactly!"

He wipes his eyes and clasps his hands together, stealing one more glance at me with a deep giggle coming from his belly.

"My Gods," he croons. "You should have seen your face."

"Oh, blood be all, and all be damned." I plant my hands on my hips.

He stands and licks his lips before pressing them shut. Our laughter dissipates. I bite my tongue and look away from him as he draws nearer. His hands reach for me the way they reached for the harp strings, and I drive my stare back into his.

"Very glum song, don't you think?" he asks as his hands find their place on my waist.

I squint up at him and can't deny him a smile. "Fitting. You're a very glum man."

His mouth drops open with laughter again, and he leans forward, placing his head on my shoulder. Of course, I can't bear the weight of him and grab onto him, faltering to hold us up.

"Are you drunk, Draven?" I squeak, which only makes him roar with laughter again.

He melts into me, and his arms surround me. He laughs into my shoulder and then presses a tender kiss against my neck before standing upright.

"No, I'm not, Adrasteia."

His laughter retreats back into a smile. His eyes sparkle, as if the somber music had opened a vein of mirth inside him. He looks like he'd bleed it all out if he does not laugh. I try to keep a straight face, but my lips tremble and give way. Yet again we're hysterical. I don't know what about.

He walks back toward the harp and plops down on the seat once more. I follow him, but this time I stand on the other side, across from him. He holds up his hands at a disciplined angle and meets my eyes as he strums the harp again.

Every note holds his smile and swells with a sound like his laughter. He doesn't sing, but lets the song bubble up between us. With every touch, the song cascades from its crest, down toward me in its still bright depths. He pulls it back toward him and pushes it out toward me. An exchange of our energy. It rings out louder than the last song, swelling and swirling with triumph and clarity.

It draws his eyes away from me and I let him go. Standing beside it isn't enough. In some of its phrases, I feel I need the song inside me. I want its warmth and brilliance where I feel heavy.

I've heard nothing like it. I've seen nothing like him... playing. Wishing and then spinning that wish into song, like a tapestry on a loom. Every strand stretched from every string he touched, creating something there between us. Listening, I can see it—feel it—knotting around us. I watch him spin and spin this magnificent song, tied up in it with him. This song feels like a celebration. A moment of joy that we don't deserve, but that I desperately need. I move from my side of the harp and draw closer to him. At his shoulder, I watch. He plays with his eyes closed. His body relaxes, and he wears a new, unfading smile. His arms surround the harp, his hands take from it all the beauty it can give. The moment is beautiful.

Suddenly, I'm hoping nobody finds us like this—that no one else is listening. I don't think anyone understands us. Even those of his people who are kind to us. *I* don't even understand us, but right now I don't want anyone to. I just listen and love every second of this song.

Forgetting the threats, the war, the pain. For just a moment—with my strange red-winged angel.

I pass him and come to stand behind him. I watch his muscled back, his movements tightening his shirt. The tilt of his head, every swirl of his black hair. I hear his heartbeat with a liveliness—a song I never imagined could live within him. I touch him, resting my hand lightly on his shoulder. He perks up, and the song falters.

"Don't stop," I whisper.

He picks the pace back up.

His body thrums with excitement. I let both my hands wander over his shoulders, feeling the rise and fall of his breath. The energy within him is intoxicating. I trace my fingers along the nape of his neck and twirl the ends of his hair. The harp's song trills and blooms, scintillating through him and up my arms.

Each hand seems in competition with the other, one stroking softly and the other picking out sharper notes. It makes me think of how he touches me. I feel the reverberation running along my bones. The glimmering notes fill my head with sounds that remind me of the way he makes my body feel.

Touching him feels like touching the song. I laugh softly to myself and keep close to him. Him, unguarded and unburdened—for just a moment, it feels right.

By the song's end, I feel... I just *feel*.

He turns on his seat and looks at me. I brush his hair back from his face and rest my once broken hand on his shoulder. His eyes are gold when it's just the two of us. Bits of blue remain, but this—it's magical.

He smiles and asks, "Do you think you could be happy here?"

My smile fades and so does his, as I draw back from him. I search the room for my memories of this feeling. He watches me quietly from his chair. The last notes of the song fade and I stop searching.

"Every happy memory I have has been distorted in some way." I turn and face him. "Because of Death or War. Something in this world seems to chase away any happiness that finds me."

He straightens up. Former celebration is gone from his eyes. Reality cools them to a darker, muter shade of blue. Still, he stands and reaches for me.

The way he looks at me makes me stand up taller and lift my chin. He's looking for his Queen in me. I offer a small smile. He returns it with a look that stings like pity. I'd ruined the moment.

"Many dark memories plague my mind, and I still find beauty. In secret mostly, I make my music. It's a way for me to turn my memories and feelings into art. Some are as the first song you heard. Rather glum."

A coy smile plays at his lips.

"And some are more startlingly honest, like the one that played between us just now. When you just touched me, I felt you and you felt it in that song. Didn't you?"

I nod.

"You commanded me not to stop, and in that song, you felt my obedience. How I wanted to obey you. Did you feel that?"

His hands drift up to my throat.

"Yes."

"I can show you how to get everything you want. With you, I believe in heavenly things I felt too damned to deserve. We can have this too. I'll show you. One drop at a time, until your thirst for blood—the thirst I understand so well—is replaced by a thirst for life and all its riches. And it's time I show you something I've been hiding."

84: SATED

Keres

"Walk through," he says.

He snaps his fingers and blue sparks jump to all the candles in the room. The room is a dark green, filled with nothing but standing, golden mirrors. Only a dozen or so, facing in different directions. "What is this place?"

"There are few things in life that torment mortals so much as the unknown. We fear what we do not understand or cannot control. Predict. These mirrors show possibilities."

As I pass each mirror, I see a different reflection. Then I look over my shoulder at him. "Are they from Illyn?"

He presses a finger to his lips and walks past a mirror. "It's a secret."

I lick my lips, watching him inch closer with the sly smile on his face.

"You got them from the Goddess of Vanity?" I ask.

He laughs. "If only." He touches the golden frame of one mirror but keeps his eyes on me. "The God of Punishment and Torment. The hunt for knowledge—for secrets—can be torturous. Men drive themselves to madness pursuing genius. They lose sight of themselves. These mirrors can show all the things you might have been and what you are based on choices you could have made or did. To reflect on."

"I get it. Because they're mirrors. Can they show future versions?"

"No, my girl. They're mirrors. Not telescopes."

"What's a telescope?"

He smiles. "I'll show you another time. Look around."

Versions of myself find me peeking in at them. Twists of my fate.

Myself, in other forms, called to other destinies, entangled in other webs of truths and lies. Versions of myself, so different from who I am. Strangers with my face and name. One of them has the black hair I was born with in my first life. The girl I would have lived to be if I had not died, probably. I did look like Herrona, but with bright green eyes. It made me wonder what Mrithyn saw in me before making me His. Because the look in that reflection bespoke untapped power.

As if I stood in a corridor, a passage of time, with every reflection moving in sync with me. Belonging to a different reality. There's a version of me—a dead child. What I would have remained if Mrithyn hadn't spared me. Beside that reflection, another mirror holds the Coroner behind its glass. My Godling form.

"Divine," he says, coming up behind me.

A torq of shadows around her neck trails down over her shoulders and wraps her in inky darkness, playing with the green Brazen burning around her edges. She is Death. From her horns down to her toes. An omen incarnate. Her presence in the mirror hits the same vibration as her existence within me. I feel most exposed looking at her than I did looking at the others. The mirror, a vial for the poison. But she doesn't scare me. I look at her with pride.

And so does Draven.

The shadows swirl around her, licking every inch of her armored body and smoking up the mirror. Draven rakes his eyes over her, and I turn to face him. She turns too as my gaze travels from her to him. He's in the reflection beside her now, just as he is beside me. His hand touches my waist and hers. I like the look of him touching me. He doesn't need to shift; I see his wings in the mirror. Scales claim places on his skin. The power in me and the power in him… coming to life behind the glass. A flare of red light builds up in his chest, pulsing.

His smile widens. He takes my hands by the wrists and turns me to face the mirror. He presses against me, moving me toward it. I look at him in our reflection and smile. He's hard and his eyes are darker. He touches the glass, wiping away the reflection of the Death Spirit. I see us as we are now.

"I want to take you right here, this way. While we both watch. I want you to see what I see when I fuck you—the way your eyes light up only for me."

Heat pools between my legs at his words. His hand drops to lift my night dress—giving him a glimpse at the lace panties I have on underneath. He runs his hands over my hips, my ass, and squeezes. "But first, close your eyes. I want to show you something else."

I do as he says, and I hear him take his shirt off. "Open."

I look in the mirror at him, then spin around when I see it.

A tattoo. On the left side of his chest, on the side of his ribs. Tucked under his arm—against his heart: A wolf swallowing the moon.

"My little wolf," he says and flexes. He moves his arm so I can see the whole thing. "I got it done this morning while you were with Hadriel. I heal quickly, though, so you can touch it."

I run my fingers over the soft black lines. Tracing the snout of the wolf, the circle of the moon between its teeth. "It's beautiful."

"You're beautiful," he says with a smirk. "Now turn around and let me make you feel beautiful."

He spins me back around, and lifts my nightdress off as I watch the fabric pass slowly up my legs. Revealing the lace, then my midriff. My breasts drop when they're free of the dress. He presses his face into my hair and inhales my scent. I watch the way he looks at me. He holds onto my hips, holding me as he looks down at the lace. He touches it, feeling it grate against his skin.

"Every inch of you..." he breathes and then curses. "I think the Gods took their time. Now, I'm going to take mine."

My nipples harden, cold without my clothes. I watch his hands travel over my body, his gaze following. He brings them around me and watches our reflection as he lifts my breasts and squeezes them. His palms warm my chest, his fingertips pinch my nipples. I bite my lip, and he smirks again. He keeps one hand on my chest and the other brushes over my belly. Passing down slowly.

"You're right," I say. "I am small compared to you."

He chuckles. I love how his eyes brighten when he laughs. My spine arches for him so that I'm pressing against him. I love the way I look naked in his arms.

"Yes, you are, my girl. A perfect fit."

He touches my hair, tracing his fingertips over my ears as he pulls my hair back. Then he touches his scar on the back of my neck. I watch the goosebumps crawl over my skin. My face flushes.

"I love how you blush," he whispers against my ear, and traces lazy lines over my face and neck. "Your sweet blood paints the image of an angel but heats your body with need like hellfire. Your body invites both worship and punishment. What a blessed devil I am that you're mine."

The Death Spirit purrs in my chest, and he presses himself against me. I lock eyes with him in the mirror, seeing how mine darken as my Godling comes out to play.

"Mm," he sighs into my hair, keeping his eyes on mine. "My Darkstar."

I turn and face him, my fingers going to his pants. He allows me to undress him. I move to the side and look at him in the mirror, next to my naked body. Trailing my fingers over every muscle in his abdomen, his arms, as I watch.

He turns my face and kisses me hungrily. My head falls back as he bows over me. His hands lock around my throat and give me some pressure that makes me sigh. He touches his way down, kneading my breasts, my hips, bringing his erection flush against my belly.

I pull out of his kiss to lick his neck. Passing my hands behind his neck and knotting my fingers in his hair. He lets out a soft breath as I graze his skin with my teeth.

My fangs sink into him and draw a deep, rumbling moan from his chest. I hold his head, angling it so I can drink from him. His blood is sweet and hot. I lick away the bites. He bends down, picking me up under my legs and holds me up. I wrap my legs around his waist. His cock touches where I want him to fill me.

"Let me in, little wolf," he says huskily.

I reach down and guide him into me. He lifts and lowers me, controlling my movements on his cock. He turns his back to the mirror, so I watch him over his shoulder.

I hold on to him around his neck and watch his hips as he thrusts into me. His perfect ass tightening with the movements. My core tightens around him as he strokes me. I watch my fingers move through his hair. I bare my fangs at my reflection and bite into him again. Watching my eyes change as I drink from him. I feel him shudder and kiss away the bite.

Blood stains my lips, and I lick them.

He picks up his pace, and I lean back to look at his face. Grinding against him, I allow my wings to spread out. Watching them, wrapping us in them. His flare out as well, brushing against mine, and I watch the shadows play around us in the mirror.

His wings graze against mine and the most unexpected, pleasurable feelings lights up my center. He thrusts harder into me, and I toss my head back, bouncing on his cock as he holds me. My apex grinds against his pelvis and lower abdomen as we move. A climax builds and I see the feelings shift through my expression. My lips part as I moan. His mouth claims mine and I close my eyes. Moaning into his mouth as my pleasure crests.

My arousal soaks our sex, and his fingers dig into my legs, my ass, as we still.

He sets me down and spins me toward the mirror. I tuck my wings away, but he keeps his, holding them out with pride as he bends me forward. I flatten my palms against the cold mirror, arching my back for him to mount me. He grabs my hips and enters me, biting his lower lip as he watches. My head drops forward as he sets a slow and steady rhythm.

He takes my hair in a fist and pulls my head back, forcing me to watch. He leans into me, reaching into my core, driving pleasure into me. I tighten around him, pulsing and pulling him in deeper. His hand pushes my back down, forcing me to arch for him more.

I spread my feet apart. Holding myself against the mirror, watching my breasts swing and bounce with our movements. As he pounds into me harder, I push my weight back into him, meeting him stroke for stroke.

His face tightens, and he growls, looking at our reflection and then down at my body. He spanks me hard and the shock that crosses my expression is quickly wiped away by excitement. He does it again and then reaches a hand down between my legs, leaning closer to the mirror. I feel him moving against my ass as his thick cock strokes my pussy. His fingers play against my sex as deftly as he touched the harp. Gods, he brings sounds out of me I didn't know I could make.

My inner walls contract around him again, the sensation intensifying. As he pounds into me, every stroke feeds my craving for him. Watching his brow furrow and the sweat beading on his skin.

"Look how beautiful you are when I fuck you. Now, you see what I see."

And I feel beautiful. On fire. Burning in his stare. He withdraws, and I whimper. He smiles at the sound.

"Look at that pretty little pout." He dives back into me, making me gasp. My breath fogs the mirror. I wipe it away quickly to watch.

"See? When I leave you empty and wanting?" He pulls back out again, and I groan. Every time he withdraws from me, the more I crave it. Another climax builds in my core.

I bite my lip when he pushes back into me. "The hunger in your eyes as I give you what you want, makes me want to give you everything, Keres."

I whimper again. "Please, don't stop."

He smiled, his fangs showing and his eyes brightening.

"Fuck. Don't stop," I say again. He keeps hitting that place deep inside me. Something shifts in my eyes, drawing my attention. Black swirls with green—then with violet light.

"There you are, my love. Now, I won't stop until you come for me."

I snap my attention back to him and purr. He thrusts harder, never stuttering. Pushes me toward my next orgasm. I focus on that feeling, on his eyes and mine. My climax soars through me and the brightness in my eyes intensifies. His mirror it. That amber and gold light fills them. His hand strumming my sex quickens, drawing out the pleasure, and my eyes roll back as I cry out.

He thrusts faster, and I push off the mirror to bring myself closer to him. He hits another angle, and another sound escapes me. My skin is on fire, my core is melting, soaking us so that it runs down my legs, and my eyes are glowing. His eyes burn amber, shifting into gold and even into red, then blue. Like fire. I reach my arms up behind me, holding on to him as he slows his pace.

Watching the mirror as he bares his teeth and bites my neck, I meld into him as his teeth break through my skin. It stings, but incredible warmth follows it. I rock against him as he drinks from me, his cock still buried inside me. The pressure—the pull of his drinking feels erotic. My heart is wild for him, thriving as he demands the blood from my body.

His arms snake around me, massaging my breasts and my sex as he drinks deeply. It's like a kiss that goes deeper; I feel it beneath my skin. I quake with pleasure when he locks eyes with me. He smiles with me between his teeth. Right where I belong.

"You thought you were the only one who sees? I see what I do to you, my King. The animal in you—my beast."

He closes his eyes and kisses my neck. Running his tongue over my pulse and suckling at the bite marks until they close and are clean.

"I love it when you call me yours," he whispers.

His breath warms my skin, gliding up my neck. He licks behind my ear. I moan and watch him in the mirror. My full breasts are tightened, and my nipples peaked from arousal. My supple curves writhing against his hardened, muscular form. My eyes are full of promise and power. His just as so.

"Now, I'm going to give it to you again." He pushes me down to my knees and kneels behind me. His hands smooth over the goosebumps on my arms and then trail down my back. He pushes me forward so my head is in my hands and my ass is in the air. He grabs onto my waist and guides me back onto his cock. Bent over, I look up at him in the mirror, and he sinks into me again.

From this angle, he's deeper. I want to scream. Stretching my hands out on the floor. My breasts swing under me, and he reaches to hold on to one. His other hand stays on my hip as he fucks me even harder. My body bucks against his as he hits a wall inside me. I arch my back as he pushes me down. My breathing is as rapid and heavy as his thrusts. I try to keep my eyes on him, but I can't, focusing on the feeling of him breaking my body. I growl, unlike I ever have, until my voice shatters into a scream.

"Open your eyes."

My eyes spring open and lock with his in the mirror. He doesn't let my gaze go. Even as I bounce against him, even as I cry from the overwhelming tightness and burning in my core. Even as I bare my fangs at him, wild with hunger for that power. No matter how hard he hits me from behind, no matter how deep inside me he buries himself, my hunger burns. Now, he is holding back!

"Don't you fucking hold out on me." I retract my power from him.

"You're learning, hungry girl." He laughs. "I want you to watch yourself come again on this cock."

"Yes, please." I smile.

He jerks my head back to look at him and thrusts deep, holding himself there inside me and rolling his hips. Licking at me from the inside, touching every inch. I lick my lips and moan as he watches my face. His power rumbles in his chest and he leans down to grab my neck. I gasp as his grip tightens.

His power surges into me. "Burn, beautiful girl."

My body catches fire. The Brazen kissing, chilling my skin. Darkness closes around us. Leaving only us and the mirror. My green fire lights up the night. I tremble, my breath fluttering against the flames as they slither against us.

My flames lick at his skin, reflecting in his eyes. Then he meets them with his own. Consuming me in heat that exudes from my core, where his cock strokes that perfect spot. Delicious heat pooling inside me and pouring out. Tears line my eyes from the intensity of the sensation. Molten, burning me from the inside out.

"Thank you," I gasp.

His hand covers my throat as I fight for breath. It moves to my mouth, and I bite into his hand. He growls into my neck, biting me back. He's fucking me so hard, lacing every stroke with his Spirit's energy. Giving me what I want—himself. I surrender to him, giving him all I have.

We are torches, burning for each other in our hellfire, in our precious darkness. His eyes burn even brighter than before when he pulls away and looks at me. Colors flash through his eyes. A kaleidoscope of radiant power. The way he stares into mine, I know he is just as hypnotized. Knowing we give each other what we need. Sated.

"Come again," he whispers.

His expression softens as he watches me. His hand slides back down to my throat and presses against the bite marks he left behind. My pulse pounds in my head. His cock pounds between my legs. And steadily, another orgasm swells inside me. My eyes roll, and the colors in his eyes blur.

"That's it. Look at me, my love. Let me see those beautiful eyes while I make you come."

Tears blur my vision as he feeds me more and more of that heady power.

"You take my breath away," he says huskily. I moan loudly as the orgasm crests. My body jerks into his and his eyes soften again. "Tell me you love the way I make you feel."

I nod my head against his hand. "I do. I love it."

"Come for me again. Right now."

Obediently, another orgasm rips through my body. I crumble in his arms, but he lifts me back up and rides me through it. Kissing my neck. I reach my hands back and hold on to him, crying out from the relentless intensity. He smiles and wipes away a tear streaming down my face.

Still shaking from my climax, my core still throbbing, I catch my breath. "Your turn, my King." My voice is layered with the Death Spirit's. Laced with desire.

His eyes widen with surprise, and I lift off his body. He runs his hands through the wet mess between my legs and licks his fingers. I turn, kneeling, so I can kiss him. Our eyes close and his tongue gently sweeps over mine. He kisses me softly.

Then, I bow down and take his cock in my mouth, tasting my arousal on him. He groans, running his hands through my hair as I move up and down, stroking him with my lips, my tongue.

I hold my hand around the base of his shaft, unable to wrap my entire hand around him but giving him just enough pressure. I rest the tip of him against my lips and smile. Lifting my eyes to find him glowing. That amber color radiating beneath his skin and pulsing with every heartbeat, bright through the blue fire.

My tongue chases the fire against his skin. I suck him into my mouth and moan against him. Allowing my fangs to graze him. As I withdraw, he pops out of my mouth. I turn my head and bite his inner thigh. He hisses and laughs, twirling my hair as I lick his leg.

I look back up at him.

"Finish with me," I say and lick him again, pulling him back into my mouth and drinking in his taste with a satisfied hum. I swallow him hungrily, like the tattoo of the wolf consuming the moon.

When I release him, we shift, lowering down to the floor so I can ride on top of him.

As he had done for me, I feed him everything I have left. I feel some of my power leaving me and flowing into him. Invigorating him. My body moves with his, leading him to his pleasure. Stroking him with neediness. I roll my hips, lifting onto my feet and bouncing on him.

His hands wander up and down my body. I toss my hair back over my shoulder so he can feel every inch of me. He runs his thumb over the sensitive peak between my legs as I ride him. I grab his hand, bringing it to my mouth to suck on his fingers.

"This is for you, Draven." I lean over him, knotting my fingers in his hair and working my pussy on his cock. Kissing his handsome face, his neck. Licking him where I'd bitten him. Running my hands over his muscled chest, the tattoo. Digging my claws into his arms. I nuzzle into his neck, loving the way his stubbled jaw feels against my cheek.

"I want you to watch yourself come inside me." I turn his head, so he watches in the mirror. His hands play along my torso as I lift back up and ride him with abandon.

He gives me his attention, pinching my nipples, looking at where we connect. Watching his cock as I lift to the tip and drop back down on him.

"Fuck," he hisses and looks into the mirror again. His head arches back and he moans as I work my core, milking him hungrily. He promised every drop of blood in him is mine—I want every drop of his pleasure, too. I crave it above all else.

He climaxes inside me, watching himself and then looks into my eyes, resting his hand over my heart. The look in his eyes is the holiest thing I've ever known.

I smile, relishing in the feel of his cock pulsing between my legs. I slow and sink onto him. I don't let go of him until his breathing and his heart rate slow, taking mine down with him.

We both lie down on the floor beside each other, and watch the colors shift and change in each other's eyes until they eventually fade back into their usual shades of blue and green.

85: SUNDERLANDS' WOLF
Keres

"Sire." Blyana kneels before us in the throne room. "What would you like us to do with the survivors of Wolvens?"

"Have they been questioned to our satisfaction?"

"Yes, my lord," Malyn replies with a grin.

Draven looks at me, and I nod.

Hadriel and Liriene cross gazes in the audience. The King turns back to his spy master and assassin.

"Bhaltar, Nilsine, and Gydaeon, step forward."

The three warriors join Blyana and Malyn in the center of the room. These two men and woman are Draven's most trusted champions. Commanders in his army—most of which, I learned, lives in the Krypt. In Illyn. Although a good number live here, within Mannfel, or in unmarked places in the Baore. Small villages—military families. Not dissimilar to the clans of the Sunderlands.

A hushed stillness possesses everybody present. They hang on the King's next words.

"Please recount what you found in Wolvens."

"We found the houses of men who are known members of an order that sells people into bondage. To be slaves, for sex or labor. Sometimes to fight in their petty skirmishes, or are bought by dark witches to be used as sacrifices in rituals," the first man says. The one named Gydaeon.

"The King of Hannor does not heed his people's cries for help. Eagland and Wolvens are constituted of deserters—safe harbors for war criminals and other kinds," Bhaltar adds.

"Were there not families in Wolvens too?" someone asks. A valid question.

"There were very few, and the women and children were not hunted. In fact, they probably escaped. Whether they fled to Eagland or Falmaron, it's not sure," Nilsine assures us.

"Were no victims recovered?"

"In the fray, a bunch of children who they'd taken escaped. There was a young man among the victims. He led them away. We didn't pursue them."

That was a relief. But with the Ressid and the Cenlands against us, the Sunderlands in limbo, and the Heralds heading toward us, we were ready to make our next moves.

Wolvens was just the beginning. The Ressid province is corrupt. I think about the Elves Yarden taught me about—the notorious. I wonder whether they were involved in such heinous activities as trafficking. Ryu and Roderick, our political figureheads and ambassadors, conveyed rumors of their peddling harmful substances to the public of Falmaron. The village, Falten, which used to be beautiful and safe, had fallen into ruin. Which surprised Draven, being that it was so close and connected to the Shadow Guild. Either way, the Baore and the Ressid are at war, and I have no problem with our plans to move against them.

Them or us. My people are here. Their people are harboring evil. If they could come into our city and abduct me, they can do it to anyone. Stopping them is important.

"How many men are there?" Draven asks.

"Fifteen, my lord," Nilsine responds. I like her. Her voice is strong. She disarms lesser men. Her light blue eyes remind me of Ivaia's.

"Bring them to the Atys Grounds," Draven orders.

I take a deep breath but school my expression into one of stone. Liriene's mouth drops open with horror. Looking at her, I send her a thought.

"You weren't there. You didn't see what I saw. Children, Liri. Ripped apart. Raped, beaten, sold, and killed. If that happened to my child—I'd demand the worst fate."

"Judge and executioner, now?" she questions.

"Coroner." I lift my chin and sharpen my glare.

She straightens her spine, balling her fists.

We watch the execution, but Liriene hides in her room. The men's bodies are pushed on to the spikes slowly. We would reserve impalement and crucifixion for the most wicked. I made him swear it—while he was inside me this morning.

I watch, unflinching. The stench of their blood and excrement taints the air. Draven and I stand side by side. Crowned. Exacting justice. It's horrific, but so were their crimes. Their screams crack the silence, and in my Spirit, I feel nothing but satisfaction.

The voices of the ghost children haunt me, in harmony with the sickening sounds of the torturous execution. The things they endured. Avenged. I was not created to tolerate perversion of Mrithyn's power. These men raised their hands against innocent people, did horrible things to them. I was created to question the guilty and to answer the cries of innocent blood.

If that makes me a monster—fine. It takes one to destroy one.

"They got what they deserved," I say to Draven as I watch.

"Yes, little wolf."

🔁🔁🔁

At the next meeting, I make a motion for my people. Also, innocents. The people of Bamidele listen and they side with me. Over the next few days, we release them from the dungeons of Dale into one of the military villages in the Baore. Closer to Bamidele. I encourage Liriene to consider moving into the town with them, but she doesn't want to discuss it with me.

Our people are going to train, to be sifted by skill. Every survivor would find a place in this new era. Eventually, I'd move the King to allow them to repopulate the Sunderlands. Let them rebuild—make the Sunderlands stronger. Under our banner. We can still control the border and they won't have to suffer.

Draven's plans for Illyn are complicated and would take time, but he will find places for the good people who are stuck on the other side of the border. Alongside our people. Queen Hero is on board, but the King of Elistria is not. He'd need to be persuaded—or subdued.

Draven's war proved the Sunderlands was not strong enough, not supported. Until now. If he ever made a move against my people, he'd answer to me. I was his little wolf, but I was a wolf of the Sunderlands foremost.

86: STRONGER

𝔎𝔢𝔯𝔢𝔰

"You're stronger. You may even be ready to play in the land of monsters with me." Draven wipes the sweat from his brow and flourishes his sword, circling around me.

I ready my blade and smile. "Good thing you gave me my other powers back, then." I stomp the ground and it answers my magic, rumbling. A crack runs from under my foot to his and he loses his balance.

"Careful, creature," I say with mock concern.

He smirks at me.

I'm getting the hang of sword play—he's a good teacher. I hear Liri whimper in pain and look over. Hadriel is trying to teach her the basics of combat in the next ring over. She looks beaten down. Like she's got no fight left in her. I notice her, shivering and making small movements, as Hadriel tries to lead her through moves.

"Hold on." I hand Draven my sword.

"Liriene," I call, then jog across the training grounds. We've had a few snow-free days, and the dirt is frozen beneath my boots. I reach her and she straightens up.

"Come on, Liri. Show him he's fucking with a Demi-Goddess." I mirror Hadriel's stance. "Like this."

"I'm not interested in fighting," she says.

"What?" I scoff. "Liriene, we're at war. Our people are training. You need to learn to fight. What if we're attacked? You do realize there are many people against us right now."

"We shouldn't be on this side of the war, Keres. I don't want to fight the other side. They're right. You and Berlium—you're dangerous for this world."

"This world is dangerous, Liriene. Which is why you have to accept where you are. You have to." I punched the air, throwing a ball of Brazen flying at her.

She shrieked and dodged.

"Liriene!" I scream and throw another fiery hit. "Did you just dodge my fire? You're literally the fucking Sun incarnate, woman. Learn to burn. That's what Ivaia taught me, not Berlium or Hadriel."

"I don't burn like you, Keres," she shouts back. Weaving and dodging my attacks.

"Then burn your way, for fuck's sake. Show me you're still alive." I throw myself at her. I hold back a little, but I swing at her. My fist collides with her shoulder. She cries out in pain.

"Fight me. You're angry," I growl. "You hate it here? You hate me? Show me!"

She sinks back into a ready stance and returns my hit. I dodge her, backing away and drawing her forward.

"Again."

She lurches for me, and I don't miss the tears lining her eyes.

"Let it out." I attack her again.

She lights on fire and roars as she throws herself at me. I tear through the flames she shoots at me, pushing them aside with my hands coated in Brazen. She kicks—actually lands it!

"Fuck yeah." I laugh. "You're in pain. Make it useful or it will make you weak. You can't just shrivel up and die. I won't let you. If you don't fight, you're going to join the dead. I will not let that happen."

"What if I want to?" She breaks down.

"What?" I lower my hands. We both extinguish our fire, and she drops to her knees. I run to her and kneel with her, grabbing her by the shoulders. She won't meet my eyes as she covers her face.

I look at Draven and Hadriel. They come closer.

"No!" she screams at them.

I hold my hand up.

"Liriene, talk to me," I say in a soothing voice. "You've been through so much. You can't just hold it in; it will poison you."

"I can't let it out. It will be a raging fire."

"I can take it." I push her hair back and lift her face. "I'm not afraid of any darkness—any fire. I love you. All the broken and burned pieces. If you feel weak, I can be stronger. I can take it; let me help you."

She pushes me away and gets up, running past the King and the magister. Back to the castle. I nod to Yarden, and he follows her in. I wipe a tear from my eye.

"At least she's angry," I say. "It's better than nothing. Numbness—despair is dangerous."

"She'll open up in time," Hadriel says.

The next day, Liriene comes down to breakfast. Clean, well dressed. Calm.

"You look better. Are you feeling better?" I ask as we make our plates. She piles hers high and eats like she hasn't in a month.

"Let's just enjoy our meal," she says. I watch her shovel her food into her face. Her eyes are far away, but they're not dull. Not empty. I touch her hand, drawing her attention. She stops eating, slows her chewing.

"I love you, Liriene."

She swallows and lowers her gaze.

"I know. I'm sorry."

I slap her arm. "Don't be sorry. You're my sister. No matter what happens, you're allowed to kick me and scream. You're not allowed to go silent. Don't be sorry—just be here."

She turns back to her plate. A tear drops into her food, and she won't give me anything else.

87: Save My Soul

Liriene

Katrielle—the other eight. Mother. Father. Ivaia and Riordan. Attica. Maro. I feel like I'd died with them.

How many more lives will be lost in this war?

Keres was the only person to die and come back—had she, though? What she is... I don't recognize her anymore. Maybe I'm just not being honest with myself, wanting to see something she isn't. Not trusting her the way she isn't trusting me. But I can't see past the pain.

The visions. The flashbacks.

Every time I strip naked, I see the scar from the arrow that pierced my chest. The scar in my hairline from where the mallet hit me. I get headaches. The brand on my shoulder. I feel Varic and Karmic on my skin, hissing in my ear, telling me I'm not what I am. Threatening to rape me.

I hear Berlium snapping Keres' bones. I feel him draining my power. His blood curse. I can still feel the burning in my hand sometimes—when I look at the scar.

Then I see him next to her. The day they visited Tecar. Her matching scars. Her ring. Him, passing his coat around her after she gave me hers. I see her leaving with him. She came back from Wolvens changed. She tries to make me understand her. I just don't.

I see her looking at him. I see more visions. I see Katrielle. Alive and naked beside me, hidden and safe in our secret world. Dead. Impaled. Armor split open. Had Keres forgotten that? As she watched Berlium's champions torture and impale the criminals. How did she not see the past—Kat? Staked and bleeding out of her mouth, choking on her blood.

In excruciating pain.

Did the past not haunt her? How did she look forward—did she ever look back?

Even when I close my eyes, I see it. Images stalk my mind. Clamoring with Oran's voice. I feel like I'm going mad. I feel like the noise, the visions, are carving out the safe spaces of my mind. No matter how far I retreat, they find me. Clawing at my eyes. And I feel cornered.

She's trying to help me, but I'm so scared. How does she see in this darkness? I see nothing and everything. Oran shows me His revelations and I don't want to see them. I don't want to see anything. I want to be with Katrielle, and I know it would be better if I joined her. So Keres doesn't have to worry. To fight for me.

I don't want to fight for myself. It's not worth it. Like she said, the pain can make you weak. Well, I can't be stronger. I tried. Too much pain. My spirit has atrophied. Every vision bores into my skull—like the nails driven into Maro's body. Hadriel sent tea to my room to calm my nerves, and I dumped it into the potted plant in the room.

The plant died.

I'm not here anymore. Holding onto the shell of who I am... I want to let go.

Keres went with Hadriel to study. I go to the roof.

I've considered many ways to end my life. I could steal a weapon. I could cut myself. After watching Keres train with blades, I knew where to strike. If I slit my throat, it'd be over fast. I could attack a guard or Keres or the King, force someone to fight me. Take another arrow to the chest. I could steal something from Hadriel's lab, or something from the alchemists to poison myself. I even considered storing the teas he sent me to drink in a large quantity. Maybe I'd go to sleep and never wake up.

I feel plagued by exhaustion. Unable to truly rest. I just want it to end.

As I look over the battlements we'd walked with the King, my legs tremble. I'm afraid—it isn't enough to save me. Knowing Keres' heart will break, it makes my stomach hurt. Just more pain. And anger. I shouldn't be angry at her, but I am angry at the world. That should save me, but it makes me want to throw myself over the ledge. I hold on to that anger.

Oran flashes into my mind, telling me not to do it. I feel his bright eyes train on me. The cold light of the High Winter sun. My stomach feels like water. I vomit. Wipe my mouth, looking up at the Sun. Chills course through me, though I'm sweating. I'm dizzy enough that I know once I'm on the ledge, I'll probably fall before I can jump.

I am weak. This... this is the death I deserve.

I know I might scream. I know I'll be scared every inch I fall. I don't want to be alone as I fall, but I am alone standing here. I feel alone every day. Despite Keres trying to force her way in.

I don't burn like you do.

My God made me into a woman on fire. I used to be on fire. For a moment, in Tecar, I was aflame. Keres was beside me. We were flying. Burning that place. I smile as I press my hands against the stone ledge and hoist myself up. It's funny. I laugh. As chaotically as I laughed in the cave before we met the wretched King. Laughter that breaks into tears until my feelings turn to ash.

I have wings—wings I don't deserve. So, I'm going to fall.

Every moment of every day, everyone has the option of doing something horrible. To change or ruin their life. Even to end it. Ever since we reached Dulin, I've thought about it every day. I looked up at the Dragons and felt fear. I stared at the walls and felt small. Stuck. I wanted to escape, but there's been no way out. Except this.

What if I just jumped today?

Tomorrow?

And then I ask, *what's the point in waiting?*

At every point in time, the ledge was here. Death is always an option—a choice. For being broken, I choose to shatter myself. For being weak, I choose to punish myself.

My God will probably hate me, but if He feels anything... maybe He'll save my soul.

I'm too tired to care—to ask Him to, so I step off the ledge.

88: SLIP

Draven

I love watching Keres read. She devours books. I love watching her eyes move over the words. The curve of her lips as she focuses. The way she tilts her head closer to the pages.

Hadriel is a lucky bastard—getting to watch her read every day. Hearing and answering her questions. It's a bit of jealousy I love feeling. At night, she tells me about what she's learned. Sometimes she shows me her notes, reads me a part of the book, and then looks at me with wide eyes.

"Look, isn't this amazing? It's my favorite part…"

Everything impresses her. Gods, I haven't felt that way in a long time. I've spent my life studying in solitude. Except when I trained with Hadriel. I never got to look up over the edge of my book and see someone across from me. Until now.

My sexy little monster.

I rake my hands through my hair and look up from my book. She should be done with her lesson soon. My feet dangle over the window platform and I look out at the mountains. A blur above draws my attention.

A rush of blue fabric and red hair. Wingless. Motionless. Plummeting.

I throw myself over the edge, my wings and shadows following me into the fall. Lengthening my body, keeping my wings close to fall faster.

I reach out and grab at her dress. She screams and flails, slipping out of my grasp. I curse. The ground is getting too close. I shift. Lengthening my hand into claws and I catch her.

Her body jerks as I flare out my wings. Stopping our fall with barely enough time. We slow, but we still almost hit the ground.

With her in my arms, I run my feet along the ground until we collapse and roll.

Shaking my head like a wet dog, I push up and look toward her body. I lurch toward her, turning her body over, pushing her hair off her face. She has a scratch on her cheekbone. Her eyes flutter open—she bursts into tears.

I know she hates me, but I wrap her in my arms, pull her into my lap, and I hold her while she weeps. I look up at the battlements. I know she didn't slip. She shakes as she sobs. Her hands dig into my arm, and I hold her just as tight.

"Why?" she asks. "Why did you stop me?"

I hold her back and look into her mercury eyes.

"Why?" I repeat her question. She looks up at the battlements and tears blur her eyes again.

"Liriene, look at me."

I call my shadows out of the Void, and they surround us. "Don't look there. Just listen to me. You're not finished. You're tired and you're hurting. But you're not fucking finished."

She cries. She cries until she loses consciousness. From shock—sheer exhaustion. I look into her mind. The nightmares—she grimaces while she sleeps in my arms.

So, I wrap my cloak of darkness around her thoughts, shielding her from the visions.

Her face relaxes, and she's limp in my arms. Giving into the weight of her exhaustion—allowing the darkness to envelop her. As I carry her back into the castle, I play music into her mind—songs I made when I felt alone too. Music that understands the long nights and soothes the waking nightmares.

🔳 🔳 🔳

I hate seeing Keres cry. She unleashes her emotions. Sadness. Pain. Anger. I hate watching her eyes move over her sister, asleep on the bed. The frown hanging on her lips as she crawls into the bed next to her. The way she touches her sister's hair with shaking hands.

Liriene was lucky. I was lucky I caught her. If she had died, Keres— I didn't want to think about what Keres would do.

I listen to Keres crying. A bit of anger fraying that knot in my chest. A confusing feeling. She turns her head and thanks me. Eyes wide with so many fucking feelings. Everything in her eyes hurts me.

I haven't felt this way—ever.

Two hundred years. I've spent my life trapped in my mind, knowing I was a monster. Knowing I was alone, and that's what I deserved. I never got to look up and see someone across from me that made me feel like… something else. Until now.

89: SURVIVE
Keres

Choose to live. Choose to fight.

Almost two months ago, I stood before King Berlium and considered giving up my life. He offered me two options. Save my people or die. For a moment, I considered welcoming oblivion. Relinquishing—giving up the fight. Abandoning my role, my people. It was easier than facing what I was and what had happened. Easier than losing and hurting.

But my inner monster was angry and hungry. I wasn't fucking done.

Even when he hurt me—I wasn't done.

No matter how he tried to break me, I never turned back to those thoughts. I pulled myself up and pushed forward. Even when it felt wrong, even when it was hard, I looked for something to anchor me. To connect to. I chose my people. I chose power. I also chose him.

I'm not perfect, but I'm not fucking done. I fight. I live. Yes, I still feel pain and fear… but now I know how to use it. I don't walk a path of righteousness, but I walk. I'm ready to march.

If I had been on the ledge with Liriene, what would I have seen?

Would I have been able to pull her back?

I don't burn like you do.

There is no perfect answer to every question that haunts us in moments of despair:

Why me?

When does it get easier?

What if I just… stopped fighting?

Different people need to hear different things. But everyone needs to hear the words—Live. Fight. I will not leave you.

I didn't know if Liriene could hear me while she slept, but while I lay next to her, I bridged my thoughts with hers. And I told her those words repeatedly until she woke up.

Sometimes all we can do is survive. There's no perfect path to healing. Over the next week, Liriene sank into herself and then resurfaced. In an ever-changing pattern of emotions. She screamed at me one moment and cried the next.

But I told her I could handle it and I did. "Good. Fight."

Sometimes fighting looks like that. It doesn't always look like strength. That's okay. "You're here. I'm with you," I tell her.

I make her drink her fucking tea. It helps her calm down. Draven told me about her visions, her nightmares. She told me about her flashbacks. When she started talking, we found things to help her. Something is still different, though. She still hates it here. She still wants to believe in some savior. I just want her to believe in something.

We walk together down the halls, on our way to the library. Today, I sense something's wrong. She's lost in thought, but she stops walking. I stop next to her.

"Liri?"

I send a quick thought to Draven, asking him to meet us at the library.

"I'll be right there."

"You know, I sense the Veil. What the King said is true—it's thin here," Liriene says and waves her hands. The air—it moves. Like a curtain being pulled away.

"Liriene, I don't think you should—"

"I can touch it." She turns and looks at me. "Thanks to Hadriel's lessons, I can rend it."

Blue and green and white light shimmers through the air as the Veil answers her touch. I take a step back, watching. An unnatural breeze filters down the hall, rushing against my skin. Every hair on my nape stands and my skin pebbles. My eyes trace the line her hands make. A tear—she pulls it apart. Light flashing under her fingertips and a howling wind breaking through. The tear widens until it's a massive wound between our world and the Other.

Liriene steps aside, and behind her stands Thane.

90: SEPARATED

Keres

The corridor seems to move between us, lengthening and shortening. I sink into a fighting stance. My claws rupture through my fingertips, my fangs sink into my mouth, and my horns swirl out of my skull.

"Well, aren't you pretty," Thane says and steps over the threshold of the Veil. "Thanks for opening the door, Liriene."

"Liri—why?"

"I told you he was coming. The Baore is protected. He couldn't channel us when we were in Dale. But here, it's thinner. He reached me while I dreamed. After I jumped. He told me he was nearby."

"I took a stroll through the Godlands," he says, crossing his arms over his chest. He's dressed in all black. His black hood pulled up over his head. A loose strand of long brown hair hangs in front of his face. His teal eyes are startlingly bright, compared to his golden-brown skin. He drags his gaze over me, noting my trousers and crimson tunic—Draven's shirt.

"You smell like him," Thane sneers.

"Jealous?" I pull my sword out of its sheath on my back. Thankfully, I still carried it from training this morning.

He holds up his hands and steps aside as another man steps out of the Veil behind him. A black-haired, fair-skinned man with two different colored eyes.

"I know you," I say. "I saw you—In Ro'Hale! You were there. Juggling in the streets. By the temple of Mrithyn."

"I also dressed up as a wolf in the Court of Beasts," he says, and bows. "My name's Rivan."

"I don't want your names. I want you to leave. You're not welcomed here."

"Oh? The King and I are good friends. Oh, wait. That changed when he took you. Didn't it, Draven?"

Liriene's brows furrow with confusion as she turns. She doesn't recognize his true name.

I sense him behind me. Every hair on my body stands, and I inhale his scent. His wings ruffle. I take steps backward, not taking my eyes off Thane and his men. Three more men wait on the other side of the Veil.

Draven's hands snake around my waist.

"Hello, Thane. Two hundred years of courtesy, and you couldn't even knock at the front door," he says casually.

"Was hoping you weren't home, brother."

Brother?

Draven's grip tightens as he pulls me to his side, under his wing. I look at Liri, and she draws closer to Thane.

Thane cracks his knuckles, the movement drawing my attention to the tattoos on his hands. "We can do this the dramatic way or the peaceful way."

"I'm not going with you," I say.

Thane smirks. "I see you love drama. No wonder you bound yourself to Draven. This hallway is so cramped. Do you really want to fight here?"

"I'll fucking tear you to shreds if you try to take me by force," I snap.

"She's not lying, Thane. She's got such pretty little fangs."

"Fuck yeah, she does," the red-headed man on the Other side says.

"Morgance, silence," Thane shoots back at his companion.

Shadows cover Thane's face, obscuring him, and they crawl out from under his cloak, dripping from his arms like smoky tendrils. I remember the version of myself that I saw in Draven's mirror. The torq of shadows around me—and I call for them. I don't know where they come from, but they answer. Draven looks down at me and grins. Running his fingers along the shadows that sigh at his touch.

"Ah, how precious. She carries a piece of me," Thane says in an inhuman voice.

I swing my attention back to him. "You wish."

He laughs—his voice splitting the same way Draven's does. Yarden comes running down the hall, sword singing as it's unsheathed.

"God of Fury, what the fuck is going on here?" Hadriel files into the corridor next.

"We have a visitor," Draven says, his own voice splitting, too. It sends a shiver down my spine. Such a turn on.

"She purrs for you, brother," Thane notes.

"He makes me do a lot more than purr," my Godling's voice growls through mine.

Draven chuckles.

"Liriene," I plead. "If you really want to go with him, I won't fight you. But please don't. Look at him! You don't know him."

"I'm sorry," she says and steps into the Veil.

"Alright, Keres, be a good girl and come with me, and I will spare your mate."

Mate.

"Don't speak to her that way," Draven snarls.

His scales bloom on his skin, covering him from head to two. Like armor. He hulks forward, black sharp horns growing through his hair. His claws lengthen, bigger than usual. He opens his mouth, revealing rows of jagged teeth.

"Brother, you've gotten ugly—your breath," Thane says, waving his hands in front of his—well, he looks faceless. *King of Shadow.*

Draven pushes me behind him, shaking his wings. They shiver and he fucking rattles. And they're not the beautiful, red-feathered wings. But shiny, leathery black. Like dragon wings.

"I wonder how prepared you are to fight me for her. How far you'll go. Make no mistake, I will not hold back, brother. She's mine, and I'd rather die than see her fall into your hands," Draven says in a dark, growling voice.

My heart is beating so hard, I'm sure it's bruised my ribs.

Yarden's hand touches my shoulder. I turn, finding his eyes full of bronze fire. His brows are pushed forward with anger. In one hand, he wields a sword and in the other, a whip made of fire. He passes me backward to Hadriel—whose eyes are a storm of swirling dark silver. His own fangs express, and he turns into that Nightmare Warrior that I saw on the battlefield of Ro'Hale.

Thane and Draven charge at each other.

Thane's shadows split and stretch, sharpening and tearing through the air like swords. Draven twists and jumps onto the wall, crawling along it like some kind of spider demon. Yarden steps in front of me, winding up and then lashing out with his fiery whip. It cracks through the air and light erupts, scattering the shadows.

They retreat to Thane's hands. Swelling beneath him, rushing through his clothes and lifting him into the air.

"Cerberus," he hisses at Yarden. Another onslaught of shadows reaches out as Thane shoots his hands toward us.

They scissor through the whip, but it regrows. Another lash and the hall lights up. Draven uses the flare to pounce on Thane. Shredding into him with his claws—Thane disintegrates! Sinking into our shadows cast on the ground. Clones of his body appear in front of each of us, popping up out of the darkness.

A sphere of blue light pulses through me, expanding and severing Thane's hold on me. I wheel around and see Hadriel, lifting only one finger to cast the ward. He sets glyphs on the floor, covering our shadows, like shutting trap doors. Thane aims at Draven. By the time I'm turned around, they're rolling in a cloud of winged darkness. One of them cries out and blood splatters the wall. Thane hits the floor.

Fire blasts out of the tear in the Veil and Liriene jumps back into the corridor. Her fire distracts Draven, and he claws through it. Thane uses the chance to jump back. She shoots more fire at him, but I turn it into Brazen, bending it toward Thane. He dodges, but Draven lunges at him again. Summoning his blue Brazen as well and creating a wall of flames between us and the Veil.

Liriene tears through them and orbs of fire float around her.

She shoots them out, pelting Draven. Yarden pulls away from Rivan and jumps in front of the King. His whip transforms into a shield of flames.

He pulses it forward, as if he were battering through a wall, and light bursts out of it.

Searing light that knocks Thane back.

Rivan—where the fuck did he go? He pops up behind Hadriel and I. We both whip around, noticing he got through the ward.

"How?" I shout.

"Fight, child!"

I imitate Thane, flaring my shadows out like swords, readying my actual blade. Rivan stops them with his hand, bending them, dulling them, and even bites through one of them with his fangs.

"What the fuck?"

"Fangs! He's a servant?" my Death Spirit hisses.

I throw myself toward him, thrusting my sword. He disappears. Pops up behind me.

"Fuck." I spin and strike again, but my sword cuts through shadows. I encase my body in fire and push it out of me in a forceful burst.

Hadriel holds up a hand, stepping through it, but it knocks Rivan back. He dusts sparks off his black jacket.

"Ouch, Keres."

I close my eyes and reach my consciousness out along the Veil, locking in on his Spirit.

"Horror," I say under my breath.

Draven is a monster and so am I. He wields power over the mind, but he taught me, through bridging, I too can touch the mind. I can do more than send messages. He taught me to call upon Atys, the God of Punishment and Torment. The same way I can summon Brazen, I can summon Affliction. My spoken words became hexes. The same way he can command me and make me see things, I can make Rivan see his worst fears.

He shrieks as horror overcomes his mind. He falls, clutching his hands to his head.

"Gods below, Coroner—did you just?"

I smirk at Hadriel. "I knew I'd make you proud one day, my dark minister."

Hadriel smiles, baring his own fangs. My eyes are probably rounder than coins. He licks his lips with a split tongue as he turns toward Rivan. I stumble over my surprise.

"Marvelous girl. You'd make your mother proud too," Hadriel says.

He flicks his wrist and builds a cage-like ward around Rivan. He screeches and his shadows swallow him. Transporting him back to the Rend.

We turn back and see Thane and Draven circling each other. Yarden's clutching his arm, bleeding, against the wall. Liriene's wiping blood from her lip, standing closer to the Rend. The men on the other side seem to be barred, like they can't pass through.

"Hey!" I shout and run forward. Thane turns toward me—fool. Draven slashes at him. Time slows.

Thane sinks slowly, desperate to evade Draven's claw, which looms within inches of his head. And then I see Liriene.

On fire from head to toe—lunging into the space between them.

Time hits us as Draven's claw sinks into Liriene. She screams and falls into Thane. With inhuman speed, he pivots, catching her and throwing her through the Veil.

Draven catches his balance, realizing he's hit my sister. As he watches her soar through the Veil, Rivan catches her. I snatch control of Rivan's blood and pin him to the spot before he can take her. He struggles against my hold. Liriene's eyes lock with mine. She sees I'm doing something to him and punches fire at me. I drop the reins on Rivan to tear through her flames. She just fucking attacked me. I push a gust of air down the hallway, blowing distance between everyone as Rivan throws Liri through the Veil.

Thane's shadows spear into Draven, forking into his shoulder, bicep, and wing. Pinning him to the wall.

I coat my blade in Brazen and sever the thick shadows that pierce him. He stumbles and Hadriel turns his attention to Draven. I attack Thane, but he pulls the same shit Rivan did, popping in and out of sight.

"Pain," I hex him, but it doesn't work, and he laughs. "Fuck."

Draven's scaly claw lands on my shoulder and Thane materializes in front of us again. Winged shadows jump out of the corner of the room, forming a vortex around me. I lift off the ground, tumbling as I'm thrown backwards.

The darkness disperses, and I roll to the floor. Looking up to see I'm further down the hall, behind Draven and Hadriel.

Thane's shadows bloom, darkening the hall, crawling along the walls and gobbling everything up. Draven and Hadriel disappear in the inky blackness that spills toward us. Yarden falters backwards, holding up his shield of light, keeping the shadows from touching me.

Everything goes dark around us

"Draven!" I scream and grab onto Yarden, tucking myself in close to him. The shadows snap at us like jaws, but he deflects them. He pulses his shield out again, only breaking through the wall of darkness a few feet. It's heavy, unnatural darkness. Absolute. We're in a void.

A loud hissing sound behind me spins me around so I'm back-to-back with Yarden. I make a dome of Brazen around us, but a seam of green light tears open the darkness behind us.

The Veil splits again and the darkness shatters.

"Keres!" I hear Draven.

Two large hands reach through the veil, grabbing me, not even bothered by my fire. I scream and lash out my sword, but it goes through the arms without harming them. Like they're made of air.

I look up into abysmally dark eyes—at the fanged smile of the man from my nightmares. The man bearing a Death Spirit.

"Keres!"

The man flips me like I'm feather-light, spinning me around so I can see Draven jumping toward me. Yarden's fire behind him like a bronze halo of light. His winged shadows reaching for me—his hand held out, glowing with blue fire. Mine, burning green, reaches out and our fingertips almost touch, but he's pulled back as Thane's shadows spear through his chest and the Veil slams shut.

EPILOGUE

THE SHARPEST SHARD

"My story is a battle cry.
When I scream, the world hears my bloodline.
When I march, the blood of innocents
Awakens and shakes the very earth it stains."

—Keres' Journal

EVEN IN DEATH
Keres

My eyes linger on the empty air in front of me. Still, I'm on all fours where the man dropped me moments ago. My hands still aflame, fingernails digging into the dirt and scorching it. The man stands behind me, but I can't look away. Trying to make sense of what just happened.

Draven's blue eyes wide with shock. The blood dripping from the sharp tip of the shadows' spear. Did I imagine his heart had stopped beating?

"*No,*" my Death Spirit's voice breaks through mine hoarsely. "*No, no. It didn't stop. Please, it can't—he can't...*"

"Are you crying?" the man asks in an r-tapping accent.

I swing my attention to him and snarl, jumping to my feet and brandishing my sword again. I open my mouth to speak, but realization replaces the curses.

"Hello, Blood Drop," he says with a wry grin.

His blackened eyes lighten into pools of doe brown. His mouth curves into a fanged smile, and he pushes his long, ashen hair back with clawed fingers.

I look him up and down and wipe the tears from my face. From his bare feet to his black leather pants. I note the belt full of knives and chains. His tunic is dirty, stained with old blood. The black jacket he wears over is bumped up where, I guess, more weapons are concealed. A green-bladed longsword with a silver hilt is strapped to his back. Like mine.

"You're Geraltain."

My dark predecessor's smile widens. "So, you have heard of me.

Funny. I was supposed to be forgotten."

"You're dead."

"Really?" He looks down at his body. "I think I'd know if I died, Blood Drop. I would have been there when it happened." Streaks of violet and red light flash through his eyes.

"Yeah, you would have been there—two hundred years ago." I dismiss him, turning back around. Willing the seam in the Veil to reopen. I need to get back to Draven. I hold up my hands like Liriene did. Trying to touch the unseen fabric that separates us.

"Are you trying to Rend?"

"Shut up," I snap. Sweat beads on my brows as I extend my senses. "Why isn't it working?"

"Mrithyn doesn't want you to leave. Not yet."

Two swift footsteps stomp into the black earth and a hand grabs my shoulder, spinning me around. I shove Geraltain away from me and he steps back with his hands held up. The tears don't stop coming.

"I have to go back. My—"

"Your?"

"He's hurt." My voice breaks, and then a growl erupts from my chest. "What the *fuck* do you mean Mrithyn won't let me leave?"

I shove him again and he just lets me. My mind feels torn in two. The Death Spirit's howling and growling, enraged and pained. Every hollow part of my Spirit is reverberating with the need to know he's okay. I ball my fists at my side. The air suddenly feels too thick, and my chest feels heavy.

"Hey." Geraltain reaches a hand out. "Get it together, Blood Drop. I'm sure you know how hard it is to kill the King."

I stare at him unblinking, seething. I know Draven can heal, but will he? I don't know his limits. And Thane....

Fucking Thane. He attacked my husband and stole my sister. I'll hunt him down and kill him with my bare hands. Even if Draven is alive—you don't fucking touch what's mine and live.

"I need to go back. Now."

Logic isn't winning this argument. My Spirit wants her creature more than she wants her God right now, and that should really fucking terrify me, but nothing does more than the thoughts of Draven cold on the floor, blood pooling under his body. His war-drum of a heart, silenced. My heart. My blood is on fire. Every drop of my blood is burning for him.

She's mine, and I'd rather die than see her fall into your hands. My stomach twists with the thought of what Draven said. He was prepared to fight for me... even if it cost him his life. He put himself between me and Thane, like a stone wall. Knowing Thane would try to tear him down. That meant more than anything either of us had ever said to each other. If it was the last thing—no. It wouldn't be the last thing. We weren't fucking finished.

I turn and hold out my hands, still shaking and burning with green Brazen. Trying to touch the Veil again.

Geraltain claps a hand down on me. "No can do, missy."

"Get your paws off me." I swat at him and then wipe another rebellious tear away. "I'm not just going to leave him behind."

"You're not going anywhere, Blood Drop. Not until Father says so. He's shielding you."

I turn and glare at him. *Shielding me.*

"From Thane?"

He smirks. "I'll let him explain that."

I take one last look at the empty air. Wishing that the seam would reopen, but it doesn't, and Thane's fate is sealed with it. No matter what bond we share, he has designed a rift between us.

I look around, seeing nothing except rolling, dark-soiled plains drenched in hazy, dim light cast by the Black Sun. Liriene... She went through a tear, but she's not *here.*

"So, we're in Mrithyn's realm?"

Darkness corners my vision and the Brazen creeps up my arms, flaring out as Geraltain catches my attention and raises a brow. As if he can't believe I just asked that.

He tilts his head back and laughs—a sharp sound that makes me shiver. "Everywhere is Mrithyn's realm. Tell me of a place Death does not touch."

I swallow hard, and movement behind him catches my eye. I step to the side and see—Osira! She tilts her head and smiles. Her huge brown eyes *seeing* me. Soft brown fuzz has sprouted on her head.

Dumbfounded, I gape at her.

"What—how? Are you dead?" My voice is a shredded rasp at this point.

"No. We're just in the Godlands, Keres."

She walks up to me and hugs me. I squeeze her and then hold her back, looking at her. The world beyond her. Behind her, in the darkened sky, the Black Sun is outlined in silver light, gray clouds pass over us.

"Why? I'm happy to see you, but do you two even realize what just happened? Liriene was hurt—"

"Father's waiting," Geraltain says, pointing in the opposite direction.

A massive black mountain tears through the horizon. Violet stars shroud the peak and a blood-red moon rests behind it.

"Mrithyn," I breathe.

Geraltain latches onto my wrist and Osira's. His next step forward jolts into some kind of rushing stream of power. The world blurs by. I feel dizzy and catch my footing, as we stop at the foot of the mountain.

I jerk free of his grasp. "Wait!"

Geraltain grabs me again.

"You really don't understand what paws off means, do you?" I snarl.

"You can't go back there. Not yet."

"But—"

"Rule number one in the Godlands: you can only Fade Step toward your God. Want to get anywhere else? Got to go the old-fashioned way. I brought you where you are meant to be right now—at Mrithyn's feet. He wants to speak with you."

Guilt gnaws at my stomach.

"Ah," Geraltain says and crosses his arms over his chest. He looks me in the eye.

"Seems we sink our teeth into the people we depend on, don't we?" he asks.

I narrow my eyes to slits.

"You've made an interesting choice with the King, Keres. I wonder at the consequences."

I look away from him, up at the mountain.

"You can't go before Father looking like that. Shift all the way, Blood Drop. Let's see how beautiful you are. Wings and all."

I look at Osira again. "It's okay," she says with a smile.

My Spirit flows through me. I feel the coldness uncurling through my veins. The weight of my claws hanging from my fingertips. My vision sharpens as the darkness overtakes me. My fire answers my call, burning green and violet. Shadows swirl at my feet.

"Fuck yeah," Geraltain crows. "I've never seen another Coroner shift."

My wings flourish, but I don't feel the satisfaction he does. My Spirit is torn in two. Part of me wants to get away from here. Part of me feels pulled toward the mountain, toward Geraltain, too. The Death Spirit feels like a howling wind inside me.

A grin breaks open his face and he cheers. "Bloody brilliant!"

"Your turn."

In big guy fashion, he flexes his muscles. His huge hands morph into beastly claws with red-tipped talons. Where mine are spindly, his are bone thick. His eyes hold streaks of the colors of the stars above us in darkness, blacker than the Sun.

A silver light traces the outline of his white-haired head. Drawing my eye up as he seems to grow. As if barely coming up to his chest didn't make me feel small enough.

The air rushes away from us, swirling our hair, as his massive wings erupt from his back. Black like mine, but more skeletal. The violet starlight seems to reach toward him, bathing the dark plumes with an ethereal sheen.

"Your flowers are cute." He snickers. "Wither Maidens?"

I flare my wings with annoyance and nod.

"I bet you had quite the experience if you drank that stuff."

I snort. "Titillating."

"You should try dragon's blood someday. Talk about ecstasy. Alright, enough dallying. Let's go."

I widen my eyes and look back at the mountain

"Cesarus, come," Osira said. Cesarus appears at her side. His eyes are glowing the same way they had in my vision.

"Were you truly there with me, Osi?" I reach out and she grabs my hand. She's really here. Questions swarm me, followed by guilt.

She beams at me. "I was with you in Spirit. You have no idea what I had to do to get here, though. But I sensed you were in danger. So, I came to Mrithyn in person to ask for help. The world is turned against you now, Keres. I couldn't sit and do nothing knowing that."

I smile at her, but that statement worries me. Without further explanation, she climbs on Cesarus' back and approaches the mountain.

The Mountain is like a smooth obsidian steeple that reaches toward the Blood Moon, crowned with stars. Geraltain beats his wings and lifts into the air, smirking down at me. I shoot upward to meet him where he hovers. Together, we fly up the face of the mountain. Reaching its peak, I look down and see it's hollow. The inside is a void of darkness.

"How do I know I can trust you?" I ask him. I trust Osira, but him?

He shoves a sleeve up his arm and scratches his skin open with a talon. Black light bleeds out of the cut. He grabs my arm and does the same before I can protest.

The same thing—the same black light oozes out of me.

"Your Spirit is the same as mine. Mirk-blooded—like a bloodline all Coroner's share."

"They call you the Blood Waker," I say as my skin closes, sealing the strange light inside me.

He smirks at me. "It's a great nickname. They'll be calling you that soon enough. For now, you're Blood Drop. Until you prove you're as badass as me."

I just nod, unable to take his bait.

Cesarus carries Osira up the side of the mountain, to the brim, and then runs down into the darkness. Geraltain nods his head in their direction. "Race you down."

Reluctantly, I follow, breaking through the darkness like a cloud of smoke. Inside the Mountain, we land in a brightly lit throne room. A massive black and silver throne takes up the center. We land in front of Mrithyn.

He turns around, opening his long arms. His eyes are just as I remember. Swirling with darkness, red, green, violet, silver. Other colors I didn't know the names of.

An iridescent river runs around His throne and down the ivory aisle that stretches back to a gate. I hear the growling and panting of a hound, glimpsing its massive body as it paces on the other side of a gate in the farthest wall.

I turn back to Mrithyn and bow, suddenly noticing the state of my appearance. I probably look ragged and crazed, in Draven's crimson tunic and my worn trousers. Clutching my Illynic blade like it's tethering me to him. I keep my eyes on the hem of Mrithyn's black silk robes. I notice the thin, silver embroidery that meanders at the edges, in a continuous line that folds back on itself. I trace it slowly up to His collar, and finally meet his gaze.

"Fairer than ever," He preens. His voice is soft, like the sigh of the wind after a storm. His words drop into my mind, chilling my blood, like raindrops soaking your clothes.

"Rise, my faithful servants."

Geraltain and I both stand.

Mrithyn is also very tall, but slender, unlike the big guy next to me. His arms seem too long and impossibly graceful. His facial features are sharp. His eyes are set high in His long face. His lips are thin, stretched in a slight smile that doesn't seem to budge. His long white hair reaches His waist, braided in places with silver thread that's as bright as the stars above the Mountain. He smiles wider as I appraise Him, baring His fangs.

"Made in my image—a masterpiece. Life, my lover, made you oh, so fair. It makes the game more fun."

"What, am I not pretty enough for you?" Geraltain sighs.

Mrithyn glances at him and snorts. "You're my demon. Keres is my angel."

"Ah, yes. Father, son, and unholy ghost," big guy says.

"Aye, what about me?" Another voice preludes the thud of heavy feet.

I turn and look at another ashen-haired man who's just jumped down off a ledge. Like a fucking gargoyle come to life. I notice the rows and rows that circle up the walls of the mountain. Like shelves and ivory statues of people frozen on them.

The other big guy, though not as big as Geraltain, strides over. "I'm Isaldor."

"He's the boring one," Geraltain says under his breath.

"I thought you said you've never seen another Coroner."

"Not in Godling form. Izzie here can't shift anymore."

"Oh yeah? Just because I didn't kill a God like you doesn't mean I'm boring, and excuse me for dying. We couldn't all be raptured by Father."

"You *what?*"

Geraltain shrugs and opens his mouth to speak, but Mrithyn silences us all. Wordlessly. We all whip our heads around as if He'd made a sound our Spirits heard, but our ears didn't.

"Keres, you made a peculiar choice in Draven," He comments.

I shouldn't be surprised that my God knows my husband's real name.

"That's what I said," Geraltain says and walks over to a table laden with food—had that been there a minute ago?

Osira joins Geraltain and Isaldor at the table.

"Is the King dead?" I ask.

If anyone knows, it's Mrithyn. He just walks around me in a circle, smiling. His silence makes my skin crawl. What if Draven was dying still? Slowly or painfully. Rage still blazes through my blood, but in Mrithyn's presence I feel His chill competing for my attention.

"My beauty, there is a great game at play. You—you are a rarity. Designed by the Gods. You've touched the darkness of the Void through Draven. That was... unexpected."

"I did what I had to do," I say, straightening my spine and clasping my hands behind my back, under my wings. Mrithyn rounds to face me and smiles wider.

"I wonder—do you love him?"

I meet His eyes with tears in mine.

"She better fucking not." Another voice shreds the silence. I spin toward the voice—the quick footsteps.

Cut through by the glare of diamond eyes.

Catching the attention of a set of azure blue eyes.

Gasping as my gaze settles on eyes like my own—emerald green.

"Oh, come now, Ivaia," Mrithyn purrs. "The rules… There are no rules. I wonder what the Kings will do. If Draven survives, of course."

His words set my already racing heart into a frenzy. I look down at my feet, and then slide my gaze toward the hem of Mrithyn's robe.

"Keres between the two of them." He chuckles darkly. "Now, Queen of the Baore—how endlessly fascinating. Wouldn't you agree, Resayla? Your daughter proves worthy of your prayers."

My mother's eyes glow and tears flood mine. "Yes," she says with a smile and holds out her arms. "She does, indeed."

Ivaia softens, and she wraps her arms around both of us. Herrona lingers in the periphery. Geraltain and Isaldor watch us, licking their fingers as they eat and look at my family. Their gauzy white dresses. Their ethereal auras. Beautiful. Even in Death.

That chill seeps into my bones, siphoning some of the angst out of me. I turn back to Mrithyn with them surrounding me and find Him smiling. I step forward and hold my wings out to their full breadth. My Death Spirit, heralding her loyalty under the watchful gaze of her Maker.

"You brought me here for a reason."

He chuckles softly and takes a seat on His massive throne. Reclining, He holds out His hand and black fire blooms in his palm.

"Mortals wage war on the Gods and on each other. The Pantheon casts their lots with their Instruments. Power locked away for centuries— rattles its cage. The Veil is torn. The Grave of the Forsworn—the stone shall be rolled away from the tomb, and Illyn awakens from its slumber. The Thrones of the Void are Vacant. Godlanders walk among mortals. And you—you have stepped into the arena. Playing with Gods and Monsters. You've taken the King and put the other in check. You have become a Fate, so dark and lovely. And this game, for the first time in centuries… it's finally worth playing."

THE END FOR NOW

This lush, sexy, dark fantasy series continues in...

World of Aureum Series, Book Three

BLOOD WAKER

THE ANDRETHEORAN CALENDAR:

month	ruler	constellation	sign	season
1 Skythe	Mrithyn	Sickle	Axis	High Winter
2 Reanthen	Adreana	Raven	Guide	Mid Winter
3 Morth	Nameless God	Trenches	Twin	Mid Winter
4 Elymarth	Elymas	Staff	Wand	Low Winter
5 Tarinth	Taran	Mountain	Ram	High Spring
6 Genethary	Imogen	Cup	Knight	Low Spring
7 Orbinth	Oran	Torch	Pentacle	High Summer
8 Entich	Enithura	Tree	Vertex	Mid Summer
9 Nerrathen	Nerissa	Fish	Ness	Low Summer
10 Aramath	Ahriman	Horn	Herald	High Autumn

KERES' JOURNAL:

Bridging- Communication in the more immediate mental space.

Channeling- Connecting two minds across a long distance. In a level of the subconscious.

Rending- Creating rifts in the veil. Passable doorways or chasms.

Transformation- Expression of one's Godling form

Summoning- Splitting the Veil and Calling elements from the Godlands. For example, Brazen Fire, Shadows, etc.

Mapping- Tracing the threads of the Veil to navigate items or people.

Warding- Veil Reinforcement

Notes

The Pantheon rules the Principalities, the Instruments. The caste system of the Instruments is divided by scope of power. Instruments are more closely related to the Gods and Monsters than other mortals. On the plane of the First Children. Other mortals, in any dominion, are the Second Sons. Examples of different dominions: Humans, Elves, Daemons, etc.

Death and Life, the Preeminent Deities. Their servants are called Fates: Coroners & Wardens

Light and Darkness, the Reigning Deities. Their servants are called Seers & Shades

Elemental Gods are the Composing Deities. Their servants are called Phenomenals.

The God of Magic is a Magnifying Deity. His servants are called Wonders, they're children.

War and peace, the Orchestrating Deities. Their servants are the Mediators.

Oracles are considered gilded mortals. Accessories, mouth pieces for the Gods.

The Nameless God... does he have servants?

Geraltain used to be called the Blood Waker or Soul Eater. Some even called him a Godlander...

Special Thanks

First and foremost, thank you to my readers. Those who have been awaiting this book for more than two years. Those who have just discovered the World of Aureum and are here to stay. Being here with you means everything to me.

Thank You to my Beta Readers:

My sisters, Emily and Michelle. For always being a phone call away, always ready to listen to me rant about this story. For loving it as much as I do. For standing by me and always keeping it real.

Sophia B. For staying up into the ungodly hours with me to make sure this book was the best it could be. In the robe bond we trust!

Ossiris G. For being the baddest bitch a woman could ever want in her corner cheering her on.

Adreanna S. For loving Aureum from page one.

Megan, Erin, Dani, and Montse, thank you for stepping up and putting so much loving energy into this book.

A *very* special thank you to my Sensitivity Readers, Emil T. and Kinsey, whose strong voices helped me craft this narrative with mindfulness and courage.

Major thank you to the Goddesses lending me their powers, Micaela Alcaino, our artist, and Mackenzie Letson, the editor.

All my love and thanks to the Scorpio King, Zachary James, my precious friend and formatter. You truly light up my life.

Last but not least… thank you to my father, Aaron. For saving my life. For holding me back from the edge, for never leaving my side when I was at my lowest. For putting the phone in my hands and sitting with me while I called the suicide prevention hotline. For listening to my darkest stories. I'm still here telling my stories because of you. I love you for infinity.